Margohot

Harpy Parenthood, Volume 1

Keith Melo

Published by Keith Melo, 2024.

This is a work of fiction. Similarities to real people, places, or events are entirely coincidental.

MARGOHOT

First edition. November 14, 2024.

Copyright © 2024 Keith Melo.

ISBN: 978-1966243076

Written by Keith Melo.

Table of Contents

CHAPTER 1 1
CHAPTER 2 27
CHAPTER 3 48
CHAPTER 4 68
CHAPTER 5 98
CHAPTER 6 129
CHAPTER 7 147
CHAPTER 8 167
CHAPTER 9 193
CHAPTER 10 222
CHAPTER 11 240
CHAPTER 12 258
CHAPTER 13 284
CHAPTER 14 316
CHAPTER 15 347
CHAPTER 16 372
CHAPTER 17 401
CHAPTER 18 422
CHAPTER 19 442
CHAPTER 20 469
CHAPTER 21 489
CHAPTER 22 516

Dedicated To The Loving Memories Of

Inay Soledad & Tatay Faustino

Grandma Everil & Grandpa Carl

Uncle Bruce

Ate Rachel

Kuya Jojo

Tita Dory

And Ate Amy

We miss you all dearly

"God gives every bird its food,

but He does not throw it into its nest."

—Josiah Gilbert Holland

CHAPTER 1

Red Desert sandstorms are among the most vicious a traveler could encounter. Living in America's far West would never have been possible without locomotives that made transportation a safer and more comfortable experience for traveling Americans.

Despite how hard the storm blows the sand, the train is sturdy enough to be unfazed by the sands that collide with these trains. The only thing louder than the sandstorm is the train whistle, which always grabs anyone's attention close to the railway.

Even the passenger car keeps passengers safe from the brutal sandstorms. This train traveling through Wyoming has fewer passenger cars than most since only a few folks go this far west, especially visiting smaller towns. It's hard to get a good view of the Red Desert from the window of this train in Wyoming's sandstorm. All anyone can see is the dreadful desert storms covering any good view. The only thing any of these passengers can see are some dead plants and tumbleweeds within close distance next to the rails.

Since this is one of the trains that's traveling very far, the interior quality feels like that of a third-class car despite being connected right behind the locomotive. Only a married couple sits in the first-class car, perfectly safe from the brutal weather outside.

The wife, sitting next to the window, doesn't dress like she is going west. Instead, she dresses like one of the city girls, wearing a thick ballgown that reaches the bottom of her boots. The black jacket the wife wears has the shoulder portions puffed upward. To show her sense of fashion, she has a jade scarf wrapped around her neck, gloves as white as her dress, and a bonnet covering her bright brown hair.

The husband, sitting on her left, is wearing an off-white peach suit. Black bowtie and black shoes, losing their shine, are the only things remotely different in color from his bright suit and white shirt. The husband has a nicely groomed red beard and short red hair. He takes out his pocket watch to see that it is five past two, then puts it away and crosses his arms impatiently.

"Oh, Monty," says the young wife, "if I'd known there was going to be a sandstorm today, I wouldn't be wearing this dress. There goes dressing to impress your family."

"Samantha, my darling," the husband says, "I think my parents would appreciate the thought of putting this much effort into seeing them."

"I know, Monty," Samantha says, turning to the window. "I wish I had met your family before we got married."

"Don't feel bad, my darling. You know they cannot leave their ranch when they have that many sheep to feed."

"By the way," Samantha turns to Monty, "you've never told me why you're the only family member who decided to move to Arkansas. You didn't run away at a young age, did you?"

"Of course not," Monty says, startled. "I just didn't want to spend the rest of my life being a shepherd and cutting sheep wool. It's not meant for me. The amount I make from selling watches is twice what my whole family makes."

"Right. Other than your parents, do you have other family members helping out?"

"Nobody. I'm the only child they have."

"You mean to tell me you left your family to work hard at the sheep ranch?"

"Hey, now." The husband leans away from his wife. "They gave me their blessings, and they have plenty of dogs guiding those critters to wherever they need them."

"Right. I'm just disappointed you kept me from meeting your family for so long. It's not right that you've decided that now's the time for me to meet my in-laws," Samantha sighs and turns to the window. "I just don't know how we're going to raise a healthy family if you're still keeping secrets from me."

"Come on, Samantha. It's not like that at all. It's just that...," the husband looks away and stares out the window on the other side of the car, "... maybe you won't like them."

Samantha turns to Monty with her arms crossed and looks more upset. "Monty. What makes you think that I won't like them? Don't you think I'm a person who gives others fair chances?"

"I know, my darling, but my family—well, you came from an upper-class background, and my family isn't of the same stature." The husband looks down, feeling uncomfortable about where the conversation is turning.

Samantha quickly changes her expression after noticing her husband's change of mood. She puts her hand on his. "Sweetheart. I'm not like other girls who judge the less fortunate. I just want to meet your family because I think it's fair to meet the ones who raised the man I love so dearly."

Monty turns to his wife with his undivided attention.

"I promise you, my love, that whatever happens over there, I will love you no matter what."

"Are you sure about that? Can you handle some of their unique lifestyles, loud noises, and gross sense of humor? They're not like most families, who are concerned about manners and etiquette."

"Well, if that's the case, I'll just follow your cue and—"

A loud bang sounds as something hits the window next to Samantha, causing it to crack. Samantha and Monty turn to see what has happened, but only Monty sees what has hit the glass. By the time Samantha turns around, it's too late to see what Monty has seen.

Startled, Samantha exclaims, "What was that?!"

"I don't know. It looked like a buzzard... or some sort of bird flew into our window."

The couple feels the slight breeze blowing through the crack in the window. Samantha feels the window weakening from the sand hitting it while her husband leans forward to examine the crack. There's a small drop of blood in the center of the crack on the exterior of the glass.

"Oh, the poor fellow." Monty touches the window. "That bird really did hit himself hard against the window."

"A bird? What kind of bird would even fly through a sandstorm like this?" Suddenly, the door behind them opens. A tremendous amount of sand comes in from the back door as it opens. The conductor is boarding the first-class car. He urgently enters and slams the door to prevent more sand from coming in.

"Golly," the conductor says. "It's been a while since I've seen a storm like this."

A slightly overweight conductor, older than the young couple, wears a dark blue suit and round hat. His uniform is dusty, but his gold buttons and pocket watch chains are spotless. He dusts himself off, wipes his glasses, and fixes his mustache before addressing the only passengers in the first-class car. The official sees the crack in the window next to Monty and says, "Hey, what happened to the window?"

"Sorry, sir," Monty replies, "but I think some sort of bird flew right into the window and caused that crack."

"Sir. Is it alright if we sit in a different seat?" Samantha asks. "I'm afraid the window might shatter if the storm worsens."

The conductor nods. "Suit yourself. You two and one in the last-class car are the only ones on board this train. No one will be taking any of these seats anytime soon."

"Thank you, sir," Samantha responds with gratitude.

The young couple moves back to the seat close to the conductor. As they take a seat, the conductor walks to where they sat and examines the cracked glass. "So you say a bird just flew and hit this window?" the conductor shouts across the car.

"Yes," Monty responds loudly. "It happened so fast. I only saw that a black bird hit the window. It was hard to see with so much sand blowing."

"Interesting. I have never seen a bird fly through a sandstorm, but seeing blood outside the window lets me know you're telling the truth."

The husband sighs with relief. "Oh, and sir. How much longer till we reach Rawlins?"

The conductor takes a seat across from the young couple. He removes his hat and wipes more sand and dust off his uniform. "I'd say it won't be very long. So where are you two coming from, if you don't mind me asking?"

"Russellville, Arkansas," Samantha responds.

"That's quite a long way. What brings you two to the West?"

"Just family," Monty answers. "My wife here never has met her in-laws, so they'll be meeting each other for the first time."

Upon observing two individuals displaying an affectionate gesture, the conductor reciprocated with a smile. The official was visibly moved by the presence of the young lovers, a sight that exuded a luminous aura. The brief exchange between the trio was abruptly interrupted as the whistle of an approaching train resonated, followed by the perceptible movement of the conveyance.

"Sounds like we're arriving soon," the conductor says. "I must be going." The conductor gets up from his seat and heads to the door leading to the locomotive. As the official exits the car, the couple gets up and waits for the train to stop. The dust storm has not only not settled but also developed into a reddish fog, making it even harder to see. Samantha and Monty watch the window intently as the train slows down. Through the dusty fog and blowing sand, they can only make out the silhouettes of buildings and the wooden platform of the train station.

The couple exits the train as soon as it comes to a stop. The moment they step out of the passenger car, their bright clothes get filthy from the dust blowing at them. The husband's suit and wife's dress become as red as the desert sand outside. The couple shields their eyes and noses as the sand blows in their faces.

The conductor approaches them and shouts, "Follow me! I'll lead you two to your luggage."

Samantha and Monty follow the conductor to the baggage car. It's a short walk, as the train only has three passenger cars. Through the window of the last-class car, Monty sees the only other passenger sleeping in his seat as the conductor opens the baggage car door and climbs inside. The conductor hands the passengers their bags, locks the baggage car, returns to the locomotive, and disappears into the dusty fog.

The husband struggles to carry both suitcases, one in each hand, as sand pelts his unprotected face. The wife pulls out her umbrella to shield her husband from the sandstorm hitting his face. Monty is grateful for the umbrella, as it provides much-needed relief from the sand and wind. The train whistles as they exit the train station and look for someone to talk to.

"Darling," Samantha says. "Did you tell your family that we're arriving today?"

"Yes, I did. I sent the family a telegram telling them to meet us here today, days before we set off."

"Did they send you a telegram to confirm they'll be here?"

"No, darling. They live far from the station, so I don't expect a telegram from them. Plus, they're not rich, so it's going to cost them more for the Pony Express to travel that far. I'm trying to be considerate of their budget."

"Oh, I can't take this sandstorm anymore. Let's find a place to stay."

"What about my family? They might be around here somewhere."

"Please, Monty. I can feel the sand in my shoes right now. No one will wait for anyone in a situation like this. I need to get away from this storm."

The husband looks around and sees a building in front of them. He gets closer to read the sign on top of the building and says, "Hey! That general store. I know someone who works there. The store owner is a good friend of my family."

The couple hurries to the store. Samantha opens the door for her husband, who is still carrying the luggage, and closes it behind them. Inside the general store, the whole place is made out of wood. The store has plenty of open space in the middle for customers to walk around. The counters are like a bar, separating customers from the items on the shelves. Next to the counters are barrels labeled with the names of various goods, such as salt, pepper, and other items. Samantha pulls out a chair to sit on and removes her boots to pour the sand into an empty bucket beside her, seeing that there's more sand than she expected.

"Garner!" Monty calls out, rushing toward the cash register. "Mr. Garner. It's me. Monty. You know, Pete and Patty's kid?"

Monty takes a moment to wait for a response. There is no answer. Monty then hops over the counter and heads to the hallway like he owns the place.

"Monty!" Samantha says. "What are you doing? The store owner is going to get mad."

"It's fine, my darling. I know Mr. Garner is okay with me just paying him a visit. I've done this plenty of times, so don't worry."

Samantha shakes her head over her husband's cockiness as she removes her other boot and pours more sand into the metal bucket. She hears him repeatedly call for his former employer's name at the back. While Monty continues searching for his former employer, Samantha notices that the sandstorm outside is dying down. She looks out the window and sees the train they had been on leaving. After the train whistles and departs Rawlins, she looks around the town.

In frustration, Monty steps out of the owner's space walks around the counter and complains. "Gee. I couldn't find Mr. or Mrs. Garner anywhere. It's not like them to leave the store open and have it unattended."

"Hey, Monty," Samantha says, staring at the window. "Is that normal right yonder?"

"What do you mean?"

Monty joins his wife at the window. As the sandstorm abates, the dusty fog slowly lifts, revealing a scene of desolation. Feathers are strewn across the road, and more are seen on the rooftops. But there is no sign of life.

"That's strange," Monty responds. "I've never seen this many feathers around here." He steps out of the general store to examine the town. "Hello? Is anyone there?"

"Monty," Samantha says, putting her boots back on. "Wait for me."

One of the piles of feathers on the ground in front of the store has Monty kneeling on one knee and picking up a large feather. The feather is thirty inches long, the same length as Monty's forearm. Its vane is black but has an unusual red reflection. Perhaps it's the reddish atmosphere that's causing the unusual reflection. The calamus that Monty is holding has an ivory color, like old bones. Monty rubs the feather's vane with his index finger, feeling its stiffness and firmness compared to a normal feather. He rubs it more until he touches the edge of the vane, which cuts his fingertip. He lets out an "ouch" as his wife approaches behind him.

As Samantha catches up to her husband, she asks, "What is it, sweetheart?"

"I don't know. This looks like feathers from eagles of some sort, but I've never seen feathers this big before."

Monty looks up as he hears the sounds of horses ahead. He sees two horses that are connected to a wagon. The husband grabs his wife's hand and leads her to the wagon. The horses look healthy despite enduring the sandstorm. As Monty tries to see what is in the wagon, one of the horses jumps up out of fear and moves hysterically.

Soon, the other horse starts panicking and moves uncontrollably with the other horse. As the husband backs away for safety, Samantha comes in, calming the two horses down by gently stroking their heads simultaneously. Both horses quickly calm down upon feeling her gentle touch, ensuring their safety. "Gee, I almost got kicked by one of them. How are you able to do that?"

"I grew up with horses. I have a way of calming them. By the way, horses wouldn't act this way unless they've been in danger."

"I doubt it's the storm," Monty says. "But I think it has something to do with why Rawlins has so many feathers."

Monty circles around the tall wagon and examines it closely as Samantha caresses the horses. When he gets behind the wagon, he sees a massive pile of feathers covering the entire surface of the wagon. Monty gets on board and carefully picks up one of the feathers. Upon closer examination, he realizes blood is on the feather he's holding as one drop of the red liquid falls off the sharp vane. The husband drops the feather out of fright. As he steps back, he notices a hand sticking out of the feather pile.

With much bravery, Monty digs out the feathers by using his suit's sleeve to push away the feathers and prevent any cuts. Some feathers poke through his sleeve, but Monty pulls them out by holding the quill and clearing the feathers with his suit. It doesn't take long for him to realize a corpse is in the wagon. When he pushes a feather off the corpse's face, he sees it's someone he recognizes. The husband screams out of shock, which gets Samantha's attention.

"What is it, darling?" the wife shouts.

She walks around the back of the wagon where her husband is. She then sees the same corpse, covered in blood, with her eyes opened wide and lying motionless. Monty holds on to his wife as they both are in shock. As Samantha regains control over herself, she notices her husband weeping.

At that moment, Samantha understands that Monty knows this dead person. He lets go of her, jumps on the wagon, puts his head down on the corpse, and starts to grieve. The young wife can't help herself from shedding a tear over her husband's sudden change of emotions.

After giving him time to grieve, she asks, "Darling... who is it?" Monty catches his breath. "It's...it's my ma. My ma is dead."

Hearing that, Samantha goes into shock once more. She takes a couple steps back to step away from the gruesome scene, both hands covering her mouth and nose. Too much anxiety overtakes her self-control, so she covers her mouth and screams as loudly as possible.

The husband lifts his head from his dead mother's chest. The red mist is gone, but he can see something in the distance past the farm behind his wife covered in sand and feathers. A figure that looks like a bird is flying toward them. As it draws nearer, it becomes less bird-like and more human-like, with wings that match the color of the feathers that were all over town.

Samantha notices her husband staring at something strange as he stops sobbing and stares wide-eyed into the distance.

The wife is too late to see what her husband is seeing, feeling a gust of wind blow past her as she turns. She doesn't notice the sudden wind blowing her hair and dress. The disturbed lady doesn't see anything but the farm covered in feathers.

"Monty?" Samantha turns to her husband. "What did you—"

At that moment, she sees her husband is headless, and his body falls on his mother's corpse, spilling blood all over his dead parent. The gruesome sight gets worse, and Samantha can't regain self-control. She falls to the ground and screams out of distress. After what she just witnessed, she can't return to her feet.

In her most unfortunate circumstance, Samantha hasn't been given time to grieve, as she feels a sharp pain coming through her right shoulder. Her grieving screams suddenly turn into physical pain screams. Incapacitated by the pain, she reaches out with her left hand to feel the sudden injury. She feels the grip of a giant bird of prey, the talons larger than any bird she had ever felt. She opens her eyes to see her deceased husband and mother-in-law in the wagon at her feet and that she is many feet above the ground.

She tries to go back to the earth by shaking her legs, but the pain from the stab wound in her shoulder and being pulled aloft make the situation even more agonizing. The horses are frightened again and run off with Monty and his mother on the wagon. Whatever is holding the suffering wife isn't bothered by the animals making their escape. Samantha sees a wing from the corner of her eye, but it's too quick for her to process what she is seeing.

With all of her might, she looks up to see whatever is abducting her. As soon as she makes eye contact with her kidnapper, she feels another giant talon grabbing her by the throat. The unknown flying fiend quickly and effortlessly rips her throat, and Samantha's screams go silent. Her blood spills from the air to the ground as she's being taken away.

The horses race as though the wagon is weightless, galloping so quickly that the feathers are blown off the wagon. They race out of Rawlins and into the Red Desert. The fearful animals run off the road, and their path gets so bumpy that the two corpses fall off the wagon. The horses make their escape, still pulling the wagon. Monty's headless body and his mother's corpse collapse onto the ground, and their remains roll on the desert's sand.

After the momentum stops, two corpses lie together, gathering sand as the sandstorm and the sandstorm makes its return. It doesn't take long until the same mysterious monster flies in and collects their remains. Like a bird of prey, it swoops in and snatches one of the corpses. There's another creature as well, the same species as the flying beast that slaughtered the married couple, carrying the second corpse off the ground. With the corpses taken away by the beasts flying away, Rawlins is left a ghost town devoid of any sign of life.

THE BOSTON POST OFFICE Square and Sub-Treasury Building are always busy during opening hours. Constructed with three stories, an additional two stories above the center, and a grand entrance, this complex facilitates the sending and receiving of letters, enabling long-distance communication across the many states of America. The recent expansion of postal services to international destinations further enhances its significance. Within the post office complex, the grand lobby boasts one of the largest interiors in the country, adorned with intricate artistic elements from the flooring to the finely crafted ceiling illuminated by radiant lights. The mail clerks' counter, spanning almost the length of a football stadium, divides the office spaces behind it, each located within pillars supporting the roof of the first floor.

In this bustling environment, a customer dressed in a matching brown plaid suit and pants, accompanied by a black bowler hat, approaches one of the open mail clerks. Appearing to be in his mid to late twenties, the customer is cleanly shaved but exudes an air of paranoia as he glances around the lobby with anxious eyes.

"Good morning, sir," the mail clerk greets. "How may I serve you?'

As the customer approaches the clerk, he turns his head to the left, avoiding eye contact. He then places his hand in his suit pocket and speaks in a thick Boston accent.

"Hey there," he says, passing a letter to the clerk. "I need you to mail this for me."

The clerk retrieves the letter from the customer and notices that both the mailing address and the return address are the same. The customer continues to act suspiciously, turning his head constantly. After a longer-than-usual silence from the clerk, he begins to pay attention to her. He notices her frowning as she reads the letter.

"Is there a problem?" asks the suspicious customer.

"Your return address is 4851 South Nottingham Boulevard, Boston, Massachusetts," the clerk replies, "I've never heard of this address before."

"Oh, it's a real place, toots. Just gimme the bill and send it out, will ya?"

"Okay, will you wait here for a moment? I just need to double-check on that address for you."

The customer looks over his shoulder, "Thanks, toots."

Rushing to the end of the hallway, the clerk embarks on a lengthy journey from her central station in the lobby. The paranoid customer keeps a watchful eye on her until she disappears through the back door. Once the door closes, he turns around, leans against the counter, and assumes a calm and collected demeanor. While waiting, he begins to whistle loudly, much to the annoyance of nearby customers and clerks. No one confronts him directly, but they glare at him and look away whenever he catches their gaze.

Minutes pass, and still, the same clerk has not returned. Growing suspicious, the customer realizes that the service is taking longer than usual. He ceases his whistling but continues to lean against the counter. Checking his pocket watch, he notes the time: 9:43 AM.

"Gee, what's taking her so long?" the customer mutters. "I never had to wait this long for the mail to get out."

He turns behind once more and notices a man standing in line behind him. The man is tall and well-dressed, wearing a dark gray coat, lighter gray pants, polished black shoes, and a brown Boston felt hat. He is estimated to be in his forties, standing at six feet tall. His face is clean-shaven, revealing a long shape with thin lips and a prominently shaped nose. The customer notices the man's intense dark eyes fixed upon him.

"Hey. Ya sendin' out mail?" The cocky young one asks.

"Yep," The man in line responds in a soft-spoken, mid-Atlantic voice. "Just trying to send a birthday letter to a relative of mine."

"That's thoughtful of ya," the one with the Boston accent replies, then looks at the other lines in the same lobby. "Why don't cha go to the other line and get better service? The mail clerk is taking her sweet-ass time over here."

"Eh, I'm a patient man. I have nothing better to do now than mail this birthday letter to a family member of mine."

"So, huh, your relative is having a birthday, huh? Where ya' mailing that birthday letter to?"

"My aunt? Well, she lives at 4851 South Nottingham Boulevard."

The cocky individual says "Well, wish her a happy birthday for me, will ya," and turns to face the clerk's desk in front of him. He takes a moment to process the information, realizing that the address the man has just mentioned is the same one he has written on the letter he has handed to the clerk. A wave of confusion washes over him as he ponders what the man has just said. Slowly, he turns back to face the man, one hand in his pocket and the other reaching inside his coat.

"You wouldn't happen to be Benjamin Stanley, would you?" The man in line pulls a couple of already-opened letters from his brown coat and waves them to him. "We have a couple of clerks working here that reported that you've been sending fraudulent documents through mail."

He pulls out one of the letters and reads it out loud, "Here's one that says, "Mrs. Welks, it comes to our attention that you did not file your taxes this year. We hate to inform you that since your taxes are overdue, you must pay the exact amount of $150 and a late fee of $10. If you do not send back the exact amount on July 23rd, 1899, to the returning address, you'll be asked to go to your nearest court to explain your reasoning for tax evasion. Signed, the Boston Internal Revenue Service." Ah, you've done an excellent job getting this letter written on a typewriter."

The mysterious man retrieves another letter from a different envelope and proceeds, "In contrast to the one I presume is in your handwriting," he reads aloud," 'Dear Mr. Gubbernick, this is a notice from the I.R.S. informing you that we have not received your tax return this year and are requesting–'" He pauses his reading. He directs his attention to Benjamin Stanley, "I apologize, but your handwriting is exceedingly difficult to decipher." He retrieves yet another letter from yet another envelope, "It is the same with his letter. May you read this one out loud for me?"

The suspected fraud begins sweating and counters, "Y-Ya got the wrong guy– I did-didn't send out those letters. Who are you, anyway?"

The man puts the letters back in his coat, "Oh, where are my manners? Allow me to introduce myself—"

In a gesture of courtesy, the mysterious man reaches into his coat, retrieving a badge. The badge he presents is unique in its design, featuring a six-pointed star shape. Adorning the top of the badge is a circular plate bearing the inscription "U.S. Post Office Dept. Inspector" along its circumference. The center of the plate exhibits an intricate eagle design, symbolizing authority.

"I'm United States Postal Inspector Jed Pluck," he declares, "Benjamin Stanley, I place you under arrest for fraudulent documentation and impersonating an Internal Revenue Service official."

Stanley, realizing the gravity of the situation, attempts to escape by swiftly moving to his left and rushing towards the exit. In his haste, he shoves a customer who is being assisted by a mail clerk out of his way. Reaching the open front door, Stanley is met with a disheartening sight: police officers heading up the entrance stairway outside.

With no other escape route in sight, Stanley turns around, desperate for a way out. However, Postal Inspector Pluck anticipates this move and quickly catches up to the fraud. With a well-executed tackle, Pluck brings Stanley to the ground and promptly handcuffs him. Police officers promptly enter through the front entrance. Working swiftly, they pull the apprehended criminal up from the ground and escort him out of the post office.

Exiting the front stairway, Postal Inspector Pluck watches as police officers place Benjamin Stanley in the police wagon. With his arms crossed, the postal inspector smirks at the fraud, who stares back at him through the caged window. As the door at the back of the wagon secures, police officers mount the driver's seat and whip the reins of the horses, causing the sturdy animals to pull the wagon and transport the fraud to the nearest police station.

"Another fine job you did here, inspector," the police officer in charge states, watching the wagon move away, "Tell me, how long did it take you to find this guy?"

In response to the policeman's question, Postal Inspector Pluck remarks, "With over a decade of experience, catching individuals who carelessly leave their return addresses on letters becomes increasingly straightforward. In this specific instance, it only takes three days from the time the letters are reported fraudulent." He turns to the chief and adds, "To make matters even more convenient, the individual chooses to mail these letters in the same building as my office, making apprehension effortless."

A chuckle escapes both the officer and the postal inspector as they struggle to maintain their professional demeanor on duty. However, their brief moment of mirth is interrupted by the sound of a bicycle bell, signaling the arrival of a mailman. Dressed in a traditional navy blue coat and pants adorned with large golden buttons, a round hat with a flat top, and a Western Union badge, the mailman dismounts his bicycle and approaches the two officers on foot. The inspector and the chief immediately turn their full attention to the messenger.

"Telegram for Inspector Jed Pluck," the mailman declares.

"Yes, that's me." Pluck replies, "Who's it from?"

The mailman retrieves the letter from his bag and reads aloud, "The Postmaster General has assigned you to a case in Wyoming involving recent disappearances in the North West region. Post Inspector Louie Secoli will be your partner. He'll meet you in your office by noon today. Signed, John Wanamaker."

The mailman put away the letter. "That'll be thirty-five cents."

UPON RECEIVING A TELEGRAM from the Postmaster General, Mr. Pluck eagerly awaits the arrival of his newly assigned partner in his office situated on the uppermost floor of the Boston Post Office Square. As the noon hour approaches and boredom threatens to overcome him, a knock resounds upon the door of his office. With alacrity, Mr. Pluck hastens to open the door and beholds a man of comparable stature. This individual adorns round spectacles and possesses a brown goatee beard, characterized by a mustache that surpasses the thickness of the hair adorning his chin.

His facial hair makes it difficult to tell what face shape he has, but the rest of his heart-shaped cheekbones and downturned eyes make him come off as friendly to Pluck. The man wears a gray coat, a matching blue plaid suit and pants, and brown shoes. He removes his brown homburg hat when Jed opens the door for him.

Pluck notices that the man is carrying a wooden suitcase in one hand and a round birdcage in the other. Inside, the birdcage contains a budgerigar with yellow feathers on its head, green on its body, and black and yellow spots on its wings and the back of its head. The small parakeet seems content in sitting on the swing hanging in the cage's center, no matter how much the cage shakes with every.

Noticing the man holding the birdcage, Pluck gets confused by what he's seeing and has him say, "I'm sorry, but can I help you?"

"Glad to meet you, Inspector Pluck," the visitor says, dropping his suitcase on the floor to retrieve and show his badge from his coat. "I'm US Postal Inspector Louie Secoli. It's nice to meet you, partner."

The inspector shakes Jed's hand as soon as he puts his badge away. Jed receives an awkward smile from his new partner, still bothered by the birdcage he's holding.

In the midst of giving his surprise partner a firm handshake, Pluck replies, "It's a pleasure." Still bothered by the birdcage, he releases his handshake and points at the cage that Secoli is holding. "What's with the birdcage? Is that a present for me?"

"Oh, Chap?" Secoli laughs. "He's my companion. I bring him wherever I go. Are you going to let me in?"

Jed stops being distracted and says, "Oh, my apologies. Please step in."

Inspector Secoli sees Jed's office has two desks; one is an executive desk placed in the middle of the room, and the other is a rolltop desk that's against the window with a good view of Boston Square. There is a carpet underneath the executive desk, a trash can that still needs to be emptied, and four wooden chairs with armrests. Two are facing the executive desk, and the other is behind the desk. Jed sits behind his executive desk while Secoli sits in the visitor's chair, places the suitcase on the floor on his side, and sets his birdcage on the other chair next to him.

"This morning, I received a telegram from Postmaster General Wanamaker that said you have all the information I need to know about this case," Pluck says, getting comfortable in his chair. "I rarely get any communication directly from the president's most trustworthy executive, so this is certainly a high priority. So what of these disappearances that are happening in Wyoming?"

Secoli takes a paper out of his jacket pocket and passes it to Pluck. Pluck sees the letter has the US Postal Inspection Service stamp on it and reads:

Washington, D.C. Inspector Secoli:

I'm assigning you to Inspector Jed Pluck in Boston to investigate Wyoming's mysterious disappearances. Inside this package is one of many pieces of evidence of what's left of this series of disappearances. Keep this case and its evidence confidential, stop the perpetrators, and report back to us if you find any survivors.

John Wanamaker: 11:13 P.M.

"For the last couple of days," Louie says, seeing Jed putting down the letter, "many in the North and Southeast have had trouble communicating with anyone in Wyoming. We haven't had a single response from that state through telegram or telephone for days, and it's getting Congress worried despite the neighboring states reporting that they're doing fine."

"You sure it isn't telephone lines being cut by outlaws or some hooligans?" Pluck says, putting the letter on top of his desk.

"If it was, Western Union would have already fixed the damage days ago. Their workers said the connections to Wyoming are fine, but there hasn't been any mail coming out of the state for over a week. However, the last train that came back from the West reported that many of the towns with a railway and train station are ghost towns."

"Ghost towns?" Jed leans forward with a brow raised. "What's the cause of these disappearances? Do we have any eyewitnesses or evidence of the cause?"

"We have no witnesses other than the last train to Wyoming. The conductor assigned to search for people couldn't find life in the towns of Cheyenne, Laramie, Rock River, and Rawlins. However, when the conductor went farther to Rock Springs and Lemonstown, those were the only towns with the population gone unharmed."

"Wait. I thought you said no one could reach any of the towns in Wyoming because of the disappearances. How are those two the only towns still with people in them?"

"Well, that's because the farthest town with a telephone line or telegram is Rawlins. I checked it on the telegraph line map. Wyoming is one of those states where telegraphic communication is still under development."

"Has that conductor warned the citizens of those towns of the other towns' disappearances?"

"I hope so. The report did say that those operating those trains to Wyoming couldn't go any further to see any survivors since the sandstorms had become too much for the train to handle, and they had to turn back."

"Okay, so when is the effective time to set off to Wyoming?"

Secoli pulls out train tickets and places them on Jed's desk. "The effective time is this afternoon at three."

"At three? Aw shucks, Louie. I need to call my family to let them know I'm leaving Boston again."

Pluck turns to his rolltop desk behind him and grabs the telephone. The telephone is a candlestick model. Jed lifts the receiver off the switch hook and places it against his left ear. He then uses the rotary dial to enter each of the numbers to enter the phone number of his family. After entering the number, he leans forward and puts his lips close to the carbon microphone.

Louie then puts his attention on his bird, Chap. He sticks his index finger between the bars and rubs the budgie's head. It's a relatively small cage, so he can reach the small bird's head. The bird doesn't mind Louie patting its head, making the bird's owner smile. As he does that, he overhears Jed speaking on the telephone.

"Hello? Allie? Yes, this is your father. Listen, I need your mother on the telephone—yes, this is urgent."

As Jed waits for his wife to get on the line, he looks over his shoulder to see Louie playing with his pet. Seeing the bird being very calm and trusting, his owner distracts him. Then he hears his wife's voice on the line. He turns back to his roll-top desk.

"Yes, Clara? It's me, Jed. Hey, listen. I have a case in Wyoming. I know, darling. It's only been a week since I resolved the case in Georgia, but this case is coming from the postmaster general. I cannot say no to that order. Yes, it's in Wyoming. Yes, it's far, but this is an emergency. Apparently, I'm being asked to investigate a series of disappearances. That's right. So how long will it take you to pack up my luggage? I'm leaving today at three this afternoon. I know it's so soon. I just need one suitcase with clothes that will last me a week. Hold on for a second."

Pluck pulls away from the phone.

"Hey, Louie. Which train station are we going to?"

Louie stops playing with the bird and replies, "The same one I got off at. South Station."

"Thanks." Pluck turns back to the microphone. "It's South Station. Yes, the one that was just opened recently. Yes, I'll meet you there. Oh, one more thing, my love. Can you please bring the girls so I can say goodbye to them before my train departs? Thanks, darling. Should I send someone to give you and the children a ride to meet me there? I won't have time to stop by at home. Okay, you tell Darla that I owe her one when I get back. See you then. I love you."

Pluck hangs up the phone.

"Oh. There's one more thing I almost forgot to tell you, Jed."

After putting the telephone away, Pluck turns to his partner and asks, "What is it?"

"I almost forgot the evidence that the conductor brought back. One common thing that all the disappearing towns have is that they're covered in feathers."

"Feathers? Now, that's ridiculous. What do feathers have to do with these Wyomingites' disappearances? Do you think it might be outlaws or Native Americans using the feathers to leave their mark?"

Louie pulls up his suitcase to his lap and opens it. He pulls out a thirty-inch feather, colored black, with a red tint as the light from the window touches it. Louie holds it by the quill and shows it to Jed. Jed is in awe of what his partner is holding and leans closer to the bizarre object.

"Is that feather real?" Jed tilts his head. "No. It isn't, is it?"

Secoli hands the feather to Pluck. Pluck gets up and reaches for the feather's tip.

As he touches it, the edge of the vane pokes his thumb and startles him from the unexpected pain. Louie simultaneously is startled by his partner's reaction of pulling back the feather. Jed uses his other hand to cover his injured thumb.

"Sorry," Secoli says. "I forgot to tell you to be careful. The edge of the feather is razor sharp. Nothing like I've ever seen before."

"Damn. Well, please be less forgetful ahead of time, won't ya?"

Louie places the evidence next to the tickets. Learning from his lesson, Pluck holds the calamus of the feather. As he receives it, he sits back in his chair and closely examines the evidence. Inspector Pluck is distracted by the size of the evidence and how the light touches the feather, as its highlight is red while the rest is nearly silhouette. He uses his other hand to touch the vane, avoiding the edges.

"Good Lord," Pluck says. "This thing is so uncanny. And the feathers feel like needles. This thing is just unreal."

"I couldn't say it better myself. Take a look at how dangerous this thing is." As Louie closes his suitcase and puts it on the floor, Pluck sniffs at the feather. The feather's stench is so foul that the postal inspector pulls his head back and nearly lets go of the feather. While examining the feather, Secoli gets up and takes a piece of paper from Pluck's desk. Pluck then pays attention to what Secoli is doing.

As his partner still holds on to the feather, Secoli places the top center of the paper under the bottom of the vane's edge. Instantly, he pulls the paper upwards, cutting the paper in half. Pluck is surprised he doesn't lose his grip or feel any push back of the feather splitting the paper. Louie points at one half of the paper that he's holding while the other falls to the ground.

"See how dangerous this thing is?" Louie throws the split paper he's holding into the trash next to Pluck's desk. "Whatever this thing is, it can cut like a knife. Why it's all over Wyoming is beyond me. Whoever or whatever this belongs to or where they came from tells me this is no ordinary case."

Louie sits back down. Still holding the feather, Pluck pulls a small knife from this desk drawer and attempts to cut the feather's vane. The feather is durable, as the knife hardly leaves a scratch on the evidence.

"This feather... it can't be real. Do you suspect it could be some kind of giant eagle? Because no bird I know of has a feather this size. Not to mention a feather as sharp as this."

"I gave up my childhood dreams of finding Bigfoot a long time ago, so I don't believe in fairy tales or ghost stories any more. But I don't know what to make of this."

"This is one giant bird that I like to see myself."

THE GOVERNOR MICHAEL S. Dukakis Transportation Center at South Station is the largest train station in the United States, possibly the biggest in the world. The giant train station opened this year, replacing the several terminals once all over Boston into a singular hub for long-distance travelers. Jed is with his new partner and his family at the terminal. Standing in front of them is the train, which remains at the terminal. Some people are boarding now, but there's still time for Jed to spend what's left of it with family. It's still crowded at the terminal's dock, leaving only elbow room to move around.

Jed's four daughters are all hugging Dad tightly right now. His oldest child, Jessie, is a teenager who dresses older than her fifteen years of age. Strong similarities exist between her and her mother, Clara, with the exception that she shares her father's long raven hair.

The second-oldest, Julia, who is twelve years old, shares her mother's light brown hair but more closely resembles her father due to his long face and round eyes. Allie, the second-youngest, shares Julia's appearance, but she is shorter and two years Allie's junior. Janet, the youngest, still maintains some baby fat at age six, giving her chubby facial features. Little Janet wears more stylishly, similar to the doll she is carrying, in contrast to her three sisters, who dress in outfits suited for their ages.

The family always delivers really tight hugs as they say farewell. While the others are giving him front, back, and side hugs, the one in the middle is invariably the one who is departing. Janet, however, receives a consoling hug because she is the youngest and lightest. The girls release simultaneously, and Jed sees them all crying, upset that he's leaving so soon.

"Daddy, why do you have to go?" cries Janet. "You just got back."

"I'm sorry, sweetie." Jed puts the littlest one down. "But it's my job, and America needs me again."

"Daddy," Jessie says, "how much longer will you be a postal inspector? It's just not fair that you've been gone for weeks, and you have to leave us again."

Jed tries hard not to shed a tear, unable to fathom his girls' sadness. "Oh, come on, Jessie. You know our country needs me. Someday, when you get a job, you'll realize how much you're needed."

"But you're needed here! Allie's birthday is next week."

"Are you going to miss my birthday, Daddy?" Allie asks.

"No. Of course not, Allie," Jed says. "I know how much your ninth birthday means to you. There's no way I'm going to miss it."

"You promise?" Allie says. "You missed Jessie's birthday a month ago, and she isn't too pleased with you."

Jed is unable to respond to Allie. He turns to his wife, who looks upset but not as sad as the children. Clara approaches her husband as the girls give their parents some space.

Clara says, fixing the lapel on Jed's brown coat, "Please take good care of yourself, hun. You've never been to Wyoming, and you don't know what it's like out there."

"I know that, Clara. And don't worry—no postal inspector has ever been harmed in the line of duty, and I won't be the first either."

"Yes, Jed. But I can't help worrying about you whenever you're not around."

"There's nothing to worry about. Just watch our girls while I'm gone, and I promise to treat you to a good restaurant when I return. It's been a long time since you and I went out on a date, hasn't it?"

As Clara and Jed continue their conversation, the girls focus on Inspector Louie Secoli. The four are in awe of the budgerigar in the cage that he holds. The bird's presence cheers the sisters up.

"That's a cute bird you have there, Mr. Secoli," Allie comments.

"I've never seen a bird like this before," Janet says as she holds her doll. "What's your bird's name?"

"Oh, this little guy?" Louie responds. "His name is Chap. He's a budgerigar."

"What's a bu-budge..." the youngest struggles to say.

"It's pronounced 'budgerigar.' They're a small breed of parakeet from Australia."

"Chap is so cute!" Allie says. "I love his yellow head and striped wings."

"How long have you had Chap, Mr. Secoli?" Julia asks.

"Chap and I have been since he hatched out of his egg. That makes him seven years old."

"Ooh. That's wonderful," Jessie responds.

"I want a parakeet!" Allie turns to her parents. "Mommy! Daddy! Can we get a parakeet for my birthday? I want one that's as big as an eagle! Just like the one on your badge, Daddy!"

The train whistle's piercing sound cuts through the terminal and interrupts everyone's conversations. The conductor rings a bell to tell the passengers to board the train. Jed and Clara break away from their conversation. As Jed turns to pick up his suitcase, the girls run behind him and give him one more group hug.

"Where's my soon-to-be birthday girl?" Jed turns around, picks Allie up, and hugs her. "I'm going to miss you. I'll do my best to make it to your birthday this year."

The whole family gives the father a tighter hug than the last. Louie reaches his assigned car and puts his luggage and the birdcage on the platform leading to the car's door. As he gets to the back of the car, he sees his partner still being embraced by his family. The man feels guilty about involving their father in this case after seeing how much the family loves each other.

The Plucks release their family hug as the train whistle blows once more. Jed catches up with Louie, who's already in the passenger car. Louie picks one of the two-person seats closest to the car's door. Jed gets into the passenger car, and Secoli places his birdcage on the seat. Jed sees his partner pick the seat next to the car's back door as he crouches down and puts his suitcase underneath their assigned seat.

Secoli gets up and says, "Sit by the window to wave your family goodbye." Louie moves aside for his partner to put his suitcase underneath his seat, next to his luggage. As Jed takes a seat, he sees his family through the window and waves at them. Once Louie places the birdcage on his lap, he sees Jed's wife and daughters through the window waving back. The train pulls away, and as it picks up speed Jed's family becomes lost in the crowd of the train station.

The two passengers see that the train passes the dock and exits the terminal's interior. Jed continues to look through the window, seeing six tracks in front of him and many trains passing by. Once the train moves at top speed, Jed turns to Louie, who's petting his budgie on the head with his index finger. "Hey, Louie. Do you ever think maybe it's a bit unprofessional to bring

that bird along?"

"You're not the first who's told me that. Don't worry. I got approval to bring Chap while on duty. This budgerigar gives me a lot of joy and helps me do my job well."

"What if someone decides to—forgive me for saying this—take your bird hostage when you're in a line of duty? What will you do?"

"Funny that you brought that up." Louie takes his index finger out from between the cage bars. "I was in a case where someone had committed mail theft. When I tracked him down and confronted him, he snatched Chap from me as his hostage. He stuck a knife at Chap..." He takes a moment before continuing. "And threatened to kill him if I didn't let him go. You know what I did, Jed?"

"What?"

"I pulled out my pistol and shot him in the shoulder."

"Good God! You didn't get in trouble for that, did you?"

"The suspect was armed and held my muse hostage, so I considered it justifiable to make that decision."

"Did your supervisor ever take issue with you taking Chap everywhere you go?"

"He did for a while until he noticed I couldn't perform well on duty without him. When I showed him how much better I am with Chap around—well, I shoot better, get the paperwork done twice as fast, and solve postal cases better than anyone in Washington."

"I see... but don't you worry about others not taking you seriously? I mean, Americans are relying on us postal inspectors to do their job well... and you're carrying that bird around."

Louie gets annoyed with the comment and replies, "Let me explain this to you, Jed Pluck. I'm one of the best on the East Coast. I've locked up so many crooks and solved so many cases that many of my peers would never have figured out if I hadn't been involved. I bring Chap with me almost everywhere I go, and even when he's in danger, I make it clear, time and time again, to never mess with my muse. Whenever that happens, I demonstrate what happens, even if he's in danger."

Louie grips the birdcage tighter. The budgie chirps louder as it notices his owner getting emotional.

"I've been through some very tough times in my life," Louie continues, "and the only thing keeping me going is having Chap by my side. It's not that I want Chap with me—I *need* him. Do you understand where I'm coming from, Jed?"

Pluck sees this as a sensitive topic for his partner. Louie's straight eye contact and serious look make this conversation uncomfortable.

"Okay, okay," Pluck says. "I got the picture. I'm sorry, all right?"

Secoli loosens the grip of the birdcage. The budgie feels his owner calming down and stops making loud chirps.

"Good." Louie turns away. "I hope we'll never have this conversation again."

Pluck feels guilty about how south the conversation has gone. He stares at the little parakeet standing on the birdcage's swing in a different light. He looks at Louie, who appears to be wishing to be somewhere else, as he looks away. This is no way for postal inspectors to behave. If Pluck still has issues with Secoli carrying his bird around, how will they solve this case?

"Well, if it makes you feel better, I'll ensure Chap will be protected." Louie raises an eyebrow. "Do you mean it?"

"If Chap means that much to you, I'll defend him at all costs so you can do your best job here."

"You mean it, Jed?"

"You have my word. I'm considering getting a bird like that since my girls love him. Say, where did you find a bird like that?"

"Seven years ago, when I used to live with my ex-wife in England. Budgerigars are quite popular in that country despite them coming from Australia. We had a set of budgerigars in the house, and I love those birds to death." Louie sighs. "But because I put way more attention on them, it affected my marriage—well, that's one of the reasons. Though she claimed the budgerigars in court, I managed to take one of their eggs. Then he hatched and became mine to keep. Since then, Chap and I have become inseparable."

"Isn't that sweet?" Pluck genuinely smiles. "Hey, Louie. You think I can get a budgerigar somewhere in America?"

"I haven't seen any budgerigars in any pet store or state I've been in. You're better off visiting England and getting one there since it's a better option than traveling to Australia."

"Drat." Pluck puts his head down. "Looks like I'm going to have to get Allie a different bird in Wyoming then. You've been to Wyoming before?"

"Nope. Never. You?"

"This is my first time as well." Jed sighs. "Looks like I'm going to have to figure out what present I should get for Allie. God willing, we get this case solved and get back home before August 15."

CHAPTER 2

A day has passed since the two postal inspectors left Boston, and they are now on the railway leading to Wyoming from Chicago. Jed Pluck and Louie Secoli, the only passengers on the train, stretch their legs and lounge on the separate two-person seats. While Pluck is asleep with his felt hat covering his face, Louie continues to play with Chap. The budgie has been removed from its cage and is now perched on its owner's finger. Upon Louie hearing the door of the car they're in open behind him, he puts his little parakeet back in the cage and sits back up. He glances over his shoulder as the conductor closes the door, then walks down the aisle of the train car.

The conductor looks to be in his early fifties and has a noticeable brown handlebar mustache and gray beard. From where Secoli is sitting, he can tell that the train official is shorter than him, appearing to be standing five feet, seven inches tall. "Excuse me, Mr. Conductor, sir," Secoli says. "How much longer until we finally get out of Nebraska?"

"We should be past the border by now," the conductor answers.

"Thank you. One more thing. Are there other passengers on this train?"

"No, sir. You two there are the last ones on board. Which station are you
 getting off at?"

"We're stopping station to station in Wyoming on this railway. Would you kindly hold the train at every Wyoming station and depart only when we return?"

"Sorry, sir. I can't do that. This train is on schedule, and we can't stop or hold this train for anyone."

"Oh, I almost forgot." Secoli places his birdcage on the floor and pulls out his badge and shows it to the conductor. "I'm United States Postal Inspector Louie Secoli. We're on a mission to solve the disappearances happening in Wyoming." He then pulls out a paper. "And here is a telegram signed by the Postmaster General from Washington, D.C., who sent us on this case."

The conductor retrieves the telegram and reads it. Secoli observes the official's expression changing as he reads, realizing that he's understanding what it says.

"Furthermore, I checked the train schedule for the state of Wyoming, and I saw that this train is the only one on this railway," Secoli continues. "If there are any passengers in Wyoming getting on this train, they can wait by order of the government."

"I'm on it, sir." The conductor passes the telegram back to Secoli. "Just let me inform the engineer about this. Excuse me, Inspector."

"Thanks, Mr. Conductor. You're doing a great service to America."

The official heads to the door that leads to the locomotive. As soon as the door ahead of them closes, Louie gets up from his seat and shakes Pluck's shoulder. Pluck isn't too pleased to be awakened by his partner.

"Hey, Jed. We're almost at Cheyenne. Get yourself ready."

Pluck removes his flat cap from his face, repositions it on his head, and rubs his eyes. The lack of curtains on the car window makes it hard for him to adjust to the sudden brightness when waking up. Upon waking up, he looks out the window next to him to see many dead orange grasslands stretching for miles beneath the horizon. He sees no clouds in the sky and notices the sun is soaring above them. Pluck then pulls out his pocket watch; he sees it's six past twelve.

"Am I in a dream?" Pluck yawns, looking out the window. "Because it looks like hell out there."

"Haven't you ever been in a rural state before?" Louie asks, seeing his partner across the aisle from where he sits.

"I have, and I hate it." Pluck yawns and stretches. "I'm more of a city boy than an open-field guy. You?"

"I'm flexible. I have no preference for either rural or urban. Now, back to this case." Secoli says as Pluck continues to rub his eyes, fighting to stay awake. "I asked the conductor to stop and hold the train within every town we'll visit. I let him know we're postal inspectors on a case."

"Good. Our badges are always useful when we need to get something done. I can't imagine us riding horses in this hot and humid weather." Jed yawns. "I hope this will be more exciting than our standard postal case. How anyone could take down an entire state capital is impress—"

The shrill sound of the train whistle cuts through their conversation, signaling the two postal inspectors to arrive in Wyoming's capital. As Pluck stretches once more to fully wake up, a loud slapping sound from outside the window startles everyone. Pluck and Louie both turn their heads in time to see a large black feather flying out the window. The normally silent bird begins to chirp incessantly in response to the same noise.

"Was that..." Pluck pauses for a second, getting up from his seat. "...one of the feathers that we have as evidence?"

Louie has no response, anxious as they approach the crime scene. He can feel his heart pounding faster as the train reduces speed. Jed hunches over to the window where the feather flies. They both see a couple more feathers lying on the dead grass fields, then a couple more drifting from the wind. As the train reduces its speed, the first buildings they see have more black feathers covering the rooftops and sticking to the walls.

"Hey, Louie." Pluck shakily points to him, staring at the window. "Hand me the feather in your suitcase, will you?"

Secoli kneels to grab his suitcase, unable to take his eyes off the town covered in feathers through the window. He then focuses on what he's doing as he takes out his luggage and opens it. He holds their evidence by the quill and hands over the oversized feather to Pluck. Pluck turns around and carefully takes the feather by the quill. After Pluck takes the feather, Secoli clutches his birdcage to calm his nerves. Quickly, he feels safer, and the budgerigar stops his chirping.

While Secoli is distracted by the parakeet, Pluck creeps closer to the window with the feather in his hand. A feather suddenly smacks against the window next to the seat in front of Pluck. The feather's lodged in the window, its sharp edge wedged between the window and the frame. Inspector Pluck seizes the opportunity to move closer, places the feather he's holding against the window, and positions it in the same spot as the other feather hanging on the outside of the window.

" My God," Pluck mutters. "It's a match."

The train whistle blows again and reduces its speed even more. Secoli sees Pluck staring at the window, then realizes Pluck is comparing the feather he's holding to the one outside. Secoli sweats heavily while witnessing the matching feathers, indicating evidence of the same culprit. Pluck and Secoli stop getting distracted once the train comes to a stop. The conductor emerges from the front door, startling the postal inspectors with his loud coughing.

"Are you all right, Mr. Conductor?" asks Secoli.

"Inspectors..." The conductor clears his throat. "We're here. It smells quite bad out there. What's with the feathers all over this town?"

"That's why we're here," Pluck responds. "My partner said you're helping us. Can we leave our luggage here while we investigate?"

The conductor nods. Pluck gets out of his seat, bringing the evidence with him. Secoli brings his birdcage while following Pluck and the conductor out of the passenger car. Instead of holding the cage by its ring on the top of the cage, Secoli holds it by the bars. Chap only sees where his owner is going since Secoli's hands block the sides, and Secoli's stomach covers the back of the cage. Upon exiting the train, the stench of the evidence is now everywhere.

"Good Lord!" Pluck shouts, covering his nose. "You weren't lying about how putrid it is out here! It smells like an aviary!"

Secoli sees the conductor in front of his partner, holding his nose over the malodor. Secoli isn't too bothered by the smell outside the train. The man has been surrounded by birds for most of his life, which gives him a nostalgic feeling. While the conductor and Pluck cough, Secoli seems to be the only one paying attention to how empty the train station is.

The station is fairly small, as are many in rural areas. The docks are gathering dust, indicating there has been a long absence of anyone in the area, putting Secoli on full alert. Secoli only hears the wind and the sound of feathers rustling like tumbleweeds, in addition to the coughing of the men behind him. When Secoli gets to the docks, he sees the conductor retreating into the passenger car, unable to take any more of the malodor.

Pluck removes his handkerchief from his coat and wraps it around his mouth and nose, then ties it at the back of his head. Secoli smirks over how his partner looks like a bandit with his nose and mouth covered. Secoli turns his attention back to the scene and places the cage back against his chest, obscuring Chap's view from inside. Astonished that Secoli is impervious to the reeking town, Pluck gets off the train and follows him.

The train engineer comes down the locomotive with his nose held. He looks younger than the conductor, with no gray hair on his black sideburns or mustache. His overalls, face, and cap are covered in coal smears. As he approaches the postal inspectors, he removes his blue-and-white-striped engineer's cap and thick, filthy gloves, looking confused.

"Just when I was about to quit my job because of the daily smell of burning coal," the engineer says, "now I smell something much worse. Why isn't the conductor ringing the bell? And where is the station master?"

"Your conductor had to run back in our car because the smell was too much for him," Secoli replies. "As for the station master, who knows?"

"Right. I was told you two are postal inspectors, and you need my train?"

"Yeah. We were sent here because of the disappearances occurring in this

state. Seeing all these feathers all over—well, it's why we're here."

"So, what exactly happened to this place?"

"How should we know?" Pluck replies. "We just arrived. Stay put till we get back, okay?"

"Will do, sirs."

"Thank you," Secoli says. "Remember. You're doing your country a great service."

The conductor leans against the coal car, seeming to be getting used to the smell since he's not holding his nose. The two postal inspectors alight from the docks and onto the asphalt main road that runs between two rows of wooden buildings. The buildings range from two to three stories high from where the eye can see. There are no wagons, horses, or signs of life anywhere in sight. The dark feathers pushed by the drift appear to replace the tumbleweeds that usually symbolize the emptiness of any location.

The gush of sandy wind doesn't do much to cool his temperature or calm the postal inspectors down. Secoli chooses a more spontaneous route by walking down the main road, but Pluck feels more vulnerable traveling this way, especially considering how preternatural the town is.

Just when Pluck is about to say something to his partner, Secoli points at one of the buildings and whispers, "There's a telegraph office. Let's try reaching headquarters and tell them what's happened here."

"Good idea," Pluck replies.

The postal inspectors head to the building. Pluck turns the door handle. "Dang it," Pluck mutters. "It's locked. We don't have time for this."

With all patience lost, Pluck pulls out his revolver. He holds the handgun barrel and aims the grip panel toward the door handle. He slams it against the handle with all his might to separate it from the door.

"Jed," Secoli whispers angrily, "that's public property."

With a couple more hits, the door handle breaks and detaches from the door. As the handle falls onto the porch floor, Pluck pushes the door open.

"Don't worry," Pluck says. "The government will reimburse the damages."

As Pluck heads inside, Secoli sighs with annoyance and follows his partner inside.

The whole place appears to be clean, with no dust, sand, or feathers inside. The one-room building is long and narrow despite its small width. Behind the wooden counter are a large round table, file cabinets against the end of the wall, and two rolltop desks on the side of the walls. Those desks have telegraphs on them.

This is the only location where Secoli feels safe enough to let go of the birdcage he's been holding on to. He heads toward the back of the office area and places the cage on one of the rolltop desks. Secoli turns around to see Pluck opening the file cabinet and looking at previous letters.

Pluck hums to himself and mutters, "Seems like the latest letter on record was August 5, 1899. That was four days ago."

"Hey, Jed," Secoli says. "Do you know Morse code?"

While investigating the file cabinets, Jed replies, "Of course. Every postal inspector should be familiar with its use beforehand. You are familiar with the telegraph, correct?"

"I do. But I asked first, so you should do it."

"Honestly, Louie...," Pluck stutters. "I haven't used the Morse code in a long time. I lost practice since I've been using the telephone."

"Fine." Secoli sighs. "While I'm telegraphing, you should investigate the town."

"Okay. Ask to send the cavalry for assistance."

"I will. But first, I need to check if this thing is still functional and if the connection is good."

Secoli sees that the telegraph machine is still on. How long it has been on is anyone's guess. Once he removes his homburg hat and puts on the headphones, he hears beeps on the headset. Someone is using the telegraph to contact someone in Cheyenne, and he just happens to tune in halfway through someone's message. Secoli quickly grabs a piece of cardstock paper and a pen next to him to jot down what he's hearing. Pluck turns from the cabinet, noticing his partner is writing instead of tapping on the telegraph key.

"Hey," Pluck says. "Who's that messaging?"

Secoli shushes him and says, "I'm trying to transcribe."

Pluck walks behind Secoli and looks over his shoulder. He reads what Secoli wrote down, which says, "...anyone in Cheyenne there?" Secoli stops writing as soon as the beeping on his headset ceases.

"Seems like someone is trying to contact someone in this town," Pluck comments. "Ready to give them the unfortunate news?"

"Whoever is messaging this telegraph office won't be pleased to hear the news," Secoli responds.

"While you're doing that," Pluck exits out the door, "allow me to investigate." Secoli turns on the machine's indicator, which is shaped like a small film reel that unrolls a paper tape. The machine's ink roller is ready to stamp ink on the tape with every press of the transmitter key, like a typewriter. As the paper tape rolls, Secoli removes his headphones to focus on signaling back to

the messenger with the Morse key.

"Cheyenne <stop>," Secoli telegraphs. "Everyone has gone missing in Cheyenne <stop>. We are postal inspectors <stop> trying to investigate what happened <stop> Just arrived in town <stop> No sign of life <stop>."

As soon as he finishes the message, Secoli puts the headphones back on. It doesn't take long for Secoli to hear beeps from his headphones again after he completes messaging through the Morse key. Secoli takes another blank cardstock and writes down the Morse code.

"Chicago. Hello, postal inspectors. A husband from Illinois couldn't reach Mrs. Godfrey for two days. Are you unable to find anyone in Cheyenne or someone whose last name is Godfrey?"

The beeps from the headphones go silent. Secoli uses the transmitter key again, "Cheyenne <stop> Cheyenne is a ghost town <stop> Let everyone know that Cheyenne is in danger <stop> United States Government is on high alert for Wyoming's safety <stop> Please reach out to Washington or government officials <stop> Send out the cavalry if possible <stop>."

In town, Pluck walks alongside buildings on the left side of the main road. The direction where he's walking has signs for what each building is, and he heads to the general store. He notices that the windows between the front door are smashed, and pieces of the frames are on the porch. Pluck peers inside and sees that the store is infested with feathers and broken pieces of wood.

Pluck mutters to himself, "A giant bird must have attacked the people in the store. But what would a bird be doing in a place like this?"

As he jumps through the broken window, he notices scattered pieces of glass on the wooden floor. The postal inspector turns around to find something to clear the feathers to see what's underneath it. It doesn't take him long to find a broom in the corner next to the broken window. Pluck then sweeps the feathers and some broken wood and shards out of the way.

Once he has cleared everything out of the way, he kneels down to see that the dark spots on the wood have turned into dry, red stains that were actually bloodstains. When Pluck feels the pressure of the blood marks on the wood with his palm, he notices that it's soft, showing that the darkened wood spot has gone uncleaned for days. There are many of them, yet no sign of anyone's remains besides the imbrue.

"Whatever this thing is," Pluck continues, talking to himself, "it must have taken the people. But who or what can even take a person away and not leave a trace?"

The general store brightens, making the inspector look up. Pluck notices a large hole in the ceiling and sees the clouds moving away from the sun, which explains the sudden brightness. The large hole in the ceiling appears bigger than Pluck in diameter.

"My God," Pluck mumbles. "What kind of animal is big enough to do this much damage?"

Pluck turns around and sees a rifle lying next to the broken window he had gone through. He approaches the Henry repeating rifle surrounded by empty powdered brass. Upon picking it up, the postal inspector opens the chamber and sees the barrel's interior is oily from the bullets' powder. As he examines it, the amount of filth lets him know the one who owned this repeater used it a lot. "Poor fellow," Pluck mutters. "No matter how many bullets he used against it, it seems that it's not enough to put it down with this. Just what was this thing the people of Cheyenne were fighting against?"

The postal inspector puts the repeater back down and looks out the window he came through. The building across the road has bullet holes all over. Though the sign of the building has damage from gunfire, he sees the sign "Sheriff" on top. Pluck jumps over the same window and approaches the building across the way.

As Pluck crosses the main road, the wind blows toward the train station, carrying feathers along in its current. A nearby feather grazes Pluck's left cheek, causing the postal inspector to recoil. Then, another feather flies in the same direction and pokes through his pants, having the feather's edge puncture the side of his left thigh. This causes the postal inspector to fall on his right side.

As he lies on the ground, Pluck realizes what has hit him and hears the whoosh of feathers flying toward him. With little time to react, he cups his hands over the back of his head, uses his arms to shield his face, and holds on to his Boston felt hat to protect his head. He lies motionless on the asphalt, dodging the razor-sharp feathers drifting above him like ducking gunfire. The postal inspector seizes the opportunity to get across the road as soon as the feathers drift past him before the wind blows them back.

Pluck extracts the feather from his left thigh, gets up and limps to the sheriff's office. He leans against the wall, just an arm's reach from the doorknob. As he catches his breath, he twists the doorknob and finds the door unlocked. He makes his way in and slams the door with frustration.

"Sheriff! Deputy!" Pluck shouts. "Is anyone in here?!"

The place is dark, but once Pluck's eyes adjust to the dim light, he sees that the scene is much worse than what he found in the general store. The first thing he sees are wooden chairs on the ground and a desk that is split in half. The concrete walls are riddled with bullet holes, and bloodstains mar the walls and floors.

It is still too dark to see clearly, so Pluck takes out a box of matches from his gray jacket and strikes one. He now sees the extent of the bloodstains on the surfaces that lead to the darker part of the room. He witnesses something surreal while following the blood trail to where the prison cells are located. The jail cells are in disarray, with doors torn down and bars bent. Blood is splattered everywhere, from the floor to the ceiling.

The bloodstains here and in the general store have the same dark hue, indicating that the blood was spilled on the same day. That much damage against metal is inhuman, especially how far the jail bars have been bent. Even though he has seen crime scenes of all kinds throughout his career, this one is too much for him to handle. Pluck drops the lit match and limps out of the door with vomit in his mouth. He doubles over and vomits over the edge of the road, holding on to the porch fence for support. Overwhelmed, he sits on the porch's platform and leans against the fence.

"Christ," Pluck swears. "What kind of abomination caused all that?"

As Pluck catches his breath, Secoli runs across the main road, avoiding the razor-sharp feathers drifting all over. He holds on to his homburg hat from blowing away while using his gray coat to shield Chap in his birdcage from the wind. Unscathed, he makes his way to the sheriff's porch, where he sees his partner looking unwell as he sits against the porch's fence.

"Jed?" Secoli asks. "What happened?"

"Whatever you do, don't go in there. That crime scene is grotesque, I tell you."

Despite being warned, Secoli takes a peek through the cracked door. The match on the floor is still lit, revealing the crimson interior of the sheriff's office. It doesn't make Secoli nauseous, but it startles him, making him leap backward and hit the porch's fence. Chap, held by Secoli while inside the birdcage, moves off his swing and bumps into the bars.

"Just what the hell are we dealing with, Jed?"

"Something completely inhuman," Pluck responds. "I don't suppose you've ever seen anything like this, have you?"

Secoli can't answer his question, unsure if it is genuine or rhetorical. Pluck struggles to get back up as he uses the fence for support. Pulling himself up from the ground takes longer than usual for Pluck. Secoli notices Pluck has some blood on the handkerchief covering his mouth, then sees more bleeding on the left thigh of his pants.

"Jed, you're bleeding!" Secoli gasps. "Did something happen back there?"

"No, not in there," Pluck responds in frustration. "I got hurt crossing the road, and one of those damn feathers stabbed me in the leg as the wind blew."

"We've got to bring you somewhere safe and treat your wound."

"No, I'm fine."

As Pluck tries to walk away from his partner, his limping says otherwise.

Secoli doesn't look pleased with what he's seeing.

"Jed, if we're going to work together, we need to look out for each other. I've worked with too many tough guys who always push themselves too hard and put me at risk. If one of us can't take care of ourselves, what good are we?"

Pluck takes one more step before trembling onto the fence, holding it for support. "Okay," Pluck says. "You made your point. Let's find somewhere safe, okay?"

Secoli places Pluck's arm around Secoli's neck and guides Pluck to safety. Carrying the birdcage and providing Pluck support puts a lot of strain on him. He guides them down the aisle, taking Pluck's pace into account. While moving farther away from the train station, Secoli is looking for a place where he can treat his partner. The two postal inspectors continue on their way until they come across a building with a sign that reads "Lucky's Fashion" and a creaky front door.

Upon entering, the two inspectors find the clothing store filled with dusty and sandy dresses. As they move farther in, they see less filthy clothes and more of them on display covered in bloodstains. Then, they see the blood-soaked floor, indicating that the attack had taken place days ago. Despite the gruesome scene, the two men do not smell the stench coming from outside. Pluck finally removes his handkerchief, which he had been using to cover his nose and mouth, revealing a gash on his cheek.

Secoli leads his partner to a chair next to an open toolbox. He places his birdcage on Pluck's lap as soon as he takes a seat. Secoli then tears a sleeve from a nearby delicate dress and uses it to bandage Pluck's wounds.

"Put this on your cheek," Secoli said. "Apply pressure to stop the bleeding." While Pluck uses the ripped cloth to cover the cut on his cheek, Secoli folds Pluck's left pants upwards to see the wound on his thigh. Fortunately, the cut is not deep, but Secoli sees a piece of the feather embedded in his thigh. The black needle is visible from the blood pouring out of the wound. Secoli looks in the toolbox to see if there's anything that could be used to remove the needle. "How bad is it, Secoli?" Jed moans.

"Well," Secoli answers while pulling out tools from the box, "you seemed to forget to remove a piece of the feather from your leg. But I can get it out for you."

While Secoli takes out items from the toolbox, Pluck gazes at the budgerigar in the birdcage on his lap. The budgerigar is clearly anxious about being so close to Pluck instead of its owner. The injured postal inspector brushes it off, not thinking much of the little bird before seeing Secoli pulling out sewing needles.

"Hold still," Secoli says. "I don't know how much this will hurt, but these two needles are the smallest tools I can find to pull out that piece of the vane."

"It's fine. This is nothing compared to getting shot in the Civil War." Pluck doesn't notice Secoli giving him a look of surprise at what he said.

As Pluck turns to him, Secoli brushes off what he's thinking and begins removing the sharp object with the two needles. With a needle in each hand, Secoli uses both of the tools' points to hold on to the tip of the sharp object sticking out of his flesh. Though getting both needles to make contact with the tip is tough, he manages to get them to hold on to the sharp object. With good timing, Secoli pulls the needle out of his partner's thigh.

Having the small sharp object slip out of the wound makes Pluck react strongly to the stinging feeling. His reaction is so intense that it startles Chap. As Pluck clutches his wound and groans in pain, Secoli drops the needles and picks up his birdcage, which had fallen off his partner's lap. He then sets the birdcage down on the floor and quickly bandages Pluck's injured thigh with another torn cloth.

"How do you feel, partner?" Secoli asks.

Pluck gets up from his seat and walks around a little. He's no longer limping like before.

"As good as new," Pluck responds. "Thanks, partner. Oh, by the way, who did you contact on the telegraph?"

"Someone from Chicago who's been trying to reach one of the locals here. I informed him of everything we knew and that we were still investigating Cheyenne. Did you happen to see anyone around?"

"Nope. The only buildings I investigated are remains of what looked like a gunfight. Have you requested military assistance?"

"I did," Secoli says. "The person I was communicating with said they'll try to get military assistance. However, there are no known cavalry near this state."

"Drat. Looks like we're going to stay put till we get military support.

Someone—or something, rather—has caused damages that I've never seen before. Things like causing holes in ceilings and bending the jail cell bars—there are even bullet holes all over the town that show that gunfire does not slow this thing down. Plus, I haven't found a single body anywhere."

"What do you suppose would have this many feathers scattered all over Cheyenne?"

"My guess is it might be a giant eagle," replies Pluck. "But what animal would want to massacre a town this big when they need to just hunt for a meal?"

"Well, look around you, Jed. We haven't seen any animals in these dead

grasslands, and any inhabitant out here would kill anything for a meal."

"But an entire town? How's that even possible?

"Maybe there's not just one giant eagle," Secoli says. "Perhaps we've got an entire flock. Plus, the chances of it being an eagle are slim considering that eagles are independent species."

"Do you think a giant eagle would be different from other eagles in that it would rely on others of its kind and form a flock?"

Secoli shrugs. "It's still an eagle. Growth in size would mean the eagle would be more independent. There's no way a singular being could make the entire town disappear."

"So what should we do since we lack military support?"

"I suggest we find the town's gun store and collect what we need for our investigation. Seeing how the citizens fought these things shows we need as many guns and ammo as possible. Plus, we need to visit the other towns up ahead and see if we can find any survivors. Hopefully, we're not too late in reaching out to the other towns farther west."

"Good idea, but first, I'd like to send a telegram to my wife."

"Jed, remember, this case is confidential. If this goes public, it will not only cost us our jobs but also put both of us in Federal prison."

"I know. I know. But I promised to send them a telegram. I'll let them know this case might go longer than anticipated and leave it at that."

AFTER A LONG DAY OF playing, little Janet Pluck and her older sister Allie lie on the front lawn, exhausted. The children look up at the clouds, their young minds filled with wonder at the shapes they form and the stories they could tell. They both enjoy the feeling of the grass being blown in the wind as they lie on the ground. Allie's so excited about her upcoming birthday that she is seeing animals in the cloud formations and imagining what kind of pets she will get. However, this moment of relaxation gets interrupted by hearing their mother scream "Goddamn it!" from the house. The two of them jump up from lying on the grass when they hear their mother shouting.

"What did you do this time?" Allie asks as she gets to her feet. "I didn't do anything!" Janet shouts. "What did you do?"

"Nothing! I swear!"

Like good girls, Allie and Janet rush to the front door. The Plucks' house is a two-story blue farmhouse with a pitched roof and windows all over the front. The porch has a white fence and pillars, which match the white window frames. Most families in Boston can hardly afford a standard house, yet Jed's job as a postal inspector has made this house luxurious.

The two young sisters rush up the porch steps and head for the front door. Allie, the older of the two, runs faster than Janet and reaches the door first. But before she reaches the doorknob, the front door opens and a post office telegram messenger steps out. He has an embarrassed look on his face, looking like he'd rather be delivering a different message to Mrs. Pluck if he could. Janet and Allie stop and watch the messenger fix his tie and straighten his blue hat, which says "Western Union," before he notices them.

The man changes his expression to a jolly one and says, "Oh, hello, little girls."

"Ooh, it's the telegraph messenger," Janet says. "Did Daddy send us a message?" Allie asks.

"He did, and I think it's better if you hear it from your mother." He fixes his uniform once more. "Well, back to work for me. Have a nice day, little misses."

Allie and Janet watch the telegraph messenger step off the porch and hop onto his bicycle. As the messenger rides away, the two girls put their attention back on the house when they hear someone crying. Allie creaks the door open, and they both peek inside the foyer. While Allie stands, Janet crouches, both looking through the same doorway. No one notices the little ones eavesdropping.

Allie and Janet see their mother, oldest sister Jessie, and second-oldest Julia sitting on the stairway, appearing distressed. Clara has her head down while Jessie reads the telegram as she caresses her mother. Allie and Janet showed up in time to hear their oldest sister read the message aloud.

To the Pluck family,

Hello, my darling and my four adorable ones. It's Daddy. I hate to give you all the unfortunate news that my case will take longer than expected. I'm unsure when I'll be back home, but if I don't make it back next week, I wish Allie a happy birthday.

Love, Daddy

The whole room goes silent. Jessie crumples the telegram into a paper ball and throws it across the room. The oldest sister puts her chin up to take a deep breath before shedding a tear.

"He did it again," Jessie says as her tears come down. "He missed my fifteenth birthday, and now he's going to miss Allie's ninth birthday. Mom, what are we going to do?"

"I don't know," Clara responds, her head still down. "Just give her a birthday celebration without your father around, I guess."

"But you know Allie wanted Daddy to be here for her birthday more than anything," Julia says. "Just what are you going to tell her?"

"We're not going to tell her anything." Clara picks her head up. "Look, I'm as upset about this as you both are." She holds Jessie's and Julia's hands. "If he can't make it, he can't make it."

"Why are you okay with this, Mother?" Jessie raises her voice. "He even missed his own birthday when his case was here in Boston, and twice he forgot about your anniversary. Doesn't he know his career is tearing this family apart?"

"No. It's not tearing this family apart," Clara calmly says. "It's just one of

those times when his country needs him the most."

"More than we need him the most?" Jessie gets up from her seat on the stairs. "Do you ever suspect he makes his own schedule or works slowly to get away from us?"

"That is not true!" Clara yells. "You know your father loves us very much and has the whole country depending on him regardless of whether anyone ever knows it. And we're not the only family who has an absent father. Think about others who abandoned their families or are enlisted in the United States military and must leave their families to fulfill the government's commands."

"Well, none of those military families had their fathers disappear as much as Dad does. For crying out loud, Mother. Can't you convince him to get a different job?"

"I've asked him that many times." Clara stands up to Jessie's level. "I've been married to that man for seventeen years, and he's one of the hundreds who's been selected for this job and does a very good job at it. It's hard for even me to understand, but knowing that he works hard and gives us a house that others wish they had is enough to show how much he loves us."

"But what does having a good home even mean if the one providing is barely present?" Jessie walks down the stairs.

"Jessie Jane Pluck." Clara follows her down the stairs. "Don't you walk away from me and speak ill of your father like that."

"And are we going to remain silent about Allie's birthday?" Jessie turns around as she gets off the stairway. "Give her a celebration and pretend Dad will still show up, just like my birthday?"

Suddenly Janet interrupts the argument by bumping her head into the door. It's loud enough to make Jessie and Clara stop arguing and notice the two eavesdropping from the front door.

"Ow, my head," Janet whispers, rubbing her forehead. She then notices something wet touching the area where she hit her head. "Allie, I think the plumbing upstairs is leaking again."

As Janet looks up, it is not a leak that's dripping on her head. Tears are coming down from her older sister's eyes. Allie is also having difficulty breathing and trembling over the sudden news. Even though Janet does not understand what Jessie and her mother are arguing about, Allie does and it is having a profound effect on her. Clara knows that Allie is outside sniffing and upset over what she just heard.

"Allie?" Clara says, opening the front door.

Janet gets up and makes way for her mother going through the front door. Clara sees Allie is clenching her fists and has her head down. She tries to not show that she's crying by having her hair cover her face. However, the loud, short breaths make it obvious that Allie is upset. Since Janet is still young, she cries whenever her sister cries, despite not understanding why she's crying. Clara can tell by her reaction that Allie is having a hard time accepting that her birthday will be unfulfilling.

"Oh, Allie..." Clara kneels and reaches out to her. "I'm so sorry, my darling."

"Let go of me!" Allie cries, pulling away from her mother's grasp. "Daddy doesn't care about me! Daddy doesn't care about Jessie! He doesn't care about us!" Instead of yelling back, Clara pulls Allie to her chest and hugs her tightly.

The child submits to her mother's embrace. Allie continues to cry on her mother's shoulder, having difficulty catching her breath as she breathes through her snotty nose. Clara can feel her daughter's grief affect her breathing as she holds Allie in her arms.

"It's not fair, Mommy," Allie cries. "I need Daddy more than anything right now."

"I know." Clara lifts her up. "We all need him, Allie."

Clara carries her daughter back inside and places her on the lounge room's sofa. As she lies there, Jessie fetches her a cup of water. As Jessie helps Allie drink it, Janet approaches both of them.

"Allie," Janet says, "I'm sorry Daddy isn't coming home for your birthday.

Since he's not coming, I thought I'd give you an early birthday present." The youngest one pulls out a small present, fully wrapped with a bow. "Janet," Clara says. "You're not supposed to give it to her until her birthday."

"I know, Mommy," the youngest replies. "But I feel so sorry for Allie that

I thought she should have my gift to make her feel better."

"Mommy…" Allie wipes her tears. "Can I open it?"

It's hard for Clara to say no in this situation after being devastated by Jed's absence on the most important day for Allie. Clara also sees Janet in tears, which is heartbreaking as well.

"Okay," Clara responds, "this is the only present you can open. After that, you'll have to wait for the rest till your birthday next week. Is that understood?"

Allie nods, which brings a smile to her face. "Fine." Clara sighs. "You can open Janet's present."

Janet gives her sister a big smile as she hands over the present. Allie removes the bow and opens the box. She pulls out an object and sees that it's a wooden box. It has a winding key on the right-hand side. It doesn't seem particularly special to the soon-to-be birthday girl.

"What is this, Janet?" Allie asks.

"First wind the key on the side," Janet instructs. "Then open it, and you'll see that it's one of the best presents in the world."

Allie winds the key, then slowly opens the top of the box. As the box opens halfway, jingles of music play. Inside there's a small metal disc where the jingles come from. There's also a metal piece that keeps the disk centered and rotating to make the music go. As Allie opens the box all the way, the top of the opened box reveals a picture. The picture is a black-and-white photograph of the entire Pluck family and says "Happy Birthday, Allie."

Seeing Jed in the photo with her, her sisters, and her mother has Allie tearing up again. Having a music box as her present is indeed a surprise— and a meaningful one. Though the thought of her father's absence returns, everyone in the living room assumes Allie is crying tears of joy. Allie just stares at the photo and listens to the slow tune coming from the music box. She thinks this is the tune that represents the importance of her family.

The mother and the rest of Allie's sisters are listening to the tune. Though they had already seen the customized present, Allie's reaction toward the gift and the song fills their hearts with joy. Allie doesn't dare close the box. She keeps the music box open to let the tune repeat.

"Thank you, Janet," Allie says through her tears.

Clara then hugs Janet on her left arm as she still lies on the sofa while she hugs Janet on the other.

"You know that's what I want to see," Clara says, holding back her tears over this tender moment. "I want you four to be close together as sisters. Your father and I won't be with you forever, so I'm asking you all to stay strong as a family no matter what happens. Promise?"

"We promise," Allie and Janet respond simultaneously.

"This goes for you too, Jessie and Julia." Clara turns to them. "Though you two are looking ahead to your futures, they still need to be part of your plans as well."

Julia nods. Jessie, however, has her hands on her mouth and nose over how adorable Janet is in making Allie happy. Clara doesn't repeat herself as she takes the hint that she understands.

"Well, then," Clara lets go of the hug and gets back on her feet, "I'm going to clean up upstairs before preparing supper. Hope you enjoy your present, Allie."

"I do, Mommy," Allie responds. "Thank you."

"Don't thank me. Thank your sister for getting you the gift." Allie turns to Janet. "Thank you, Janet. I love this present."

"You're welcome, big sister," Janet responds.

Clara heads up the stairway, still able to hear the jingles from the music box. No one is making any noise downstairs as they enjoy the calm, slow tune that gets the four sisters emotional. Clara also feels emotional from the sound of the music box. It isn't just jumbled noise to keep the children amused. Though she had already heard it when she bought the present, she initially didn't think much of it. However, hearing this now, she sees why it makes her think about her family a lot more, especially her absent husband.

As she enters the bedroom she shared with Jed, her thoughts are consumed by him. Clara closes the door, and all those tears she held back immediately pour down her face. She immediately jumps into the double bed and lies on her stomach. The wife then weeps on the comforter, saddened and angered over her husband's decision to keep going with his career. She always tries to show how strong she is in front of her daughters, but in the bedroom, especially when her husband isn't home, Clara can let go of everything she's feeling.

Once Clara Pluck catches her breath and calms down from her quiet sobs, she can only say, "Damn you, Jed," feeling the hurt once again over his unavailability.

CHAPTER 3

The morning sun gives the Red Desert the same orange scenery and heats up last night's cool temperature. The citizens of Lemonstown are up before sunshine appears over the horizon. As business hours begin, offices and stores unlock their doors to welcome potential customers. Lemonstown is similar to Cheyenne, where there is only one main road between two rows of buildings. The only difference is that the place is half the size of Wyoming's capital and the only town in the middle of Wyoming's Red Desert.

Despite being located in a hostile environment, Lemonstown has a couple of strategies to help its citizens survive. The town has two wooden water towers that pressurize water from the well and collect rainwater. The fact that this town has two wells in the middle of a desert is considered a gold mine for the locals. All the buildings' porches are knee-high to prevent sand and small wildlife from entering their homes.

And, of course, Lemonstown never would have a chance if it didn't have a railway passing through, delivering goods to keep the town operable. The tiny train station is the only connection to the rest of the United States. Passengers board and disembark from trains at ground level, as there is no platform in this town. Not to mention, what travelers pay during their visits is making Lemonstown's economy thrive. The citizens anticipate a train to stop by soon with potential customers on board.

A train whistle is heard coming from behind a plateau. Citizens quickly sweep their front porches and fix their store displays to attract these visitors. The townspeople have always been quick to set up before the train arrives, and this time's no different. The train chugs along the sandy plain before coming to a stop in front of Lemonstown's main road. Minutes pass until the train finally stops, and the locals finish tidying up.

The train engineer is looking for the train station's dock and realizes Lemonstown does not have one. Inspectors Pluck and Secoli alight from the first-class cars with their luggage. They're careful not to fall, as the ladder from the car to the ground is quite high. Pluck heads toward the locomotive while his partner takes his time climbing down, holding his birdcage in one hand.

"Nice to finally see a town full of people, huh, Inspector?" the train engineer shouts, popping his head out of the locomotive's window.

"Hey, we're going to be here for a while!" Pluck shouts back as the locomotive pumps steam. "Why don't you and the conductor just relax in Lemonstown while we take care of business?"

"With pleasure, sir." The train engineer puts his head back inside.

When Pluck turns to his partner, he sees his partner talking to one of the locals. A morbidly obese man in a high hat, white shirt, maroon vest, navy blue pants, and leather boots talks to Secoli. He has gray hair and light brown mutton chops.

"Hey, Pluck," Secoli says as Pluck approaches him. "This man says he's the mayor of Lemonstown."

"Good morning, gentlemen," the mayor says with glee, shaking Secoli's hand. "I'm Michael McLusky, the mayor of Lemonstown." He then shakes Pluck's hand. "Thank you for visiting my town. You two are the first visitors we've had in days. Enjoy each of our services, as we provide beer, souvenirs—"

"I'm sorry, Mr. Mayor," Pluck interrupts, pulling out his badge. "We're United States postal inspectors. My name is Inspector Jed Pluck. This here is my partner, Inspector Louie Secoli."

Secoli pulls out his badge as Pluck continues. "We're on a case of missing people—and towns in Wyoming turning into ghost towns."

They both put their badges back in their pockets before Pluck then pulls out a telegram and passes it to the mayor. The mayor reads it.

"Lemonstown seems to be the only town still left unharmed," Secoli adds to the conversation. "It's a good thing that we got here before any disappearances start happening in your town."

"Are there any missing people in your town, Mayor?" Pluck asks.

The mayor has a disturbed look on his face as he finishes the letter. He lowers the telegram and looks at the two postal inspectors.

"What's the meaning of this? Is Wyoming having a series of kidnappings or some sort of invasion? And why have I been informed of this crisis just now?"

"Mr. Mayor," Secoli leans toward Mayor McLusky. "Are you missing anyone?"

"No. Every morning, I check to see if all the buildings are presentable during business hours, and I haven't noticed any disappearances."

The two postal inspectors both sigh in relief.

"Is there a place where we can discuss this privately?" Pluck asks. "Yes. To my office. Right this way, Inspectors."

The mayor leads the two postal inspectors down Lemonstown's main street. As they walk, the visitors take in the sights of the town. On their left, closest to the railway, they see the saloon, the largest building in town and one of the few two-story buildings. Next to it is the two-story hotel, slightly smaller than the saloon. After that is the bank, the smallest building on the left side of town. It looks like it is squeezed between the sizable hotel and the equally large Town Hall. At the end of the left row of buildings is a livery stable where horses can be heard inside, and wagons are parked outside.

The right side of the main road, in contrast, is lined with one-story buildings. The train station, the smallest structure in town, is the closest building to the railroad. Despite its size, the train station also serves as the post office, which makes sense given that there is no platform for the trains to stop at. The trading post, the largest building on this side of town but still smaller than the saloon and hotel across from it, is the next building down the row.

The next buildings on the right side are in order: the bathhouse, hardware, mining supplies, and the jailhouse on end. There is an empty desert behind the building on the right of the main road. However, the houses where the locals live are behind the buildings on the left side. As the postal inspectors stroll down the main street, the owners and workers of the buildings wave to them. Pluck and Secoli wave back, pretending to be regular visitors. After spending the previous day in ghost towns covered in feathers, they appreciate the welcoming atmosphere. They both noticed that the mayor was not heading to his office on the left, but instead to the jailhouse.

"Please wait here," Mayor McLusky says, turning to them. "I'm going to fetch the sheriff and the deputy."

Unbeknownst to Pluck and Secoli, children have been following them as they wait for the mayor in the jailhouse. They sneak up to Pluck and surprise him with the old boo trick that nearly makes him drop his luggage. Pluck and Secoli realize what has just happened and smile as the children laugh. The children's odor, while unpleasant, is preferable to the stench from the ghost towns from yesterday. The young locals then turn their attention to Chap, who's carried in a cage by Secoli.

"Wow," says one of the children. "What kind of bird is it?"

"How does it have yellow and green feathers?" another child asks. "Where did you find this bird?" asks another. "And why are you carrying it around?"

Before Secoli can respond, the jailhouse door opens, and the mayor ushers in two men in matching black cowboy hats and vests, each with a star-shaped badge pinned to their chest.

"Beat it, children! Shoo!" The mayor raises his voice. "I told y'all not to get anywhere close to the jailhouse."

The children race off like it's a game to them. They all run behind the hardware and mining supply store on the next block. They can be seen peeking out from the end of the porch and the edge of the building.

"Inspectors," the mayor says, "here is Lemonstown's law enforcement. This is Sheriff Butch Wood."

Sheriff Wood of Lemonstown has a light blond horseshoe mustache and a big hooked nose. His face is triangular, and his eyes are almond-shaped. He looks slightly older than the postal inspectors, with tucked-in lips, a deep nasolabial fold, and wrinkled eyes. He wears a red scarf around his neck, a blue shirt under a black vest, and a brown leather holster belt around his blue pants. "United States postal inspectors, right?" the sheriff asks with a thick Southern accent. "May I see your badges?"

Without hesitation, Pluck and Secoli pull them out. The sheriff takes a look at the badges and reads them both before continuing.

"It's a pleasure to meet both of you." The sheriff glances back at the visitors as Secoli and Pluck stow their badges. He pulls his hand out to Secoli for a handshake. "I'm Sheriff Butch Wood. I've been Lemonstown's first law enforcer since Wyoming became a state. Gosh, that's nine years. Well, it's an honor to have a Federal agent come to our town."

"The pleasure is all mine, Sheriff Wood," Secoli says as he shakes his hand. "I'm Postal Inspector Louie Secoli."

Pluck then shakes the sheriff's hand. "And I'm United States Postal Inspector Jed Pluck. Nice to meet you, Sheriff Wood."

"And here's his deputy," the mayor says, continuing his introductions. "Deputy Gordy Hall."

The deputy, who is a few inches taller than six feet, wears the same outfit as his superior except for his pink sleeves. He has a five-o'clock shadow that makes him look like he has been on duty overnight. He has a Roman nose, droopy eyes, and thick lips. His face is relatively wrinkle-free, indicating that he is in his mid-thirties. He has a smug expression as he stares at the postal inspectors.

"Howdy," the deputy says. "I'm Deputy Gordy Hall. I've been protecting Lemonstown for a good five years."

"Now that we're done with introductions," the mayor says, "can we move this conversation to the Town Hall, where we can speak about your case privately?"

"Certainly, Mr. Mayor," the sheriff responds.

The five men cross the main road and walk up to the Town Hall. The two-story building is strikingly white against the other buildings, with a balcony supported by porch pillars and a giant clock above the Town Hall sign. A bell tower rises above the clock, taller than any other building in Lemonstown.

Pluck turns around to see if the children are trying to play another trick on him and his partner. A little girl steps off the porch of the hardware store and stops when she sees Pluck watching her. She scurries back to her friends, hiding and observing from across the street. The sight of the little girl trying to get his attention makes him think of his daughters back in Boston, and he immediately feels homesick.

Upon entering the Town Hall, they see that the whole place is made of wood, and the long wooden seats look like they belong in a church. The middle row seats are the longest, while the left and right rows can only fit two people. All the seats face what looks like a judge's bench in a courtroom. Having a Christian cross built against the wall and the two American flags standing on both corners of the room gives mixed signals to the postal inspectors.

"Welcome to our Town Hall, gentlemen," the mayor says. "This is the sanctuary. Don't let the name fool you because this is a multipurpose facility. We use this place for town meetings, private meetings, church services, stage plays, and court cases."

The lawmen and the mayor head straight to the judge's bench while Pluck and Secoli analyze the place. When they turn back to where they came from, they see a ladder that leads to the second floor that leads to the bell tower. The mayor and lawmen take the visitors through a door behind the judge's bench. The room is cramped but tidy, with only an executive desk and three chairs.

"And this here is my office," the mayor says. "This is where I hold private meetings, which is why I would like to continue our conversation here, my dear inspectors." He sits behind the desk. "Please take a seat."

The two Federal agents put their luggage next to their seats. Secoli sits on the chair on the left, and Pluck takes the one on the right. Secoli places his birdcage next to his briefcase on the floor while the mayor organizes his desk. Deputy Hall closes the door and stands behind the mayor, next to Sheriff Wood. "So..." McLusky stops arranging the items on his desk and sits back.

"What is going on in the other towns in Wyoming?"

Pluck nods to Secoli, who signals him to open his briefcase. Secoli takes out a wrapped package from his luggage and places it on the mayor's desk. He unwraps it to reveal a ten-inch black feather with pointy vanes.

"I strongly advise you to be careful with it when you hold it, Mr. Mayor," Secoli says as he closes and puts away his briefcase. "The edges are pointy as needles, and the feather is as durable as bones. Hold it by the quill if you want to pick it up."

The mayor does as he's instructed and analyzes the evidence.

"This is just one of the many feathers left all over the towns in Wyoming." Secoli continues, "We found no one, not a single person in Cheyenne, Laramie, and Rawlins. But all three towns we were in yesterday are covered in these deadly feathers."

The mayor picks at the edges of the vane and feels its stiff points.

"We have no idea who or what took these Wyomingites," Pluck adds. "And we don't know why or how they disappeared. Yet, it's amazing that such a thing has successfully made even the capital of your state a ghost town."

The mayor is giving the two inspectors a disturbed look as he hands the plume to the sheriff, who examines it.

"We have every reason to believe this threat is heading to Lemonstown," Pluck continues. "We want to do all we can to protect your town."

"How are we supposed to do that?" the mayor asks. "We're a small town that hardly has any trouble coming our way. What in heaven's name did we do to deserve this?"

The deputy points to Secoli's birdcage. "And what the hell is that thing in the cage for? It's no bird that I've ever seen. Does that weird bird have anything to do with this?"

"No," Secoli answers. "Chap—I mean, this bird—has nothing to do with this case at all."

Secoli struggles with coming up with an answer to make the mayor and the lawmen understand why he carries Chap with him everywhere he goes. Pluck notices he's having difficulty explaining the budgerigar's purpose.

"That's a budgerigar," Pluck improvises. "It's an entirely different case involving us delivering this delicate bird breed to its destination."

Pluck flashes his partner a brief smile, signaling to Secoli that he has his back as the officials buy the story. In return, Secoli gives a grateful nod.

"Mr. Mayor," Secoli asks, "how much experience do your people have with guns?"

"I'm sorry, but Lemonstown is filled with nice common folks. Like I said, we rarely have any trouble in this town, so we've never been in a position of combat."

Sheriff Wood passes the evidence to his subordinate behind the mayor while the mayor speaks. Despite paying full attention to the conversation, the deputy doesn't pay attention to his hand's location. He yelps when he accidentally touches the edge of the plume that cut his finger. Everyone in the room sees blood on the tip of his index finger. Even when he's covering it, they can see that the cut on his finger went pretty deep, judging by how much blood is pouring into his other hand.

"Hey, Hall," Sheriff Wood says, "you're bleeding. Why don't you go to the trading post and get yourself a bandage."

Hall moves from his post and exits the mayor's office. Sheriff Wood kneels and picks up the evidence lying on the floor by the quill. He puts it back on the wrapping paper on the mayor's desk.

"As I was saying," the mayor continues, "we have no combat experience. Any potential danger outside this town has been out of our reach because we're in the Red Desert. Criminals would rather put more effort into robbing and causing trouble to other towns, but being in a desert has benefited us."

"Have either of you two telegraphed or given a telephone call for additional help?" the sheriff asks. "Maybe the cavalry can help us as they should."

"We have," Secoli answers, pulling out a telegram from Chyenne and passing it to the mayor, "but it seems that the government is using the National Guard and the cavalry for other purposes. Where's the closest telegraph we can use to confirm that Lemonstown is safe and request your protection?"

The mayor finishes reading the telegram. The sheriff reads it over his shoulders.

"We don't have one. The end of Wyoming's telephone line is back at Rawlins."

"Oh, Gawd," Pluck comments, "we were just there. We might as well turn our train around and go back there. You would have thought that manufacturers would have come up with trains that can reverse by now."

Looking exhausted, McLusky puts both hands on his face. Everyone in the room can feel the mayor's fear and stress getting to him.

"So now that military support is out of reach," the mayor says, "what's our next move?"

"Well, my partner and I brought some rifles on our train," Pluck answers. "We're planning to arm the first town with the weapons we collected from the towns we visited. Apparently, yours is the first we found alive."

"The baggage cart is filled with rifles and crates of ammunition for those guns," Secoli adds. "We can make the citizens use it and fight off whatever this demon is."

"I'm not taking that risk," the mayor interrupts. "Lemonstown is a peaceful town, and trouble hardly ever happens here. You're asking me to make my citizens become gunmen and risk their lives against this giant bird. Sorry, but that's not worth it."

"If that's the case, Mr. Mayor," Secoli continues, "I have another idea. How about bringing all your citizens on board our train and having them evacuate this town? I'm not risking any lives to stay in this state."

"You know," the sheriff responds. "I like that idea better."

"Good thinking, Louie," Pluck says. "Mr. Mayor, how long will it take to gather all your citizens and get them to board the train?"

Before McLusky can answer, the conversation is interrupted by a train whistle heard from outside. It first became noticeable a minute ago in the conversation. However, a minute passes and the mayor becomes annoyed.

"Damn it," the mayor swears. "Won't someone tell that train engineer to stop that noise?"

The two postal inspectors notice that the sound of the train whistle is coming from somewhere other than the direction where they got off; it sounds like it's coming from the opposite direction and farther away. Even more unusual is that the train whistle isn't stopping its alarm and, in fact, gets louder with each passing second.

Everyone in the room turns to the only door in the office, and a loud knock sounds on the door. Deputy Hall barges in with an apprehensive expression.

"Sheriff!" Hall shouts. "A train is running full speed to this town! And it ain't slowing down! It's going to crash into the inspectors' train!"

Everyone gets up and follows the deputy out of the office. Secoli brings his birdcage with him and is the last to exit the room. They rush through the sanctuary and out of the Town Hall. The nonstop train whistle is much louder when they all rush out of the building. They can see burning smoke soaring above the buildings in front of them—much darker than the usual locomotive steam.

The citizens of Lemonstown are blocking the main road, facing the source of the noise. The five of them rush across the main road and alleyway between the jailhouse and hardware store. Standing at the back of the jailhouse, the five officials see the runaway train following the railroad circling around the desert terrain.

The sheriff takes out a pair of binoculars to get a better view of his current position. The other four can see in the distance that the locomotive is on fire. The fiery train is only pulling a cargo train, carrying fifteen boxcars. The five are only a little over a mile away from where the train is turning right. "Inspector..." The sheriff removes his binoculars from his sight and hands them to Pluck. "You have to see this."

Secoli takes the binoculars and peers through the ocular lenses with one hand while holding his birdcage in the other. He's astonished by what he sees, making Pluck eager to see what he's looking at. Secoli takes a few seconds to look through the ocular lens before passing the binoculars to Pluck.

When Pluck looks through the lens, he sees that the fire is coming from inside the locomotive. Though he can't see any closer, he sees familiar silhouette shapes flying out of the front of the train. Judging by how fast Pluck turns his head, the train is going around sixty miles an hour. He then wordlessly hands the binoculars to the mayor.

When Pluck turns to his partner, Secoli no longer stands beside him. Pluck makes a full turn when he hears Chap's chirpings and sees Secoli running through the alleyway to where their train is tethered.

"Louie!" Pluck screams.

The mayor and two lawmen immediately turn to Pluck. "He's going after our train."

A frantic Pluck chases after his partner, followed by the mayor and two lawmen.

Pluck makes it out of the alleyway and down to the main road. The sheriff and his deputy get out of the alley before the mayor, as he's out of breath from running so much.

"Hall," the sheriff says, "get to the bell tower and ring the damn bell." The deputy returns to the Town Hall as the sheriff runs down to the tied-down train.

As Secoli sprints down the main road, he goes straight to the baggage car behind the last-class car, where guns and ammo are kept. Seeing where Secoli is heading, Pluck knows he's trying to save the weaponry from getting damaged by the incoming train. Despite the weaponry car being two cars ahead from the rear, the fiery locomotive can potentially crash and burn the guns and bullets. Secoli makes it to the third baggage car from the back and places the birdcage on the ground.

He then tries to slide the car door open as the bell from the Town Hall rings. The bell signals everyone in Lemonstown to run to the Town Hall for safety. Unable to budge it open, Secoli sees a lock. He recalls telling the conductor last night to lock the cart to secure the guns, and now he regrets ever doing so.

Pluck pulls Secoli away from the tracks just as Secoli sees the fiery runaway train approaching. Secoli then realizes that he left his birdcage by the railway, so he frees himself from Pluck's grasp and immediately runs after it. As he picks it up, Pluck grabs Secoli's sleeves again and pulls him to safety as the train's whistle blows louder. They hurry back into the main road before the two trains collide.

When the two postal inspectors pass the saloon, the runaway train makes a hard collision and explodes through the caboose. The momentum of the train behind and the locked brakes ahead make the railroad cars in between push up in the air. The busted caboose and the two baggage cars nearly fly into the saloon, but the weight of the cars leans in the opposite direction, and they fall into a ditch.

Upon impact, the exploded locomotive is still in motion as it is also pushed up in the air but leans in the opposite direction, crashing through the saloon. The postal inspectors are several feet away from getting hit by the unstoppable machine. They both fall for cover as the train goes through the building. Having run off the tracks, the train has ceased moving, and the train whistle finally stops blowing. The fire spreads from the train and engulfs the saloon in flames. The baggage cars are connected to the tie-down train, which drags five passenger cars into the ditch. While the hand brakes are locked and the wheels are chocked, the coal car and locomotive still drag into the same ditch and break apart. The citizens outside the Town Hall spring into action by heading to the water tower behind the saloon. The owner of the saloon passes wooden buckets and empty barrels to those who are helping. A saloon worker assists in gushing water from the water pump underneath the water tower into everyone's buckets and barrels. Without wasting time, the citizens carry the water-filled containers and pour them into the fire. While the citizens are pouring water behind the burning saloon, the postal inspectors get up from the ground and hear someone screaming.

"There are still people in there!" Pluck exclaims.

Pluck rushes to the saloon's front door. The hard fall Secoli took is preventing him from keeping up with his partner, who barges through the door. As Secoli walks up the porch's stairs, one of the pillars falls and blocks the entranceway. Louie can't see where his partner is inside the scorching building. He hears Chap chirping with fear, so he gets off the porch and stands in the middle of the main road.

Secoli screams, "Jed!" multiple times, hoping he's still alive. He's hugging the birdcage while he's in a state of panic. Chap is also trembling after having been in the cage, which fell over multiple times and getting too close to the flames. While Secoli continues to scream his partner's name, Sheriff Wood and two locals approach him.

"Inspector!" yells the sheriff. "We've got to get to a safer place."

"No!" Secoli responds with urgency. "My partner is in there! We have to help him!"

Secoli and the sheriff suddenly hear a familiar voice screaming, "Louie!" from the second-floor window. Pluck sticks his head out of the window.

"I've got three people who need help getting down!" Pluck exclaims. "Get a ladder!"

Sheriff Wood turns to Secoli. "I know where to get a ladder. Follow me."

Staring out the window, Pluck watches Secoli carry his birdcage and follow the sheriff back to the alley between the jailhouse and the hardware store. He then turns to the two saloon girls and the conductor in the room, knowing why he is with them. Fire hasn't made it to the bedroom that they're in yet, but smoke is all over the room, making it hard to breathe. Even with the window open, all of them are coughing from the fire's smoke that's beneath them.

Pluck peeks out the window again to see that Secoli and the sheriff are both carrying a wooden ladder that looks to be around twelve feet long. The sheriff is carrying the ladder at the front, and Secoli is lifting it at the back. Since Pluck cannot see the birdcage from his point of view, Secoli must have put his budgerigar in a safe place. The sheriff puts the front ladder down and rushes back next to Secoli's end. They lift the ladder and place the top underneath the window where Pluck is. Pluck assists by placing the top of the ladder firmly under the window frame.

"Is the bottom of the ladder firmly on the ground?" Pluck shouts.

Secoli kicks the ladder's feet on the ground and shouts, "It's good to go!"

Pluck turns to everyone in the bedroom. They're all eager to get on the ladder and climb down.

"Ladies first," says Pluck, helping one of the saloon girls out the window. "One at a time, Inspector!" shouts the sheriff. "We don't know how much weight this ladder can hold. The last thing anyone needs is for this ladder to break."

Pluck, while helping the lady on the ladder, gives the sheriff a nod from the window. The woman gingerly descends the ladder as the sheriff and Secoli keep it steady. After a long struggle, she finally reaches the ground and asks Secoli and the sheriff to help the woman from collapsing. Once Pluck sees that the first saloon girl has safely reached the ground, he turns his attention to the next girl. However, the woman in the bedroom panics as she sits in the corner, trembling and coughing.

"Hey, it's your turn," Pluck says.

"I can't!" The lady coughs and screams. "I'm afraid of heights."

"You'll be much safer down there. If we don't start moving, you'll burn alive. I'm not leaving until everyone is safe."

"I can't," she continues coughing. "I'm too scared."

Impatient and panic-stricken, the conductor runs to the window and gets on the ladder. The second person climbs down quickly, but no one notices because they're all distracted. The ladder starts to wobble as the conductor moves too fast. The ladder rotates when the conductor makes it to the halfway point. Everyone turns to the conductor as they hear him yell and hear pieces of wood crashing.

Pluck immediately gets up and looks out the window to see that not only did the ladder fall on the porch, but the conductor went through it. The old man is painfully groaning as he lies on the broken wood. The sheriff and Secoli run to the conductor and carry him out of the hole he made. The locals join in and carry him to safety. Pluck worries about the poor old man who may or may not be alive from the accident.

With the conductor out of their hands, Secoli and the sheriff bring the ladder back up and put it back in position. Pluck then turns to the distressed worker, still trembling at the corner. The smoke gets heavier, making them both cough. Pluck can feel that the fire has reached the second floor and is behind the bedroom door. With little time left, the selfless postal inspector pulls her out from the corner and to the window.

Knowing that there's no other choice for her, the saloon girl gets on Pluck's back in a pack-strap carry. She wraps her arms around Pluck's neck and her legs around his waist as tight as she can as he slides both of them through the window and onto the ladder. As Pluck continues down the ladder, the saloon girl covers her face against the postal inspector's back. It doesn't take long for him to make it to the main road's curve and collapse.

The young lady lets go and lies on the concrete with her rescuer. She and Pluck take a moment to catch their breaths and get to their feet. Secoli gives Pluck a pat on the back while the two saloon girls hug each other. Pluck looks at the window and sees that the bedroom is on fire, thinking it would have been too late if they stayed there longer.

"Goddamn, Jed," Secoli swears joyfully. "You're a real hero!"

"Thank you so much, Inspector," the sheriff adds. "Without your help, who knows what would have happened to Miss Bell and Miss Winston?"

Pluck catches his breath. "How's the conductor? Is he okay?"

"We don't know," Secoli said. "He's unconscious from his fall. We took him to the Town Hall to get someone to treat him."

"Louie," Pluck continues, catching his breath. "Where's Chap?"

"Oh, right." Secoli rushes to the hardware store to retrieve his budgerigar. "I'll be right back."

"Just what the hell happened here?" the sheriff asks.

"I don't know, but that train shouldn't be here. We got confirmation from headquarters that all trains scheduled to Wyoming were seized."

"Even so," the sheriff continues, "how in the world did that train end up on fire?"

Pluck watches the saloon burn while the workers continue to try to put out the fire.

He circumnavigates the burning building to examine the exploded locomotive. He then stops immediately when he feels he has stepped on something. The sheriff sees Pluck kneeling down and pulling a black feather he showed everyone in the mayor's office.

He and Pluck turn to the connecting boxcars and see more black feathers on the railway. Secoli runs back to Sheriff Wood and his partner with his birdcage in time to see more evidence. Pluck turns to everyone, holding the burnt feather in his hand.

"Whatever is responsible for those ghost towns," Pluck declares, "is getting close to Lemonstown."

"Then we're going to need those guns more than anything," his partner replies. "We might still be able to save what's left of those guns. We need to get the keys from the conductor to unlock the baggage car."

The postal inspectors and the sheriff rush to the Town Hall where the conductor is. The sanctuary is filled with women, children, and a couple of men, leaving little room for the three to walk through without bumping into someone.

"Deputy Hall," the sheriff calls. "Where is the conductor? Is he all right?"

"He's lying on a table in front, Sheriff," the deputy answers. "He's unconscious, and we don't know how badly he's hurting." He then raises his voice for everyone to hear. "Make way for the lawmen, please!"

The crowd parts to let the officials through to the conductor, who lies motionless on a rectangular table. Secoli sees the tip of a key protruding from the man's left pocket and quickly snatches the chain of keys. With urgency, Secoli and the men with him rush out of the sanctuary and back to the railway. The mine car and first boxcar are overturned, and the second boxcar's coupler is detached, leaving a large gap between the cars. They walk through the gap and head to the ditch where the postal inspectors' train collapsed.

The four officials watch from the edge of the ditch as the fire from the saloon, which is ignited by the burning locomotive, spreads to the front of the passenger car and continues to engulf the following cars. It would have been easy to just head down to the third baggage car behind the last-class passenger car. However, the fire in the damaged caboose in the opposite direction spread to the baggage cars. The weapon stash is caught between two infernos.

"Hurry," Secoli says. "We gotta get the guns and ammo out of there."

"Hall..." Sheriff Wood turns to his deputy. "Help the inspectors out. I'm going to get additional help to get those guns out of the baggage car."

"Yes, sir," Deputy Hall responds.

The sheriff hurries back to the main road in search of help. Despite how much heat is felt, the three still head toward the third baggage car. The distance between the edge of the ditch and the slanted cars is large. Secoli decides to safely slide down the ditch and climb up to the car's door. Pluck and Hall do the same, while Secoli places his birdcage on top of the car's side and starts looking for the right key for the lock.

As soon as Pluck and Hall reach the top of the baggage car, Secoli finds the key that unlocks the door and slides it open. The three of them see the rifles and bullets that break through the crates all over the interior. Secoli quickly gets in the car just before the sheriff returns with backup. Lawman's seven men threw water from the caboose onto the fire right away. It doesn't take long for the fire at the back end of the train to be put out.

"Sheriff!" Pluck shouts. "We're going to pass you guys these weapons."

Inspector Pluck and the deputy collect the items from Secoli and toss the weapons to the group at the edge of the ditch. Some are in good condition, and others are obviously bent but are still passed on to the group with no time to waste.

It's already past the twenty-gun mark, yet no one is paying attention to the birdcage. The birdcage slips down the narrow surface of the baggage car. Pluck notices that Secoli's budgerigar is in danger again and grabs it before it falls off the car.

Already annoyed with Secoli's neglect of his muse, he passes the birdcage to the locals, retrieving the items. Pluck continues helping Deputy Hall to pass the rifles before he notices. Even as they continue to get everything out of the baggage car, the fire in the saloon gets worse. It's already making the sheriff and the assisting locals feel unsafe. Everyone has successfully taken more than sixty rifles out of the car.

"Jed!" Secoli shouts. "That's all the rifles! I'm passing you the crates now!" Secoli doesn't answer and pushes one of the crates out. Pluck and Hall then pull another crate out and toss it to the group. More townspeople are showing up to help by bringing guns to town. After the fifth crate has been retrieved, the saloon collapses into the railway, spreading the flames even further.

The collateral damage is only a few feet from hitting the baggage car they're in. Pluck and Hall are so caught off guard by the blazing impact that the crate they were taking out falls back into the car. Though it doesn't land on top of Secoli, the crate hits the ground, and bullets spill all over the floor. Realizing the passenger train next to them is on fire, Pluck and Hall see how much closer they are to danger.

"Louie!" Pluck shouts, and he reaches down to him. "We gotta get out of here. The saloon fell on the train, and it's on fire!"

Secoli is picking up the bullets from the floor and trying to put them back in one of the opened crates. He doesn't respond back. Pluck loses all patience and gets down inside the baggage car. He grabs his partner by the sleeves, dropping some of the bullets he has in his hands.

"Let it go, Louie!" Pluck shouts. "We're in grave danger! We're all too damn close to the fire! We're not picking up anymore! Now get going!"

Secoli doesn't know how close to the danger he is, but he hears his partner lashing out at him for the first time. Pluck lets go of Secoli's sleeves and climbs out of the car.

Hall pulls Secoli out of the car and sees how much closer the fire is spreading. One by one, the three of them jump out of the car and land on their feet on the edge of the ditch. The sheriff and the locals help prevent the three of them from having an accident as they leap over to them.

Exhausted from everything they've done, Pluck is the last to jump. Instead of having his feet land on the ditch, his chest lands on the edge, and he almost slips down the ditch. The two lawmen and Secoli immediately pull Pluck up, and everyone runs to safety. All of the guns and crates of bullets are carried to the trading post, where they can be secured. When Pluck and Secoli run past the cargo cars on the main road, they see everyone applauding them. While Secoli feels admired for his efforts, Pluck is confused over this celebration that he feels he doesn't deserve.

The mayor approached with his arms raised, saying, "You two saved my town! What you two just did today is incredible. We can never repay you enough for all you've done."

"This is no time for celebration!" Pluck shouts.

Everyone goes silent over his sudden response as he pulls out his badge. "I am United States Postal Inspector Jed Pluck. I'm a Federal agent sent by the United States Government. My partner and I have come to this town to inform you that Lemonstown is in danger.

"Other towns in the state of Wyoming have had massive disappearances, turning each of them into ghost towns. Rawlins, Laramie, and even your state capital, Cheyenne, they're all ghost towns. Slowly but surely, Lemonstown will be next. We didn't risk our lives because it was a heroic thing to do. We did it to save the guns we brought to you in preparation to defend yourselves for what is to come."

"What's causing all of these disappearances?" a man in the crowd asks. "We don't know…" Pluck clears his throat. "Neither my partner nor I know or have seen what caused these disappearances."

Pluck kneels and picks up a black feather close to his right foot. He gets up and raises it in the air. "But this is what's been left behind in these ghost towns. This is a very unnatural feather capable of slicing anyone and anything." Pluck puts down the feather and points to the destroyed saloon. "And whatever is causing these disappearances has done that to your town. Imagine what this demon can do when it gets here."

Pluck drops the feather and finishes, saying, "I suggest that those who want to save this town go to the sheriff and deputy right now to learn how to wield these guns that we risked our lives for. If you have any further questions, please ask Mayor McLusky."

The crowd quickly turns their attention to the mayor and his lawmen, overwhelming them with panic. Pluck walks away and heads to the alley between the trading post and the bathhouse. Secoli follows his partner and immediately stops.

"Oh, no!" Secoli gasps. "Chap! I left him back on the train."

"No, you didn't," Pluck responds angrily.

Pluck stops and changes his direction to the trading post. Secoli watches as Pluck passive-aggressively heads to the crates and pulls out the birdcage that was placed behind the ammo boxes. Secoli so exhilarated over the safety of Chap, walks up to Pluck and grabs the birdcage. He hugs the cage and rubs his fingers on the budgerigar's head between the bars. After being near the fire several times, the parakeet is unharmed.

"Oh, thank you, Jed," Secoli says with delight. "Thank you so much for saving Chap. How can I repay you?"

"Save it," Pluck responds. "We'll discuss your lack of professionalism after I take a nap. It's still morning, and it's already been a long day."

Pluck walks away and heads straight for the hotel. Secoli watches his partner walk through the crowd to the hotel's porch, confused by his change in attitude. Even across the street, over the noise of the crowd, Secoli hears Pluck slam the front door as he enters. The crowd doesn't notice it, but Secoli hears that door slam clearer than anyone in Lemonstown. He stands in front of the trading post, confused by Pluck's behavior.

CHAPTER 4

The Town Hall is filled to capacity, with every seat taken and many more people standing in the back, all eager to hear what Mayor McLusky has to say. Everyone except Deputy Hall is facing the empty judge's bench, waiting for the Town Hall meeting to start. The sanctuary remains calm despite the townspeople's loud and agitated voices. The door behind the judge's bench bursts open, and Mayor McLusky, Sheriff Wood, and the two postal inspectors emerge. "All rise for the Honorable Mayor McLusky," the deputy calls.

The sanctuary immediately falls silent and stands up when the mayor arrives at the judge's bench. Before McLusky sits down and strikes the sound block on his desk, Pluck, Secoli with his birdcage, and the sheriff walk around the bench, stand in front of the judge's bench, and face the audience. The banging noise makes everyone sit back down except the lawmen and inspectors, who remain standing and attentive.

"Thank you all for coming," the mayor says. "For those who helped out clearing the railway and putting out the fire, I want to thank you for helping out the town in this unfortunate circumstance. Since we had that train accident this morning, we don't have any trains to transport us out of Lemonstown. The postal inspectors have confirmed that the US Government has seized all trains from coming into Wyoming. This explains why we haven't gotten a visitor, a cargo train to deliver the goods or a pony express that handles our mail for days now."

The mayor clears his throat. "We just had two accidents. One victim is unconscious, and the other is healing from severe burns. Unfortunately, we won't be rebuilding the saloon any time soon." McLusky sees the owner of the saloon and his employees sitting together, appearing dismayed. "Businesses in Lemonstown will be closed until further notice, and weekly taxes will be waived during this time. Given the current lockdown and curfew, it is not feasible to expect you all to be able to afford this month's payment."

Whispers sweep through the room as the mayor continues his announcement. The saloon's owner gets up from his seat from the second row on the mayor's left, next to the aisle. He is wearing a black derby hat, vest, and western-style bowtie, contrasting with his white shirt. He is an older fellow with a gray beard and a chubby round face that matches his overweight body. The saloon manager doesn't look all too happy.

The saloon owner shouts, "How are we gonna repair my saloon without 'em taxes?"

"I understand your frustration, Mr. Benjamin," the mayor politely answers. "But that's not a priority right now. Right now, we're focusing on how to counteract whatever is threatening this town."

"Not a priority? That's my entire livelihood you're talkin' about!"

"Please, Mr. Benjamin. We'll take care of your saloon after this is all done.

We can't do anything about it right now because we don't have the resources to rebuild your saloon, nor is there any nearby town available to help us out."

"And how would you know about that? None of you here have left Lemonstown to know if what the postal inspectors said is true. You've collected taxes monthly to not reimburse the damages caused by..." Mr. Benjamin points at the postal inspectors. "...these two. Why the hell are you collecting taxes anyway if they're not going to be used for public service? In fact," the man continues, "I pay more taxes, have the most employees, and have more success than any business in town. And this is what I get? Without my saloon, Lemonstown will not be as attractive as it used to be."

McLusky bangs his gavel to silence the troubled business owner. Mr. Benjamin stops his rant. Everyone attending the Town Hall meeting seems like they could be more pleased with what he said to everyone.

"Now, Mr. Benjamin..." The mayor puts down his gavel. "That is no way to treat the United States Postal Inspectors. They are Federal agents with more authority than my lawmen and me."

"You know, Mayor McLusky?" Mr. Benjamin replies. "You said the exact same thing to me years ago when that riot happened in my saloon. I eventually had to pay for the damages since I couldn't wait any longer for your empty promises. Repairing those damages almost got me out of business, but this time... I can't do business here anymore." He turns to his employees, who are mostly saloon girls and a few men, who are bartenders and musicians. "C'mon, y'all. Our business is done here."

The mayor uses his gavel again. "Order in the court, Mr. Benjamin."

"I refuse to take any more orders from you, McLusky! Ever since you've been elected mayor of Lemonstown, this town's gone to shit!"

"Sheriff," the mayor turns to his official, "show Mr. Benjamin his way out the door."

Sheriff Wood approaches the distressed businessman. Mr. Benjamin pulls his arm away when the sheriff touches his shoulders to lead him out of the sanctuary. "Get your damn hands off of me, Sheriff!" Benjamin yells. "I know my way out the door. C'mon, y'all. We ain't needed here."

His employees leave their seats and follow their employer down the aisle and out the door. The long bench is now empty as they all head out the door. As the saloon crew walks out, the two girls Pluck saved from the fire give the postal inspector a quick glance. Although Pluck remains still, he acknowledges the girls' embarrassment at being forced to leave. Upon the saloon crew's departure, folks from the back move up to take those empty seats.

"Now then," the mayor says, calmer now, "everyone, please remain silent until I open up the floor for questions. I hate to inform you that the original plan was to evacuate everyone out of Lemonstown. Still, since we have no train, we must defend ourselves from whatever is causing Wyoming's disappearances. Now that daily business hours are closed until further notice, during this time, everyone in Lemonstown will be on guard all day and night. We'll be keeping track of every person in town. Each man will be given a rifle and ammunition to defend Lemonstown and their loved ones.

Those who don't know how to properly use a rifle must see Sheriff Wood or Deputy Hall for proper training. I have on record that we have forty-two men in Lemonstown, including Mr. Benjamin and his five men, who will all be handed their rifles and take the role of guarding Lemonstown."

McLusky sees the train engineer who drove the postal inspectors' train. He's changed into a different outfit, blending in the crowd. The train engineer, though not a local, is aware that he's noticed and expects to be chosen to defend the town. McLusky takes his attention away from him to subtly say he's off the hook.

"Actually, Mr. Mayor," Secoli interrupts, "we only have twenty-eight good rifles."

"Only twenty-eight? I thought we saved a lot more guns than that from your train, Inspector."

"We did, Mr. Mayor. But that train crash damaged many of the rifles we brought in. We only have twenty-eight good rifles, sir. The rest are either bent or have missing pieces. We don't have a gunsmith; we can only settle for what we have. And the revolvers that my deputy and I carry are something that we never let anyone touch."

"So, in doing the math..." McLusky takes out a piece of paper and does his calculations. "Forty-two minus twenty-eight. Okay. So that makes it fourteen who are relieved from wielding a gun. Does anyone in this courtroom know how to wield a rifle?"

The mayor pauses for a moment, hoping that someone will speak up, but the room remains silent.

"Umm, Mayor..." A voice is heard from the audience, with a hand raised. Everyone in the room stares as he stands up. He's wearing round glasses, a dark brown coat with a black bowtie wrapped around the white collar covering his entire neck. He has frizzy whiskers and a beard that doesn't appear as groomed as his long hair, which reaches his shoulders. He places his arm down to pull up his Bible to his chest level.

"I'm sorry, Mr. Mayor," the same man continues, "but as a man of God and preacher of this sanctuary, I'm going to need to be pardoned from wielding a gun."

"I'm sorry, Father Jenkins," McLusky responds, "but the paper says you're

forty-four years old. You're not exempt from wielding a gun."

"But, Mr. Mayor, it's against my principles to take another man's life."

"You're a preacher, right?"

"That's right."

"Do you consider yourself a warrior of God?"

"Yes, sir. I do."

"And if the devil were here, would you grab a gun and shoot him down?"

"I...I would if I could, sir. For the Lord's sake, especially."

"Then that makes you the perfect candidate to be on guard with the rest of us."

Father Jenkins doesn't say another word. Mayor McLusky is too witty for him to handle the debate. Being called out as a man of God and not fighting his enemies would make him look like a hypocrite to everybody in the room. "Moving on. Twenty-eight men who are fifty and younger will have to meet my two officials at the jailhouse tomorrow for gun training at eight o'clock sharp. No exceptions." He puts down the paper. "Women and children will have to remain here in the sanctuary. You'll be asked to leave your homes and share living space for your own safety."

"But what about when we need to get out, Mr. Mayor?" A woman raises her hand. "For something like using an outhouse or picking up food?"

"I was getting to that," McLusky responds. "The only reason anyone not wielding a gun needs to get out of the sanctuary is to use the outhouse, pick up something, or pay a visit to someone who must do so not only quickly but be accompanied by someone who is on guard duty. Anyone who disobeys this order will be personally meeting with me over violating safety protocols."

Straight away, female voices are yelling in the room. Many are not too happy about the sexist rules being made. The mayor continues to bang his gavel to calm the angry women in the room. The last voice is heard as the noise quiets down, saying, "So the men are allowed to stay out while the rest of us have to be trapped here? It defeats the purpose for us women to move to the West to have more freedom than in the East."

"I understand that many of you aren't too keen on this new rule," the mayor continues, "but please consider that whoever is responsible for these series of ghost towns spared nobody, including women and children.

While we're on curfew and outdoor restrictions, the water tower behind what used to be where the saloon is completely dried up. Anyone who needs to get water has to go to the water tower behind the bathhouse. However, the bathhouse is off-limits since we're down one water tower. There is a restriction of one full bucket of water per person—"

The mayor notices that people at the back are facing the opposite direction. From where he's sitting, he can hear ragtime piano playing with the sounds of banjo and violin. Everyone in the room also hears it, placing their attention away from the mayor and onto the doorway behind them.

"What is that racket?" the mayor comments.

The music being played outside distracts some of those who are sitting. Some get out of their seats and head out the door. Moments later, more people grow curious and follow everyone else out the door.

McLusky bangs his gavel. "Everyone, return to your seats! We have important matters to discuss! Hey! Aren't any of you listening to me?"

The audience's attention has drifted away from the mayor, leaving their seats and exiting the door. The lawmen and postal inspectors remain standing on stage despite how curious they are about the music being played outside. Annoyed with everyone gone, the mayor gets out of his chair and moves down the judge's bench.

Following McLusky out the door, the officials hear ragtime music outside that's usually heard in saloons. The five of them see everyone surrounding the trading post building. Festival lanterns are lit to showcase the saloon crew members performing on the trading post's porch. As the mayor, lawmen, and postal inspectors walk down the approaches, they see one saloon girl dancing before the men playing the piano, violin, and banjo.

The mayor wordlessly heads to the performance, with the officials following and providing him protection. When they get closer, people are already in front of the porch, given room to waltz to the ragtime-Western music being played. The mayor pushes away the waltzers about to bump into him and gets up on the porch.

McLusky attempts to stop the musicians by pulling the violin out of the player's hand and slamming it on the porch. Then he does the same with the banjo player and throws the string instrument onto the porch as well, then pushes the pianist off his seat. Everyone watches as Benjamin gets on the porch and confronts the mayor.

"That is no way to treat my employees, McLusky!" the saloon owner shouts. "Are you mad? This is no time to celebrate when Lemonstown is supposed to be on guard!" the mayor shouts back.

"I know what you're trying to do." Benjamin points at the mayor. "You're trying to make me go out of business. Do you actually think that since I can't have a saloon, I can't do business? Well, you're wrong!"

"No. You're the one who's wrong here! Playing music out here is only attracting unwanted attention! You're making Lemonstown the next ghost town!"

"Geez, McLusky! Ever since you became mayor, more restrictions and rules have been created out of the blue! Are you really that hungry to control everyone here?"

"Out of all the citizens in Lemonstown, you're the only one being unreasonable. Don't you even stop to think about the safety of Lemonstown?"

Benjamin clenches his fists and is about to give the mayor one on the face. He holds back when he sees the sheriff get on the porch and stand behind the mayor. Benjamin turns and notices that the deputy is standing behind him. As much as he wants to give the mayor a piece of his mind, he releases his fist.

"Forget it," Benjamin says. "I don't see the point in being here anymore. Come on, crew. We're leaving Lemonstown. Let's grab our bags and get the hell out of this town."

"But, Mr. Benjamin," one of his men says, "all our belongings were burned up in the saloon. We don't have anything else."

"And we don't have a train to catch a ride," another of his male employees says, "and there won't be another one coming since trains are no longer entering Wyoming."

Mr. Benjamin looks at the two postal inspectors standing before the crowd. "You two did something to prevent all trains from coming into this state, didn't you?"

Pluck and Secoli remain silent as they glare at the reckless old man. Secoli holds his birdcage tightly, resisting the urge to strike him. Having Chap close to him is what's helping him maintain his composure, no matter how much he feels the man deserves a good smack. Conversely, Pluck wants to crack a smile, seeing that this businessman is a head shorter than he and his partner.

"No matter," Benjamin says. "Let's just go to the stable and a wagon. Com'on, y'all. We're leaving tonight!"

"But what about the monsters out there?" a saloon girl asks. "It's better to be safe here than to be sorry goin' out there."

"I've heard enough about these stupid superstitions and ghost towns. If any of you are smart like me, you will start leaving Lemonstown for something better." Mr. Benjamin steps down from the porch and approaches the owner of the stable. "Mr. Madison," he takes out his wallet, "here's a hundred and fifty dollars for a wagon and two horses."

The stable owner takes the money. "I'll get a pair of horses drawn to a wagon right now, sir."

As the crew descends the porch, the men descend first before helping the saloon girls safely down the main road. All except for the small ginger whom Pluck recognizes he saved from the fire.

"Anabelle!" Benjamin shouts. "We're all waiting for you."

"Mr. Benjamin…" The saloon girl pauses, appearing fretful. "I decided I don't want to work for you anymore."

"Oh, come on!" her employer whines. "Don't tell me you're just like the rest of these brainwashed nutjobs who believe these stories."

The young woman takes a deep breath. "No, Mr. Benjamin. I'm done taking your orders from you. You've been cutting my pay for far too long, and I'm tired of working for a man who cares very little for his employees. You can go on without me. I'm safer here than being with you."

"You know, she's right," another saloon girl responds. "You've been taking our tips and cutting our salary for months. We have no reason to stay with someone as sleazy as you."

The rest of the female employees cheer her response. Benjamin is already embarrassed that everyone is hearing his secrets while his female workers spew accusations against their employer.

"How is it that the men who work for you not only get higher pay," another voice yells, "but they never had cut pay?"

"You can't deny it, Mr. Benjamin!" a fourth woman yells. "We heard from Bartender Harry that he and the rest of your men never had a problem with the money they're owed. You tell him, Harry!"

The bartender can't find the right words to say. Benjamin gives his bartender the death stare like he's been betrayed.

"What's wrong, Harry?" the same woman asks mockingly. "Are you too much of a coward to admit the truth?"

Mayor McLusky walks on the edge of the porch, looking down at Benjamin. "Funny that you complained earlier about me not using the tax I collect for the better good. Yet, here I am hearing that you're cutting your hardworking employees' pay. And taking their tips?" The mayor gets down on the porch, shaking his head as he approaches him. "That's a new low. If you want to get out of here, then get on. Get! I don't think you've made any friends tonight with how you've insulted this whole town."

The mayor and the businessman exchange intense stares. The mayor can feel Benjamin's rage as he looks down to see his rival clenching his fist and taking a swing at the elected official in the left eye. The crowd gasps over the strike, and the lawmen swiftly move down the porch and grab Benjamin by the wrist.

"Stop, Sheriff," the mayor says, picking himself back up. "Let him go."

The mayor gets up, wipes the dirt off his sleeves, and returns to standing before Benjamin with his swollen eye. Even giving him a free shot when the mayor let his guard down didn't keep the elected official down. Everyone is impressed that the overweight leader could take a punch. The mayor spits on the ground, looking like he wants to hit Benjamin back.

"Well, you got what you've always wanted," the mayor continues. "Too bad you blew any chance of me reimbursing you with a new saloon. I sure hope you have the money to start a new business elsewhere. Now, get the hell out of my town. Don't bother coming back to Lemonstown. I'd hate seeing you return, wishing you had stayed and behaved."

The mayor walks away, and the crowd in his direction makes way for him to bypass. Despite always wanting to get physical with the mayor, Mr. Benjamin knows he lost. Years of waiting for him to do it made him look like the bad guy instead of the other way around. Before Benjamin turns to the opposite direction where the stable is, people in his way are already leaving the main road. The townspeople have had enough of the sleazy businessman, who's been insulted and is ashamed of what he's done.

"Remember, men!" Sheriff Wood shouts as the crowd walks to their houses. "Those under fifty years of age must meet us at the jailhouse at eight o'clock sharp. For the rest of you, curfew begins tonight. Pick up your belongings and move to the sanctuary!"

Benjamin and his men are being escorted by Mr. Madison and the Deputy. Seems, though, that he lost more than half of his crew since all his saloon girls quit. Pluck and Secoli watch the saloon crew make it to the wagon Benjamin paid for. Though the stable owner is old, he still has a way of caring for horses by getting two out of the stable that just woke from their sleep. As he helps attach parts of the wagon to the horse, Pluck turns and notices the same girl he helped carry out of the burning saloon standing in front of him, trying to come up with the words to say to him.

"Mister—I mean, Inspector Pluck," Anabelle says while playing with her hair, "it was a mighty brave thing you did to rescue me from the fire. I never got a chance to thank you for what you did for Bianca and me when we were... you know, trapped up there."

Pluck sees the ginger is only as tall as his chest level and looks like she's half his age. Her diamond-shaped face and blue eyes weren't noticeable when they both were covered in smoke. Now, in a better circumstance, he can't help but be attracted to how Anabelle presents herself. Only a sleazy employer would make her dress in high heels, a tight bodice, and a skirt that only covers one leg and exposes the other.

However, seeing how the young lady dresses reminds him of his daughters trying on their mother's dress, which Clara only wears whenever she gets romantic with him. This instantly makes him lose interest and focus on her as a person.

"I'm always trying my best to do a great service for everyone, ma'am," Pluck responds. His accent can't be any more non-Western if he tried. "If you ever need any help, just let me or my partner know, and we'll gladly help out any way we can. Now get your things and head to the Town Hall. It's curfew."

"But inspector," a female voice is heard behind Pluck, "the saloon was our home. It was where we worked and slept."

"You mean to tell me Mr. Benjamin never let you girls leave that place?" The two women shake their heads. The rest of the former saloon girls approach the inspector for guidance. Pluck takes off his Boston felt hat and scratches his hair.

Pluck puts his hat back on and says, "You ladies deserve to be treated much better than how that dirtbag treated you. I'll see to it that you get shelter and your own rooms in the hotel."

"Aren't we supposed to live in the Town Hall during curfew?" a lady asks. "Who's going to pay for our hotel rooms, Inspector?" another saloon girl asks.

"Well, the mayor said business hours are closed," Pluck answers, "so I'll make sure that the hotel owner will give you seven ladies the space you need to be protected like everyone else in town. If he still expects payment for your stay, I'll assure him that the government will reimburse the hotel owners for your stay as long as you need it."

The seven ladies gasp and scream with joy. This makes Pluck smile, knowing he's done a good deed. The ladies' reaction reminds him of how his daughters have the same reaction whenever he makes it back home from a long absence—which only makes the postal inspector more homesick.

"Thank you, Inspector!" Anabelle cries. "You're like an angel that God sent for us. How can we ever repay you?"

"No need to," Pluck responds. "Just do me a favor and be safe during curfew. Lemonstown needs you all more than you can realize. Now go check yourselves in, and have a good night's sleep."

The ladies run straight to the hotel, giggling as they make their way through the door like they never had a gentleman spoil them. Pluck then sighs, both happy to do them a favor and sad about how much he's missing family. It's the feeling he gets whenever he communicates with any woman half his age. Most of his contemporaries would go after innocent ladies, but Pluck remembers his commitments. However, despite his commitments, the married postal inspector gets tempted, especially since he's repeatedly away from his wife.

As the ladies enter, the postal inspectors see Mr. Benjamin and his men are two buildings down the same side of the main road. From where they stand, they can see what's left of the crew set off. Despite how dark it is outside, the stable's only lantern still shows everything going on over there. Another lantern is lit from inside the wagon, showing light through the cover.

"Are they really going to leave when it's pitch-black outside?" Pluck asks. "Mr. Benjamin must either really hate McLusky's guts that much," Secoli responds, "or he's that stupid."

Neither of the postal inspectors wants to stop the crew from leaving this late, still insulted by Mr. Benjamin's transgression. The businessman is adamant about leaving despite the dangers of driving through the dark desert. The stable owner gives the driver a thumbs-up and the wagon storms into the desert. Despite how far they drive east into Rawlins' direction, the lantern's light seen through the wagon's covers is the brightest thing in the darkness.

Mr. Madison disappears into his stable. Pluck and Secoli turn around to see that everyone but the two lawmen are in the Town Hall. The deputy approaches the postal inspectors from the south side of the main road and the sheriff on the opposite.

"Well, gentlemen," Sheriff Wood says, "it's late, so we'd better get some sleep to start guard duty tomorrow."

"Don't worry about me, Sheriff," Pluck responds. "I took a nap this morning, so I can stay up a little longer in pulling security."

"I appreciate the help, Inspector, but I can't afford to have you pull guard duty all by yourself. You need someone to pull guard with you tonight."

"I don't think it's necessary. Everyone is exhausted from everything today, and it would be inconsiderate of me to take up any more of someone else's time when they would be better off getting some sleep."

"Actually, I'll volunteer to pull guard with my partner tonight," Secoli says, making Pluck turn around with a look of disapproval. "I agree with Sheriff Wood. You can't be on watch all by yourself, Jed. You need someone to have your back in case something goes wrong."

"Louie," Pluck counters, "you've been up all day. These people need at least one postal inspector in charge to be fully awake tomorrow."

"Well, since you're volunteering," the sheriff replies, "I think both postal inspectors can sleep in the morning. The people here don't know you two very well, so they'll listen to me. I'll take charge for tomorrow till you two wake up. We'll keep these street lanterns lit for you two to see. If you need an extra lantern, oil, or any other tool, don't hesitate to pick one up at the trading post. Have a good night, Inspectors."

Wood and Hall give the postal inspectors a hat tip and head home. Pluck and Secoli remain silent as they watch the lawmen enter the alley between the hotel and the bank. Pluck is already feeling a little uneasy being alone with his partner. A part of him feels a little regret over how passive-aggressive he was to Secoli in their last interaction. Since waking from his nap, Pluck can feel that his partner holds a little resentment toward him.

THE CANDLELIGHT IN the street lanterns has died out, leaving the only light in the pitch-black Lemonstown coming from the two lanterns the postal inspectors carry. Their tension toward each other has them pulling security separately. Secoli regrets volunteering to guard the town tonight since he's feeling dozy. Secoli's tired mind isn't making him think straight as he wants to know the time.

While having his hands full, he puts down his lamp and takes out his pocket watch while still holding his birdcage with his left hand.

"Damn," Secoli says. "It's only been two hours since I started guarding this place."

He puts his pocket watch away and then turns his attention to the bird in the cage.

Chap is sleeping in a unique position, standing on the base's wire grille with his head turned almost 180 degrees and his head resting between his feathery back and the back of his wing. Even though the bird is off the cage's swing and sleeping on a steadier bottom bar, the postal inspector realizes he's been moving the cage all night, not giving the little bird a chance to sleep well.

Already exhausted, Secoli places the birdcage and lantern on the Town Hall porch.

He watches Chap for a while to see that the budgie no longer opens its eyes and can finally slumber. This comforting sight is putting Secoli to sleep. However, that doesn't last long as he feels his body lose balance, which makes him open his eyes again. Immediately, he places his foot where he's about to collapse, finding that he's falling asleep while standing.

The exhausted postal inspector can't take any more of it, submitting to taking a seat on the porch next to his birdcage. He crosses his arms and stares at whatever the lantern's light touches. The night's cool breeze gives him even more comfort, having Secoli doze off, hoping to end this incredibly long day. This moment of peace inevitably ends once he hears his partner's voice.

"You should go to your hotel room and get some sleep, Louie."

Secoli gasps as Pluck's voice awakens him. Pluck gets down from the porch and stands in front of him.

"I won't deny it," Secoli says nervously. "I've been up all day, keeping the mayor informed and answering as many questions to the locals as possible."

"Which is an even better reason for me to be the only one on watch."

"I can't let you be by yourself, Jed."

"I appreciate your concern, Louie, but like you said when I got hurt in Cheyenne, what good is this mission if neither of us isn't being taken care of?"

"True..." Secoli pauses, making Pluck eager to hear what he has to say. The uncomfortable silence grows, making Pluck impatient.

"Well, Louie," Pluck changes his tone, "you have something you want to say?"

"You know, I don't get it, Jed," Secoli says aggressively. "You're very inconsistent in acting professionally, and other times, you're having too much fun with this job. And times like now and this morning, you're acting like a different person."

"And your point is?"

"My point is, you're not really cooperating as a partner, and it's...getting difficult for me to carry out this case."

"Difficult for you, is it? Gee, I can't believe you're oblivious to how much I had to carry both of us, and you have the audacity to complain about my so-called lack of professionalism."

"And you call that professional when you rudely walk away to your hotel room to sleep on the job? You left me to carry the rest of the weight by handling the worries of everyone in town. Even when I need you the most, I let you sleep till the sunset."

Pluck sighs before saying, "You know, Louie, I've tried my very best not to worry about you and your bird since we had that conversation when we left Boston."

"So you're blaming Chap for your problems? So, you do have a problem with me carrying him wherever I go. Is that it?"

"I don't mind you carrying your parakeet wherever we go. But my worrying about that bird has gotten in the way of this case."

Secoli gets up from the porch. "Really? How so?"

Pluck reacts strongly to his question by pointing his finger before saying, "Haven't you been paying attention, Louie? Look at what happened today. You've put both our lives in danger by putting that bird in a dangerous position. Haven't you noticed that whenever you've left Chap, you've almost gotten killed by having to go back and rescue him? Twice this morning! Not to mention that you left me at the saloon when I had to rescue the girls and the conductor."

"Now, wait a minute," Secoli intervenes. "I have an excuse for that. When you entered the saloon, fire blocked my path, and I couldn't get inside."

"Okay. But why didn't you hold on to the ladder when the conductor climbed down? Because you were distracted, he fell and landed on the saloon's porch. Now, the poor man is still unconscious and may never walk again."

Secoli looks away, offended by Pluck's criticism.

"Like I said," Pluck continues, "it's twice that you put that poor bird in danger today. And both of those times were because you'd rather take the chance to save those guns instead of keeping yourself or that poor animal safe. You haven't been doing me any favors by bringing your pet to places it shouldn't be."

"Hey, Chap is no pet! He's..." Secoli struggles to find the right words.

"Go on. I'm listening."

"Chap is my emotional support."

"Emotional support?" Pluck laughs mockingly. "You? A Federal agent needing emotional support from an animal? How did someone like you get qualified to be a postal inspector?"

"You shut up!" Secoli raises his voice. "The poor bird has nothing to do with this."

"Wrong! You brought this bird, and it's both slowing us down and putting us in danger. What happens if we face this feathered beast out there where you have a gun and I'm being attacked? Will you pull the trigger and save me, or will you run to your bird because the beast is too frightening for you to emotionally handle?"

"Do you really think that poorly of me? Do you really think I won't save you if you're ever in danger?"

"Well, you haven't proven to me that you can stand on your own without that bird."

"I...I..." Secoli stutters. "I can. Give me credit. I was able to get almost everything out of the baggage car and help provide the weapons needed to give this town a fighting chance against this unforeseen threat."

"Really?" Pluck lowers his voice. "Well, let's put that to the test."

Pluck walks around his partner and picks up the birdcage. Chap wakes up from the cage being moved. Realizing that Pluck is carrying its cage, the budgerigar chirps out of fear.

"Just what are you doing to Chap?"

Pluck turns to his partner. "Nothing. I'm just going to just go in front of the stable and hold on to this birdcage. Don't worry. I won't harm your bird or do anything funny with him. I just want to see how you can handle yourself without this bird. I'm giving you two minutes to stand on your own without this bird. I want to see if you can handle yourself without bringing your muse everywhere you go. If not—" Pluck walks down the main road, shaking his head, "—I don't know what to say."

Secoli can see Pluck holding his lantern with his right hand and carrying the birdcage by the ring with his left. The lantern's light helps him see his partner walk past the Town Hall and to the next building, where the stable is. As he walks down, Chap can still be heard chirping. Already, Secoli's heart starts beating faster. Pluck stops and turns around, facing his partner.

"Your time begins..." Pluck raises his voice loud enough for his partner to hear. "...now."

Pluck then opens his lantern's door and blows out the candle inside. Secoli can't see his partner or the birdcage despite still hearing Chap chirping with fright. The parakeet, too, is having separation anxiety.

"Okay," Secoli mutters. "Just two minutes—that won't be a problem."

Secoli finds himself overestimating his capabilities. Hearing his budgerigar making distressed noises urges him to run after his troubled muse. His heart is beating faster, making him tremble where he stands.

It's completely dark, his lantern on the Town Hall porch being his only light source. It hasn't reached a minute yet, and Secoli is already breaking a sweat.

Secoli turns around, hearing a cannon fire. The distressed postal inspector can no longer hear Chap in front of him as he sees himself in a familiar place on a grassy field, with men screaming at the top of their lungs. He looks down to see fallen men wearing Union uniforms lying motionless. When he picks his head back up, the screaming of hundreds of men gets louder. Coming out of the darkness, Secoli sees Confederate soldiers running toward him, all holding rifles and the Southern flag. This post-traumatic episode has made the distressed postal inspector lose his balance.

Landing on the porch makes Secoli come back to reality. The screaming is no longer heard, and the soldiers he just saw have disappeared. The troubled agent hears Chap again. Unable to bear it any longer, Secoli grabs the lantern from the porch. He runs toward the darkness in Chap and Pluck's direction like his life depends on it.

Suddenly, Secoli hits his boot on a rock, causing him to slip and fall to the ground. He drops his lantern, almost putting out the candle inside. While it still has a flame lit, Secoli crawls toward the lantern while it has light. He picks up his lamp and stands up. Before he continues to run in the same direction, he sees the light from behind him.

Secoli realizes that he ran past Pluck, who remained still the whole time.

Pluck walks up to his partner and passes the birdcage to him. Instantaneously, Secoli grabs the cage and hugs it. Pluck can see his partner take a knee as he weeps while wrapping his arms around the bars. Chap stops making those noises and hangs on the bar where Secoli presses his face onto it, and the bird rubs its head against his owner's cheek.

Pluck stands watching, seeing how much the animal and his master cling to each other. Never before has he seen a bird capable of loving a human as if it were a dog. Pluck feels guilty that he tormented his partner when his intent was to carry out a simple test. A feeling of despair is hindering his ability to perform his job.

Pluck says, "I'm sorry, Louie..." before walking away, unable to look at Secoli, disappointed over being paired up with a non-ideal partner. Secoli doesn't bother looking at Pluck or saying anything to him. The test is overwhelming, and he's too exhausted to continue arguing. He picks up his lamp to help find his way back to the hotel on the first floor. Secoli doesn't bother to change or get under the blankets, as he's so desperate to end this long day and rests up for the next one to come.

WAKING UP TO THE SOUND of gunfire is not the way anyone wants to start their day. Secoli had an episode last night, and hearing actual gunfire makes him relive the Civil War again. The first fire round makes the traumatized agent bolt out of bed, landing on the wooden floor and crawling under the bed for safety. Chap, who's also rudely awakened, chirps from the noise while trapped in his cage on top of the nightstand.

Coming to his senses, Secoli crawls out and grabs the birdcage, taking it with him under the bed. While in his cage, the parakeet is confused as to why the noise is happening and why his owner is underneath the mattress with his face on the floor.

Seconds go by, and the traumatized agent anticipates more gunfire. He listens closely for another gunshot or footsteps approaching his hotel room door. It surprises Secoli to hear people walking slowly and steadily down the first-floor hallway and to hear their voices speaking at a normal volume. This makes him pick his head off the floor and wonder why no one is panicking like him. The inspector ducks again and covers his head with the birdcage as another round of gunfire rings out.

Upon the second round of gunfire, Secoli hears the sheriff shouting outside and then remembers firing practice is scheduled this morning. Secoli raises his head again to see his pocket watch on the floor next to the nightstand. Wanting to know the time, he grabs it and sees it's three past eight. The postal inspector sighs with relief to know that there isn't a battle going on. A chap can sense his master calming down, making the parakeet stop tweeting.

Secoli gets out from underneath his bed and leans against the wall while he sits on the floor. He's hugging his birdcage while catching his breath to treat his panic attack. The third and fourth shots are fired, but those don't faze either the owner or his bird.

Thankfully, no one has seen Secoli having an episode except Pluck last night. It would have made him look bad in front of the townspeople, who are entrusting him with their lives. The thought leads to thinking about what Pluck said and put him through last night.

Secoli's heart races again as he grows angry, thinking about what Pluck did to him.

He disapproves of his partner's stance on bringing Chap with him, yet it's hard to disagree with what Pluck said about the many times Chap was in danger. What Pluck said plays over and over in Secoli's mind, angering him over being criticized and questioned for having Chap with him. Finally, he opens his eyes and looks at Chap.

The birdcage is on his lap, with the budgerigar standing on its swing. Seeing how adorable and innocent Chap is makes it hard for him to resist. Thinking again about what Pluck said about how Chap almost got killed twice yesterday reminds him of the previous cases where Chap was in grave danger. Somewhere in Secoli's mind, he thinks he might have to let go of his muse. But if it comes to that, how will he mentally cope?

Another sound of gunfire startles Secoli again, nearly knocking the birdcage off his lap. It doesn't bring him back to having an episode, but it makes him sigh and lean his head against the wall. Secoli takes a deep breath to pick himself off the floor. As he stands up, Secoli sees a mirror in front of him and realizes that he is still wearing the clothes he had worn the day before. Remembering what the locals smelled like, he thinks it's okay to wear the same clothes for another day.

After fixing his hair with his saliva and putting on his brown homburg hat, Secoli heads out of his hotel room with his birdcage. One of the girls who used to be in the saloon crew walks past his hotel room as he opens the door, heading up the stairs. He walks past his partner's hotel room, that's next to his, thinking that he's finally asleep. No one is in the small lobby as he exits through the front door.

Secoli turns left to the jailhouse, where the sheriff teaches twenty-eight men how to fire a gun properly in the open desert. Already, he's lecturing a young man on how to wield a Mannlicher M1890 Carbine but stops the lawman when he sees Secoli approaching. Everyone else aims their rifles down.

"Ah, Inspector," Sheriff Wood says. "Shouldn't you be resting after pulling guard last night?"

"I think you're confusing me with Jed," the postal inspector responds. "Inspector Pluck gave me an early night, and he's asleep now."

"Actually, he went to Rock Springs with my deputy."

"He what?" Secoli raises his voice. "Why in the world would he do that?"

"He told us you pulled guard duty, and he went to sleep. The mayor asked

him to go and see the town down west and warn everyone there."

"Oh, no," Secoli responds with a worried tone. "But what about the danger he's in? Sheriff, I've got to get a horse and go after him."

"Don't worry, Inspector. Rock Springs is only forty minutes away by foot and twenty by horse. He should be back any minute now."

"When did he leave?"

"Around six in the morning, when the mayor gave him the order."

"Damn it!" Secoli swears. "Do you realize how much danger Jed and your deputy are in? You sent my partner off on a dangerous search without telling me. How do you expect me to help you protect Lemonstown if everything is done without my consent?"

Sheriff Wood doesn't have an answer for him. He looks away as the Federal agent frowns upon him. In this direction, he turns his head and sees someone approaching. Secoli notices the sheriff's expression change. The mayor crosses the street. Though his black eye is darker and more swollen than last night, McLusky looks jolly.

"Inspector Secoli!" McLusky calls. "A fine morning we're having, aren't we?"

"Mayor." The postal inspector lowers his aggressive voice. "Did you send my partner out to Rock Springs without me?"

"Of course," he answers, unfazed by his strong reaction. "We needed to—"

"You, of all people, should know that it's dangerous out there!" Secoli interrupts. "No postal inspector has ever died in their line of duty, and if anything happens to him, I'll see to it that you're removed from your position as Lemonstown's elected official. Now fetch me a horse so I can go after him."

"I'm sorry, Inspector, but I cannot allow you to go out on your own. Like you said, it's too dangerous to be out there."

"So it's okay for Inspector Pluck and the deputy to leave, but I can't?"

The postal inspector walks around the mayor and heads directly to the stable across the road. He keeps his birdcage steady on his chest as he picks up the pace, knowing the mayor and sheriff are chasing after him.

"Inspector," the mayor shouts, "I beg you to stop this instant!"

Secoli stops immediately. He doesn't do it to obey the mayor. Instead, he sees something black in the distance that pops out from the orange desert.

"Geez," the mayor continues, getting right behind Secoli. "For once, someone is listening. Look, I understand how you're feeling ri—"

Secoli shushes the mayor. Both the mayor and sheriff look in the direction Secoli is facing, now noticing black figures coming in their direction. Two of them, in fact.

Immediately the lawman and the Federal agent place their hands on their pistols in their holsters. Mayor McLusky sees what they both are doing and immediately moves behind Sheriff Wood for protection.

"Sheriff," Secoli says, "can I borrow your binoculars?" There is no answer from the sheriff.

The postal inspector turns to the lawman and sees he's already using his binoculars before Secoli asks for them. "What do you see, Sheriff?"

"I can't make it out since it's still far," the sheriff says, "but I think I'm seeing Deputy Hall and Inspector Pluck heading in this direction."

Wood hands the binoculars to Secoli. Through the lens, Secoli can almost tell it's exactly what the sheriff described. Who else wears a brown Boston felt hat in the West or has the same outfit as the sheriff? Both of them appear dark because they ride on non-fading black horses. He's relieved that not only is his partner returning safely, but also there isn't a dark beast approaching Lemonstown, as they feared.

"It's them," Secoli unenthusiastically says.

Secoli hands the sheriff back his binoculars and walks in the direction where Pluck and Hall are. While traversing through the sands, Secoli moves his birdcage on his shady side to shelter Chap from the scorching sun.

"Inspector!" the mayor shouts.

"Y'all stay put!" the sheriff shouts at his firing trainees. "We'll be back. And don't any of you dare pull that trigger until I come back, ya hear!"

The mayor and sheriff run after Inspector Secoli. Despite appearing flat, the Red Desert's sand is uneven. Secoli has difficulty moving at a normal pace as his shoes go through the sand with every step. Secoli perseveres in his pursuit of Pluck and the deputy despite the desert's inhospitable terrain. McLusky and Wood, however, catch up with Secoli, used to walking in these sands.

"Inspector!" the mayor shouts. "What do you think you're doing?"

"I'm going to have a word with my partner," he answers without looking at them. "Please don't do what I think you're going to do."

"Do what?" Secoli looks back in annoyance.

"Now, Inspector Secoli, I know you're upset with Inspector Pluck, but it's stupid of me to be convinced to allow him to go off like this. But I want both of you to act civilized. We already had one act of violence last night, and I won't stand having any more of it."

Secoli gets interrupted by stepping on deep sand. "Damn this desert," he mutters, pulling his foot out of the deep spot and continuing walking. "Do you think someone like me, who worries about my partner's safety, would dare harm him?"

It doesn't take long for the three to start seeing Pluck and Deputy Hall. As they draw nearer, they can see that Inspector Pluck and the deputy are covered in dust from the desert. As they all get several feet away from each other, Pluck and Hall get off their horses, and Secoli stands before his partner.

"You've got a lot of nerve leaving Lemonstown without me," Secoli says. "Good God, Jed. Your eyes are red. You didn't get any sleep at all, did you?"

"Nope," Pluck says calmly as he brushes off his shoulders and sleeves. "Don't you think it's unwise of you to go to Rock Springs without me tagging along? How can I be your partner if you keep leaving me out and making me worry about you?"

"After what you went through last night, I thought you needed a good sleep."

"The least you could do is wait for me. What would have happened if you'd gotten killed there?"

"Good thing that didn't happen. And speaking of killing, we got some bad news."

"It's really bad, Sheriff and Mr. Mayor," the deputy pipes in. "Everything about those other towns being ghost towns...I-I couldn't believe my eyes."

"Oh, no," Secoli responds. "Not Rock Springs, as well. Have you found anyone left behind?"

"Nope. No one. It's another ghost town filled with feathers." Pluck angrily throws his hat on the ground. "Damn it. It seems this demon went past Lemonstown and headed farther west. It's too late to save everyone else in this godforsaken state. All we've got is Lemonstown."

"No. Say it ain't so," says the mayor shakily.

"It is so," Pluck picks up his hat and brushes the sand off.

"He's...he's telling the truth, Mr. Mayor," the deputy responds. "Rock Springs ain't like it used to be. It was so eerie, and feathers were everywhere. The whole place smelled way worse than the smell of the feather these two brought in yesterday. And even worse, there's blood and destroyed buildings all over Rock Springs."

"Oh, Lord." McLusky hopelessly falls on his knees to the sand. "You gotta be kidding me."

Pluck takes a wrapped paper from his jacket pocket and hands it to the mayor.

McLusky gets up and wastes no time unwrapping it. Inspector Pluck and Deputy Hall hold their noses, anticipating what will happen. There are many layers of paper, but he eventually opens them to show what's inside. Several black ten-inch-long razor-sharp feathers fall and land on the sand in front of McLusky.

The new evidence is fresh, and the odor smells much worse than the other evidence in the mayor's office. McLusky, Wood, and Secoli hold their noses. Even Chap, inside its birdcage, chitters over how unpleasant the smell is. Unable to bear it anymore, the mayor buries the evidence with his foot in the sand.

"Jesus…," the mayor mutters. "And it's a miracle that we—figuratively— dodged that bullet."

"Now, what are we going to do?" the sheriff asks.

"Were you able to find a telegraph office in Rock Springs, Jed?" Secoli asks.

"Don't forget, the end of the telephone line is in Rawlins, the opposite direction," Pluck replies. "Since neither Rock Springs nor Lemonstown has a telegraph or telephone line, the only way to contact anyone is if we go east back to Rawlins."

"Then we have no other choice," the mayor says. "We must head to Rawlins and tell everyone that Rock Springs is a ghost town, and we need military support at once."

"Oh, for pity's sake, Mr. Mayor." Pluck raises his voice. "I pulled the night's watch last night and just came back from Rock Springs. At least let me get some rest before I carry out another—"

The conversation halts when the five hear a single gunshot echoing through the Red Desert. All of them react by turning in that direction.

"Jesus Christ," Sheriff Wood says. "I told those idiots not to pull the trigger until I got back. Excuse me, Inspector Pluck. I'm going to have to ride your horse to see what's going on. You're coming with me, Hall."

The sheriff and his deputy get on the black horses and hurry back to Lemonstown. Worrying about what just happened, the mayor and the postal inspectors go after them on foot. Knowing how to walk through the soft sands, the mayor walks faster than the two Federal agents struggling to bypass. Secoli switches hands to hold his birdcage to shelter

Chap in his shadow. The postal inspectors finally make it to harder ground and can run in the direction where gunfire is heard. Near the jailhouse, the men circle around the sheriff and the shot victim. All of them surround a middle-aged man. Everyone sees the bullet wound on his chest when they open his coat, with his shirt covered in blood. The deputy runs to the sheriff with a leather medical bag and opens it to find the right tools.

"Talk to me, Mr. Humphrey," the sheriff says. "You're doing great. Just keep breathing, and let us do the rest."

The fallen victim is breathing heavily, looking dazed and confused. Father Jenkins puts his rifle down and begins praying over the injured man. The preacher speaks in tongues to cry out to God for mercy while the deputy takes out a pair of forceps and attempts to take out the bullet. Realizing Hall is using the wrong tool, Pluck intervenes.

"No, Hall," he says. "That's not the right one. It's the other one that you pulled out. Here. Let me take the bullet out. Once I take the bullet out, you put that cloth on the wound, and we should immediately wrap a bandage around his chest. You got it?"

The gruesome sight makes Secoli look away. His Civil War experiences are being recalled for the third time since last night. Secoli walks away without anyone noticing. His surroundings drastically change from standing in the open desert to being trapped in a medical tent. Everywhere he turns are wounded and fallen Union soldiers on stretchers and tables.

This post-traumatic stress feels much more real than the last two incidents and is getting to Secoli. His shortness of breath becomes more apparent. He starts hearing screams that are all too familiar to him, which worsens his panic, making him hug the birdcage for dear life. Trapped in its birdcage, Chap chirps as he can feel the cage bending. Secoli's overactive imagination subsides when he hears Chap chirping.

The budgerigar's pleasant sound immediately makes the tent, stretchers, and screaming soldiers disappear. Secoli realizes it is all in his head, and everyone is still watching his partner remove the bullet. Everything becomes quiet. Even the preacher has stopped his prayers.

Secoli turns to the wounded man to see Pluck put a towel over his head. Everyone watching takes off their hats and mourns over Mr. Humphrey. Pluck takes off his Boston felt hat to show his respect. Realizing what's going on, Secoli does the same. The sheriff gently places Humphrey's head on the ground, taking off his black cowboy hat while still kneeling.

No one says a word for a good long while. Not even Father Jenkins can pray while in shock and grief. The only thing everyone hears is the wind blowing and Chap's chirruping out of confusion over the silence. Despite Pluck and Secoli never knowing the man, they join the mourning to represent themselves as compassionate authority figures. The sheriff gets up and turns.

"Didn't I tell you not to mess with your rifles till I get back?" the sheriff asks quietly but furiously. "So, who was the one that pulled the trigger?"

The men look around and then move away to reveal the shooter. Everyone remains silent and glares at the shooter. He appears to be in his twenties, has curly blond hair, and has no facial hair. The kid's eyes are so watery that he could start crying at any second. He's holding his rifle by the barrel with both hands and quivers as Sheriff Wood approaches him.

"Jeremy Payton?" Sheriff Wood says.

"It…" The young man struggles to come up with something to say. "It… was an accident, Sheriff. Really. I swear."

"Even if it was, boy," the sheriff responds calmly yet intimidatingly, "you murdered Mr. Humphrey."

"Oh, God," the young man cries.

The deputy snags the kid's rifle off his hands. The sheriff pulls out his handcuffs and cuffs the boy's wrists. He and his deputy pull the kid directly to the jailhouse next to them. Over and over again, Jeremy keeps crying, "I'm sorry," as he's being taken away.

"I don't want to do this anymore," a man still holding his rifle says. "I'm too damn scared to hold a gun."

He drops his rifle, and immediately, the gun fires. Everyone backs away from the rifle, trying to avoid another accident. Thankfully, the rifle is pointed toward the desert, where no one is in the way of getting hit. The sheriff steps out of the jailhouse.

"Who the hell fired that rifle?" the sheriff shouts. "Is anyone hurt?"

"It was me, Sheriff," the man anxiously admits. "I just put my gun down, and it fired."

"No one is hurt, Sheriff," Pluck answers. "It went off when he dropped the rifle."

"Caleb Walsh." Sheriff Wood picks up the rifle. "You shouldn't throw your gun down like that. Do you know what the postal inspectors went through in risking their lives to save these rifles? You could have wound up in the same jail cell with Jeremy."

"Oh, please, Sheriff," Caleb Walsh cries. "I don't want to be a guard. Knowing I could accidentally kill someone..." He drops to his knees and pleads. "Please, Sheriff. I've never held a gun in my entire life, and today was way too much for me. It's too loud. I can't shoot straight. I'm shaking when I hold that rifle. Can't you please let me off—"

"No exceptions," the sheriff interrupts and turns to everyone. "Now you all know Lemonstown is in grave danger. We're down by two men, and we haven't had this monster arrive in town yet. Now that's embarrassing. Deputy Hall and Inspector Pluck just returned from Rock Springs, and it is now..." He pauses, knowing he's about to bring everyone the unfortunate news. "...a ghost town."

All the men gasp and look at one another.

"Now then," the sheriff continues. "The fact that this...threat skipped past Lemonstown is nothing but a sheer miracle. But there's no guarantee they won't come back and finish what's left undone. All these towns in Wyoming are being slaughtered and having their citizens taken away because they were unprepared."

He pauses to temper his aggressive tone. "But we're prepared. It's alright if you feel scared. It's all right to feel like you're unfit to wield a gun. I'm surprised many of you call yourself Americans and have never shot a gun. That is impressive, if you ask me. But that's all right. At least you all know you're holding a dangerous weapon and care about being alive. At least y'all are smart about that."

"Now let me teach you all how to shoot like true Americans so we can fight off this devil that dares to take this town. I need four men..." The sheriff looks at Caleb. "...except for you, who can help me take Mr. Humphrey to the Town Hall. The rest of you, pick up your rifles and follow my direction." The men grab their rifles and return to line formation, facing the open desert. Before anyone approaches to carry Mr. Humphrey, the postal inspectors and Mayor McLusky are already taking the dead body to the stables next to the Town Hall. The trio considers taking him to the Town Hall, but they decide against it because they don't want to disturb the peace as everyone is sharing the same space. Secoli, while lifting the legs, is also carrying his birdcage by the ring with his left index finger. Mr. Humphrey is a bit overweight, making it difficult for the three to carry him across the main road.

Then Father Jenkins joins in, helping them carry the dead man to the stables. The four settle him down on a haystack next to the door but away from the horses. They all take a moment to mourn in silence.

"Did you get to know him, Mr. Mayor?" Secoli asks.

"Of course," the mayor answers. "This is a small town, so I had to get to know everyone in my town. Mr. Humphrey," McLusky sighs, "is one of my best friends in this town."

"I'm so sorry. What does he..." Pluck pauses to correct himself. "I mean, what did he do in this town?"

"He ran the hardware stone next to the jailhouse."

"I've been meaning to ask," Pluck says, "that hardware store also sells mining supplies—said so on the store's sign. Why does anyone need mining supplies in the middle of the Red Desert?"

"When we used to have trains coming to Lemonstown, we had miners stop by our town to have a good time in the saloon and get supplies. Many come to Wyoming to get a taste of that goldmine and try to become rich. In return, their search for gold and gemstones is what's used to help this town economically. Besides the saloon, of course."

"Interesting. I never knew Wyoming was famous for mining. My partner and I have never been to this state, so my apologies for asking stupid questions."

"It's not a stupid question at all. We're glad to have that store helping Lemonstown economically. Mr. Humphrey..." The mayor starts choking up. "Do you need space, Mr. Mayor?" Secoli asks as he puts a hand on the mayor's shoulder.

"Yes." McLusky nods and sobs. "I don't know how to tell his wife, Martha, about this."

"Can I get you something to drink?" Secoli asks. "Anything to make you feel better?"

"No." The mayor sniffs. "Please leave me with him."

"Yes, Mr. Mayor."

"Not you, Father." The mayor stops Jenkins as he faces the exit with the postal inspector. "Can you give this man a prayer for me?"

"I will, sir," the preacher responds, returning to where he was.

The postal inspectors can hear the preacher pray as they leave the stables. Neither knows the man, so they leave the mayor and preacher to mourn. They exit the stables and see the men in line, pointing and firing their rifles at the empty desert.

"Damn," Pluck swears. "The bad news just won't stop coming, Louie. Since yesterday, things have been getting worse."

"Jed," Secoli says, "you should get some sleep. You've already pulled guard, ran off to Rock Springs and back, and tried to save that man's life. You're only killing yourself by staying up longer."

Pluck sighs before saying, "You're right. How did you sleep last night?"

"Like hell. I just want to go back to bed."

"At this point, I could sleep through the gunfire happening right now." The postal inspectors head back to the hotel. Both of them are too exhausted to say anything along the way. When Secoli returns to his hotel room, he feeds Chap with birdseed and pets him before crashing to bed. Despite hearing gunfire outside, the traumatized agent is able to sleep through it and put his worrying mind at ease.

CHAPTER 5

"Rawlins <stop>," Secoli telegraphs. "Postal inspectors still alive and return to Rawlins to telegraph <stop> Lemonstown is alive <stop> However, Rock Springs is now a ghost town <stop> No one left alive <stop> Urgent request <stop> Lemonstown in grave danger <stop> Please help <stop>."

Secoli finishes his Morse code on the telegraph machine and pulls out a blank cardstock paper and a pen. Secoli still listens carefully for any beep to be heard from his headset. With a pen in his dominant hand, the postal inspector prepares to transcribe the incoming message. Eager to start writing, he's already making small scribbles on the top-right edge of the paper. The postal inspector then scribbles on the bottom-right and left of the paper's corners.

Secoli places the pen on the center of the card, hearing what he thinks is an incoming signal. He immediately stops when he realizes it's his imagination. He then takes a deep breath, already disappointed at hearing nothing.

The postal inspector then looks at the edges of the cardstock, noticing there's no room to write words on the paper. He finds himself losing self-control over being impatient again. He pulls another card from the desk's drawer but doesn't throw the old one away. He scribbles on every area of the old card to prevent himself from wasting another piece of paper, going autopilot again, and waiting impatiently for any beeps from his headset.

Minutes go by, and the written paper is entirely filled with ink. There is barely any white spacing on the old card. Secoli stops when he realizes he's wasting the pen's ink. Secoli then pulls out his pocket watch. The time is twenty-five past seven in the evening.

"Geez," Secoli says. "It's almost been a half-hour since we came back to Rawlins.

And it's been twenty since I sent the message. Why isn't anyone answering?" He looks over his shoulders and sees the sun coming down through the windows. He raises his head to see over the counter. The feathers outside aren't as black as when he first came to Rawlins two days ago. Earlier, Secoli and Pluck saw the feathers left in Rawlins were dirty from the dust from being blown outside for so long.

Secoli then turns to his birdcage. He sees Chap sleeping peacefully at the base. This is the first time he sees Chap in his sleeping position at this time of day; it's usually sundown when the bird starts getting tired. The postal inspector thinks his parakeet has the same disjointed sleeping schedule and leaves him alone. Louie then grabs his pen and places it on the blank cardstock paper. Again, he realizes the beeping is his imagination again. The headset remains quiet. "God," Secoli mutters. "The wait is killing me. Has anyone received my message?"

Secoli checks the receiver in front of him. Seeing the machine's indicator still rolling and marking his message shows there's still enough battery power on the machine, and the ink hasn't dried up yet. Secoli then looks at the amount of paper tape rolled out of the reel and piled onto the floor. Judging how slowly the reel moves the paper out of the receiver and seeing the paper tape on the floor shows how long he's been waiting.

Seeing that the reel is running out of paper, he removes it from the receiver. He reverse-rolls the reel by hand to pull the paper tape back in. When he sees the inked portion with dots and dashes, he stops rolling and rips the paper off. The postal inspector places his inked Morse code on the desk and puts the reel back on the receiver. The reel continues to move slowly.

Losing all patience, Secoli uses the telegraph and sends out the same message. Resending the message takes a while, as do all Morse codes. When he finishes resending the message, Secoli takes out his pocket watch to see it's fifteen till eight.

As he stares at his watch, seconds feel longer than they usually do. Having the headset tightly on his ears makes him hear every breath he takes. Secoli has had enough of waiting. The postal inspector removes his headset, puts on his brown homburg hat, and heads out the door.

He turns around the building and looks at the telegraph line attached to the rooftop. Secoli sees that it looks perfectly normal. Then he moves his eyes to where the telegraph poles lead, from the train station and following the railroad on the side. The postal inspector sees a gap between the two telegraph poles not too far from the train station docks.

Secoli says to himself, "That wasn't there before. Who cut the line?"

"Louie." Pluck's voice is heard from the opposite direction.

Secoli turns and sees his partner walking down the main road. Pluck isn't wearing a handkerchief covering his nose and mouth like last time. He's holding the reins of two brown horses pulling a wagon. Those horses weren't the ones the postal inspector rode to Rawlins, as their non-fading black horses were strapped to the telegraph office's hitching rail. As Secoli looks behind Pluck and the brown horses, he sees the wagon's roof cover torn apart.

"What are you doing with that wagon, Jed?" he asks, raising a brow.

"I think this must be the wagon Mr. Benjamin and his men rode on when they left last night."

"What?" Secoli reacts in shock. "How'd you know?"

"Look..." Pluck pulls the reins to stop the horses from pulling the wagon. He gets to the driver's seat and pulls out a black derby hat. "You recognize this?"

"Oh, no!" Secoli gasps, recognizing the bowler. "Not Mr. Benjamin."

"Yeah. This must be his. And look inside the wagon."

Secoli walks around his partner and looks over the driver's seat. There are black feathers all over the wagon. Upon closer inspection, it becomes more apparent to him that bloodstains are on the wagon's cover. The powerful stench of the wagon makes Secoli step back out of nausea.

"It took him and all his men as well," Pluck says. "I wanted to bring the evidence to you instead of having you walk out of town where I found it."

"Good God. This beast came back to Rawlins and finished the job."

"I don't think that's the case, Louie. The feathers all over the town are the same as when we were here. All of them are dirty, and some have lost their edge somehow. But these look fairly new. They must have been attacked in the Red Desert when it was pitch-black that night."

"Then what's it doing here in Rawlins?"

"My only guess is that these horses ran like hell across the Red Desert and eventually made it here. When I found them, they collapsed on the sand while still drawn to this wagon."

Secoli turns to the brown horses. "Then why didn't the beast take them?" Pluck shrugs. "Your guess is as good as mine."

While examining the horses, Secoli sees black needles on the mares' backs. The poor animals look exhausted and in pain with those razor-sharp feathers on their backs and necks. He touches one of the needles on the horse closest to him. This makes the horse jump and move in place hysterically.

"Whoa!" Pluck yells as he pulls the horse's reins. Pluck touches and caresses the horse's head to calm it down. "Shhh. Shhh. Shhh. It's okay, girl. It's okay." He turns to Secoli when the horse settles down. "Don't touch it. Remember how much it hurt me when a piece of the feather went through my leg? These two must be hurting like hell."

"I'm sorry," Secoli responds. "I'll be more careful. By the way, did you find anything else here in Rawlins?"

"Besides this wagon and the horses? Not really. The town is the same as when we last left it. Have you heard anything back on the telegraph?"

"That's what I was about to tell you. I think we are disconnected. Look over there." Secoli turns and points at the telegraph poles. "There's a gap between the poles. I don't remember seeing a gap the last time we were here, so how did the line snap?"

"Your guess is as good as mine."

"Right. So, do you know how to repair a cut wire from the telegraph pole?"

"I don't have the slightest clue. I usually get someone from Western Union to take care of it. Please tell me you know how to fix something like that?"

"Neither do I, Jed." Secoli sighs, kicking a rock down the slope. "Even if we found the tools, I wouldn't know where to start in reconnecting those wires.

We're much more stranded now. We better get back to Lemonstown before it gets dark."

"Hold on, Louie. These horses haven't had water all day. I'm not going to be cruel and neglect these innocent creatures. First, let's unhitch them from this wagon and bring them to the water trough next to our horses before heading out."

"Fine." Secoli sighs.

The postal inspectors loosen and remove the harnesses from the two horses. They do so carefully to avoid touching the needles and puncturing their backs. The one on the left is released first as Pluck raises the horse as high as possible for the mare to walk underneath it. Secoli pulls the mare out and leaves her in place to help remove the second one.

The next one is more challenging, considering the horse has a feather sticking in its back. As Pluck tries to raise the harness above the mare's back, the breeching strap touches the wound. The pain makes the horse run, pulling Secoli, who's holding its reins. Secoli falls to the ground, pulling the mare's head with the reins, trying to keep it from making a run for it. Pluck rushes to the troubled horse and caresses the poor creature while his partner puts all his weight down to prevent the animal from going farther.

Once again, Pluck successfully calms the horse down. Secoli picks himself back up when he feels the horse stop resisting, then brushes off the dirt all over his clothes. Pluck is already guiding the horse that pulled Secoli to the water trough. Secoli then grabs the lonely horse by its reins and follows. Both horses identify water in the trough and rush over to drink. Neither one slows down their drinking as the postal inspectors tie their reins to the hitching rail with their horses.

"Thirsty girls, aren't they?" Pluck then looks back at the telegraph pole gap. "Wait a minute. Something is off about the poles."

"What about them?"

"Look at the poles again. See the pattern of each of them connecting to each other in that distance? Notice that the gap between those poles where the wire snapped is a lot farther apart than the rest of them? Unless there's a wire long enough to reach that distance, there's supposed to be one more pole in between those two."

Secoli observes where his partner points and notices they're twice as far apart as the other poles. This realization makes him wonder how he didn't notice it before until Pluck pointed it out. Because the buildings block their view from the ground, they head toward the gap to look closer. While the wind blows gently, the postal inspectors watch out for incoming black feathers. They pass through the train station, seeing the docks dustier than ever.

When they reach the disconnected poles, they both notice that a pole that should be in between them has been knocked over. The broken pole lies atop the railway, and the wires lie on the gravel. The postal inspectors examine both the broken end of the pole and the half still attached to the gravel. The other half is only a knee-high from the ground.

"Oh, my God," Secoli mutters. "Why would anyone cut this pole down?"

"A better question is, *how* is anyone or anything able to knock a pole down?"

"What do you mean?"

"You see where the ends break? There's no sign of it being chopped down." Secoli sees both ends of the broken pole and sees that both ends show no signs of it being cut. Instead, they have twigs and fibers sticking out like spikes. "If this pole was chopped," Pluck continues, "then the lumberjack would normally cut that area horizontally in order to tear this pole down like a log.

However, seeing these fibers sticking out of both ends instead of a straight cut... it can only mean that it's been knocked down."

"It's been snapped in half like a twig," Secoli says. "Do you think the wood gave out and collapsed?"

"That's not how wood works, Louie. The other poles are still standing, but this one is torn down."

"Do you really think that giant bird knocked it down?"

"I can't imagine it being anything else that caused this. I saw the other ghost towns having holes in roofs, walls crashed down, and jail bars bent. Unless there's an elephant on the loose that's grown some feathers, this has got to be the strongest goddamn bird in the world."

"But if this pole was standing up with the wires attached when we first arrived two days ago, either it was knocked down yesterday, or it must have happened today."

"Or it might still be here.... That means that we're not alone."

Pluck takes out his revolver. Secoli becomes anxious when he sees his partner preparing for combat this suddenly. He clenches his fist and then immediately looks around. When Secoli pulls out his gun, he realizes he doesn't have his birdcage with him. The traumatized agent begins to tremble.

"Um, Jed," Secoli whispers.

While looking around, Pluck slowly whispers, "What is it, partner?"

I forgot Chap."

"Are you serious?" Pluck whispers angrily.

Pluck looks at his partner and now notices he has been empty-handed this whole time. Secoli's face is starting to look pale. Pluck frowns at his timid partner and says, "Damn it, Louie!" he swears, still keeping his voice down. Pluck pinches the bridge of his nose and tries to calm down. "Go get your bird and meet me back here."

Secoli nods and immediately sprints back to the telegraph office. In a high-alert state, Pluck moves in the opposite direction. Secoli makes it back inside and catches his breath. He then walks toward the birdcage on top of the desk, where the telegraph's transmitter and receiver are. He assumes Chap is still asleep, but as he gets closer, he realizes the birdcage is empty.

Secoli gasps at the sight of the open birdcage door, and Chap is no longer inside. Anxiety escalates into shock for Secoli. The postal inspector runs to the empty birdcage. He trembles as he grabs the birdcage to see that his eyes don't deceive him.

A federal worker is experiencing a panic attack. He starts sweating and has shortness of breath. When he looks around the room, Secoli sees that he left the front door open. His first immediate thought is Chap flew away. The postal inspector's heart is racing, and he is wheezing. It's unlike Chap to fly away, especially when a budgerigar is clingy to its master. Secoli is so scared of losing his muse that he's going numb, not knowing if he's inhaling or exhaling as his lungs feel clogged. Tears are coming down his eyes as he slowly exits through the main entrance.

Each step he makes feels like a prickling sensation worse than he had earlier. The worst he's ever had, in fact. The one thing that has kept him sane is now gone.

As he makes it to the porch, he nearly collapses as he holds himself onto the pillar. No matter what, he held on to the porch's pillar with all his might. Secoli's trembling and paresthesia get him on his knees. His lungs are so tight that he can't cry out loud if he wants to.

Secoli tries to look up, and somehow, the pillar he's holding turns into a flagpole waving an American flag. Confused about what's going on, he looks around and sees himself no longer in Rawlins, and he's starting to hear gunfire and explosions. He keeps turning his head, seeing himself surrounded by Union soldiers. The Union army is facing forward in Secoli's direction, where the Confederate army is charging.

The incoming confederates outnumber the Union squad, who are still firing and retreating from stampeding enemies. Secoli can't move, still holding on to the flagpole, supporting him from falling over. Though some Union soldiers fired at their enemies, many more bullets fired back in Secoli's direction. Secoli sees his fellow soldiers getting hit left and right, feeling too real when he hears bullets fly past him and the cries of agony everywhere.

Secoli looks to see if he got shot. Unable to tell if it is his or another soldier's blood, he sees that his uniform is not entirely blue. He looks up and sees that the soldiers, still able to stand and fight, have left him. He's all alone, wheezing over being surrounded by his fallen comrades and others wearing the same uniform he never knew. Secoli looks ahead and witnesses the countless gray coats climbing the hill he stands on.

The enemies in front of him cease climbing and point their rifles at Secoli, who's still leaning on the flagpole that carries the Union flag as the standard-bearer. Secoli finally lets go of the flagpole when the incoming bullets hit him in the stomach. The pain is so excruciating that he drops to his knees and places his forehead on the ground.

The pain in his forehead is the only feeling he has; he doesn't even feel the grass he stands on. He opens his eyes and sees his homburg hat off his head and lying on the floor beside his face. From the corner of his eye, Secoli catches a glimpse of the porch's pillar and looks down to see he is lying on the wooden floor. He realizes he's been on the porch this whole time. Even now that the hallucination is over, his symptoms have worsened.

Secoli can't get back up from severe numbness. His lungs are so tight that it's preventing him from breathing. He continues to hold on to his tight chest and has his head on the floor, feeling like he could die at any minute. No matter how much the traumatized Federal agent refuses to accept it, Chap is gone.

Unable to move or breathe, Secoli is feeling his life slipping away without his irreplaceable budgerigar. At that moment, he feels that he's not dying from being unable to breathe but rather from grief. This hapless situation he's in is too overwhelming to bear. He closes his eyes, wishing it will be over soon.

Believing all is lost, Secoli hears a chirping noise similar to that of Chap. Hearing its pleasant sound helps his lungs to reopen and take a deep breath. So much air comes into his lungs, giving him the feeling of living again. He exhales, sees that his lungs are no longer tight, and is now able to breathe normally.

Unsure if it is real or his imagination, hearing what sounds like a budgerigar brings his head back up from the ground. The feeling of a bird's presence gets him to control his breathing and recover from his numbness. Realizing the bird's noise is coming around the pillar next to him is a good enough reason to get back on his feet.

Secoli regains normal feeling and puts his homburg hat back on his head. As he gets back on his feet, he sees his budgerigar on someone's finger. He wipes his tears to see better and be certain if it really is Chap and who's standing before him.

"Ah, you must be the one this budgerigar is looking for," a soft-spoken Southern female voice says.

Secoli regains his vision and is surprised that a woman in a purple dress is standing in front of him. She's also wearing gloves, a scarf, boots, and a Victorian hat with fake feathers in the same black tone. The lady's face shows that she has porcelain skin and curly, titan-red hair tied underneath her small Victorian hat. Her facial features stand out for having sharp green eyes and thick lips that match well on her freckled, heart-shaped face and thin, straight nose.

Secoli breaks from analyzing the woman when the budgerigar jumps off the mysterious woman's hand and flies into Secoli's chest. Realizing that Chap has returned to him, he catches his bird. He moves the bird away from his chest to see that this is the same one that entrusts and loves him. Once more, the presence of Chap shakes off any sadness and fright Secoli possesses.

"Thank God," Secoli whispers as he catches his breath. He places his forehead over the bird's head. "I thought I lost you, Chap."

"It's wonderful to see that this bird trusts and loves you," the woman comments.

Just when Secoli starts shedding a tear, he focuses on the woman.

"You got a lot of nerve taking my budgerigar out of his cage," the postal inspector angrily says while catching his breath. "This bird means the world to me, and you had no right to take him without my consent."

"My apologies," the woman responds calmly, "however, I had nothing to do with your budgerigar flying out of his cage. All I did was catch him and befriended the little fellow when I got here. If this bird got loose, leaving him unattended is probably your fault."

"Who are you, anyway?" Secoli asks suspiciously. "And what are you doing here in this town?"

"Oh, yes. Where are my manners? I'm Dr. Fiona Fletcher. I'm an ornithologist."

"Orni-thologist?" Secoli interrupts. "Never heard of that before. What exactly do you do?"

"Well," Dr. Fletcher continues, ignoring his tone of voice, "ornithology is the scientific study of birds. I travel around the world and do a tremendous amount of research on them."

"That's quite interesting." Secoli starts to calm down a little. "I don't suppose all these feathers all over these towns and the missing people are what brings you here, Doctor…"

"Fletcher," she fills in for him. "And yes, that is precisely why I'm here. To find and figure out what species is taking away the citizens of Wyoming. And you are?"

The postal inspector shows his badge to her and replies, "I am United States Postal Inspector Louie Secoli. My partner and I are on the case of finding these missing citizens of Wyoming as well. You wouldn't suppose you found the monster that harmed and kidnapped these people, would you?"

"I'm sorry, Inspector. I haven't seen what is responsible for these recent disappearances. I've just come from Sundance, Wright, and Casper—from the Northeast by wagon." She turns and points to her two horses drawn to her wagon. "Sundance was alive and well when I was there a couple of days ago. However, Wright and Casper are just as dead and grim as Rawlins."

"Damn. Are Wright and Casper full of feathers like here, Cheyenne, and Laramie?"

"Oh, my word." The ornithologist covers her mouth. "Wyoming's capital has fallen as well?"

"Unfortunately, yes. Can you please answer my question?"

"Which is it? Oh, yes. The last two towns are infested with these monstrous feathers like here. You're the first person I've seen in days. And your budgerigar is also the first bird I've found since I left Wright. What is a postal inspector doing with a budgerigar? Their natural habitat is in Australia, so seeing yours here in this desolate state caught me off guard."

Secoli doesn't answer. Instead, he heads back inside with Chap in his hands. The ornithologist can feel his mood shift after asking the question. Dr. Fletcher realizes that she has asked a personal question as she follows him inside. She sees the postal inspector around the counter and puts Chap back inside his birdcage.

"Inspector Secoli," Dr. Fletcher says. "I apologize if what I said offended you."

"No, you didn't," Secoli says softly, putting Chap in his cage and shutting the door. "But it's confidential."

"I understand."

An awkward silence falls over the two. Secoli focuses on Chap, thinking about how close he was to losing him. Dr. Fletcher remains standing next to the entrance door, waiting patiently for him to continue the conversation. Suddenly, a voice is heard from outside.

"Hey, Louie!" Pluck's voice gets louder as he enters through the front door. "What's taking you so long to—"

Pluck notices his partner with a new face. Unlike Secoli's first impression of the ornithologist, Pluck is enthralled by seeing Dr. Fletcher. The both of them make strong eye contact from several feet away. While Secoli is recovering from his post-traumatic episode and unable to say anything, Pluck can't take his eyes off the ornithologist, especially one that appears so stunning to him. The ornithologist, however, is more intimidated by how strong Pluck comes across.

"Oh, Jed." Secoli breaks the awkward silence in the room, still focusing on Chap. "This is Dr. Fletcher. She's a…" He turns to her. "What is it again?"

"An ornithologist," the doctor answers. "The scientific study of bir—"

"The pleasure is all mine." Pluck, not realizing he interrupted her, approaches Dr. Fletcher. He takes her hand and kisses it.

"Oh, I'm flattered," she responds with hesitation. "And you are?"

"United States Postal Inspector Jed Pluck, at your service, Dr. Fletcher."

He lets go of her hand. He quickly rethinks what the doctor said. "Wait a minute. Studying birds? Do you work for the government?"

"Oh, no," Dr. Fletcher answers. "I'm coming from Cornell University in New York."

"New York? You have an interesting Southern accent, coming all the way from New York. Where are you originally from?"

"It's a long story, I'm originally from Hattiesburg, Mississippi. I went to Cornell University to study birds, and now I am a professor who teaches about birds there."

"Wait a minute." Pluck's tone becomes suspicious. "How is it that our case just opened recently, and it took us a day and a half to get from Boston to here by train? There's no way that you've traveled from New York to Wyoming before we did."

"Yet somehow, you're conveniently here," Secoli adds to the conversation, which turns into an interrogation. "Did you have something to do with knocking down the telegraph pole?"

"Louie!" Pluck interrupts. "That's a stupid question. No way a woman could knock down the pole, let alone a group of men." He turns to the ornithologist. "My apologies. My partner says silly things when he's distressed."

"Telegraph pole?" the doctor nervously answers. "No. I just arrived at Rawlins just recently by wagon." She turns to the window behind her and points to her horses drawn to the wagon. "I just wanted to see if someone was at the telegraph office who could send a telegram back to my university. But all I found was your budgerigar flying around the porch."

"Flying around?" Pluck frowns at his partner.

"Look...," Secoli says, intimidated by Pluck's angry expression, "Chap just got loose. She found him, and that's how we ended up meeting each other."

"If you say so." Pluck turns back to Dr. Fletcher. "We're the first to investigate these disappearances. As far as I'm concerned, reports of missing people in Wyoming haven't been made public yet. So how did you know of the disappearances?"

"Funny you asked," Dr. Fletcher says. "I was studying birds in Montana. Right now is the best time of the year to study them. Then I received a telegraph from my university that said they received a telegraph about missing people in Wyoming and that feathers were left behind. Luckily, being at the right place at the right time, I drove my wagon to Wyoming. That's why I'm here, Inspector...Pluck, is it?"

"Yes, ma'am. It is," Pluck answers.

"Thank you. And please call me 'Doctor.' Anyway, that's why I'm here, Inspector Pluck, to find out what's causing these disappearances."

"Do you have the telegram from your university with you?" Secoli asks suspiciously.

"Yes, I do," the ornithologist responds. "Can you show it to us?" Pluck asked.

"Why do you want it so badly?" she counters.

"Just to make sure you're telling the truth," Pluck replied. "We just want to see the telegram and see what it says. That's all."

"Sure. It's left in my wagon. This way, please."

The postal inspectors follow Dr. Fletcher out the door and head to her wagon. Secoli stops and turns around to bring the birdcage with him. He catches up to them before they notice he almost forgot to bring Chap along. There are two white horses drawn to the topless wagon. The wooden vehicle has luggage, a few barrels, and crates. Dr. Fletcher climbs on board before either one of the men asks her for a hand. She opens one of the crates and pulls out a cardstock.

"Here," she says as she passes the telegram to Pluck.

Secoli looks over Pluck's shoulder, and they both read the telegram. It says:

Ithaca, New York

Dr. Fiona Fletcher: We received a message that an unknown bird species is taking citizens in Wyoming. We know that we sent you to Broadus, Montana, to study black-billed magpies, but we have a change of plans for you since you're close to Wyoming. Please see what type of bird is taking these people away and message us about Wyoming's status.

Prof. Jeremy Campbell, 2:45 P.M.

The two Federal agents see that the message is typed and the telegram title is on the card. The stamp date says August 7, 1899.

"This doesn't make any sense," Secoli says. "How did Cornell University know of the disappearances at the same time the United States Postal Inspection Service did?"

"I don't know," Pluck answers, "but telegraphs go faster than we can imagine. I can only imagine the newspapers have published articles about Wyoming's disappearances by now."

"And how did this Prof. Campbell know where to send you this message?" Secoli asks.

"They arranged a hotel for me to stay in Broadus," Fletcher explains. "When I returned to my hotel room, the receptionist gave me this telegram from the Pony Express."

"So you came from Montana, right?" Secoli asks. "That's right, Inspector." Dr. Fletcher nods.

"Have you seen any survivors or someone—or something—responsible for all of these disappearances?" Pluck asks.

"Like I told your partner, the only town I found that has unharmed citizens is Sundance. However, Wright and Casper are as empty as Rawlins."

"Damn it," Pluck swears. "Forgive my language, Doctor. We had a long day returning to Rawlins and trying to use the telegraph, which isn't working. Unfortunately, this is the only telegraph office farthest to the west in Wyoming. Lemonstown is the only town here that hasn't become a ghost town. Unless we go east to use the telegraph office at Laramie—"

"No way, Jed," Secoli says. "I'm not letting you risk our lives to get to the next town. It'll be too dark and dangerous by the time we get there. Plus, we'll be much farther from Lemonstown. We're going back to help the others."

"Lemonstown?" the doctor asks. "Is everyone there safe?"

"So far, yes," Secoli replies. "But my partner here went to Rock Springs this morning and found the town had just been attacked. For some reason, this...beast, which is what we're calling it, flew past Lemonstown and continued west."

"At least we know that the suspect is moving west," Secoli adds. "The feathers are all over these towns, but we've seen one of them outside these ghost towns. Do you know what bird or animal has the size of..." Secoli turns around and looks at a feather on the ground closest to him. "...feathers like these?"

"There are no species on record capable of growing such lengthy feathers," the doctor says. "Nor have I ever encountered one."

Pluck sighs before saying, "What do you think it might be, Doctor? Is there a possibility of a giant bird whisking people away?"

The ornithologist smiles, trying to resist laughing. "There is a possibility, but I speculate there's a new species that may or may not be a bird."

"If that's the case," Secoli strokes his facial hair, "how will we take this giant down? We've seen bullet holes and evidence that showed citizens have struggled with taking this beast down. And now it knocked down a telephone pole, and we cannot contact anyone. How about you helping us with the case, Doctor?" Secoli asks.

Pluck and Fletcher turn to Secoli, and both simultaneously say, "Really?"

"Why not? Neither Jed nor I have as much bird expertise as you do, and we need as much help as we can get. Besides, you're the first person in this country that has known Chap is a budgerigar. That's proof that you really do study birds. So, are you in? You'll be doing a great service for your country by helping us out."

Dr. Fletcher smiles. "Sure. I'll help you two out on your case."

"That's great," Secoli responds. "It's getting dark. We'd better get back to Lemonstown before the sun sets. It's not safe to go out in the dark."

"All right," Pluck says. "Let's get the horses, and we shall get movin'."

The ornithologist looks at the horses standing before the telegraph office and says, "You're riding on four horses? Why did you bring so many?"

"We came here with one horse each," Pluck answers. "We just found two more that were abandoned here. Tell me, Doctor. Do you know if birds attack horses?"

"Not to my recollection, Inspector. Usually, birds of prey attack animals their own size and prey only on smaller species or when they have to defend their nest."

"MA'AM," SAYS A TELEGRAPHIST. "I'm sorry, but we're closed."

"I'm not leaving," Clara Pluck shouts as she waves her receipt, "unless I get a good reason why my message to my husband hasn't been received! It's not like him to not message back a telegram after I send one to him."

"Right. Can you tell me where you're sending him this message again?"

"Oh, my." She looks away in frustration. "I told you and your coworkers

many times over to telegraph this message to Cheyenne, Wyoming."

"And are you sure your husband is there?"

"I'm positive! Even if he isn't there, they would pass the message one town over and make sure he receives it. Are you sure that you telegraphed that message to Cheyenne?"

"We have, ma'am," another telegraphist says, sitting on his desk. "It's just that we're not hearing back from anyone from Wyoming."

"Nothing at all?"

"Nope. Nothing at all."

"Is there a connection problem or something?"

"If there is, then someone from Western Union will take care of it." Janet and Allie are running behind their mother while she's arguing with the workers. There's enough space in the telegraph office's lobby for the little girls to play without bumping into anything. Except the two sisters aren't playing. It's more like one of them is chasing the other. The youngest one is upset and is trying to take her doll back from her older sister, who's bullying her. Frustrated that her older sister is faster than her, Janet stops running and turns to her mother.

"Mommy! Mommy!" Janet yells as he pulls on her mother's dress. "Allie took my Bella!"

"Did not!" Allie yells back, hiding the doll behind her. "Did too!"

"You two..." Clara turns to her daughters. "Stop it right now. The adults are talking here." She puts her attention back on the telegraphist. "Okay, so how will you know when communication will work again?"

The daughters stop squabbling and wait still behind their mother.

"As soon as we receive a Morse code from Wyoming," the front desk receptionist answers. "Then we'll know they fixed it."

"Then you'll send them my message again?"

"I'm sorry, Mrs. Pluck. We have to charge you for another message."

"You've gotta be kidding me. Are you telling me that the message I sent yesterday didn't go through? And you're charging me to have that message sent again?"

"I'm sorry, ma'am, but it's Western Union policy that every message sent by telegraph has to have a fee. I can't resend your message without payment."

"That was $2.80 I paid! I could have bought my family an entire meal with

that kind of money!"

"I know your frustration, Mrs. Pluck, but messaging all the way to Wyoming from here is a really long way. Have you tried calling your husband on the telephone?"

"Don't you think I tried that already? The operator said the exact same thing you're telling me. Saying no one can take or receive calls."

"My apologies. I forgot that telephones and telegraphs have the same connection, so you won't be able to reach anyone in that state until someone fixes the issue here."

"Since my husband didn't receive the message, I demand a refund!"

"Sorry, Mrs. Pluck. Western Union doesn't issue refunds for telegrams that have already been sent."

"I refuse to accept that! You give me back the exact amount right now before I have a word with your manager."

"I am the manager, Mrs. Pluck, and I'm telling you I cannot refund your money."

Janet turns around and sees Allie running out the entrance door. Seeing her doll behind Allie and tied to her waist makes the little one chase after her older sister. Their mother doesn't realize her daughters are no longer inside the building and continues arguing with the telegraphists. Outside the telegraph office, Janet finally snags the doll off her sister. Allie turns around. The little one tightly holds on to her doll while Allie gives her a mocking smile.

"Gee, Allie," Janet says. "Why do you have to be so mean!"

"Well, Janet," Allie responds, "maybe you should stop bringing that stupid doll with you wherever we go. Everyone is making fun of me for having such a baby for a sister."

"I'm not a baby!" Janet yells.

"Then prove it. Let go of that doll right now and grow up."

"But I don't want to leave Bella. She's mine."

"Geez, Janet. Don't you care what everybody is saying about you?"

"I don't care. I just want to be with Bella forever."

Allie laughs at her little sister. Janet looks away as she can't take any more of her bullying. Her older sister hears her sniffing, sensing that Janet is starting to cry. Allie is getting scared, not about Janet's feelings, but about what her mother will do when she finds out.

"Janet," Allie says, "I'm sorry. I didn't mean it."

The youngest starts sobbing, covering her face with her doll. Allie tries patting her sister on the back to make her stop crying. She can't think of anything to stop Janet's mewls from getting louder. The older sister looks around and notices she's getting looks from the locals. The trouble escalates when her mother comes out of the telegraph office.

"Terrible, terrible service," Clara rants as she tosses her receipt on the sidewalk. "That is the last time I'm ever coming to this telegraph office." She grabs both of her daughters' hands. "C'mon, girls. We're going home."

Janet still has her doll covering her face as her mother pulls her along.

Her crying gets louder. Clara stops and kneels down to her youngest one. "What's the matter with you?" Clara asks.

"Al-Allie was mean to me again," Janet answers, wiping her tears. "She took Bella from me and called me a baby for carrying her around with me."

Clara turns to Allie and gives her a scowl. Allie is terrified by her mother's expression, imagining what she will say.

"That's enough out of you, Allie. She's only six years old and doesn't need you to be picking on her."

She squeezes Allie's wrist. "Ow, Mommy," Allie reacts.

"Your birthday is coming up in four days. Do you want to be grounded on your birthday?"

"No, Mommy."

The mother lets go of her wrist. Allie immediately holds and rubs her painful joints as soon as Clara lets go.

"Now, be good. You hear me, Allie?" Clara continues scolding. "Otherwise, you won't get a birthday party. Got it?"

"Yes, Mommy."

"C'mon, Janet." Clara picks up Janet and carries her onward. "Let's get home and have supper. Your sisters made meatloaf for us. Cheer up now. You love meatloaf, don't you?"

The youngest one doesn't say anything as she lays her head on her mother's shoulder. Allie follows them without saying a word. It's not too far to make it to where the horse bus makes its stop. She puts Janet down when they arrive at the stop, and the three of them wait for the public transportation to arrive.

Clara looks around to search for the horse bus, then glances at the newsstand next to her. As the store owner closes his shop and puts away the newspapers, she pays attention to the front cover of one of the papers. She sees the bold title that says "Wyoming" under "The Boston Post" as the owner removes the paper from the shelf.

"Excuse me." Clara approaches the newsstand owner, pulling her children with her. "How much for that?"

"Well, since it's considered old news at closing hours," the owner replies, "I'll give you half off."

"Thank you so much, sir," Clara says.

She pays the owner and receives her copy. Clara begins to read the front page article. It says:

Wyoming In Danger And Off Limits August 11, 1899

The United States Government has ruled that the state of Wyoming is under restriction from entry for America's safety. This lockdown began when telegraph offices trying to send messages to Wyoming received no response in the past couple of days, and mail had mysteriously gone missing. Investigators entered the state and reported no sign of life in many of the towns they visited.

All of the citizens of the state capital, Cheyenne, have disappeared. The latest reports were from the same investigators, saying that Laramie, Rock River, and Rawlins have the same issue of sudden disappearances. However, the investigators who sent the reports through telegraph have yet to give any further reports. The reasons for these disappearances are unknown.

Reporters and officials have wanted to hear from DeForest Richards, the Governor of Wyoming, regarding these disappearances. However, since he has not made any contact or appearance, many believe he has disappeared like all the locals.

President William McKinley has put Wyoming on state lockdown until further notice. All borders of Wyoming are on high surveillance for any suspicious activities and those at the border have been put in interrogation. Montana, South Dakota, Nebraska,

Colorado, Utah, and Idaho are on the watch of Wyoming's borders but are understaffed. Despite reinforcements entering Wyoming to retaliate against possible suspects, none have returned or been contacted since yesterday.

Citizens of Afton, Alpine, Jackson, Lovell, and Sheridan have been rescued and evacuated out of the state before they fall victim to these mysterious disappearances. The concern is rescuing the other towns and locals farther from the border.

Criticism of President McKinley for not taking aggressive action rises. His reason is that nearly all mountain states' National Guards are deployed to war in the Philippines and need as much manpower there as possible to win the war. Many have questioned the president's focus on colonizing the indigenous island being more of a priority than protecting Americans in the West. Many Americans have families and loved ones left in Wyoming and are worried about their safety. Gregory Godfrey from Chicago, Illinois, was the first to hear about the disappearances. He claims that since he went on a business trip, he has been trying to reach his wife back in Wyoming since last week. That is when his telegraphist finally got contact from the Federal agents to give him the unfortunate news of her disappearance.

Many are saying the Natives are attacking and kidnapping the Wyomingites. While others suspect it might be Canadian forces who have snuck past Montana and are preparing another war against the United States. What is certain is that whatever is happening in Wyoming threatens our national security. If we do not act fast now, who knows how and when the disappearances will spread to other locations in the United States.

"Oh, Jed," Clara mutters. "Why didn't you tell me?"

"Mommy...," Janet says.

Clara puts down the newspaper and looks at her daughters. Janet has stopped crying. Both she and Allie are eager to know what their mother just read.

"What did the news article say?" Janet asks. "Does it have something to do with Daddy?"

Clara can't come up with a response that won't upset her children. Seeing both of their sad eyes is already too much for her to bear to tell them the truth. She hears a bell ringing from the driver of the horse-drawn omnibus.

"I'll tell you later," Clara says. "C'mon, children. We have a bus to catch." She folds the newspaper and places it under her arms, next to the purse she's carrying. The mother grabs her daughters' hands and brings both children on board. She moves around the long carriage to tell the driver where their destination is and pays him the transportation fee. Clara then moves inside the bus and sits between her children.

The horses pull the bus, leaving the troubled wife to hold on to Janet and Allie and watch out the window.

"Mommy," Janet says. "You didn't tell us if the news said something about Daddy."

"I'll tell you two and your sisters after supper." Clara looks out the window next to her and quietly says to herself, "Oh, Jed…I pray to God that you're okay."

THE SUN SETS TO THE point where little light is seen in the Red Desert. The travelers would have moved faster to Lemonstown, but the two horses the postal inspectors rescued are still hurt from the pieces of the sharp feathers that are still sticking on their backs.

They're lucky to still be able to travel with Pluck and Secoli, riding on their horses. Dr. Fletcher's horses pulling her wagon are also slowing down from all the traveling they did today. Pluck moves the horse he's riding on closer to the ornithologist on the wagon's driver's seat.

"Sorry for the slow travels, Dr. Fletcher," Pluck says. "I don't want to push these rescued horses more than they should. I just can't leave these beautiful creatures back in Rawlins. I hope you understand."

"I do, Inspector," the ornithologist replies. "I admire your care for animals, which is something not all men do."

"Out of all the professions, why choose ono-on…you know, studying birds?"

"It's called ornithology." The doctor laughs. "I love and adore animals. At first, I wanted to be a zookeeper, but like many professions, it wasn't a job where they hired women. So, when I went to Cornell University, the study of birds intrigued me. I've been birdwatching my entire life, and the studies somehow became easy for me to learn."

"So, did your major make you study every bird species, study their bodies, and try to distinguish each bird?"

"That and much more. Scientists everywhere are still discovering new species and are trying to figure out how life works. It's almost impossible for a biologist to keep track of all of life, so science organizations divide the fields. My field of work requires me to keep track of known bird species and keep discovering new ones wherever the university wants me to go."

"Sounds like an easy job. Doesn't it, Doctor?"

"On the contrary, Inspector. Photographing birds is a challenging task for ornithologists. They need photos to prove their findings, but birds often mistake cameras for guns. Sometimes we think we take a good shot, but when we print them, it ends up being unclear, making us go back in hopes that we find this again."

Jed nods. "Oh, I didn't know."

"Also, it's not enough in my field to just look at a bird in the distance. Many times, I have to catch one and physically examine the species. Since birds come in all shapes and sizes, not all traps catch all of them, especially when I need them unharmed. Do you know what it's like to catch a bird and ensure it can fly when you let it go free, Inspector Pluck?"

"No, but I have shot down a couple of birds when I went hunting at a young age."

She hums in disapproval over the postal inspector's remark. Dr. Fletcher whips the reins to make the horses pull her wagon faster. Inspector Pluck doesn't bother to make his horse catch up with her. He can feel that she's not interested in talking to him.

So he follows behind the ornithologist and his partner, keeping a steady pace to guide the two injured horses. Feeling the horses' reins pulling Pluck's hand, he realizes the injured animals are falling back from exhaustion.

Pluck sees Dr. Fletcher catching up to his partner and starts conversing with him as they journey. Pluck is annoyed at how Secoli seems to get along with the ornithologist better than he does. The distance between him and those two makes it hard to listen to their conversation, and the horses he's guiding are slowing him down. Pluck looks away when Dr. Fletcher plays with Chap in his birdcage and laughs.

The travelers are now moving up a sand hill. Once Pluck and his horses reach the top, the group is able to see the view of Lemonstown in the distance as the sun sets below the horizon. The ornithologist's wagon and Secoli's horse move down the sand hill first, while Pluck allows the rescued horses to catch their breaths. As Pluck makes it to the bottom and approaches the group with the horses, he makes the horses speed up and take the lead.

It's already dark to the point where he can barely distinguish the color of the desert's sand. Straight ahead, there's already light in Lemonstown, with lanterns being carried and moved around the main street. Hearing the ornithologist giggling influences Pluck to look behind, and the horses proceed forward. With what little light there is, he can see Secoli smiling and enjoying having his birdcage on Dr. Fletcher's lap. Seeing that his partner trusts the ornithologist in handling his parakeet makes Pluck turn to Lemonstown and shake his head with a cringe.

Facing forward toward the town, the postal inspector hears someone screaming in the distance. It becomes more apparent to Pluck as he gets closer to town. Secoli and Fletcher stop amusing each other as they hear what sounds like an older woman yelling at someone. The group approaches behind the east side of the building, noticing so much light is seen from the other side of the jailhouse. Curious to see what's happening, Pluck moves his horse faster and lets go of the reins of the rescued horses.

"Hold on to these horses, Louie?" Pluck says.

Secoli catches up to the rescued horse and takes hold of its reins as Pluck gallops back to town. Pluck's horse rushes around the jailhouse for him to see the commotion. Ten guardsmen stand on the jailhouse porch with their torches in one hand and their rifles in the other. They all stand firm, preventing the middle-aged woman from entering the building as she holds a hatchet.

"I'm telling you, Sheriff!" the woman yells. "Let me through!"

"Mrs. Humphrey," the sheriff responds. "I know you're very upset that your husband passed away. But avenging his death won't solve anything."

"So what? Are you just letting Jeremy Payton stay in his cell and live?

You're just going to let him go after a few days, ain't 'cha?"

"Ma'am, it was an accident, and all of us saw it." The sheriff sees Pluck and his group approaching with horses. "You can ask the postal inspector. He saw it, too."

Everyone turns to Pluck.

"Accident or not," the widow cried, "my husband is dead because of that boy. I demand justice!" She turns to the postal inspector, shedding tears. "Please, Inspector. I cannot let this go unresolved. Tell these men to step aside."

"And what will happen if I let you in, ma'am?" Pluck responds. "More unnecessary deaths in Lemonstown?"

"You don't know Jeremy Payton like I do." The old woman shakes the hatchet at him. "That kid is nothing but trouble, always fooling around since he was a little boy. You gave him a gun, and he killed Henry—my Henry. Do you know what it's like to be married to a man as good as him for thirty years?"

"Please..." Pluck gestures to her, lowering his hands. "Let go of that ax. We don't want any more killings right now."

"And what of Jeremy Payton? Is he going to just stay there to make him think about what he's done? That isn't justice!"

"And what does justice look like to you? An eye for an eye? What do you think his mother will do if you have your way with him?"

"I-I-" She starts trembling, struggling to find an answer. She still points her hatchet at the postal inspector, losing control as she shakes it some more. Pluck can see how emotional she is, sympathizing with her. He gets off his horse and approaches the troubled widow.

The postal inspector is within arm's reach of her. He gently grabs her wrist and removes the small ax from her hand. Mrs. Humphrey releases the handle and looks down. Tears drip on Pluck's shoes. He hands the hatchet to the closest person and lets her place her head on his chest. Pluck puts his hands on her shoulders, letting her cry out.

"I promise you, Mrs. Humphrey," Pluck whispers. "You will get justice.

Payton will get a trial. Whatever the mayor decides, it's his decision."

"When-when will my Henry get a fair trial?"

"We don't have a set date. But it isn't safe out here, do you understand? You need to go back to the sanctuary—get some sleep and let us do the rest. Sheriff!"

"Inspector?" the lawman says, stepping off the porch.

"Have one of your men escort Mrs. Humphrey back to Town Hall."

"Yes, sir." The sheriff points to a man to his left. "You. Help her get home." The chosen guardsman steps out of the crowd and approaches the widow.

Pluck lets go of Mrs. Humphrey as the guardsman pulls her away from his chest. Everyone watches the widow being escorted away from the main road. "Oh, Inspector Secoli," the sheriff says, making everyone turn in the other direction. "I see you brought some visitors. More horses and...a lady?"

Pluck's partner and the ornithologist get out of their vehicles and approach the crowd after watching what happened. Dr. Fletcher needs clarification about what's going on. Secoli is looking more concerned than the ornithologist with him. He's still holding the reins and guiding the two brown horses.

"Oh, my word," the stable owner says as he walks up to Secoli. "I recognize those two horses. That's Paisley and Dawn." Mr. Madison reaches for one of the horses.

"Hold it!" Secoli raises his palm at him. The stable's owner stops.

"Please be careful! These horses are covered in those black feathers we've seen in these ghost towns. They're badly injured. Any sudden movements toward their injuries will make them run away."

Another guardsman approaches one of the horses and uses a torch to get a better look. The needles and feathers sticking on the horses' backs and other areas of their bodies become more apparent.

"What happened?" Mr. Madison asks with his eyes wide open.

"We cannot say for sure," Pluck answers, "but when we found these horses in Rawlins, they were still drawn to the wagon we suspect is the one the saloon owner bought from you."

"Wha-what happened to Mr. Benjamin and his crew?"

Pluck shakes his head. "The only thing we found in that wagon is piles of feathers—and Mr. Benjamin's hat." He walks to Fletcher's wagon and hands the sheriff a black derby hat. "And now they took him and his men, but the horses were spared."

"Now I don't know anybody else in Lemonstown who wears a hat like this, Sheriff," Secoli comments. "But whoever attacked those men, they struck them down when they were out in the Red Desert. They might be closer than we think."

"My God...," the sheriff mutters. "Mr. Madison, bring these horses to the stable.

And please be careful in removing the needles and feathers off of them."

"Will do, Sheriff," the stable owner responds before taking the horses' reins and heading inside the stable.

"Did you send a telegram and ask for help?" The sheriff turns to the inspectors.

"We tried, Sheriff. But someone tore down a telegraph pole and cut the wires."

"What? How did that happen?"

"We don't know." Secoli puts his head down. "The connection was just fine the last time we were in Rawlins, but our guess is that the giant bird did it. Even if we found someone that could reconnect the wires, a broken pole is damaged beyond repair."

"And who is she?" Wood looks at the woman standing next to Secoli.

"I'm Dr. Fiona Fletcher, Sheriff," the ornithologist says. "It's a pleasure to meet you—and the rest of you. I'm an ornithologist."

"Orni-what?" the sheriff asks with a slightly confused expression.

"I study birds. I came from Cornell University to investigate what kind of bird is attacking Wyoming."

"Ah, I see." The sheriff rubs his chin. "So it is a giant bird behind all of this, huh? You know what kind of bird might be attacking our state?"

"There has never been such a large or powerful bird in our records. Which is why I'm here. To discover this phenomenon and put it on record."

"So, how did you end up with these two postal inspectors?"

Fiona turns to the crowd, who's watching and listening. "Well, we bumped into each other in Rawlins when I needed a telegraph. Since Inspector Secoli couldn't fix it, I decided to tag along and see these birds myself. I hope my expertise will benefit your fight against whatever is responsible for these disappearances."

"That won't be necessary, ma'am. Since you're here, you need to either sleep in the Town Hall or get yourself a room in our hotel. It's curfew time for you."

"Curfew? Now, Sheriff..." She turns to Pluck and Secoli and tones down her voice.

She looks at Sheriff Wood and gives him a smile. "Surely you wouldn't want an ornithologist who traveled all this way here to miss out on a discovery of a lifetime."

"I'm sorry, Doctor," the sheriff responds, "but no woman or child is allowed to step out of the shelter until we bring this thing down."

"Bring it down? You don't mean you're going to shoot—shoot the bird, do you?"

"Look, Doctor..." The lawman walks closer to Dr. Fletcher. "We're doing all we can to protect our loved ones from danger. I'm following orders from the mayor and the postal inspectors who made this curfew."

The ornithologist turns to Pluck and Secoli with an annoyed look. "Is he serious, Inspector Secoli? You too, Inspector Pluck?"

"Dr. Fletcher," Pluck responds, "please understand. We don't want anyone who can't wield a gun to be running around in this town."

"I can handle a rifle. I'm quite a good shot."

Secoli raises an eyebrow. "Since when did you learn how to shoot, Doctor?"

"Since I was young—that doesn't matter right now. Look. I did not come

all this way here just to miss out on this chance of a lifetime to see this species. Maybe we can understand what's troubling them."

"Nope," Pluck says. "We're not risking it. These birds have wiped out entire towns. There's no way I'll let them take you away."

"And if I refuse?"

"Then we're just going to lock you up in your room. Secoli, please take Dr. Fletcher to her hotel room."

"Don't touch me, Inspector." The ornithologist shrugs her shoulders away from the postal inspector. "I'll bring my luggage to my room by myself. If I'd known you'd keep me locked up, I'd never even consider coming to Lemonstown with you two."

She moves past the men and heads to her wagon. The two postal inspectors follow her. Secoli takes his birdcage off the driver's seat as Pluck still focuses on Dr. Fletcher.

"You need a hand with those?" Pluck asks.

"Since you're insisting." Dr. Fletcher takes a French leather travel bag off the wagon. "Why don't you tell your men to bring everything to my room?"

Pluck turns to the crowd. "You heard the lady. Grab all her things and take them to her room. Place your rifles on the porch and your torches on the gravel." The guardsmen do as told, and it takes all of them to empty the wagon.

The sheriff stands back on the porch and watches the men following Dr. Fletcher and the postal inspectors to the hotel. Secoli grabs the keys from the clerk's desk and opens a hotel room right across from his room. Once he opens the door, all the men enter the room and place her belongings on the floor.

"Okay. Now, everyone, get back to your line of duty," Pluck commands.

The guards bolt from the hotel and cross the main road to retrieve their rifles and torches. They all move with urgency. The postal inspectors stand in front of the ornithologist's hotel room.

"Have a good night, Dr. Fletcher," Pluck says. "I'll check up on you in the morning."

"Thanks," she unenthusiastically responds, slamming the door on both of them.

"Well, that went smoothly," Secoli quips.

"Yeah, well, goodnight, Louie," Pluck says, heading to his room.

"Wait a minute. Isn't one of us supposed to be on guard for this shift?"

"Since you're the one who remembered, why don't you join them?"

Secoli sighs. "Fine. But you better be ready when it hits midnight when we change shifts."

CHAPTER 6

The first night of guard duty is an uneasy experience for all. Though the men assigned to this shift are inexperienced for the first time, this will be Secoli's second time on watch. The men are all struggling to stay away as they spend all day learning how to shoot, being taught how to maneuver between the aisles when under attack, and how to get information as a firing squad against the enemy. However, the one who's having the hardest time staying awake is the preacher, who's been doing all that and praying with many mourners who knew Mr. Humphry.

Exhausted after a long day, Father Jenkins sits on the hotel porch, leaning against the fence and closing his eyes.

"Father," the postal inspector says, "this is the second time I've had to wake you."

"I'm sorry, Inspector," Jenkins replies, rubbing his eyes. "I didn't get a chance to sleep at all."

"Speaking of which, how many bullets have you guys used for training?"

"We—we finished an entire crate of bullets."

"Damn it! We've only got four more crates left."

"Hey, now. I will not have you swear in front of me."

"My apologies, Father. I'll try my best to not have that happen again."

"Don't ask me for forgiveness, son. Ask God for his forgiveness. I didn't write the Ten Commandments, you know."

"Look, Father. I can't let you fall asleep on us when this shift needs you to watch over this side of town. What do you think will happen if one of those demons comes and snatches you away? You know that devils are merciless, especially to a man of God, such as yourself."

"Right. Right. Right. I'll go find a barrel of water and splash myself." Father Jenkins gets off the porch and walks to the bank's alley. He stops just before he enters. "By the way. How much more time till our shift ends?"

"We've only got..." Secoli places his birdcage on the bank's porch and pulls out his pocket watch. He brings his torch closer to see the time. "We've only got ten more minutes until midnight. Then you can get that deserved sleep."

The preacher makes his way between the bank and Town Hall, unable to walk straight. Secoli turns around to see that the only light in Lemonstown is coming from the guards' torchlights. Not a single building has a lit light. Even better is that this shift is as quiet as it can be. However, everyone in this shift isn't taking it as seriously as they should. For a town filled with a non-combative population, pulling guard duty is the bravest thing these locals have ever done.

Secoli then pulls away from viewing the town to see how Chap is doing in his birdcage. As usual, the budgerigar is resting in its sleeping position on the cage's base wire grille. To resist the urge to sit down and fall asleep, the postal inspector continues to stand. While he does so, Secoli admires his bird whenever he gets a chance.

However, Secoli gets interrupted by a sudden stick snapping from the hotel's alleyway. Secoli turns to the sound's direction and pulls out his handgun from his holster. The Federal agent then sways to the alleyway between the bank and the hotel. The torch he's holding shows the end of both buildings.

"Don't worry, Inspector," a female voice says. "It's only me."

"Dr. Fletcher?" Secoli says, lowering his gun.

The ornithologist approaches the postal inspector. "The one and only."

"Hey, now." Secoli puts his handgun back in his holster. "You're supposed to be on curfew. Get back to your hotel room, Doctor."

"And do what?" She steps out of the alleyway. "Miss out on finding a new bird species? I won't let you do that to me, Inspector."

"C'mon now. We're trying to keep you protected."

"Geesh. You men are so overprotected that it's no longer cute at this point.

Not that it ever was to begin with."

"And what should I do when that thing takes you away?" Secoli asks. "I suppose you're going to have to let that thing carry me away then."

"Are you nuts? Do you know how much danger we're in right now?"

"As a matter of fact, I do. But what fighting chance do you and Lemonstown have if we don't even know the enemy? When you and Inspector Pluck told me about the other towns where you two have shown evidence of gunfire, it showed that this species knows how to combat firearms. Please. Have a seat so we can discuss this."

"I'd rather not. I'm supposed to pull shift with the rest of these men."

"For how much longer?"

"Less than ten minutes."

"Then I say it's the best time to discuss these matters." The ornithologist walks past the postal inspector and sits on the porch next to his birdcage. "So are you going to answer my question earlier of why you carry Chap around?"

"I'll answer your question if you answer mine first."

"Sure. Ask away, Inspector."

"Remember when we first met this afternoon. You said something about Chap looking for me when he left his cage today. How did you know that?"

"Easy. Chap is a domesticated bird. You've had him since he hatched out of his egg, right? Well, there are some species, like this budgerigar, that are docile by nature and others that are born to be free in the wild."

"Docile? What does that even mean?"

"It means being submissive and comfortable to be in the presence of people or a person as its owner. Some birds, like owls, are incapable of living in a cage since it's in their nature to be out in the wild like other birds of prey. But even for Chap here, it's quite rare to find a bird so attached to you."

"And how did you know he was looking for me?"

"Normally, when a birdcage opens, any bird will fly out and make a run for it. On the other hand, Chap flew around the porch as if it was missing its nest. Since I'm quite good at catching birds, it was easy to grab hold of him when I needed to use the telegraph office."

"I see." Secoli strokes his mustache and beard. "I'd never expect someone with such expertise in birds to give such a profound answer."

They both giggle over the joke.

"Now it's your turn to answer my question, Inspector," the ornithologist says. Secoli stops stroking his facial hair. He then pushes his glasses up to the bridge of his nose and swallows his saliva. Dr. Fletcher remains still and patient

while the Federal agent feels anxious regarding what he's about to say. "I-I-" Secoli stutters. "I-I need Chap."

"Need? Like how?"

"I suffer...mentally...without him."

"Please elaborate, Inspector. I don't understand."

"Promise me..." Secoli crouches to her level and looks her in the eyes. "Promise me that whatever I tell you, it's strictly just between you and me. I wouldn't let Jed know about my condition, even though he's aware of my breakdowns."

"Don't worry, Inspector. You have my word."

"Okay. I fought in the Civil War. I was fighting for the Union Army and..." Secoli stops himself and examines her facial expression. She remains wide-eyed and watchful. "You weren't for the Confederates, were you?"

"Oh, me? I grew up in a family that was from the Confederates. However, I stood for the Union's cause when I studied and taught at Cornell University. That's in New York, of course. And yes, I'm for the Union."

Secoli sighs with relief. "Oh, thank God. It's just too uncomfortable to mention to anyone that I was a Union soldier. Even though it's been years since the war ended, the country is still divided over the North's victory."

"Yes, I'm very aware of that. But what does that have to do with you bringing Chap wherever you go?"

"Right. I was getting to that. I-I was in many battles with the Union and was shot more than once—three times total and survived. I was young, and my job was to be the color bearer. In case you are unaware, it is the person carrying the flag."

"You had to keep hold of the American flag on the battlefield?"

"The Union flag, yes. I remember getting shot for the first time in my third battle carrying the flag. But after my wounds healed, I had to return to the battlefield for my fourth one. That was my last battle." Secoli looks away. "It was horrifying.

"I-I was ambushed by a Confederate fleet. I still remember being left alone.

Abandoned even. I kept hold of the flagpole...," Secoli shuts his eyes, "... sur-surrounded by my dead comrades. Many were close to me. And I remember feeling so vulnerable as the enemy approached me. I remember feeling a bullet go through my stomach and being stomped on so many as I bled to death. Then I blacked out as if I'd died."

The traumatized agent stops speaking and stares at the bathhouse across the main road. He is so lost in his mind that he loses grip on his torch, which falls into the gravelly curve of the main road. Secoli holds on to the birdcage with a tighter grip, even shaking it. Chap wakes up from his sleep and starts chirping out of worry. Dr. Fletcher realizes that he's mentally breaking down. She places her hands on his hand that's holding the cage.

"Hey. Hey. It's all right, Inspector." The ornithologist caresses his hand and forearm. "You're not there anymore."

"I know," Secoli continues, unable to stop shaking. "Whenever I'm reminded of that near-death experience, it gets worse as time passes."

"Then what in the world are you doing being a postal inspector?"

"Because..." Secoli swallows his saliva. "My country needs me. I'm very good at bringing criminals to justice. And I can't do it without Chap by my side."

"So are you telling me you're using Chap to cope with your trauma?" Secoli takes a brief pause before answering. "Yes."

"Oh. I never knew anyone would ever use birds for psychological purposes."

"Psycho-what?" The Federal agent turns to her.

"Psychological. It's the study of how people think. For your condition, it's—quite severe, by what you're telling me. I'm no psychologist." Dr. Fletcher sees from his expression that he doesn't know what that means. "Oh, that's someone who's expertise in how the brain works. As I was saying, what you're dealing with is sad—but extraordinary."

"How so?"

"Well, psychology is a fairly recent study, and it's pretty close to ornithology when I'm trying to understand how birds think based on their behavior. But no one in the educational field I know of has ever used birds to treat a mental diagnosis. Tell me, Inspector. When this series of disappearances gets resolved, would you like to be my personal test subject for this discovery?"

"What would I have to do?"

"Just show up with Chap, follow my instructions, and let me do the research." Secoli hums to himself, saying, "I'll think about it, Doctor."

"So, how long has it been since you've been using Chap to cope with your trauma? Oh, wait. I almost forgot. Since he was born. So how old is Chap now?"

"He was born in 1892 when I got him. So that's—"

"So he's around seven years old? Louie!" she raises her voice, pulling her hands away from him. "I mean, Inspector. Do you know what the lifespan of a budgerigar is?"

Secoli looks into her eyes and shakes his head.

"They live up to eight years of age," the ornithologist continues. "What will you do if Chap passes away from natural causes?"

"I..." Secoli looks away. "I don't know. I never really thought about it since I had him since my divorce."

"Divorce, you say?" She returns her hands to his hand and continues caressing the troubled postal inspector.

"That's right," Secoli sighs, "I've been divorced since Chap was born."

"Don't you have family members or loved ones that you can talk to about your trauma? It's unhealthy to continue ruminating over those events during the Civil War."

"I would. However, I am uncomfortable about talking about my experiences with the war. Since the war ended, this country is still divided into the North and South. I'm very cautious about who I share my experience with. My ex-wife was from a Confederate family. At first, she could look past that I fought for the Union, but after a while, it damaged our marriage whenever we talked about politics."

"I'm so sorry, Inspector. You've been through a lot."

"Yes..." Secoli quickly wipes off a tear. "Yes, I have."

"Don't you have children?"

"I do, but I lost custody of my two young boys."

"Boys?" Dr. Fletcher stops caressing his forearm and hands.

"That's right. My oldest one, Maximillian, must be around nine, and my youngest, Timothy, should be seven."

"I see." She puts her hands on her lap and looks away. "So why do you want to keep all this information away from Inspector Pluck?"

"I just heard him briefly mention serving in the Civil War. But because I have bad experiences with those still attached to the Confederates, I'm too scared to ask."

"Well, judging by his accent," Dr. Fletcher turned to Secoli. "I think it's a bit mid-Atlantic like yours, Inspector. Where is he from anyway?"

"Boston."

"Well, there's your answer. Massachusetts was a free state during the Civil War.

The likelihood of being from a state that far north and being a Confederate is very unlikely."

"Perhaps. However, I want to be apolitical about this. Nothing makes me more uncomfortable than talking about that war and politics."

"I understand. So, how long have you known Inspector Pluck?" Dr. Fletcher asks.

"A couple of days ago, we got assigned to this case." Secoli breaks eye contact, staring off into space. "I feel sorry that Jed had to say goodbye to his family."

"He has a family?" the ornithologist turns back to him. "That's right. He has a wife and four daughters."

"Daughters?" The ornithologist raises an eyebrow. "You don't say. Tell me. What are they like?"

"They were the most adorable family that I've ever seen. I don't know much about them other than saying goodbye to them when we got on our train to this state. But—" Secoli stops momentarily and looks around. "Hey. Where did my torch go?"

Dr. Fletcher points out, "You dropped it on the gravel down there."

The postal inspector gets up from the porch and picks up the torch. It still has fire, but luckily it didn't spread on the ground. When Secoli gets back up, he sees torchlights approaching his direction. Men's voices are heard in the distance. "That reminds me," Secoli continues. "My shift is about to end. Go back to your hotel room before anyone sees you."

"Okay, Inspector." Dr. Fletcher gets up from the porch and returns to the alley between the bank and the hotel. "Have a good night."

She disappears into the darkness. Secoli grabs his birdcage and joins everyone, gathering in the center of the main road. A circle is formed, and inside are Inspector Pluck and the two lawmen. Secoli moves through the circle and makes it to the center.

"Ah, Louie!" Pluck calls out. "How was your shift?"

"It was fine," Secoli answers. "Sheriff, is everyone accounted for?"

"The fourteen that are on my shift are all accounted for. How about you, Hall? Is everyone from your shift accounted for?"

The deputy finishes his counting. "I only counted thirteen."

"That's okay, Deputy Hall," Secoli responds. "I'm here."

"No, Inspector," Hall replies. "That's also including you. We're missing someone."

"Hold on," Wood says. "Are you sure Henry Humphrey and Jeremy Payton are off the list?"

"I'm positive, Sheriff. I updated the list before we began tonight's first shift."

"Everyone from the deputy and Inspector Secoli's shift, stand over here,"

Sheriff Wood points in front of the bathhouse, "so we can get everyone counted, and you all can get some sleep."

The men break out of the circular formation and stand in front of the bathhouse, facing the authorities. The deputy counts again.

"Sheriff," the deputy says, "we're still missing one person."

"What? Deputy Hall, put your torch closer to me so I can have a better look at the list." The sheriff pulls out a scroll. "I'm gonna call your names, and you all say 'Here.' Y'all got that?" The sheriff rolls it open and reads it aloud. "Chuck Madison."

"Here, Sheriff," the stable keeper responds. "Caleb Walsh."

"Here, Sheriff," he responds as well.

The sheriff continues reading off the list. "Patrick Newsome!" "Angus McKinsey!" "David Graft!" "George Brunt!" "Julian Cunningham!" "Gallus Kennedy! Joe Diamond!"

They all respond with "Here, Sheriff!" after hearing their names being called.

He continues until he sees someone new on the list. "Nick Carter!" The sheriff looks closer at the list. "Who's Nick Carter?"

"Here, Sheriff! I'm the train engineer that helped the two postal inspectors to Lemonstown before—that train accident."

"Okay, glad that you're helping us out." Wood continues down the list. "Val Jenkins!"

There is no answer.

"Val Jenkins!" he repeats. "Are you even paying attention?"

The group looks at each other, searching for that person. All of them are unable to find him.

"Where on earth is Father Jenkins?"

"The preacher?" Secoli responds. "The last I saw him was when he was going—"

Secoli immediately runs off to the alley between the bank and Town Hall. Everyone follows the postal inspector rushing across the main road and into the alley. The sheriff and everyone else shout, "Father Jenkins!" as they search for him. Sheriff Wood is leading everyone through the alley. Behind the bank, Secoli stands next to the preacher. Jenkins lies on his stomach next to a barrel of water on the ground. The sheriff kneels and everyone circles around the body.

"He's fine," Secoli says. "He passed out. He's so tired from staying up all day."

The sheriff gently taps the preacher on the cheek, helping Jenkins open his eyes.

"What are y'all looking at?" the preacher says, getting up from the ground. "I was...getting comfortable. That's all. I have to conduct a funeral tomorrow, so cut me some slack."

"You made us worried, Father. Now, get some rest. You got yourself a big day tomorrow." The sheriff gets up and turns to everyone standing behind him. "All right, everyone who pulled the deputy's shift is dismissed! Meet us back here at six A.M. Those who are going to Mr. Humphrey's funeral in the morning are allowed to participate. The rest of you! Get to your posts and keep watch! If I catch any of you falling asleep on my shift, you'll be wishing you hadn't!"

SECOLI LOOKS AT HIS pocket watch to see that his shift for today is nearing its end. The postal inspector doesn't participate in the funeral that's being held. Instead, he guards Lemonstown with the very few on the same shift who don't know Henry Humphrey as well. Besides, there has to be an official in charge while the deputy participates. The funeral lasted about an hour, making it fair that those on his shift this morning did an acceptable amount of time in their line of duty. It would be selfish of Secoli not to let those on his shift pay their respects to Mr. Humphrey.

The bell tower rings, and the mourners come out of Town Hall. This is the only time the curfew has been lifted. It takes a little while for the main road to fill up. The main road hasn't been this crowded since the postal inspectors arrived. Everyone makes way for Mr. Humphrey's casket to be carried out of Town Hall and to Lemonstown's cemetery, located farther north of town. Secoli sees the grieving widow following her husband, who's being carried by four men on his shift. Seeing them do more than attend the funeral proves they aren't trying to escape guard duty.

They make it in front of the stables and put the casket on a wagon. The driver whips the horse's reins, and the horse pulls the wagon at a walking pace so the mourners can follow the hearse on foot. Besides the driver, the only one on top of the hearse wagon is Martha Humphrey, sorrowfully sitting beside her husband's casket.

Seeing how heartbroken the widow is, Secoli looks away and focuses on the birdcage he is holding, which continues to comfort him as always. Being reminded of death makes Secoli think about his conversation with Dr. Fletcher. Taking off his glasses and pinching the bridge of his nose, he thinks about how long Chap has left to live and how he'll cope without his muse.

From behind, Pluck says, "So, how's your shift going, Louie?"

"Oh, Jed," Secoli says. He puts his glasses back on, blinks, and shakes his head rapidly to conceal his emotions. "Please don't sneak up on me like that."

"Sorry. It's just that you should have shown up in the meeting when we

counted heads before switching shifts. Is the funeral distracting you?"

"No, it isn't. I'm just saddened about what Mrs. Humphry is going through."

"Speaking of which, should someone be carrying a rifle to the burial?"

"Jed..." Secoli pulls his head back in surprise. "I don't think that's appropriate."

"Appropriate or not, they're going out of Lemonstown, and there's no telling if those monsters are out in that direction. They're all entering dangerous territory."

"If you're that concerned, I'll walk with the mourners and guard them."

"Denied, Louie." Pluck places his hand on his partner's shoulder. "Your shift is over. You need to head back to your hotel room and rest up for your shift tonight."

"I'm fine, Jed."

"No, you're not." Pluck shakes his head. "Your eyes are pretty red right now. It's either you didn't sleep well, or you're teary-eyed. Did something happen?"

"No. I'm not getting teary-eyed, and I'm feeling healthy. But if you really want me to, I'll head back to my hotel room. But who will be guarding the burial?"

"I'll take care of that." Pluck looks at someone carrying a rifle walking past the jailhouse's porch where he stands. "Hey, you. Jacob—um, Neilson, is it?"

The man stops and turns to the two postal inspectors. "Yes, that's right, Inspector. What do you need, sir?"

"Which post did the sheriff assign you to?" Pluck asks. "Between the trading post and the train station/post office, sir."

"I'm reassigning you to protect the mourners at the cemetery. Get one more person on our shift and tell them they're resigned to post to the cemetery with you. Tell them it's the postal inspector's order. I can't trust that these folks are safe when monsters are still out there."

"What about the sheriff? Won't I get in trouble with him for leaving my post?"

"You let me worry about Sheriff Wood. That's an order directly from me. And make sure that you have everyone come back to Lemonstown as a group. Understand?"

"Oh, I hear you, sir. Let me fetch Berk Hartman. He's more comfortable using a gun than I am?" The man runs across the main road and through the alley between the bank and the hotel.

"As for you, Louie," Pluck turns to his partner, "you get some sleep."

"All right. See you at six tonight." Secoli leaves the porch and heads to the hotel.

Pluck watches the last mourner exit Town Hall. The bell stops ringing as everyone participating in the funeral heads north into the Red Desert. Pluck sees Jacob Neilson bringing someone, and they both chase the crowd, heading to the burial ground.

Everyone from the funeral is off the main road and into the sands of the Red Desert.

Pluck watches the two guards until they both get off the main road before entering the jailhouse. The penitentiary only has a single desk with a couple of wooden chairs: one behind the desk, one against the wall behind the desk, and one at the front of the desk. On the left side of the desk are the jail cells. The jail only consists of two cells, each with an uncomfortable bed, a single barred window, and a very narrow space.

Inspector Pluck sees Jeremy Payton sitting on his bed in the left-hand jail cell. "They hate me, don't they?" the prisoner says with his head down.

"I won't lie to you and say they don't. As much as I had to argue with Mayor McLusky, he insisted on having the funeral and burial today. I hope that nothing will happen to those folks in the cemetery. Otherwise, it's more blood on your hands."

The young man starts to sob. "I told you it was a mistake. An accident. I swear. Isn't anyone out there able to forgive?"

Pluck pities the inmate, realizing his words once again are hurting others. Even when he's supposed to have a whole life ahead of him until his pending trial. Seeing poor Jeremy cry has Pluck head out the door. Pluck then looks in the direction where the mourners are moving. Though it's hard to see the cemetery from where he stands, everyone dressed in black makes them all transparent against the orange sands. The postal inspector is hoping everyone makes it back to Lemonstown safely but is not willing to go since he isn't the emotional type.

Suddenly, a female voice is heard from the opposite direction from where Pluck is looking. "Looks like someone is being the sheriff and deputy's replacement."

Pluck turns his head. "Dr. Fletcher? Hey now. Unless you're going to the outhouse, you're not supposed to be out here."

She approaches the postal inspector from the main road's curve. "That's not what I was told, Inspector. I heard that curfew is lifted."

"It's only lifted to those participating in the funeral. First of all, you never met Mr. Humphrey when he was alive, so you have no excuse for coming out here unprotected."

"Gee, I never met a man as stubborn as you, Inspector. Can't you just have little ol' me get to experience Lemonstown for once?"

"Nothing gets by you, Doctor, does it? I'm really running out of things to say to convince you to stay in your room. Just what am I going to do with you?"

"Trust me, of course. I promise to not get in your way."

Pluck then says, "Follow me," walks down the porch, and enters the alley between the jailhouse and the hardware store. The ornithologist continues following the postal inspector until he stops behind the buildings.

"Now, what is it that you want, Dr. Fletcher?"

"I just wanted to apologize for my behavior last night. It's not normal for me to be rude to you and Inspector Secoli, who have been so gentle and kind to me. Without you two, I'd not be making it safe in Lemonstown."

"Oh...I-I didn't...," the postal inspector stutters, surprised by this sudden apology he's receiving. "You're welcome, Doctor."

"Please, Inspector. Call me Fiona."

"Oh, um…. You're welcome, Fiona."

"That's better. While we're here, how about I show you I'm worth being an exception from being under curfew?"

"How in the world are you going to do that?"

"How about I show you how well I can shoot? If I hit all the targets, I'll be exempted from the curfew."

"And if you miss one target, you will stop resisting and do as you're told."

"Sure." She gives the postal inspector a handshake. "You got yourself a deal."

"Deal." Pluck shakes her hand gently. "Some guards on my shift participating in today's funeral left their guns at the trading post. It's this way."

"Can't I use your gun instead?"

"Oh, no. A handgun is too easy to handle. If you want to convince me that you're good with a gun, you've gotta use a rifle, which everyone else is using."

"Fine." She gives him an annoyed look. "Hand me one of those rifles, and

I'll show you what I got."

The ornithologist follows Pluck behind the buildings leading to where the guns are being stored. The postal inspector sees the trading post's back door open.

"Well, that's irresponsible," Pluck comments. "Who leaves the weapons unlocked? When they return from the cemetery, I'll have a word with them." Pluck enters the trading post's back entrance and heads to the store area.

He takes one of the rifles and a couple of bullets from an already-opened crate. The postal inspector exits from the back door and hands the ornithologist the rifle and three bullets.

"Now show me how you load these bullets into the rifle." She examines the rifle. "This is a carbine, isn't it?"

"Good. Now show me how you load the rifle."

Dr. Fletcher pulls the bolt handle and inserts the bullets into the chamber. Once all three bullets are in, she closes the handle. When she shows that she can load the gun without trouble, Pluck picks up two tin cans from the ground. He places one on top of a wooden fence and one on top of a stack of logs.

"That's two targets," Dr. Fletcher says, "what about the third?" After looking around, Pluck then says, "I have an idea."

The postal inspector pulls out a wrapped object from his coat. He unwraps it and takes out one of the black feathers. Pluck pulls out one of the logs from the stack and makes it stand upwards. He stabs the quill on top of the log firmly on the wood's top surface. He then gets behind the ornithologist standing next to the back door.

"Now, I want you to shoot the can on the log pile first," Pluck instructs. "Then the one on the fence. And lastly, the feather right in front of you—in that order. You're exempt if you can hit all your targets in less than thirty seconds. Got that?"

"Won't everyone hear gunfire and think that we're being attacked?" Fletcher asks.

"You let me worry about that. Now show me what you got."

Dr. Fletcher takes a deep breath and points her carbine at the can on logs. She pulls the trigger, and the can flies out. With no time to waste, Fiona pulls the bolt handle and pops an empty shell out. She pushes the handle back and aims for the can on the fence. That, too, hits and gets knocked out by a bullet. The ornithologist pulls and pushes the bolt handle back.

Pluck counts fifteen seconds pass in his head and is impressed with how good Fiona is with that gun. The ornithologist points her rifle at the feather on the log before her. She takes a deep breath and pulls the trigger. The feather flies out of the log.

"Sweet Lord! That was twenty-two seconds, and nothing was missed. Who taught you how to shoot?"

"My father. So am I exempt from the curfew?"

Pluck walks to the feather. "Well, it sure looks like you're exempt. I must say that you've made a fool outta—" He stops and picks up the black feather. "I'm sorry, Doctor. I think you missed the feather."

"What?" the ornithologist responds with surprise and upset. "That's impossible!"

"Then explain why this feather doesn't have a bullet hole through it."

"You-you placed that feather so firm on the log that it couldn't be pushed out without a bullet hitting it."

"Maybe the wind blew the feather out of the log. C'mon, this thing is about ten inches long. How could you possibly miss this?"

Fletcher raises her voice. "I'm telling you that I know it shot the damn thing. You are not keeping me in the hotel because the feather doesn't have damage on it. You-you must have switched the black feather I hit with the fresh feather!"

"What? Now that's a ridiculous accusation, Doctor!"

"I know you did, Inspector. You have an issue of women capable of handling a gun and joining guard duty with the men in this town."

"Now I've done no such thing! These things are so dangerous that they can literally poke through my jacket! There's no way I'm carrying more than one of these damn things."

"Okay, show me that you ain't hiding another feather. Hand me your coat!"

"Fine." Pluck puts the feather down and removes his jacket. "Here, search it! There isn't anything in there but my bullets, a notepad, my badge, and a box of matches."

Dr. Fletcher takes his coat and checks the sleeve, pocket, and inside of the clothing. It is exactly what Pluck said was in his jacket.

"Well, what about your pants?" she asks angrily.

The postal inspector pulls out the insides of his pockets. The only thing that comes out is his wallet and some coins. He rolls up his pants to his thighs. Dr. Fletcher watches carefully while her face turns red.

"See." Pluck straightens his back. "Face it, Doctor. You lost the bet."

"Horseshit!" she screams. "I hit that perfectly! How about you try shooting that feather and see if you can make a hole in it?"

Pluck grabs the feather from the ground and places the quill firmly on the log's surface. He crouches and blows the feather to see if it's steady; the feather doesn't fly off. He gets in front of the ornithologist and turns around. The postal inspector draws his revolver from his holster and shoots the feather; the feather flies off the log. Both Pluck and Fletcher rush to the feather. When Pluck picks it up, both of them are in shock that there isn't a single bullet hole or any damage on the feather. Pluck drops the feather and fires another shot at it on the ground and sees his bullet ricochet off the side of the roof.

"Oh, my God," Pluck responds in disbelief. "This is impossible!"

Subsequentially, two guardsmen appear from the trading post's alleyway, and one of them says, "What's going on? Are you two okay?"

"Jed! Are you...." Secoli arrives carrying his pistol and birdcage. "Dr. Fletcher? What are you doing here?"

"We-we were doing an experiment," she answers, "and Inspector Pluck and I found out something you all need to know."

Pluck again puts the feather's quill through the log. "Now, you three stand in line and point your guns at the feather. Don't shoot at the feather until I give the count to three."

Pluck and Dr. Fletcher hide behind Secoli as the two guardsmen aim their guns at the feather. The wind blows, but the feather is held in place by its quill, demonstrating its strength.

As soon as the wind stops blowing, Pluck shouts, "Fire!"

Secoli pulls his trigger at the same time the other two do. Three bullets hit the feather, and it flies off the log. Chap, inside its birdcage, reacts negatively toward the gunfire. Everyone notices that one of the bullets ricochets in the fences and sand. Everyone examines the bullet hole in the wall and is both surprised and confused.

"How did one of the bullets get there?" asks one of the guardsmen. "Gentlemen," the ornithologist says as she picks up the feather, "it looks like the feather deflected your bullets."

"What the hell?" one of the men replies. "How is that even possible?"

Dr. Fletcher hands Pluck the feather. There's not a single bullet hole on the dark plume. The only damage the bullets did was to create a dent in the vane and a chip on one of the edges. The feather feels heavier to Pluck than it ever did. He turns to the others.

"This-this explains why we saw bullet holes all over those ghost towns and found no survivors. This beast's feathers—they're bulletproof."

"Jed," Secoli says timidly, "we're gonna have to rethink our strategy on taking this thing down."

CHAPTER 7

No matter how crowded it gets, there is always some space to claim and sleep in the sanctuary. Under these uncertain times, Lemonstown's citizens have never been as communal, forcing everyone to live together. Everyone pitches in to prepare meals, and no one stays alone. Some are eating, others are napping, and others kill time by playing poker on the floor. Although the townsfolk find gratitude in difficult times, they find it inconvenient to be escorted to the outhouse one at a time.

The position of Town Hall guard is the least desired, as all they do is escort those who need to use the outhouse throughout the shift. Though Lorette Brown waits a while for her turn, she's the eighth person that Moses Williams has to take to the privy. Because of the nets with bells set up in every alleyway, he is taking her the longer route around the stables instead of going through the alleyway. Just as they make it around the corner, Dr. Fletcher walks in the opposite direction. All of them nearly bump into each other.

"Oh, excuse me," the ornithologist says. "Have you seen Inspector Pluck?"

"Who the heck are you?" Miss Brown says. "And why is she walking outside without a guard?"

"This is Dr. Fletcher, ma'am," Williams responds. "She's exempt from the curfew because she's helping us out."

"Helping us out?" Brown says. "With what? Wooing the men while you keep the rest of us locked in the Town Hall?"

"That's no way to treat our guest," Williams interrupts, "especially when she's working as hard as anyone to take this devil out." He turns to the ornithologist. "I'm sorry, Doctor. Miss Brown overreacts when she gets jealous."

"Jealous?" Brown punches him on the arm. "Now, you take that back!"

"It's all right." Dr. Fletcher walks away, ignoring the insult. "I'll just find my way to the trading post."

"It's close to the railroad, Doctor!" he shouts as she walks away. Feeling embarrassed, Williams grabs Miss Brown's wrist and leads her to their destination. "As for you, Miss Brown, you oughta learn some manners if you ever want to get married again."

Dr. Fletcher walks down the main road. She notices that she's getting plenty of attention from the other guards. Aware of her attractiveness, the ornithologist doesn't want to attract unwanted attention, but it's unavoidable. She smiles and waves after each greeting but moves faster. She would have gone through the alleys to avoid this much attention, but they're all blocked with nets.

Up ahead, she sees Pluck giving the men instructions on the trading post's porch.

The men he's leading are carrying crates from the building. They all stop what they're doing and gaze at Dr. Fletcher. The postal inspector turns around to see what everyone is looking at.

"Dr. Fletcher," Pluck says, approaching her. "What can I do for you?"

"Oh, um..." The ornithologist stops moving so fast. "The mayor and the sheriff sent me to pick up some more bells for the nets. Do you have any more?"

"Sorry, ma'am. We're all out of stock, and there's none in the hardware store."

"If you don't mind." She then whispers, "I seem to be gathering unwanted attention from the men. Can you kindly escort me back?"

"Oh, sure." Pluck jumps off the porch. "My shift is almost over." He looks at the rest of the guards. "Y'all bring the rest of those boxes to the hotel lobby, ya hear?"

All of them simultaneously respond with a "Yes, Inspector."

"This way, Doctor." Pluck stops her from going in the same direction. "We'll go around this burnt building."

"What happened to it?" Fletcher asks, approaching the derelict building. "This used to be the saloon. It caught on fire after a train accident a couple of days ago."

They make it around the burnt saloon and on the railroad. The ornithologist sees the broken train lying on the ditch next to the tracks they're walking on.

"Was this the train that burned this building down?"

"Yes. It took an entire water tower to put out the flames. Thank goodness they have a second water tower. Otherwise, we'd have to risk our lives in migrating out of this town on foot."

"Wow." Fletcher giggles. "Look at you being a tour guide of Lemonstown."

"Naw. I just got here a couple of days ago. I'm no expert on this town. Changing the subject…. How long have you been an orni-ornithologist?"

"Almost ten years."

"Studying birds for so long, I don't suppose you ever get tired of studying the same birds. Ever thought of studying different animals?"

"No, never. No other animal kingdom is as interesting to me as birds."

"Because they can fly, right?"

"Not all of them. There are flightless birds, you know. But what I admire about them is that they're the only other warm-blooded species that aren't mammals, and they have unique beaks, lay eggs, and have intelligence. If only you've been out of this country and seen birds worldwide, you too would be fascinated."

"Do you have a favorite bird?" Pluck says as he steps off the railroad and moves to the neighborhood road.

The ornithologist follows him off the railroad. "I cannot say. I love them all."

"Okay, then, what is your least favorite bird?"

"I think you're asking the wrong person, Jed. No bird will ever be seen as inferior or superior to me. How about you? Do you have a favorite bird?"

"I really don't think much about animals. I just ride horses, and that's pretty much it. But my family loves birds."

"So you have a family, Jed? Where are they?"

Pluck puts his left hand in his jacket pocket. He removes his wedding ring with his thumb and pinky finger. The postal inspector then takes his hand out of his pocket, leaving his ring inside. He looks around as he and Dr. Fletcher continue down the neighborhood road. He sees guards setting up nets between houses with no bells attached.

"I only have siblings who have kids, which are my nieces and nephews," Pluck continues. "I see them from time to time on holidays like Thanksgiving and Christmas."

The ornithologist raises her brows and looks at Pluck from the corner of her eye with suspicion. "So you're not married?"

"No." Pluck puts his head down. "I mean, I was."

"And do you have any children? Daughters, perhaps?"

"Daughters? No, it didn't work out between my ex-wife and me."

Now, both of her brows are raised. "Have you ever thought about settling down and having a family one day, Jed?"

"Maybe one day, I suppose." The postal inspector clears his throat. "How about you? Ever thought of having a family one day and settling down from putting all that attention on birds?"

"I do want children." Her expression turns happy. "In fact, one day, I want to have many children and make them all enjoy birdwatching with me."

"Really? So, how many children do you plan to have?"

"Twenty."

"That's not humanly possible." Pluck stops walking, examining her facial features and seeing her roughly as old as him. "If you start now, you'll be past your sixties to reach that goal. By that age, you'll risk your child's life and your life."

Dr. Fletcher stops when she notices that she's ahead of Pluck. "Well, if I had triplets each time, that would speed up the process, wouldn't it?"

"But you've been studying birds for a decade, and you should have planned it out decades ago."

"How ironic that you judge me for remaining in my expertise for so long, yet here you are, married to your career as a Federal agent. Besides, you don't have to worry so much about me and my plans, Jed." Fletcher gets close to the postal inspector and looks him in the eyes. "It's just ideal."

"Inspector Pluck." The mayor's voice is heard in the distance.

Dr. Fletcher slowly backs away and turns to the mayor. Pluck shakes off his intense conversation with the ornithologist as he sees McLusky and the sheriff approach. The mayor doesn't look too happy.

"Do you have any more bells to put on these nets, Inspector?" the mayor asks.

"I don't see the point of attaching bells in these nets when we can use all we have in the main road, Mayor. I'd say keep those bells where they're at. There is no point in having the guards spread out in the neighborhood area when everyone's in Town Hall."

"That still doesn't explain why the nets in the main buildings have so many bells when we can have one bell attached to each net."

"Mayor, one bell will not be loud enough for everyone to hear in the distance. You saw it yourself—one touch of those nets will ring all of those bells."

"Then there's no point in setting up these nets between houses."

"It is necessary. We don't want them to run and hide between buildings.

We have to keep them visible on the roads."

"But what if they can fly over the buildings?" Sheriff Wood intervenes. "Then what?"

Pluck doesn't respond. This is the first time he finds himself unable to win an argument with the mayor or the lawmen.

"Sheriff," McLusky says, "get your men and start taking those bells from the main buildings and make sure each of those nets has no more and no less than one bell each."

"You got it, Mayor," the sheriff responds. "I'll tell that to the next shift since it's almost time for us to switch shifts."

"Is it six o'clock already?" The mayor turns to his lawman.

"Yes, sir. Meet you at the rendezvous. Oh, Pluck. You don't have to make it to formation. I got you accounted for already."

The sheriff takes the long way to the main road.

"One more thing," the mayor adds. "Dr. Fletcher, I know you're exempt from curfew with Inspector Pluck's approval, but I want you to be careful. I can't bear the thought of someone as pretty as you getting hurt."

"Don't worry about me, Mayor, but thank you," Fletcher responds. "With my involvement, Lemonstown has a great advantage to stand up against these giant birds."

Pluck and Fletcher watch McLusky get to the railroad and disappear. There's still sunlight at this hour. The neighborhood road is empty now that the guards are on the main road for their headcount, leaving Pluck and Fletcher alone.

"Well, you heard it from the mayor," Fletcher says. "For now on, you're going to have to escort me wherever I go."

"Correction," Pluck says. "He said a guard or two will have to escort you. He said nothing about me being with you all the time."

"C'mon, Jed. I don't trust anyone besides you and Louie."

"Look, Fiona," Pluck says. "Louie and I have big responsibilities to keep this town safe. You don't know how much responsibility that is or what kind of danger we're really in. This isn't some birdwatch event. We are the prey here. No woman should be risking their life like we are. Why don't you get yourself acquainted with the ladies?"

"They're a gossipy 'n envious bunch. Ain't no way I ever get along with them."

"And you're much less safe with the men staring at you. Gee, why can't you understand the situation we're in here, Fiona?"

The ornithologist goes silent and looks away in disappointment. Pluck sees himself again, upsetting another person. It makes him even more guilty for doing it to someone he's highly attracted to. Dr. Fletcher walks away without saying a word before Pluck can apologize.

Pluck remains in place as she heads in the same direction the mayor went. Pluck puts his hand in his pocket when she disappears and takes out his wedding ring. The temptation to violate his commitments continues to get harder to resist.

Deserts are known for their humid weather, yet many who haven't been in one for long aren't aware of how cold it gets at night. It explains why many homes and buildings in deserts have furnaces. Although the Midwest folks wear clothing that protects them from the harsh sun, it doesn't keep them warm enough on frigid nights. The guards on shift are struggling tonight, as it is the coldest night in Lemonstown since the end of spring. As for the men on break, they're sharing the same space with the women and children in the Town Hall.

Everyone in the sanctuary has brought their blankets from their homes. The husbands on break stay warm by sharing blankets with their wives and children. It would have been ideal for others to have a blanket by themselves. However, the lack of additional body heat makes it challenging to endure the cold. Even the candles lighting up the sanctuary aren't doing much to make the citizens sleep more comfortably. If there's ever a time to be communal, it would have to be sharing body heat on cold nights like this.

"Damn," a woman swears as she shivers. "Why is it freezing in the middle of August?"

"August is the last month of summer, after all," says another woman beside her. "Seems like the season is changing sooner than anyone expected."

"Fall has arrived this soon? Oh, dear, Pearl. I gotta clean out the furnace once we're allowed to—oh, I forgot. We don't live in the saloon anymore."

"Good riddance."

"Hey. Ain't no way to speak ill of the dead like that. Sure, Mr. Benjamin was a pig to us, but no one deserves to die the way he and his men did."

"Okay, I'm sorry. What I don't get, Anabelle is why we have to move out of our hotel rooms while the postal inspectors and that new doctor are still sleeping there. We could be a lot warmer there than over here."

"Well, they'd better not be taking the whole hotel for themselves. What could they possibly need from an entire building?" Anabelle wraps her blanket tighter. "And why is that birdwatcher getting special treatment anyway?"

"I'm sure it's for a good reason. Everyone thinks it's a giant bird taking all the other towns. If that's the case, then it's God's mercy for sending Dr. Fletcher here. When this is over, what do you want to do?"

"What do you mean?" Anabelle raises her brows.

"What I mean is, once they take care of that giant bird, what are you going to do with your life? We got no job. We need food. And this town is damaged beyond repair."

"That's a bit of an exaggeration, don't you think? I'd be happy staying in Lemonstown."

"You really want to stay here? I mean, after all we've been through?"

"It's not that bad, Pearl." Anabelle looks down, not wanting to argue with her friend. "At least we're being fed and taken care of. Also, not everyone here hates us. If they did, we wouldn't be sharing space with everyone and be attacked by those birds."

"Speaking of birds, you don't suppose the birdwatcher doctor and Inspector Secoli have something going on between them, do ya? You know, the bird obsessed and the bird owner? Seems like the best way to catch a lady like her."

Anabelle giggles. "Without that bird, I doubt Inspector Secoli would even have a chance with someone as pretty as Dr. Fletcher."

"By the way, what did she say she was? An oni-orna... the job that studies birds?"

"I know what you mean. I can't even remember what it's called either."

"Well, whatever it's called, once this damn curfew is all over, I'll ask if I can join Dr. Fletcher and be her assistant."

"Is that your plan? You're really going to leave Lemonstown with her?"

"Why not? She seems to have an exciting life that's full of adventure. And look where she is now. She's telling these men what to do as much as the inspectors. Who knew someone who studies birds could have so much power? It's...quite inspiring."

"Pearl." Anabelle puts her hand on the same shoulder where she hit her. "Please don't go. This town won't be the same without you."

"At least for you, it won't be. When I leave, no one will even remember that I was here. Being with Dr. Fletcher is a good enough reason to get out of here."

"And if she refuses?"

"I'm not someone who takes no for an answer, Anabelle. Wherever she goes, I'll follow her. As long as I'm not with another man telling me what to do, it's better for me."

"That's dedication and all, but," Anabelle moves her hand from Pearl's shoulder to her hands, "you might creep her out. You better practice how to approach a lady like her. It ain't the same as charming a man in the saloon."

"This is great and all," Pearl yawns, "but it's getting late." She lies on her side on the long chair they're sitting on. "You should get some sleep as well."

"I will." Anabelle gets up and leaves her blanket on her seat. "But first, I need to use the outhouse."

"Hold on a sec." Pearl gets up from her seat and follows her while still keeping her blanket on. "I need to go too."

"Weren't you just falling asleep a second ago?" Annabelle looks at her as she heads to the front door.

"I was," Pearl says, catching up to her. "But I need to go to the outhouse as well."

"Mr. Newsome!" Anabelle calls to the guard as she and Pearl exit through the front door. "We both need to go to the outhouse."

"Sure," the guard standing in front of the porch says. "But I'm only allowed to take one person at a time."

"But we saw you earlier escorting Mrs. Graft and her child out of Town Hall."

"A woman with a child is an exception, Miss Larson." Newsome places

his rifle against the wall and crosses his arms. "I can bring only one person at a time. So, which one of you wants to go to the outhouse first?"

"Oh, c'mon, Patrick." Pearl stomps her foot on the porch. "If you take both of us there, it will save you an extra trip."

"You've got a point," the guard says, releasing his arms and looking around. "Okay, follow me. If the deputy or postal inspector catches us, we'll all get in trouble. So we better move fast, okay?"

Both Anabelle and Pearl nod with a smile just as Newsome lights his torch with a match, which quickly ignites. The guard then grabs his rifle and leads the two ladies through the dark main road. Anabelle and Pearl can barely see in front of them, except for some of the torches carried by other guards. Both of their dresses are blown by the strong wind, and the flame on Newsome's torch can barely contain itself from the gusts. If the torch he's carrying was thinner, the fire would have been put out immediately.

Once they make it around the stables, both ladies run to the outhouse. Anabelle goes in first, Pearl waits outside for her turn, and Newsome turns away from the latrine. The bathhouse owner is so uncomfortable with the women doing their business that he moves a couple more steps away from the outhouse. Anabelle finishes using the latrine, and Pearl goes in as soon as she comes out.

Upon exiting, Anabelle is confused as to why Newsome is farther away and facing the opposite direction from her. She remains standing where she is, unsure what the man is thinking or if there's anything in front of him.

Pearl steps out of the outhouse and notices her friend and escort looking away and standing still before asking, "Hey, what's going on?"

Anabelle shushes her. "I think something is in front of us."

Newsome hums over what he hears and turns to the ladies. "You two done? Let's head back inside before we get caught."

"Oh." Anabelle is caught off guard by his upbeat tone. "Yes. We're done here." The three move quickly out of the backway and around the stables. Before returning to the main road, Newsome looks around to see the torchlights from the other guards on duty farther down the main road. He signals Anabelle and Pearl to continue moving, yet he doesn't move as fast as when he took them out of Town Hall. The wind isn't as strong as earlier, making the return to the sanctuary easier. Walking down the main road gives Anabelle an eerie feeling as she hears a horse from behind her. It isn't coming from the stables but from outside and is moving toward them.

Anabelle can feel this unstoppable force heading right behind her. She hears the stomps and noises of what sounds like a wild horse. Her immediate reaction is to pull Pearl toward the main road's curve. Just as she saves her friend from being hit, she sees a horse just mere inches away from hitting her best friend. Pearl doesn't understand why she was pulled to the side but then hears their escort take a bump and collapse on the ground. Newsome's fallen torch illuminates the scene, revealing that the mysterious horse has also fallen upon contact with Newsome.

"Mr. Newsome!" Pearl yells as she frees herself from her friend's grasp.

The ladies run after Newsome to see if he's okay but stop when the horse gets up and gallops around in a frenzied state. Newsome's torch is on the ground, showing that this black horse has feathers all over its back. Pearl and Anabelle recognize that it's the same black feathers that the postal inspectors showed to everyone are all over the horse's back. While the animal circles around the unconscious Newsome, the two ladies notice something attached to the horse's saddle.

They both look down to see the stirrup tied to a strap attached to someone's foot.

A person in a military uniform is covered in the same black feathers that the horse is covered with. No one could identify who the person is since the body is facing away from the only light source. The body's weight keeps the horse from running away as it gallops in place. If the horse's screams hadn't alerted those around, Pearl's screaming over the horrifying sight surely would have been heard by everyone in town.

Anabelle covers Pearl's mouth, but it's already too late. All the guards on duty are heading in their direction, and others who are resting step out of Town Hall. The men run and try to settle the wild horse down.

Many are kicked to the ground, failing to grab the reins to calm it down. After the horse knocks down the third man, one of the men on the ground gets in front of it and pulls its reins down to try to get it to stop.

The horse refuses to obey the command and stands on its hind legs, sending the guard holding its reins to go up in the air. While the horse is rearing, the other guards grab hold of the reins and together pull it down. Anabelle and Pearl pull the unconscious Newsome away from the horse as he's close to getting stomped by the horse's hooves.

As the horse's head is pulled by the reins, Inspector Pluck intervenes by caressing it and whispering gently to calm the troubled animal. The horse finally stops being hysterical.

Inspector Secoli cuts the leather strap and frees the horse from the body. Dr. Fletcher runs toward the military person covered in feathers. She checks the body and feels a pulse. The fallen soldier is breathing.

"Good Lord!" the ornithologist exclaims. "This man—he's still alive!"

"Chuck Madison," Pluck turns to the stable owner, "put this horse in your stables and keep it there."

"Yes, sir," the stable keeper responds, guiding the injured horse to join the other horses in the keep.

"The rest of you, keep an eye out and guard the Town Hall and hotel. There might be something out there, so be prepared to shoot whatever approaches." Pluck turns to the men who came out of the Town Hall. "The rest of you who aren't on shift, help me bring these two unconscious bodies to the hotel. Burnt, get your hotel keys, and open a room for both of these men."

The hotel manager nods at the postal inspector and rushes to fetch the room keys to his hotel. Pluck, kneeling next to Pearl and Anabelle, looks at Newsome, who's unconscious and bleeding from a head wound caused by landing headfirst on the ground. Pluck picks him up from his arms, and men from Town Hall run in to help him carry Newsome to the hotel. Carrying the other body isn't any easier since the fallen soldier is covered in razor-sharp black plumes. One of them carrying him has his forearm cut from the feathers, causing him to release and flee from the pain. Pluck sees what's happening, so he lets the men carrying Newsome take over, bringing him to the hotel and rushes to help carry the unconscious military man.

The postal inspectors and lawmen carefully carry the soldier to the hotel with Newsome and his carriers. Anabelle and Pearl follow them to the lodge, wanting to do more to help. Dr. Fletcher sees them hurrying to the hotel and stops the two ladies.

"You shouldn't be here," the ornithologist says, pulling both of their arms.

"We just want to help them out," Pearl tells her. "We can't just sit around and do nothing."

"You're right." Dr. Fletcher changes her mind and lets go of their arms. "We need all the help we can get. Are you both willing to do everything that I tell you?"

While Anabelle gives her a serious nod, Pearl nods while smiling. She is thrilled to have the chance to prove herself worthy of being the ornithologist's assistant.

"Good." Dr. Fletcher points to both of them. "Now stand beside me and follow my lead. One slip-up from either of you, and it's back to the sanctuary. Got it?"

"Yes, ma'am," the both of them reply as they follow her to the lodging.

The three ladies enter the lodging as the men head up the stairs. They follow the group carrying the soldier to his room. The men open the door to a room and place the man on the bed. Newsome is placed in a nearby hotel room, where he's getting his forehead bandaged. Dr. Fletcher sees that the bedrooms upstairs are smaller than the downstairs bedrooms where she and the postal inspectors sleep.

"Does anyone have anything to help remove the feathers and needles from this man?" Secoli shouts while sitting on a chair, catching his breath.

"I've got some tools in my office, Inspector," the hotel owner answers as he heads out of the room.

"Thanks, Mr. Brunt," Secoli responds as he leans back in the chair out of exhaustion.

Exhausted as well, Pluck examines the soldier. He doesn't have a hat or emblem to indicate which military division he belongs to. Despite how much blood is on the uniform, Pluck recognizes that the soldier's blue uniform and yellow gloves mean he's from the United States Army Cavalry. His upper arm sleeve has two large yellow V-shaped patches that indicate he's a sergeant. He's someone this town desperately needs but is in very bad shape.

He is punctured by black feathers throughout his scalp and face, down to his shoulders and chest. It is hard to see how bad the sergeant is outside, but with the lamp inside, it's clear how much blood is all over his face and body.

"Goddamn," Pluck swears as he examines the soldier. "It's a miracle this man survived. Now we know this giant bird is ruthless."

The soldier says something in a low, whimpering voice. Nobody in the room can hear what he's saying.

"Excuse me?" Pluck moves his head closer. "Can you please repeat that?" Pluck hears the soldier struggling to say, "Water...."

The postal inspector turns to everyone in the room and asks, "Does anyone have some water for him?"

"I have some," the sheriff responds.

The lawman passes him his canteen from under his coat, opens the cap, and helps the poor soldier drink the water from the canteen. The sergeant keeps drinking without catching his breath until it's empty. The hotel manager returns to the second floor with a box of tools. He places it on the hotel room table and opens it. There are surgical tools like scissors, tweezers, screws, and saws. Dr. Fletcher takes out a tweezer and turns to Anabelle and Pearl.

"Okay." A serious look spreads across the ornithologist's face. "We have to remove the feathers from this soldier. I need you two to hold this box and hand me the tools I need when I ask for them. You got it?"

"We're not familiar with any of these tools," Pearl says as she grabs the box and looks inside. "Can you quickly tell us the names of each of them?"

"Never mind. Just stand beside me and let me pull out whatever tool we need." Dr. Fletcher turns to Secoli. "Inspector, I need to borrow the chair for a minute."

"Yes, ma'am." He gets out of his seat and places the chair beside the bed. Dr. Fletcher sits down and attempts to pull out one of the feathers from the man's face. Instantly, the sergeant rears up and screams. Pluck immediately pulls the soldier back to his bed, and the rest of the men hold him down.

"Quickly." Fletcher turns to the ladies. "Pass me that towel. He needs something to bite on to endure the pain."

Pearl passes the ornithologist the towel hanging on the doorknob. Fletcher then places the towel in the sergeant's mouth as he struggles. She uses the tweezer again and pulls out another feather. His screams sound loud and painful, even with a towel covering his mouth. The men holding him down struggle to keep his limbs from moving.

"You—" Dr. Fletcher points to Pearl. "See that bucket in the hallway? I need you to bring it here so we can put these feathers away."

Pearl runs out of the bedroom and fetches the pail. When she brings the bucket, Dr. Fletcher drops the plucked feather in the pail. The ornithologist pulls out another one. Witnessing the gruesome sight makes Anabelle put the box on the only table and head out of the bedroom. Pearl doesn't bother going after her but remains to assist.

Anabelle can't take any more of the bleeding and the screaming, covering her ears and cowering on the floor. The men who carried Newsome to his bedroom then rush into the sergeant's room to restrain him and complete the operation. The screaming becomes so loud and disturbing that Anabelle rushes downstairs to leave the hotel. She remains outside, waiting for Pearl as she catches her breath.

Though she can still hear the screaming outside the hotel, she refuses to go back to the Town Hall until Pearl is done. None of the guards outside are bothered that she's sitting on the porch's stairs alone when the rest are under curfew. Pearl is the first to emerge from the hotel after the soldier's screaming stops after half an hour of treating his wounds.

"Are you alright, Annie?" Pearl walks out the front door and stands on the porch. "I'm sorry, but Dr. Fletcher needed my assistance."

"It's all right," Anabelle replies, sounding like she's okay, but her body language says otherwise. She walks up to the hotel's porch. "I'm not meant for that kind of stuff. How's the soldier doing?"

"He's doing great. We got all the feathers off him, and he's fully bandaged up."

All the men from the sergeant's room leave the hotel and pass the two ladies. They all walk straight to the Town Hall to get back to sleep before their shift begins. In the darkness, the two ladies see the guards on duty pointing their rifles toward the Red Desert. None of them want to get anywhere close to this giant bird and end up like the soldier after hearing him from the hotel. The two young women turn around to see Sheriff Wood and Deputy Hall walk past them without saying a word.

"Well, since it's over," Anabelle covers her mouth as she yawns, "how about we get some sleep?"

"Not yet." Pearl walks to the hotel's entrance door. "I need to see how the soldier is doing."

Anabelle follows Pearl back to the hotel. The two ladies arrive at the stairs and see postal inspectors coming down, who do not acknowledge their presence in the hallway.

"Jed," Secoli says in an exhausted tone. "I know my shift won't end till half an hour, but I haven't seen Chap in a while." He puts his hands on his knees to catch his breath. "I don't feel like myself right now."

"You've done enough, Louie," Pluck says, giving his partner a pat on the shoulder. "But I'm glad you're doing better for yourself without Chap."

Secoli enters his hotel room and locks his door. Pluck walks past Anabelle and Pearl, not saying anything to them. They both turn and look at the postal inspector leaving the lobby and into the main road.

"Gee," Pearl complains as she puts her hands on her hips. "Do these men not even acknowledge that we helped them?"

"Give 'em a break, Pearl." Anabelle places her hand on her friend's shoulders to comfort her. "They did all the heavy lifting, and they're exhausted from helping the soldier. C'mon." She turns to the stairs. "Let's see how our patient is doing."

As they reach the second floor, they peek around the soldier's door, which is wide open. They see the soldier's clothes have been removed, and his head is entirely wrapped in bandages, with only his eyes, nose, and mouth exposed. Dr. Fletcher places her hand on his forehead to check his temperature. The soldier's blood is on her hands, so she slowly licks it off.

"Dr. Fletcher." Pearl startles the ornithologist as she rushes to the bedroom. "Don't do that. You're going to get sick if you do that. Here, use a towel." She turns to her friend, who's still standing in front of the doorway. "Anabelle, fetch some water to clean the blood off her hands." Anabelle rushes downstairs. "How is the soldier doing?" Pearl asks as she cleans Dr. Fletcher's hands with the towel.

"He's doing fine," Dr. Fletcher says as she allows Pearl to wipe her hands clean. "I'm glad he's finally asleep." She releases her hands, leads Pearl out of the bedroom, and closes the door. "He's not in a condition to be interrogated, but in the morning, the postal inspectors and I will ask the soldier what happened to his division and what exactly he saw. If I need anything, I'll fetch you. Also, I didn't catch both of your names."

"Oh, I'm Pearl." She blushes. "And my friend is Anabelle."

"I want to thank you and Anabelle for your help." She fixes Pearl's messy raven hair and gets a better look at her blue eyes and freckled face. "I just want to show my gratitude for your bravery and selflessness in helping Mr. Newsome and Sergeant West."

"I'm happy to hear that." Pearl's face turns even redder. "I'm always glad to help you out."

"I almost forgot. I left the bucket of feathers inside. I need them for my research."

Dr. Fletcher re-enters the bedroom and retrieves the pail full of black razor plumes from the chair and the bed. Even with every step that makes the wood floor creak, the ornithologist manages to not wake the soldier.

"I don't want to take any more of your time," Fletcher said. "I will need all the help I can get from you and Anabelle tomorrow, so please get some rest."

"Really?" She joyfully raises her head.

"Yes." Dr. Fletcher walks past Pearl and descends the stairs. "Have a good night."

"Goodnight, Dr. Fletcher." From the second floor, Pearl hears her close her hotel room door.

Pearl smiles as she walks down the stairs and heads out of the hotel. When she's about to go down the porch's stairs, Anabelle appears and brings in a bucket full of water. Pearl stops on the main road's curve as Anabelle stands in confusion.

"What?" Anabelle puts the bucket down. "She doesn't want water anymore?"

"Not anymore." Pearl heads back to the Town Hall. "But we should get to sleep."

SERGEANT WEST WAKES up from a nightmare. Even in his dreams, he still remembers the events from earlier tonight. He looks around and sees he's still in the same hotel room. He catches his breath from the attack he's been through. He then lies back down and tries to get back to sleep.

However, the soldier is still in a lot of pain. There are still severe excruciating punctures all over his face and body. None of his rescuers know it, but he has additional injuries, including a broken rib and a twisted ankle from falling off his horse when arriving in Lemonstown. Each time he moves, he's in the worst pain he's ever felt. Sergeant West cannot help but think about how his cavalry was slaughtered in the ambush.

West can't recall what attacked him, but he was lucky to get out of it. The bed he's lying on isn't comfortable. Even if he wanted to move around and get comfortable, his pain would only get worse. The one thing an injured person cannot stand is cold temperatures. Even being covered in a blanket and having his entire face bandaged up, he can't find any warmth from the objects touching him.

He closes his eyes to get back to sleep. Even when he closes his eyes, he sees the moonlight through the window through his eyelids. Suddenly, through his closed lids, the light flickers like a shadow moving past the light. Sergeant West opens his eyes and moves his head toward the window. There's nothing but the nightly clouds that are almost covering the moon. He closes his eyes again and can see the moonlight through his eyelids.

For a while, everything remains normal, but the light is no longer seen through his closed eyes. At first, the soldier thinks he's asleep but still thinks to himself. He opens his eyes and notices the room is dark. He turns his head and sees why the moonlight isn't giving the room a little bit of light. Something is standing outside the window, staring at him.

Sergeant West notices the figure has feathers and immediately knows what it is.

He wants to scream, but he is petrified. The pain in his ribs and ankles makes him unable to get out of bed. He can only shake timidly and watch the dark figure stare back at him.

But the staring doesn't last long. The figure uses its talons to open the window and reach for the escaped victim. When Sergeant West attempts to scream, the talon grabs him by the throat and pulls him off his bed. The claws go deep into his vulnerable neck and do not let go.

The claws go deeper and deeper until the tips of the claws touch and pierce his throat. All the soldier can do is squirm from the pain. With all its might, the dark figure rips out the soldier's throat, blood gushing everywhere. The sergeant holds on to his exposed neck and trembles from the agony. He moves his legs so much that he kicks the bedframe's legs so hard that it moves the bed.

The figure notices how much noise the victim is making. To put him out of his misery, the figure places its talons firmly on his chest. It uses its hallux at the back of its foot with all its might to piece the sergeant's sternum and reach for his heart. With the big claw that it has, it stabs, and stabs, and stabs until it hits the racing heart. The sergeant stops moving and bleeds profusely on the floor where he lies.

The mysterious figure doesn't take its talons off the man's chest. Instead, it grasps inside the body. With the strength of one foot, it can lift the entire body up. As it carries its prey on one talon, it uses the other foot to hop its way to the window. The feathered fiend flees through the window and flies away with its prey. The moon is now covered by clouds, making it so dark that no one in Lemonstown can possibly see that they've had an intruder tonight.

CHAPTER 8

Patrick Newsome's rest is disrupted by loud stomping and people yelling from the hallways, making his head injury feel worse. There's barely any sunlight coming through the window, but it's nowhere as bright as the light seen underneath the door in front of him. The light outside Newsome's hotel room flickers as shadows from the hallway pass between the lamp and his doorway. When the noise gets louder, someone bangs on the door and barges in. The room becomes so bright that Newsome covers his eyes and endures the migraines.

"Oh, thank God," a familiar voice says, approaching Newsome in his bed. "Patrick, you're still here."

More men enter Newsome's room. One of the men removes his blanket and puts a lamp over the bed he's lying on. The injured bathhouse owner moans and holds the side of his head as his migraine worsens.

"No sign of blood or any injuries," says another familiar voice.

"Logan? Daniel?" asks the bathhouse owner, recognizing their voices. He keeps his head down and covers his eyes from the bright lamp. "What's going on?"

"It's us, Pat," one of the guards says, pulling Newsome's blanket back on.

"You know that cavalry soldier bumped into you tonight?"

"What soldier?" Newsome asks after he pulls his blanket up and covers his head. "I don't remember how I got in this bed."

"Well, it's nothing for you to worry about. Just stay here and get some rest."

"But what's with all the noise?" The bathhouse gets out of bed.

"Whoa there, Pat." His friend grabs him by the shoulders. "You're in no condition to help. You need to stay in and rest."

"Excuse me." Someone walks into the room carrying a birdcage. "Why is Mr. Newsome out of his bed? Is he all right?"

"He is, Inspector." Smith lets go of his shoulder. "Pat is just confused. I'm trying to put him back to bed."

"Well, it's good to see that he's safe." Secoli walks out the door. "Go back to sleep, Mr. Newsome. We'll handle everything here."

Newsome no longer resists as Logan helps him go back to his bed. The injured man gets under his covers just as the guards finish their search.

"There isn't anything unusual in this room, Logan," says one of the guards standing next to the door. "We need to check the other hotel rooms and see if anyone has been in there."

As the door shuts, Newsome lies back down to settle his migraine. The noises and stomping through the walls make it difficult for him to get back to sleep. He moves to his side and covers his ears with his pillow, but it doesn't help at all. The bathhouse owner's curiosity is piqued by the commotion coming from the hallways. With all his might, Newsome gets out of bed again. Though still lightheaded and aching, he slowly approaches the door.

He cracks the door open to see Inspector Secoli talking to Sheriff Wood. He doesn't make out what the conversation is about, no thanks to the racket that's occurring. However, he does hear the inspector say, "It found us because it followed that soldier." They both head to the stairs as the sheriff says, "We gotta put the guards in a perimeter from the hotel to the Town Hall."

Newsome opens the door and peers down both ends of the hallway and finds no one in sight since they're in the other hotel rooms. The bathhouse owner quietly leaves his room, getting ready to move down the stairs. Upon reaching the steps, he sees a door to the abandoned room next to his hotel room open, and a lamp is on inside.

As Newsome walks into the room, he is appalled to see that it's a crime scene. He sees a long bloodstain across the pillow to the edge of the bed. The trail of blood continues to the floor, where it spreads even wider.

The trail doesn't stop there. It continues up the wall and ends at the window that's still open. The recognizable stench of the black feathers is all over the room, yet he sees no feathers anywhere.

Newsome is perturbed that this happened next door and so recently. He steps backward over the disturbing sight, unable to take his eyes off the room. The bathhouse owner has his back against the hallway wall and can still see the bloody scene in the distance. Newsome averts his eyes and clutches his knees before vomiting on the hallway floor just as his friends make it back to the hallway.

"Oh, my God, Patrick."

Logan and the other three go toward him. They all catch him before he collapses, nearly landing on his vomit.

"You should have stayed in your room."

"No!" the bathhouse owner exclaims as he's held by the guards. "Please don't send me back to my room! I'm too damn close to that-that…" He struggles to finish as he points to the crime scene. "…that blood!"

Logan knows how disturbed his friend is now that Newsome knows he's near the murder location. As the guards are holding Newsome, they all feel him quivering. He is so afraid that he keeps watching the bloody room, unable to stand properly. Despite being pulled back into his room, Newsome refuses to return to his bed. Once freed, he leans against the wall, cowering for dear life.

"It's no use, Logan," one of the guards says. "Pat is hysterical. He's seen too much."

"What is the meaning of this?" Secoli says, going up the stairs. "I thought I told you to put him to bed."

Smith says, "Patrick Newsome snuck out of his room and saw Sergeant West's room. He's so scared that we can't put him back to sleep. He refuses to return to his room, knowing he's so close to the crime scene. Would it be all right if he switched rooms to calm him down?"

Secoli stops midway up the stairs and sees Newsome trembling and his vomit on the floor.

"There should be one more room at the bottom floor that isn't taken. I think the one next to Dr. Fletcher's room is still vacant." Secoli rushes back downstairs with Sheriff Wood and Logan Smith. "I'll grab the keys from the clerk's desk. You and the rest escort him to his new room."

"Right away, sir," Smith responds, grabbing his friend from behind.

Secoli puts his birdcage on the clerk's desk as he goes around it. Chap wakes up as the postal inspector pulls out the drawers and takes the keys to all the hotel rooms. He grabs his birdcage and hurries down to Newsome's new hotel room. It's easy for Secoli to find which key unlocks the door next to Dr. Fletcher's room, as it has a small carving with the room number on each of them. Upon unlocking the door, everyone hears Newsome screaming as he's carried downstairs.

Secoli focuses his attention on the lobby's direction, where he sees the guards carrying the traumatized bathhouse owner. Two guards hold Newsome's back while the other two hold his legs and walk backward. Dr. Fletcher comes out of her hotel room in her sleepwear with her boots on. The group passes her door and enters the bathhouse owner's new room. Curious to see what's happening, she follows everyone entering the new room next to hers.

Realizing he's in a new room, the bathhouse owner stops yelling and catches his breath. The guards put him in his bead and put him under the covers while Inspector Secoli checks on his bandaged scalp.

"It's okay, Mr. Newsome," the postal inspector says. "You're safe and in a better place now. Just lie down and rest. Just hang on tight, and we'll—"

The postal inspector stops as he hears an unnatural sound coming from outside. Secoli sees everyone in the room startle and pause over what they just heard. It sounded like a combination of a woman screeching and an eagle's peal call.

"What the hell is that?" Newsome swears as he grips his blanket and covers his mouth with it.

"Oh, no—" Secoli mutters, looking at the ceiling and the window next to the bed. "Don't tell me they found us."

The second time they hear the screeching, everyone leaves the room. Dr. Fletcher follows the men running through the hallways and out of the hotel, leaving Newsome alone, hiding under the blankets. The group sees it's nearly dawn, yet it's still dark outside. They all run down the main road and head to the Town Hall.

Guards struggle to keep women inside the building while getting the rest of the guards who are resting to come out and help defend Lemonstown. The men who just woke up still have their pajamas on, each wielding a rifle. The women rush back inside the sanctuary when they hear the same screech for a third time. All the men on the main road aim their rifles up, ready to fire at any moment, but they don't know where the noise is coming from.

Secoli crouches and places his birdcage on the ground, not knowing that Dr. Fletcher is behind him. The ornithologist takes in her surroundings while the men keep their guns pointed in the same direction. Everyone grows quiet, anticipating the noise for the fourth time and waiting for the beast to finally appear. The only noise heard is Dr. Fletcher slowly walking to the alley between the bank and Town Hall. As Secoli hears her footsteps, he immediately points his gun at her. He nearly squeezes the trigger after realizing it's the ornithologist.

"Goddamn it, Doctor," Secoli angrily whispers as he points his pistol down. "I told you not to come out here when there's danger. Go inside the Town Hall, where you—"

Secoli gets interrupted after hearing someone collapse on the ground and drag themselves across the dirt. He feels the wind brush past him and smells the same foul odor of the feathers from the ghost towns. The wind blows so hard that Secoli's birdcage is knocked over, and his homburg hat flies off his head.

Turning around for a split second, the postal inspector sees a bald humanlike head with black-feathered wings carrying a guard by the head with his talons. Since the mysterious invader is flying so fast, he can't comprehend what he saw. There isn't a lit torch in the southern direction to allow them to fully see the black figure in the darkness. Everyone immediately fires in the flying figure's direction. Chap cries from being shaken down from inside the cage. Secoli doesn't pay attention to his muse's worries as he puts all his attention on taking the flying fiend down, wherever it is.

The men stop firing when they can no longer see the monster in the darkness.

After a short time, it flies back in the guards' direction without the body it was carrying. When it gets closer to the men, everyone briefly looks at the demonic entity now that it's seen in the lights. The flying fiend falls after more shots are fired.

It lies motionless after rolling from a rough landing. The guards approach the monster with their guns pointed at the black-feathered beast. One of the guards walks to the body and gently kicks it, with his thick books preventing the sharp feathers from piercing through. The mysterious monster lifts its talon and slashes the guard across the chest. The guard collapses on the ground and screams in agony.

The group fires their guns again as the birdlike being that's getting up and covers its body with its giant long wing. None of the bullets pierce its thick layered feathers; instead, they're deflected toward the buildings and the sand. The gunfire is heard less and less as seconds go by until they run out of bullets.

While they reload, the feathered monster sticks its head out from beneath its wing. Secoli and Dr. Fletcher get a good view of the monster in the distance, and its face resembles that of a human. It stands six feet tall, has a torso shaped like a skinny man, and has pale skin from its head down to its belly. Meanwhile, its crotch, thighs, and arms are covered with overgrown, ravenlike feathers, and its yellow talons are larger than any bird has ever had. The ones closest to the monster can hardly contain themselves from the horrid smell coming from the beast.

Seeing that its enemies are reloading their guns, the monster grabs its injured victim by the ankle with its talon. It then flaps its wings and flies up with the guard upside down. As the creature rises in the air, the captured prey screams for dear life as he is lifted through the dark sky. The monster flies so high that no one can see the fiend or their taken comrade in the darkness above. The guards fire indiscriminately in the air, unable to tell who they're shooting. The men continue firing until they no longer hear their captured comrade but hear the monster screech for the fifth time.

This loud shriek catches everyone off guard and makes them cover their ears. The high-pitched noise lasts half a minute, leaving many on the main road to collapse from the unbearable volume. Even the windows on the main road are cracking from the extreme noise coming from above. Once the screeching stops, everyone outside suffers tinnitus and struggles to get back on their feet.

Then, the fiend is seen flying into the light with its talons reaching out to its next prey. It wears an evil, sadistic grin as it grabs hold of two guards' shoulders.

Secoli shakes off the ringing in his ears and hears the two men scream in agony.

He turns toward the screaming and sees the two men are pierced by the monster's talons and are being carried off from the ground. Secoli points his pistol into the fiend's chest in mere seconds and pulls the trigger. The demonic bird lets go of its two prey when a bullet strikes the side of its kidneys. Though it's barely a missed shot, it's painful enough for it to flee back into the night sky. When it is no longer seen, it shrieks for the sixth time but in a lower pitch than the last.

Secoli attempts to shoot in the direction where the screech is heard, but his pistol is out of bullets. He quickly reloads his gun as everyone gets back on their feet and picks up their rifles. He recovers from hearing loss when he hears Chap chirping out of fear. The Federal agent looks down and sees the birdcage has been tipped over. He straightens the cage back on the ground and Chap calms a little.

The postal inspector looks at Dr. Fletcher getting up from the filthy ground and recovering from hearing the high-pitched scream. Secoli picks up his birdcage and then grabs the ornithologist by the arms, and takes both of them inside the Town Hall. The women and children who are hiding under the long chairs, still hurting from the earlier loud noise, startle when Secoli barges through the sanctuary's front entrance. He immediately puts Dr. Fletcher on the edge of the long chair and leaves his birdcage next to her. Realizing where she is, she notices Chap is next to her and sees Secoli run back outside.

When Dr. Fletcher is about to chase after him, Anabelle Larson and Pearl Herbert grab the ornithologist's arms, keeping her from going back outside. Despite Fletcher's desire to see the species, the women refuse to allow her to do so. The door is locked, and there is no way of getting out of Town Hall. The opportunity to get a better look at this monster is out of Dr. Fletcher's grasp.

The ornithologist refuses to be confined in the sanctuary, but there's no way of escape. She angrily moves to the front of the room, close to the judge's bench, and sits alone. There's no more gunfire or screeching coming from outside. Everyone in the sanctuary remains quiet and keeps their heads down, worried the feathered monster could crash in and attack innocent bystanders. However, nothing happens.

Dr. Fletcher glances at the windows to see what's going on outside. However, the windows are all nailed with wooden boards to prevent intruders from coming in. The only thing she can see between the boards is the darkness being eliminated from the break of dawn. The ornithologist can't get her mind off of the man-bird hybrid, and it drives her mad as she remains seated. She turns to look at the only exit, the front door, but sitting right behind her are Anabelle and Pearl.

"Whatever you're thinking about, Dr. Fletcher," whispers Anabelle, giving her an intense stare, "it's not worth it."

"It is worth saving this town," Dr. Fletcher whispers and turns away from the two former saloon girls, "if you only knew what's out there."

Hearing her remark has made Pearl conflicted. She knows it's too dangerous for anyone to head outside, yet remaining sheltered and relying on the men to risk their lives seems counterproductive. Pearl, however, has a strong gut feeling that Dr. Fletcher can save the town.

"Anabelle," Pearl says as she turns to her friend, "Dr. Fletcher seems thirsty. Can you fetch her some water while I watch over her?"

"Really?" Anabelle replies rhetorically. "At a time like this?"

"Yes. We can't let her die of thirst after what she's been through."

"Fine." Anabelle rises from her seat, averting her eyes from both of them. Seeing Anabelle walk toward the barrel filled with water near the entrance,

Pearl leans forward to Dr. Fletcher and whispers, "I know a secret way out of the sanctuary. Follow me before Anabelle gets back."

Suddenly, gunfire is heard outside, causing everyone in the sanctuary to scream and cower. The noise outside startles Anabelle so much that she drops the water-filled tin cup on the floor. She is too scared to clean up the spilled water and crawls underneath the closest long chair. Pearl pulls the ornithologist off her seat, leaving the birdcage behind. She takes Dr. Fletcher around the judge's bench and into the mayor's office.

The door to the mayor's office is unlocked. Immediately when they make it inside, Pearl moves the chairs and rolls up the carpet. There is a square floor hatch in the center of the room. She opens it to reveal a wooden ladder leading to a secret basement.

"How did you know there's a secret exit here?" Dr. Fletcher asks.

"When I was a saloon girl," Pearl says as she assists Fletcher down the hatch, "I had to do special favors for customers, including the mayor. He got away from getting caught by his wife when he sent me down there."

Dr. Fletcher makes it to the bottom of the ladder and replies, "I'm sorry you had to go through that."

"Just follow the path, and you'll find the other hatch out of here." She starts closing the hatch. "Also, Doctor, please be careful."

Pearl closes the floor hatch and puts everything where it was just before Anabelle appears. More shots are heard from outside.

"What are you doing here, Pearl?" yells Anabelle as she barges into the office in a state of panic. "Where's Dr. Fletcher?"

"I'm looking for her." Pearl cowers with her friend as they both hear more shots coming from outside. "She made a run for it the moment those guns started firing."

"Forget about her." Anabelle grabs her friend's wrist and pulls her away. "We gotta get to a safer place."

As they leave the office, everyone hears the screeching from outside. It goes high-pitched once again and hurts everyone's ears in the sanctuary. The women, children, and elderly all covered their ears from the painful noise. Pearl and Anabelle collapse behind the judge's desk and cover their ears. The noise lasts more than a minute, causing some to have a headache and squirm on the floor. Since the volume coming from outside is so extreme, the sanctuary's glass-stained windows vibrate so much that some crack.

Suddenly, the high-pitched shrieking stops after a gunshot. Pearl, who recovers quickly from her tinnitus, hears wings flapping away next to the barred window. The next thing she hears is tumult from the men from outside. Pearl doesn't wait for Anabelle to recover and neglects everybody's well-being. She heads straight for the front door, curious about what's happening outside and hoping that Dr. Fletcher isn't hurt.

No one notices Pearl removing the wooden chair jammed under the front doorknob. It's the perfect opportunity for her to step out despite knowing she'll be sent back in. When she exits and arrives on the porch, she sees all the men picking themselves back up. Pearl wonders why the men are still yelling at each other. She approaches Caleb Walsh as he gets up from the ground.

"Caleb." Pearl touches his shoulder. "Are you all right?"

"What?" the bathhouse worker yells. "Did you say something?"

"I said—" Pearl raises her voice, "are you okay?"

"What?" Walsh sees her lips move. "Oh, God!" He touches his ears. "I can't hear!"

At that moment, this clears the confusion regarding the yelling going on. The men are deaf and struggle to communicate vocally with one another. As excruciating as it is to hear the monster's shrieking inside the sanctuary, it has to be worse listening to it up close outside. Not to mention the added noise from the guns that are fired.

Pearl wonders how Lemonstown will survive if its defenders cannot hear. The helplessness continues to grow with Pearl when she searches for Dr. Fletcher.

Pearl runs down the main road, looking for the ornithologist. When she notices the brighter sky, she sees a silhouetted birdlike figure flying off, carrying another person. She stops, witnessing the petrifying sight of seeing the monster for the first time and taking away one of the town's citizens.

Pearl can't distinguish who the monster is carrying since it's rather far away. Seeing the body lifted upside down and so high up in the air is the eeriest thing she's ever seen. She stands still, unable to take her eyes off the monster and its captured prey. This feeling of hopelessness and terror makes her hug herself due to the goosebumps all over her body. Pearl stops feeling immobilized when she feels something touch her shoulders. Her immobilization doesn't last as she feels someone touching the back of her shoulder, which causes her to startle.

"You shouldn't be here!" yells Inspector Secoli. "This is no place for a woman."

"I can't, Inspector. Dr. Fletcher has disappeared. I need to look for her."

"Dr. Fletcher is what? She's gone? Where is she?"

Before Pearl gives him an answer, she stops and notices everyone outside has stopped yelling. She glances over the postal inspector's shoulder, catching Secoli's attention and causing him to turn around. Coming out of the alleyway between the hotel and stables is Dr. Fletcher with a rifle and Inspector Pluck carrying Gallus Kennedy together. The ornithologist and Pluck look exhausted from doing a two-person carry for Kennedy and drop the trading post owner on his back. Everyone approaches the two and circles around the trading post owner.

"Mr. Kennedy!" Pluck shouts, examining his injuries. "Are you okay?" There's no response from him even though he appears to be conscious. Pluck turns to Fletcher. "Doctor, what happened?"

"He was too close to that harpy that's been screeching." The ornithologist kneels to Secoli's level and replies, "Gallus would have gotten his head blown off if I hadn't shown up and shot the harpy away."

"Harpy?" Secoli responds as his hearing recovers. "Is that what that thing is? How can you be so certain?"

"Yeah," says a man standing behind him, who's also recovering from hearing loss. "How do you know it's not an angel of death?"

"I saw too," says another man next to him. "That was definitely a death angel. No man or animal fits closer to what the Bible described."

"Then it's true," Father Jenkins says. "The time of God's judgment is upon us all."

"No. That wasn't an angel." Dr. Fletcher turns to everyone. "I'm telling you, it was a *harpy*!"

"Enough!" Pluck shouts, still kneeling to the trading post owner. "Gallus, if you can hear me, say something."

Kennedy does not respond. He keeps looking at everyone surrounding him while lying on the asphalt road. He starts getting uncomfortable with the attention he's receiving and sits up from the ground.

"What's everybody looking at?" Kennedy asks. "Is something wrong with me?"

"Gallus," Secoli replies. "Are you okay? Answer if you can hear us."

"Why is everyone so quiet?" Kennedy continues. "Quit playing around.

Why isn't anyone saying anything?"

Kennedy looks at the two postal inspectors in front of him. He can't hear anything either of them is saying but sees their mouths moving. He faces Dr. Fletcher as she moves her lips, but no word is heard. Gallus Kennedy sweats anxiously as he realizes something strange about him. He flicks both ears and faces the awful truth.

"Oh, God!" Kennedy screams, holding his ears. "I can't hear! I've gone deaf!"

Gallus struggles to hear his own voice to the point that he screams as loud as he can, but he can't hear his voice. Everyone, however, hears his sorrowful cries. The ones watching pity him for suffering this new fate. Kennedy is so hurt by this realization that he rolls onto his stomach and weeps even louder to see if it's possible to hear himself.

Pluck gets to his feet and does his best not to shed a tear in front of everyone. He turns to the closest person beside him and whispers into his ear. The guard then helps Kennedy up and escorts him to the Town

Hall. Everyone on the main road can still hear him weep uncontrollably from inside. Secoli sees that the man's circumstance so disheartens Pluck that he's unable to lead right now. He stands up and faces everyone.

"All right, men," Inspector Secoli says, "line up so we can get a count. Sheriff, count how many men we have left."

Sheriff Wood moves to everyone standing in a single line in the center of the main road. He starts counting from left to right. As everyone pays attention to the headcount, Pearl approaches Dr. Fletcher.

"Doctor," Pearl whispers, "tell us what happened to Gallus?"

"When I got out," the ornithologist replies, "a harpy stood beside him, screaming into his ears. With all my might, I grabbed his rifle and shot the harpy."

"You shot the monster?"

Dr. Fletcher nods while looking Pearl in the eyes. "Wow, Doctor. You're a real heroine if I ever saw one."

"Inspector." The sheriff stops counting. "We're missing two people. That excludes Gallus. I don't see Wesley Simmons or Berk Hartman in this formation, sir."

Secoli walks before the sheriff, facing the guards in line. "Has anyone seen them?"

"Inspector," Pearl says, "I saw the monster carry someone. It must have been one of them."

"You did? Then why didn't you say anything earlier?"

"I... don't know, sir." Pearl puts her head down in embarrassment. "Did you get a chance to see who exactly that fiend took?"

"No, sir," she answers and looks away, feeling useless. "It was so high and far away that it was hard to see who it was carrying."

"Damn it," Secoli swears. "And was the monster carrying two or one person?"

"Only one, sir."

"Then that means one of them is still in Lemonstown. Which direction did the monster fly?"

She looks up in the sky, recalling that the sun was rising to the left of the flying monster, and points in that direction north of the main road.

"Are you sure they went that way?" She nods nervously.

"Okay, all of you start looking for either Simmons or Hartman around town. Inspector Pluck and I will head south to save whoever the monster took." Secoli turns to his partner. "You ready, Jed?"

Pluck snaps out of pity for Kennedy when he hears what his partner says. He pulls out his pistol and starts reloading his gun with new bullets. He pushes the cylinder back in his gun, turns to Secoli, and replies, "Ready as I'll ever be."

"HELLO. IS THIS THE United States Postal Inspection Service? Yes, this is Clara Pluck. Yes, the same one who called yesterday. I want to know if you've heard anything about Postal Inspector Jed Pluck. I want to know if you heard anything from him lately."

Janet and Allie scamper through the hallway after hearing their father's name. When they both peek at the edge of the archway to the living room, the two sisters see their mother using the house's only telephone. Clara stands facing the living room while she holds the receiver against her ear. The other hand holds the telephone to put the microphone close to her mouth. Despite wanting to know, the sisters sense nothing positive will be said.

"Still nothing yet?" Their mother raises her voice. "How in the world is the government neglecting a Federal agent? Then why haven't you sent the military to save my husband yet?"

She pauses to listen for a response.

"That is unacceptable! Your organization could have picked any other postal inspector, but you always have to pick *my* Jed! *My* husband! He has given so much to this country since the Civil War and up until now. You never let him settle down and let someone else take the job! Not only is Inspector Pluck going to miss another one of our daughters' birthdays this year, but no one knows if he's even alive."

Clara takes a deep breath to rant some more. "I'm incredibly dissatisfied with and disappointed in how the Postal Inspection Service neglects my husband's safety. The same organization that has been taking advantage of *my* husband for many years. The same organization that is tearing *this* family apart. And the same organization that took my husband away—possibly permanently. "I hope you're proud of how you ruined this family! I hope to God you won't take advantage of another married postal inspector before you ruin another family as well. Good day, sir!"

Clara hangs up the phone very hard and slams the telephone back on the table.

Allie and Janet, still eavesdropping, see their mother catching her breath. They also see that their mother sheds some tears as she slowly turns. Clara looks up from the floor to see her two youngest daughters peeking from the edge of the archway. They, too, look as distressed as their mother.

"Allie," Clara whimpers, dropping some tears, "I'm so sorry. I don't think your father will be coming home anytime soon."

Instead of running away at the unfortunate news, Allie races to her mother, needing a parent more than ever. Clara kneels with open arms to give her a hug. She grasps her second-youngest child and holds her tightly, knowing her ninth birthday will be far from ideal. Clara can feel tears coming down her neck as Allie rests her head against her shoulders. Janet runs toward her mother as well to also get a hug.

Clara lifts her head after briefly crying with her two youngest children to see her other two daughters standing before them. Julia has watery eyes, feeling the heat of her breath as she covers her nose and mouth with her hands. Jessie has her eyes closed, dropping some tears with a scowl. Clara lets go of Allie and Janet and gets up to give her two oldest daughters a hug.

While Julia accepts her mother's hug, Jessie remains distant. Clara reaches for her oldest daughter as she has Julia wrapped in one arm. Jessie moves away as she feels her mother's hands. Despite turning away, Clara hugs Jessie from behind, stopping her from running upstairs.

Jessie breaks down and cries like all the other times she receives a family hug instead of the other way around. All of them can feel her frustration and despair that their father may never return home. Her mother and sisters guide her to the stairs to sit down. They all sit on the stairs with Jessie, seeing that she's taking it harder than the rest. To comfort her, the family rubs her shoulders and arms as she cries loudly.

Everyone breaks away from their moment of grieving when they hear knocks on the front door. Clara gets up and opens the door to see who it is.

"Hello, Mrs. Pluck," says a young man around Jessie's age who takes off his flat cap to make a good first impression. He stops smiling when he notices Clara's red eyes. "Is everything all right, ma'am?"

"I'm sorry, but can you come back another time?" Clara says as she closes the door. "Now is not a good time."

"Jacob!" Jessie calls out. She approaches the front door just as Clara is about to close it. "I'm sorry. I completely forgot that we're supposed to go out. Can we do it another time?"

"Okay," the handsome blond boy replies, seeing her red eyes. "Did something happen, Jessie?"

"Nothing that concerns you." She places her hands on his through the doorway. "I'll tell you all about it on our next date."

"Sure thing." He gently swings her arms left and right. "Should I pick you up tomorrow?"

"Tomorrow isn't a good time. My sister is having a birthday tomorrow. How about the day after?"

He stops swinging her arms and shrugs. "Sure. I'll reschedule our picnic together.

I'll see you next time, Jessie." He's about to give her a peck on the lips until he notices Clara watching him intensely. He lets go of Jessie's hands and puts his flat cap back on. "Have a wonderful day, Mrs. Pluck."

Clara slowly closes the front door as Jacob steps off the porch. Jessie's red face starts turning pale again as the door closes. When she looks at her mother, Clara doesn't seem too happy.

"Since when were you going to tell me you're in a relationship, young lady?" Clara scolds her oldest daughter. "I've told you you're too young to start dating."

"Oh, c'mon, Mother." Jessie raises her voice. "Father isn't around to take care of me. I can't just be sitting around the house waiting for him when more exciting things are out there."

"I'm telling you, Jessie, you're not ready to start dating."

"And will I ever be?" Jessie cries angrily. "It's not fair that you found Dad when you were my age, but I can't be in love."

"Jessie, you're not mature enough to dedicate yourself to a man. And this boy... Jacob. I don't trust him, and I don't think he's good enough for you."

"You're always like this whenever I'm with a boy. All my relationships have been broken because you forced me to end them. I'm not letting you keep me from Jacob. I do have a whole life ahead of me. And it's being with him."

"Aren't you even aware that you're throwing your life away for that sleazebag?"

"Don't you dare talk to Jacob like that when you don't even know him."

"I know enough to know that he can't take his hands off of you."

"Damn it, Mom!" Jessie opens the front door and steps out. "Why don't you understand?" She slams the front door and chases Jacob down the street. "Jessie!" she yells, rushing out the door. "Get back here this instant! I forbid you to see that boy!"

Her eldest daughter runs past the front yard and into the street. Clara watches from the porch to see Jessie catching up to her boyfriend. She watches her receive a hug from him and sees him clear away her tears with his handkerchief. Clara remains silent and watches them walk in the town's direction. She lets them go when she remembers that she did the same thing when she was Jessie's age.

Watching her daughter with that boy reminds her of how much her mother disapproved of Jed. She used to see Jed nearly every day before he joined the army when the Civil War broke out. Back then, she was impressionable and madly in love with her children's father. Just seeing Jessie and Jacob together makes her long for the romance Jed used to provide her. Now, she fears that the cycle continues with Jessie.

Just as Jessie and her date are no longer seen, Clara turns around and sees her other three daughters worried about her. Janet, Allie, and Julia are recovering from grieving a moment ago and see that their mother is very upset.

"Mommy," Janet says, "is Jessie leaving us too?"

"No, dear." Clara walks back into the house. She closes the door as all three get inside with her. "She just wants to be with her friends right now. She'll feel better when she gets back."

"Will Jessie make it to my birthday tomorrow?" Allie asks as she wipes her face.

Clara kneels to Allie's level and holds both shoulders. "Unlike your father, I promise she'll be there for your birthday tomorrow. You know Jessie. She has her priorities, but one of them is to make you happy, Allie."

AFTER SPENDING ALL morning searching for the monster, the two postal inspectors ride back to Lemonstown, hoping they can still save the abducted one. The humidity is getting to the two. Even their horses struggle to transport the Federal agents back to town.

"Damn it," Pluck swears as he removes his brown Boston felt hat and wipes the sweat off his forehead. "It was a waste of time looking for that missing man. That saloon girl may have pointed us in the wrong direction."

After taking off his coat and covering his birdcage on his lap to provide shade for Chap, Secoli says, "She didn't. We did find some fresh feathers the monster shredded. It's just that the wind has blown away the only trail that could have led us to the beast."

As the postal inspectors get closer to Lemonstown, they hear a woman's cries.

Worried over what's causing her to cry so loud, they whip their horses to speed up. Since the alleyways are still netted, they move around the row of buildings. Inspector Pluck and Secoli get off their horses when they see the townspeople circle around the grieving woman. They're so focused on the commotion that they ignore their horses rushing to the closest trough for a drink.

The two Federal agents walk through the crowd to reach the center. They see a woman and a young girl both hugging a corpse. Neither can recognize the person since his entire face is so scarred and covered in blood that he's unrecognizable. The postal inspectors aren't familiar with any of the guards' loved ones either, making it difficult to tell who the town found. Pluck and Secoli turn to Sheriff Wood, standing beside them with his hat off.

"That's Wesley Simmons," the sheriff whispers. "We found him hanging halfway to the water tower."

Secoli mutters, "That means Berk Hartman is the one that's taken."

Secoli removes his homburg hat and places his birdcage on the ground to mourn the fallen guard. The cries of the widow soon turn into sorrowful screams. Her only daughter snivels as she grieves silently, appearing old enough to understand the concept of death. Nobody dares to stop the family's grieving. Then, an older woman steps out of the crowd and approaches the postal inspectors with a worried look on her face. The lady places her hands on Secoli's arm and almost knocks over the birdcage beside him.

"Inspector," says the old lady, yanking his sleeve, "have you found my son, Berk Hartman? Please tell me you at least found him."

Louie swallows his saliva before he can give her an answer. He knows whatever he says will break her heart. The postal inspector can feel it in him that she'll break down like Simmons' widow. He can see how watery her wrinkled eyes are getting like she already knows but wants to hear it from him.

"I'm sorry, Mrs. Hartman," Secoli replies, placing his hands on hers. "We looked everywhere and didn't find him. I hate to tell you this, but… he's gone."

The mother then places her face on Secoli's chest. She takes a deep breath while hugging him before she weeps. Secoli wraps his arms around her to comfort her, but nothing can ease her pain. Her sobs become as loud as those of the widow on the ground with her dead husband. Secoli feels awful to be the one to give her the bad news.

Pluck startles at seeing the monster returning when gazing up at the sky, only to realize it's a figment of his imagination. The thought of the monster returning makes him desperate to control the situation. He then rushes to the grieving Mrs. Simmons, trying to help her and her daughter back up, but she refuses to let go of her husband.

"For pity's sake, Jed!" Secoli shouts at his partner. "Let them mourn!"

"I'm sorry for doing this, but who knows if that monster will come back and strike again when we're most vulnerable."

"He's right," Dr. Fletcher says, popping out from the crowd. "A carnivore shows no mercy to its prey. That monster knows where we are, and there's nothing else out here for it to feed on. There's no telling when it will come back."

"Right," Pluck continues. "Let's put Wesley Simmons in the trading post. I need some volunteers to help us carry him there. Anyone who wants to pay their respects to Wesley can do so, but only briefly since we're still under curfew."

Mrs. Simmons rose to her feet and took her daughter's hand, allowing the guards to carry her deceased husband. Everyone follows them to the trading post, where the mourning will take place.

"Does anyone have something for my partner and me to drink?" Pluck asks as everyone moves off the main road.

He snatches a water canteen from someone and drinks it all without paying attention to who gave it to him. Exhausted from the attack earlier that morning, he's reluctant to start his shift, which is now tempting him to sleep through it. He turns to his partner, who's drinking from a canteen also given to him. Louie wipes his mouth after he empties the canteen and thanks the person who offered him water. He notices Jed isn't in a good mood and knows his partner hasn't rested enough. As a good-hearted person, Secoli picks up his birdcage and places his hand on his partner's shoulder.

"Hey, Jed," Louie says, "if you're really that tired, maybe we should switch shifts."

"It's fine," Jed replies, avoiding eye contact. "I can handle this. I'd hate to make a change and screw up both of our sleeping schedules." He makes eye contact with him. "Besides, I suspect this is the kind of monster that strikes at night, so I like for you to be at your most awake when it comes back."

"Well, that's reassuring," Louie sarcastically responds.

"He's right, though," Dr. Fletcher pipes up. "Plenty of birds of prey prefer to hunt at night when it's difficult to spot them."

Both Inspector Pluck and Secoli turn to the ornithologist and notice she's carrying a thick book.

She continues by saying, "Sorry for interrupting, but there's something I need to tell both of you in private. You know a place where we can discuss—" she lowers her voice, "the harpy?"

Pluck looks around and sees everyone moving off the main road before he replies, "Let's continue this discussion in the hotel. So, which room will our meeting be held in?"

"Since you're proposing the idea, Inspector," the ornithologist replies, "why don't we continue this conversation in *your* hotel room?"

Fiona's directness makes Pluck pull his head back. He swallows his saliva and says, "All right. Meeting in my room then."

Jed leads his partner and the ornithologist to the hotel. He feels tension over the doctor's suggestion to be in the same place where he sleeps. Before entering the hotel, Pluck places his hands in his pocket, where he keeps his keys, and quickly removes his wedding ring. Once he feels his ring finger is free, he pulls out his hotel key. It's an unusual feeling for him to take off his wedding ring, but he still wants Fiona to think he's available, regardless of the outcome. Pluck unlocks his hotel room and rushes inside first. Before Secoli and Fletcher enter his room, he grabs a picture frame of his wife and daughters from the nightstand and places it under the pillow. He turns around to see his guests closing the door upon entering, not noticing what he's doing. Pluck then pulls out the only two wooden chairs in the room for the both of them and faces them toward his bed, where he'll be sitting.

"Dr. Fletcher," Pluck says, sitting on his bed, "I forgot to thank you for what you did earlier stopping that monster. It was probably the bravest thing any woman had ever done when that monster screamed so loud that we couldn't shoot back."

"You're welcome, Inspector," she says, blushing at his compliment. "But I'm sure there are other women who are far braver than me if you look hard enough."

"Speaking of which, do you know if Mr. Kennedy has his hearing back?"

"No, Inspector," she sighs. "When I checked up not too long ago, he's deaf now.

The harpy's high-pitched screams seem to be its greatest weapon against its prey."

"Damn it," Pluck swears and rubs his chin. "How are we going to fight off this monster if we can't protect our ears?"

"I have an idea," Secoli adds. "I saw cotton on display in the hardware store. If we get everyone to put it in their ears, we won't have to worry about another person going deaf if that monster decides to use that strategy again."

"Good idea," Pluck replies. "That should protect our ears well."

"I suggest telling your men to keep your distance from the harpy as much as possible," Fiona adds. "We can't completely rely on our ears being protected if the monster is too close. You saw what happened to Mr. Kennedy when he got too close."

"Speaking of which," Secoli turns to her and raises a brow, "how did you get out of Town Hall? The last I checked, the building only had one door out, and the windows were nailed with planks."

"One of the ladies showed me a secret exit," she answers. "There's a hatch underneath the mayor's office."

"Don't you think you should have stayed and watched over Chap like I told you?

Staying out there when we're being attacked isn't the safest idea for a wo—"

"That's enough, Louie," Pluck interrupts. "We've had this conversation with Dr. Fletcher many times already. She proved capable of firing a rifle better than all these men who were inexperienced with shooting. Besides, without her help, who knows how much this place could be."

"But we still don't know how to take that monster down," Secoli replies. "We shot it many times, and none of the bullets penetrated the damn thing."

"That's why I wanted to speak to both of you in private," Dr. Fletcher says. "To kill this monster, we first have to know what it is."

The ornithologist takes the book off her lap and gets up. She then places it on Pluck's bed. The title on the cover says *Greek Mythology*. The postal inspectors look over as Dr. Fletcher then opens the book and turns the pages filled with illustrations of monsters and hybrids on the pages she turns. She then stops at the page that illustrates a woman with exposed breasts and wings and feathers all over her body. Despite how disproportionate the illustration is and how it appears female, the depicted illustration fits the description of the monster they saw. Above, the illustration says "Harpy" as the chapter's title. Both Jed's and Louie's eyes are glued onto the page.

"This is what I wanted to show you, gentlemen," Dr. Fletcher says. "What we saw this morning was a harpy. I'm flabbergasted; it was as if the page had just come to life."

"Then what is this...harpy doing in Wyoming instead of being in Greece?"

"I honestly don't know," she replies, "but I hypothesize that harpies exist in every region in the world or they're flying to someplace warmer."

"But it's still summer," Secoli says. "There's no way that birds start moving from north to south when the season is still humid around the world."

"Plus," Pluck adds, "why are we discovering harpies for the first time? How have they been hidden so well after all these years?"

"I still don't know, but based on what this book says about them...," she picks it up and reads a paragraph, "Harpies are wind spirits. Their names translate to "snatchers." Whenever there's a disappearance, a harpy has carried someone away from Earth. They are agents of punishment who abducted people and tortured them on their way to Tartarus.'" She stops reading and looks at the postal inspectors. "That's Greece's version of hell." She continues reading. "'Harpies are seen as hounds of the mighty Zeus.'"

"Zeus," Pluck says. "Who's that?"

"That's the ancient Greek god of lightning, the skies, and all the other gods. I'm glad I brought this book with me on this trip. I knew somehow it would be handy."

Fiona sees Louie's hand over her shoulder in a receiving gesture, signaling that he wants to read it. She hands him the book, and he reads it independently while standing. She is quite annoyed that she's unable to read the rest of the harpy's description to both of them.

"So, is a harpy a bird or a man?" Pluck asks, not realizing the annoyed expression she has just made.

"It's a hybrid," she answers. "Meaning it's both. After seeing that harpy this morning, I wonder what other creatures in Greek mythology are actually real."

"Jesus Christ," Pluck mutters. "How does a thing like that even exist?"

"Funny," Secoli says as he turns the page, "this book doesn't have enough description about the harpy. It doesn't even say if its feathers are impenetrable or give any further details about the monster than what's on two pages." He puts the book on Jed's bed. "You wouldn't happen to have another book about harpies, would you?"

"Sorry, Inspector," Fiona says. "That's the only one I brought with me. We'd have to go to a library to read about what the Greeks say about the creature."

"Right. It looks like now we know what we're up against. We'd better get everyone some cotton to protect their ears."

Secoli picks up his birdcage and wastes no time heading out the door. Since he moves urgently, he shows that he cares for the townspeople's safety. He doesn't even stop when Pluck says, "Louie? Where are you going?" When he gets up to go after his partner, Dr. Fletcher pulls his sleeve, preventing him from leaving his room.

"Jed," the ornithologist says. "You need to get some sleep. Your eyes are very red, and you look so exhausted. When was the last time you slept?"

"Since midnight last night."

"Jed..." She grabs his shoulders and makes him sit on his bed. "You must take better care of yourself. You can't protect this town when you don't rest."

"But what about Louie? He and I can't switch shifts. It's going to mess up both of our sleep schedules."

"Well, you already messed them up when looking for Berk Hartman. I'll tell Louie you need rest, and he'll take your shift."

Dr. Fletcher places her hand on the postal inspector's shoulders, stimulating Pluck with her touch. Pluck rubs his own neck and looks away out of embarrassment. He then feels the stiffness on the back of his neck, realizing how exhausted his body is. The ornithologist then helps Pluck by removing his coat and boots before she helps him lie in bed. Pluck feels very comfortable under the blankets and can't stay up for much longer.

"Don't worry," Fiona says gently. "I'll handle everything."

The ornithologist leans toward the exhausted postal inspector and kisses him. Surprised over what she's doing, Pluck opens his eyes and pulls his head against his pillow. He feels something hard through the pillows and remembers his picture frame of his family is still underneath. The kiss from Fletcher lasts longer than a simple peck. She opens her eyes, makes strong eye contact, and takes her lips off his.

"I'll see you when you're fully rested, Inspector Pluck," she says flirtatiously.

She gives him a wink before heading out of his hotel room. She slowly closes the door like she doesn't want to leave. When the door closes, Pluck gasps over this flustered and alluring moment. Already he has butterflies in his stomach, the same feeling as when he first met the beautiful ornithologist. Before he gets carried away with the tender moment, Pluck can still feel the discomfort of the picture frame under his pillow.

He then takes the picture frame out without having to get up. His beating heart and adrenaline slow down when he flips the frame around and sees the picture of his girls in Boston. Though he's not in the picture, Pluck imagines his wife and daughters watching him as he stares at the photo of them. He then wipes his lips to remove any lipstick marks on his lips. After viewing his family photo for a long while, he puts the picture down at his side.

Although it felt great to receive a kiss from one of the most beautiful women he'd ever met, he felt awful about it. He holds his nose to relieve some stress, then realizes his ring finger is free from his wedding ring, which is still in his coat's pocket.

Remembering that he removed his wedding ring to hide evidence that he's married makes him feel even more guilty. Even though he received the kiss, he believes that it did not constitute an affair. As he thinks about what to say to Dr. Fletcher about stopping this liaison, Pluck finally drifts off to sleep and gets that deserved rest.

CHAPTER 9

People inevitably get less sleep as they get older, despite how tired they become when awake. For Jed Pluck, five hours of sleep is the most he gets in his forties. It's even harder for him to get back to sleep when he can still see sunlight behind the curtains. Whenever he wakes, he lies in bed, ruminates about the past, and overthinks about the future. Since getting up an hour before his new shift, Pluck can't get the kiss he received from Fiona Fletcher off his mind. Why she did it and whether he should pursue this affair is what's distracting him from this case.

Having someone as attractive as her being interested in someone like him keeps Pluck awake and ashamedly keeps him aroused. He imagines how much he always wanted a ginger just like her; however, he still remembers his marital vows and his responsibilities as a parent. Pluck knows how much it would tear his family apart if they knew about that kiss or his lustful fantasies about the ornithologist. He ponders the repercussions of being caught with Dr. Fletcher but wonders if there would be any consequences since he is so far away from his family.

It's not like having a little fun and giving in to temptation will change how he feels about his family, will it? After all, once this case is over, Pluck plans to simply return to his family and separate from everyone related to this case. Returning to the mundane life of raising his family will be monotonous and unfulfilling, as it has been for a long time. Perhaps this case is a blessing in disguise for him to escape his responsibilities and is an opportunity to have fun one more time.

As he thinks about all the things he's been doing since arriving in Wyoming, he realizes this case of taking charge of defending Lemonstown is the most excitement he's had since fighting in the Civil War. Why not take it further with Dr. Fletcher since there's no guarantee that anyone is coming out of this alive? So far, nobody stands a chance against that harpy, which Dr. Fletcher calls it, and Pluck predicts that's the way he's going out. He'll regret not committing to his lustful desire for Fiona if she dies sooner. His moment of fantasizing gets interrupted by a knocking coming from the door. The whole room breaks its silence from whoever wants to see Inspector Pluck.

"Jed," a familiar voice says through the door. "It's me. Louie. We need to talk."

Pluck gets up and realizes he's wearing the same clothes from last night before heading to the door. When he opens the door, he sees his partner with a blank look on their face.

"Sorry for bothering you, Jed," Secoli says while struggling to make eye contact.

Secoli walks past the doorway and grabs one of the chairs in the room. As he pulls it to the center of the room, Pluck realizes his partner has come empty-handed.

"Lou?" Pluck asks. "Where's Chap? You didn't lose him, did you?"

"No," Secoli answers as he sits down. "He's with Dr. Fletcher."

"Oh," he says with surprise. "Seems like you either trust her that much, or you're getting better at standing on your own two feet."

"Have a seat, Jed. There's something you need to know."

Pluck grabs the second chair in the room and sits down. "Sure. What's on your mind?"

His partner takes a deep breath and sighs before saying, "Jed, please don't take this the wrong way. I acknowledge your efforts in doing so much for Lemonstown. And I'm only bringing this up because I care about you." He pauses again, expecting the conversation to turn into an argument. "But a lot of folks here think you're a slacker."

"Slacker?" Pluck responds by pulling his head back, feeling offended. "And who specifically is saying these things about me?"

"Everyone who was on your old shift right now. Many mentioned how much they appreciated my attentiveness during your old shift. At first, I was offended that the guards on this shift thought so poorly of you. But when they explained that they only see you only at the beginning and the end of their shift..." Secoli clears his throat to delay where this conversation is heading, "they accused you of taking advantage as they work so hard and risk their lives out there."

"Is that what they're saying about me?" Pluck gets up from his seat.

"Hold on, Jed." Secoli grabs his sleeve, preventing him from heading out of his hotel room. "It won't do you any favors if you confront them when you've already created enough animosity with the town."

"I've done no such thing." He pulls his arm away from his partner's grip and sits back down.

"Jed. After talking to all of them, I see their point of view. You..." Secoli looks away to sigh some more. "You don't seem to be as interested in protecting them as you should."

"And now you're siding with these bozos? You disappoint me, Louie."

"Well, you disappoint me more, Jed," Secoli raises his voice. "Have you forgotten why we're here?"

"To help save this town? You think I'm that stupid?"

"Yeah, I do. When you had a hissy fit about me putting Chap in danger, you embarrassed me in front of everyone when you handed me his birdcage and marched right into the hotel. I admit it's my fault that I put you in danger when neglecting Chap. But you've made a bad first impression with your unprofessional behavior."

"Is that all?" Jed asks dismissively.

"There's plenty more. You were disruptive toward Simmons' and Berk's families when they were grieving. For God's sake, you didn't let them mourn, much less give them any sympathy. And now I'm hearing you're disappearing from your shift from your guards. Just what are you doing whenever you're on shift, huh?"

"You know what I'm doing. I'm guarding and looking for that...harpy."

"Even so, you aren't engaging with the folks doing their damnedest to save their home and families. If your family were here, wouldn't you do the same?"

"What kind of question is that? I'd be doing the same as I'm doing right now."

"By leaving your post and risking everybody's lives when they depend on you? You're lucky to be a Federal agent because no one would tolerate your behavior if you were anybody else. Do you have any idea how vulnerable and inexperienced these people are? We lost two men to only one harpy, and several injured as well. Also, where the hell were you when we were all facing that thing on the main road?"

"I was…trying to catch that thing behind the buildings."

"Really? Or were you sleeping when everyone was out there risking their lives? How did Fiona shoot the harpy away when she was in the same backway with you?"

Pluck remains silent. He can't come up with anything to say to Secoli. He remains sitting, unable to look at his partner. Secoli grows even more suspicious of the lack of eye contact from Pluck's end.

"Jed," Secoli continues in a calmer tone, "I know you probably want to be elsewhere right now. I, too, hate being in Wyoming. It's too hot during the day and too cold at night. Even the food could taste better. The West just isn't my place either.

"But we can't just show these people we don't want to be here. It gives them the impression that fighting off that monster isn't worth a damn. How would you feel if that thing took someone you love dearly?"

Pluck, still looking away, swallows his saliva and blinks profusely before replying, "I would be horrified."

"These loved ones dealing with their loss are feeling exactly that. I know you miss your family a lot, partner. But we've got a job to do. It's really bad out here. I need you to help me save this town. I'm also doing my part in becoming a better partner for you. I mean, I'm doing better at everything without Chap always being with me."

Secoli gets out of his seat when he realizes how long this conversation has been going on. He finishes the conversation by saying, "Now that you know your old shift hates you, please try to prove them wrong by being more attentive and proactive with your new shift. Rumors against you have grown fast in this town, but this is your opportunity to be more communal with these new faces you haven't spoken to yet."

Louie heads out of the hotel room. As the door closes, Pluck remains in his seat.

As stuck-up and prideful as he is, it takes a while for the postal inspector to concede. Overanalyzing what his partner brought up made him discern how selfish and inconsiderate he's been toward everyone in Lemonstown.

The whole time he's been putting more attention toward the women that he's been attracted to than to everyone else who's giving their all. Pluck never wanted to become that kind of leader, but having so much authority for so long has made him forget what it means to be a Federal agent. In the simpler cases he's been in, he creates some fun out of catching criminals. But saving a whole town against a harpy is an entirely different scenario with more at stake than he originally thought. The stakes are high, and he must put aside his personal desires to save everyone.

Jed remains seated until he hears everyone gathering up for a head count at the main road, loud as ever. He doesn't need to check his watch to know it's time to join his new shift. As Pluck heads out of his hotel room, he thinks about Secoli's advice on building relationships with those on his new shift. He locks his hotel room and turns to find Dr. Fletcher in the same hallway carrying his partner's birdcage.

The ornithologist calls for Pluck, but he pretends she isn't even there as he leaves the hotel. The sun is still out, and it's the hottest that it has been since the two postal inspectors arrived in Lemonstown. When he steps off the porch, Sheriff Wood finishes calling everyone's names. Pluck sees the guards who are being relieved from their shift walk past him, and some of them give him uneasy looks.

Pluck is more aware of how much they resent him. He then looks at where the relieved guards are heading, seeing the folks in the Town Hall differently. Though it wasn't his idea to put everyone in the Town Hall, he now understands how important it is to keep people safe right after seeing men hugging their wives and children on the porch.

As they all head inside the Town Hall to rest, Secoli approaches Pluck and places his hand on his partner's shoulder. "You got this, Jed," he whispers. "Now go out there and make a good impression with these guys."

Secoli lets go of his shoulder and heads to his hotel room. Pluck turns to his partner, gets on the porch, and takes his birdcage from the ornithologist. As he enters the lobby, Fletcher stares at Pluck, looking worried. When he sees her staring at him, Pluck pretends she's not there by turning to the guards on his new shift, who are standing in formation as each of their names is called for headcount. It is evident to some that Pluck is feeling insecure, and he can tell in return that the guards on this shift already miss Secoli as their leader, and the rumors about him have reached them. When the sheriff finishes calling the last name, the lawman turns to Pluck.

"Nice of you to join us, Inspector," Wood says. "Don't worry about us.

Everyone will remain at their post like they always have."

Jed swallows his saliva before asking, "So, which post is available for me to guard?"

"That won't be necessary, Inspector. You're free to walk anywhere you please."

"I am willing to fill in for any position in this shift that is currently understaffed."

"Well, whatever you decide, inspector," Deputy Hall says. "Here's some cotton for your ears. The last thing anyone wants is another one of us becoming deaf."

JED PLUCK SEEMS TO easily adjust to the new schedule but struggles to remain in one location for so long. The postal inspector isn't very patient, which makes waiting mundane for him. Since he slept, the last shift in Lemonstown took down the nets in the alleyway. They know that the fiend is too smart to fall for a simple trap, and it is a waste of time to go around the town just to get in and out of the main road. Pluck keeps to his word not to leave his post to find the monster alone.

He guards the trading post and the small train station building with two other men, Patrick Newsome and Chuck Madison. There has been no communication between the guards guarding Lemonstown's southeastern part since Pluck joined the post. For someone as extroverted as Jed, he's cautious about making his reputation worse than it already is by remaining silent. It doesn't help that one of the buildings, the trading post, is now being used as a mortuary. So far, Wesley Simmons is the only corpse being kept there, but there's a high possibility of more sharing the same space with him.

However, Pluck is more concerned about how the town thinks of him instead of being next to the corpse. Being aware of what the town thinks of him makes it difficult to befriend any of them. Jed's relationship with any of the townspeople is limited to giving orders and expecting them to be carried out. While they are obedient, it is clear that they are not happy to carry out his orders and prefer Louie Secoli to be in charge.

Since it got dark, Pluck and the other two guards in his post have walked around with their torches, paying close attention to any sudden noises or suspicious activities. It could be more efficient since the flames on their torches can only light up a short distance. Not to mention that the monsters lurking in the dark can see those holding their light source, making them easy targets. All that any of the guards can do is constantly move circles around in the same buildings. Pluck has been going on the same path for hours now, and the lack of anything happening is putting him on edge.

The only thing Pluck can find interesting are the two men in the same post circling around the same buildings but in opposite directions. Each time he passes the bathhouse owner or the stable keeper, Pluck notices their aloofness and tries to ignore them. Not once has the postal inspector tried to start a conversation with either of them. The only time Pluck even speaks is when Deputy Hall, the lawman in charge of this shift, walks around the posts to check up on everyone on duty. Their conversations are brief, as there's nothing to report.

These hours of circling in the same path are the longest six hours he's had since pulling guard duty during the Civil War. Walking at a very slow pace and going around the same buildings countless times makes him dizzy. Pluck lost count of how many times he'd crossed paths with Chuck Madison in going around the trading post. As Pluck circles around the trading post, it is a surprise that the back alley is dark, as he expects to bump into Patrick Newsome.

Perhaps the bathhouse owner's torch got put out, so it's best for Pluck to walk slowly and try not to bump into him.

Pluck walks across the backway of his assigned post, anticipating to see Newsome walking through the darkness. He sees some light coming around the other side of the trading post. Perhaps the bathhouse owner is just slowing down from exhaustion. Pluck, too, is feeling as tired as anyone out here putting this much energy into staying high alert for so long. Pluck starts to calm down a little, knowing he'll bump into Newsome at any moment. He makes it to the alley between the trading post and the bathhouse but is surprised to see the stable keeper instead.

"Wait a minute," Pluck says to Madison with his hand raised. "Have you seen Patrick?"

"No, sir," the stable keeper says. "You're the only person I've seen in three rounds around our post."

Pluck widens his eyes over Newsome's disappearance. Has it been three rounds around his post since he saw the bathhouse owner? The postal inspector starts to worry about the guard missing in action.

"Quick!" Pluck rushes down the alley. "We need to find him."

Calling Newsome's name, Madison follows the postal inspector to the main road. The guards from the other posts hear them and rush in their direction. Everyone in this shift gathers around Jed, trying to figure out what to do.

"Don't just stand here!" Pluck shouts anxiously. "Find Newsome!"

The guards spread out to town, all of them calling for Newsome. Everyone sleeping in the Town Hall wakes up from the noise. Deputy Hall runs up to Inspector Pluck, looking as worried as Pluck is.

"How the hell did you lose Newsome?" Hall shouts. "Did you or Madison hear or notice a monster flying by your post?"

"I didn't hear a goddamn thing," Pluck replies in a panic.

"Neither have I," the stable keeper answers. "I just noticed him gone when Inspector Pluck and I kept crossing paths without seeing Newsome in between."

The three of them run back to their post. They look around to find anything the bathhouse owner might have left behind. In front of the buildings, nothing is unusual, so they move to the backway. The three of them continue shouting.

Newsome's name but then hears another voice shouting something else in the distance. Pluck and the other two follow where the voice is coming from.

The three make it past the trading post and behind the bathhouse. The voice comes from the outhouse next to the eastern water tower. Pluck and the other two shout Newsome's name again, and someone steps out of the outhouse.

"For the last time, I said I'm in here!" Newsome shouts, closing the outhouse's door. "God. How can none of you hear me?"

"Damn it, Newsome," the deputy swears. "Didn't I tell you that you must let your colleagues know when you need to be excused?"

"Gee, I'm sorry, Deputy," the bathhouse owner replies. "It was an emergency."

"If you disappear on us again, Pat, I'll put you behind bars with Jeremy Payton."

Deputy Hall walks through the alley between the bathhouse and the hardware store to where everyone else is. The deputy repeatedly shouts, "We found Newsome!" for everyone to hear. The nonstop call for the bathhouse owner quickly silences, and Lemonstown becomes quiet again. As Newsome picks up his carbine beside the outhouse, Pluck sees how embarrassed he is for leaving his post like that.

Pluck sees himself in Newsome's situation, but with the key difference that he is able to leave as he pleases, while others, like Newsome, face consequences. The postal inspector can certainly tell how sorry the bathhouse owner is with his head down and eyes getting watery. As much as he has the urge to be hurtful, Pluck stops himself and remembers why he put himself in the same post with him.

"Hey, Mr. Newsome," Pluck says calmly while walking back to the southeastern section of town with his post mates. "You know how soon you're going to open your bathhouse? It's been days since I bathed, and at this point, I'm willing to pay double your asking price."

"You serious, Inspector?" Newsome replies in surprise. "You don't have to do that. After all you've done for this town, you deserve a free service."

"No. I insist. My body is getting a rash from being covered in dust, and I need to wash it off so badly."

While Pluck and Madison await for Newsome to make a response, they turn to him and realize he disappeared. Pluck turns behind him and gets a glimpse of a body being lifted in the air and taken to the darkness. Almost before Newsome gets engulfed in darkness, the postal inspector sees him being grabbed by a giant talon around the neck. Then, a gust of wind blows in their direction, and he and Madison smell a familiar stench.

As Madison and Pluck cover their noses from smelling the miasma, the postal inspector draws his pistol and blindly fires in that direction for everyone to hear.

The stable keeper exclaims in surprise, "What was that?"

Immediately, a familiar loud, high-pitched scream is heard, making Pluck and Madison cover their ears in pain. The other guards who ran to their rescue hold their ears from the excruciating shriek. Many guards outside had cotton covering in their ears before their shift began. However, it isn't enough to endure the agonizing screeching. With no other choice, Inspector Pluck blind fires in the same direction, losing his balance as he lets one ear open. After he fires his last bullet in the barrel, the harpy stops its screech.

While his hearing recovers, he turns to Madison and sees his ears are hurting. Jed takes cotton out of his pockets and places it in his ears and some extras onto the stable's keeper. The postal inspector then reloads his pistol as fast as he can and pulls Madison out of the back to the main road, abandoning their torches on the ground. Arriving in the center of town, Pluck and Madison see guards from the other shift running out of

Town Hall to add more to the defense. All the guards aim their guns in multiple directions, knowing the fiend can attack in multiple directions with all of their ears covered with cotton.

While all the guards stand on the main road, aiming their guns in the air, Pluck sees his partner exiting the hotel. As Secoli runs to join the group, Pluck notices he doesn't have his ears protected as he gets closer to the group's light.

"Louie," Jed whispers while he's able to hear, "protect your ears."

While Louie applies the cotton, Pluck sees large talons reach behind his partner. With no time to waste, he tackles Secoli, and they both land on the asphalt just before the harpy can grab the postal inspectors. The guards aiming in the fiend's direction see the man-bird hybrid flying toward them and fire their weapons for dear life.

The men closest to the postal inspectors get knocked down from being smacked by the harpy's talons. Luckily, the harpy had its talons closed when it attempted to grab one of the postal inspectors. After knuckling a couple of guards in the way, the fiend flies higher, knowing it's in a dangerous position, flying over the guards and firing their weapons. It goes so high that it disappears in the darkness, without anyone knowing if any bullets hit the fiend. Even if they could no longer see the harpy, the guards continuously fire their guns above their heads in hopes of taking the creature down.

The sheriff and his deputy pick the postal inspector up. The two lawmen speedily check to see if they spot blood on either of the two before resuming their defensive position. Thankfully, the harpy doesn't harm either Pluck or Secoli. The firing stops when they all have to reload their rifles after attempting to give their target everything they have. Since the flying monster didn't fall from getting hit by bullets, everyone anticipates the man-bird of prey is still hunting for them.

They all quickly get their guns fully loaded to prepare for another strike. As quick learners, none of them fires their guns unless one of them sees the enemy. Pluck is impressed by how orderly and cooperative all the guards are without anyone giving a command. It's as if each and every one of the men were so affected by the first attack that they can't afford to make any mistakes. Pluck then puts his attention on their enemy, who's hiding in the darkness.

The anticipation of its next move has his heart racing. The postal inspector notices he's shaking as he aims his pistol at the darkness. He anticipates the fiend to show up so much that he's struggling to keep himself from pulling the trigger too soon and misleading everyone.

Through the cotton covering his ears, Pluck suddenly hears a man screaming. Guns fire again as he turns around to see a harpy carrying someone by the shoulders. From where he stands, he sees that the victim not only has his shoulders pierced by the beast's talons but also is getting hit by bullets. The guards have no idea what they're shooting at but are shooting based on a knee-jerk reaction to spotting the beast.

The postal inspector shouts at everyone to cease firing. However, the incessant gunfire and everyone's ears being covered makes it impossible for anyone to hear Pluck's command. It's like the harpy is using its victims to shield itself from the bullets, and Pluck is the only one to notice it. How can no one see that it's their comrade's blood dripping in the air? It becomes more apparent to Pluck how intelligent this nightmarish species truly is.

The harpy flies into the darkness with another victim. It's far too late to save the second person it has taken tonight, whoever that may be. Even though the harpy has yet to be seen, Pluck has a gut feeling that the fiend is using a strategy against them. When the gun firing ceases, he turns around to see everyone putting their guns down and putting more bullets in them. Pluck sees that all of them aren't moving at a fast enough pace, and no predator has ever given its prey the time to prepare to fight back.

"Hurry!" Pluck exclaims in a panic, loud enough for everyone to hear. "The damn thing is coming back! Reload! Reload! Reload!"

No one is fast enough to fill their guns with ammunition as the harpy makes its return. While the guards are defenseless, the harpy carries back the dead body and throws the victim back at the gathered guards. A couple of men from the crowd get knocked down by the tossed victim. The harpy emerges from the darkness, screeching again, causing the guards to wince in pain despite the cotton they deeply stuffed in their ears. The harpy flies with high momentum in the same direction where it hurled its victim.

Pluck ducks for cover, narrowly avoiding the razor-sharp talons that rake the men in front of him. The men on the sides aren't so lucky either, with the fiend's razor-sharp feathers slashing as many victims as they can reach. When the harpy makes it through the center of the crowd, it stops its high-pitched shrieking to fly higher. It flies into the darkness and is out of sight again.

Pluck gets back up to see the casualties. A great number of guards in the middle have gashes on their chests. The others on the left and the right suffer lacerations on the stomach and legs from the harpy's razor-sharp wings. Pluck can hear all the casualties scream in agony through the cotton in his ears, uncertain if any died from that strike. The only tactic is the ones in the back, which the fiend flew over. Now that the harpy has disappeared behind them, they're the next in line if the beast has plans for another attack.

Many of the unharmed guards get out of position to treat the wounded. This turns out to be a bad move on their part, considering that the town's defense has weakened. Pluck, the only one to notice that it's too soon to help the casualties runs behind the crowd where the harpy flies through. He also notices he's the only one who hasn't shot his gun yet, and everyone who fired still hasn't fully loaded their guns either.

"What are you doing?!" the postal inspector shouts. "The harpy is still out there! It's going to strike again! Reload! Reload! Reload!"

Not everyone hears Jed, as many of them can only hear the victims screaming in pain through the cotton covering their ears. Only those closest to Pluck can hear his command and follow it to prepare for a counterattack. Pluck anticipates the harpy will be using the same tactic again.

With great luck, Pluck predicts correctly by moving away from Newsome's body being thrown in his direction. The body instead lands on another guard standing behind the postal inspector, causing little effect on the crowd, who have spread apart yet are still disorganized. The harpy's screeching is heard again, but it isn't coming from the direction where the body was thrown. As it gets louder, everyone holds on to their ears. Even the guards in critical condition wake from hearing the painfully loud noise.

No one can stand still, nor does anyone know where the ear-piercing screaming is coming from. As analytical and fast-thinking as Pluck is, even when he's in as much pain as everyone else, he notices the noise getting louder because the harpy is getting closer.

But from where? Struggling to see where the beast is approaching from, Pluck cannot locate the harpy. He then looks up and sees something falling directly above him.

Seeing the harpy above their heads, Pluck does his damnedest to point his pistol at the fiend. The man-bird of prey moves so fast that it lands on top of a guard, treating one of the casualties, and pierces him with its talons. The feathered beast stops its screaming as it stands on top of its latest victim. The guards closest to the enemy have to switch from covering their ears to covering their noses due to the stench coming from the harpy.

With his hands covering his ears, Pluck takes a good look at the harpy. Judging by its pale skin, black feathers, silky long raven hair, and the human face with no facial hair, it's the same harpy that attacked this morning. Pluck is unable to aim and shoot the fiend since it's screeching so loud that he has to cover his ears with both hands. Just as it's about to use its ear-piercing voice to make everyone go permanently deaf, gunfire is heard coming from the Town Hall's porch.

The harpy grows silent as it collapses on top of its victims on the ground. When Pluck gets up and looks around to see who shot the harpy, Gallus Kennedy walks down from the Town Hall's porch and aims his rifle directly at the fallen angel. As the trading post owner approaches the harpy, the monster takes one last breath before screeching as loud as it can as its last resort. All nearby windows shatter as everyone struggles to protect their ears, but Kennedy is unfazed. The harpy did the man a favor by making him go deaf earlier, and Kennedy is now using his deafness to his advantage.

Kennedy sees movement from its jaws, telling him the harpy is still alive. He shoots the man-bird of prey directly at its exposed back again as it lies on its stomach. The harpy finally remains silent and stops moving. The trading post owner uses the barrel of his rifle to push and roll the harpy onto its back. He sees the fiend lying motionless.

In complete frustration and fear, Pluck takes out his pistol and fires at the harpy, just in case if somehow Kennedy's shots didn't kill the fiend. The guards, still recovering from becoming temporarily deaf, grab their rifles and join Pluck, adding more bullets for good measure. The firing squad keeps firing till their guns run out of ammunition again. From the creature's head to thighs and knees to talons, there are many bullet shots all over its body. Not a single guard has any remorse when they overkill the harpy.

When they stop firing, the harpy receives so many bullets that its body is mutilated. Its right wing is detached from its shoulder, and its left leg is dismembered. The harpy's human-like face is no longer recognizable, as it is disfigured to the point that it is beyond gruesome to look at. No living organism could possibly survive this act of ruthless violence. Everyone on the main road remains silent, uncertain what to do now that they've mangled the beast.

Seeing that everyone who fired at the beast is calming down from the adrenaline, Pluck turns around and focuses on the casualties. He picks one of them up, and the unharmed guards do the same with the other casualties. While the torches still have light, Pluck counts eight injured and three dead. No one rejoices in their victory over the harpy, even though they have defeated their predator. There are too many casualties and deaths for that.

While everyone carries the wounded into the Town Hall, Dr. Fletcher exits the hotel and heads directly to the harpy's remains. The gruesome sight makes her tear up. As she cries, Secoli approaches to comfort the saddened ornithologist, but she pushes him away as she feels his arm around.

"What was that for, Doctor?" Secoli says angrily and confused.

"How could you?" the ornithologist wails. "How could any of you be so heartless toward this creature?"

"Are you nuts, lady?" says one of the guards. "Do you realize how many we've lost fighting this thing?"

"Yeah, we're lucky to come out alive," another one comments. "If that death angel were still alive, we'd all be dead by now."

Noticing there's an argument occurring, Pluck stops what he's doing and intervenes. He sees Dr. Fletcher is upset and doesn't know what the bickering is about. The argument settles down when Pluck moves between the guards and the ornithologist.

"What's going on here?" Pluck says. "This is no time to fight each other."

"This crazy woman is saying we did the wrong thing by killing this devil," says one of the old guards, pointing at her.

Pluck turns to Fiona and tries to cool his temper by saying, "Fiona, I know it's hard for you to understand, but what other choice did we have? The harpy wasn't going to let any of us live."

"You didn't give it a chance to live," Dr. Fletcher says as she weeps. "You didn't let me have a chance to study it. I would have figured out how to tame the beast, just like other ornithologists have done with every other bird of prey. I hope you and everyone in Lemonstown are happy that you've massacred one of the greatest scientific discoveries in the history of evolution."

"Evolution?" a man responds. "Isn't that some kind of weird religion that believes in constant changes or something?"

Fletcher gives the preacher a look of disapproval. "None of you uneducated idiots knows what science even is. If any of you did, you would have known how important it is to keep this species alive for the benefit of society." She sighs. "Never mind. What's done is done. And so is my business here."

"Wait!" Pluck says. "You're leaving?"

"I have no business being here, nor shall I be reminded of the greatest missed opportunities of all time. I'm leaving in the morning. Goodnight, Inspector Pluck. I hope to never see you, Inspector Secoli, or anyone in this damn town again."

"If the damn harpy was so special to you," Pluck replies as she starts heading back to the hotel, "then why didn't you help us keep it alive? You were the one who chased off that thing the first time it attacked us, so why didn't you help this time?"

Fletcher stops in her tracks and turns to Pluck, saying, "Why don't you ask Louie about that yourself? He locked me inside my hotel room and violated the deal you made for me. Oh, and Louie..." She looks at him. "Good luck finding someone else to take care of your budgerigar. Because I ain't gonna do it for you no more."

Dr. Fletcher flees to the hotel to escape everyone after she insults them, and no one follows her. What could Jed do when a dangerous animal like a harpy couldn't be reasoned with and was difficult to take down? Though he saved Lemonstown and brought down the culprit, his relationship with Dr. Fletcher has never been as sour. It may be for the best, though, considering Pluck still loves his family in Boston. He turns to his partner and scowls at him.

"Louie," Pluck raises his voice. "Did you really lock Fiona in her hotel room?"

"Jed," he replies, "you and I both know a battle is no place for a woman."

"Even so, she proved useful by helping us fight off the harpy the last time."

"Do you have any idea what you're saying, Jed? She would have let that harpy escape and have us spend many more nights fighting that damn thing. Are you willing to risk more lives to appease her demands?"

"You don't know that. She's smarter than any of us out here, and maybe she could have figured out how to stop the harpy using a different method."

"Don't be putting all this on me, Jed. If I recall, you started overkilling the harpy when it was already dead. You took the pleasure of continuously shooting the damn thing till it became nothing more than splattered meat like the rest of us."

That remark leaves Pluck speechless. Seeing the harpy's remains proves that Louie is right about Pluck's actions. He then holds the bridge of his nose to relieve some stress, feeling embarrassed that he's fighting his partner in front of everyone.

"What the hell are we doing fighting each other?" Secoli continues, now calming down. "We solved the case and saved Lemonstown. It's a job well done if you ask me. C'mon, Jed. Let's help the casualties before you're relieved from your shift."

"Do we still have shifts now that we've taken down the beast?" Pluck asks. Secoli pauses for a moment before replying, "You know. You're right. There's no point in doing shifts anymore. I'll tell the mayor that the job is done."

Pluck is tempted to leave right there and return to the hotel. Taking down the harpy is the most tasking thing he's done in a long time. However, from many years of being a postal inspector, a case solved doesn't mean the job is done. This case is no different except for having many more casualties than it should have. The sight of casualties being carried to Town Hall helps him remember why he's here.

It's difficult for Pluck to even look at his partner while helping the injured men who fought so bravely. It takes time for him to get over a heated argument with Secoli and even his love interest, which feels like it has zero chance of happening. He can't get his mind off being insulted by both of them while he bandages up the victims. The women are available to help treat the wounded. Understandably, the casualties' wives and families are the first ones to treat their injuries. Their love and worries for their men are prioritized before giving others additional help. Even the children's tears at seeing their fathers in such bad condition make it difficult for Pluck and Secoli to stay strong. However, the families of the three who fell from this attack are harder to comfort.

As Pluck helps one of the ladies bandage up a casualty, he overhears that not only Patrick Newsome died but nineteen-year-old Bartholomew Black, too. His mother weeps ever so loudly, unable to cope that her only child didn't make it. In equally bad shape is the town's preacher, Val Jenkins, who had his skull crushed from the harpy's landing. The preacher, being one of the harpy's victims, is seen as a spiritual attack on the town's religious folks.

The three who didn't make it are covered in a white sheet and brought to the trading post. Wesley Simmons is now one of several sharing the trading post. Now that Lemonstown is no longer in danger, all four deserve a proper burial soon enough.

Although where the harpy left Berk Hartman remains a mystery. Pluck hopes he won't be asked to continue searching for Mrs. Hartman's boy.

At this point, Pluck just wants to go home, hoping he won't get assigned to a case like this again. He's disappointed that the case didn't have a better outcome. It also doesn't feel as rewarding to help the casualties and deal with their grieving families at the end. Leading during a depressing time is a heavy burden for the hero, even with help.

ALL THINGS CONSIDERED, the townspeople can't be happier to have Lemonstown's curfew over. Though business hours have been reopened, there is a lot of damage to clean up and less help since last night's casualties were high. Despite everyone being happy that life is getting back to normal, it is too soon to have business resume to normal. There won't be any customers or visitors stopping by Lemonstown anytime soon, but business hours are reopened to keep people busy to cope with the casualties.

Pluck watches Lemonstown back in operation as he sits on the bank's porch, eating his breakfast prepared by the women. This meal is the last time free food is offered to the community since giveaways don't make a profit during business hours. The postal inspector enjoys a dish of warm grits. As he licks his plate off, thinking no one is looking, his partner walks behind him. Jed startles and pretends not to have bad eating habits when he hears Secoli call his name.

"Sorry for startling you, Jed," Secoli says, putting his birdcage on top of the porch's fence and leaning against it. "You wouldn't happen to know if Dr. Fletcher is still in town, do you? There's an extra plate of grits just for her."

"Don't even bother. She'll just turn down the offer like she did to us. Now that the harpy's dead, she's useless."

Secoli turns north of the main road and sees the ornithologist's transportation parked in front of the stable before replying, "I'm surprised she hasn't left yet. By how she acted last night, it was as if she'd leave immediately when the sun rose. I wouldn't dare talk to her after she insulted everyone. Why can't she understand that abomination needed to be put down for everyone to live? Even if she somehow captured it, she would have been as deaf as Gallus Kennedy."

"Speaking of which, what did you guys do to the harpy's remains?"

"We got the remains boxed up for evidence while you went to your hotel. We're taking the harpy's remains for the government to research and conceal. It's too dangerous for it to be in the wrong hands, especially when it still has those razor-sharp feathers attached to its wings and lower half of its body."

"And where's that box now?"

"We placed it in the jailhouse, next to Jeremy Payton's cell. It's the only place where the sheriff and his deputy can watch it."

"Good thinking. And thanks for taking care of that. If only I were more awake…." Pluck yawns.

"Don't worry about it. You did a good job leading everyone last night. You deserved a good rest."

"Thanks. And you did a good job by not bringing Chap with you in our fight against the harpy. Now that Dr. Fletcher won't be watching over your muse anymore, who will watch over Chap?"

"Well, it's…weird that I haven't had an episode without Chap lately. I mean, here and there, I feel some anxiety when I'm separated from him, but I'm doing better at standing on my own, one day at a time."

Pluck chuckles joyfully and says, "I knew you could do it. It's not so bad when you start believing in yourself."

"Thanks, but changing the topic…" Secoli pauses as he holds his nose. "Don't take it the wrong way, but when was the last time you took a bath?"

"Excuse me?" Pluck responds in an offended tone.

"There's no other way for me to ask. Sorry if I insulted you, but do you know how bad you smell? Why don't you help yourself to the bathhouse?"

"How can we? Newsome is dead, and the bathhouse isn't open."

"Not true. I got myself a bath before I went to bed last night. Apparently, workers like Caleb Wash have opened the bathhouse for everyone. Get yourself a deserved bath before we set off, all right?"

"Right." Pluck gets up from the steps and heads to the bathhouse. He turns around and tells his partner, "One more thing, Louie. The next time you say anything about my hygiene, you'll be sorry that you did."

Secoli can't say anything after being intimidated by his remark, unable to tell if that was a threat. Pluck can tell from his partner's silence that he got the picture. Though he knows he needs a bath since last night, Pluck dislikes it whenever anyone hints at his poor hygiene. As he crosses the main road, he quickly regrets what he said to Secoli. As his usual stubborn self, he's using this time of separation to cool off his temper.

Jed enters the front door to find no one in the public bath building. Now that Patrick Newsome is no longer around, his employees are without a leader. Are they still employed if the owner of the business is dead? If so, who's running the business? The thought of Newsome makes Jed feel guilty about being in his facility, feeling like he's taking advantage of the equipment and unattended service left behind. He then gets a little choked up when he thinks about the owner's wife and children, who have been grieving since last night.

After ringing the desk bell for a minute, Pluck is convinced that Newsome's bathhouse is abandoned. Still conscientious, the postal inspector takes out his wallet and places two dollars on the front desk. Two dollars is a lot of money and several times the amount the business charges for bathing services. Whoever claims the money receives an act of generosity from the bottom of the Federal agent's heart, hoping this act of magnanimity will help lift someone's spirits.

While the place remains unattended, Pluck slips past the front desk and enters through the door before him. Pluck sees a spacious room where a wooden tub that looks like an oval-shaped barrel is placed in the center. As he looks around, he sees a fireplace at the end of the room and many large steel pots on the tables. On the other side of the room, where the fireplace is located, is the trough where the water is kept. Who knows how long the water has been there since the trough shows signs of water damage.

Pluck isn't bothered by how old the water looks. He badly needs a bath. He fires up the furnace and fills one of the larger pots with water from the trough. When the pot fully fills, he places it under the fireplace to warm the water. Even despite how humid it is outside, the postal inspector hates to take a cold bath. He waits a while, checking the water multiple times till he's satisfied with the temperature. He then uses one of the smaller pots to scoop the water and pour it into the wooden bathtub.

Once the tub is full of warm water, Pluck throws some soap in the bath. The bath looks so pleasant that Pluck can't wait to soak himself in it. He disrobes to nude and relaxes in the bath. Having gotten fully wet, the postal inspector enjoys his soak, completely relieved of the stress of helping this town. This is the first time since arriving at Lemonstown that he finds peace with himself.

However, his moment of relaxation doesn't last as long as he hears footsteps coming from the other side of the room. Pluck is already feeling uncomfortable about one of the bathhouse workers stepping through the door and is coming up with what to say when that door opens. The postal inspector is insecure about anyone seeing him nude, so he keeps his entire body underwater, keeping his head above the surface. The door creaks open, and he prepares for a confrontation.

To his surprise, Dr. Fiona Fletcher enters the bathing room. Pluck is completely caught off guard to see her here, especially in an uncomfortable circumstance. The ornithologist stands before him, embarrassed to see the postal inspector in the nude. She looks away, with her face turned red.

"Sorry, Inspector," Dr. Fletcher replies, trying to hide her face, which she knows is turning redder. "I just…I just wanted to say goodbye."

"Well, couldn't we say farewell a little later? I'm in the middle of something."

"No, we can't. I find it rude to leave without saying goodbye, and I need to get it out of the way before I'm on my way."

"And you don't find it rude not to knock before entering or starting a conversation when someone is nude? You'd be in more trouble if you were a man and I were a woman. Furthermore, I don't see why I should say goodbye to you after your unacceptable behavior last night."

"If only you could grasp how important it is for professionals like me to know more about that species, you would have kept the series alive. Never mind. We've discussed this many times already. I know when I'm not wanted."

"Actually, you are wanted," Pluck interrupts before she closes the door. "And what can I do since there aren't any birds in this godforsaken town?

Except for Chap, but he's domesticated by your partner."

"It's not that. It's just...." Jed can't find the right words to say to her. He takes his time to think about what to say before making things worse. Fiona waits patiently before he says, "I know I can't take back what I did to the harpy, and I'm so sorry. Really, I am. I don't expect you to forgive me for what I did." The ornithologist crosses her arms and asks, "Then what do you want?"

"I don't know. Your expertise might still be of good use to the government. I don't know how, but..." Jed sighs and stops resisting further. "There's no other way for me to put this, Fiona. I just need to know. Why did you kiss me yesterday?"

Fiona's face turns red again. "Oh, that? I don't know what came over me. I felt bad for you over how restless you were. You couldn't settle, so I thought that was the only way to get you to sleep."

"It did the opposite. Quite frankly, it kept me awake wondering why you did it."

"Did it feel that good, Inspector?" she says flirtatiously. "What?" Pluck asks in disbelief.

"Do you like that kiss?" Fiona approaches Jed, still sitting in the tub. She notices the postal inspector's nervousness. "Please be honest with me, Inspector."

"I-I can't," he says, looking away from her.

"Well—why not?" She kneels next to the tub at his level. "Don't you like a girl like me?" While Jed looks away, she looks at his body through the water. "Oh, I see that you do like me based on what's growing down there."

"Please, Fiona! I just can't!" Pluck raises his voice to intimidate her, fighting the urge to give in to temptation and struggling to resist how turned on he is.

He pauses for a moment, thinking he scared her off. When Pluck finally turns to her, she doesn't even sway. Dr. Fletcher looks straight at Inspector Pluck. She loves seeing his brown hair wet, his handsome oval-shaped face, and his beady eyes as blue as the ocean. It's gotten so quiet that she can almost hear his heart pounding over this tender moment for her but an awkward moment for him.

To finish what she started, the ginger wraps her arms around the postal inspector and kisses him. The ornithologist's arms hold Jed tightly, and her lips are locked on his. She doesn't care how wet her clothes are from touching him. Jed's body is enjoying this moment so much that his mind drifts from resisting the beautiful doctor to succumbing to lust for her. Slowly he closes his eyes, then holds on to her. Gradually, it turns from a kiss he's receiving from her into a kiss for each other.

The moment she lets go of his lips, Fletcher releases him and removes her clothes. Jed gazes at her body as she removes her dress and undergarments. He's in complete awe over her thin hour-class shape that surpasses his libidinous curiosity. When he gazes down, he sees Fiona take everything off except her boots, which reach up to her knees. When Jed expects her to remove her boots, she leaps into the tub and lands on his naked body, splashing water all over the floor.

Now he can feel her body physically contacting him; there is no possibility of resisting; Jed is completely under Fiona's spell. They continue kissing and embracing each other in the tub, committing to this affair like nothing else. After days of fearing to pursue the ornithologist, it all slips out of his mind. All that's left in Pluck's mind is to fulfill his fantasies with Dr. Fletcher to relieve the stress from being a Federal agent.

ANABELLE LARSON CAN'T be happier to be back in the hotel. After days of sharing the same living space with the townsfolk, sleeping uncomfortably on the sanctuary's long chairs and the floor, and being confined to the Town Hall, it feels sweet to have her freedom back. She slept so well in her hotel bed that she overslept and woke up feeling well-rested. Realizing how long she's been in bed, Anabelle quickly gets up to meet her peers in their hotel rooms. She dresses up as quickly as she can and heads out of her room.

When Anabelle enters the hallway, she sees Pearl looking well-dressed and carrying a briefcase. "Pearl," Anabelle says, "why are you carrying a briefcase? You're not leaving, are you?"

"I'm sorry, Anabelle," she replies, blinking rapidly to resist shedding a tear. "I heard Dr. Fletcher is leaving soon. I'm going with her."

"So soon? Does she know you're coming with her?"

"Honestly, no. But I'm not taking no for an answer. I will be her assistant, regardless of whether or not I get paid. I want to be with someone as amazing as her."

"Oh, Pearl," Anabelle starts choking up. "Haven't you taken the time to think these things over?"

"I have, Anne." She looks down, sad that it has come to this. "I'm tired of staying in Lemonstown. I want to see the world. There ain't nothing left for me here."

Pearl turns around and quickly receives a hug from her dear friend. She feels Anabelle's tight grasp and tears coming down, dropping onto her shoulders. Hearing her dear friend sob makes her unable to hold back her tears longer. Feeling guilty that she's hurting Anabelle, Pearl cries and hugs her back. The other girls who worked with the two stepped out of their hotel rooms, confused over Anabelle's and Pearl's crying. They approach the two to get some answers.

"What's going on, Pearl and Anabelle?" asks one of the former saloon girls. Anabelle lets go and wipes her tears before she answers, "Pearl—she's leaving Lemonstown with Dr. Fletcher."

All of them gasp over this news, followed by one of them replying, "No, Pearl. Say it ain't so."

"I'm sorry, girls," Pearl says with her head down, trying not to show her watery eyes to her peers. "Now that we're no longer under Mr. Benjamin's protection, I feel vulnerable here." More tears poured down her face.

The others get choked up, empathizing with what she's saying.

"I want to see the world and be with Dr. Fletcher. She's the most amazing woman I've ever met. I can't miss sharing the same adventures with someone as brave and smart as her."

"Pearl," the same woman says, "I understand that you hate the perverts all over this town, but you hardly know Dr. Fletcher."

"Even so," Pearl continues, "Dr. Fletcher has opportunities I want. Someone like her is filled with a lot of adventures, things to learn, and…and…."

Pearl can't finish what she's saying. She covers her face and falls to her knees. All the ladies kneel to give Pearl a big hug. After all these years of putting up with the men of Lemonstown and the hardships they endured together, one is leaving them. None of them resent Pearl's decision, but the thought of separating from a dear friend is always a hard pill to swallow.

"Pearl," the oldest woman says, "take good care of yourself. If you feel Dr. Fletcher isn't treating you right or is putting you in a dangerous position,

don't hesitate to walk away. You hear me?"

"I hear you, Jolene."

"We love you, Pearl," another girl says. "I want you to remember that you helped us get through those tough times. You were always the sister I never had." Pearl weeps loudly over how much she means to her peers. This whole time, she thought they only stuck with each other because that's what women do to protect themselves from degenerate men—but it was more than just that.

This makes it harder for her to say goodbye than originally planned.

Pearl gives each of them a hug. She saves the last one for her best friend, Anabelle, who's standing in front of the stairs that lead to the lobby. Anabelle cries some more when Pearl stands in front of her and gives the tightest, most meaningful hug she has given anyone. All the girls watch the two best friends giving what looks like their last hug together.

"I promise that when I find the first telegraph office," Pearl says when they both let go, "I'll send you a telegram to keep in touch. Okay?"

Anabelle nods, unable to say any more goodbyes to her. She doesn't even watch Pearl go down the stairs. The girls don't follow Pearl down the stairs because they have difficulty accepting that one of them is leaving. Instead, they comfort Anabelle, who is sadder than anyone else.

Pearl, too, can feel the girls' grief as she realizes they're not following her down the stairs. She leaves the hotel and tries to hide her emotions from everyone. Pearl walks to the stable to find that Dr. Fletcher's wagon is still there without her present. She turns to the stable keeper, who's guiding one of the horses. "Excuse me, Mr. Madison," Pearl says, putting her briefcase in the wagon.

"Have you seen Dr. Fletcher?"

"Last I saw her, she said she needed to bathe before she set off. Are you going with her, Miss Herbert?"

She nods and heads to the bathhouse. "I am. Thanks for letting me know.

And, Mr. Madison, don't let her go without me. You hear?"

She then rushes down the main road, never being so excited and happy to start moving on. Pearl knows exactly what to say to Dr. Fletcher and will never accept no as an answer. So excited to see her new idol, she runs faster to the bathhouse, feeling so much adrenaline. When Pearl gets into the building, she hears something unusual. Pearl recognizes the ornithologist's voice, along with moaning as creaks from the wooden floor, go in rhythm.

Given her experience as a saloon girl, she knows this can only mean one thing. The thought that the ornithologist would even be having sex with any of the perverted men in Lemonstown appalls her. After all, why would an educated and respected woman stoop to the level of any of these uneducated men? She worries when Fletcher's moans get louder with the man on the other side of the door. The thought of her being violated against her will makes Pearl enraged.

Before she lets her assumptions get the best of her, Pearl has to see it for herself.

Using her experience from watching her peers in her old saloon job, she creeps to the door and opens it without being seen. In the corner of her eye, she sees Fiona completely wet, wearing only her boots, and bending over someone. The ornithologist is facing away from the door, allowing Pearl to open the door more to see who's penetrating her.

She slowly looks around the door to see a man fornicating with Dr. Fletcher. Hearing the ornithologist shout "Harder!" repeatedly is a sign that this is within the ornithologist's consent. Her curiosity gets the best of her, as she wants to get a good look at who she's fornicating with. It's difficult to see who it is since he, too, faces the furnace, completely nude and wet. Hearing him say "Yes" repeatedly confirms who he is.

Pearl is shocked that Inspector Pluck is having an affair with the woman she admires. She knows by word of mouth that the postal inspector is married. She covers her mouth to keep herself from making any sound and slowly moves back to the waiting room. Witnessing this sexual scandal immediately changes her views on the two from good role models to sleazy degenerates. Pearl quietly exits the bathhouse, feeling upset over what she saw.

This whole time, she has seen them as people to look up to, but they've changed into individuals no different than everyone else. This disappointment has affected her tremendously, telling her that degeneracy, which she's trying to escape from, will continue to follow her wherever she goes. Pearl has sadly put the ornithologist at a high standard of being above men's demands and expectations, which was a mistake on her part. It makes her feel worse to abandon her friends, as she's reminded of their hardships in satisfying male customers. Despite her disappointment, Pearl sticks to her plan to leave Lemonstown with Dr. Fletcher.

Sitting on the bathhouse porch, she can see Anabelle stepping out of the hotel, waving at her in the distance. Pearl's embarrassed that she has not left yet after the emotional goodbye, unable to wave back. She's very uncertain about telling anyone what she just saw. Perhaps it's best to keep it confidential and let sleeping dogs lie to avoid the consequences. Nevertheless, covering up this affair like she did with the others at her last job will only exacerbate her bad mood. She continues thinking things over as she sits alone on the porch, waiting for Dr. Fletcher and Inspector Pluck to finish their adulterous acts.

CHAPTER 10

It's August 15, and Allie is having her biggest birthday party yet. Many of her neighbors, classmates from last school year, and relatives are attending this celebration. The party is bigger than her sisters', but she's the only one not enjoying herself as much as she would like. Even her mother knows Allie is upset that her father isn't with her on her seventh birthday. While the children run around in the house, Allie plays only a little, as she's constantly reminded of her father's absence.

After playing games and opening presents, Allie's older sisters, Jessie and Julia, bring in the birthday cake. As everyone sings "Happy Birthday," Allie sees how colorful and decorative the cake is. Knowing the purpose of blowing out the candles, the birthday girl can hardly wait to make a wish. When the cake is placed on the table, Allie stares at the candlelight and thinks about how much she misses her father. Everyone stops singing the birthday song and waits for her to make a wish and blow out the candles.

Allie stares at the candles for a while, then weeps for her lost father. The mother then intervenes to calm the troubled birthday girl after the guests start whispering to one another.

"It's all right, Allie," Clara says, putting her hands on her daughter's shoulders.

"Make your wish, and it may come true."

"But Daddy's dead," Allie replies, already shedding tears.

"We don't know what's happened to your father. Maybe he's still alive, and he'll be back home any day now."

"But not today, will he?"

"Not unless you continue to believe that he's okay. If you wish for something that may not come true, that's okay. At least, it's the most you can do to make a difference. From the bottom of your heart, it might come true."

Clara wipes Allie's tears, and the birthday girl thinks about how badly she wishes for her father to return today. It's impractical, though, and she's been disappointed by her father's absence for a long time. The possibility that he might never come back is all that she can think about right now, but this wish might be the only way to change that.

Allie inhales as much as her lungs can and blows the candles as hard as possible. The guests give her applause for finally blowing out the candles. As everyone gets a slice of cake, Allie can only think about her wish coming true. If Jed is a good father, she expects him to come home as soon as his case ends.

Pearl Herbert remains sitting on the bathhouse's porch, waiting for either Inspector Pluck or Dr. Fletcher to come out. A couple of locals want to use the facility for a bath. Still, she prevents anyone from entering the facility, considering she's trying to cover up the sex scandal, telling the lie that the building is under maintenance. Thankfully, all of them believe her, despite knowing she doesn't work there. Even the employees supposed to be working seem to have abandoned the place since Patrick Newsome tragically died. Even though Pearl doesn't like protecting Fletcher and Pluck's reputations, she protects them after all the good they have done for the town.

After a long while, Pearl gets up and turns to the front door when she hears footsteps on the porch, and out comes the postal inspector. Pearl and Jed stared at each other intently, Pearl frowning and Jed looking guilty. Pluck surmised from the expression on her face that she knows what he had just done. Pearl gives Pluck a piercing stare as he walks away; paranoia is evident in his movements. He heads straight to the Town Hall, where Secoli, the train engineer, and the injured conductor are waiting for him before they leave Lemonstown.

She stops glaring when she hears Dr. Fletcher coming from behind her. Though upset over Pluck's decision, Pearl is sad for the woman she idolizes. The ornithologist doesn't even notice her admirer's despair, feeling very satisfied with the adulterous acts. After taking a deep breath, she notices Pearl standing before her.

"Oh, I'm surprised to see you again," Fletcher says. "Do you know I'm leaving pretty soon?"

"Yes," Pearl replies, clearing her throat to forget what she witnessed. "And I'm coming with you."

"What?" the ornithologist responds in a surprised tone.

"I insist, Dr. Fletcher." Pearl holds Fletcher's hands. "I know we don't know each other very well, but I want to come with you and be your personal assistant." The ornithologist is about to say something, but Pearl interrupts, "I won't take no for an answer. I don't care if I'll have to work for free. Anything is better than remaining here. I can cook, clean, do your laundry, organize your things—anything. Since you're a busy and respected woman, you can't be doing all the work. That's why you need me."

Fiona briefly pauses, thinking about Pearl's eagerness to join her before replying, "I suppose I need some help. A lot, actually. Come along. It's going to be a long trip."

"Thank you, Doctor." Pearl gets so excited that she squeezes Dr. Fletcher's hands.

She realizes she has hurt her idol as Fiona pulls her hands away. "Oh, I'm sorry!"

"It's all right." Fletcher rubs her hands. "We'd better get going, Pearl. I'd rather head out first before the postal inspectors do."

"With pleasure, ma'am…Doctor." Pearl follows Dr. Fletcher to where she left her wagon and horses. "So where are we going?"

"We're heading back to Montana. Since the harpy is dead, I have no business being in this godforsaken desert."

As the two of them make it to the wagon in front of the stable, the crowd surrounds the building, blocking their way. The two ladies are confused over this sudden gathering as they give applause. The cheering isn't for them but for the postal inspectors and the two train workers. The four exit the stable with a wagon with a crate on board.

While Inspectors Pluck and Secoli wave to everyone in the driver's seat, the two train crew sit atop the crate, covered in bandages from their injuries. As Pluck waves to his audience, he sees Dr. Fletcher and Pearl giving him different receptions. The ornithologist winks at the postal inspector while her assistant crosses her arms and looks away in disgust. Never before has Pluck wanted to leave as much as he does now. He looks away from the two and whips the reins of the horses pulling their wagon. The horses move forward toward the mayor and his lawmen.

"Inspectors. Gentlemen," Mayor McLusky says, "I don't know how we can repay you four for all your help in saving Lemonstown."

"Sir," the conductor says, "it's these three who saved your town. I was out of action from falling off the ladder, so I missed the whole fight against the harpy."

"Still, you brave men came all this way to save our town, and since we prevailed, I give you my most sincere gratitude."

"Aw, shucks, Mayor," Secoli says, putting his birdcage between him and his partner. "We're not looking for any reward. We're just doing our job helping out our fellow Americans."

"And for that," the mayor continues, "we're forever grateful. From here on out, Lemonstown is no more. I hereby declare this town shall be renamed Point Postal."

The mayor turns around and takes out a carved wooden sign that says "Point Postal" with a subtext underneath: "In memory of Postal Inspector Pluck and Secoli for saving our town." The audience applauds louder as the two postal inspectors are overwhelmed by this gesture. The mayor passes the sign to Sheriff Wood, who's already on his horse, and gallops to the end of the road for the men to hang up the sign high on a stake. A local climbs up the ladder, removes the old Lemonstown sign, and hammers the new one to establish the change for the town. While the Federal agents feel overwhelmed and proud, the ornithologist and her new assistant aren't too happy.

Dr. Fletcher is jealous of the credit that Pluck and Secoli are receiving. Pearl, however, is the only one who knows her idol's efforts are being neglected and pities her hero. Both ladies can't take this celebration for these men anymore and head to their wagon. While the crowd moves closer to the men on their wagon, the two ladies have enough room for their wagon to start moving without anyone in the way. They both get on their wagon and leave Point Postal with a cold shoulder.

Pluck is the only one who notices Fiona Fletcher and Pearl Herbert departing town. He can tell both are unhappy with his and his partner's reward, and he feels offended by their pettiness. Instead of chasing them, Pluck lets them go, feeling they should separate and hopefully not see each other again. He puts his attention back on the crowd as the sheriff rides back to join them.

"Mayor, Sheriff, and the rest of you all!" Secoli yells for everyone to hear. "I'm...I mean, we are very thankful for all of this. We certainly won't forget our time here with you all." He elbows Pluck, who's staring into space. "Right, partner?"

"What? Y-yes, that's right." Pluck clears his throat. "Thank you, everyone, for all of this. Thank you for your cooperation and hospitality. We won't forget this."

Everyone cheers and gives way for their wagon and horses to leave town. Pluck can see that the women's wagon is ahead of them in their direction. Seeing how far away they are, Pluck realizes they're rushing to get out of there, which might exhaust their horses. When he whips his horses' reins, they pull the wagon quickly to save the animals' stamina. As they head north and away from Point Postal, everyone on the wagon waves back to the locals behind them, cheering their well-deserved farewells.

Minutes pass since leaving the town, and Pluck sees that the wagon the women were on has collapsed. As they draw closer, everyone on board sees that the two women are off from their overturned wagon, which has a broken wheel and are unable to move. Dr. Fletcher and Pearl Herbert see the men's wagon approaching and feel embarrassed that they see their accident.

"Good afternoon, ladies," Secoli says mockingly. "I would have told you to slow down, but you were so far ahead that you couldn't hear us."

Pluck lightly slaps his partner on the shoulder and says, "That's no way to treat these ladies, Louie."

"Why do they deserve any respect?" Secoli asks rhetorically. "Fiona insulted me last night, and to add insult to injury, they ran off out of pettiness that we weren't getting any praise. And now karma has caught up with them."

"Fine, Louie," the ornithologist replies. "You win. I'm sorry. It was stupid of me to get so emotional from last night until now. Can you share some space on your wagon?"

"Apologize all you want, Doctor," Secoli says, "but you're not hopping on this wagon. You've been a pain for all of us and look where it got you."

"Why are you acting like this, Louie?" Fiona asks. "The Inspector Secoli I know would be more of a gentleman than this."

"Except when the lady ticks this gentleman off. That's where I draw the line."

"Jed…" The ornithologist faces him. "You're not leaving me out here, are you?"

Though Pluck still feels for Dr. Fletcher, he wants to get rid of her and return to his family. He feels conflicted because it will make him look like a jerk to have a sexual relationship with her and run away. However, he doesn't want to look suspicious to the others on board by playing favoritism. The only one who knows about the sex scandal is her new assistant, who's giving him a mean look. Just as Pluck is about to reply, he's interrupted by a familiar scream echoing in the distance.

"What the hell is that?" the conductor reacts.

"Impossible…," Pluck murmurs in complete shock. "This can't happen."

"Oh, no," Secoli says to himself in disbelief.

"Oh, my God," Dr. Fletcher says with glee. "There's more of them?" Everyone faces the plateau where the familiar shrieking is coming from.

It doesn't sound like a single harpy approaching, but rather multiple. Chills come down Jed's spine when he sees four dark figures flying over the plateau. This is the first time they have seen black-feathered hybrids in daylight. The harpies are flying in their direction and are coming in fast.

"Everybody!" Pluck shouts. "Get under the wagon!"

The men jump off the wagon and hide underneath their transportation. Dr. Fletcher runs back to her broken wagon and hides with Pearl. When Pluck looks around to see if everyone is hidden, he sees that the conductor isn't below their vehicle. He immediately pops his head out to see the old man moving very slowly. He appears to still be hurting from his fall. When Pluck crawls out from the back of the wagon to help the old man, it's too late for him.

One of the harpies sticks its talons out and decapitates the conductor. The harpy that struck flies past the wagon before the conductor's head hits the ground. Pluck remains motionless, horrified to see the old man's head bouncing and rolling before him. It worsens when his blood pours down from the back of the wagon, causing the men underneath to panic.

The other three harpies fly past the wagon, and neither one turns around to attack. Carter crawls out to check on the decapitated body while Pluck watches the harpies fly away. While the train engineer swears over how gruesome the conductor looks, the postal inspector slowly walks out of their vehicle and sees the harpies heading to town. Immediately, Pluck runs back to the wagon.

"Everyone!" Pluck shouts. "We gotta save them!"

"But what about Mr. Polaski?" Carter cries. "We can't just leave him like this."

"We got no time, Nick!" Pluck hops into the driver's seat. "Everyone in town will be dead if we don't make it on time." He looks around but doesn't see his partner. "Secoli? Where are you?"

He gets off the wagon and looks underneath their vehicle. Pluck sees his partner sitting motionless on the ground, holding his birdcage for dear life.

"Louie!" Pluck shouts. "Snap out of it! We need you!"

Secoli is unresponsive being in a state of panic. Losing patience, Pluck slaps his partner across the face and pulls him out from underneath the wagon. Now that he's back to reality, Secoli immediately puts his birdcage on board and gets in the driver's seat next to Pluck.

The ornithologist boards the wagon as it makes a U-turn. She grabs her assistant by the hand, but as the wagon starts moving faster, Pearl has her boots dragging on the ground. Carter, who's already on board, helps Dr. Fletcher pull Pearl on board. Pearl gets pulled into the moving vehicle and lands on the conductor's decapitated body. She screams, touching the headless corpse and having his blood all over her clothes. Pluck knows the two ladies are on board but doesn't bother to tell them to get off, as he's more focused on getting back to town to save everyone.

As they get closer to town, pandemonium is heard. Everyone on board can hear the harpies screeching, the Town Hall's bell ringing, the townsfolk screaming, and guns firing. Pluck whips the horses to pull the wagon faster and draws his pistol. Seeing what his partner is doing, Secoli places his birdcage behind him and draws his pistol. He's terrified to fight more of these fiends again, knowing this case, unfortunately, isn't over.

Pluck can see from where they're at that people are getting lifted up in the air by the harpies and thrown to the ground like ragdolls. He keeps whipping the horses to go faster, but considering all the weight on the wagon they're pulling, they can't go at top speed. Everyone on the wagon gets more anxious the closer they get back to town. The silhouetted wings of the harpies stand out as they swoop in one by one. From where Pluck can see, these monsters are more organized and tactical than the confused townsfolk below them.

Once the wagon goes past the welcome sign, everyone gets off and spreads apart.

No plan is made, as Pluck and everyone improvise while the town is attacked. Secoli follows him, birdcage in hand. They both run toward the center of the main road.

The two are horrified that the women and children are lying and bleeding on the ground. The whole town is in turmoil, with bystanders running around and even the injured men firing their guns randomly in the air. Judging by how the predators are still circling above them, none of the bullets seem to be hitting any of them. One of the harpies drops from the sky and slashes one of the injured shooters into critical status. As the attacking harpy flies back up, all the shooters below it try to shoot the fiend down but to no avail.

At the top of his lungs, Pluck yells, "Everyone, listen to me! Get the women and children inside the Town Hall! The rest of you circle around the front of the building!"

Some people hear Inspector Pluck amid the hysteria, and they carry out his command. The men stand and form a circle, and the women and children rush inside the sanctuary. The others who didn't hear Pluck notice the ones following his command and quickly join them. The main road gets under control, but not so much for the others elsewhere and farther away. As the crowd gathers in front of the Town Hall, the harpies find them formidable and target the others in the housing area instead. They swoop in and attack anyone seen on the other roads.

"Inspectors!" shouts a man standing behind Pluck and Secoli. "There are more people on the other side of town. We gotta go rescue them."

"No," Pluck replies, "those monsters want to lure you out of formation so they can strike you down."

"This isn't right!" yells the same man. "Women and children are still out there. We're sitting ducks." He runs off. "I'm gonna go save them."

"No!" Secoli shouts at the man. "Get back here!"

Secoli speaks too soon as a harpy drops and pounces on the man trying to be a hero. Pluck orders the guards to fire at the harpy, but it quickly flies out of the way, lifting its prey in the air by the head. The fiend throws its victim through the bathhouse sign on top of the building and returns to its circling position in the sky. Everyone in position knows how dangerous it is to leave the formation. As much as everyone wants to save those who aren't within the parameters of the Town Hall, they know to listen to Inspector Pluck's directions for their survival.

Everyone in formation can hear the screams from the other side of town go quieter. It's very tense seeing the three harpies circle around in the sky like buzzards do, knowing they're preparing to finish what they started. Coming out of the alley between the hardware store and bathhouse is Mayor McLusky. Everybody can see the horrifying sight of him holding his intestines dangling out of his stomach.

McLusky limps toward the guards in formation and continues to bleed profusely while holding his guts. Everyone gasps to see how strong, yet gruesome, the mayor is and panics when he collapses to the ground. Unable to take any more of it, Sheriff Wood breaks out of formation to go after the mayor.

Pluck sees what the sheriff is doing and runs after him and tackles him to the ground. Pluck and Wood feel the wind blowing and smell the stench above them when they both hit the asphalt road. They both realize they're inching close to having contact with the harpy's talons as it flies past the two authorities and back in the air. It happens so fast that the guards aren't quick enough to draw their weapons and fire at the attacking harpy. Immediately, Pluck pulls the sheriff by the collar and drags him back to the formation where it's safe.

"Dammit, Sheriff," Pluck says, releasing the lawman as he returns to formation. "It's too late for the mayor. They're just using him as bait. Don't you see they're trying to lure us out so they can strike?"

"But the mayor," Wood replies. "He's—"

"Sheriff!" cries a pained voice in the distance.

Everyone looks up to see the mayor calling toward them.

"W-when you see my ex-wife and children, tell...tell them I'm sorry. I wish I had been a better father and..."

He can't finish his sentence. Everyone can feel the mayor's life slipping away in front of them. The sheriff attempts to run to him, but Pluck and the others hold on to him from leaving the formation again. Wood's sworn duty as the town's lawman is to serve and protect the mayor, but seeing him suffer like this makes him feel like a failure. It affects him so much that he starts to cry over his employer, who's beyond saving.

Pluck lets go when the lawman weeps and stares at the harpies soaring above them, wondering what they'll do next. Again, they're circling in the air like vultures, watching and waiting for anyone to leave the formation. Pluck is getting thirsty, and the air outside is getting too humid for him to bear. While the formation keeps them from being attacked, the men guarding outside can't do this forever.

"Everyone," Pluck raises his voice, "reload your guns and get ready for them to strike again."

"I'm sorry, Inspector," replies one of the guards, "but we're not carrying any additional ammo. "

"Shit!" Pluck swears. "I know we've got one more full crate of ammunition."

"We do, sir," answers another guard. "Two, in fact, but they're in the hardware store."

Pluck looks at the building behind where the mayor's body lies. Considering how fast the harpies are and how close he was to getting hit by one of them, it's too dangerous to make a run for it. He looks around to see what he can do. The postal inspector then sees the jailhouse next to the hardware store and remembers someone is still jailed. While it's still quiet, Pluck decides to call out to the prisoner.

"Jeremy Payton!" Pluck shouts. "Payton. Are you still alive?"

"What are you doing, Inspector?" Sheriff Wood says. "That boy is no good to us."

A voice responds from the jailhouse, saying, "Yes, Inspector. I'm still here."

"Do you want to redeem yourself, Jeremy?" Pluck shouts back. "How about you help us out?"

"What can I do, Inspector?" Payton peeks through the barred window of his jail cell.

"You know, there's the hardware store next door. I want you to run over there and bring two crates of ammunition to us."

"I wish I could, but I'm still locked in here."

"Sheriff," Pluck lowers his volume and turns to the lawman, "I need you to pass me your keys."

"Like hell, I will," the sheriff replies. "That's my prisoner, and he ain't leaving his cell under any circumstances."

"Sheriff, you know we're sitting ducks if we dare cross the road. There's nobody else alive on the other side that can help us."

"Even if he somehow sneaks by and makes it to the hardware store, how do you suppose he's gonna bring two crates over here? He's going to slow down while crossing the main road with all that weight he has to carry."

Pluck then looks at everyone in the same formation as him. "Okay, how many of you have some ammunition left with you? Raise your rifles high."

The ones that do, did as they were told. There are only eleven out of nineteen who have their rifles and pistols up. Pluck swears over the lack of loaded arms they have left.

"Okay, so here's the plan," Pluck continues. "I need someone good at throwing to pass it on to Payton. Once he exits the jailhouse and opens the hardware door for us, we all head inside the store as fast as we can. Once we make it across, we bring the crates of ammo back to Town Hall, load up our guns, and get ready to give those bastards everything we got. So, who's good at throwing things far?"

"I can throw pretty far, Inspector," says a familiar voice, someone who works in the hotel.

"What is your name, and how far can you throw?"

"The name's David Graft. The farthest I've ever thrown is several meters in a game of horseshoes. I can throw those keys to the jailhouse's window."

"He's right, Inspector," says a person next to Pluck. "David Graft is the best horseshoes player in this here town. He's managed to hit the stake more times than not, better than anyone here."

"Sheriff," Pluck says, "hand Mr. Graft your keys. This is our one chance to get our ammunition."

The sheriff takes a moment to reconsider, then passes a set of keys to Graft.

Pluck turns around and shouts at Payton, "Jeremy! Stick your hand out of the window and keep it still. We'll pass you the keys to unlock your cell and help us out."

The prisoner sticks his hand between the window bars and opens his palms. The barred windows are so high that it's difficult for Payton to see. Pluck gives some room for Graft to make a good throw. The hotel worker focuses on Payton's hands across the street and takes a couple of deep breaths. With all his might, he throws the set of keys, going high and fast.

When Payton feels something land on his palms, he grasps the keys and brings them into his cell. Just as much as Graft is a good thrower, Payton is a good catcher. Pluck gives Graft a pat on the back as Graft sighs with relief. Young Payton quickly leaves jail and steps onto the porch. Fortunately for him, the harpies can't see him with a roof over the porch.

"That's good, Jeremy!" Pluck shouts. "Now, quickly. Go to the hardware store."

"What is he waiting for?" comments one of the guards watching him.

Payton remains still, thinking about how intimidating it is for him to exit the jailhouse. He hasn't seen the harpies during his time imprisoned, but there's no denying they exist based on how ear-piercing their screeches were when the last one invaded the town. The prisoner panics as he sees the shadows of the harpies moving on the ground. The young man sees everyone in front of the Town Hall yelling at him and pointing for him to go to the hardware store. He's so uncertain about what to do that he drops the keys and runs in another direction.

"Payton!" Sheriff Wood shouts with rage. "You little bastard!"

Payton sprints as fast as he can, thinking he can outrun the harpies since he has so much stamina. However, the escapee can only make it a few meters away from town before he feels a sharp claw pierce his lower back. Everyone can hear him scream, but no one can save the foolish kid. Then, two more harpies join the massacre, ripping and tearing the poor boy barbarously. Though the men watch in horror at how awful Payton's fate is, Pluck glimpses the single harpy in the air.

This is an opportune time to cross the road and retrieve the ammunition crates. He shouts to get the men's attention, and half of them run to the hardware store with him. They run as fast as they can, just as the third harpy in the air swoops down to strike one of them. Pluck is the first to the door and opens it for everyone with him to make it inside. The last man has his ankle caught by the harpy.

While being pulled up in the air, the caught victim holds on to one of the porch's pillars for dear life. Pluck immediately draws his pistol and takes an open shot at the harpy's talon holding its victim's ankle. Once a bullet hits the fiend's foot, the harpy lets go of the victim and flies away. The postal inspector saves the man's life and assists him inside the store. Through the window, Pluck sees the three harpies finish mutilating Payton and fly back into the air. While his remains are far away, he can see Payton is torn apart so much that his insides are exposed. "Have you fellas found the ammunition?" Pluck shouts, turning to everyone inside the store.

Four men bring the two crates full of bullets to the postal inspector. Pluck immediately opens both crates and sees all of them are made for the carbines the guards are carrying. Despite not having a single bullet made for his pistol, this is the most that Pluck can do to keep the guards armed.

"So these are the last crates we got, huh?" Pluck comments. "All right. Start reloading. Get ready to head back outside, and give the remaining ammo to the rest outside. If you see a harpy coming, give them hell."

The men take bullets from the crates and fill their rifles with them, still having more than enough bullets left for everyone else waiting outside. Pluck then closes the crates and gets next to the front door. Knowing they'll strike whenever he goes out alone, how will the harpies fare against a whole squad coming out running together with loaded guns? He then assists the man he just saved, limping from his ankle injury, and signals everyone to head out and start crossing.

Pluck makes it out first with the injured man, followed by the two men carrying the crates and everyone else with rifles aiming their guns at the soaring foes. There are so many at once that the harpies have difficulty spotting a weak link in the moving squad from that high above.

Pluck and everyone else successfully returns to the circular formation unharmed, with ammunition. Pluck opens a crate, and everyone immediately takes the bullets they need and reloads their rifles. A guard, whose gun is full of ammo, notices something different happening above them and shouts, "Incoming!"

Everyone hears the spotter's call and aims their guns at the harpy descending. Before they can fire, the harpy makes an ear-piercing screech, catching all the men off guard, holding their ears from the unbearable shriek—all except for the deaf Gallus Kennedy, the only one firing at the enemy. The harpy sees who's firing at it. While the deaf businessman still misses hitting the fiend's weak spots, the man-bird of prey lands directly on Kennedy's skull, splattering his brain all over the ground upon impact.

Standing on top of his body, the harpy screeches more, the painful noise so unbearable that the men who are too close to it are becoming deaf. No one has cotton in their ears to protect themselves from the ear-piercing experience. The pain in Pluck's ear is so severe that he is becoming dizzy and deaf as a result. Then, the harpy's screeches are interrupted when another of its kind swoops down and stops the shrieking one. As Pluck's dizziness subsides, he looks around to see all the men fighting with him, lying in agony. As he endures his tinnitus, he sees the harpies standing in the middle of the crowd.

Standing before Pluck is the black-feathered harpy with a masculine body and short hair; this one has stopped attacking. Instead, it's having a conversation with another harpy strikingly different from the ones he's seen. This one has a voluptuous body with human female breasts and crimson feathers. Pluck can't get a good look at this harpy variation as he's standing behind it. As he regains his hearing, Pluck can make out that they're speaking a language that sounds European, but he cannot recall what it is specifically.

Their conversation doesn't last as they both fly to the sky. Pluck rolls onto his back and sees that there are now five harpies in this flock. The harpies stop circling around the sky and leave Point Postal. When Pluck gets up, he sees the enemies fleeing back to the direction where they came from.

"What the hell happened, Jed?" Secoli says very loudly, having no volume control from his deafening experience. "Why did they suddenly leave?"

Pluck turns to his partner in a panic and says, "Louie! Did you see that?

There's a fifth harpy!"

"What?" Secoli shouts, still having trouble hearing anything clearly. "I said...," Pluck raises his voice, "there's a *fifth* harpy on the loose."

"A fourth harpy?" Secoli yells in complete shock. "Where the hell did that other one come from? Are you sure you weren't double-visioned or something?"

"No, I'm positive I saw another one. This one looks different. It appeared and..." Pluck puts his attention back to the harpy's direction, who disappeared in the plateaus. "...they all left."

"They appeared, and what?"

Pluck sighs before raising his voice. "Never mind. I'll tell you what I saw when your hearing gets better." Pluck looks at the guards getting up. "Let's first help these people and see how many are still with us."

CHEYENNE ISN'T AS COVERED in feathers as when the postal inspectors left. So many have drifted away from the wind, buried under the sand, or decomposed. It remains empty because rescuers from Colorado and Nebraska have been attacked by the harpies. One of them watches over the town, standing on a rooftop. Its long hair from its head and its exposed breasts show that it's a female harpy.

Her feathers are black and sharp, and her talons are deadlier than those of any bird of prey. Though she's all alone, she has successfully slaughtered any visitor that has arrived in Cheyenne. She has made this ghost town her territory, waiting to strike the next person who comes. It's been days since she struck and ate her last prey, and she's starving. A pile of bones is gathered on the same roof she's been living on, and there isn't any meat left on any of them. Then, the female harpy sees someone walking across the dead plains. Her eagle-like eyes can see how far the person is. The female-hybrid is in the ready position before she starts flapping her wings and taking her prey down with a single strike. She feels the wind's current perfectly blowing into her prey's direction. She knows she'll be at top speed when she starts flying toward her next meal.

The harpy then flaps her wings and lets the current direct her to the poor visitor. She extends her wings as far as she can to get the most out of being pushed by the wind. It only takes several flaps of her wings for her to make it past the buildings and out of town. She lifts her talons directly at her prey, approaching at top speed. The female harpy is so excited to feel her prey's flesh in her talons and can hardly wait to eat it.

Just when the harpy can make contact with its prey, an arrow hits the beast in the chest. The pain is so excruciating that she collapses on the ground. She screeches in her ear-piercing voice to defend herself as she struggles to get back up. Before she could turn around to see who had shot her, another arrow pierced the harpy's throat. Immediately, she becomes quiet and falls back to the ground.

As the harpy lies and bleeds to death, she sees what's supposed to be her prey carrying a crossbow. It's difficult for the harpy to identify her killer, no thanks to the person's hood that's covering and shading their face. The visitor reloads the crossbow and fires another arrow through the skull to end the harpy's misery.

The person in the cloak kneels and places their fingers on the harpy's neck to check her pulse. There is no more sign of life from the fiend. The mysterious hunter pulls the arrows out of the dead harpy and puts them back in their quiver. The hunter then gets back up on their feet and pulls out a map and pen.

"Well then," the cloaked individual says in a female voice and a thick European accent.

The map is of the state of Wyoming. Already, there are markings all over the map that mark the locations where the hunter has been and the number of harpies she has killed. The map shows that the hunt began in Sundance, then down to Newcastle, Lusk, and Torrington. Numbers are written between and on charted towns to mark how many she has killed. The cloaked individual writes the number seven above Cheyenne and X'ed out Wyoming's capital to mark that there's no life found in this ghost town.

The hunter finishes writing and heads west of Wyoming, free from harpies. She folds her map and puts her pen back in her pocket. The cloaked individual then reloads her crossbow and heads west on foot. The hunter follows the railroad that leads to the next town. She walks slowly and remains silent as she journeys, waiting to rid more towns of harpies. Though she hasn't found any sign of life besides the harpies she's killed and other animals the harpies spared, the hunter hopes to find human beings who might still be alive.

CHAPTER 11

The town, now called Point Postal, is having one of its worst days. Never before has the town had this many casualties in a raid like no other. Point Postal would have been the next ghost town if the postal inspectors hadn't come back and saved the town again. They long for their homes after staying in the town longer than expected. The Federal agents and the survivors spend the remainder of the day gathering dead bodies and treating the injured victims they could find.

There are a great number of dead citizens, so many that there isn't enough room in the cemetery to bury them. It's a health risk to have so many corpses all over town, so the postal inspectors make a tough decision to gather all the dead bodies and have them cremated at a funeral. The cemetery is so far from town that there is no way anyone alive could leave town to dig so many graves. Those who died earlier and were kept in the trading post will no longer have a proper burial as originally planned and will join the cremation with the rest. Everyone gathers around the pile of bodies; the fire is started, and the funeral begins.

The bodies are piled from bottom to top in no particular order. The postal inspectors, however, honor the town's former chairman by placing Mayor McLusky's body at the top. No one argued over this decision, considering that he was the town's leader and did his best to protect the town. As the cremation fire reaches the corpses on top, the mourners cry. It becomes harder for Jed and Louie not to cry over the dead women and children whose bodies joined the burning.

It's bad enough that the postal inspectors didn't keep the conductor and the train engineer alive. However, Jed Pluck breaks into tears when he recognizes Wesley Simmons lying on top of his dead wife and daughter. As he's a family man, it's hard for him to bear to see the whole family cremated together. He feels guilty over how unfair it is for the entire family to die while Pluck still has his. From that moment, the postal inspector fully understands the gravity of the situation. Everyone watching the cremation feels self-defeated or laments over the fallen.

While he mourns, Pluck hears Miss Herbert crying the loudest. Pluck knows why she's grieving since he found Anabelle and the other six of her friends before anyone else did. Pearl Herbert's heart breaks as she watches Anabelle Larson's body burn in the same fire as the other six former saloon girls. She and Jolene are the only two alive who experienced the hardship of being Mr. Benjamin's saloon girls, and they whimper over the deaths of those they considered family. Considering Pearl's knowledge of Pluck's affair, Pluck keeps his distance from her by not saying or doing anything that might upset her, especially when she's sorrowful.

It becomes too much for the former saloon girl that Jolene has to guide her away from the cremation. When the two girls leave the funeral, a fight breaks out. Pluck and Secoli head to where the commotion is taking place and witness the widow, Mrs. Humphrey, and the mother of Jeremy Payton at each other's throats and hitting each other. The postal inspectors struggled to pull the two ladies apart.

"I'm glad your son is dead, you ol' bitch!" Martha Humphrey shouts as she's pulled away. "The harpies did me a favor by taking that lil' bastard of yours out."

"What did you say, you old hag?" Mrs. Payton replies viciously, being carried away. "You talk that way about my son again, and I'll have you cremated with the rest of the fallen victims. That way, you'll never get buried with your dead husband."

Hearing them spew insults at each other, Pluck understands what the fighting is about. Martha's husband's death enrages her, and she is taking it out on the mother of his killer. Their actions are upsetting the mourners, who find their behavior to be inappropriate. The postal inspectors are having such a hard time keeping them away from each other that they pull the two ladies out of the funeral. Mrs. Humphrey is sent to the Town Hall, while Mrs. Payton is sent to the hardware store across the street. Neither of them dares to leave the places they've been sent to for the remainder of the funeral.

By sundown, the bodies become huge piles of ashes and piles of burnt bones. Since the town's only preacher, Father Jenkins, is cremated with the others, no one is taking charge of the funeral, nor has anyone said any word of comfort to calm the bereaved attendees. Deputy Hall sweeps all the ashes and bones and puts everything in empty crates. The plan is to have everyone that died from the harpies' attacks to share a grave together. Sheriff Wood gathers everyone and checks all the names to properly get all the fallen citizens' names. Those who don't respond are declared dead, and their names are engraved on tombstones. The two postal inspectors and the deputy stand next to the sheriff as he calls out everybody's names individually. Each time someone is called and that person replies Pluck gives a sigh of relief deep down inside. However, the silence becomes uncomfortable when no one responds when a name is called.

By the time Sheriff Wood makes it to the last name on the list, Pluck looks over his shoulders and sees the list.

Once the sheriff finishes the list, Pluck asks, "So how many on the list are still alive, Sheriff?"

Sheriff Wood counts the names before replying, "That's a total of thirty-five we have left, Inspector. We only have ten men alive. That's not counting you, Inspector Secoli, my deputy, and yours truly. The rest on the list are women and children. Make that twelve since we have two more men in the Town Hall and are in critical condition."

"And how many children did we have, and how many did we lose?" Secoli asked.

The sheriff swallows his saliva before answering. "We lost eight children, and we only have five still alive."

"Damn it," Pluck swears in defeat. "Those poor kids. We've lost more than half the town's population. We don't have enough men to pull guard."

Pluck notices something wrong on the list. "Wait. Do you have Fiona Fletcher on the list?"

"That's right," Pearl Herbert says, standing in formation with everyone else. "I don't recall Sheriff Wood mentioning Dr. Fletcher's name."

Wood calls out for the ornithologist again, and everyone in the line falls silent and looks around for her to respond. The silence makes Inspector Pluck anxious; in fact, he's already breaking a sweat over her absence.

"Has anyone seen Dr. Fletcher's body being brought to the pile before the cremation began?" Pluck shouts for everyone to hear.

He stays silent to hear a response from someone, but no one answers. This prompted Pluck to run down the main road, calling out her name. All the townsfolk immediately break out of formation and search for the ornithologist. Even those too tired and hurt comb the area for Dr. Fletcher as commanded. Pluck and his partner join the search by starting with the trading post since no one has yet looked in the old store. Although all the corpses were cremated, the stench of the Trading Post left behind remains unbearable.

When they can't find anything, the postal inspectors leave the building and see a lady running to the Federal agents and says, "We found her!"

"Where?" Pluck asks so eagerly.

"She's in one of the houses. She's alive but unconscious. Let me take you there." The two postal inspectors follow her back to the neighborhood area where citizens are circling a house. The woman leading the Federal agents stops to catch her breath, and they run past her to see what is grabbing everyone's attention. Pluck and Secoli push their way through the crowd to get a closer look at the damaged house. Right before them, they see that one side of the house's walls has collapsed, with Dr. Fletcher lying incapacitated on top of a pile of wood.

The unconscious ornithologist is being held by her assistant, Pearl, who hugs her tightly. Pluck shoves her out of the way to evaluate the ornithologist's condition. Though she's breathing, her clothes are ripped, and her forehead is bleeding.

"How did none of you notice Dr. Fletcher was here this whole time?" Pluck shouts.

Everyone remains silent, not knowing what to say.

"Never mind. Help me carry her back to the Town Hall. She needs medical assistance."

Four men run to the ornithologist and pick her up. Pluck walks back to the Town Hall, and everyone follows him. Arriving in the sanctuary, she's placed on an empty long chair next to two critically injured individuals who've been lying there since last night.

One of the ladies with medical experience bandages the ornithologist's head and checks for further injuries. Both postal inspectors stand behind the woman, who's working fast in treating the unconscious Fiona.

"How is she?" Pluck asks, struggling to stay calm. "Will she be all right?"

"It's hard to say for sure," the woman replies while checking Fletcher's pulse. "I'm not good at telling if there are any internal injuries, and I need her to be conscious to tell me where she's hurting. The only thing I can find is the cut on her forehead. If that's the extent of her injuries, then Dr. Fletcher is the toughest woman I've ever seen."

"Thank you," Secoli says. "Please look after her well and get us when she wakes."

Secoli then turns to his partner and whispers into his ear, "Pluck, what are we going to do? We only have half the population left to defend this town."

"Then we have no choice." Pluck claps his hands to get everybody's attention in the sanctuary. "Everybody, gather around. We're going to have a mandatory meeting."

The folks inside the sanctuary immediately walk out to inform everyone else outside. Pluck gets up on the judge's bench and sits on the chair where Mayor McLusky used to sit. While he waits for everybody to sit, Secoli gets on the small stage and approaches Pluck.

"I take it you appointed yourself the one in charge of town now," Secoli comments, approaching the judge's bench. "Do you have a plan?"

"Don't worry," Pluck replies. "I have one."

"Would you mind sharing your plan with me first before you tell everyone?" Pluck doesn't respond, focusing more on everyone coming into the sanctuary and taking a seat. Sheriff Wood and Deputy Hall stand in front of the small stage, facing everyone as though Pluck is the new mayor of Point Postal. Secoli remains on the stage, standing next to the judge's bench like how he used to in McLucky's Town Hall meetings.

The sheriff counts everyone in the sanctuary and tells Pluck, "Thirty-five. That's everybody, Inspector."

With half the town's population gone, there are more empty seats than usual. There are more women than men in the room. Pluck's heart races as he struggles to start the Town Hall meeting, unsure how everyone will react. Everybody remains silent, eager to hear the next plan to counteract the harpies.

"Everyone," Pluck says after a moment, "thank you all for coming. Lemons—I mean, Point Postal—has seen better days. Knowing there are more harpies out there and the harm they caused has put us in a dire situation.

"The number of men we have left is smaller than we can imagine, and fewer are in acceptable condition. I never thought I'd ever be doing this, but to save this town and all of you..." Pluck pauses for a brief moment. "...I ask for women of all ages to start guarding the town with the men," Everyone in the room gasps over this decision as Pluck finishes by saying, "Even the elderly have to participate. The only ones who are exempt are the children and the three who are in critical condition."

Secoli turns to his partner and asks, "Are you nuts, Jed?"

"No way am I ever letting our women fight those godforsaken harpies!" yells a man sitting in the center of the room.

"The women are incapable of fighting!" yells another man sitting farther back. "We'll all be dead if they fight alongside us men. We might as well have no replacements rather than fight alongside them."

"What did you say?" screams a woman sitting across from the man. "Do you really think we're incapable of helping you fight those demons who killed my husband?"

"I'll have you know everything a man is capable of," another woman shouts from the opposite side of the room, "a woman is capable of, too!"

"I agree with Inspector Pluck's decision to fight alongside the men!" yells another woman next to the front door.

The arguing between both sexes intensifies. The men and women in the sanctuary can't agree to fight together and end up fighting one another.

"Even if the women are willing to fight," Secoli shouts, "we don't have enough time to train these women to properly use the rifles!"

"By a show of hands," Pluck asks, "how many of you women have ever used a gun?"

Not a single hand is raised, nor a voice is heard. The silence again brings a sense of hopelessness to everyone in the room.

"Well, that says it all," a different male voice says, breaking the silence. "We're all doomed."

"Shut your mouth, Angus McKinsey," says a woman sitting behind him. "Your criticism and pessimism aren't helping anyone. We wouldn't be in this mess if we learned how to use those rifles."

"It's not like we wanted to remain at the Town Hall while you men risked your lives," a woman says, turning in McKinsey's direction. "There weren't enough weapons to go around, and now that we have more than enough unoccupied rifles, I'd say we're done hiding and ready to fight those damn harpies together."

"If Dr. Fletcher was able to fight the harpies," Pearl Herbert adds, "why can't we all do the same? With our help, we can save the town."

"All right. Order." Pluck finishes banging the gavel. "So it's settled. The women will be joining the fight with us men. So that's twenty-seven men and women total on guard duty. Like before, we will all take shifts, and there will be fourteen total per shift."

"Actually, Jed," Secoli interrupts, "one of the shifts will be thirteen people assigned since fourteen plus thirteen is twenty-seven."

"Right," Pluck continues, "but don't forget that the lawmen and us two will be doing the same shifts as before. And like before, all of us will be doing six hours per shift. I'll get Sheriff Wood to assign everybody to either one of these shifts. One more thing: all the women in this room, meet Sheriff Wood and me outside so we can give you your rifles and teach you all how to use a rifle."

"Jed," Secoli interrupts once more, "we only have a crate and a half of ammunition left. We have to conserve as many bullets as possible. You know how many bullets we used to take the first harpy down as well as I do. It's hard to fathom how much more ammunition we need to take out the rest of those damn things."

Inspector Pluck grows silent over his partner's objection before replying, "You're right, Louie, but I don't want to leave the ladies clueless about using a rifle while they can help us save this town."

AFTER COMPLETING THE women's training, the guards resume their shifts as before, now including women. The nine women assigned to the first shift are intimidated by being out in the dark after spending a week protected indoors. It doesn't help that they're assigned to be on the same shift with five other men who disapprove of Inspector Pluck's decision. Inspector Pluck and Sheriff Wood, both in charge of this shift, are aware of the tension between the sexes on duty and hope they can cooperate for everyone's sake.

All the guards have to watch and protect only within the parameters of the Town Hall and go no further than from the bank all the way to the stable. Even though the harpies haven't attacked any horses, Pluck still wants the stable to be guarded. Everyone remains in a particular spot to defend the northwest section of town. The only ones who can move away from their post are those in charge of the shift and those who need to use the outhouse. Pearl Herbert is assigned to guard behind the Town Hall with her only friend left, Jolene.

Despite feeling intimidated by being out in the cold night and carrying live-round rifles for the first time, they're relieved they no longer have to get a guard to escort them to the outhouse. As long as they return to their post and inform someone that they're doing their business, they can go to the outhouse whenever needed. Pearl suspects that her friend Jolene is taking full advantage of this privilege. It's been only two hours since they began their shift, and Jolene has gone to the outhouse for the third time. Jolene didn't go to the outhouse many times when they were kept in the Town Hall, so why is she doing this so many times already?

Pearl sees Inspector Pluck walking by, checking on everyone on shift and tries to be more attentive to those on his shift. It's just unusual for him to do so for both sexes. So far, he's made a great impression of giving the women a chance to help the town more, except for Pearl Herbert.

Jed still avoids Pearl for knowing of his adultery with Fiona Fletcher. If he had not given Sheriff Wood the authority to assign people to shifts, he would have transferred Pearl from her current shift to the one that Inspector Secoli and Deputy Hall are on. However, that might bring suspicion if he did. After encountering Pearl for the third time in this shift, Pluck stops avoiding her and says, "Hey. Have you seen your friend? What's her name?"

"Her name is Jolene," Pearl replies aloofly. "She's still in the outhouse."

"Still there?" Pluck responds. "Never mind. Carry on."

When Pearl calls out "Inspector," Pluck stops and listens to her. "Just to let you know…your affair with Dr. Fletcher is kept secret with me. But if you harm Dr. Fletcher in any way, so help me, God, I'll let your secret out."

"Why do you resent me so much?" Pluck turns to her. "Didn't you used to get involved with other men in your old job at the saloon?"

"I'm trying to move on from that. However, I'm not the one with a wife and kids."

Pluck briefly becomes numb over that remark. This blackmail against him becomes more consequential after hearing that from her. With no choice, Pluck removes himself from the uncomfortable situation he's in. Jolene returns after Pluck leaves, looking confused as she sees where Inspector Pluck had gone to Pearl's upset expression.

"Did something happen between you two?" Jolene asks. "What did he say?"

"Nothing," Pearl replies with her arms crossed.

"Sounds to me like a whole lot of something. Did Inspector Pluck do anything to you?"

"No." Pearl looks away from her.

"I don't understand what's happening between you and him, Pearl. He's taking care of Dr. Fletcher and doing the best he can to save this town."

"It's nothing for you to worry about." Pearl faces her friend. "Also, why on earth do you need to go to the outhouse so much? Are you having some problems?"

"I think it's something I ate." Jolene puts her rifle on the ground and leans against the wall, trying to relax after having bladder problems.

"Hey, Jolene." Pearl chokes up, trying not to break into tears. "When I was leaving this town, I had a gut feeling I wasn't going to see you and the rest of them again. But never did I imagine Heather, Charlotte, Carol, Sherry, Nancy, and..." She takes a deep breath as tears pour down her cheeks. "... and Anabelle would go out like that."

Pearl covers her face and falls to her knees, still hurting since the funeral. It's not a good look while trying to prove that a woman can pull security, but she can't brush off the pain. There's a tremendous amount of guilt within as she realizes her farewell this morning was their final goodbye. She feels worse over ignoring Anabelle while she is distraught over the postal inspector's and the ornithologist's affair. To have that as Pearl's last memory of her alive gives her a heavy heart.

Jolene kneels to her level and hugs her grieving friend tightly. Pearl's head and hands lie on Jolene's chest for dear life. Her friend, too, is going through the same pain over the loss of who she considers family. She makes shushing noises to help her not cry so loud while also shedding tears with her. The last thing she wants is for someone to find her feeling vulnerable when being asked to protect the town.

"It's okay, Pearl," Jolene whispers gently. "We'll find a way to stop those..." The sudden pause makes Pearl want to hear the rest of what Jolene is saying, and she feels the hug she's receiving from her get tighter. Something feels off as Pearl still has Jolene's head against her chest. She feels other textures from the necklace worn around Jolene's neck and chest that don't feel like anything she's wearing. For some reason, it feels sharp and wet, touching her forehead. When Pearl hears her only friend making unusual gurgling noises, she tries to release herself from Jolene's tight grasp.

Once Pearl releases the hug, the little light from her torch reveals a couple of sharp black objects protruding from her chest. There's more blood pouring down from her neck down to her dress than the bleeding from the mysterious, short, sharp points. When she looks up to see what's happening to her friend, she sees blood coming out of her mouth and a glimpse of enormous wings behind her. It becomes more apparent that her worst nightmare is right before her, already piercing the only family she has left.

Pearl is so shocked that she can't move over the horrifying sight of her dying friend being lifted into the air. Though she is one of the townswomen who wants to save the town, she can't stomach how appalling it is to be so close to the enemy and what they're capable of. Jolene cannot make a sound nor show any sign of movement as she's being lifted higher. When she finally sees her friend's killer's face, Pearl immediately leaps for her gun and rolls on her back to fire at the harpy.

She fires three rounds, but there's no telling if she hit the harpy flying into the nightly sky with Jolene. Everybody on the shift runs to where they heard the gunfire. Nobody, not even Inspector Pluck, asks what happened as they see Pearl covered in blood, still pointing her rifle in the air and trembling. The evidence on Pearl is already enough to tell everybody that the harpies are invading again and have taken another one of its citizens. Pluck immediately picks up the rifle Jolene dropped and points the gun in the same direction where Pearl is aiming.

"Wake everyone in the sanctuary," Pluck commands, aiming his gun at the sky. "Ring the bell, protect your ears with cotton, and get into your assigned positions!"

Inspector Pluck pulls Pearl to the sanctuary as everyone executes his order with urgency. While Pearl's sudden loss still shocks her, Pluck guides her to safety. Everybody in town is inside the sanctuary, many underneath the long chairs in the room. Others are on the rafters holding nets, preparing to drop them on the harpies that dare enter the building.

They all anticipate any one of them to barge into the sanctuary and set a trap upon them. Everyone closely watches the clerestory windows to the front entrance—the only way the harpies could possibly break in. Underneath one of the long chairs, Pluck and Pearl both see Dr. Fletcher is still unconscious while this is all happening. The ornithologist is placed underneath the long chair next to them, protected by two bandage-covered men wielding rifles and willing to keep fighting.

Everyone startles when they hear two harpies crashing through the clerestory windows. The first harpy crashes through the left window while the other enters the opposite side. Before anyone opens fire at the fiends, the townsfolk on the rafters drop the nets at the enemies below. Once the net lands on top of them, the men and women closest to it hold down the nets to prevent the harpies from flying away. Others who are farther away open fire on the harpies with their rifles.

The two harpies react strongly over the bullets hitting them, making it difficult for those holding the nets down. Neither of the beasts can take a deep breath to make their ear-piercing shrieks to free themselves from the pain they're enduring. As they struggle to free themselves and scream from getting shot at, the guards holding the nets try to avoid touching their black, razor-harp feathers as they move so hastily. One of the guards holding the net notices feathers is cutting and ripping the nets. Upon multiple shots firing at them, the two harpies refuse to be held down, not realizing they're breaking free from their nets.

Once the shooters reload their rifles, one of the harpies notices the nets are torn.

The shooters can't fully reload their weapons in time as the fiends slice the nets and break free. Everyone can see both of their bodies covered with bullet wounds and blood. Despite hitting the harpies in all directions, especially in the head, they're alive and still have the strength to stand on their feet. One of the harpies uses its ear-piercing shriek before any shooters can aim after reloading.

As before, the cotton protecting the guards' ears doesn't do much to keep them from hearing that painful noise. As Inspector Pluck covers his ears for dear life again, he catches a glimpse of the other harpy that's not shrieking and is suffering from the ear-piercing noise as everybody else.

Does this mean other harpies that feel the same painful noise from their kind whenever one of them shrieks so loudly? The other harpy can't take the high-pitch screech any longer and knocks its ally down to the floor for it to stop. Both of them briefly argue with each other in their foreign language before fleeing the sanctuary and getting shot at again. Everyone in the sanctuary recovers from the deafening experience and aims their rifles at both broken windows they went through.

Then, a gun is fired, and everyone turns toward where the shot was heard.

It isn't a harpy, but old Mrs. Payton standing above Mrs. Humphrey, who's bleeding on the floor. She's trembling at the sight of a bullet shot at the back of the widow's skull. Sheriff Wood and Inspector Secoli both run to check on Mrs. Humphrey. Where she's been hit, no one could have survived.

"Mrs. Payton," Sheriff Wood says. "Do you realize what you've done? You murdered Mrs. Humphrey. Why? Why did you do it?"

"I told her," she explains shakingly, "that she'll wind up dead if she ever speaks ill about my son again. She should have kept her comments to herself in a time like this."

"You know the difference between what you and your son did? Jeremy made a mistake that led to Mr. Humphrey's death. You committed first-degree murder over your hatred toward Mrs. Humphrey. At least your son could have come out innocent."

Suddenly everyone's attention is back on the harpies just as they hear something crash above their heads. As pieces of wood fall from the ceiling, they see the guards responsible for dropping the nets attacked by another harpy crashing through the wooden ceiling. A woman gets pushed off the ceiling joist and crashes onto a long chair below. Everyone runs to the fallen guard to see how badly she's hurt. The attacking beast strikes another male guard above and abducts him. Pluck recalls that the guards throwing nets from high up are unarmed.

Seeing how vulnerable and fearful the four unarmed guards still on the ceiling joist are, Pluck runs straight to the ladder that leads to the ceiling. The lawmen and Inspector Secoli see what Pluck is doing and follow him to the rafters. While the three climb the ladder, Pluck gets on the rafter and slowly approaches the three women and the only man on the ceiling joist. Though the joists are wide and aren't far apart from each other, it's the worst time for him to start having acrophobia. The sanctuary's ceiling is twenty-plus feet from the ground, and Pluck struggles to keep himself from looking below and instead focuses on the guards who need saving.

Just as he lends a hand to one of the ladies closest to him, the same harpy crashes through the wooden rafters and strikes another victim behind the woman Jed is trying to rescue. Pluck grabs the lady before she becomes the next person to fall, but he can't save the other one who's being abducted. Secoli arrives on time to help the damsel back up to the ceiling joist. Knowing how much weight is already on the wooden platform they're on, both of the lawmen wait to assist the ladies to the ladder. Deputy Hall leads the rescued woman to the ladder, and Sheriff Wood waits for the Inspectors to help the other two guards farther away from them.

Thankfully the last two who need rescuing waste no time, and both approach the sheriff and the two postal inspectors. They both watch their steps and make it past the postal inspectors to the sheriff. Wood leads the second woman, and then Secoli leads the only man to the ladder. As Pluck is about to follow everyone back to the floor, he hears the victims screaming outside and turns around to look through the opened ceiling created by the harpies. When Secoli becomes the last person on the ladder, he sees his partner not following him but still moving across the rafter.

Pluck ignores his partner calling for him, but he wants to save the victim, who's screaming from outside the broken ceiling. He peeks to see where the victim is and sees the kidnappee and the kidnapper on the bank's roof. As she screams, the moonlight shows a harpy gutting her with its talons and throwing her insides away. It's too gruesome for Pluck, so he puts his head back inside to keep himself from vomiting.

As soon as the woman stops screaming, Jed can tell it's too late to save her. What is the reason or motivation for these harpies to be so violent toward these people instead of just eating them? Do they want vengeance over the harpy that was killed, or are they killing for amusement? Never before has Pluck seen a species toss aside their prey's carcass as they do. Pluck realizes this is the only time he's seen any of the harpies at their most vulnerable.

The postal inspector pops his head out again and aims directly at the harpy that's stuffing its face in the woman's guts. He pulls the trigger, but then a black wing briskly gets in the way of the bullet and Pluck's target. Another harpy flies right in front of Pluck, ascending higher. Seeing that this harpy has no bullet wounds or injuries on its body shows that this fiend is not the same one who broke into the sanctuary earlier. Pluck shoots all the bullets in his handgun at the beast's chest and abdomen.

Though the harpy he fired at flies away, the other harpy, on the bank's roof, sticks its head out of its prey's body and glares at Pluck. Seeing what he did to the member of its flock, the harpy flies right at the postal inspector. Pluck pulls the trigger on the harpy, but the cylinder is empty. He becomes immobilized by how fast it's flying toward him and how nightmarish it is to see its talons reaching him. Just when it seems like all hope is lost, a figure in a dress leaps from the Town Hall's roof and knees the harpy in the face.

The person who saved Inspector Pluck falls with the harpy into the alley. It happened so fast, but Pluck catches a glimpse and sees the person who saved him is wearing a purple dress and had ginger hair. Could it be Dr. Fletcher who just saved his life? Immediately questions pop into his mind, such as how did the ornithologist get up the rooftop, how long has it been since she regained consciousness, and whether she's in danger from attacking the harpy. Despite being saved, Pluck becomes concerned for the lady who knocked the harpy down.

Pluck can't see or hear what's happening in the dark alley from where he stands, no thanks to the direction of the moonlight. He turns around and looks down to where he last left the ornithologist. To his surprise, Dr. Fletcher is no longer with the two fully bandaged men. Did Fiona really risk her own life to save him? If so, she's out there in danger with the harpies.

Pluck immediately heads back to the ladder. Secoli is right before him, slowly and carefully trying to get back to safety by watching his steps on the ceiling joist.

"Have you lost your mind, Jed?" Secoli asks rhetorically. "You could have gotten yourself killed. Hurry. Let's get back down before—"

"Louie," Pluck interrupts. "It's Fiona! She's out there fighting those damn things by herself!"

"What?" Secoli looks below and sees that she's not where she's supposed to be. "Impossible! What the hell has she gotten herself into this time?"

"We've got no time to lose," Pluck replies impatiently.

He moves around Secoli and carefully gets to the ladder. Both postal inspectors return to the ground and immediately head out the front door. Seeing what they're doing, everyone follows Pluck and Secoli out of the Town Hall and into the alley where the ornithologist was last seen. Torches are lit for everyone to see through the alley, but the harpy and the ornithologist are no longer there.

"What the hell are we looking for, Inspector?" Sheriff Wood asks, not knowing what's going on.

"Dr. Fletcher," Secoli replies. "She's not here. Are you sure you saw her, Jed?"

"I'm posi—" Pluck turns around and sees something approaching him, causing him to exclaim, "Take cover!"

Everyone hears Pluck through the cotton in their ears and does as he commands.

They all drop to the ground just before a harpy swoops down. Pluck sees the harpy fly past them and through the alley.

"Everyone," Pluck continues shouting, "get back inside! Move! Move! Move!"

Everyone immediately gets back up and heads back to the sanctuary. The postal inspectors and lawmen are right behind everybody, rushing back inside. As the officials head to the porch, another harpy is spotted and flies toward them fast. None are quick enough to draw their weapons and defend themselves. The talons are stretching toward Pluck's direction, preparing a strike. Just as the postal inspectors and the lawmen are about to get hit by the incoming harpy, an arrow pierces the harpy's leg. This sudden turn of events sends the fiend to fly above the four men and have a rough landing on the main road. The harpy quickly gets back up and looks at its injured leg. It recognizes the silver steel arrow pierced through its limb and then flees. Another arrow is shot at the harpy but misses it by an inch as the harpy flies away and

calls for the others.

The sound the harpy is making isn't ear-piercing or anything that's been heard before. It sounds more eagle-like with a scared tone to it. Whatever it meant, it made the other three harpies fly out of their hiding spots and follow the one with an arrow in its calf. While everybody steps outside to see the harpies flying away, Pluck looks in the opposite direction, trying to see where the arrows came from. Coming from the desert is someone wearing a greenish cloak and carrying a crossbow.

"Hey!" Pluck shouts at the mysterious person. Everyone pays attention to who Pluck is talking to. "Seize that person and bring him to me."

The men and women run after the cloaked individual and pull him to Pluck.

Pluck, and everyone with him remains still as the mysterious person is being brought to him. Despite having his arm bent to his back, the visitor cooperates with the guards without showing any signs of resistance. He doesn't even resist his crossbow being taken away by a guardswoman. Once the guards bring the unexpected visitor to Pluck, the postal inspector removes the hood from the individual's head. A torch is brought closer for everybody to look at the visitor.

The cloaked individual is a Caucasian woman with a scar on the right side of her face, reaching from her brow to the bottom of her lip. Besides her noticeable scar, the rest of her face is well structured, with a sharp, precise jawline accentuated by a long, slim, pointy nose. Her Mediterranean skin tone and long silky brown hair make her stand out as someone not from the Wild West, maybe not from this country. While Pluck is surprised to see someone he didn't expect underneath the hood, the lady gives him a charming smile.

"A pleasure to meet you," she says in a thick European accent. "It's been a long since I last saw human life."

"That accent," Secoli comments. "Who are you, and where did you come from?"

"My name's Zephyra Klouví. I came all the way from Greece. And you are?"

"Greece?" says a guardsman holding her from behind. "Never heard of it. What is your business being here?"

Pluck becomes so irritated by the citizen getting involved that he interrupts by saying, "This is no place to interrogate her. Sheriff. Bring Miss Klouví to your jailhouse. She's got some explaining to do."

"Jailhouse?" She recognizes the first word and immediately stops smiling. "Jail? Why am I going to jail? Am I not allowed to save your lives?"

"Sorry, ma'am," Pluck replies. "But we're in danger right now, and we can't trust anyone. It's the best place to get to know each other without interruptions." Pluck catches a glimpse of Mrs. Payton peeking from a group of women on the porch. "Oh, and Sheriff, arrest Mrs. Payton over there for murdering Mrs. Humphrey."

"With pleasure, Inspector," Sheriff Wood replies. "I almost forgot about you."

Sheriff Wood gets on the Town Hall's porch and pulls Mrs. Payton toward the jailhouse. Already, the old lady regrets her decision to commit murder, as tears come out of her eyes. Zephyra Klouví is confused over why this woman is being taken into custody with her. Everything is happening so fast that she's unable to comprehend what's going on. Even so, she remains cooperative and calm. As she's being led to the jailhouse with Mrs. Payton, she reminds herself that these people aren't her enemies despite how unwelcoming they are to her.

CHAPTER 12

Zephyra Klouví never imagined her first contact with another human would take place in a prison, believing that saving lives from the harpies would make her an ally. She sits on a wooden chair, handcuffed behind her back. Inspector Pluck and Sheriff Wood sit opposite her at the desk, while Inspector Secoli sits next to her with his birdcage on his lap. Klouví is fascinated by the budgerigar, wondering how such an exotic bird had ended up there. She keeps her thoughts to herself, finding it to be the most intriguing thing she has seen in days. Mrs. Payton sits in the same jail cell where her son was held when he was still alive, listening to the interrogation in the worst emotional state she has ever been.

On top of the sheriff's desk are all the equipment and items Klouví brought with her. Her standard crossbow with a quiver filled with steel arrows is located on the far left of the desk from where Klouví is sitting. The arrows' shafts are mixed with bronze and silver from the tip to the very end of the arrow. There is no sight of wood on these arrows, but there are black, razor-sharp feathers on the end of each of them, making it feel similar to the ones the harpies have. There is a lot of interest from all the men in the room as they examine her weapon of choice and are captivated by its uniqueness.

Besides a canteen and a bag full of standard traveling supplies, the officials dug out the Wyoming map with many markings. All of them are intrigued to know what each of the markings on the northern and eastern sections of the state is indicating. They can only see numbers and crossed-out sections in many of the towns marked on the map. Klouví analyzes what these men do with her possessions and reads their expressions over each item they inspect.

The authorities in the room haven't yet asked Klouví anything as they have their full attention on the unique items she brought with her. The interrogee is doing her best to make a good impression on the authorities, given that she is a foreigner traveling in parts of America where foreigners aren't as welcome. She tries to continue to make a good first impression with the ones in charge despite not getting a fair chance upon their first greeting. She can only project a fake smile while they are intimidated and confused over her sudden appearance. As they talk among themselves over each item on the table, Klouví eagerly awaits to explain herself and try to convince them she's a friendly, trustworthy person who can be useful to them.

The entrance door creaks open from behind, startling her. She looks over her shoulder to see Deputy Hall walking around her, placing cups and a jar full of water on the edge of the desk's surface. Secoli then pours some water into one of the cups and helps the handcuffed Klouví drink. Even though she wishes for a warmer welcome, at least her captors help her hydrate. As Secoli helps the prisoner drink another cup of water, the deputy is surprised to see this many items on his supervisor's desk. The other three men in the room wait patiently for Hall to say something, as he's too distracted with the unusual confiscated objects.

"Hall," the sheriff says, "how many people do we have left?"

The deputy replies, "We have thirty left, sir. That includes Mrs. Payton, sitting in her cell. All the casualties in this attack were women."

"Damn it," the sheriff swears. "Who did we lose, exactly?"

Hall takes out his list and reads it aloud. "As already mentioned, we lost Mrs. Humphrey, no thanks to her." His remark is heard from Mrs. Payton's jail cell, making her feel worse. "Then we lost Jolene Henderson, Lorette Desmond, and Clarice Brown. Darla O'Hare, who fell from the ceiling, didn't make it."

"That's awful," the distressed sheriff says, putting his head down and placing his hands on his forehead. "I wish we'd done more to protect them."

"Give 'em credit, Sheriff. The women fought just as bravely as the men," Pluck interrupts. "The women still standing are proof that they could hold them off with us men. Were there any signs of Dr. Fletcher anywhere, Deputy Hall?"

"No, Inspector," the deputy replies. "Everyone is doing all they can to find her, but it's dangerous to be lookin' for her this late. Are you certain she jumped from the Town Hall's roof and knocked down one of the harpies, Inspector? That doesn't seem possible unless she had some sort of death wish."

"I saw it with my own two eyes, Deputy. The fact that she's no longer lying in the sanctuary proves that she's awake and…somewhere out there."

"But where could she be?" the sheriff asks. "I hope she wasn't taken away or…." He stops himself from mentioning the unwanted possibility.

"I saw four harpies fleeing town when Miss Klouví here scared one of them off," Secoli says. "I didn't see them carry any victims. Dead or alive, Dr. Fletcher has to be somewhere in this town."

"But if she's alive," the sheriff interjects, "then why hasn't she shown herself?"

"That's why we're still looking for her." Pluck sighs. "She's our only chance to fight these harpies."

"Not true," Secoli says. "Miss Klouví here saved all our lives by shooting one of them with her crossbow before they fled. The fact that those monsters flew away after one shot from her tells me they probably know our suspect and are afraid of her."

Wood and Pluck both turn to Klouví, still smiling and trying to make a good impression on the two in charge.

"So, Miss Klouví," Sheriff Wood says after clearing his throat, "sorry for appearing hostile toward you. The state of Wyoming has been attacked by these monsters lately, so we're on high alert and suspicious over everything right now."

"That is understood," Klouví breaks her silence, "but after saving your lives, I do not understand why I am in trouble."

"Sorry," Pluck adds. "It's just that you come across as suspicious by carrying a weapon like this…intimidating."

"I have to have my crossbow with me," she replies. "It is the only weapon that is powerful enough to help me hunt the harpies."

"So you are aware of harpies roaming around and terrorizing Wyoming," the sheriff comments. "Out of all the animals you hunt, why harpies?"

"Before answering that question," Secoli interrupts with an aggressive tone. "First, tell us what you're doing all the way out here, where you got all these things, and how you managed to smuggle these dangerous possessions into the United States."

Intimidated by the sudden response from the aggressive postal inspector, Klouví brushes it off and says, "Harpies originated from my home country, and Greece would never have survived against the harpies if it weren't for us harpy hunters. Greece has no more harpies, but the last harpy flock migrated to your country and attacked the West. That is why I'm here, to kill the last harpies."

"Well, that answers the first of my questions," Secoli says, still in the same aggressive tone. "Tell us how you managed to smuggle unauthorized items into this country."

"Louie…" Pluck intervenes over his partner being hostile to the interrogee. "I…" Klouví drops her smile, struggling to admit the truth. "I brought all my things by sailing all the way here."

"Obviously," Secoli interrupted, "But there's no way that you've come all the way here without any paper or proof of entry from the Federal Immigration stations. So how did you manage to come to America without having to go through immigration?"

"I traveled here on a private boat…so I could bring my items to stop the harpy population from growing in your country."

"So you arrived here illegally and smuggled weapons into this country," Secoli continues. "Just how did you manage to bypass the Coast Guard? Where and when did you arrive here in America?"

"Coast Guard? I don't even know what that is. I arrived in America twenty-six days ago…in Florida, I believe. Since I came here, I have been exterminating harpies."

"I don't understand," Pluck says. "Are you telling me you've been hunting these harpies from Florida all the way to Wyoming?"

Klouví nods while humming. "Other harpy hunters who came with me have been killing harpies and destroying their nests. Each time we kill them, they call their flocks and fly away, knowing who we are. We chased them north, and now they fly west."

"Fly farther west?" Secoli says, pulling his head back with a frown. "So you're telling me you brought these harpies to Wyoming?"

Klouví gets more nervous over such an accusation. "Me? Bring you harpies? I didn't bring you harpies. They fly farther west to escape from us, harpy hunters."

"And the other harpy hunters. Did they come here illegally like you? How many came with you?"

"There are only three of us. One of them died from a surprise harpy attack in—what was that name of the state?—Kentucky. The other went a separate way to hunt harpies in the North."

"So you mean there are harpies in the north?" Pluck asks calmly, yet eager to know.

"I told him that harpies went west, but he didn't believe me, so he went north to Ohio. But I tell him, no, the harpies moved west. They create fake scents to put us off track. Since we could not agree, we separated."

"And who is your friend?" Secoli says. "I want their names!"

"Hold on, Louie," Pluck interrupts, trying to calm his aggressive partner. "My apologies, Miss Klouví. We've had a long week fighting these harpies and lost so many people since they came to Wyoming."

"It is all right, sir." Klouví starts to relax a little since at least one interrogator isn't antagonistic toward her. "Since coming to Wyoming, the harpies have taken more lives than usual. In every town I have been in since coming to this state, no one has been found alive until now. I am surprised to see that Lemonstown is the only town to survive. How did you survive?"

"Oh, Lemonstown changed its name, ma'am," Sheriff Wood corrects her. "It's now called Point Postal."

"Point Postal? Since when?"

"That doesn't matter right now," Pluck replies. "And to answer your question, yes, we faced a single harpy all by ourselves. It took so many lives to take one down, but then more showed up today."

"And the rest of its flock wants revenge for what you have done to one of their own. So, how did you manage to kill that one? You couldn't have beaten them with bullets, could you?"

"Yes, we did. And it took so many bullets to take just one down."

"Oh, no. Bullets won't do. Using a gun on a harpy is like throwing stones at them. Harpies have very thick, strong skin. The only way to easily kill one is with a steel arrow with harpy feathers attached, making it go faster than bullets."

"Hot damn," the sheriff swears, taking the arrow from the desk. "We'd never guessed that this would be the solution to our harpy problem."

"Tell us, Miss Klouví," Pluck says, "how do you find these harpies? We tried tracking one harpy that took one of the citizens from this town, but they moved so fast. There has to be some way you can track one, right?"

"Of course there is. See that item in the middle?" Klouví looks directly at an object that looks like a small horn on the sheriff's desk. "That is a scentascope. We place it in our noses to smell harpies. Since they smell bad, they leave an easily traceable smell in the air."

Inspector Pluck picks up the metal device. He examines it and sees a black metal cover with two holes. He flips the device around to see where the end of the horn-like device has a nasal section where two metal pieces with holes stick upward. The postal inspector places both his nostrils on the metal pieces and inhales. Pluck immediately pulls his head away from the device after sniffing it.

He realizes he smells wood coming from the jailhouse's wall. Pluck is so impressed with the device that he puts his nostrils back up to it and inhales while he moves the scentascope around. Pluck smells the sheriff, his deputy, and the rest of the room. He can't believe what he's smelling straight from the device. It's as if he's close to the objects and smells them all so clearly. Everyone but Klouví is intrigued by Pluck's reaction as he uses the scentascope.

"This device," Pluck says in awe. "It's very neat. Where did you get it?"

"You cannot find it anywhere," Klouví replies. "Harpy hunters made that device, and I was assigned the scentascope."

"May I?" Secoli reaches his hand out to try the device.

Pluck hands over the scentascope, and Secoli uses the device. He, too, strongly reacts to it and pulls his head away from the device. Realizing where the device is pointing to when he inhales, Pluck frowns at his partner. Secoli then remembers Jed's insecurity over his hygiene when he notices his partner's peeved expression.

"Oh," Secoli says, pretending to not smell his partner with the device. "This device...is incredible." He uses it on Chap and can smell the bird exactly like he does whenever he kisses his budgerigar. "If the Postal Inspection Service had something like this, we'd be saving a lot of time opening suspicious mail being sent in post offices."

Secoli then passes the device to the two lawmen who want to try it themselves. Each has the same surprised and impressed response once they sniff the scentascope properly. While they check out the device, Pluck glances at the map of Wyoming that's laid flat on the sheriff's desk. He's interested in the towns he and his partner have already visited being marked down.

"These markings on this map," Pluck said, "I can't really make out what is written down all over this map, so can you please explain to me what you're indicating on each of these locations?"

"This is where I keep track of all the harpies I've hunted down. The numbers written down are the number of harpies I personally killed. The cities that are crossed out are the ones I visited too late to save. No one was in any of those towns."

Pluck grabs the map from the desk while the sheriff looks over his shoulder and says, "Interesting. So you started all the way up northeast at Sundance. I assume you killed two, as written down next to the town that's X'ed out. Am I correct?"

"Yes. That is correct."

"And then you traveled down to Newcastle and killed a single harpy. Then you went to Lusk, marked zero, which means you found no harpies."

"Yes. Yes. That is correct."

"Then you went to Torrington and killed a single harpy. And you've been to the capital, Cheyenne, and indicated that you killed one, but what does the letter *F* mean?"

"The *F* stands for 'female harpy.' Those are the crucial ones."

"Why are the female harpies so important to kill compared to the others?" Secoli says.

"The females are the ones responsible for repopulating the harpies from going—what is that word?—extinct. That is the harpy hunter's objective. Once all the females are eliminated, there is no chance for harpies to procreate."

"Interesting," Pluck comments. "Seems to me you've encountered more males than female harpies. It's almost like they're very hard to find."

"Hold on," Secoli says. "How long ago were you in Cheyenne? Because we were there about a week ago and saw no harpy in sight."

"I arrived in Cheyenne yesterday, in the morning."

"You mean to tell us that we dodged a bullet from encountering a harpy when we were in the state capital?" Pluck asks.

"Harpies are not stable enough to stay in one location," Klouví replies, "except when they lay a nest or if they're hurt so badly that they need to take time to heal."

"And how can you tell the difference between a male harpy and a female harpy?"

"Simple. Since their bodies are the only things that resemble humans, you can tell based on their chest shape. Males have pecks, and females have breasts. While the male harpies are the hunters and scavengers over other human beings, females are the same but are seducers by nature."

"What do you mean by seducer?" the sheriff asks. "Don't the females and male harpies just mate with each other to repopulate the harpy race? You know, like every animal and person do?"

"Not exactly. Male harpies don't have genitalia. They're only called male harpies because they aren't females. On the other hand, female harpies are called sirens for a reason. They can only mate with male human beings."

"What?" Pluck reacts with doubtfulness. "That's disgusting."

"It is true. Females only target human males to reproduce more harpies since they aren't so different from each other. Harpies cannot reproduce with each other."

"If that's true," the sheriff says. "Then why are the harpies slaughtering everybody they encountered instead of reproducing?"

"Female harpies are always the leader of every flock. When a flock has no female present, the male harpies go crazy. They end up killing every human being in sight until they encounter a female harpy that gets them under control. Male harpies are always submissive to the more powerful and orderly females."

"I never heard of a female ever taking charge," Pluck says. "Especially in the animal world. How can there be a group of males that allows a female to take charge?"

"I think a better question," Secoli interrupts, "is why harpies only attack humans? Do they ever attack animals?"

"Harpies rarely attack any other species," Klouví answers. "They fly a lot and require a lot of fatty nutrition to make up the energy required to fly. No other species besides humans have as much required fat as a harpy needs to consume. Harpies are disinterested in harming any species they see beneath humans unless provoked."

"I'm intrigued to know about the harpies' way of reproducing," Secoli says, being less hostile. "You mentioned harpy ladies are seducers, and they can't...do it with male harpies. But somehow, they can mate with male humans. Say if a female harpy is present, how does it seduce a male human?"

"A female harpy doesn't just mate with any human male. They seek one with the required genes to help them reproduce healthy harpy chicks. If she chooses a male human with bad genes, they become abnormal harpies. That is why you'll see female harpies murder or spare a human male based on his value to her. But once she finds that male human, she kidnaps and then uses him to mate in order to lay eggs."

"What are the genes a female harpy requires from a male human that will make a successful reproduction?" Secoli asks.

"A harpy won't just settle for just a healthy-looking man. Females look for males with no genetic disease and guarantee their offspring will always be female."

"Seems to me like that's gonna be hard for the female to find," Pluck comments sarcastically. He looks up at his partner, who's giving him an awkward stare. "What are you looking at me for, Louie? Do I have something on my face?"

"Jed...," Secoli says cautiously. "Has anyone on your side of the family died of cancer or any sort of genetic disease?"

"What? No," Pluck replies. "All my relatives died from either natural causes, war, or accidents. Anyway, what does that have to do with the harpies?"

"Jed...," Secoli starts talking nervously. "I think you fit the description a female harpy is searching for."

"Seriously? You're not believing every word that's coming out of this woman's mouth, are you?"

"Even so. The last thing we want is for any of those damn things to take you away and know the truth about you."

"Are you listening to yourself?" Pluck raises his voice. "You're acting like a damn fool by falling for the lies she's spewing. You disappoint me, Louie."

"I interrogated hundreds of suspects in my career," Secoli says. "I can easily tell the difference between a liar and someone who's telling the truth. I examined Miss Klouví's behaviors, mannerisms, and body language. She has not once contradicted herself or stumbled over her words."

"You kidding me? This is some sick and twisted bestiality we're talking about."

"If what Miss Klouví says is true," the sheriff intervenes, "shouldn't you be worried, Inspector Pluck? I mean, you did say you saw a fifth harpy and claimed that it was female-looking."

"That's right," Deputy Hall says. "Didn't you say the fifth harpy had red feathers instead of black like the others?"

"Where did you see the female harpy?" Klouví asks earnestly. "Do you know where she is?"

"Jed here claims to be the only one who saw it when they attacked us in broad daylight yesterday," Hall replies. "He said its feathers are red. Nobody else saw it after we nearly had our ears blown off from their screams."

"You..." Klouví turns to Pluck with a serious look. "Tell me what happened. When did you last see *that* harpy?"

"I only saw it once in the morning when we were all ambushed by the harpies," Pluck answers. "One of them with black feathers screamed so loudly we all almost became deaf. The fifth one showed up, stopped all the harpies from fighting us, and fled town. But tonight's harpy attack...I didn't see that one. Why is she so important?"

"Are you positive that the harpy that you saw was not only female but also had crimson-colored feathers?"

"I saw what I saw. Do the red feathers mean it was female?"

"No. Other females have black feathers, but that red one is no ordinary harpy, sir. That is Margohot. She's the queen of the harpies."

"So harpies have individual names, huh?" the sheriff comments. "So what makes this...Margohot so important?"

"The Harpy Hunting Federation in Greece has been chasing Margohot for generations. She is hundreds of years old, and she is said to be the eldest of the harpies. Right now, she is the last female alive. If we kill her, it's the end of the harpy line."

"Okay, seems simple enough," Hall says. "All we have to do is use these arrows and this...scenta-majig, and we can take care of the harpy situation. Easy as that."

"It is not as simple. Margohot is the most clever, vicious, and cunning of all the harpies. Living so long has made her more experienced and wiser than her children. I am a fifth-generation harpy hunter, and my family and I have never successfully taken her down. If you all struggled to eliminate just one harpy, you won't have a chance against her." Klouví looks at Pluck in the eyes. "You better hope you don't encounter her again and find out who you are. Otherwise, the harpies will repopulate."

"Oh, there we go again with this bullshit," Pluck swears. "There's no way that harpies come all the way to nowhere just to fulfill some—"

"Can it, Jed!" Hall interjects. "Miss Klouví. How does a female know if a man has good genes? That's what I'd like to know."

"You do not know that harpies can disguise themselves as humans?" Klouví asks in astonishment.

Immediately, everyone in the jailhouse becomes immobilized with that remark.

"You're kidding me, right?" Pluck rhetorically says. "Now you're telling me harpies can disguise themselves as humans? That's not possible."

"It's true. You've been to other towns, right?"

"What of those towns?" Secoli sits back down and picks up his birdcage from the floor.

"All those harpy feathers are all over those towns because when they turn into human form, all their feathers fall off their bodies."

"Really?" Secoli reacts. "Are you saying harpies have been disguising themselves as humans, and that's why those feathers are all over those ghost towns?"

"Ghost towns? I don't believe I saw any ghosts."

"It—it's slang for empty towns. There's not really any ghosts."

"Then yes. Sometimes, it's not just a disguise. They turn into humans to spread their feathers to mark their territory and signal that they killed everybody in sight."

"Jesus," the sheriff says. "It all makes sense now. Miss Klouví. What is the possibility of a harpy living among us right now?"

"You too, Sheriff?" Pluck gets up from his seat angrily. "First, the female harpies are taking charge, then only reproducing with other human males, and now they can disguise themselves as humans? What's next? Harpies can talk to the dead? What about you, Deputy? Do you believe her story like these two fools?"

"You and everybody else in this town know nothing about these monsters, Inspector," Hall says. "But I've learned so much about them by letting her talk. What she said does sound suspicious, but I didn't believe these harpies existed until I saw them with my own eyes. Now, what Miss Klouví is saying does match everything together."

"So you too, huh?"

"Jed," Secoli says, "we're not your enemies, and I doubt she is either. But I can tell from Miss Klouví that she's sharing her experience with us because she wants to help. I have no reasonable doubt that she's been genuine during this interrogation."

"You're all nuts!" Pluck shouts. "Those harpies are proof enough that monsters do exist, but this is all too far-fetched, even for me. I expected all of you to be better thinkers than blindly believing what's been said by a stranger like her."

Too peeved that this interrogation is going in the suspect's favor, Pluck heads to the door, leaving Secoli to shout, "Jed! Where do you think you're going?"

Pluck doesn't give his partner an answer and needs to avoid everyone to cool off his temper. He knows he's losing control, and his emotions aren't making him look professional, especially in front of the suspect. It's best for him to remove himself from everyone's presence to think things over.

As he opens the jailhouse's front door, Pluck is surprised to see the townsfolk standing before the porch. The light from everybody's torches certainly takes his mind off the argument. Standing in front of the crowd is Fiona Fletcher, wearing a torn and filthy dress.

"Sorry if we're disrupting you, Inspector," says Pearl Herbert, "but we didn't know when was the appropriate time to tell you."

"Fiona?" Pluck yells joyfully, running off the porch and heading directly to the ornithologist.

Once he jumps off the jailhouse's porch, he surprises Fiona with a hug. Despite everybody watching, Fiona lays her head on the postal inspector's shoulder, feeling appreciated for how much she's been needed by him. It's no longer a secret that they have personal feelings for each other as everyone on the main road watches. However, the only person who knows how personal those feelings are is Pearl, looking away in disgust over this public display of affection.

Inspector Secoli and the two lawmen step out of the jailhouse to see Pluck and Fletcher hugging. Secoli jumps off the porch with his birdcage and approaches the two. The physical affection they're giving each other doesn't even enter this postal inspector's mind. Rather, he's more surprised that she survived the harpy she fought against. As soon as Pluck lets go, Secoli hugs her platonically and forgets their past animosity.

"Good God, Dr. Fletcher," Secoli says, letting go of the hug. "How the hell did you survive? Better yet, where did they find you?"

"We found her in the alley between two of the houses," replies one of the guardswomen. "Seems like she fought hard and survived yet again."

"Are you hurt, Fiona?" Pluck asks. "Did those monsters injure you?"

The ornithologist laughs as he checks for her injuries and says, "No. I'm fine. I can handle myself. It's you I'm worried about. You almost got yourself killed back there, Inspector. I don't know how many more times I must save your life."

"I'm glad you're okay," Pluck replies. "I thought we lost you for good. Look. There's someone I think you need to see. She claims to be an expert on harpies, but I need your observation to know if she's telling the truth or is straight-up lying."

While everyone pays attention to Inspector Pluck's conversation with Dr. Fletcher, the handcuffed suspect looks between the lawmen, blocking her view from the doorway to see what's happening. Klouví is left shocked to recognize the ornithologist's skin tone, titan-red hair, sharp green eyes, and freckles all over her face. Despite panicking to see who's in front of everyone, she attempts to run after her, attempting to strike Dr. Fletcher even with her wrists cuffed. The sheriff and his deputy see the suspect trying to jump off the porch but grab her before she even gets close to Dr. Fletcher.

Everyone stares at Klouví being pulled back into the jailhouse.

"What the hell do you think you're doing?" the sheriff says, trudging to pull her back inside. "I didn't give you the authority to leave my jailhouse."

"It is her!" Klouví exclaims, using her feet against the doorway to push herself from entering through the front door. "It is her! That is Margohot! She is the female harpy!"

"Hold on, Sheriff!" Secoli shouted. "What are you saying?"

Sheriff Wood and Deputy Hall stop attempting to put Klouví back in the jailhouse but still hold on to her arms as she watches everyone from the porch. "I am telling you the truth, sirs." Klouví raises her voice in fright. "She

isn't who you think she is. She is really Margohot."

"What?" Pluck replies. "You're more nuts than I realized, Klouví. How much more are you willing to go with this insanity?"

Dr. Fletcher becomes so anxious that she starts walking backward, away from the two postal inspectors. Secoli catches a glimpse of the ornithologist slowly walking away. He becomes suspicious that Fletcher is hiding something from everyone and is attempting to escape. He then turns around and grabs her by the wrist.

"Going somewhere, Doctor?" Secoli asks antagonistically.

"Let go of me, Louie!" the ornithologist screams, attempting to free herself. "Louie!" Pluck shouts. "Are you out of your mind? Let her go this instant." Secoli does as his partner commands, and Fiona starts running. However,

the townswomen block her way, growing suspicious over her sudden change in behavior. The ornithologist looks around and sees all the townsfolk circling her. A man gets behind the ornithologist and holds her in the full nelson.

"Have all of you gone mad?" Pluck shouts. "Let her go!"

"Ignore that command!" Secoli exclaims, joining the angry mob. "We need to see who she claims to be." He then turns to the harpy hunter still held by the lawmen on the porch. "Klouví. How can we tell if she's really a harpy?"

"Take off her shoes!" the harpy hunter shouts for everyone to hear. "A harpy can disguise themselves as human, but they cannot change the shape of their talons."

Before Secoli can make the order, the townsfolk immediately surround Dr. Fletcher, attempting to remove her boots while she's being held against her will. The only ones who object and fail to calm the angry mob are Inspector Pluck and Pearl Herbert, who believe in Fiona's innocence. Dr. Fletcher screams for mercy, scared over the town's hostility against her. Once both boots slip out of her feet, the crowd immediately steps away in fear, except for the man still holding her in a full nelson, who can't see from his angle.

Everyone but he can see the awful truth about Fletcher. Underneath her skirt, they all see talons that look just like the ones the harpies have but smaller. The postal inspectors and Fletcher's admirer are appalled by what they see. Pluck especially becomes numb and nauseous over not seeing proper human feet from her and feels like a complete fool for not suspecting it sooner. Everyone is too afraid to approach the ornithologist, except for the man who's holding Fletcher steady.

Knowing her disguise has been revealed, Dr. Fletcher changes her behavior from being fearful for her life to finding the scenario she's in amusing. She has her head down while still held against her will, making whimpering noises that slowly change to laughter. Hearing her laughter sound more sinister as she gets louder shows the real side of her that no one has seen before. Pluck hears Fletcher's laughing accent change from Southern American to Mediterranean. She puts her head up and gives Klouví a minacious grin in the distance.

"Everyone," Klouví exclaims, "get away from her! Get out of the way before—"

Before she can finish her warning, Fletcher abruptly grows spikes from under her shoulders to her wrists. Somehow both of her pinky fingers extend a couple feet. So many ten-inch-long spikes grow in an instant. The man with her in the full-nelson position has his arms, torso, and neck pierced by the spikes. It becomes too late to save him as each of those spikes instantly blossoms with razor-sharp feathers.

As the spikes grow into feathers, parts of the man's body are pierced into gore. The crowd standing behind the transforming harpy has the poor man's blood and organs land on them. The transforming harpy notices how disgusted the townsfolk behind her are with her victims' body parts landing on top of them. The female harpy twirls around like a ballerina as she distributes all her victims' blood and organs to everyone around her.

Her feathers are left spotless when she stops twirling. Her red feathers move like cloth dangling on her arms. Pluck and Secoli do not wipe blood and organs off them like everyone else, as they are petrified at Dr. Fletcher's true identity. The dress she wore is torn apart, exposing her fully nude. Her crotch to her knees is covered in the same crimson-colored feathers as her wings. Her talons doubled their size and are as sharp as those of the other harpies they've seen.

When Pluck looks at the female harpy's face, she still has red hair but has grown so many wrinkles, resembling an elderly woman. Her evil grin gives both postal inspectors shivers down their spines, making them petrified. Now that her feathers have grown out, a new stench arises, arguably worse than that of the black harpies.

This new, powerful, foul smell makes everyone move away while they clean the remains of the guard off them.

"Well, Jed?" the female harpy says in her real Mediterranean accent. "Do I still look beautiful with this new look?"

She laughs at her own joke, knowing how disgusted and horrified Pluck and everyone around her are. In her harpy form, the harpy queen can see in her bird's-eye vision and see her surroundings better. She even sees several townsfolk pulling out their rifles, aiming straight at her from her front and sides. Before they can pull the trigger, Fletcher raises her wings as high as possible and promptly flaps them down, sending her immediately up in the air. With a single flap of her wings, she flies into the dark sky and disappears.

"Everyone!" Pluck snaps out of shock. "Quick! To the sanctuary!"

No one wastes any time running back to the sanctuary. Even Sheriff Wood escorts Klouví inside the Town Hall, being very protective of his captive. On the other hand, Deputy Hall heads back inside the jailhouse and picks up Klouví's crossbow and quiver filled with steel arrows. As he heads out the door, Mrs. Payton is scared out of her mind, remaining in her jail cell, and grabs the deputy's arm through the jail bars.

"Please!" the prisoner cries. "Don't leave me. Get me out of here!"

Hall pulls his arm away from her and hurries out the door, leaving the jailbird hopeless and defenseless in her cell. Even when she cries louder for help when he leaves the jailhouse, the deputy does not look back. He is the last person to enter the sanctuary, seeing everyone underneath the long chairs. Everyone has rifles, ready to shoot when they see the female harpy. Despite having enough room to hide underneath any of those long chairs, the deputy decides to stand to use the crossbow.

Hall kneels on an aisle, takes out an arrow from the quiver, and attempts to load the crossbow. Hall has trouble pulling the latch to properly set the arrow on the flight groove. The issue is the razor feathers on the arrows, which make it difficult to properly load the crossbow, as it pokes his fingers. The crossbows push the arrow out of the flight groove, as Hall cannot get a proper grip. After the fourth attempt, a feather cuts his index finger.

"Sir," Klouví whispers loudly from underneath a long chair, "you need my gloves to avoid hurting yourself from the arrow's feathers. It's the only way to load that crossbow with those harpy arrows."

He then drops the crossbows and quiver on the aisle and slides them underneath with the harpy hunter and the sheriff.

"Release me from my cuffs," Klouví says. "I can kill Margohot and save us all."

Hall tries to take the keys out from the belt on his waist, but he doesn't feel his keychain where he normally puts it. He then remembers where he placed them.

"Sheriff," the deputy says, crawling to him, "I left my keys in your desk drawer. I don't suppose you have your keys with you."

The sheriff swears as he feels nothing on his waist or his pockets. "I left those spare keys in that damn desk of mine. How the hell are we going to release these cuffs?"

"No way is anyone going back to the jailhouse to get those keys."

"Dr. Fletcher...," Sheriff Wood mutters. "How the hell did none of us suspect she was a goddamn harpy this whole time?"

"Jesus. It all makes sense now. Why those harpies left when Point Postal was about to become the next ghost town. All her absences. Her skipping meals. And why has she been against us killing any harpies. It was Dr. Fletcher."

The sheriff shushes his deputy to stop him from talking. Deputy Hall notices everyone is holding their rifles steady, anticipating something foreboding from the female harpy. Despite how quiet the sanctuary has gotten, all of them are frantic over the female harpy's ploy to strike. While aiming their rifles at the opened ceiling and windows, none make sudden movements to startle or create a false alarm. All of them grow uncomfortable over the fact that at any moment, Margohot might pick her next victim, and none of them wants to be the next person to die.

HOURS HAVE PASSED SINCE everyone got underneath the long chairs. Dr. Fletcher hasn't been seen since she flew away, but the survivors are expecting her to attack at any time. After posing as a human and living among them for so long, she learned the postal inspectors' self-defense strategies. Despite how tired everyone is, everyone pushes themselves to stay awake and keep their rifles pointed all over the room. Never has the town had this much tension and so few people alive.

Inspector Pluck lies underneath the same long chair with his partner and his birdcage. Even though his sleep deprivation is taking a toll on him, watching Dr. Fletcher become a harpy continues to haunt him. Though her transformation as a harpy was truly disturbing, that's not the only thing troubling him. Not only is everything Klouví said in the interrogation true, but he also realizes having an affair with Fiona is the worst thing he's ever done. Is he now responsible for saving the harpy race by committing an affair with her? He's been able to resist other more beautiful-looking women than her, so why did he allow her to seduce him so easily? Having that joyful memory turn into regret is making him feel nauseous.

After hours of fighting off this ill feeling, Pluck feels like he's going to regurgitate. He gets up from under the long chair and runs straight out the front door. Everyone is still awake and grows concerned over Pluck exiting the sanctuary without saying anything. While everyone is left confused over what's going on, Secoli gets up and goes after his partner.

When Secoli exits the Town Hall, dawn is breaking. He sees Pluck puking in the alley next to the bank on one of the empty barrels. Secoli steps off the porch and checks to see how his partner is doing and avoids seeing what Pluck spewed out. Never has he seen his partner look so pale and sickly.

"Jed," Secoli says, "you need to get some sleep. You've been up since six in the evening yesterday, and I've never seen you look this bad."

Both of the postal inspectors turn to see Klouví exiting Town Hall, still handcuffed but somehow escaping from the lawmen who are supposed to be watching over her.

"Did you do it?" Klouví asks bluntly before the sheriff and his deputy grab hold of her. "Did you fornicate with Margohot?"

"What?" Secoli responds strongly to her remark. "What makes you think that? Pluck is a loyal husband and a good father. There's no way that he'd ever commit adultery. Isn't that right, Jed?" He turns to his partner. "Jed?"

Pluck is too petrified to say anything. His guilt is making him sick and preventing him from speaking up. His long silence makes Secoli even more concerned and suspicious.

"That's enough out of you!" The sheriff pulls the harpy hunter back inside. "You should know better than to ask an inappropriate question like that."

The postal inspectors are alone outside.

"Nothing is going on between you and Dr. Fletcher, is there?" Secoli asks.

Pluck struggles to maintain eye contact before saying, "I'm sorry, Louie."

"How?" Secoli raises his voice. "How could you?... When did this happen?

And how long has this affair been going on?"

"We had…." Growing paler, Pluck swallows his saliva. "We had sex when I went to the bathhouse. She was being so direct with me that I…I couldn't help myself. Even when I tried scaring her away, she was too irresistible for me to handle."

Secoli doesn't say another word to him when Pluck breaks down. This is the first time he's seen his partner look so defeated after all the bravery he has shown. He can see how truly sorry his partner is. Secoli grabs Pluck just as he starts losing his balance over feeling so ill and emotional and takes him back to the sanctuary. Everyone, even Klouví being held by the two lawmen, watches as Louie assists his partner.

Secoli covers his partner's tears from everyone as he walks down the aisle and heads straight to the mayor's office. They both get around the judge's bench and open the door to find the children still hiding in the room. Upon entering the mayor's office, Secoli sees the children still hiding under the mayor's desk.

"Children," Secoli says. "Go to your parents. It's safe to come out now." All of them leave the office, leaving Secoli and Pluck alone. Secoli places Pluck on an empty chair, and he grabs himself a seat. He looks his ill partner in the eyes before saying anything to him. Pluck's anxious and sickly, anticipating scolding from Secoli.

"Jed," Secoli says, "why the hell did you do such a thing?"

"I—I don't know what came over me, Louie," Pluck says sorrowfully as tears pour down on his face. "She approached me when I was preparing a bath for myself. She wouldn't leave, but she got physical with me. Somehow, her sweet kiss just…made me change my mind and give in to temptation."

"Did she take off her clothes? Did you even notice that she has talons?"

"She removed all her clothes except for her boots, which reached up to her knees.

I didn't bother asking her to remove them since I was already into her."

"Damn it. She was too clever. If you'd taken off her boots, we'd probably know who she is sooner. So, how long has this been going on between you two?"

"Okay, I'll come clean," Pluck starts speaking more clearly. "I keep taking my wedding ring off each time I see her. She was just so stunning when we found her in Rawlins. She was like the ginger so many men like me always wanted to have. Wherever you weren't around, I tried to get intimate with her, but we just kept arguing with each other. I gave up on pursuing her around the time you and I switched shifts."

"Now that you mention it," Secoli interjects, "what I don't get is if she's trying to hide from her true identity this whole time, why didn't she share the harpies' identity with us that day instead of keeping it a secret?"

"I don't know. Since Ms. Klouví told us about the female harpies looking for someone with good genes…does Fiona even know that my family line never died from sickness or that I have daughters? I never told her, so how did she find out?"

Secoli thinks hard before saying, "I think I hinted to her that you were married and had four daughters."

"What? When did you tell her that?"

"As I recall, she snuck out one night when you tried to keep her under curfew. We talked about you until I had to change shifts."

Pluck wipes his tears and becomes upset. "So you're the one who let her know. I tried keeping my family a secret from her. You just had to blab about me when you two had nothing to talk about."

"Don't put the blame on me, Jed," Louie lashes out in anger. "It's your fault that you fucked her and gave the harpy race a chance to survive. Goddamn it. Of all people you could have had an affair with, it had to be her. Weren't you even thinking about your wife and children whenever you encountered that jezebel?" Pluck goes silent, unable to come up with anything to say to him. Despite being insulted by his partner, he knows Secoli is right about everything he's saying. Saying anything back to him would only make the situation worse than it already is. All he can do is look away and take the insults like he did during their last argument together.

Secoli tries to take a deep breath over how much his partner is hurting right now. Seeing how unhealthy and exhausted Pluck is makes Secoli sympathize with him.

"So what's next?" Pluck asks, wanting to change the topic and break the silence. "Fiona has got to be back with the other harpies, building a nest to prepare to lay eggs."

"Well, we've seen how Klouví's crossbow and arrows are the only thing that can kill them. And we know how that scentascope works. Why not use both of them to our advantage, go after them, and end those harpies?"

"You're right. We have no other choice but to go after them and stop her from bringing any more harpies into this world. I can't stand seeing another woman or child get slaughtered by those damn things. It's a big mistake for me to get women involved in the fighting. So, it will be just us men that will end this once and for all."

"Okay. And the women?"

Jed shakes his head. "That's simply out of the question. No way are we ever going to bring women to dangerous grounds after how many we just lost last night. But what about Zephyra Klouví? She seems to claim to be an expert harpy hunter. She showed that she was knowledgeable. "

"Honestly, Jed. Even though what she told us about the harpies turns out to be true, I don't trust her."

"What are your reasons for not trusting her?" Pluck asks, tilting his head.

"There's something about her that rubs me the wrong way about separating from the other harpy hunters. Why did she come alone if the harpies are so dangerous?"

"Yeah. That is suspicious," says Jed. "Plus, it is unusual to see a woman carrying a crossbow and traveling the desert all by herself."

"What if she killed her peers herself?"

"Now, that's a bit too much speculation, especially coming from you."

"What if she really is a harpy?" says Secoli, staring at the door. "What? If she really is one, why would she betray her own kind?"

"It's better safe than sorry."

Pluck gets up from his chair, but Secoli stops. "Whoa, Jed. Let me take it over from here. You need rest. I suggest you lie down in the long chair and get some sleep."

Pluck gives his partner a nod, eager to finally get his deserved slumber. Both postal inspectors get up from their seats and head out the door. Before the door opens, everyone in the sanctuary is eavesdropping on the conversation between Pluck and Secoli through the door. When they hear Secoli and Pluck approaching, all the men, women, and children move away from the door and pretend to still be on guard. They both leave office, assuming everyone is on high alert, but don't suspect a thing.

Pluck goes to the long chair where his partner's birdcage is placed and finally lies down. Before Secoli heads out of the building, he turns around toward the citizens standing next to the office door over a thought that comes to his head.

"Everybody," Secoli says, "take off your shoes and show me your feet. I need to make sure we don't have any harpies among us."

Everyone does as told and removes their footwear. The little ones have their parents remove their shoes for them. Despite having podophobia, Secoli is relieved that there are no talons in sight.

"Good." Secoli looks away with disgust. "No one is a harpy here. Where's Miss Klouví? Did the sheriff and his deputy bring her back to the jailhouse?"

All of them give the postal inspector a nod, and some answer yes. Secoli heads out of Town Hall, leaving his partner behind to rest up. Upon arriving at the jailhouse, Secoli sees the deputy and sheriff asleep in their chairs, so he lets them rest after their hard work. Mrs. Payton is lying in her cell's bed, snoring loudly. The next cell contains Klouví, still awake and sitting on her bed.

Secoli approaches Klouví and whispers to her, "Do me a favor and take off your shoes. I need to make sure you're not a harpy."

"As you wish," Klouví replies. She removes her leather boots and socks to show him she has human feet. "Now that I proved I'm no harpy, can you please release me from jail?"

Secoli swallows before replying, "I'm sorry, Miss Klouví. You're going to have to remain here. It's for your safety."

"*Malákas*!" Klouví swears, raising her voice and hitting the jail bars. She wakes up everyone in the jailhouse. "What the hell did I do to deserve this? I helped you and everyone, and this is how you repay me?"

"Miss Klouví, you've done a great job in helping us find the harpy living among us and providing useful information to help us fight the harpies."

The two lawmen get behind Secoli.

"However, you haven't shown any proof that you came to the United States legally. As a postal inspector, it's my job to uphold the law and protect the American people. Because you're an illegal alien, I cannot let you leave. When I get back from killing those harpies, I'm going to have to send you back to your home country."

"You? Kill those harpies? You won't stand a chance. You need me to help you kill those last harpies. Please." She leans closer to the jail bars. "Let me help you finish off those harpies first. I couldn't care less about being sent back to Greece, but I won't let you do that unless all of them are dead. You will die out there without me."

Wordlessly, Secoli heads out the door as she attempts to shake the jail bars. She screams for his and the lawmen's attention, but the sheriff and deputy follow the postal inspector out the door to remove themselves from her. Amid her ranting and raving being heard from outside of the jailhouse, Secoli turns to the lawmen on the main road.

"Sheriff Wood, Deputy Hall, I suggest getting some sleep in the Town Hall. We're going to need all the men this afternoon to finish off those harpies with that crossbow and smelling device of hers."

"Then who's going to take charge of the town, Inspector?" the sheriff asks. "Without the men, the women and children are defenseless."

"You let me worry about which one of the ladies I'm gonna pick to take charge while us men are gone," Secoli replies. "You two need to rest up before we head out."

"And Miss Klouví?" Hall says. "Are we really going to leave her in jail?"

"I'm not risking it with her tagging along. She might make a run for it after we kill the harpies. I have no other choice but to keep her in her cell until we return."

The two lawmen head inside the Town Hall, and Inspector Secoli returns to the jailhouse. He goes straight to the sheriff's desk and takes all of Klouví's things to bring with him on the hunt. While he's putting her belongings in her bag, the postal inspector notices Klouví is silent. When he looks at her cell, she remains sitting on her bed, with her head on her knees and arms around her legs.

She heard what Secoli and the two lawmen said from outside. Klouví feels absolutely hopeless remaining in her jail cell and is furious that the men get to go after the harpies. She knows none of them have enough experience to fight off the harpies, and they're going on a suicide mission. All the harpy hunter wants is to help her fellow human beings, but they won't give her a chance. For a country seen as the land of opportunity, America hasn't been a pleasant experience at all for her.

Secoli finishes gathering Klouví's belongings and walks out the door, disregarding how hurt Klouví is by his words. Secoli realizes how insensitive he's becoming and hates himself for it. The most difficult aspect of being a leader in difficult times is that you must make decisions that will upset people but are in the best interests of everyone. This experience has taught Secoli what it's truly like to be a leader who isn't loved by all but does so with love and care that no one will ever know about.

CHAPTER 13

Clouds are covering the entire sky over Point Postal, the first in months. For once, the citizens go outside without having to squint from the brutal light of the sun or feel the overwhelming humidity. A day like this has made the restless people in Point Postal enjoy a moment of ease in this time of danger. The remaining seven townsmen are well-rested and ready to join the postal inspectors and lawmen on this dangerous task.

The seventeen women and five children alive remain in town while the men are about to deploy out to the desert in the cool temperature. The women are all armed with rifles, so they won't be vulnerable when the men are gone. They take what they're given because the men are bringing the rest of the ammunition onto one of their two wagons. In addition to seven rifles, three barrels of food and water, and camping and traveling equipment, both wagons are carrying enough supplies for the expedition.

The men in this deployment aren't the best compared to the ones who unfortunately died too soon. Caleb Walsh and the banker Moses Williams are as cowardly and in poor shape as they come. Despite being an expert on horses, Chuck Madison is too old and a bit senile for this deployment. The hotel worker David Graft is the youngest and most inexperienced in this expedition, and the middle-aged Logan Smith is unhurried and past his physical prime. The only ones who seem capable and suitable to partake in this harpy hunt are Angus McKinsey and Julian Cunningham, yet their drawback is that they hate each other as coworkers at the trading post.

If only Mark Johnson and Jim Bush weren't in critical condition and wrapped up in bandages, they could have easily benefitted the expedition for their loyalty and excellent marksmanship. All the men are on board both wagons except for the lawmen and the postal inspectors riding their horses. They're using eight horses from Madison's stable on this journey, and four are pulling the wagons. Some may say it's unfair that the officials get to ride horses individually. Still, considering that the officials are responsible for protecting the men on this expedition, they need plenty of room to maneuver.

Pluck rushes inside the jailhouse to collect the crossbow, a quiver full of arrows, and thick gloves from the sheriff's desk. As he grabs everything and turns to the door, he catches a glimpse of the two jailbirds. Mrs. Payton, whose cell is closest to the door, sleeps in her bed, making the loudest snores ever heard from anyone. The second and last cell at the end of the room contains Zephyra Klouví, who's staring at him and holding on to the jail bars. Pluck stops as he anticipates her telling him something.

"You will die out there without me. Please," Klouví says. "Let me join you."

"I'm sorry, Miss Klouví," Pluck replies. "Inspector Secoli and I decided to keep you here, where it's safe."

"Don't you think I know how to handle myself against the harpies?"

"Sorry, but we won't risk one more woman dying under my leadership."

"You are just as much of a fool as your partner. You'd rather go on suicide than have an expert fight alongside you and get you back home safely."

"For your information, I'm not just a Federal agent. I'm also a Civil War veteran with more than my fair share of killing and surviving."

"Compared to fighting harpies, that will never be enough. Once Margohot finds you, you will be responsible for repopulating the harpy race."

"We shall see. Goodbye, Miss Klouví. If you need anything, Mrs. Bell will take care of you and Mrs. Payton while we handle our harpy problem. Have a good day."

"Before you go, I need to know if you fornicated with Margohot. Show me your chest, and let me see if you've got something on you."

Pluck heads out the door, not even looking back at her. Not a single word she said to him made Pluck rethink his decision to bring her along. As Pluck steps off the jailhouse's porch, he encounters Pearl Herbert in his tracks. She isn't giving him a nasty look like before but shows signs of remorse.

"Inspector Pluck," the young Herbert says, "I want to apologize for my behavior as of late. Since I defended and idolized Dr. Fletcher for so long, I have become resentful toward you. I hope you find it in your heart to forgive me."

"I do, Miss Herbert. I know you're going through a lot of unfortunate circumstances, from finding out Fiona is a harpy to the loss of all your friends. My condolences. You have my deepest sympathy."

"Thank you, Inspector." Pearl's eyes get watery over his sincere sympathy. "And don't worry. I don't look up to Dr. Fletcher no more. I look *through* her now."

"The feeling is mutual, Miss Herbert. Take care now."

Just as Pluck heads toward the men, ready to set off, Pearl catches a glimpse of the postal inspector's shirt unbuttoned and notices something blue underneath his clothes. She grabs him by the shoulders when he moves past her and makes him face her. She then quickly unbuttons the rest of his shirt.

"Hey," Pluck says. "What are you doing?"

Pearl exposes his chest before replying in shock, "Inspector. You've got some unusual spots on your chest. It looks like blueberries from a muffin."

Pluck looks down at his chest and sees what she's seeing. He's petrified over his sudden and unusual skin condition. Now seeing the sort of blue chicken pox, he has the need to scratch the tingling sensation on his chest, but his hands are full with the crossbow and quiver.

"It doesn't look right, Inspector," she continues. "We need to treat those spots. Does this have something to do with you having sex with Dr. Fletcher?" Pluck's eyes go wide at what she just said. Committing adultery with Fletcher is more consequential than he ever would have imagined. This extramarital affair not only gives the harpy race a chance to survive but also is taking a toll on his health. The thought makes Pluck feel nauseous again. Herbert wishes there was some way she could make him feel better and change his mind, but the sickly he is is too stubborn to stop.

Pluck gives her a look of helplessness before returning to the men waiting for him. As he gets closer to the group, the crossbow and quiver feel heavier, and he breathes more heavily from being suddenly light-headed. As he passes all the equipment to the men on board, Pluck immediately buttons up his shirt and coat to hide his unknown condition from everyone. Though no one suspects his skin condition, they notice his heavy breathing and slow momentum. Even Pluck's partner is concerned over this sudden change in behavior as he struggles to get back on his horse.

"You all right, Jed?" Secoli asks. "Did something happen back there?"

"No. It's nothing you should worry about. I'm just…a little nervous. That's all."

"We all are, Jed. We all are."

Secoli takes out the scentascope lying next to his birdcage on his lap. He points the device in the direction of the desert and puts his nostrils on the end of the device. He sniffs the device, and he can smell the desert's sand. However, that isn't what he wants, so he keeps sniffing as he moves the tool around. After he moves the scentascope higher, the harpy's familiar stench becomes apparent. The strong scent makes him react strongly by pulling his head back and taking his nose away from the device.

"All right, men!" Secoli calls out. "The harpies' trail is leading that way. We're off."

Secoli whips his horse's reins, and he leads the expedition to the Red Desert. All the women and children wave at them goodbye as they all remain on the main road.

Many widows and fewer women married to the men boarded on those wagons watch as they leave, hoping they'll return home safely. There is a feeling of awfulness among the townswomen as they watch the men go farther up to the plateaus. For the town's coolest day in what feels like weeks, the chills in the air have changed from comforting to ominous now that the ones who are supposed to protect them are gone.

THE HARPIES' SCENT leads the expedition past the cemetery and the first plateau. The men are so far up north from Point Postal that they can no longer see the town on the horizon. After hours of picking up the monsters' trail and leading the expedition, Secoli is nauseous over smelling the same stench from the harpies. However, he's not the only person who doesn't feel too well at the start of this journey.

Since finding out about the blue spots on his chest, Pluck hasn't gotten any better.

The lightheadedness he's enduring has been a constant struggle since the expedition began moving north. He tries hard not to make it obvious to the others, but everyone notices how he's keeping his head down and pulls his head up constantly. If it weren't for the horse he's riding on knowing how to travel, he wouldn't be able to keep up with everyone. Pluck is lucky to be riding on an animal that knows how to keep up and follow cues from those it's traveling with without having its rider tell it what to do all the time.

Each time Pluck is asked how he's doing, he denies being ill, but the two lawmen follow behind the drowsy postal inspector regardless. They watch him closely, making sure he doesn't fall off his horse or go off course. Pluck remains firmly in the saddle throughout the expedition, even on the roughest terrain and steepest slopes. Though this is a very dangerous way of travel, no one dares to tell him that he should get off his horse and hop aboard one of the wagons. His partner's too engrossed in tracking the harpies' scent and watching their footing as they followed him up the steep terrain to get around the second plateau.

The men on the wagons have their own conversations. The first wagon has David Graft driving the horses pulling the vehicle, and Angus McKinsey and Caleb Walsh as passengers who are watching over the crate of ammunition and one of the barrels full of water. The other wagon has Chuck Madison in the driver's seat, with Julian Cunningham, Logan Smith, and Moses Williams on board, watching the rest of the equipment. The men are lucky to be traveling in two separate wagons to keep Cunningham and McKinsey separated. "I shouldn't be here," Williams says, feeling timid as usual. "I'm just a simple banker. I'm not fit for this. I gotta go back to town."

"Sit back down, Moses," Smith says, pulling him back down. "You don't want to desert the group and have everyone catch you."

"I can't stand having to fight no more, Logan. We're all gonna die."

"Oh, quit your bitching, Moses," McKinsey aggressively whispers while

driving the wagon. "All that bellyaching is just bringing everyone down."

"Y'all have a better chance to survive than I do," the banker continues venting. "I'm telling y'all I'm not the right guy to be helping. I'm just gonna be in the way and ruin everybody's chances of survival."

"If that's how you feel," McKinsey replies, "you should stay behind. Besides, you never fire your rifle whenever we see a harpy."

"That's not true," Williams says. "I fired my rifle like y'all did."

"Bullshit. Whenever the postal inspectors ask if anyone still has ammo, you're the one who still has a full round and refuses to raise your hand."

"That's a lousy accusation if I ever heard one. I'm telling you that I fired all the ammo given to me right at those harpies as much as you and everyone else did."

"If that were true, why are you backing out from fighting some more right now?"

"Cut it out, Julian," Smith says. "You're not helping by instigating Mr. Williams."

"Oh, and I suppose you're going to hide with the banker and start a pity party," Cunningham says mockingly. "Boy, we're completely screwed if we're relying on you two old coots for this last fight."

"Hey, Angus," McKinsey shouted from the other wagon ahead of them, "quit picking on them and shut your mouth! No one wants to hear you at a time like this."

Cunningham wants to say something back to his rival, but he catches a glimpse of Inspector Secoli and the two lawmen looking back at him as they head up the alluvial fan. The two rivals' open hostility toward each other in front of the Federal agents was a first, and it left everyone feeling uncomfortable. Since their employer, Gallus Kennedy, fell victim to the harpies, everybody keeps an eye on both of them. Cunningham remains silent and looks away, preventing further fuel to the fire that would lead to another bloodbath like the one between Mrs. Payton and Mrs. Humphrey.

While everyone minds their business and focuses on getting up the alluvial fan, the confrontation flies over Inspector Pluck's head. He's so ill right now that he's losing consciousness as his horse carries him upward. Jed's illness is taking so much of a toll on him that he starts losing his balance. His horse panics from its rider's unusual movements and rears up, sending the sickly Federal agent off his saddle and rolling down the alluvial fan.

Deputy Hall dismounts his horse and slides down the steep hill, grabbing Pluck's arm to prevent him from rolling to the bottom. As Sheriff Wood and Inspector Secoli turn their horses back, the wagons' drivers pull their reins to see what's behind them.

It's a bad decision to stop in the middle of a steep hill, considering that the horses are still pulling the wagon and are being pulled backward by the wooden vehicles.

Secoli catches a glimpse of the wagons pulling the horses backward and shouts, "It's too steep! Keep heading up to the top."

The wagon drivers whip the horses' reins for them to continue to go uphill and prevent an accident.

"We'll meet you up there, where it's safe. When you reach the top, wait for us there."

As the wagons continue their way up, Secoli gets off his horse with his birdcage and slides down directly to his partner. Pluck has his arm around the deputy's back, being pulled up the hill. As Secoli nears the two, he feels raindrops pelting his skin. He's so worried about his partner that he doesn't stop to notice how fast it starts pouring.

Still on his horse, the sheriff looks up to the clouds and comments, "So that's why it's been so cloudy today."

Upon reaching his partner, Secoli immediately puts Pluck's other arm around his neck to help the deputy carry him upward. Thunderstorms are then heard, and the rain starts getting heavier. The wagons reach the top before they can slip from the steep terrain, which is now soaked and slippery. The men refuse to wait for the authorities to make it to the top, as some of them get off the wagon and help them.

Caleb Walsh grabs the three horses' reins while Angus McKinsey heads directly to Inspector Pluck. Being nearly seven feet tall and brawny, McKinsey takes the ill postal inspector off Secoli's and Hall's shoulders and gives Pluck a fireman's carry. The young man doesn't seem bothered at all, carrying Pluck up the slippery alluvial fan, moving faster and more carefully than the deputy and Secoli. Now, all Secoli has to worry about is keeping Chap as dry as possible and getting to the top safely. McKinsey brings the unwell postal inspector to the top while everyone catches up. Cunningham looks away, annoyed at his rival's help, seeing this as a way for him to show off.

McKinsey places Pluck on his rival's wagon since they have more room. Secoli approaches his sick partner, lying in the wagon, and places his hand on his forehead. His body temperature is colder than it should be, shivering and breathing heavily.

"Jed, out of all the times for you to start feeling sick," Secoli says, "why now?"

"We can't turn back to town," the sheriff replies. "We've traveled so far. Traveling through a rainy desert is dangerous. Especially now that the desert's sands are too wet and soft for the wagons to bypass."

"Not to mention that it's getting dark," the deputy adds. "I suggest we start building tents and keep ourselves dried."

Secoli then looks around and sees how much of a godsend it is that the top of the alluvial fan is flat ground for the men, horses, and wagons to rest. If there's ever a place to camp in such a craggy location, this would be here where they stand. Secoli realizes how miserable everybody is over the storm and that it's a good time to finally rest after hours of traveling through these rough grounds.

"Everyone, start building camp," Secoli commands. "We'll keep moving forward once the rain finally settles—hopefully in the morning."

All the men are happy to hear the command, so they grab the tents from the other wagon and waste no time building them. As they make camp, Secoli takes off his coat and covers his birdcage with it before using the scentascope again. He sniffs in the direction that they're heading, but for some reason, he can't smell the harpies' stench in that direction. He turns the device around and smells through it some more but still can't find the harpies' pong. Secoli continues turning around and searching for the stench he's been smelling all day, but all he can smell from the scentascope is the moist sand in the distance.

"We got the tents all set up, Inspector," Sheriff Wood says, then notices Secoli using the scentascope. "Do you still have the harpies' trail?"

Secoli continues to use the scentascope a little longer before replying. "No. I can't smell anything but the wet desert and a couple of objects in the distance. Sheriff, is it possible that the rain can take away the scent in the air?"

"I wouldn't know, Inspector. When I was tracking a runaway years ago, I used our ol' dog to track its scent in a storm like this and found the crook. I think the ability to track someone's trail from the ground lasts longer in the rain than tracking it in the air."

"Damn it," Secoli swears, finally putting down the scentascope. "How the hell are we going to find those damn monsters if we lose their trail?"

"We'll think about that later, Inspector, but first, we need to get out of this rain and keep ourselves dry. Help me bring Inspector Pluck into one of these tents, will ya?"

As both men turn around, they see Cunningham has the ill postal inspector on his shoulder and is carrying him to a vacant tent. He's almost the same size and strength as McKinsey, so he has no trouble carrying Pluck by himself. He places Pluck inside one of the tents and tucks him under the covers. He then gets out and stares at his rival, showing off that he can do as well—if not better—than him. As Secoli retrieves his birdcage covered by his coat, he sees the two rivals glaring at each other.

McKinsey and Cunningham have their eyes blazing at each other and fists clenched. Everyone stops and watches this silent confrontation occurring, anticipating this feud will escalate into a fight. This confrontation between these large young men could turn violent if either of them makes any sudden movement. McKinsey and Cunningham's eye contact is finally broken by the sound of Pluck moaning from his tent. Secoli then rushes to his partner's tent, running in between the two rivals, which then makes Cunningham walk away. McKinsey joins Secoli inside the tent to check on Pluck, pretending the stare-down never happened.

Secoli puts his birdcage next to Pluck and removes the coat covering the cage. He checks Pluck's temperature and sees that he's as cold as ever. Graft comes in and brings an ignited lantern inside the tent, giving Secoli light to better see his partner.

"I feel so cold, Louie," Pluck moans shakingly. "So cold. I need something warm."

"Don't worry, Jed," Secoli says. "I'll build a campfire to warm you up."

"But, Inspector," Graft replies, "a firepit is flammable. His tent might catch fire.

Even if it doesn't, smoke will fill up inside the tent, so it will be toxic to breathe."

"Okay. Hand me the lamp so at least Jed can have something warm next to him." He reaches for the lantern from Graft and places it close to his partner's face. "Please hand me my sleeping bag. We must warm him up by putting him in two bags."

"What about you, Inspector? We didn't bring any more sleeping bags."

"I'll be fine. It's him I'm worried about. Now hurry."

As Graft and McKinsey exit the tent, Secoli then opens Pluck's sleeping bag and begins removing his drenched clothes. As soon as he removes his wet coat and shirt, Secoli is appalled to discover blue spots on his partner's chest. Since it's only on his chest and not anywhere else on Pluck's body, it disturbs Secoli so much that he doesn't bother to remove the rest of his clothing. He then hears Graft returning, and Secoli puts the cover back on to hide Pluck's gruesome spots and tries to forget what he saw.

"Here's your sleeping bag, Inspector," Graft says, entering the tent and handing him the sleeping bag. "Help me lift Inspector Pluck up so we can double cover him."

"No. No. No," Secoli reacts strongly. "I'll—I'll take care of it from here."

"Gee. Sorry if I scared you, Inspector. I'm only trying to help." Graft tries to calm himself from being startled. "If you need any of my help, I'll be sharing a shelter with Logan and Angus. Have a good night, Inspector."

"Mr. Graft," Secoli stops the man from heading out. "Tell everyone that whoever needs to step out to do their business should be carrying that crossbow and make sure it's loaded. It's too dangerous to go out this late at night in the desert."

"Where should the crossbow be kept, Inspector?"

Secoli calms down and thinks while stroking his beard before saying, "Have the crossbow ready in your tent. Have it placed in the corner next to your tent's entranceway. Also, are the horses' reins tied to something steady?"

"We have them all tied to the edges of the tents. Even the horses that pulled our wagons have been released and have their reins tied like the rest. Anything else?"

"I think that's all. Thank you. Don't forget to tell the others where the crossbow is when they need to do their business, okay?"

"Will do. I hope Inspector Pluck gets well soon. Have a good night."

As soon as Graft leaves the tent, Secoli slowly opens Pluck's covers to examine his marks. The spots all look like pimples colored light blue and reach from his sternum to his nipples. Secoli notices that even when he's asleep, Pluck's still breathing heavily. It doesn't help that there's probably no doctor left in Wyoming, nor has he ever seen a skin condition such unusual and disgusting as this.

Secoli covers up Pluck's body to keep him warmer and puts him in the additional sleeping bag. Though Pluck awakes for a brief moment as he stuffs him into another sleeping bag, he is so exhausted and fatigued that he quickly goes back to sleep as he gets double-covered. Secoli is feeling cold from the temperature dropping and from his soaked clothes. He removes all his clothes except for his undergarments, which are the driest clothing he has left. He sits on the other side of the small tent while watching his partner remain snuggled in those bedsheets.

Luckily, the lantern's flame is the only thing warming up the tent, which Secoli keeps on until the oil runs out. Before the Federal agent closes his eyes, Secoli brings his birdcage closer to him, only to see Chap sleeping peacefully at the bottom of the base wire grille. Despite how uncomfortably cold it is to remain sitting on the wet ground, he knows his partner needs to keep warm more than ever. The logical thing to keep himself warm is to huddle with his snugged-in partner since he has no covers.

This is an issue for Secoli, considering that not only is he uncomfortable touching another person—not just a man—but he refuses to risk touching Pluck in case his condition is infectious. So he puts his head on his knees and tries to sleep while sitting. Despite not usually sleeping this early, there's nothing else to do as he remains in the same tent with his partner. Hearing the heavy raindrops land on the tent over his head suddenly becomes relaxing.

The warmth from the lamp and the cool breeze from everywhere else initially felt like an issue is now comforting. Secoli thought he had left behind the days of sleeping without a bed or blankets during the Civil War, but he could sleep anywhere as long as he was dry.

POINT POSTAL'S FIRST rain in nearly two years is immense, with floods and puddles all over town. Despite this long-awaited pleasant yet overwhelming weather, the women and children remain high maintenance. Though it's unlikely any creature could fly through this amount of rain, there's still that ominous feeling that the harpies could still come in and attack again at any moment. Since the harpies left a lot of damage in the sanctuary, living under the same broken Town Hall roof is unfeasible. The consensus is that it is in the best interest of everyone to relocate to the hotel, where there are ample rooms.

The hotel, however, isn't the only building standing that keeps the townswomen dry. The jailhouse remains intact and well protected without the sheriff or his deputy present. Lorraine Payton and Zephyra Klouví remain imprisoned in their jail cells, unsupervised by anyone. It seems there wasn't anyone assigned to watch over the jailhouse, and none of the women would want to volunteer to watch over the felons.

Everyone in town grows paranoid about getting anywhere close to the murderer and the mysterious harpy hunter.

Lorraine Payton has calmed down a little since the men left town. There's something about being controlled by the opposite sex and having them make decisions that have always rubbed her the wrong way. She hates that nobody takes her seriously, so she remains unmarried. Raising a clumsy son on her own when he was alive was a challenging task for her. Likewise, she was never well-liked by the townsfolk.

Now, she sees firsthand what it is like to be in the same jail cell that her lost son was once in. Even in confinement, Mrs. Payton continues her bad habit of being blunt and making negative assumptions, especially toward the only person imprisoned with her. Since the men left, Mrs. Payton has attempted many times to make Zephyra Klouví open up, especially since they're the only ones in the jailhouse.

The harpy hunter, however, remains silent in her jail cell. Though the harpy hunter dislikes how loud and abrasive her neighbor is, she has a lot of patience and discipline not to fall for Lorraine's pettiness. Despite hearing and knowing so much about her from last night's interrogation, there's a lot about the harpy hunter that remains mysterious.

Both jailbirds hear footsteps coming from the porch, and Mrs. Bell appears, soaked but carrying two plates of supper. She doesn't say a word to either of the prisoners as she leaves their meals and silverware on the floor next to the jail bars. Seeing that this is the second time Bell is doing this today irritates Mrs. Payton.

As Bell fetches a jar of water on the sheriff's desk and fills two empty cups for them to drink, Payton says, "It would be nice if you give us our meals by opening the jail door and handing it to us, Samantha."

"You think I'm that stupid to fall for that trick?" she says, placing the cups on the floor next to their dishes.

"And how am I supposed to eat supper when the plate is wider than the length between the bars? Beef jerky and beans? And not only that but the food is all wet from the rain. Y'all having better food right yonder and giving us the scraps, aren't ya?"

Before responding, Mrs. Bell catches a glimpse of Klouví sitting on the floor with her legs crossed and her hands between the jailhouse bars. She has her plate still placed where it's left and starts to use her utensils to cut and lift the food from her plate and eat properly. Seems as though the harpy hunter is resourceful enough to eat her meals while in this circumstance. Payton looks over to see what her neighbor is doing. Samantha smiles over what she sees from the other jail cell.

"See?" Mrs. Bell says. "Why can't you be more like her? You wouldn't be in this mess if you cooperated with us. We took her to the outhouse twice today, and not once did she attempt to escape. What do you have to say about that?"

Payton can't make a response after being compared to the harpy hunter. While standing, she picks up the plate from the ground and tilts her dish to go through the bars so she can eat inside her cell, but stops when some of her beans spill. Lorraine then uses her fork to bring her food between the bars and into her mouth. As expected, she is unimpressed with the taste, knowing the townswomen make better food than this.

Just as Lorraine begins eating, Samantha grabs a chair and waits for the two prisoners to finish supper. Just as she sits down, Klouví empties her dish and finishes drinking from her cup. Seeing that the harpy hunter ate and drank so fast, Bell is impressed while Mrs. Payton takes her third bite from her plate.

"Excuse me," Klouví says. "I would like to use the outhouse, please."

"Sure." Samantha gets up from her chair and heads out the door. "Just let me get the others to help me escort you."

Zephyra Klouví and Lorraine Payton are alone again. The harpy hunter remains still while her neighbor makes so much noise chewing her food. As annoying as it is to hear her smack her lips with every bite, Klouví tries not to let it get to her. If it weren't for the sound of pouring rain coming out of the jailhouse or the cool air, she'd be having a much more difficult time coping in the jailhouse.

"So when are you gonna stop being so quiet?" Payton asks with her mouth full. "You won't make it out here if you keep giving people the silent treatment, ya know."

Klouví lets her take another bite off her plate before asking, "Would you like to share why you are here with me?"

"Huh?" Lorraine swallows her food and realizes Klouví finally said something to her. "Oh, now you're talking to me. Why is that? Is it because your stomach is no longer empty?"

"No." Klouví doesn't notice she was mocked due to the cultural differences in how she communicates. "I am curious as to why you ended up locked here with me."

Lorraine swallows her food too fast and coughs from almost choking. She even drops her plate, causing it to shatter and spill the food. Payton tries to clear her throat to breathe properly once more. Before she says anything, Mrs. Bell barges in through the front door and brings in Pearl Herbert and Wendy Morris. They are soaked and perturbed, pointing their rifles as soon as they enter.

"What's going on here?" Bell shouts, then looks down at the floor. "Look at what you've done. I've only been gone for a minute, and this happens."

"Shut up, Sam," Lorraine replies, still clearing her throat. "I almost choked from eating your God-awful cooking."

"Do you want me to pass that on to Mrs. Smith, who makes your meals? You're lucky that we still feed an awful murderer like you. If it weren't for the sheriff not wanting me to take care of you, I wouldn't even bother."

Mrs. Payton holds her tongue again, knowing she might not get fed if she talks back at the guardswoman. The silence makes Bell turn her focus on the other prisoner. Without speaking to her, Klouví follows the procedure of stepping away from the bars and placing both hands on the wall. Morris, responsible for the keys, unlocks the door, handcuffs the harpy hunter from behind, and pulls Klouví out of her cell and out the door. Samantha and Pearl follow them and grab the lanterns they left on the porch to see through the dark and rainy night.

The outhouse where they're bringing the harpy hunter is behind the jailhouse. As Morris holds on to Klouví, Pearl enters the outhouse and quickly inspects the latrine with her lantern. Once giving the nod to signal that the outhouse is clear, Klouví then gets uncuffed and is freed to use the latrine while her escorts wait for her to finish.

"Can you believe this weather?" Morris comments, enjoying the rain. "If we had this much more often, I'd save so much money from going to the bathhouse."

Bell laughs while trying to cover her face from getting wet with her arm on her forehead and replies, "If it rained this often, then I'd have a good reason to bring an umbrella. I'm glad that it only rains once every year or so."

"You don't like the rain, Sam?"

Samantha shakes her head. "Not at all. I moved west to avoid getting wet. Gosh, this weather is dreadful." She wants to change the topic but sees Herbert looking a little distant. "Hey, Pearl. So what do you think of this harpy killer?"

"What's there to think about?" Pearl replies. "She is what she is."

"What I mean is, do you think Miss Klouví is a real harpy hunter?"

"If she really is, why isn't she with the men on their expedition? I mean, there's a reason why she's held in jail, right?"

"You know, that's what I've been wondering," Morris adds. "Why is she even under arrest? She doesn't come across as someone that has any criminal intent."

"Especially compared to Mrs. Payton," Bell snarks. "What she did to Mrs.

Humphrey—that was just inhumane."

"I can only imagine Angus McKinsey and Julian Cunningham doing something similar to each other out there. It's a big mistake that the postal inspectors brought those two along."

"You don't really believe that, do you?" Pearl says. "If they hate each other as much as Mrs. Humphrey and Mrs. Payton did, then one of them would have shot each other days ago when they were guarding this town."

"God willing, nothing bad will happen to those men. They're our only hope." Bell gets more annoyed with how long she's been standing in the rain, "Gee. What's taking her so long? She'd better not just be sitting in there." Bell then raises her voice. "Hey. Are you almost done? We're all wet and miserable out here."

Bell and the other ladies wait for a response. Considering how loud the heavy rain is, it's hard to tell if Klouví is making any sound. Herbert approaches the outhouse and knocks to see how the harpy hunter is doing there. Since she hasn't answered, Pearl opens the door and puts in her lantern. Nobody is there. Not only is Klouví gone, but Pearl sees the wall in front of her busted open.

"Oh, my God," Morris says, watching over Pearl's shoulders. "She's gone." Herbert exits the outhouse and looks behind the privy, where the wall is busted open. She looks down and puts her lantern closer to see. The other two join her, and they all see footprints flooding with water that leads up north, lying next to the broken pieces from the outhouse.

"Follow the trail," Morris says, grabbing Pearl's rifle. "She's making a run for it."

Pearl leads the way as she gives light for everyone to see through the darkness. The wet soil and sand traces haven't been washed away by the rain. While they follow the tracks, there are signs that Klouví twisted her feet and fell several times. It shows how much of a disadvantage the harpy hunter has, being unable to see where she's going. It doesn't take long until the three see the light touching someone ahead.

"Hey. Stop!" Morris shouts while running after her.

The person ahead refuses to stop running. Since she hasn't turned around, there's no clarity if it's really Klouví ahead of them since she's covered in mud. Already irritated, Morris decides to stop running and fire a warning shot to her left, then aims directly at the runaway. Upon hearing gunfire, the escapee stops and raises both hands. She then turns around, and the three chasers identify Klouví.

"Hold it right there, jailbird!" Morris yells as she grabs the harpy hunter's wrists and cuffs her. "You turned out to be as bad as Mrs. Payton."

"Please," Klouví says, getting cuffed and brought back to town. "Let me go! The men out there are in terrible danger! I need to save them!"

"And how are you going to do that, huh?" Pearl replies, still carrying the lantern and leading everyone back to Point Postal. "The men took all the horses and your equipment. It's too wet, dark, and dangerous to be out here. Just how stupid are you?"

The townswomen return to town with the prisoner and head to the jailhouse. While imprisoned, Mrs. Payton sees everyone with mud all over their clothes and is left confused and speechless. What catches the prisoner off guard is Klouví is being brought back with her escorts being belligerent toward her. "Wait a minute," Pearl says, stopping her peers from sending the harpy hunter back to her jail cell. "Check to see if she's carrying something."

As Morris stands behind Klouví and holds on to her cuffs, Bell checks her pockets and under her shirt. Bell feels uneasy searching for the harpy hunter because she doesn't dress like other women. The harpy hunter is wearing men's clothing, giving Samantha mixed signals like she is inspecting someone who's male when she is, in fact, female.

"I think I found something," Morris says, feeling something in her boot and pulling a chisel. "Ooh. So that's how you've managed to escape. You thought you were so smart."

After Morris feels nothing on the other boot, she leaves the jail cell and locks up the door. Defeated, Klouví sits on her bed, averting her gaze from her captors.

"I bet all the times when she supposedly was using the outhouse today," Morris comments, "she must have kept using the chisel to cut the wood."

"I hope you feel proud of yourself." Pearl confronts the harpy hunter in front of her cell. "Here, we thought that you might be innocent. But you ended up being as deceitful as Dr. Fletcher. Actually, not as bad as her. At least you ain't no harpy. Never mind. I should stop being impressionable to strangers because all of y'all just keep taking advantage of the good people in this town. Let's go, girls. We're done here."

Pearl storms out of the jailhouse and back into the rain. When the other two leave the jailhouse, Klouví's once again alone with Mrs. Payton. Despite being an adventurer, the harpy hunter hates being filthy and refuses to sleep while being covered in mud.

Klouví disrobes to her undergarments and then pushes her bed to the barred window so high up in her cell. The harpy hunter then grabs the cup she left next to the jail bars. She stands on the headboard and sticks her cup out of the window for the rain to fill it up. The rain is pouring so hard that it quickly fills up the cup with water.

The harpy hunter then gets down and pours all the water on her hair. Since a full cup isn't enough to wash the mud off her hair and the rest of her body, she gets back up and uses the rain to refill her cup and repeats the process of resourceful bathing. Klouví doesn't care how much mess she's making all over the floor. She wants all the mud off her long, dark brown hair.

"What are you doing?" Payton asks, unable to see her neighbor from her jail cell.

"I am taking a bath by using a cup," the harpy hunter replies.

"That's pretty smart. Speaking of which, did you really try to escape?"

"It doesn't matter," Klouví responds as her cup is refilled from the rain.

"My plan has failed. And the men are going to die without me."

Klouví continues pouring more water on her and focuses on removing the mud off of her. Her cell's floor has filthy water all over. Seeing that the harpy hunter is hated by the townswomen, Payton stops being antagonistic toward her. After hearing what the girls say to her, she starts to pity the young woman.

"To answer your question from earlier," Payton says, "I'm in here because I killed a woman. I know what I did was wrong, but she wanted my son dead because he accidentally killed her husband."

Klouví stops to listen to her.

"Even despite witnesses saying it was an accident, they didn't allow me to see my son," Payton continues, "I didn't even get to say goodbye when the harpies took him away from me. Since then, the whole damn town doesn't give a damn. And how Pearl Herbert compared you to Dr. Fletcher was uncalled for."

"You and I have loved ones who were taken away by harpies." The huntress starts drying herself with the blanket on the bed.

"You lost someone special to those monsters?"

"Yes. First my mother, then my fiancé on my wedding day back in Greece."

"Oh, no. I'm so sorry to hear that. My condolences for your loss."

"Thank you." Klouví lies in bed and closes her eyes.

LOGAN SMITH, MOSES Williams, and Angus McKinsey, who share the same tent, decide to stay up longer and play five-card poker. The three can't sleep this early in the evening despite everyone else taking an early night while remaining dry in their tents. They're using the second lantern the group brought with them to see their cards. Since everyone went to sleep in their tents, they felt enjoying themselves was necessary. The men are in their twentieth round in the game, and the rain hasn't settled down since it began.

All of them are decompressed and in the perfect environment to play as many card sessions as to their hearts' content. Since the tarp over their heads is heavy-duty, there isn't a raindrop hard enough to get inside. Though they don't have any poker chips, they place money and other personal possessions they brought with them as replacements. They even gamble over the bullets they've been given.

"Remember how much fun we used to have when the saloon was around?" Williams asks while exchanging cards. "There was no better place to play poker."

"Yeah, it was nice and all, but," Smith replies, receiving a card from McKinsey, "playing in the tent while it's raining outside isn't half bad."

"Yeah, minus the music, women, and drinks. I'd kill for some ale right now."

"Okay, are we ready to show hands again?" McKinsey interrupts.

"You betcha," Smith replies. "All those bullets are going to be mine with this hand."

"Wait," the banker interrupts, "what happens to the ones that lose this bet? How are we going to kill those harpies without ammunition?"

The tent becomes silent over this moment of realization. Each of them feels stupid over what they're trying to put on the line. All three of them look at each other awkwardly over gambling away each of their ammunition.

Smith shrugs his shoulders and replies, "We can always get more from the crate."

"I don't know," McKinsey opposes. "Everyone keeps saying that's the last ammunition we have left. We'd better gamble with something else instead of these bullets. I hate to take more when we're supposed to."

"I agree with Angus," Williams replies, "I think we should put something else on the line besides these bullets. I-I don't want someone to have the most bullets while we take more from the crate without permission."

"But I have nothing else to draw," Smith groans. "I got nothing but the clothes I'm wearing."

"I'll bet you my wallet and the photo of my wife for your undershirt," McKinsey replies, placing the items he named on the center and taking his bullets back. "That's a fair deal, right?"

"While you're making your decision," McKinsey says, "I'm going to take a leak."

Angus lays his cards face down on the ground and puts his bullets back in his pocket. Considering his height, he gets on his knees to avoid hitting his head on the tent's ceiling. As he crawls out of the tent, Smith remembers something important.

"Angus," Smith says. "Don't forget to bring the crossbow with you."

"Oh, thanks for the reminder." McKinsey takes the crossbow and an arrow from the corner of the tent. "You'd better not look at my cards." Williams replies, "Of course not," unable to hide his grin.

Smith frowns at Williams as McKinsey exits the tent with the crossbow. The tall young man finally gets up from the ground and stretches from being in such a small space. He feels his back making cracking noises and gets soaked after finally getting himself dried. As he searches for a good place to urinate, he sees someone standing beside the tents. Since it's so dark outside, he can't see who it is.

Taking aim at the dark figure before him, McKinsey slowly approaches it with his crossbow. His heart races as he approaches the mysterious figure, and he breathes slowly but heavily to lower his heart rate. He catches a glimpse to see the crossbow loaded and places his index finger on the trigger. The rain is getting lighter, and the raindrops aren't so loud. This all makes it easy for McKinsey not to miss this shot.

He immediately stops and carefully watches the mysterious figure. It looks human, and the clothes are soaked. With the lighter rain, it's more apparent that whoever is standing in front of McKinsey is slowly moving his head as he stands. Since it's less noisy, he hears what sounds like sucking air from some kind of pipe or tube.

When the mysterious figure turns around, McKinsey looks at who it is. "Oh," McKinsey says, lowering his crossbow. "Inspector Secoli. It's only you." Secoli puts down his scentascope and looks at the tall young man. "Shouldn't you and your friends be getting some sleep?"

"It's only a little past nine, Inspector. None of us can sleep this early. What are you doing out here by yourself?"

"I'm trying to see if I can get the scent of the harpies. It seems as though the rain made their trail disappear. I smell nothing but what I think is wet sand."

"Why don't you wait till the rain stops? Sent will be back by tomorrow."

"I doubt their scent will reappear when the rain stops. Damn it. We came so far, and now we're lost."

"Inspector. It's not good for you or anyone to keep pushing yourself to find the harpies. It's too dark to see anything too. By the way, how's Inspector Pluck doing?"

"He's fine for now. He... he's a little dizzy from dehydration. I'll make sure he drinks more water when he wakes up."

"That's good to hear." McKinsey walks away. "Have a good night, sir."

"Angus," Secoli says, making him stop in his tracks, "can I ask you something?"

The man turns around and replies, "What's on your mind, Inspector?"

The postal inspector sighs before saying, "I can't help but notice the tension between you and Mr. Cunningham. Is something going on between you two?"

McKinsey swallows his saliva over the topic he wants to avoid. He tries his best to keep it from affecting the expedition, but everyone except the postal inspectors is aware of their history. Now that Secoli wants answers, there's no escaping this sensitive topic.

McKinsey sighs and finally says, "When I came to Lemonstown, I wanted to start a new life away from my family and experience the open West that everybody was discussing back home."

"Where are you from?" Secoli interrupts.

"I'm originally from Vicksburg, Mississippi, sir. It was a tough decision to leave my family and live independently, but I decided to go to Wyoming. Don't ask why. I don't remember. But when I got here, I took a job from Gallus Kennedy and became his stock boy. This is before Cunningham came to town, and the workers there were much different compared to before we were attacked."

"How long have you been living in Wyoming?"

"Seven years. I moved here when I was seventeen years old. Even though the pay is good and the town is home to me, that's not why I decided to stay here for so long. I-I was in love with Mr. Kennedy's daughter." McKinsey looks away.

"Did Gallus approve of you pursuing his daughter?"

"Malorie? No. No, he didn't. She and I were—we were in love with each other. We had a secret affair behind everybody's back for five years. It wasn't until one of my coworkers found out about her that Kennedy said he would fire me unless I stopped seeing her."

"Why was he overprotective over his daughter from a suitable man like you?"

"She was in an arranged marriage."

"To Cunningham, right?"

"Long story short, she wasn't in love with Cunningham. Her trading post and all her family possessions were going to be inherited by him. When he moved to town and became my coworker, he showed his colors by being a real jerk to her. Malorie wanted me to come back to her, but I couldn't do it. I moved on and planned to leave town to forget about her and stop creating so much tension between her father and her fiancé. That is until you and Inspector Pluck appeared and made us stay under curfew."

"Were you two seeing each other in the Town Hall?"

"I tried avoiding her, but Cunningham kept forcing himself in on her. I kept minding my own business until—until she met up with me during my shift."

"And what happened? It's all right. We're not on curfew anymore, and it's just you and me talking."

"We made love."

"During your shift?"

"Yes, Inspector. I confess. We had sex when I was supposed to be at my post."

"What's done is done." Secoli sighs aggressively. "Then what happened?"

"Cunningham walked to my post and found us together. He pulled her away and was this close to shooting me on the spot. If it weren't for her stopping him, I would have gotten killed. Since Cunningham didn't want her to get caught sneaking out during curfew, he sent her back and pretended like none of it had happened. I'm surprised you're hearing about this for the first time, Inspector."

"So Malorie Kennedy—is she still alive?"

"No..." McKinsey sniffs, starting to whimper. "She was one of the victims that got killed by the harpy's third attack yesterday. The fact that she and her father died that day—it was truly heartbreaking. It was bad enough to see Malorie despondent overseeing her father go permanently deaf, and then that happened. Seeing her and her father cremated together was the hardest thing for me. And since then, Cunningham blames me for their deaths."

"So that's what's been going on between you two. The sheriff has always told me what's been happening in the town but never really has talked about the townsfolk. If only he told me about you two sooner, I would have let you stay back in town."

"But that wouldn't be fair to anybody." McKinsey wipes his tears. "I'm one of the few who didn't get hurt, and I can still fight."

"Even so, this animosity between you and Mr. Cunningham might jeopardize this expedition. Maybe I need to talk to him and—"

Someone from McKinsey's tent interrupts the conversation and calls out, "Angus, what's taking so long? You said you were just going to...." Smith stops shouting as soon as he gets out of the tent and sees McKinsey with Secoli.

"Oh, my apologies, Inspector. I didn't know you two were talking to each other."

"It's fine," Secoli replies. "We were just finishing our conversation."

"I'll be with you shortly, Logan," Angus says.

Once Williams heads back in the tent, Secoli says to McKinsey, "Thanks for letting me know. I'll see if we can get this resolved tomorrow."

"Thank you, Inspector. Have a good night."

The two go their separate ways. As McKinsey puts down the crossbow and starts doing his business, Secoli makes it to his tent. Before he enters, he looks at the scentascope he still carries. He wants to amuse himself by smelling through the device again before sleeping. The postal inspector puts his nostrils on the holes and makes one more inhalation.

Suddenly, Secoli smells something familiar. He pulls his head back over how strong it smells. Then, it occurs to him that the familiar stench he's been looking for is finally detected after hours of smelling rocks and wet sand through the device. He puts his nose back on the device and smells a trace. Suddenly the reeking smell gets stronger and stronger like it's approaching.

Secoli then realizes McKinsey is still peeing and vulnerable. The postal inspector runs toward the young man. In the corner of his eye, Secoli catches a glimpse of feathers flying directly at McKinsey. As he extends his arms to the young man, he tackles McKinsey before the harpy strikes the kid.

"Hey! What are you doing?" McKinsey shouts as they land on the ground. "The harpies!" Secoli replies, getting up. "They're here! Where's the crossbow?"

Secoli and McKinsey look around to find the weapon. It's too dark for either one of them to see.

"Oh, no. It was right here." McKinsey touches the stone and ground where he left it. "I swear. It was here."

Both of them are on their knees, looking for the crossbow on the ground. McKinsey is disgusted that he's touching urine and tries to wipe his hands with his shirt. Through the rain, Secoli sees talons flying around the camp in what little light there is.

With no time to waste, the postal inspector takes his pistol out and starts firing at the harpy. The fiend then flies back into the darkness, where it's out of its prey's sight.

The gunfire wakes everybody up. The first to come out of their tents are Logan Smith and Moses Williams, both armed with rifles. It doesn't take long for Caleb Walsh and Chuck Madison to join the rest outside. Then the lawmen run out of their tents and draw both pistols, ready as ever. Everybody who's now outside wastes no time for the rest to come out of their tents and face the enemy. The only one outside who doesn't have a weapon is Angus McKinsey, who's still searching for the missing crossbow.

Everyone else is looking in all directions to where the harpy might be. Only McKinsey's tent provides light, and the rain is getting heavier again, making visibility even worse for everybody. Then David Graft and Julian Cunningham finally get out of their tents, fully clothed and armed with rifles. As they join the group on high alert and prepare to shoot on sight, Cunningham sees his rival crawling around.

"Hey, jackass," Cunningham whispers. "Quit fooling around and help us fight."

"The crossbow," McKinsey replies, "I can't find it."

"Shit," Cunningham swears, then gets on the ground to help his rival find the harpy hunter's weapon.

While they both continue looking for the crossbow, Secoli realizes Pluck isn't outside. His partner is still ill and too weak to leave their tent. He starts to panic when he remembers Chap is in the same tent. Knowing they're both in grave danger, Secoli immediately runs to his tent. The sheriff sees what he's doing and catches a glimpse of a harpy swooping out of the darkness toward the postal inspector. Secoli is so far from the group that the lawman has no choice but to shoot at the incoming fiend, making Secoli immediately drop to the ground.

The gunfire has everyone firing in the same direction. However, no matter how many bullets hit the fiend, the harpy doesn't slow down and flies over everyone's heads. As all the men turn around to see where the harpy went, another harpy appears from the same direction, flying toward the men looking away. Secoli sees the other harpy and draws out his handgun in a last-ditch effort to stop the incoming beast from hurting anyone. He takes the shot as soon as its wings rise and its body is exposed.

The postal inspector sends a bullet through one of the harpy's ribs. This catches the harpy off guard, and it misses the sheriff as its closest target. Upon hearing gunshots firing in his direction, the fiend disappears into the darkness as soon as the men turn toward Secoli.

Everyone surveys their surroundings as the harpies are again out of sight. Secoli tries getting up but realizes he landed too hard on his left knee. With no other choice, he crawls to his tent. Luckily, he doesn't crawl far or go around the tent since the entranceway is ahead of him. The postal inspector makes it inside and sees his partner struggling to get out of the double sleeping bag. He's also a little relieved to see Chap in his cage beside Pluck.

"I feel awful," Pluck says in a groggy voice. "Go on without me. Save yourself."

"Jed," Secoli replies, crawling toward him and grabbing his birdcage. "We gotta get you out of here. There's no telling when—"

Secoli gets interrupted by shots being fired from outside. As the firing continues, he tries to get his partner out of the sleeping bags. As soon as Pluck slips himself out, suddenly, the tarp somehow goes up in the air. The postal inspectors feel the pouring rain as they see a harpy pulling the tarp, soaring so high that the ropes attached to the pegs come off the ground.

Despite the pain in his left knee, Secoli pushes himself up and carries Pluck with his partner's arm over his shoulder. He also grabs his birdcage and starts limping back to safety. Chap is chirping so loudly over this rude awakening and getting wet, while Pluck feels dizzy and nauseous being carried to the men. Everyone then runs toward the postal inspectors and circles around them for protection. It was good planning for Secoli to teach everyone in this expedition this tactic before they left Point Postal.

Even being surrounded by all the men, Secoli has his hands full by still having his shirtless partner over his shoulder and holding Chap in his birdcage. Despite being in an uncomfortable predicament, he's doing his all to protect both of them. While all the men keep their eyes up in the dark and rainy sky,

Secoli catches a glimpse of Julian Cunningham and Angus McKinsey still looking for the crossbow.

"Forget the crossbow!" Secoli shouts. "Get over here now!"

McKinsey is the only one who hears the postal inspector's command from the loud raindrops and runs toward him. There's no telling if Cunning is ignoring Secoli's command or if it's too loud outside for him to hear. He continues looking for the crossbow as his rival runs to the group like his life depended on it. McKinsey immediately stops when he hears Secoli shouting but has trouble comprehending what he's trying to tell him while all the men call for him all at once.

"What?" Angus shouts for clarity.

Wood shouts at the top of his lungs, "You left Julian behind, goddamn it!"

McKinsey hears that loud and clear. He turns around and sees his rival still next to the stone, searching for the missing crossbow. Considering how hard it is for him to hear from all the loud raindrops hitting the rocky ground, especially since Cunningham is on his knees where the splashing is loud, McKinsey doesn't bother calling for his partner. He makes the impulsive decision to run back to Cunningham and try to pull him to the group instead.

McKinsey runs back as fast as he can, ignoring Secoli, who's shouting, "Come back! It's not worth it!"

Just as he reaches to Cunningham, gunfire is heard from behind. His immediate reaction is to fall to the ground, lie on his stomach, and put his hands over the back of his head for cover. In the midst of dropping to the ground, he then feels something grab his boot by the ankle. In a split second, he thinks it's Secoli grabbing him by the foot to pull him to safety. However, he can feel something sharp poking his boots, lifting him upside down.

At that moment, McKinsey finds himself being caught by one of the harpies as his lower body is being ascended. The young man finds himself hanging upside down as his hands are out of reach from the rocky terrain where he stands. McKinsey screams for help, and the men use all their ammunition to make the harpy let go. The fiend ignores the bullets hitting its body and holds on to its prey tightly, soaring higher into the wet air. The harpy has the poor kid above one of the tents and flies in place as the shooting stops.

McKinsey hears one of the men below shouting, "Reload!" which explains why the shooting stopped.

Suddenly, he feels something grab his other ankle. When McKinsey looks up, he sees a second harpy has his other leg. Then, the two harpies start pulling the young man's legs in opposite directions. It is as though they're playing tug-of-war with his body. This truly feels like the end for him. Never before has he ever felt this much pain, feeling his crotch and inner thighs being pulled apart from each other.

All McKinsey can do is scream wildly, feeling the muscles that connect his upper legs to his lower body being detached. This torturous method of dismemberment is producing the most severe pain the young man has ever felt. While the men do everything they can to inflict bullets from below, the harpies add more pressure to their pull by flying in opposite directions and flapping their wings faster. As the harpies indulge in their worst impulses, McKinsey can feel that his body will split in half at any moment. It is so painful for the poor kid that he can no longer scream or breathe.

Just as the harpies are about to have their way with their latest victim, an arrow flies through the heavy rain and hits one of the harpies in the sternum. It lets go of McKinsey's right foot, having the other harpy fly in the opposite direction, thinking it succeeded in splitting its prey in half. When the other harpy releases the other ankle, it sees its comrade falling with McKinsey, with his limbs still attached. With its eagle-like eyes, the flying harpy sees the member of its flock has a steel arrow through its chest.

McKinsey makes a hard landing on top of a tent, and the fallen harpy lands headfirst on the ground. With quick reflexes, the harpy sees another arrow coming after it and dodges the steel reed by mere inches. Knowing exactly what is firing at him, the harpy flees back into the darkness and is heard screaming farther away. All the men come to McKinsey's rescue, moving the parts of the tent away to carry the young man out. The rescuers then bring him to the circular formation, still aiming their guns at the dark sky and ready to shoot the harpy on sight.

"Angus," the sheriff says, checking on him, "are you all right?"

The lack of response tells Wood that McKinsey is unconscious. Since it's too dark and wet to check for his injuries, the lawman pulls the kid by the shoulders and brings him to his tent, where there's still light from the lantern. Secoli takes his sick partner and his noisy budgerigar in the same tent, which is wider than the one he was in. He places Pluck on the opposite side of Angus in the tent.

"I'm freezing, Louie," Pluck says, chattering his teeth as he shivers. "Don't worry, Jed," Secoli replies, putting his birdcage down to help his partner get in one of the sleeping bags. "I'll get you warmed up."

"Th-thanks, partner." He gets tucked, still shivering.

Hearing his partner's gratitude makes Secoli smirk. He covers Pluck's chest with the sleeping bag to hide his condition. When his partner closes his eyes, Secoli turns to Sheriff Wood, who removes McKinsey's pants. He looks over the lawman's shoulder and sees that the kid has blue marks on his inner thighs and knees. The sheriff removes both of McKinsey's boots and sees blood around his ankles.

"Poor kid," Secoli comments. "Those harpies did such a great number on him that his inner thighs turned blue."

"If we had Miss Godfrey with us, tell us how we can treat his legs," Wood replies. "The harpies pierced through his ankles, but the blue marks—I can only imagine if they're strains or some sort of torn muscle. Whoever shot that arrow saved Angus's life."

"Speaking of which, I must see if that harpy is dead."

Before Secoli leaves the tent, he checks to see Chap in his birdcage. The budgerigar isn't happy about being soaked. While on the swing, it uses its beak to suck the wetness from its feathers and continuously shakes its body to dry itself. Despite the bird having a miserable time, Secoli is happy that his muse is safe from harm. The last thing he sees in the birdcage is the bottom of the cage, and underneath the wire grille is a huge chunk of rainwater.

Secoli leaves Chap next to Pluck, exits the tent, and limps to the fallen harpy. A couple of men are looking at the beast on the ground, the rainfall washing its blood away. While David Graft brings in a lit lantern, everyone can see the harpy lying on its back with the end of the arrow sticking out of its chest. The postal inspector places his fingers on the harpy's neck and doesn't feel a pulse.

The postal inspector takes out his handkerchief and wraps his hand with it to avoid cutting himself with the razor-sharp arrow at its end. With all his might, he pulls the arrow out of the harpy's chest, and a huge amount of blood gushes out as soon as he removes it. He almost falls down from pulling so forcefully. Secoli looks at the steel arrow and sees that it's not damaged at all. Secoli turns around and sees Cunningham stepping into the light and reveals himself carrying the harpy hunter's crossbow. He chortles with glee at how powerful he feels after defeating the harpy.

"You did an excellent job, son." Secoli laughs loudly with joy and pats Cunningham on the shoulder. "After all the bullets we gave this damn thing, it only took one of these bad boys to finally kill it. Since you made the perfect shot, I'm assigning you as the expedition's crossbowman."

Cunningham smiles over the overwhelming compliment and replies, "Thanks, Inspector. I'll do my best not to disappoint you. I'm glad to save Angus' life."

"Speaking of Angus..." Secoli changes his mood. "There's something I want to discuss with you."

"Really?" Cunningham replies, put off by this sudden change of tone. "At a time like this?"

"If I'm going to trust you with all our lives, you need to hear this from me."

CHAPTER 14

The morning is just as grim, and rain is pouring down harder than ever. Who knows when the state of Wyoming last had a morning as dark and moist as today? The men are not accustomed to dawn without sunshine or feeling this cold. In addition to the harpy attack last night, all this contributed to the exhaustion everyone is experiencing on this expedition. Despite how grim the morning feels, at least everyone on this expedition can see the desert from the top of the alluvial fan.

Inspector Secoli is still using the harpy hunter's scentascope to find the trail of the harpy from last night. Though the scent is still present when using the smelling device, the postal inspector is confused about where the actual trail is. The harpies circled the camp last night, making their trail feel like it was going in circles. Not to mention that the morning rain is making the scent trail disappear. The only time their scent is strong is when Secoli has the scentascope pointing in the direction of the dead harpy still lying on the ground. Secoli removes the device from his nose when he sees the sheriff approaching and says, "Howdy, Sheriff. Is Angus McKinsey awake yet?"

"He is." Wood sounds distressed but calm. "But I'm afraid I got some bad news. Angus can't walk."

"What do you mean? Are his legs hurting really bad?"

"He can't feel his legs, nor can he move them. The harpies hurt him so badly that he may be permanently paralyzed."

"How is that even possible? Those monsters couldn't have pulled his legs so hard that his muscles snapped, could they?"

"It's either that or he landed too hard onto one of those tents. Either way, his legs are bluer and darker than before."

"Damn it," Secoli swears frustratingly. "How's the poor kid taking it?"

"He's taking it hard. He's depressed about what happened to him."

"We've only got ten men left in this hunt."

"Angus isn't the only one who's down, sir." Secoli swallows his saliva, guessing where the sheriff is taking this conversation. "It's Inspector Pluck."

"It's those blue spots on his chest, isn't it?"

"Not just his chest, sir. It's on his shoulders and on his armpits as well."

"What?" Secoli reacts, eyes wide. "Oh, no. It's spreading."

"How long have you known about this, Inspector?"

"Butch," Secoli looks at him in the eyes, sounding serious as ever, "this is just between you and me, okay? We're after the harpies because of the possibility that Dr. Fletcher is laying eggs and repopulating the harpy race. He had sex with Dr. Fletcher before we all knew she was a harpy. We don't know if she's pregnant or laying eggs like birds do, but if what Miss Klouví says is true, then he's responsible for giving the harpies a chance to repopulate."

"My God." The sheriff feels vomit coming out from the breakfast he ate earlier and has to swallow back in. "This explains why Miss Klouví asked Pluck that inappropriate question. Is that why he's so ill?"

"I honestly can't think of any other reason he has those blue spots. I mean, I have never seen spots as unusually blue as his. Have you?"

"This is my first time seeing it as well. What do you suggest we should do, Inspector? If we continue to bring Inspector Pluck and Angus McKinsey on this expedition, they'll surely slow us down."

"Or worse, get us killed. We have no choice but to have them both go back to town. It'll be nine of us who'll have to go after the harpies and end them."

"That's too dangerous, Inspector. Who will help Inspector Pluck and Angus McKinsey if either one falls off their horses? I suggest that we leave them somewhere safe and hidden until we get back."

ONCE BREAKFAST IS FINISHED, the men pack up and prepare to move ahead. Pluck is being carried by his partner and Deputy Hall, helping him get on the wagon. Since McKinsey can no longer move or feel his legs, he's being carried by Caleb Walsh and his rival. It comes off as unusual for Angus to see Julian being approachable and nice to him since waking up. Once they both get on the same wagon that Pluck's riding on, the expedition moves onward with the sheriff leading the way to the rocky path.

McKinsey raises a brow with suspicion as Cunningham sits beside him and asks, "Hey, Julian. Can I point out something?"

"Ask away," he replies with a genuine smile.

McKinsey continues, "Why are you being so nice to me all of a sudden? You handed me breakfast, and you helped me get on this wagon. Is something going on?"

Cunningham stops smiling and leans closer to him. "I spoke with Inspector Secoli last night when you were out cold. He told me everything he knows about what's happened between you, me, Mr. Kennedy, and Malorie.

"I want to apologize for how I treated Melanie—and to you especially. She deserved a good man like you. If only I wasn't so pig-headed and accepted that she wanted you instead of me, I would have respected her wishes. I blame myself for what happened to her."

"Julian..." McKinsey makes straight eye contact with him. "What happened to her and her father isn't your fault. You know exactly who took them away."

"Yes. You're right. If I don't come back, I want to let you know there are no more hard feelings between you and me."

"I hope you're not just saying that because I'm now crippled, are you?"

"I do mean it. Life is too short to be holding grudges. I never intend to be antagonistic, and I can't go on with life like this. So what do you say? Truce?"

"You know, Julian, I didn't believe them when they told me you found the crossbow and saved my life." McKinsey smiles. "Now I see a side of you I've never seen before. We both miss Malorie, and I'm sorry you got dragged into that complicated relationship. I also want to apologize for taking your girl."

"No. No. She was yours first. I only saw her as part of Mr. Kennedy's inheritance instead of a human being."

"Gee. What did you and Inspector Secoli talk about last night?"

"A lot of things…" Cunningham looks away to hide his watery eyes. "Like a lot that I can't explain so easily."

"It's a truce then," says McKinsey, making Cunningham look back. "No more hard feelings."

McKinsey offers a handshake to him. Cunningham sees what he's doing and immediately shakes his hand. The transition from enemies to mutual allies is something they never thought would ever happen. The feeling of ending this much animosity toward each other is more overwhelming than they could ever imagine.

"I see you two finally getting along," Secoli interrupts, riding his horse alongside the wagon they're on. "How are you feeling, Angus?"

Cunningham moves to a different seat as McKinsey's attention is now on the postal inspector. He doesn't want others to know that he made peace with his former rival despite it already being witnessed. Showing weakness to others is one thing that hasn't changed about him.

"I'm fine, Inspector," McKinsey replies. "All things considered. So what's the plan? I can't be fighting without my legs working, can I?"

"No, you can't." Secoli looks at his partner, who's crossing his arms and shivering. "And neither is Inspector Pluck."

"Then why are we still tagging along?"

"We're looking for a safe place to hide you and my partner while we continue the search. Since he's too ill to ride a horse and you—you know. I can't let both of you go back to town alone."

"I feel awful about that, sir. I wish I didn't get hurt last night,"

Seeing how the young man feels, Secoli tries to cheer him up by saying, "Well, don't think about your condition as a hindrance. You're still useful to us."

"Like how? I can't even feel or move my legs."

"While the rest of us go out on this dangerous mission, you can still protect my partner," Secoli hands McKinsey his birdcage wrapped in a cloth, "and this little guy. You'll be doing your country a great service if you protect both of them."

"Thanks, Inspector. I'll protect them at all times. But I—and the rest of the town—have always wondered why you carry this bird around."

"I'll tell you when I get back." Secoli whips his horse's reins and speeds ahead to the sheriff up front.

McKinsey peeks under the cloth to see Chap in his birdcage. After the adrenaline from last night's attack, the budgerigar is asleep right now. He can't help admiring how adorable it looks now that he finally sees Secoli's muse up close. Some raindrops are splashing at the tireless bird, waking Chap up. McKinsey then covers the birdcage with his sleeping bag, keeping him from getting any wetter.

McKinsey looks at the person who is under his protection. Inspector Pluck doesn't look too good. It's hard to see someone as strong-willed, fearless, and determined and look so vulnerable. It doesn't feel right for him to protect the one who's been protecting, planning, and leading him and his peers. Even so, McKinsey realizes the ill postal inspector is just as human as everyone else, no matter his status or occupation.

Then he looks at his former rival, now turned ally, sitting next to Inspector Pluck.

Cunningham struggles to get comfortable in the drizzle, having a sleeping bag over his head. Though he appears to have fallen asleep, he's tearing up underneath the covers. Despite portraying himself as a tough guy, he doesn't want to show anyone how much of a softy he really is. The truce Cunningham made with McKinsey has taken a lot of weight off their shoulders. Despite how good it feels to stop the feud, being unable to fight alongside his former rival in this expedition adds to McKinsey's guilt.

McKinsey then stops ruminating as soon as the wagon stops. He looks around and sees a small cave next to the cliff. From where he's sitting, he can see that the cave is roughly four feet high, and he can see the end of the cave.

He hears Secoli tell the sheriff, "This is a good place, if any, to keep Jed and Angus from getting wet. What do you think, Sheriff?"

"Men. It's time to get up!" the sheriff shouts. "Help Inspector Pluck and Angus McKinsey to this cave and set up their sleeping bags."

Cunningham immediately takes the sleeping bag off his head and carries McKinsey with Secoli's birdcage out of the wagon. Since Pluck can walk on his own, he slowly follows the two into the cave. The other men grab sleeping bags and a spare rifle the men will need in the cave. McKinsey gets tucked in the bag while Pluck gets doubled up to help him stop shivering. The men move fast to settle the holdovers before Inspector Secoli speaks with them.

"This is the best we can do for both of you," Secoli says, getting down from his horse and examining the cave. "To the best of your ability, please take good care of Chap and Inspector Pluck."

"I'll do my best, sir."

"I know I'm asking you to do way more than you can handle, but please," Secoli looks at his partner lying next to him before whispering to McKinsey, "keep an eye on my partner. He's a lot sicker than he looks."

Hearing that from the postal inspector makes him realize he knows more than what he's telling him. Angus nods, understanding the task that's entrusted to him.

"If something bad happens, take this horse." Secoli steps out of the cave, pulls his horse's reins, and ties them to the cave's stalactite next to the cave's entrance. "And, Jed, get well soon, partner."

Secoli doesn't wait for his partner to respond, not that he's well enough to reply.

Secoli gets on another horse that tagged along with the group and moves forward. McKinsey sees everybody getting back onboard the wagons. He feels awful that he can't join them and wishes he could do more.

McKinsey no longer sees everyone leave as he remains in the cave. He hears the wagons' wheels rolling away, horses' hooves stomping and getting quieter, and raindrops landing on the rocky ground. When he only hears the raindrops, he's all alone with the ill postal inspector and budgerigar under his protection. It has become lonely for McKinsey since Pluck and Chap are both asleep. With nothing else to do, he picks up his carbine, watches the water pour in front of the cave entrance, and ruminates on how he could have avoided being crippled.

EVERYONE IN THIS PEREGRINATION continues moving forward tirelessly through the rain. There's nothing but a landslide on the left and a cliff on the right as they follow the downward rocky path. It seems like the path is leading the expedition away from the second plateau in the journey. Seeing they're heading back down to the wet desert is a relief for everyone, but there's still no trace of the harpies anywhere. As Secoli uses the scentascope, he finds the enemies' scent untraceable, leading the expedition to nowhere.

While everybody is happy to be back on the desert ground, Secoli's as frustrated as ever. He doesn't say a word as he leads the group and sniffs through the scentascope for any possible sign of the harpies' trail. Even with his wide field of vision, all he smells is wet sand and rocks, as he had since the rain began. After turning in all sorts of directions for the third time while his horse moves forward, he signals for everyone to stop moving.

"What is it, Inspector?" Sheriff Wood asks, pulling the reins to stop his horse.

Secoli heaves a big stressful sigh, then says, "No, Sheriff. I've been smelling the same thing for hours now. Do you know how tiring it is to focus on smelling the same thing this long? It's like finding a needle in a haystack but using your nose."

"If that's the case, you should let me use the scentascope, Inspector. Perhaps it's better if we switch roles once in a while."

"Do you even remember what the harpies smell like?"

"Do they smell anything like the feathers that you and Inspector Pluck have?"

"It's much more profound. This device is tricky because you have to focus on finding just an ounce of their scent in the distance. I've been smelling this thing for so long that, at times, I can't tell if I caught their scent or if it's my imagination."

Deputy Hall, on his horse, dashes up to the two ahead of the wagons and says, "Hey, everybody behind you two wants to know what's going on. Is there something wrong with the scenta-ma-jig?"

"No," his supervisor replies. "Inspector Secoli has been frustrated over trying to find the harpies' scent since yesterday. We think the rain indefinitely made the harpies' trail disappear."

"Then let me give it a shot," the deputy says. "I'm pretty good at spotting things. Maybe I'll have a pretty good sense of smell if I try it."

Inspector Secoli passes the scentascope to Deputy Hall while they're still on their saddles. The deputy immediately puts his nostrils on the holes and inhales deeply through the device for the second time since interrogating Klouví back in Point Postal. He's amazed when he's able to smell objects and other odors in the air using the device outside. Everything that's far from reach smells so close.

"Woah," Hall comments, removing his nose from the device. "This thing is more powerful than when I last used it."

"Just don't let yourself get carried away," Secoli replies. "We've got a job to do."

Deputy Hall nods and continues using the device. While smelling in all directions, Secoli whispers to Sheriff Wood, "He's impressed with this device now, but the novelty will wear off over time."

"All right, Hall," the sheriff says. "That's enough. We're still looking for—" Wood gets interrupted by Hall's immediate reaction when he faces the direction behind him. He says the Lord's name in vain and pulls his head back so fast that it scares the horse he's riding on. The deputy loses his balance with his horse and falls with his animal. He lands on his left side and has his left leg caught between the ground and his horse. As Secoli and Wood get off their horses to help the deputy, Hall manages to slide his leg out and back up before they can help him.

"You all right?" Secoli asks. "What happened?"

"I'm fine," Hall replies. "but I think I smelled some kind of shit in the distance."

"It might be animals that did their business back there," the sheriff comments. When the horse gets itself back up, Secoli walks over and picks up the scentascope. He points it toward the plateau where they were and where Hall pointed the device. He inhales and immediately pulls his head back. "Good Lord," Secoli said. "It's like some heinous bird poo."

"How do you know what that smells like, Inspector?" the sheriff asks. "If you've been on rooftops in many cities as long as I have, you won't forget how bad it smells. Plus, I clean out my birdcage every day, and it doesn't get any better. But this..." Secoli points in the same direction and sniffs some more. "... it's worse. Hold on," Secoli continues to smell through the scentascope in the same direction. Somehow, through the horrid smell, he then smells the harpies' scent. "Oh, my God. I..." He sniffs through the device some more. "I can smell harpies."

"You do?" the sheriff says.

"It's from the plateau we were just on! Why couldn't we smell it sooner?

Sheriff, hand me your binoculars."

Wood does what he's told, and the postal inspector looks through the ocular lenses. Secoli can see a lot of white stuff that looks like paint surrounding a cave in the middle of the plateau facing in his direction. When he adjusts the binoculars, it becomes clear that there are black feathers surrounding the mysterious white material.

"Sheriff," the postal inspector says, putting down the binoculars, "I think we found where the harpies have been hiding this whole time."

"Really?" he replies. "Let me see."

The sheriff then retrieves his binoculars, sees what Secoli's been seeing, and says, "Good God. You don't suppose that white stuff is actually harpy shit, do you?"

"If it is," the deputy replies, "then we'll have a more miserable time killing those damn monsters than we already have."

Still looking through the binoculars, Wood says, "But there's no path that leads up to that cave. How do you suppose we get up there?"

Secoli ponders momentarily and looks at the wagon. "Remember we had some ropes and pickaxes onboard one of the wagons?"

"Don't tell me." The sheriff puts down his binoculars and looks at Secoli. "We're going to climb up there. I've never rock climbed before. Have either of you?"

The postal inspector and the deputy shake their heads.

"Then I suppose we should ask the others on the wagon." He then raises his voice and approaches everyone still on the wagon. "Okay, so who here knows how to rock climb?"

Only one hand slowly rises up from the wagon farther back. When the authorities walk around to see who it is, they see Logan Smith raising his hand at the back. Secoli approaches the middle-aged man, doubting that he has any experience in rock climbing.

"Mr. Smith," Secoli says. "Do you really have experience climbing high terrains?"

"I do, sir," he replies. "I was a miner long ago when I first moved to Wyoming."

"How many years has it been since you last climbed something as high as that?" Secoli points to the plateau.

"It was almost a decade ago when I had to go up to a plateau just like that one. Nowadays, I sell mining supplies in the hardware store where I work."

"Have you had to climb on top and drop down a rope without you or anyone ever falling off?"

"I never fell off, sir, nor has any ever dropped on my watch either."

The sheriff says, "I can't risk letting this man and our lives get up there. It's been long since he climbed that high. Plus, it's wet, and he might slip and fall. Does anyone else know how to climb high terrains?"

No one raises their hand. They all remain sitting in their wagons and stare at the lawman and the postal inspector.

"Damn it," the sheriff swears. "Fine. But if anything happens to this man, don't say that I didn't warn you, Inspector."

THE EXPEDITION IS RIGHT beneath the cave that towers over them, reaching at least six stories high. Now that the rain has finally stopped, the smell of the white oversized bird feces becomes more apparent and fetid. It's almost as if the rain didn't do much to wash away the putrid smell or the defecation. All the ropes, nine meters' worth, are tightly tied together and wrapped around Smith's waist and his right shoulder. It's tough for them to tie all those ropes together when they're so close to the excrement, but it will be harder for Logan Smith to climb up to the cave with all that white feces in the way.

"I sure hope these tied ropes are long enough to reach the bottom, Inspector," Smith says, stretching his muscles.

"Okay." The postal inspector sighs. "Good luck. All of us will watch over you and will try to catch you. Whatever you do, please don't look down until you get to the top."

Smith nods to Inspector Secoli and begins climbing. There are a lot of ledges within arm's length for the middle-aged man to grab hold of and step on. Now that it stopped raining, the ledges on the plateau are much more slippery than expected. Smith slowly takes his time to get himself up. He places his hands on the first ledge he can reach, then puts his legs up.

Everyone is impressed with how flexible Smith is for his age. Some start cheering for the old man to continue his way up.

"You got this, Logan," says Graft, standing behind him. "You got this."

"You can do it!" Walsh cheers loudly.

"Can y'all shut up?" Smith says, heaving himself up on the ledge. "I can't concentrate when you're making all that racket."

"Everyone," Secoli whispers loudly, "keep your voices down. We're in the enemy's territory. The last thing we want is for them to know we're trespassing."

Everyone watches in silence as Smith climbs sideways to the next ledge. Logan Smith is extremely careful over which ledge his hands and feet should use to support him as he climbs higher, but mostly he goes sideways. He focuses on keeping his right hand and left foot in place as his left hand and right foot move to different ledges. When Smith has to do the same for the other limbs, he repeats the process and vice versa, feeling some sort of diagonal line through his center of gravity. Upon every ledge, he pulls himself higher; Smith constantly analyzes for the closest ledge above him to hold on to, then uses his feet to slowly pull himself up.

Smith climbs higher, zigzagging carefully to choose the driest ledge to heave himself onto, though his options are limited. The experienced rock climber is halfway up the cave, and he maintains a steady pace despite losing count of how many times he stops to make sure he is holding on to the correct ledge to continue his ascent. From everybody's point of view below, Smith appears to be confident, yet none of them know exactly how anxious he is. Smith is feeling exhausted, making it this far to the top, and his body is starting to get fatigued from moving as much as he did when he was a decade younger. Despite the cool and moist atmosphere, he's sweating profusely over his anxiety and surpassing his physical limitations. So far, Smith has proven his usefulness to the sheriff and to every whippersnapper below him despite becoming fatigued.

It doesn't help that he's trying his best not to touch what is assumed to be the harpies' feces. He struggles to breathe and keep up, the stench overwhelming. It's difficult for him not to cover his nose as he clung to the ledges, so close to the harpies' excrement splattered on the cliff face. To not let that get to him, he continues to breathe through his mouth and ignores how foul the white material is. Smith looks up and sees himself only an arm's reach from touching the last ledge that leads to the cave.

Now that he starts moving in a hurry, he pushes his legs up to reach that last ledge, but as soon as he grabs onto it, both feet slip. Smith finds himself holding on to the ledge for dear life, unable to find a spot for his feet to support him. Everybody below can see Smith in trouble, anticipating the rock climber to fall at any moment. Smith is already having second thoughts about his decision to put himself at risk.

Then he remembers being in this situation a long time ago when a familiar voice in his head told him to "Swing your body left and right till your feet touch the ledge." The memory of an old mining comrade instructing him to do just that makes him swing his legs left and right. The more he swings his feet, side to side, the higher his feet get, but his fingers are giving out. Just when he thinks he is going to fall, his left foot finds purchase on the ledge above him. With all his might, he puts a much of weight on his left foot to heave himself up to the cave.

Logan Smith, exhausted, rolls over onto his back by the cave's cliff to catch his breath and cool down from the exertions he has put himself through. Smith is impressed with himself for still being able to rock climb since retiring as a miner a decade ago. Logan Smith groans as he struggles to his feet, his abdomen aching and his whole body feeling weak. Instead of getting up normally, he rolls onto his stomach and uses his hands and knees to push himself off the ground. He looks for a stalactite to tie the rope that he's been carrying and sees a plethora of them on the ceiling and ground.

Despite how malodorous the whole cave is, Smith can finally cover his nose as he decides which stalactite is thick and durable enough to keep the ropes steady. There are so many of them inside the cave that he becomes indecisive. After a while, he then picks one that's the thickest one that's closest to the cave's entrance.

Smith unties the rope from his waist and wraps it twice around the stalactite, tying it tightly. As much as he can, Smith does his best not to let his fatigue bother him and try not to make any noise that could echo throughout the cave. As soon as he makes a firm knot to the best of his ability, he goes to the cave's entrance and drops the rest of the rope to his companions below. Thankfully, the tied-together ropes reach the bottom.

"Good God," the sheriff mutters. "The son of a bitch did it."

"Okay," Inspector Secoli says. "So, who will be the first to climb this rope?"

The group falls silent, none of them eager to volunteer to go first. Judging by the height of the climb, no one in the hunting party is confident enough to take the lead.

Secoli gets agitated waiting for any of them to volunteer.

"Okay," Secoli continues, "so here's the plan. Let's get the end of this rope and tie it around the waist and legs. Julian, stand next to me."

Cunningham does as the postal inspector says, having the rope wrap around his waist, then his thighs. Secoli makes a thick knot to secure the crossbowman.

"Okay," Secoli continues. "Since I'm the only one who knows how to climb a rope, I'll meet Mr. Smith up there to help me pull whoever is attached to the rope up to the cave. Whatever you do, don't make any sudden movements when you're being pulled up. Secondly, don't adjust the ropes when we drop them for the next person. Finally, once you put on the rope around your waist and thighs, pull it twice to signal that you are ready to be pulled up. Understood?"

All of them give the postal inspector a nod before he starts climbing the rope. He leaps high to catch the ropes, then pulls himself up and draws his knees to his chest. In the moments before he crashes into the steep landslide, Secoli grabs hold of the ledges with his heels while pulling upward. As he climbs the rope, he has no belay tools around his waist to keep him safe from falling. He does so well, however, that he reaches the top and gets inside the cave much faster than Logan Smith did. All of them are impressed with how well he gets himself up to the cave there with no issues.

When Secoli enters the cave, he sees Logan Smith collapsed on the ground and panting like he ran for miles. Secoli isn't half as tired as the retired miner, but he doesn't want to waste any time ending these harpies, who may or may not be in this cave. So the postal inspector goes up to Smith and helps him up.

"Great job, Mr. Smith," Secoli whispers, lifting Smith up from the ground. "None of the guys downstairs knows how to climb. Help me pull the next person up."

"You mean we're going to pull up all of them here?" Smith groans in pain. "Not all of them. Just this one person, and then you can rest as much as you like."

Secoli shakes the rope to signal to Cunningham and waits momentarily to feel the rope shake or pull back twice to signal that he's ready. Once it's been felt, Secoli and Smith pull the rope and help Cunningham up. This becomes much harder than the postal inspector predicted, considering Julian is large. It also doesn't help that nobody knows that Smith is almost completely fatigued, making Secoli do most of the pulling.

Cunningham makes it up to the cave and removes the ropes wrapped around his waist and thighs as soon as he gets up. As soon as he puts the crossbow and quiver on the ground, he drops the ropes off the cave's cliff so the next person can be pulled up.

Smith collapses to the ground again, feeling like all of his muscles will explode if he pushes himself further. Cunningham leaves Smith alone as he lies on the ground and holds on to the rope with Secoli to start pulling when they feel a tug from below.

It takes a while for both of them to feel the signal from the rope before they begin pulling. With Cunningham and Secoli now pulling the rope together, they're able to pull it faster and more easily. A moment later, they see the next person being pulled up, and Deputy Hall emerges. He wastes no time removing the ropes wrapped around him, dropping the ropes down for the next person and helping Secoli and Cunningham to pull up the next person. With more people helping in the cave, it becomes easier and faster to pull the expedition to the harpy's lair.

All the men are armed in the cave, ready to take all the harpies in their territory. Cunningham has the harpy hunter's crossbow ready and plenty of those steel arrows with harpy feathers at the end to slay each of those harpies. If he's still as good of a shot as he was last night, the harpies won't stand a chance. As they bypass the stalactites and stalagmites, the men surround the crossbowman like he's the most important person in this expedition. Considering that he's wielding the only weapon known to kill a harpy, who wouldn't?

While it gets darker as the men get farther away from the cave's entrance, they hear the rain coming from outside, echoing throughout the cave. It doesn't help that the strong stench remains consistent no matter where they go in the cave. Thankfully, Chuck Madison comes prepared by bringing a lantern that helps them see in the darkness. Bringing a lamp, however, becomes pointless when the men see a light coming from the end of the cave ahead. Everyone heads over to what looks to be a doorway with a curtain covering the entrance.

Before entering, everyone leans against the walls and faces the entrance. Secoli is the first to peek through the curtain and sees this cave section, surprising and disturbing the expedition's leader. There are ignited wooden torches standing in this room's corners that look like long tiki torches. A large haystack in the center of the room that has nothing on top of it. The postal inspector is fascinated by the Greek pattern that runs along the edges of every surface of the walls and floors.

However, the fascination is short-lived when Inspector Secoli sees bones scattered on the floor. It becomes apparent that these are human bones judging by the human skulls lying in many of the piles. Farther away, against the wall, are corpses piled on top of each other. All those piled bodies have their hands and feet removed. It doesn't take long for Secoli to find that all the hands and feet are nailed across the room underneath the Greek pattern on the wall, like some kind of ritual slaughter.

Along with the bones are a pile of feathers, blood splatters, and stains across the room's surfaces. There are also chains on the walls that make this whole room look like a torture dungeon. Considering how many bloodstains are across the room, it's evident that the harpies use this room to indulge in their worst impulses toward their captured victims. The stench of the harpies combined with the feces and carcasses of their victims makes Inspector Secoli's stomach turn. Even enduring America's most violent war and solving very disturbing cases is nothing compared to seeing the remains in this room.

Everyone waits for Inspector Secoli to devise a plan until footsteps are heard from the same room. The sheriff then peeks with Secoli, and they see naked human beings walking through the door on the other side of the room. They look male based on how flat their chests are, and both possess typically masculine figures. What is even more bizarre, however, is that these naked men have no penises, no scrotums, and no genitals between their legs, exactly how Zephyra Klouví described.

Recalling that Dr. Fletcher transformed from human to harpy that night, Secoli immediately assumes that these humans are male harpies in human form. Two of them are speaking in a language he is unfamiliar with, their thick Mediterranean accents similar to the harpy hunter's, but with masculine voices. Secoli sees scars and other marks that appear to be minor dark marks that should have taken years to heal. But how did they heal so fast since those injuries most likely were inflicted two nights ago?

When the suspects walk around the pile of hay in the center, Inspector Secoli gets a look at their feet and calves and sees they are smaller-size talons. Their feet resemble those of an ornithologist with their protruding claws and birdlike feet, indicating that they are indeed harpies. He looks at all the men behind Sheriff Wood and the rest standing behind him.

Secoli pulls Cunningham, the closest to him, and whispers into his ear, "Harpies are approaching. Get in position and get ready to kill them with your crossbow."

With no hesitation, the crossbowman immediately runs past the curtain. Secoli is too late to pull the young man back in after seeing him act impulsively. Julian, now standing before the two harpies, takes aim with his crossbow at one of the fiends and lets loose a steel arrow tipped with harpy feathers. The arrow bolts, but something much faster, ascending from the ground, gets in the way. It happens so fast that the arrow is hit and flies off course from hitting one of the harpies. In a flash, it becomes apparent that a rope connected to the ceiling snagged the arrow, and Cunningham's hoisted into the air and caught in a net.

Nobody would have guessed that the harpies are smart enough to lay traps, and now the crossbow is trapped with the crossbowman. As Inspector Secoli and Sheriff Wood spring into action to free Cunningham, all the men barge into the room and aim their rifles at the two harpies. Before a trigger pulls, the harpies elongate their pinky fingers, grow feathers, bulk their talons, and sharpen their teeth. As soon as guns start blazing, the fiends have enough time to shield their heads and bodies with their wings. None of their bullets manage to go through their razor-sharp feathers. Both harpies wait for all the intruders to stop shooting since there isn't enough space in the room to fly or maneuver their attacks.

Cunningham is panicking and struggling to free himself, making it difficult for the sheriff to cut the net with his knife without hurting the crossbowman.

"Damn it, Julian," Wood swears, holding on to the net, which is moving back and forth. "Quit squirming so I can free you."

Secoli looks at the net Cunningham is in to see why the sheriff is taking so long to free the crossbowman. The postal inspector is petrified to see the lawman is drooling blood and has his abdomen sliced by a large crimson wing. The one who struck the sheriff is standing right behind him as his body is sliced in half. Secoli is terror-stricken as he sees Butch Wood in his own pool of blood with his guts and spine exposed and detached from his lower body. Secoli then startles over a gush of blood landing on his face and hears Cunningham's scream.

When he looks up, Secoli sees the harpy with the crimson feathers continuously and mercilessly stabbing the crossbowman with her claws on her fingers. Cunningham screams in pain as blood gushes out of the net as the slashing and clawing continue.

Secoli gets temporarily blinded when the blood hits him in his eyes and glasses. As Secoli wipes his eyes and cleans his glasses, the harpy cuts the net with her razor-sharp wing, sending the mutilated Cunningham to the ground. The crossbowman is so badly mangled that he can't roll onto his stomach, so he crawls on his back as fast as he can to retrieve the harpy hunter's crossbow.

Just as he could grab the only weapon that could kill the harpies, a talon breaks the crossbow into pieces with a single stomp. Just as Cunningham looks up to see who destroyed the weapon, the same talon stomps on his face, and his eyes are gouged by its sharp claws. The crimson harpy's claws are the last things Cunningham ever sees.

The blinded Julian holds on to his pierced eyelids and cries loudly. Now that he has lost his ability to see, all he can do is roll and squirm uncontrollably over how insufferable it truly is being the harpy's victim.

Secoli quickly wipes his glasses, but he sees a red tint from the smears on the lenses. As soon as he can see again and draws his pistol, he sees it's far too late to save Cunningham. The crimson-feathered harpy puts an end to him by stomping and piercing the young man's sternum with her talons. As Cunningham no longer screams and becomes motionless, the harpy sticks her head up to reveal it's the ornithologist in her harpy form.

"Fiona...," the postal inspector mutters in sheer terror.

As soon as he points his gun at her, Secoli notices the guns have all stopped firing, and an ominous silence fills the room. The postal inspector then looks around and sees the other two harpies have finished massacring all the men with him. Seeing the dismembered and dead Deputy Hall and Moses Williams lying beside his feet makes him tremble. When he sees the people with whom he formed connections turned into corpses and dismembered body parts, it is perhaps even more horrific than what he endured during the war. Never before has Secoli wanted so badly to have a hallucination of his time in the Civil War to escape this hellscape he's in.

Secoli still has his handgun pointed at Dr. Fletcher but is having difficulty keeping his aim steady at his target. As the other two harpies get ready to make the postal inspector their next victim, Fletcher raises her hand at them and fluently speaks to them in their native language. They all stop in their tracks despite Secoli pointing the gun at her. Even knowing none of his bullets can kill her or pierce through her wings, which she shields herself with, this is his last resort before ending up like the rest, who are lying dead all over the room. Secoli fires all the bullets in his handgun with freight, but the female harpy deflects all the bullets with her wing. The female harpy then immediately runs up to him and knuckles Secoli in the gut with a closed talon. That kick to the gut hits Inspector Secoli so hard that he flies up from the ground and hits his back against the wall. He spits blood from his internal injuries while he's on his knees and holding his stomach. Secoli is in complete panic and cornered by the three harpies approaching.

"Why, Fiona?" Secoli quivers, kneeling before her. "I thought we were friends. We protected you. We respect you. We adored you. Why did you have to kill them all after all we did for you?"

"It took you a while to get here," she replies in a calm yet menacing tone. "I'm grateful for the hospitality—or lack thereof when I was living among you. Even despite how you deserve to die for killing two of my own, I'm allowing you to live for treating Chap so well. Also, please stop referring to me by that name, Louie. Dr. Fiona Fletcher is the name I took from one of my victims."

"You mean..." Secoli struggles to speak, still hurting from the kick to the stomach. "Correct. My real name is Margohot. And I am the queen of the harpies. The real Fiona Fletcher is dead."

Margohot speaks in the harpies' native language, and her lackeys then grab Secoli by the arms, bringing him to his feet. He tries to free himself, but each time he makes sudden movements, the postal inspector gets poked by their sharp feathers. He realizes how strong the male harpies are as they barely budge when he tries to free himself from their grasp. The flock members lock Secoli's wrists in the dungeon shackles attached high to the wall and his ankles to a chain ball. Secoli hangs uncomfortably against the wall, still hurting from his internal injuries.

"It's not like you to come all this way without bringing Chap with you, Louie," Margohot says in her real accent. "Boy, do they grow up so fast."

"What do you want, Fiona?" Secoli asks.

It angers the queen of the flock to be referred to by her fake name, so she slashes her captive's shins with her talons. The cut runs so deep that both of Secoli's tibias are chipped from the slash and have a gash that's exposing the laceration. Since both his calves are now broken, the experience is far more excruciating than the hard kick to the stomach. Secoli screams over how unbearably painful his lower legs are feeling now.

Margohot waits patiently for Secoli to stop his agonizing screams before saying, "If you don't refer to me by my real name, you'll lose both legs and have them nailed onto our wall with our collection. Is that understood?"

Secoli takes his time breathing heavily from the pain before replying, "Okay, Ma--Margohot.... What is it you want?"

"Has the harpy hunter not told you? And speaking of which, where is that little bitch? I thought you would have brought someone as experienced as her with you to kill me and the rest of my family." Secoli remains silent but is unable to hide the truth as she looks into her eyes. "Oh, my. You really are that stupid." She laughs. "And here I was, taking you seriously like you're highly intelligent."

"Quit laughing at me!" the prisoner cries loudly. "Tell me what you want. Why are you harpies massacring all of us?"

"Aw, don't you look so different, looking so helpless after acting so tough and mighty when you led the town?" Margohot says mockingly. "You're in the position to have only one question answered. What I really want is to know where Jed is."

Despite how red his eyes are from tearing up so much over his pain, Secoli refuses to say anything. Even being frightened by the face of humanity's most infamous threat, he won't dare give his partner's position away. His sick partner cannot make a run for it if he's found. With little time left, Secoli swiftly thinks of what to say to the queen of the harpies to divert them from finding Jed.

"Jed?" Secoli answers. "You're too late. The townswomen took him east to send him back home."

"Please..." Margohot rolls her eyes. "You're nowhere half as good of a liar as I am.

I had all of you fooled until that damn harpy hunter blew my cover. But don't worry, Louie. If I, or my flock members, have to torture you till you admit the truth, you'll be dead within minutes. That's how fragile human anatomy is. However, I have a much easier and faster method to make you confess the truth."

Margohot raises her right wing and pulls off a single feather with her left hand. The crimson feathers she randomly pulls are no different than those on her wing or anywhere else on her body. Knowing how sharp and dangerous harpy feathers are, Louie moves his head away and leans against the wall as she brings the feather closer to his face. She places her other hand over the tip of the feather, and with a single finger snap, a small flame ignites on the tip of the feather. Margohot then waves the feather back and forth to quickly put the fire out.

For some mysterious reason, the burned feather smells pleasant. She grabs the prisoner's chin and places the feather under his nose. Despite inhaling something pleasant, Secoli finds the aroma so strong that he loudly coughs.

"Now then," Margohot continues, letting go of Secoli's chin and throwing away the burnt feather. "Where is Jed Pluck?"

Suddenly, a strange sensation takes over Secoli and makes him say, "I left Jed with Chap and Angus McKinsey because he's so sick with blue spots growing on his body. Angus is unable to walk. And Chap is too precious to me, so I left all of them in a cave close to this plateau we're in."

When Secoli stops talking, he gains full control over his body. The prisoner is nonplussed over how he told the whole truth after sniffing her burnt feather. He drops his jaw and shakes his head over what he has done. How could inhaling the strange scent catch him under such a spell and do Margohot's bidding so easily? Secoli panics over this turn of events, realizing how powerful the queen of the harpies truly is.

"No!" Secoli shouts, shaking his head aggressively. "No! No! No! No! No! That isn't true. He's leaving Wyoming right now."

"A sudden change of story, Louie." The harpy queen giggles with delight. "I think the story of Inspector Pluck being nearby is far more believable. I want to thank you, Louie, for being a—"

Margohot's expression abruptly changes from one of amusement to one of pain.

She then gets down on one knee and holds on to her abdomen, shouting with agony. Two of her lackeys then run to her aid and hold onto her shoulders and wings. Secoli is confused about what's happening to the harpy queen. He looks around the room to see if someone has come to his rescue or if there's a possible survivor who struck her when she was vulnerable, but everyone is lying on the ground motionless.

One of the harpies assisting Margohot speaks to her in Greek, saying, "What's happening, Mother? Did that pathetic human do something to you?"

"No, my son!" Margohot shouts in Greek, catching her breath. "It's not him. The eggs…. It's time for me to ovulate!"

Secoli can't understand any of what the three are saying. He remains hanging and watches the harpies bring Margohot to the haystack. As soon as she gets on top of the pile of hay, the queen of the harpies squats and screams in pain. Though the noise she's making isn't ear-piercing as when the other harpies shrieked as an attack, it does alert the third black-feathered harpy, who's been absent until now, to rush into the room to witness this crucial moment for his species.

While Margohot has her back turned away from the prisoner, Secoli is witnessing firsthand what's happening. As the harpy queen screams in agony and remains scooching, something distinctively white and oval-shaped slowly emerges from beneath her crimson feathery groin. At first, the curious prisoner wonders if it's the white material seen earlier near the cave's entrance. As soon as it drops into the hay, and another just like it is coming out the same way, Secoli realizes she's laying eggs.

The eggs are roughly the size of a baby's head, covered in amniotic fluid, and are as white as any eggshell. The harpies watching their queen's ovulation see the eggs as a miracle for their race, but Secoli finds the eggs appalling. Prior to the third and last egg dropping, one of the harpies, fuming over Secoli's screams, punches the postal inspector in the face, knocking him unconscious.

All three of the male harpies give applause by slapping their sharp wings together to make a unique and loud clapping noise while making their peal calls. While the flock gives harpy-style applause to their queen, Margohot slowly walks down from her nest, exhausted from how painful this ovulation was. Two of them catch the queen as they see her lose her balance. They gently help her sit on the ground and give her space to breathe. One of them hands her Sheriff Wood's remains and helps her drink blood from his exposed intestines to quench her dehydration.

"Lord Zeus," Margohot says in Greek, wiping her mouth from drinking the sheriff's blood and tossing his upper body aside. "I've been laying eggs throughout my lifetime. And that one was one of the most difficult processes I have gone through. And here I was told that the more eggs I lay, the easier it gets."

"We're all proud of you, Mother," a male harpy says. "You've saved our race."

"We don't know if all of these will be daughters just yet, my sons," Margohot replies, still catching her breath and lying on the hay with her eggs. "We have to wait until they finally hatch. But before they do, the father must see the birth of his newborn children. Please, bring me the one who's named Jed Pluck. I need him to help me bring more harpy daughters into this world."

SINCE LYING INSIDE the small cave and getting the best rest possible since leaving Point Postal, he has kept waking up from repeated nightmares. Still, he regrets his decision to commit adultery with the supposed ornithologist. He keeps thinking about being punished for being unfaithful to his wife and family. Part of him even wonders if he enjoys working in the Postal Inspection Service just to avoid the responsibilities of being a father and faithful husband. He hates being stuck at home, but now he is as homesick as he is sick.

Thoughts of Dr. Fiona Fletcher continue to haunt him in his dreams. He notices that the more brief his sleep is, the more realistic his nightmares of her feel. The memory of seeing her turn into a harpy has affected him on such a spiritual level that he's grown paranoid. Since he is constantly being attacked by harpies in his dreams, Pluck keeps waking up abruptly, even when he's not dreaming. For the seventh time since being left in the cave, he startles McKinsey, who was lying next to him in his own sleeping bag.

"Are you all right, Inspector?" McKinsey asks. "This is the third time that you scared me."

"Sorry," Pluck replies, getting under the covers. "Just another nightmare."

"So the harpies are affecting your sleep as well?"

"You can say that. But I don't want to talk about that." Pluck then pops his head out from the covers. "By the way. Do you know what's the date today?"

"I do. It's August 17, 1899."

"Goddammit," Pluck mutters. "It's now been two days since Allie had her birthday." He sighs with distress. "Looks like I'm going to be doing a lot of explaining when I get back home."

"Who's Allie? And where are you from, if you don't mind me asking?"

"I'm from Boston. Allie is my second-youngest daughter. I was determined to finish solving the case by August 15th so that I could make it to her eighth birthday. Or was it her ninth birthday? Shit. I don't know anymore."

"Boston? That's a hell of a place to be coming."

Pluck laughs and says, "You're right. What's crazy about being a Federal agent is that you'll never know what the US Government will ask you to do. It's been my job to protect Americans within the boundaries of this country and police postal crimes across the United States."

"Out of curiosity. Why did you decide to be a postal inspector?"

"Well, it sure beats being a Pinkerton, that's for sure." Pluck expects McKinsey to laugh, but the joke flies over his head. "Anyway, since retiring from the Civil War, this was the best fit for me. Plus, I needed a job that didn't keep me stuck in offices or having a supervisor breathe down my neck. Who could have guessed that getting involved with mail fraud and other postal crimes would bring me here. If you're thinking of becoming one, the US Postal Inspection Service is very selective."

"Do you think I qualify for the job if I'm crippled?" McKinsey asks rhetorically.

"Sorry. I forgot. Forget what I just said."

"It's fine," McKinsey interrupts, looking away in disapproval.

The two men grow uncomfortably silent. Both Jed Pluck and Angus McKinsey are extroverted; however, they struggle to find anything in common. Since they both have been talking to each other, nothing between them progressed any further than McKinsey asking questions and following the postal inspector's orders. The only thing they both have in common is how they both trust and admire Inspector Secoli, as well as their hatred for harpies, but neither wants to discuss either of the topics. As soon as Pluck returns under his covers, McKinsey tries something else to engage their conversation.

As soon as he opens his mouth, McKinsey finds the sleeping back that he's dragging toward the cave's entrance. The first thing that comes to his mind is that the cave has a leak, and water is pushing him out of the cave. As soon as McKinsey places both elbows firmly on the ground to stop drifting, he doesn't slow down nor does he feel any water that would explain why he's being brought out of the cave. Then he looks at his feet and finds out what's dragging him out.

A giant talon has a grip on his feet. Since McKinsey can no longer feel his lower body, he isn't able to tell that the talons pierced him so deeply that he's seeing his own blood through the bottom of his sleeping bag. Knowing exactly who those talons belong to, he sees the harpy peeking its head in from the rain, dragging McKinsey closer to its cold stare. The rain is pouring so hard that the fiend is able to invade his sleeping ground without being heard or smelled. Although McKinsey has no physical sensation in his lower body, the psychological trauma of the torture that caused his disability is haunting him.

The horror since last night continues, making McKinsey grab his rifle and attempt to shoot the harpy before he can scream. The fiend is so quick that it lets go of the sleeping bag and flies away before a bullet can even touch it. Jed jumps out of his sleeping bag, startled by hearing gunfire out of the blue. Even Chap shrieks over the sudden gunshot.

"What the hell, Angus?" Pluck yells angrily, not noticing the harpy that flew away.

"They found us!" McKinsey exclaims. "The harpies—they're here!"

Despite still feeling unwell, the postal inspector gets out of his sleeping bag and runs after McKinsey still has his body under the covers. Pluck moves so briskly that he doesn't even notice blood bleeding through the covers until he pulls McKinsey out of his bag. The postal inspector finally lets go of him as soon as he sees gashes at the top of both of his feet. It comes as too surprising and gruesome that Pluck falls down, petrified over the lacerations. Despite not feeling anything, McKinsey is appalled to see his metatarsal bones sticking out from one of the wounds.

However, taking a moment to register the gruesome injuries proved to be a costly mistake, as the harpy quickly stuck its talon back in the cave and grabbed McKinsey's left foot again. Pluck immediately leaps toward the crippled young man and grabs hold of his left arm. He finds himself being pulled with McKinsey as the fiend pulls his victim out of the cave with full force. As the postal inspector is attempting to save him, the rain makes McKinsey's hand slippery, making it easier to let go of Pluck before he, too, becomes a victim. As a last-ditch effort, McKinsey drops the rifle he's been holding on to so Pluck can fight back.

The postal inspector sees McKinsey drop the rifle, landing next to him. Despite how much colder he feels from getting soaked from the rainfall, he hastens to get up from the ground and grabs the rifle. While Pluck aims his rifle at the harpy flying above him, the young man is lifted by the foot and hangs upside down. Almost immediately, another harpy swoops underneath the one holding McKinsey. At top speed, the second fiend extends its wing and uses one of them to slice through his neck, beheading the young man.

While McKinsey's head falls in midair, a third harpy appears and retrieves his head at the same speed. It happens so fast that Pluck can't even pull the trigger. He then finds himself horror-struck again over how fast the flock moves. McKinsey's blood pours heavily on top of him before Pluck begins blanking out with a thousand-yard stare.

Pluck's panic becomes brief when he hears a horse neighing next to him. He turns to see the black horse's reins tied to a stalactite next to the cave. Despite feeling unwell and weaker than usual, he urgently unties the reins and gets on the saddle. The postal inspector whips the horse's reins to make the black stallion run. Pluck is so fearful for his life that he abandons Chap in the cave.

There is nowhere for him to go but up the narrow path with the landslides on his left and a cliff on his right. Pluck looks up to see and sees the three harpies flying in circles above him like a kettle of vultures. No matter how fast his horse gallops, he still sees the harpies flying over him in circles. After the horse reaches the top of the path and accelerates by running down, a harpy breaks the formation and plummets right after them, moving faster than his horse.

The postal inspector leans forward to avoid the harpies' talons. The fiend misses him and flies past both of them. Pluck sees the path leading to the desert through the heavy rain affecting his field of vision. His only option is to make his horse run as fast as it can across the desert to exhaust the harpies. Pluck and his horse finally escape the gravelly path and make their way through the open desert. The frightened stallion maintains its speed while Pluck analyzes his surroundings.

As he struggles to clearly see through the pouring weather, he's only able to see how plain and spacious the desert is in front of him, with no place to hide or a means of diverting the harpies. The only change in the environment is the mountains, which are over the horizon. It'll take a miracle for his horse to have enough stamina to make it there to find a place to hide or divert the predators. The attempt to run away doesn't last as the stallion falls and collapses on its side.

As Pluck falls into the wet sand, he catches a glimpse of one of the harpies knocking down his horse. Due to the horse's momentum, the postal inspector falls off his saddle and rolls on the muddy sand with the animal. The stallion is so terrified of the harpies that it immediately gets up and runs away, abandoning its rider. Despite how awful he's feeling, Pluck picks up the rifle from the mire just before the flock lands on the ground and surrounds him.

He takes aim at the harpy standing in front of him. At five and nine o'clock, in his position, he sees the other two. All three of the black-feathered fiends remain motionless, waiting for the postal inspector to make his first move. All of them look identical and simultaneously give him a cold stare, disturbing him with their bright, eagle-like eyes. Pluck keeps switching targets, aiming back and forth at any fiends who might make the first move.

The postal inspector then looks over his left shoulder to see one of them giving him an evil grin in its human form. Since it has transformed to its human form so fast, he sees all the harpy's feathers fall right below under its talons, which have shrunk half its original size in this form. This is the first for Pluck to see the male harpy in human form, appearing as a man with long silky raven hair without any genitals, pubes, or body hair.

Pluck shoots one of his pursuers, assuming its vulnerability lies in its human form. His expectation is subverted when the bullet bounces off its skull upon impact, only causing the harpy's head to jerk back and graze his flesh. After wiping away the fiend's blood, the fiend mockingly approaches the terrified postal inspector with a sinister grin. Despite the bruise caused by the bullet, the harpy is still robust in its current state because of its extraordinary pain tolerance. Wanting so desperately not to get any closer to any of these demonic beings, Pluck screams in terror and repeatedly pulls the trigger as though his life depended on it.

As more bullets hit it, the harpy quickly transforms back to its original form and uses its wings to shield itself from further injury. Jed sees that he has used all his rifle's ammunition as soon as he hears clicking noises while he rapidly pulls the trigger. He then catches a glance at the other harpy approaching him. The postal inspector then throws the rifle at the other fiend, draws out his handgun from his holster, and fires three rounds at it. Jed sees the one behind him approaching slowly as well, and he gives that one three rounds. Unlike the others who shielded themselves with their wings, this one also wants to prove how tough it is to its prey and the other members of the flock by allowing those bullets to hit its chest and neck.

The other two lower their wings and see their own approach their prey, giving the helpless Pluck a smirk of superiority. Pluck starts tearing up as soon as he finds his last gun is not only empty but he is all out of ammunition together, sending him crying in trepidation. Even when he threw his revolver at its pursuer in the face, the fiend didn't flinch when it hit him. Once the harpy is within arm's reach, as his final resort, Pluck clenches his fist and swings at the fiend as hard as he can.

Seeing what the prey is doing, the harpy then shields his face with its wing, making Pluck punch its black-feathered pinion. Punching its razor-sharp feathers is like simultaneously punching sword blades and spikes from a porcupine. Jed cries at the top of his lungs after his fist is caught in the thorny wings. He suffers many gashes on his right hand when the harpy pulls his fist out of its wing.

The postal inspector suffers so much that he presses his mutilated hand against his chest. The injuries continue to hurt as the heavy rain drops onto his exposed lacerations. The poor Federal agent is so overwhelmed by the excruciating experience that he gets on both knees, continuing to scream some more. To stop feeling any more rainwater touching the insides of his hand, Jed needs to lean down so he can shelter his exposed wounds. The experience is so excruciating that all he can think about is how intense the affliction is.

As he hits his forehead on the harpy's scaly and warm talons, the postal inspector remembers that the harpy that severely injured him is still in front of him. Before he can open his eyes, his face is kicked by the same talon. As soon as the right hand he struggles to cover is feeling the stinging from the rain again, the same talon grabs his lacerated hand and squeezes it hard. That same hand now has a new searing pain that's piercing his palm and knuckles. It's so agonizing that Jed can't scream, especially after shrieking at his highest pitch from his previous injury.

The harpy flaps its wings, already meat hooking Pluck's right arm up. Just as he uses his other hand to reach his right arm and attempt to pull it out of the talons, another talon grabs his left wrist. The other harpy doesn't know how hard it is squeezing his left wrist joint. It's like Jed is being crucified on all sides of the wrist without a board to hold on to. He finds himself in a diagonal Jesus Christ pose before both harpies fly higher with their caught prey. Jed Pluck is in an insufferable position, being meat hooked up in the air, and he no longer has his feet on the ground.

No sooner does Pluck open his eyes than he looks down to see how high up he is before the third harpy ascends to his level and makes eye contact. It has been staring at him intently since it was on the ground with him. Seeing the third harpy hovering to his level, he anticipates that it will all end soon. He is expecting to join the many others who have fallen victim to these devilish creatures, but they keep him alive, for they have something far worse in store for him than the pain he is experiencing right now.

The harpy flying in front of Pluck turns and leads the flock with the prey back to the direction where Pluck was. Pluck looks down at the path he and his horse had taken, which looks tiny from his current height as the harpies carry him higher and around the vast upland. Despite being unable to smell the harpies with their soaked feathers, the captured prey smells something putrid on the other side of the plateau. As the flock carries him closer to the plateau, Pluck starts to see the white feces from the fiends and the feathers they shed all over the cave's entrance near the top of the plateau. Below the cave, the captured postal inspector sees horses and wagons, recognizing them from his expedition. The fact that he doesn't see any men with the animals and transportation could only mean the harpies killed all of them.

When things can't get any more unpleasant for Pluck, he sees the flock taking him to the plateau's cave. Not only does the stench from the cave smell worse as he gets closer, but it's hauntingly pitch-black inside. At that moment, Pluck realizes why the flock is taking him there instead of killing him like all the others. The female harpy with whom he had an affair is waiting for him in the dark cave. One of the last people he ever wants to see again forces him to attend her nest in the most undesirable manner. There has never been a time in Jed's life when he wanted to leave a toxic relationship as bad as this one.

CHAPTER 15

After days of pouring rain, it becomes cool in the desolate Red Desert. It is, after all, approaching autumn when local birds like buzzards and eagles start flying south. However, not all birds can migrate to a warmer location. Inspector Secoli's budgerigar is abandoned in the same small cave his partner hid from the harpies before Jed Pluck was found and captured. Poor Chap is not only neglected but hasn't been fed since the day Inspector Pluck was taken.

The bag of birdseed is on the other side of the cave, near Pluck's old sleeping bag. This poor bird is parched, and the water dish attached to the cage is empty. The bars of the cage are too strong for the little bird to break free. Shrieking for help is futile, even if someone nearby might hear the budgie. Despite how dehydrated and starving the budgie is, Chap misses his master more. Throughout this bird's life, he's been domesticated and had Inspector Secoli with him at nearly every waking moment. Despite the postal inspector's recklessness and the many dangerous situations he has put the bird in, Chap's feelings for his owner have never wavered. As much as everyone who knows Louie well knows that Chap means everything to him, nobody ever notices how much Chap loves his master. This mutual feeling between two different species goes beyond master and pet.

With the little energy he has left, Chap constantly wakes up when he hears something, only to find that it's his imagination. Usually, the imagination of hearing footsteps or someone's voice only lasts a few seconds until it becomes silent again. However, this one, the sound of footsteps approaching the cave Chap is in, doesn't stop. The famished and parched bird opened its eyes as it heard unusual footsteps slowly coming closer. The sound of the footsteps makes a tapping noise with each step. Certainly, no human would constantly be sniffing rampantly while it moves, either.

Chap peers out of the birdcage between the bars to see who is coming into the cave. Chap chirps at them regardless of who they are, seeking their attention. The bird is restless and impatient to be taken out of the cave and have its needs met. However, this becomes a great mistake on the caged bird's end. Chap immediately stops making noise when he sees that the one popping its head in isn't human.

It is full of fur, has a long muzzle, pointed ears over its head, and frightening yellow eyes staring straight at the caged bird. As it slowly walks inside the cave, it becomes more noticeable that it's a coyote. The worst part is that this coyote has skin and bones, and its mouth is drooling at the sight of Chap. Although Chap has only interacted with humans his entire life, witnessing a coyote for the first time puts his instincts on high alert.

The helpless budgerigar has his back against the cage's bars and away from the canine's snout. The caged bird can hear the coyote's sniffing, sounding so loudly with its nostrils between the bars. The coyote is so enticed by how delicious the bird smells that it is pushing the birdcage over with its head. The birdcage falls sideways and rolls away from the cave's entrance, crazily spinning Chap's whole world. The caged bird can't grasp onto anything as it bumps and rolls with the coop.

Then, the birdcage makes an immediate stop. While Chap is recovering from all the dizziness, he sees the coyote's paw placed firmly on top of the bars and its canine claws between them. The caged bird, never felt so vulnerable and terrified, shrieks. The sound of Chap calling for help makes the coyote open its mouth as wide as possible and attempt to bite through the birdcage's bars.

Chap sees firsthand how durable the birdcage bars are as the coyote attempts to bend them with its jaws and fangs. The budgerigar can feel one of the coyote's sharp teeth and saliva touching his feathers, smell its foul breath breathing over his head, and hear loud growls coming from its throat. The desperate wild dog lifted the cage off the ground and shook it violently in an attempt to free the caged bird. The coyote shook its head and then released the cage, sending it tumbling to the back of the cave.

Chap can feel his cage slam against the cave's wall and make a hard landing on the ground. The budgerigar hits his head hard multiple times against the bars and bird swing and feels dizzy from being shaken in his home. The coyote rushes over to its cage, clamps its jaws onto the bars again, and lifts the cage into the air to crazily shake it once more. The poor budgerigar squawks for help and mercy, but the starving dog cannot be reasoned with. The coyote swings the birdcage again to cause more damage, throwing it outside the cave and into the ground where the sunlight touches it.

As the cage stops rolling, Chap tries to recover from all the dizziness and pain from the bumps. Despite how much damage the coyote has made in its attempt to open the cage, it has merely bent the bars open. The intelligent bird sees that there's a wider gap between two of the bars where the coyote bites down. It is wide enough for the helpless Chap to escape and flee from danger. While slipping through the gap, the budgie hears the coyote growl as it walks out of the cave toward the birdcage again.

The coyote grabs the cage with its teeth and raises the birdcage in the air once more. After the wild dog shakes the cage for the third time, Chap slips through the bars and escapes from his birdcage. As dizzy as the poor bird is, he spreads his wings and flaps them to fly away from the coyote. The budgerigar sees the coyote drop the birdcage and give chase, realizing how much faster that coyote is than he is in the air.

The coyote leaps into the air and attempts to pounce on its prey. Aiming for a higher altitude, Chap flaps his wings quickly. By mere inches, the hungry canine misses its prey, only touching the tail end of Chap's tail feathers. The terrified parakeet flies out of the coyote's reach. When the budgerigar looks down, he can see the coyote give him an evil stare from below before it starts howling.

Not understanding why the wild canine howls, hearing it echo across the badlands only makes Chap fly even higher and out of the coyote's sight. Since the coyote is stuck in a path, there is no possibility that the hungry canine could follow the budgie flying up toward the plateau. Despite how badly the place reeks, Chap continues to go high enough to remain safe. This is the most that the budgerigar has ever flown in its entire life. By the time Chap reaches the top of the plateau, he collapses on the top surface, catching his breath from all the flying and his lack of stamina.

The domesticated bird finds out how much colder it is at high altitudes compared to how much warmer it is below. The hard winds are making Chap shiver, but he's too afraid to go back down, knowing how dangerous the Red Desert is. As he lifts his head from exhaustion, Chap has an excellent view of the desert and badlands. He scans the horizon for any sign of humans or horses, hoping to find his owner. He walks to the edge of the plateau and looks in all directions, but the area is deserted.

Not only is the bird scared and confused, but he also has no confidence in traveling alone. Spending his entire life with his owner making decisions and nurturing him is a privilege turned into a disservice to the naive animal. Chap is especially too afraid to chirp, trying to remain hidden from any possible predator nearby. After circling around the plateau and looking below at every corner, he finds no sign of life or any food or water. Never before has Chap ever felt so alone and abandoned.

The budgerigar wants nothing more than to find his master and stop his hunger pangs. As the breeze feels incompatible with his feathers, he can feel how ominous the whole location is. While still exhausted from his near-death experience, Chap gets into his sleeping position and uses the feathers on his back to cover his beak. With the cold air and the uncomfortable ground he has to stand on, it becomes difficult for Chap to rest before he uses the last of his energy to search for food, water, and his master. This is the worst way for Chap to learn that the Red Desert isn't his natural habitat.

THE LAST THING JED Pluck remembers is entering the darkness after enduring all that suffering on both of his upper limbs. He doesn't know or remember what happened right when he was brought to this malodorous cave before blacking out. The postal inspector's period of unconsciousness is unknown, but it's a blissful respite from what he had been through and what he was feeling upon waking. The pain in Jed's hand and wrist comes back, excruciating as it was before. As the feelings of his wounds return, he also feels something around his face, ankles, and wrists, like a rope tying him down. Just as much as his feeling comes back, so does his hearing, which becomes more acute and filled with echoes that become overwhelming.

The postal inspector tries to cover his ears from all the loud sounds filling the atmosphere but cannot move his hands. He hears his groaning but can't speak since he realizes his mouth is covered as well. He also hears other voices next to him speaking in a foreign language he can't comprehend.

A familiar voice is heard from behind, saying, "Jed? Jed, are you awake?" When Inspector Pluck tries to turn around, something ties him to his knees as he tries to move, but he discovers that more of his body is bound. While Pluck's eyes are still covered, he's confused if he's alive and now is a prisoner or dead and in hell with whoever is calling for him, which are both highly undesirable. The air falls silent as a woman's voice is heard. She spoke in the same unfamiliar language, commanding the attention of all the males in the room. The blindfold is removed from Pluck's eyes as the same female voice speaks in a Mediterranean language.

The postal inspector tries adjusting to the brightness by blinking repeatedly, as he's unable to rub his eyes while tied up. Pluck becomes more aware of his surroundings as his vision clears up, and he sees a room filled with Greek patterns on the ceiling but bloodstains, bones, and corpses below. His state of terror returns when he sees the remains of the victims and his abductors. His vision becomes clearer, and he sees his captors' feet are oversized talons. Glancing up, he sees the harpies towering over him.

All three black-feathered harpies make way for the crimson-feathered female harpy approaching the postal inspector. As Pluck's vision clears, he sees the ornithologist with whom he had an affair walking toward him. Seeing her in her harpy form puts him in a panic and fills him with regret over falling for her seduction.

"Well, if it isn't my lover," the harpy queen says in her Greek accent. "Why were you running away when I needed you the most?" She then looks at her underlings and speaks to them in Greek. "Untie his mouth. He and I need to have a serious discussion."

The male harpies do as commanded, and Pluck gasps before saying, "Fiona. Please let me go. I don't want to be here. I've got kids and a wife waiting for me."

"Oh, so you do have a family," she replies mockingly, changing to her Southern accent, which Pluck remembers. "Why didn't you tell me that you had one when we were together?" She then switches back to her real accent, gets on her knees, and holds his chin firmly. "Of course, I knew you had a family this whole time, Jed. Your partner told me himself." She then moves Pluck's chin and makes him face behind him. "See him standing right behind you?"

Secoli has his arms and legs chained against the wall. He is shirtless, his body is covered in scars, and his shins are gashed. Louie's eyes are red, and his face is pale as ever, looking like the harpies have tortured him. Judging by how much his facial hair grew into a full beard, Pluck must have been out for days. Louie tries to say something to him but has his mouth covered with a cloth, preventing him from speaking.

"Louie? What the hell did they do to you?" Pluck cries out before the female harpy lets go of his chin. "Release him, Fiona! He has no part in this!"

"Oh, he is very much part of our relationship, my love. And for your information, Fiona Fletcher isn't my real name. I stole that name from one of my victims. It became so convenient for me to use my lifelong experience with birds to pretend to be an expert on them and fool you all."

"Then who the hell are you?" Pluck raised his voice.

"Since your partner informed me that your harpy hunter didn't tell you everything you should know," she moves back and sits on the haystack before him, "I'll be happy to answer all your questions. My real name is Margohot, queen of the harpies."

"You mean to tell me you're behind all these goddamn murders?"

"Not all of them." She fixes her sharp claws on her fingers with her sharp fangs. "Remember that I'm not the only one. I cannot control others when I'm not around."

"What is it you harpies want?" Pluck asks, struggling to get comfortable while feeling numb from the tightness of the ropes wrapped all over his body. "What did we do to you harpies?"

"What did you do to us? It's quite simple, my dear." Margohot gets up from the haystack. "You humans have been putting us on the edge of extinction for long enough. Whenever any of us, my children especially, attempt to restore our race, you humans destroy any chance we have to live normal lives."

"What do you mean by 'us humans'? None of us has ever known your kind existed until these attacks started happening."

Margohot sighs before replying. "Well, at least this side of the world doesn't know of our existence. But back in Europe, we've been attacked by humans everywhere. We have nowhere else to go but to migrate as far to the west as we can. Admittedly, it's my fault, and my brothers' and sisters' fault as well, that we didn't control our boys before we separated during migration. Zeus knows how uncontrollable they can become without a lady in the flock." She frowns at her underlings, making the male harpies cower in shame. "Although, I would have apologized on behalf of my flock if it weren't for the fact that you mercilessly murdered Ypsipétis and Barthas."

"Yep-si.... Who the hell are they?"

Pluck's remark angers the harpy queen. In retaliation, she slashes the left side of his face with her razor-sharp claws. Though it doesn't go that deep, the swift slash from her claws is painful enough to make Pluck scream. As Pluck screams from that strike, Secoli struggles as hard as he can to get himself out of his chains, but to no avail. To stop Jed's screaming, Margohot places her sharp index finger under his chin. Pluck refrains from making noise as he feels how lethal her nails are, especially when no pressure is applied.

"Coming from you, who has been spending days respecting the dead back in that town," Margohot replies, "I expected you would do the same for the fallen harpies."

Pluck pulls his head back as her claws add pressure to his chin. She can see how intimidated he is before letting go of him.

"Now that we understand how to respect my fallen flock members, I will answer that question.

"Ypsipétis and Barthas are members of this flock I've been searching for. Ypsipétis was the harpy that you, Louie, and the rest of that town gunned down until he was completely disfigured. Barthas is the other of their brothers who got killed with that crossbow and arrow that belonged to the harpy hunter. It's good that I destroyed it before it got into the wrong hands."

"S-so you were looking for these harpies this whole time?" Pluck asks while enduring the new slash on his face. "Are they even your children?"

"Well, by how you humans organize family relations, they are biologically my nephews. But to harpies, any child our siblings have automatically become our children as well. There are no uncles, aunts, nephews, or nieces to harpies. Only parents and children. It's the dominance of prior generations, and being female is what makes us natural-born leaders."

"I don't get it. Why do women harpies get to call the shots while males are only treated as secondary beings, submissive even?"

"There are plenty of females in other species that are stronger and physically more powerful than their male counterparts. One that comes to mind is female hyenas taking charge of the pack because they're larger, stronger, and more dominant than every male hyena. That certainly gives us female harpies so much privilege to rule every flock." Margohot snaps her finger to signal one of the male harpies to approach her. "As you can see..." She grabs the feathers from the male's crotch and pulls them out. The male harpy tries his best not to react to the pain of his picked-off pubes. "Male harpies have nothing. They have no reproductive system. Male harpies cannot benefit the harpy species other than serving their queen and sisters of their flocks."

Margohot then grabs her own pubic feathers and pulls them off. She sits back on the haystack and spreads her legs to show her human-looking vagina to the two postal inspectors. She does a better job of not reacting to pain than her lackey.

"As you can see, this is the only reproduction system in the harpy race." Margohot sees Pluck looking away in disgust. "What's wrong, Jed? I thought you had some fun with her?"

"Don't you dare show me that thing, you demon," Pluck says, closing his eyes. "I already have enough regrets as it is."

"Aw, now you've hurt my feelings. Too bad you know that I'm a harpy. We could have a lot more fun together if only you could accept who I really am." Margohot switches her mocking tone back to being serious. "But since my stupid sisters couldn't tell the difference between human males with good genes and walking contaminants, I ended up with sons instead of daughters—or nieces by your logic. Now, it's my responsibility once again to lay more eggs despite having already given birth to too many children in this lifetime. We need more female harpies to help repopulate our species, our family line. I'm reaching my limit as to how many children I can bring to this world."

"And where are the other harpies now? How many of you are out there?"

"They're all dead, no thanks to those goddamn hunters and her genocidal organization." Margohot gets up, clenches her fists, and gets triggered. "That goddamn organization has been putting us on the edge of extinction for many years now. The blood of our family is on their hands."

"Why take it on us instead of those hunters? They're killing your kind, not us." Margohot calms down and returns to maintaining her composure and answers, "Because you humans on this side of the world would have done the same as them by committing genocide against harpies everywhere. I tried to give you and Secoli over there the benefit of the doubt that you would've given harpies a chance." She sits back down on the haystack. "But you two and everyone in Point Postal is no different."

"What choice did any of us have? We had to defend ourselves from those—" Pluck notices Margohot raising her eyebrows, expecting to hear him call her children something offensive. "From your children. They were the cause of all those town's disappearances, and we didn't want to end up just like them."

"True. But I did try to propose alternatives to stop Ypsipétis from harming your town. But you didn't listen because I'm a female. If only I could turn into a male human to make you and everyone listen to me, we wouldn't be in this mess."

"One thing that's not clear to me is when you made your flock flee from turning Point Postal into a ghost town, why did they come back to attack us later that night?"

"Barthas disobeyed my direct orders and decided it was better to finish you all off instead. You'd be dead if I didn't save you from him and his brothers that night."

"Should I be surprised that you tore one of the telegraph poles down and cut the connection back in Rawlins to prevent us from communicating for help?"

She laughs at his sarcasm before answering. "Very good, Inspector. Even if you somehow fixed it, I knocked a couple more down the railroad for good measure."

"And that cavalry soldier who entered the town that other night. Who took him?"

"Admittingly, it was me who took him and ended him. I couldn't last another night starving and didn't harm one of the townspeople to draw suspicion."

"So that explains why you skipped meals whenever we offered you food. How do you expect me to trust you to stop your harpies from attacking us when you committed murder and cannibalism?"

"Cannibalism? I don't recall humans and harpies being the same species. Furthermore, it's not murder if you eat what you kill. Besides, he wasn't a citizen of that town, so why do you care? You humans have already overpopulated the world and always overreact whenever a small number of you die. Not to mention, you humans also eat what you kill all the time, do you not? I say it's fair game if you ask me."

"Yeah, but—they're humans, not animals."

"I hate to break it to you, Jed. But since you humans have been so high on the species totem pole, you think human life is far more important than any other species. In fact, you refer to species that aren't human as animals to belittle them." Margohot raises the same intimidating brow. "Harpies are every bit as intelligent as you humans, are we not? Even though we can speak your language and develop our own culture, are we still animals to you? If that's the case, you humans are every bit of an animal as every known organism."

All these ideas are too new to Jed. He never thought of harpies and other species that way. Though a part of him disagrees with the harpy queen, he's in no position to argue with her. Unable to think of anything to say to her, he remains silent.

"We're carnivores, my dear," Margohot continues, returning to fixing her claws. "If we could eat anything else, we would. However, there is no organism that harpy bodies tolerate as well as humans. I'm sorry. It's just the way things are."

"Then give me a good reason why you harpies deserve to live after all the

slaughtering your kind has done to us?"

"It's simple, really. We are messengers of Zeus. We are sent to punish and kill those who anger and displease him. Without us, no one can serve him."

"Zeus...," Pluck says while pondering. "I remember you mentioning his name back when you introduced that Greek monster book to us. Are you serving the god of lightning, the skies, and all the other gods?"

"Of course. We harpies originated from his dominion. As sworn servants, we are known as the hounds of Zeus due to our utmost loyalty to him."

"How can you be so certain if Zeus—and all those other gods—are real?"

"Look at us, Jed." Margohot gets up and spreads her wings. "Do you expect any other god or millions of years of evolution to reach our glorious structure? We harpies were designed to be his perfect servants. What you call angels in Abrahamic religions, we are every bit as one and more."

"But your kind is on the verge of extinction. Why does he allow this to happen?"

"That is out of Zeus's control, but in everything else, he guides us. I would never have found this flock if he hadn't given me directions to reach Wyoming. He also fulfilled one of my prayers that led me to you."

"What do you mean? Is it because I have the genes you need to reproduce?"

"See how smart you sound right now? At least that's one intelligible thing

the hunter told you. Tell me. Where is that wench?"

"Well, the joke's on you, Margohot." Pluck starts sounding more confident despite being in so much pain. "I'm not the one you're looking for. I have four sons back in Boston. The only one who has daughters is Sheriff Wood. You're only wasting your time putting this much attention on me, so we better call quits on this twisted affair."

"Oh, that's too bad." Margohot goes back to mocking Pluck. "If only I didn't kill the sheriff and all the men that Secoli brought here to kill my children and me—"

"You did what?!"

"That's right. All those idiots thought that they could stand a chance against this flock. All of them are now part of our forage. You can see on your right that their bodies are piled against the wall over there."

Pluck turns his head in that direction and recognizes the clothing that all the men wore still on those piles of carcasses. The sight of their heads, hands, and feet having been removed makes him furious and terrified. Seeing that their remains have been so close to him this whole time sends shivers down his spine. Seeing that their clothing has bloodstains all over makes Pluck shed tears.

"Did…did you do this to them?" Pluck cries, speaking softly.

Margohot shrugs like their lives don't mean anything to her. When she follows that up by giving him a smirk, Pluck shakes his head, and more tears pour out of his eyes. The lack of empathy from the harpy queen has made Pluck cry so loudly. Just when he thought he couldn't feel any more helpless, the remains of those he tried to protect hit him in the soul.

"No! No! No! No!" Pluck cries loudly. "Why did you do such a thing? I thought we were friends."

"Friends? I thought we were more than friends, Jed. That's why we made sweet love to each other. Remember?"

"No more!" Pluck cries louder, attempting to break free. "No more, Margohot! Stop it! Stop this madness now!" He falls on his side and rolls around like a psychotic despite how tight the ropes are wrapped around his limbs. "I'm begging you to stop! Stop it! Stop it! Stop it now!" Pluck then catches his breath and stops attempting to free himself from the ropes. "No more. Stop it."

Margohot sits on the haystack and watches Pluck lie on the ground, weeping and continuously screaming, "No more." This is a side of the postal inspector she has never seen before. Torturing Secoli earlier wasn't as hard as watching Pluck being tormented. Seeing him filled with so much ego and entitlement to now pleading for mercy has made her sympathetic. She feels sorry for Pluck's feelings but has no remorse for her actions.

Margohot waits for Pluck to calm down and lets him finish his crying before saying, "I'm sorry, Jed," she turns away, trying not to show how she feels. "It's the way things are. My children and I are the predators. You and humankind are the prey." She then gets up from her seat and helps him properly sit on the ground. "But you're not prey to me. No. You're far more important than being our next meal."

Margohot gets interrupted by a rustling sound coming from the haystack. She snaps her fingers and points upward to the male harpies. Two of them grab Pluck and help him to his feet. They hold his head to make him watch the haystack from a better angle. Pluck has his eyes widened oversees three oversized eggs shaking on its own.

This whole time, he was facing a giant nest that the expedition was after. Before anyone says anything, he slowly comprehends what's really going on as the eggs continue to roll on their own faster.

"Mother," says one of the male harpies in Greek. "It's time."

"I can see that, my son," Margohot replies in her native language before she switches to English. "Let's make a bet, Jed. If these newborns are all female, then you live. If at least one of them is anything but female, it will cost you your life."

"Wha-what's all this about? What the hell is happening?"

"Can't you already tell, Jed?" Margohot says with utmost joy. "It's the birth of our children. Yours and mine, darling!"

The egg farthest away from Jed is the first to start hatching. At first, it looks like an oversized chick breaking out of its shell, until the first body parts coming through the cracked eggshells look like infant human fingers. Pluck is horrified to witness how unnaturally strong this infant is, coming out of an egg so big and thick. As its hand reaches out of the egg, he sees more of its fingers, its pinky finger being much longer than its other digits. That same hand then holds on to the cracked opening and attempts to pull itself out while the rest of its limbs try to push out from the inside.

As that unnaturally strong infant continues to hatch out of its egg, it doesn't take long for the other two eggs to start hatching with their sibling. Suddenly, the cries of what sound like a mix of human baby cries and eagle chicks screeching come from inside those eggs. It's already grotesque to see a mixture of amniotic fluid and blood soaking these newborns and spilling out of the cracked eggs. None of the adult harpies helps these infants get out of their eggs as they watch the young hatch on their own. Still being forced to watch, Pluck is petrified and starts panicking the closer the harpy infants are to getting out of their eggs.

It haunts the postal inspector to see the firstborn has its face already sticking out. The firstborn is the loudest, crying as it crawls out of the cracked opening, not bothered by the cracks scratching its body. When it has its body out of its egg, it collapses into the haystack in exhaustion.

Aside from the unnaturally long pinky fingers, the harpy chick has hock joints, a shank for calves, and chicken-like feet that show it isn't human at all.

The chick looks smaller than a human newborn, no taller than ten inches. Despite being vertically challenged, as it stretches its underdeveloped wings, it is double the length of its height. Despite being covered by fluid from the egg, its skin is flesh peach as much as Pluck's skin color. As the rest of its siblings continue hatching, Margohot picks up the newborn. As she examines it, the baby continues to make that peculiar sound that was a cross between a human cry and a bird's squawk.

"Is it a daughter?" the male harpy holding on to Pluck asks in Greek. "Or a son?"

The harpy queen smirks before exclaiming in her native language, "It's a girl! Thank Zeus, it's a girl!" She laughs with glee. "I'm naming her Sýnnefo."

"That's a miracle from Zeus himself!" the male harpy standing next to her yells. "Jed Pluck is the human male we've been looking for."

"Hold on, my son," Margohot interrupts. "There's no certainty he is the one who will help us save the harpy race just yet. We have two more still hatching." Margohot puts her newborn back in its nest, and everyone focuses on the other two struggling to hatch out of their eggs. She then glances at Pluck, who's pale as ever and giving his first harpy child a thousand-yard stare. While the harpies in the room find the birth of the newborns a triumph, the father of these harpy chicks is haunted beyond belief by what he's done. He continues to have shortness of breath, staring at how that infant resembles him. The newborn's oval-shaped face, beady eyes, and pointy nose look more like Pluck than his children in Boston.

The father of these harpy chicks starts growing numb as the secondborn emerges from its egg, followed by the other thirdborn hatching at the same pace. The anticipation excites the harpies, but Pluck would rather die than bear witness to his greatest regret. There is no denying that these three are his children. He feels more uncomfortable being unprepared for this disturbing moment. He's so perturbed that he doesn't flinch when the second hatchling starts kicking itself out of its egg, squirting bloody fluid on him.

The secondborn kicks its way out of its egg and rolls out in exhaustion. Margohot then picks up the infant and examines it. The male harpies wait for her to respond.

The harpy queen grins before saying in her native language, "So far, so good. This is also a female."

All the harpies in the room make a peal call with utter joy over hearing the news.

"You are also a gift from Zeus himself, my young one. You shall be called Dóro." She looks at the pale Pluck and says in English, "You've got one more chance, my love. Let Zeus be merciful to you and Louie."

Pluck doesn't even react or look at her. He is disassociated from the situation he's in. It's tormenting enough for the father of these chicks to see these abominations that he cannot stomach looking at them anymore. Pluck wishes that the third one is male so Margohot can end his suffering.

She places the secondborn next to her twin. They both continue to make that cry only a harpy chick can. The harpy queen grows impatient, waiting for the last one to break out of its egg; so far, it has not gone further than cracking it. She then grabs the third egg that's still hatching, making all the male harpies panic simultaneously.

"Mother, wait!" one of the male harpies shouts in Greek. "You mustn't help any of the young hatch out of their eggs. It's bad luck."

Margohot viciously squawks at her son approaching, making all the male harpies back away as she starts helping the third harpy chick hatch out of its egg. With just the claw of her index finger, she carefully creates more cracks in the eggs and digs the thirdborn out. With the help of its mother, the thirdborn makes its way out of the egg.

As soon as it shows life by sticking his underdeveloped wing out, Margohot brushes the pieces off of the triplet and throws the shell away. All the male harpies anxiously look at her facial expression as she examines the thirdborn.

She smiles and says in Greek, "I think we found the human male we've been looking for, my sons." She then changes languages and looks at Pluck, who's still motionless. "Jed, my love. I want to thank you so much for giving me the gifts I've always wanted. It's been a long time since anyone has ever given me all daughters. It means the world to me." She then picks up all three of the chicks from their nest and shows them to their father. "Meet our daughters, Sýnnefo, Dóro, and Tycherós."

Pluck finally moves his eyes and looks at the triples, who are still wet. The fact that all of them are identical and have his likeness traumatizes the postal inspector even more. He is so petrified he can't scream at the sight of these abominations. Regret is beyond what he's feeling right now. If he could free himself, he would abort all three of them and correct the biggest mistake of his life. Instead, he stares in utter fear and remains motionless while held against his will.

"I understand that it's hard to accept that you're the father of these three beautiful daughters right now." She places the triplets back in their nest and snaps her fingers for her lackey to grab her something. "But with time, you'll eventually love all three of them. Take it one step at a time, and you'll fit right in. You're part of the flock now despite not being a harpy.

"Oh, what's wrong, sourpuss?" Margohot caresses Pluck's scarred cheek. "Aren't you happy that you get to live? Neither my sons nor I will ever harm you as long as you do as you're told and keep your penis and testicles intact. The only way you're allowed to die is if the disease I gave you kills you in time."

Pluck's eyes widen over that remark before saying, "You mean... you're the one who gave me these blue spots?"

"You mean the harpy flu? Yes, Jed. Having intercourse with a female harpy is contagious. You didn't really think that being a member of my flock as a human being would be long-term, did you?" She giggles at her joke. Margohot lets go of his cheeks and takes a couple of steps back. "Come now. As a flock tradition, we watch the newborns have their first meals. We can't start without everyone in the family joining in. Our children are starving, my dear."

The male harpies pull Pluck back to his feet and make him watch his children in their nest. It now makes sense why the harpy chicks are all crying uncontrollably. They weren't just born and unaccustomed to life outside of their eggs—the newborns are all hungry after pushing themselves out of their eggs and growing a serious appetite. The male harpy fetching their meals brings in a headless body that only Pluck can identify.

Judging by the dark-collared shirt and blue vest, this is Angus McKinsey's torso.

As the clothing gets removed, Pluck can only say no repeatedly as this endless nightmare escalates. As soon as the carcass is free from clothing, the body is placed in the center of the nest, and the triplets begin chowing down McKinsey's remains. Even though the infants don't have any teeth, they somehow know how to use their tiny claws from the top of their wings to dig and rip out the meat and start gulping the pieces. The harpies celebrate by making their peal call while Pluck screams with them in horror.

Witnessing this level of unnatural brutality after they are born is Hedean and cruel. Is it really in their nature to be this violent? The newborns aren't being fed but are instead given the food, and they're helping themselves, already knowing how to scrape the meat and feed themselves. Pluck can't take any more of this bestial act. He shakes his head and struggles to free himself again to stop this endless traumatic experience. The male harpies can feel him attempting to free himself again. They throw him back to the ground before he does anything to the nest.

The same one who held him against his will puts his foot on the postal inspector's skull. His three front talons touch his face and the hallux on the back of his neck. Feeling how lethal those talons are again makes Pluck stop moving, remembering how they pierced his hand and wrist like it was nothing. Pluck lies helplessly, tearing up over how spiritually damaged he has become. He sees his partner still chained up against the wall, crying over Pluck dealing with this cruelty. If anyone is sorry for all this, it's Pluck for having Secoli bear witness to his torture.

As soon as the harpies stop their peal calls, the talons let go of Jed's skull. The same male harpies then move him to lie on his back and wrap more ropes around him, holding him on the ground. He has his mouth covered, but the ropes wrapped around his crotch oddly cut loose. He sees the harpy queen approaching him with a jubilant expression that only someone attending a party could make.

"Oh, Jed," Margohot says, standing over him. "You've made a mother like me as happy as can be. Besides not knowing proper harpy etiquette, you're truly perfect. How could I ask for more than what's been given to me? Oh, wait—"

She snaps her fingers, signaling the male harpies to leave the room. As soon as they all leave, the only ones left are the newborns still eating in their nest, Margohot taking control, Pluck tied to the ground, and Secoli still chained to the wall. With Pluck fully wrapped in ropes except for his eyes and crotch, it could only mean one thing in the harpy queen's twisted and degenerated mind.

"I want to grow an even bigger flock," Margohot continues, "and you're going to help me. Now then. Let's get a little more comfortable to your liking, shall we?"

Margohot steps away from Pluck to the end of the room and raises both wings. Immediately, all her crimson feathers collapse on the floor, and she transforms back to her human form. She's now in the appearance both Pluck and Secoli remember, but completely naked with her small talons that can never transform into human feet. The harpy queen, in her human form, slowly turns around seductively. Pluck's body is aroused at the sight of her despite her being unable to change her talons. She slowly approaches Pluck to set the mood after all that Margohot put him through.

"So do you prefer me with this look like how you remember? Or do you prefer me in my true form? Nah. I've put you through enough already. You deserve something more satisfying to your liking." Margohot walks over to her prisoner, gets on her knees, and unzips his pants. She first examines his penis and scrotum. "Nice to see that despite how rough my boys were with you, they did the right thing in taking care of...the most important part."

Margohot then gives Pluck fellatio. Pluck is trying to shake his head and scream, but he's tied down so well that he can't squirm or move his head. Despite his body's arousal, Jed hates every moment of this violation. The sexual act of having his penis in her mouth doesn't last long as she remembers Secoli is still in the same room with them. She glares at Secoli, still held against the wall, witnessing how revolting this all is.

She lets go of Pluck's penis and gets into a kneeling position, and says, "I almost forgot you're still here, Louie. But don't worry. You've got yourself a front-row seat to a show of a lifetime. Enjoy it while it lasts."

Margohot puts Jed's penis in her vagina and gets in the cowgirl position while Pluck is still stiff. She has to act quickly before his penis becomes soft again, knowing that Pluck's fighting from having an erection. But it's too late. She's already moving her body up and down, keeping his body stimulated and his erection steady.

Now that she has him where she wants him, Margohot stays in this position until he ejaculates and makes her lay more eggs. While she performs the sexual act, Pluck cries over how he doesn't want to do it again with her. Even Secoli knows how much he's suffering. Seeing his partner in tears during this sexual assault makes him cry with him. He has never seen a sexual assault, but seeing his comrade fall victim to his heinous act is too much for his strong heart to take.

Pluck's sexual violation occurring right next to the newborns feeding on their fallen comrade is aberrant and debauched. Having both postal inspectors live and be under the harpies' captivity is the vilest of circumstances. Neither of them is allowed to die or go freely. In this moment of despair, both Pluck and Secoli believe dying is the only escape from this hell.

THE SUN IS SETTING, and it's getting cold—almost too cold for a bird to handle. Chap cannot get comfortable or sleep after going up to the plateau. He's far too fearful of returning to find food after almost getting killed earlier today. The poor bird isn't accomplishing anything being so high up in high altitude when autumn's arriving. The hunger and thirst aren't making matters any better for the miserable budgerigar.

Since no one can feed the domesticated bird like he's long been accustomed to, Secoli's bird has to help himself if he wants to live. It takes a lot of guts for Chap to fly down from the plateau after getting almost eaten by a coyote. It's even gutsier for the domesticated bird to return to search for the bag of bird seeds left in the cave. Upon returning to the cave, the coyote is no longer around after the attack, but the wild animal did leave some damage to the property left behind. The sleeping bag and the bag are torn apart, leaving cotton and ripped clothes all over the cave floor.

Fortunately, the bird seeds are spilled on the ground, which makes it easier for the starving budgerigar to have its first meal in days. Even though this is the only food Chap has been feeding on since birth, the bird seeds never taste so good. The poor bird doesn't care how full he's getting; he treats this like it's his last meal. The bird pecks and swallows every seed it finds, trying to leave no trace on the ground.

While Chap munches upon the seeds, he sees a tin drum canteen lying next to the torn sleeping bag. It seems that the coyote, earlier today, was so thirsty that it tore the metal open. The parched budgie, seeing that there is still some water inside, inserts its head into the torn metal of the canteen and drinks the remaining water. Chap's hunger and thirst were finally quenched after days of deprivation.

His feast is interrupted by the sound of footsteps echoing in the cave, similar to the coyote's, but seems to be more than one. The anxiety returns to Chap, forcing him to hide in the bag near the sleeping back before anyone sees him. The bird tilts his head sideways and peaks through a hole in the bag to see who is approaching.

Entering the cave is a pack of coyotes, all four equally thin. The coyote from earlier today must have brought the rest of its pack into this cave. Seeing this many appear right in front of Chap both fascinates and haunts him. While analyzing the canine's movements, he can see they're all walking around, sniffing all over the cave's floor. One of the coyotes approaches the bag Chap's in and sticks its nose inside.

Not wanting to be anywhere close to another coyote's fangs again, the parakeet flies out and immediately makes another escape. Chap flies out of the cave as fast as he can before any of his predators can realize what is happening. As he exits the cave and flies back to the plateau, they all bark and howl over him.

Chap, with a full belly, wet beak, and renewed energy, flies to the top of the plateau faster than before. Although the Red Desert is incompatible with this domesticated bird, he has never felt so alive flying so freely as he does now. Even though it might be his last meal, it gives him another day to live. The budgerigar makes it safely back to the plateau and tries to get comfortable. Just as Chap looks down to see if he spots the coyotes, he catches a glance of a darkish brown feathered figure flying directly at him.

Without wasting a second, Chap flaps his wings to quickly move backward before getting hit. However, the dark figure swoops directly at Chap, causing gashes and fractures to his right wing. The sudden pain is so excruciating that budgerigar shrieks like never before. While the domesticated bird covers his injury, Chap looks at what attacked and what flew past him. Flying away from the plateau is a hawk eight times his size who looks as hungry as the coyotes from below. Unlike the coyotes, however, this hawk can fly and fly much faster than the little budgerigar.

The bird of prey is circling around in the air in an attempt to make another swipe at the small prey. Chap discovers in the worst possible way that he's not the only bird that didn't fly south in this cold climate. With only one good wing, Chap runs for it, desperately wanting to survive. The budgerigar's right wing drags on the ground as he runs, making it hard for him to run as fast as he usually does.

Then Chap finds himself at the edge of the cliff. He looks down to see how far down the badlands are. Knowing how bad his wing is, the domesticated bird hesitates to jump for it. That is, until the parakeet hears the hawk's hoarse call and sees the hawk flying directly at him with its talons reaching in his direction. With no other choice, the budgie decides to jump off the cliff, but another figure soars up from the plateau's cliff, startling the domesticated bird.

This new figure is three times the size of the hawk and appears more human than a bird. It quickly becomes apparent to Chap that this is one of the harpies that kept attacking his owner and his fellow humans. Since he has never been so close to his owner's enemy, seeing a harpy in front of him immobilizes the small bird. The harpy lands on the cliff's edge, and Chap sees himself between two opposing figures. As Chap focuses on the harpy towering above him, the fiend raises its wing and wraps its black feathers around the budgerigar.

The budgerigar plunges into darkness as the wing envelopes him, then the sharp feathers shake and poke it. The harpy's wing then unveils the domesticated bird, and everything is once again bathed in light. When Chap looks up to see what the harpy is doing, he sees the fiend looking up at the hawk flying away with some of the harpy's razor feathers on the bird's talons. It becomes apparent that the harpy just saved Chap from his predator, but it still remains unclear what this siren's intent is.

As the hawk flees, the fiend puts his attention back on the budgerigar. Staring straight at its yellow eagle eyes with its human face continues to put Chap off. The harpy steps back to transform into its human form. All its feathers then fall off, its wings turn into arms and hands, and its talons shrink in size. Now, in its human form, the harpy gently grabs Chap and examines the bird. It sees the parakeet's broken wing and the blood coming from the open wound.

Chap is terrified after seeing what it and its kind have done to his human allies and anticipates suffering the same fate. However, the harpy shows no signs of aggression toward the small bird. The male harpy is passive by holding Chap so gently and touching him with his index fingers in a similar way to what Inspector Secoli used to do. Even more off-putting is hearing the harpy speaking in an unfamiliar language to him. The domesticated bird is reminded of his master as he feels the fiend's human index finger rub his small scalp.

After a full minute of petting Chap, the harpy puts the bird back on the ground and steps back to where it sheds all its feathers.

Chap watches the harpy instantly transform back to its harpy form, with its pinky finger, talons, and feathers grown in an instant. Upon seeing this transformation, the parakeet becomes anxious and immobilized again. While Chap remains still, the harpy grabs him with the digits of its birdlike toes, keeping its sharp talons from contacting the small bird. Now, in the harpy's gentle grasp, Chap sees himself being carried away from the plateau, and his conveyor takes him down to the badlands.

Chap witnesses firsthand how fast the harpy can fly. The harpy is holding Chap tightly from being blown away, yet not so tight that it could crush the small bird or injure his wing further. With so much wind blowing in the bird's way, it becomes difficult for him to see where the fiend is taking him. Unable to see well, looking straight ahead, Chap can only face behind the harpy and see that it is taking him farther away from the plateau. Within minutes of being carried by the enemy, they make it to the flat desert lands.

Chap notices the harpy is slowing down its flying, making it easy to see ahead with less wind blowing in his way. Now able to see more clearly, the budgerigar realizes they're on the other end of the desert and being brought to other badlands farther away than the expedition reached. There's a cave next to the top of another, yet noticeably smaller, plateau. As the harpy places Chap in the small cave, the parakeet notices that the cave is so small that the harpy's talon can only fit in, and the bird's head can touch the roof if he jumps. As soon as his feet touch the cave's floor, the harpy flies away, leaving the budgerigar behind.

Despite everything getting colder and darker and wishing to return to his master, Chap couldn't be in a safer place. The cave is so high from the ground that no predator on foot could reach it, and the cave is so small that no bird of prey would even notice. Considering that the domesticated bird has been sheltered and protected in a cage throughout its life, Chap has no intention of making an escape, even if his right wing is in better condition.

There is so much confusion in the parakeet's mind about why the harpy chose to save him instead of killing him like all the humans it slaughtered. It's normal for any domesticated animal to worry when they're alone, but Chap has never in his life felt this isolated. The intelligent bird starts overthinking, worrying about Louie Secoli's whereabouts and what the harpy will do next when it returns. Nevertheless, in the safest place in the Red Desert, the budgerigar can only be grateful to see another day.

CHAPTER 16

Two weeks have passed since the men left Point Postal, having everyone left in town worried about those eleven brave men's statuses and whereabouts. Though some women are happy to take charge of the town after living in a patriarchal civilization, it doesn't change the fact that they all feel vulnerable without their presence. Despite the women never being as close together as they are now, Pearl is the only one in town who is not communal. The constant stress and anxiety of another possible attack is especially heavy on Pearl Herbert. The amount of work she has put into protecting and helping the town while never having time to recover from these recent events has put a toll on her.

This morning's post at the jailhouse is another time for Herbert to ruminate over the recent events. Instead of sitting on Sheriff Wood's desk and watching over Zephyra Klouví and Lorraine Payton, she stays outside to hide her feelings from everyone, as this is her only way to have space outside her hotel room. The good times all involved the girls watching over her and never leaving her alone, which is something she would love to have right now. Since everyone else is hurting and only communicating with those they're familiar with, Pearl feels neglected.

Just when she thinks she can get some time for herself, she hears what sounds like a storm coming from the distance. Pearl wipes her tears and gets up to see an army of horses approaching from behind the jail. As they all get closer to Point Postal, she sees the men all wear blue uniforms, Stetsons, yellow gloves, and scarves, just like Sergeant West, who arrived in town weeks ago. This could only mean this is the cavalry regiment, the militaristic support everyone has long been waiting for. All of them are rushing down in line formation, with an American flag and another unfamiliar flag with red on top and white at the bottom. Even though the horses' stomps are loud, Pearl can see only about twenty-five in this squadron.

The cavalry regiment slows down as they see Pearl stepping out of the jailhouse's shadow and standing right in front of them. The squadron leader halts his soldiers and then approaches Pearl, who's armed with a rifle. The soldier approaching her has a clean, shaved face like the rest of his soldiers, with a noticeably firm chin. Amid the shadow cast by his Stetson, the leader's eyes are sharp green, and his hair is dark brown.

"Good morning, ma'am," the cavalry leader says, stopping his horse. "It's not every day you see a lady holding a gun. This wouldn't be Lemonstown, would it?"

"This town used to be called that," Pearl replies, sounding timid, "but our mayor renamed it Point Postal."

"Really? How long ago did this town change its name to…Point Postal, was it?

And why wasn't the United States Government informed about this change?"

"It was a week ago when Mayor McLusky used to be alive."

"What happened to him? Was your town attacked like all the other towns? Tell me, did you get a good look at the culprits responsible for all these disappearances?"

"Tell me who you are first before I answer any of your questions."

"Ma'am, I am Captain Aaron Neilson. I'm the leader of this cavalry squadron. Now, if you don't mind telling me—"

Just as Captain Neilson starts to get down from his horse, Pearl points her rifle at him and says, "Hold it right there. How do I know you are who you say you are? How do I know you're not some sort of harpy?"

All twenty-four soldiers behind the captain retaliate by taking out their rifles and pistols and aiming them at Pearl. Hearing all the guns drawn and loaded behind him, the captain raises his hand to put their weapons away. He keeps his hand raised until he hears that all the weapons have been put away. Captain Neilson doesn't bother turning to his men, knowing how obedient they are to him.

"I'll have you know, ma'am," Neilson says, putting his arm down, "that pointing a gun at a soldier is a federal offense. Since I'm a gentleman, I'm letting this go. And what was it that you accused me of being? A harpy? What is that supposed to be?"

"A harpy. It's those monsters disguising themselves as people, but really they're demonic birds with the face of a person."

"So what you're telling me is all those feathers left behind in all the towns we've visited are actually caused by…some kind of bird people?"

"Take off your boots and show me your feet."

"What is this? Some sort of joke?"

"This town had to fight tooth to nail against those devils. We've lost so many. We all have trust issues with strangers pretending to be a person and slaughtering us when we least expect it. Now take off your boots and show me you have real feet."

"Pearl!" a woman appears and shouts from behind. "What in God's name are you doing? Don't you know this is the cavalry?"

"They may look like soldiers, Samantha," Pearl replies, focused on her aim, "but I ain't risking it if one of these men is an actual one of them."

"Stop acting like an idiot and put the damn rifle down." Samantha pushes Herbert's gun to point to the ground. "My apologies, good sir. We've been on high alert lately over these recent attacks. Miss Herbert here is a bit…on edge because of it."

"Understood, ma'am," Captain Neilson replies, "I don't suppose you got a good look at the culprits responsible for these attacks, did you?"

"We all did, sir," Samantha answers, letting go of Herbert's gun. "Two postal inspectors came to our rescue before we got attacked. Without them, we would have ended up like everyone else."

"Postal inspectors? They wouldn't happen to be Inspectors Jed Pluck and Louie Secoli, would they?"

"Yes. Yes, they are. How do you know them?"

"We received orders from Congress to find their whereabouts. Since Wyoming's national guards deployed overseas, we were taken out from Kansas to help out. Looks like you're who we're looking for. So where are Inspector Pluck and Secoli?"

"They took off over a week ago. We haven't seen them or the men who came with them since. Likewise, we haven't had a harpy attack either."

"Right," the captain says after he finishes putting his boots back on. "Is there a place where we can discuss this privately?"

"Right this way, sir."

Samantha snatches Pearl's rifle away and gives her a snarl. Pearl is left with a cold shoulder, standing in one place as the soldiers pass her. Now that she realizes she made a big mistake, Herbert has another reason to weigh her heart since she's taking it too hard. No one bothers to check on Pearl as she remains motionless, trying her best to hold back her tears. She could never have anticipated making such a poor impression on the military, which she and everyone else had been waiting on for so long.

SINCE BEING FOUND BY the harpy, Chap looks outside its tiny cave every day and waits for its master to come and feed him. The small bird is still recovering from his injured wing but now has mud covering his gash. Like every morning, the budgerigar's stomach is constantly rumbling as he waits for his master to feed him. Having said that, his master for the last couple of weeks hasn't been Louie Secoli.

Chap sees in the distance that the harpy is flying toward him from the plateau the hybrid has been going to. Since when they first met, the hybrid and bird have developed a relationship similar to Chap's with his old master, but not as close. As the harpy approaches in the air, the budgerigar jumps in place with excitement and joy. As his new master approaches, Chap can see its talons carrying two sacks filled with nourishments. The domesticated bird waits for the harpy to land on the tree branch under his small cave. As soon as it can stand on top of the branch, the new master transforms into its human form and unties the sacks, not bothered by all of its feathers falling below the landslide nor being naked in the cold weather.

The first bag that opens is the one filled with water. Immediately, Chap dunks his head in the bag and starts drinking, then bathes himself in it. As the domesticated bird soaks himself, the harpy then grabs the other bag and unties it. It doesn't take long for Chap to stop playing in the bag filled with water and focus on the minced meat pouring out of the bag and into the harpy's human palm. It's suspicious how the hybrid obtained these things in this barren desert, but being fed with it for this long made Chap stop worrying about it and enjoy having it all to himself. Once the harpy places its palm full of meat on Chap, the budgerigar doesn't hesitate to eat every piece of minced human off its hand, already accustomed to this bizarre cuisine.

As Chap eats the food on the hand that feeds, the harpy smiles over how he has earned the small bird's trust. It tries not to laugh or make sudden movements by being tickled by Chap's beak, which is pecking each piece of meat off his hand. The harpy then looks at the bird's right wing. It can be seen that Chap's wing is still recovering, making the harpy feel both pity and relief at the same time.

It has taken up to this point for the budgerigar to have a mutual feeling with the harpy, and it can tell that their time together is reaching its end. For the past two weeks, the harpy never thought that life outside of its flock would ever have something this pleasant. However, keeping this a secret from the flock doesn't last when he hears a familiar voice speaking behind it.

"What are you doing here in your human form, Yazeem?" asks the voice. The harpy then drops the bag of Chap's food and immediately turns back to its harpy form. As soon as its feathers sprout out of its skin within seconds, the hybrid turns around and attempts to slash whoever is behind it with its razor-sharp wing. Despite moving so fast, the one that startles it dodges the harpy's attempt to strike. As the harpy starts flapping its wings, it catches a glance that it's one of its brothers soaring above it and staring at the small cave.

The one named Yazeem gets in between its brother and Chap in his cave. Yazeem pushes his brother away from getting any closer, and when it tries to land on the branch, he leans against the landslide and covers the small cave. As much as it's doing its best to hide Chap from its flock members, the budgerigar shrieks in fear. The small bird is so noisy that he foils Yazeem's plan to keep his secret from the flock.

"Beat it, Ezio!" shouts Yazeem in Greek. "None of this concerns you."

"You've been acting suspicious by disappearing from the flock lately," says his brother, flying midair to his level. "Just what are you hiding from us?"

"Nothing!" Yazeem shouts, avoiding eye contact. "Go back to the lair and forget what you saw."

"No, brother," Ezio responds, flying closer, "show me what you are hiding."

As Ezio reaches him, Yazeem leans harder against the wall and kicks his brother with both talons. He has his talons clinched upon hitting him to make a less lethal attack against his kin. When Ezio gets knocked away, Yazeem quickly turns around and uses his feet to grab Chap out of the small cave, avoiding injuring the parakeet with his sharp unguis. When he feels the budgerigar within his grasp, Yazeem flies away with his muse.

Chap continues shrieking in fear, not knowing why he's being brought out of his cave. Within seconds, the budgerigar can see that the cave that he was in is now much farther away. The other harpy, who looks almost identical to his new master, is drawing near. What's even more frightening is how much faster this harpy is than the one carrying him. Yazeem flies fast, but the other harpy flies even faster.

The one chasing them is aiming his claws at Chap like he's a target. Before Ezio touches the parakeet, Yazeem twists and avoids his brother. Chap's whole world starts spinning with his new master, not knowing if he got hit by his kind. As soon as the spinning motion stops, the budgerigar can see that Yazeem is swooping down to the badlands. While still at top speed, the harpy is taking Chap through a path in the terrain to divert his brother. Since dodging Ezio's attack, Chap doesn't spot him anywhere.

As he slows down, Ezio then dives from above and lands on his brother's back, catching him off guard. Yazeem hits the ground hard and rolls over. The rescuer has a lot of self-control; he keeps himself from clenching too hard and keeps Chap safe from touching the ground. As Yazeem attempts to get up from the ground, a talon stomps on his head and holds his head down. Knowing that Ezio is keeping him from escaping, his last-ditch effort is to throw Chap, who's still within his grasp.

While he's pinning his brother to the ground, Ezio catches at the corner of his eye what Yazeem is doing with his foot. He hastily lets go of Yazeem's head and places his talons on his brother's foot in the middle of the foot's throwing motion. As Yazeem's ankle is held down, Chap falls out of his grasp and spreads his wings, attempting to fly away from danger. Despite this, Chap's wing is still injured, and the budgerigar can only fly for a short distance. Before the small bird can land on the ground, Ezio swiftly catches the parakeet with his other foot.

"Look at what we have here!" Ezio says mockingly, looking at the bird caught in his left foot. "If it isn't the postal inspector's bird."

"Leave him alone!" Yazeem screams, kicking his brother's calf to free himself, but to no avail. "It's just a bird! He's hurt and needs protection."

"So this is what you've been hiding from our flock?" Ezio responds, ignoring his brother's kicking. "And we all thought this little critter was long dead. You know the consequences of violating curfew, don't you, Yazeem?"

Threatened by his remark, Yazeem opens his talon and attempts to slash Ezio's foot, which has been standing on his ankle.

While still in high adrenaline, Ezio flaps his wings and gets several feet above the ground to avoid his brother's lethal attack. Yazeem rolls away, and he sees Ezio flying away. Yazeem, with his keen eyesight, sees Chap in his brother's talons, unsure if the budgerigar is getting hurt. The young male harpy flies off the ground and does his damnedest to chase his brother. As soon as Yazeem gets above the depression, he sees Ezio heading directly to the plateau. The rival family member is going to give Chap to the flock queen and reveal Yazeem's secret.

Knowing how loyal Ezio is to Margohot and how desperately Yazeem desires independence, the harpy has no choice but to catch up with his brother and kill him to save the bird. Worrying over the consequences, the male harpy flaps profusely to get closer to his brother, but Ezio is flying much faster with less effort. If only he was born with wings as large as his, he wouldn't have to put as much effort into keeping up.

Both the chaser and the chased are close to the plateau's exterior and are moments away from making it to the entranceway to the lair. Ezio is finally slowing down as he flies around the plateau. Knowing his limits and how close he is to losing all stamina, Yazeem makes one of the strongest flaps of his wings and attempts to dive into his brother. This attempt takes his breath away, and he makes a leap of faith, hoping to crash into his target. Just as Ezio makes it to the cave's passage, Yazeem head butts the back of his brother's skull in high momentum, knocking both harpies off course.

Both brothers take a bump against the plateau's landslide and make a hard landing on the alluvial fan. Yazeem rolls down on the sloping ground, getting dizzy from a minor concussion and all the spinning. As his body circles around, the harpy loses momentum as he rolls down the slope and comes to a complete stop when his feet are pointed directly downward. He lies on his back, tries to recover from his headache and dizziness, and gasps for air.

After quickly recovering from his dizziness and stamina, Yazeem gets up and sees that he has no serious injuries. He feels his whole world tilting the moment he gets on his feet. The young harpy then realizes he's suffering a more serious concussion than expected, having difficulty walking straight without losing his balance. It's even more difficult for Yazeem not to fall back down since the ground is slanted.

Yazeem, dizzy, barely sees Ezio, whose black feathers contrast sharply with the orange and brown desert. Another thing that contrasts with the red desert is Chap's green feathers, as the bird is up the alluvial fan next to his brother. From what he can make of it, the parakeet lies on the slope, not making any movement. Chap's critical condition puts Yazeem in a panic, and he rushes to help the small bird.

Yazeem gently picks up Chap with his fingers above his wings, preventing his razor-sharp feathers from touching the parakeet. Seeing Chap breathing up close, Yazeem notices he has new wounds across his chest and stomach, and he is bleeding profusely. Ezio's talons pulling him tightly upon impact is the only possible explanation for how he sustained these injuries. The harpy's heart sinks, seeing such an innocent creature suffer so much after taking so long to recover. The sight of Chap barely alive has put Yazeem in tears, but he acts fast to save the poor bird.

Yazeem gathers dirt and spits it up to mix into clay and to cover Chap's wounds when he's suddenly hit on the side of the head. The blow is so hard that it knocks him to the ground, and the harpy's world starts spinning again. He looks up to see that it's Ezio who struck him. There's blood pouring down the harpy's right side of the neck and right shoulder, showing signs that Yazeem did some damage to him. Despite how hurt Ezio is, the older brother approaches him with a violent look in his eyes.

Even feeling more light-headed than ever, Yazeem wastes no time to get back up and positions himself to face his rival flock member. The young harpy leaps into the air and attempts to strike Ezio with his talons. Ezio makes a quick retaliation by flying straight at his younger brother. The moment they clash, the two harpies enter aerial combat and attempt to attack each other like birds of prey fighting in the air. The two brothers are avoiding making contact with each other's wings to remain in flight, which is why they're attempting to pierce each other with their talons. Like a sword fight, both Ezio's and Yazeem's talons keep clashing, and they simultaneously struggle to get an opening spot to strike their opening spots.

As the two brothers attempt to kill each other, Chap is woken up by the harpies' shrieks for bloody murder. They both are so loud during the fight that their calls echo throughout the badlands. The budgerigar cannot cover his ears or get up from the ground. All he can do while on his side is watch the aerial bloodshed above him and endure the agonizing, violent screams. It's difficult for Chap to tell which is Yazeem or Ezio since they're both identical and moving quickly in the air.

It's even more difficult to tell who's getting lacerated as blood pours each time they collide. The domesticated bird is squeamish at any sight of blood, and witnessing the harpies' blood sprinkle to the ground where he lies is too much for the bird to handle. The injured parakeet screams for help, but the brothers' intemperate shrieks are unmatched, even at the top of his lungs.

As Chap anticipates one of the black-feathered harpies to fall soon, another harpy appears above them. While Chap is the only one to notice the third harpy in the sky, the fighting and shrieking finally cease when an even louder and more ear-piercing shriek from above echoes throughout the badlands. It is so powerfully heard that Yazeem and Ezio struggle to make a safe enough landing before using both wings to cover their ears. Even Chap is forced to move his broken wing to cover his ear. The ear-piercing shriek of the male harpies invading Point Postal was unbearable, but hearing the more feminine harpy scream is even worse. Chap and the harpies cower over the noise until the third harpy lands on the ground, standing between the two males.

While his ears ring, Chap opens his eyes and sees the third harpy has those familiar red-colored feathers. The intelligent bird recognizes that it's the same Dr. Fletcher who took care of him and is now in her harpy form. The small bird never forgot how shocking it was to see her transform that night and now is even more terrified to see her again in broad daylight. From where he lies, he sees the female harpy smacking both of the black-feathered harpies with her wings. Chap is confused that neither of the brothers fights back as she strikes them.

After a good beating, the female harpy catches her breath and shouts in her native language, "Why in Tartarus are both of you creating so much attention and fighting each other? Didn't I make it clear that we're supposed to lay low while the humans are searching for us? You could have blown our cover if any of them were nearby and put our race in danger." She waits for either of her boys to reply before asking, "Well? Which of you will tell me what the fighting is about?"

Ezio stands firmly with his back straight and replies, "Mother, Yazeem has violated curfew and kept Inspector Secoli's bird from us, and I tried to bring the bird back to show you what he's been doing this whole time, but he attacked me."

"Is this true, Yazeem?" Margohot asks calmly yet harshly. "Have you kept the bird from us this whole time? Where is Chap?"

Yazeem doesn't bother answering, knowing he cannot admit the truth, nor will he dare lie to his queen. Likewise, deciding not to speak only delays the inevitable. The sudden silence settles the echoes heard throughout the badlands, all except for the budgerigar's chirping that's being heard in the distance. Margohot and Ezio turn their attention to the Chap's soft shrieks and walk in his direction. Yazeem stops moping and looks up when he sees his mother's red feathers blowing toward him.

He sees his mother in her human form, completely naked, and picking up Chap.

The budgerigar refuses to calm down despite recognizing her as the Dr. Fletcher he remembers. While Margohot examines the poor bird, the tender memories of playing with and nurturing Chap return to her. Despite his injuries, she finds comfort in feeling his soft green feathers and tiny talons in her hand again.

"Oh, Chap," Margohot speaks in English with a fake Southern accent to calm the bird with familiarity. "What did my boys do to you?" She turns to her sons and sees how badly hurt they are. "Look at both of you. You two are covered in blood and scars. We'd better treat you all."

Once Chap is gently placed on the ground, she changes into her harpy form, gently lifts him with her talon, and flies to the cave on the plateau. Despite the injuries, both her sons follow her up in the air. It doesn't take long for the harpies to enter the cave that leads to their lair. Once they enter the cave, Margohot places the budgerigar on the ground and switches to her human form to carry him in her hands. The brothers remain in their harpy forms and follow their mother with Chap in her hands to the only light in the pitch-black cave.

Chap notices that the doorway is covered by a curtain, and what sounds like babies crying is heard from that room, sensing how off-putting the room is. As Margohot brings Chap through the curtains, the budgerigar witnesses such a grim sight. Nothing but gruesome things adorn the area below the Greek pattern, with blood all over the walls and human bones all over the floor. There's another one of those black-feathered harpies standing next to a haystack in the center where all the crying is coming from.

Margohot gets closer to her nest, and Chap witnesses three babies that look like human toddlers with pointy spikes coming out of her arms and under their bellies. Next to the triplets are three more infants that appear to be human-looking, lying next to three giant eggs in the center of the nest.

"What happened to Yazeem and Ezio?" the male harpy nurturing the nest asks. "And what's that thing that you're holding, Mother?"

"We found Louie's bird," Margohot replies, "and it's no thanks to these two that this innocent creature almost got killed." She turns and glares at both of her injured sons before returning her attention to him. "So how are my darlings, Rotzen?"

"Sýnnefo, Dóro, and Tycherós are growing so fast. Dóro and Tycherós are learning to walk on their own, but Sýnnefo is a bit behind. As for Tanzas, Majorno, and Fuschas are excellently lying beside the eggs and keeping their unborn sisters warm. By the way, have you found anything for them to eat? The children will be starving once they finish their naps."

"Nope, nothing. There hasn't been any sign of humans around the desert without having to go back to that town." Margohot takes a moment to take a deep breath. "Now that push has come to shove, we might as well hunt everyone in that town."

"We mind as well because we're out, Mother. If we want to welcome new flock members, we need to start gathering more food supplies that will last through winter."

"I have to show our friends who we found first. While we're in the torture room, please prepare some clay so we can start patching up your brothers' wounds."

Margohot walks past Rotzen and heads to the doorway on the other side of the room, which also has a curtain covering the entranceway. Once Chap gets past the curtain, he sees two bearded men being chained up against the wall, and they are pantless. Their only clothing is their torn shirts, revealing their scars between the holes. Their feces pile below them, revealing that they've never stepped out of this room, urinating and scatting where they stand. The room they're in is much smaller and has bloodstains all over every surface and appears to be recent. Chap can't recognize either one of the flock's prisoners, but they are the postal inspectors.

Not only has it been so long since they last saw each other, but Louie appears to be much thinner, has grown a full beard, has hair touching his chest, and is covered with scars. As bad as Secoli looks, he appears much healthier than his comrade, who's also chained against the wall on the other side of the room. Jed has scars all over his body as well, but his skin condition has blue spots that spread much farther than his chest to his exposed groin. The once proud and brave postal inspector is even more unrecognizable to Chap. Those ill-looking blue spots from Pluck's head to his toes disturb the parakeet and are far worse than when they last saw each other. Pluck even appears barely alive as he remains motionless, his back against the wall and his arms held high.

"Ch-Chap?" Secoli mutters with a sore throat. "Chap? Chap! Is that you?" Despite how sore Louie's throat is, Chap recognizes his master's voice. After spending this whole time remaining motionless on the harpy queen's hand, Chap finally moves and chirps with glee. Despite hurting as he moves, the parakeet has never felt so alive and relieved to see his old master again, despite wishing to be in better circumstances. All of a sudden, a noise awakens Pluck.

"Oh, thank God!" Secoli cries, already tearing up. "I thought I lost you. What happened to him? Is he all right? Why is he all muddy? What did you do to Chap?"

"The mud is covering his injuries, Louie," Margohot replies. "You're lucky Chap survived the barren desert."

Louie can't keep his eyes off Chap. After all the torture and witnessing heinous acts happening to his partner, seeing his bird is a sight for sore eyes. After so much pain and horror, seeing his parakeet again brings hope and relief.

The queen turns to her sons and says to them in Greek, "Fetch me a chair." Ezio leaves the room before Yazeem can make his first step to fulfill his mother's order. As soon as he turns around and realizes his brother is gone, Yazeem puts his head down over how disappointed he is with himself. There's no point in racing his brisk brother. All he can do is stand behind his mother

and his emotions from everyone.

"Since I know how much Chap means to you, Louie," Margohot says, "I'm for once going to be merciful by allowing you to spend time with him. But don't think that I'm doing this for you. No. I'm doing it for Chap, who doesn't deserve any of this. After all that he's been through, he deserves a happy moment."

"Thank you!" Secoli cries. "Thank you so much."

Despite language barriers, Yazeem sees Secoli's gratitude and grows jealous. His efforts to nurture and keep the budgerigar alive are ignored. Still, he keeps hold of his tongue, trying his best not to make the situation worse than it already is. After all he's done for the little bird, he cannot fathom feeling unwanted by his muse.

While Yazeem mopes again, his brother reenters the room with a stool in his hands. Ezio sees his brother holding his head down, noticing the sudden mood change since he left him. He stands next to the queen, presenting her with the wooden seat.

"Good," Margohot says in Greek. "Now, place it right in front of Louie." The male harpy gently places the stool before Chap's owner. The harpy queen approaches the stool and gently places Chap on top. What amazes Margohot is Chap's determination to reunite with his original master. Despite how damaged his body is and how much it hurts for the parakeet to move, he still pushes himself to walk directly to the edge of the stool to Louie. As the postal inspector remains chained up against the wall, he tries to pull himself closer.

Margohot sees how badly the bird and owner are trying to reach each other. This desperation for both species wanting to get in contact again influences Margohot to push the stool to touch Secoli's knees.

The prisoner finally stops squirming and is relieved to feel Chap's head rubbing against his left leg. Despite being chained up, being reunited with his loved one is the most blissful act a prisoner can ask for.

The intimate sight of Chap being comforted by his original master puts Margohot on the verge of tears before saying, "I'll leave you two alone." She then turns to her sons and switches languages. "As for you two, we've got to treat those wounds."

The brothers follow her out back to the nest room. Yazeem is the last to exit the torture room, seeing Chap intimate with the prisoner. Never in his life has he ever seen an exotic animal be so attached to a human being. The amount of jealousy is eating up the caring harpy, who wants to have the same affection from the animal. Watching the two happy be in each other's presence greatly weighs on his heart.

Unable to bear watching the love he yearns for, he slips through the curtains and tries to forget what he saw. The nest's young ones finally quiet down and sleep with the newborns. Looking over Ezio's shoulder, Yazeem sees Rotzen bring in a bowl of clay that he prepared to treat his and Ezio's wounds. Margohot takes half the clay in her hands and puts it in an empty bowl on the ground.

"Rotzen," Margohot says, picking up the bowl, "please treat Ezio's wounds at the cave's entrance. I need to have a word with Yazeem as I patch him up here."

"Yes, Mother," Rotzen replies.

The two brothers head out of the room and into the dark cave. The uncomfortable silence fills the room, making Yazeem feel uneasy. While his mother mixes the clay with her hands, Yazeem senses her anger with him and is anticipating punishment from her.

After mixing the clay to the right consistency and texture, she looks at him and says, "Sit on the stool and face the nest, Yazeem."

He turns to the wooden seat already placed next to the nest. Yazeem does as he's told and sits right before the roost. He looks down instead of looking at the rest of his sleeping sisters.

As he remains motionless on the stool, Margohot commands, "Now turn to your human form so I can patch up every wound your brother inflicted upon you."

Yazeem takes a deep breath, and the feathers on his skin fall to the ground. He is just as naked as his foster mother in her human shape. Since male harpies have no genitalia, being naked in their human form is platonic and nonsexual. Yazeem is not comfortable with this form because all male harpies see it as weak.

As Margohot starts covering the gashes on his back with clay, she says in an unusually calm voice, "Look at what's in front of you." She waits for Yazeem to bring his head up and continues, "Now tell me...what do you see?"

Yazeem swallows his saliva, doing his damnedest to not react toward the pain of his wounds getting tended, and says, "I see...my sisters."

"Right, you are," Margohot says, still treating his bloody back. "And do you know what kind of family members your sisters are?"

"Th-they are the most important ones in the harpy race?" he answers with no confidence nor certainty.

"They are. But why are they important?"

Yazeem takes a moment to think of how to answer her question. He's irritated over how painful the mud is despite how gently Margohot treats his wounds. "Because...we male harpies cannot breed or conceive?"

"Very good. I'm glad my daughter...your original mother of this flock taught you that, did she not?"

"She did." Yazeem takes a deep breath to finish what he's saying. "She taught us a lot of things."

"Do you miss your old mother?" Margohot asks without slowing down. "She was tough and directionless with where she wanted to take the flock

when we...you know, we were once a bigger flock."

"Did she treat you well?"

"I'm a male. And I had sisters who were her favorite children. I couldn't compete. I never was close to her as much as I wanted to."

"I see. How did Ezio, Rotzen, Ypsipétis, and Barthas take it when she favored her daughters over you and your brothers?"

"I can't say. All we've ever done is obey her every command and face punishment whenever we slip up."

"And how is violating curfew and keeping the bird a secret from us any different from slipping up when she was in charge?" Margohot continues treating his lower back and says, "Even though you look down upon yourself for being a male, you do have a purpose, you know?"

"And what purpose is that, Mother?"

"What else than to love, care, and protect your flock? The flock is unable to hold together without each other. Why are we on the brink of extinction, and humanity seems to have overpopulated the world?"

"Because of our mistakes?"

"You're partially right, but every human makes as many mistakes, if not more so, than harpies, but somehow they surpass every organism and manage to get on top of the species spectrum. Think about what you've done, which is no different from all the harpies who fell. Think what Ypsipétis and Barthas did that led to their deaths."

"Is it...disobedience?"

His mother hums over his answer before saying, "Obedience is always the key to survival, and disobedience surely has its consequences. But if one is in charge of the flock, who does that leading harpy obey? Think harder."

"Is it leaving the flock, Mother?"

"Yes, and do you know what that's called, my son?" she replies, nearly done treating his lower back. "It's called independence. Humanity has always remained strong because they're dependent on each other. Their willingness to work together has built civilizations and made technological achievements because they have reliability and vision. Throughout my life, I've seen our race always thinking about going off on their own and starting their own flock. Time and time again, they remain underpowered, lack resources and direction, and eventually fall for their insolence. This is exactly why we're so far behind and facing near extinction. Do you know why I'm making you look at your sisters and those eggs right now?

"Because all of them, including you and your brothers, have the potential to fall if you don't remain united as a flock." She starts treating the cuts on his right arm. "The whole world despises what we are, and that's why harpies need to stay together as a single, united flock. Is it important to abandon your flock and risk your life over that silly bird?" She remains quiet to let it sink into Yazeem's thoughts. "I don't want you to end up like Ypsipétis and Barthas. You're too important."

"How am I important, Mother?" Yazeem asks in confusion.

"A flock doesn't mean harpies born from the same mother or a union to share each other's food and living space. It's survival, my son. It's about knowing that the ones you trust will protect and keep you company, even though you might not do the same. I would rather sacrifice myself than watch you fall like the others.

"You're needed more than you realize. I can't be protecting and leading the flock forever. One day, I'll be the next one to fall, and I'll be damned if this flock becomes separated and independent. That's going to put the harpy race to extinction. And don't be disappointed with yourself that you're not a female. If we weren't so close to extinction, I wouldn't mind having more sons than daughters."

Hearing such kind words from someone he thought was as cruel and unforgiving as his biological mother makes it impossible for him to hold back his tears. Margohot can tell Yazeem has been mistreated his whole life after reacting strongly over the words she used to say to her old flock before they all died. Though she lets him cry, it is hard for her to treat his other arm while he's shaking as he tears up.

"Promise me this, Yazeem," Margohot continues, getting in front of him and looking into his eyes, "if I were to one day fall, you will have to lead the flock until one of your sisters is old and mature enough to take over. But until then, this flock needs you as second in command."

"Second in command?" he replies, feeling overwhelmed. "You mean—"

"That's right. I'm assigning you as the rightful prince of this flock. It's your responsibility to keep your queen's flock flying together and lead them to where she needs them to go. That means no more avoiding them. No more fighting them. And no more secrets because all of them will be shared and kept sacred as one flock. Now let me finish patching you up so you can get some rest so we can go hunting soon."

Both Margohot and Yazeem don't say another word to each other. It is hard to remain emotionally strong in front of her while she covers the rest of Yazeem's wounds. He continues sniffing and wiping his tears because the conversation has hit him harder than it should. This whole time of thinking there's a better life out there has made him feel more vulnerable. At this moment, he comes to a compromise, to be utterly loyal.

After his wounds are covered with clay, Yazeem sits beside the nest and leans against the haystack. He closes his eyes as Margohot leaves the nest room. While falling asleep, the young male thinks about how his life would be different if he had Margohot as his biological mother. After being undervalued throughout his life, receiving compliments and being needed is all he ever wanted from anyone.

Before he doses off, Yazeem hears Chap's delightful chirping from the torture room. After understanding the importance of remaining in this flock, Chap no longer matters to him. It's better this way, knowing that the bird prefers the company of his human master than a hybrid like him. Whatever was between Yazeem and Chap was only temporary before the inevitable truth came out. Yazeem learns that true love is the amount of effort from the other party involved instead of the other way around.

HAVING THE CAVALRY take charge of Point Postal brings a lot of sense of hope and security to the townswomen. It's only been a day since they arrived, and already Point Postal is spoiling the cavalry with so much hospitality. The women and children feel safe coming out of the hotel and treating this day as though business hours have returned to normal. The only thing that could make this day better is if the expedition made it back home and brought the good news that they eliminated all the harpies.

While the townswomen put their full attention on the soldiers, Pearl still remains behind the jailhouse. She's still embarrassed about making a bad first impression and is too anxious to see any of the soldiers. From morning till sunset, she's beating herself over, remembering how she ordered Captain Neilson to go barefoot. Sure, the likelihood of them being harpies in disguise is slim, but anything could happen if Dr. Fletcher did so well in pretending to be an ornithologist. Despite Pearl trying to cry quietly alone, Zephyra Klouví can hear her sniffing from her jail cell.

Klouví may not understand what Herbert is crying about, but she witnessed Pearl confront the cavalry this morning. Seeing it through the barred window, the harpy hunter was impressed with how brave the former saloon girl was in front of a squadron of twenty-five soldiers. Since she knows with experience how embarrassing it is to mistake an ally for an enemy, she has an idea as to why Pearl feels so forlorn. Klouví stands on her bed, peeks out of her window, and watches over her. There seems to be a reversed role where the prisoner is watching over the prison guard rather than the other way around.

Klouví sees someone in a cavalry uniform walking toward Pearl, who is having some alone time, through the window. Something was going on. Since Pearl is sitting on the jailhouse's back porch, the harpy hunter can see what's happening behind her.

"Excuse me, ma'am," the soldier says. "I believe you need this to be guarding the jailhouse."

Pearl turns and sees that the same captain she aimed her rifle at hands her the same rifle. Captain Neilson is the last person she wants to see. After retrieving her carbine, Pearl looks away in embarrassment.

"Thank you," Pearl responds, avoiding eye contact. "What is it that you want?"

Captain Neilson sits close to Herbert on the porch. "Just want to see how you're doing. No lady should be all by herself next to a jailhouse."

"I'm doing just fine." She slides farther away from the soldier. "I'm assigned to be here anyway. There's no telling when those harpies will come back to finish the job."

"Yeah...about that." Captain Neilson takes off his Stetson and rubs the back of his head in embarrassment. "Something about what you and the women are telling me ain't right. I have no doubt that any of you are telling me any lies since all the women I met are consistent in describing these monsters—I'm just having a hard time believing it."

"Can we not talk about them, please?" Pearl raises her voice, then backtracks over how rude that was. "Sorry. It's just a sensitive subject considering how many we've lost to those abominations."

"Of course. My apologies, Miss Herbert. I didn't know how it affected you."

"Please. I don't want to talk about it. I don't want to see anyone right now."

"Now, I can't let a lady be left out here when it's getting dark. If they're that dangerous, then why stay all the way out here? Why not somewhere safer?" Zephyra Klouví becomes bored with eavesdropping on their conversation.

She isn't the romantic type or even interested in other people's relationship status or love affairs. The harpy hunter has seen enough to know that the captain's intention isn't lustful but innocent romance. She sighs in relief after getting down and sitting on her bed, knowing nothing drastic is happening.

Just as she hears Klouví's bed creaking, Lorraine Payton whispers, "What did you see? What's going on out—"

Klouví interrupts Payton by shushing her and whispers, "Do you hear that?"

Payton remains quiet briefly before whispering, "I don't hear anything but those two outside. What is it?"

They remain quiet a little longer until Lorraine hears it more clearly outside. A familiar noise echoing across the desert that hasn't been heard for weeks suddenly sends shivers down their spines. Even though there is a wall between Klouví and Payton, the harpy hunter can hear Payton whimpering because she knows what is coming.

Pearl's voice is heard from outside, yelling, "Oh, no!"

"What? You've never heard an eagle's call before?" Captain Neilson replies. The noise is heard again, making Pearl say, "No, Captain. That's no eagle."

Both the prison guard and the cavalry captain get up from the porch and run around the jailhouse. Klouví hears multiple shrieks, indicating that the harpies are returning. This could only mean that the townsmen who went after the fiends have failed and are probably dead.

"No. No. No!" Lorraine cries in a panic. "Oh, please, God. No."

Klouví stands on top of the bed again and looks out the only barred window in her jail cell. There's no one in sight. This could only mean the harpies are approaching from the other side of the building. The harpy hunter starts breathing heavily, thinking about what to do, remaining stuck in the jail cell. "Zephyra!" Payton cries loudly, pounding on the stone wall between them.

"Get me out of here! I don't want to die, Zephyra! I don't want to die!"

"Shut up, Lorraine!" the harpy hunter shouts. "Give me time to think. If you value your life, remain quiet before any of them f—"

She then gets interrupted by a series of gunfire coming in the direction where the harpy's call is coming from. It becomes so loud that the prisoners can't hear each other. There's no telling what's happening outside. The pandemonium builds anxiety in poor old Lorraine, who feels absolutely helpless. Knowing this is happening all over again makes her scream for help and banging the bars in her jail cell.

Then, the firing ceases when a familiar ear-piercing shriek roars throughout the town. The two prisoners can barely hear the soldiers and townswomen scream from one of the harpies' unbearable, raucous shrieks. This won't be Miss Payton's first time hearing the fiends, but it doesn't make reliving the experience any better. She covers her ears for dear life and cowers in the corner of her jail cell.

Klouví herself has experienced this harpy tactic many times before and knows how to counteract this ploy. She immediately grabs a pillow and gets underneath her bed. She then lies on her stomach against the moldy, filthy wooden floor. She then places the pillow behind her head, covering both ears to protect them.

The harpy hunter can still hear the harpy's screaming through the thick pillow, but she keeps it tight to prevent hearing loss. If only she had her earplugs and crossbow, she would be able to withstand the violent noise and end the beasts. However, since the expedition took them, she has to think of another plan to fight the predators.

After endless shrieking, the harpy outside finally stops to catch its breath. Despite saving herself from going deaf, Klouví now hears the soldiers, the screams, and the bloodshed from outside. Even more disturbing is the townswomen and the children joining the screams of the men, who are beyond saving.

"Zephyra!" Lorraine shouts. "Zephyra! Save me!"

"Lorraine!" Klouví yells back, getting up from under the bed and running to the prison bars. "Can you hear me? Lorraine!"

"Zephyra!" Payton cowers in the corner of her jail cell. "Oh, God! Zephyra! Help!"

As she's trying to get her prison mate's attention, Klouví looks around the jailhouse's office for anything that might help them escape. She sees a pickaxe lying against the side of the sheriff's desk. Despite being too far, Payton's jail cell is the closest to that desk.

As Klouví's about to instruct her cellmate, she hears her scream, "Zephyra! Oh, Lord! Why don't you answer?"

At that moment, Klouví realizes Payton has become deaf. The fact that deafness from a harpy's scream takes a long time to recover from unless it is permanent makes it pointless to tell Lorraine to reach for the pickaxe with something. The harpy hunter slips her arm between the last jail bar and the wall. As she waves in front of the jail cell, attempting to get her cellmate's attention, Loraine continues her endless screaming.

"I'm here!" Klouví calls out, waving blindly to her jail cell. "Stop screaming!"

Then, a sudden loud bump is heard at the front door, startling Klouví to put her hand back in her jail cell. The sound of the massacre reaching the jailhouse's front porch indicates that the harpies are getting closer, and Payton's screams will draw attention. With danger being so close, Klouví quickly examines her jail cell for any points of interest. Her cell is too well structured to make an escape. The walls are made out of bricks, the jail bars are immovable, and the bars on the cell's only window aren't any weaker. After running back and forth in her confined cell, she almost trips over a soft surface.

She looks down at the center of the wooden floor and notices a weak, spongy area. A thought immediately comes to her that this area of the floor has sustained water damage. She remembers that she caused the water damage when she bathed herself when it rained weeks ago. No thanks to the cell's floor being moldy and dirty throughout, the harpy hunter never noticed the mold until now. She stomps on the same spot and feels the wooden floor being pushed down.

Knowing this is the best thing to happen right now, Klouví stomps harder and continuously, seeing pieces of the wooden floor breaking. Out of desperation, Zephyra gets on top of her bed, jumps as high as she can, and lands hard on that area. As she lands, the wooden tiles detach from each other, and pieces come out. Progress is being made much faster with this method. Klouví gets back on her bed and makes another jump onto the breaking wood. Immediately, she goes through the wood and lands on the dirt underneath.

Klouví steps out of the hole she created and moves some of the pieces of the wooden floor out of the way. She then flips the bed over and drags the mattress and bedframe upside down to the center of the room. As she gets to the lower deck, she pulls the upside-down bed over the opening to cover her tracks.

There's little space between the sandy ground and the ceiling on the lower deck.

Klouví crawls around, looking for an exit in the dark space. As she makes her way through the dark lower deck, she hears the massacre much clearer than when she was in her cell. The survivors fight back with gunfire, but the harpy hunter knows that bullets are almost useless against the hungry harpies. After crawling through the lower deck and bumping into some pillars, Klouví finally reaches a wall. She rolls onto her back and starts kicking the wooden surface as hard as possible. While she struggles to break the wooden surface ahead of her, a man is heard getting knocked down and carved alive by one of the harpies. His screams of pain and the sounds of flesh being ripped open are enough to make the harpy hunter turn around and move away from the murder occurring on the other side of the wall.

The only light ahead of Klouví is the hole she created back in her jail cell. In the same direction, she still hears Lorraine's cries for help. Zephyra kicks the ceiling to grab her prison mate's attention. The deaf woman is startled by the sudden shake on the floor she's standing on, thinking the fiends are underneath her.

"Stay away!" Payton screams, getting on her bed for safety. "Stay away!"

"It's Zephyra!" Klouví yells back, kicking the wood. "Can you hear me, Lorraine?"

It's no use. Payton remains hysterical over the invasion. The woman's deafness prevents their chance to work together and hide. Klouví gives up kicking the lower-deck ceiling and is out of ideas as to how she can make a break for it. The harpy hunter remains in the lower deck on high alert, listening closely to her surroundings, which are filled with mass hysteria and violence.

As there are fewer and fewer people screaming and less gunfire, Klouví hears footsteps above the lower deck's ceiling. Whoever enters the jailhouse is moving with urgency. Based on the sounds of the footsteps, it sounds like nothing a harpy could make with their talons in either their true or human form.

A familiar voice is heard above where Klouví lies, yelling, "Where the hell is that harpy hunter? Lorraine, where did she go?"

Payton gets down from her bed and runs to the jail bar, screaming, "Oh, thank God! It's you, Pearl! Hurry! Get me out of here!"

"I can't hear you," Pearl replies without any volume control. "You're going to have to speak louder. Tell me where she is so she can save us."

Pearl is just as deaf as Lorraine. If Klouví were to escape, she wouldn't be able to give any commands and successfully counteract these fiends. Overhearing their conversation, Klouví realizes that Pearl wants to free the harpy hunter and save the town. Klouví continues to call out to her, but she doesn't respond. After giving up on calling for her, the harpy hunter then crawls back to her jail cell to get Pearl's attention.

Still unable to hear what Payton is saying, Herbert reads her body language, how desperately she wants to leave, and says, "Oh, right. Hold on. Let me get you out."

As Klouví hears Pearl's keychain being pulled out, another series of footsteps is heard entering the room. As each step hits the floor, it doesn't sound like boots stomping but bare feet with long nails tapping against the wooden floor. The harpy hunter stops in her tracks when she hears Lorraine scream differently than previously.

"Pearl! Look behind you!" Payton exclaims. "It's one of them!"

As soon as Payton's jail door unlocks, Pearl whimpers after the sound of talons piercing flesh is heard. Klouví remains completely still on her stomach as all this is happening above her. She realizes what's going on up there as she feels blood dripping between the wooden tiles. Once she feels a body land on the floor, she knows it's far too late to save their prison guard.

The harpy slowly enters Lorraine's jail cell and pleasures itself in listening to Lorraine's screaming. It becomes worse for Klouví to hear the fiend doing a greater number on her cellmate. The sound of Payton's cries of pain mixed with organs being torn to pieces is perturbing for the harpy hunter. The only person in town Zephyra ever opened up to is being treated as nothing more than food being played by a merciless child. Once Lorraine becomes silent, she becomes another victim Klouví couldn't save.

It slowly becomes quieter not only in the jailhouse but also in the rest of town.

Knowing one of the harpies is above her, Klouví doesn't dare move a muscle. Besides the horses being spared and neighing out of shock, no signs of life are heard. Klouví can only hear bodies in the jailhouse being dragged out the front door. Even though she hears the harpies flap their wings and flee from the massacre scene, Klouví keeps still.

After a period of silence, the harpy hunter wipes the blood off of her. Klouví crawls to where Lorraine's blood slips through and starts kicking the wooden boards as hard as possible. She doesn't stop until a piece of a board detaches. Once she sees the light between the cracks above her, the harpy hunter pushes the ceiling with her back. She uses all her strength to push her way out of the lower deck and into Payton's jail cell.

While catching her breath, Klouví looks around the cell and sees Lorraine is not present. Rather, she notices parts of Payton's organs on the floor and a trail of her blood leading to the jailhouse's front door that's opened. The harpy hunter sees Pearl lying motionless on the floor next to the jail door. She slowly walks to see what the harpy did to the troubled woman. She sees four lacerations across her chest and lungs. The harpy hunter closes Pearl's eyelids out of respect and exits the jail cell. As horrifying as it is to see her lying dead, nothing can prepare Klouví for the aftermath outside.

Klouví turns and looks out the entrance door, already seeing countless black feathers left behind. She slowly exits through the front door and sees more black and crimson feathers all over the main road with all the corpses. As she walks through the new ghost town, she feels numb, and tears roll down her cheeks. Despite how poorly the town has treated her, she never wished ill toward any of its citizens. It's much too overwhelming to witness these bodies lying all over the road, as well as the shed feathers from the harpies' frenzy.

Klouví's numbness becomes unbearable when she sees a pile of feathers blowing away and revealing a dead child lying on top of her mother. It's enough to take her breath away and bring her to her knees. She turns her back to the jailhouse, directing north. In her direction, she sees four harpies fly away in the distance, each carrying prey. The fact that individuals who once interacted with her have become fresh meat is enough to get Klouví's blood boiling. Now, she is motivated to go after them and finish this once and for all. Before she starts moving, the harpy hunter hears the clicking noise of a gun coming from the stable on her left.

Klouví faces that direction and sees Captain Neilson point a rifle at her. The captain walks out of the stable, and the harpy hunter keeps still. The blue uniform identifies him as a cavalryman, and he appears to be unharmed despite being soaked in what appears to be water. Klouví is surprised to see there's a survivor from this onslaught but is confused as to why he's pointing a gun at her.

The captain places the gun's barrel on her neck and commands, "Take off your boots and show me your feet. Now!"

He's doing exactly what Pearl told him this morning when he arrived in town and is taking this advice to heart. Klouví kneels and unties her boots. She removes them and places her feet on the rough road for him to see. After seeing her feet are as human as ever, Neilson stops pointing his gun at her and takes a deep breath.

"Goddamn," the captain mutters. "I'm glad you're normal. How are you able to hear me so well when everyone else has gone deaf from those damn screams?"

"I used a pillow from my jail cell to cover my ears. How are you able to

hear me after hearing the harpy's shrieking here outside?"

"I made a smart decision in dunking my head in the water trough in the stable. I wish everyone did the same so they could hear my commands."

"Ah. That explains why you're soaked. That is a smart way to counteract."

"We have no time to waste." The captain grabs the harpy hunter's wrist.

"C'mon. We've got to get you somewhere safe."

Klouví pulls her arm away and says, "That will be a big mistake, sir. I can't let the harpies make their escape while they're on the run."

"Tell me...," the captain says. "You're that harpy hunter the women informed me about, right? I'm sorry we didn't get you out sooner when we needed you the most."

"It's too late," Klouví replies, getting up from fixing her boots. "No one can save them now. I don't want anyone else to fall victim to the harpies. I must go."

"Wait a minute," Neilson says and reaches out to her. "You're not going after them empty-handed, are you? Here. Take this carbine."

"That is no use against the harpies. Bullets are like rocks to them, and this will not be enough to take one down."

"Let me come with you."

"No. I don't travel well with strangers. You will slow me down."

"Before you go out there…" The captain takes out his canteen from the side of his belt. "You're going to die of thirst out there. Here, take this with you." Klouví takes his canteen, opens the lid, and drinks. The captain remains quiet, impressed that she's nonstop drinking it all like a man. The harpy hunter finishes every last drop, wipes her lips, and hands the captain his canteen back. "That's not what I meant," the captain says. "Never mind. If I can't join you, then what can I do to help?"

"How many soldiers are there close by?"

"My whole brigade is in Wyoming as we speak."

"Go back to your army and send every man back here. We're going to need all the manpower we can get to take all four of them down. I'll sneak in and destroy their nest. They'll chase after me once they discover what I did. I'll lure them to your army so we can once and for all destroy them. I'll meet you back here tomorrow."

"How many do you think we need to kill those four bastards?"

"Do you know how many stones it takes to kill a person? It's the same with bullets against a harpy. We need to overwhelm them with as many bullets as necessary."

The two of them get on the horses that were spared by the harpies. Klouví rides north in the direction where the fiends flew. Captain Neilson rides east where he came from. As the two separate, Neilson rides on autopilot, thinking how unbelievable this experience has been.

Throughout his militaristic experience, Neilson has never seen bloodshed as barbaric and one-sided as this. It takes one attack by harpies to change anyone's outlook on life, and he's no different. Never before has Neilson felt so powerless that he's determined to get every soldier in his brigade to take those monsters down. As the sun sets, he looks back at Zephyra Klouví going farther away, hoping she'll be all right. Now that he's seen the cause of Wyoming's disappearances, he's determined to follow the harpy hunter's plan and hopes to see her again.

CHAPTER 17

Pluck has lost count of how many days he's been held in the harpies' torture room. Having his arms chained against the wall and only being released whenever Margohot needs him to mate is undesirable, to say the least. On top of being so emotionally and physically damaged by this harrowing experience, Pluck's symptoms worsen each day. The postal inspector is so weak and unhealthy that it takes a lot of strength to open his eyes and keep them open whenever he needs to see.

To make things even harder, Pluck used to be able to easily pass out as he uncomfortably hung against the walls of the torture room with each passing day. However, since Secoli's reunion with Chap yesterday, it has been tough for Pluck to fall asleep to cope with the pain. He finds it annoying that his partner is so joyously chained up against the wall before him while the budgerigar is on the stool next to Secoli. His partner constantly makes baby-like voices and whistles, keeping the bird and himself amused. Pluck understands that they've been missing each other, but this isn't the right time or place to play around, especially when Secoli's arms are chained against the wall.

"Give it a rest, Louie," Pluck says with a sore throat. "Your amusement with that bird is keeping me up when I want to get some sleep."

"Sorry, Jed." Secoli immediately stops whistling to the bird. "It's just been so long since...well, you know. It's just a miracle that he survived and is here now."

"Well, you're keeping me awake." Pluck then gets annoyed with Chap still chirping. "And tell that damn bird to shut up, will ya? It's giving me such a headache."

"Hey!" Secoli raises his voice, unhappy with Pluck's remark. "That's no way to talk to Chap. He's not the issue here, Jed!"

Chap stops chirping and moves away from his owner on the stool, intimidated by his owner's sudden change in tone. Pluck opens his eyes and looks at his partner on the other side of the confined room and sees Secoli frowning at him.

After a brief silence, Pluck says, "I'm sorry. I should have said it better."

"No, I'm the one who should be apologizing. Who are we to fight where we've been pissing and shitting here for so long?"

Pluck snorts, then chuckles over Secoli's remark. At first, Secoli is confused over why he's suddenly giggling in a place like the torture room. As his partner laughs even louder, he realizes what he said was perfect timing and starts laughing with him. Despite being locked up for so long, the postal inspectors found themselves amused, discovering that finding humor in a hellish situation brought out their biggest laughs.

The laughing doesn't last long as they hear a commotion from the curtained doorway. They both immediately become quiet over the possibility that the harpies might be approaching. Both of their moments of escapism come back to the harsh reality they're in, changing from joy back to trauma. Pluck anxiously sweats over the anticipation of receiving punishment for being so loud. Knowing what they've already been through, the postal inspectors keep quiet for dear life.

Usually, whenever a harpy approaches, both postal inspectors can hear their talons clink on the ground with every step they make or the flapping of their wings. This time, they don't hear any of it. There's a possibility that the harpies might be playing mind games with the prisoners, but they never have since they've been held captive. Still, they've been so traumatized by the experience that they've already regretted laughing among themselves.

After a while, Pluck breaks his silence and whispers, "I don't think anyone's out there. I don't even hear the babies crying, either. Thought of a plan to escape, yet?"

Secoli sighs and whispers back, "No. Every time I think of something, I immediately think of how it could fail. Let's face it, Jed. We lost. Looks like we're going to spend the rest of our lives chained up and being fed pieces of our contemporaries. God, I hate the taste of human flesh." Secoli sighs again, places his head down, and lightly sobs. "I hate the fact that those monsters forced us into... cannibalism."

"Hey." Pluck glares at his partner. "Don't let what they forced us to do become who we are. You and I are not cannibals. Look at me, Louie."

Louie lifts his head to see Pluck's eyes gleaming in the faint light.

"You and I are not cannibals. Got that? When we get out of here, you will never again eat human parts. I've seen victims and comrades from the Civil War become their assailants because they can never come to terms with their trauma, coping to become what they hate. You're better than that, Louie."

Secoli is surprised to see that this is the boldest Pluck has been since they arrived in Point Postal. Despite his appearing ever so ailing, this is the most lively he has been in weeks. Even though everything is grim, this gives Secoli the spark he needs. What Jed says to him has a good effect on him, realizing that being traumatized by this case would consume him just like it's still doing to him from his time in service.

Secoli gives his partner a nod before replying, "There's something I've been wanting to know since you brought it up; which side of the war did you fight for?"

"I fought for the Union." Pluck swallows his saliva anxiously. "Why do you ask?"

Secoli makes another sigh, but one out of relief. "Oh, thank goodness. I wasn't sure if you were a Confederate or Union soldier."

"Is that what's been bothering you about me this whole time?" Pluck chuckles. "Have you been paying attention to my accent? I have a Mid-Atlantic voice. There's no way that I would have fought for the Confederates."

"Yeah, but have you forgotten about the damn Copperheads that were originally from the North supporting the South's cause—and they even went to war against us?"

"I forgot about those poor bastards. Which division were you assigned to?"

"I lived in Maryland and was assigned to the Eastern Theater by default.

I was supposed to be in the District of Eastern Shore of Maryland, but the Department of Pennsylvania needed a standard bearer, so that's where I was assigned to."

"Holy shit! You were a standard bearer for the Department of Pennsylvania? How the hell did you survive the First Battle of Bull Run?"

"I like to ask God about that myself. I was..." Secoli chokes up for a moment. "...shot in that battle and held as Shenandoah's prisoner until his army was ambushed by the Union in one of their battles. I can't for the life of me remember how long I was kept as their prisoner, what battle it was that got me out, or what division rescued me. I can't get my experience in Bull Run out of my head ever since."

"Shit." Pluck looks down in pity. "Now I understand why you need Chap." Secoli looks at the parakeet, rubbing his head against his master's knee. "The Army of the Shenandoah is the Confederacy's most ruthless division based on what I heard—especially to their captives. Sorry you had to go through that. I'm even sorrier that you're held as a prisoner again."

"Don't mention it. But you didn't answer my question. Which division were you assigned to?"

"I lived in New Hampshire and joined as an infantryman. But like you, I wasn't assigned to my home state's district, even though I, too, was in the Eastern Theater. I was in the Army of Northeastern Virginia."

"Hold on," Secoli interrupts. "Isn't the Army of Northeastern Virginia the Army of the Potomac? That means we could have met each other."

"I doubt it," Jed says. "I didn't join until I was old enough to serve. I came in a couple of years after Bull Run, so there was no way we could have met."

"That's a shame. Since you were part of Potomac, were you with them until...you know. When did your district surrender to the Confederacy?"

"When they surrendered to the Army of Northern Virginia, I ran off to Maryland and joined the District of Eastern Shore of Maryland before I became a prisoner for not surrendering with them. It disappointed me that the whole state of Virginia became part of the Confederacy. I was so loyal to President Lincoln and his cause that there was no way I would ever compromise."

"Thank you. It's such a relief that you fought in the Union."

"You thought I was a Confederate? God forbid I ever fought for those damn traitors. Is it really that intimidating for you to talk about the war?"

"It's not that talking about the war intimidates me. It's just that whenever I encounter a veteran from that war, I'm intimidated because the Confederates traumatized me. Even though it's been over thirty years since the war, some still believe in slavery in this country."

"I know what you mean. Despite abolishing slavery and making the people of color just as American as you and me, something we fought for still doesn't seem like a complete victory."

"What do you mean by that?" Louie asks.

"Even though there's no more slavery, people of color seem to be mistreated daily by whites. Knowing how stubbornly Americans refuse to compromise, that mentality somehow crept into the North. Instead of seeing white folks living harmoniously with people of different skin colors, I see division among communities. If Abe Lincoln were alive, he would have done more to finalize the issue I see in the North."

"You really believe he would have done more if he weren't assassinated?" Jed nods. "I do. I remember in the Boston Post Office Square when the office was short of staff years ago black Americans applied for those positions as mail clerks. But the one running the whole post office didn't even consider them despite some being qualified for the job. I asked him why none of them were hired. He responded that none of them would represent the Square well. He fought for the Union, like you and me, but it disappointed me that despite being against slavery, he didn't support non-whites."

"Is he still working there in the Square?" Louie asks.

"Yes, he's still in that position. When I brought up to the postmaster this issue of not hiring non-whites, they said it was perfectly legal to do so. What troubles me about that approach is not only does it defeat my purpose of fighting to abolish slavery, but also those candidates for the job cannot change the one thing everyone notices but is born with. Tell me, Louie. How did the state of Massachusetts fight for the Union then end up mistreating the people they fought for?"

"I-I don't really know, Jed. This is the first time this has been brought to my attention since I've avoided political discussions for so long. I never really thought about everything you said. My only guess is that there hasn't been a president since Lincoln who has paid as much attention to that aspect of this country."

"It makes me worried how the current generation will continue this mentality with their children and grandchildren. I don't know if Lincoln's vision of unionizing America will ever come to fruition. With the way things are happening now, I don't think I'll ever see it in my lifetime, at least."

There's a pause in the conversation as the two postal inspectors consider the topic being discussed. It's the first time they've had a deep discussion, and it's refreshing for both of them to get their minds off the harpies and discuss something human for once. Somehow this conversation is so personal that neither can continue the discussion.

Moments after the end of their conversation, Secoli startles Pluck by whispering, "Hey. I think someone's coming. I hear one of them on the other side of the curtain."

"Please let that not be her," Pluck whimpers, quaking with fear. "Please let that not be her."

"Shut up, Jed," Secoli whispers loudly.

"Oh, Lord!" Pluck cries loudly, pouring out tears. "Please, Louie. Don't let her take me away. For God's sake. Don't let her take me away."

"Would you please shut up? You know what happened the last time you got so loud that you woke those babies up?"

A familiar voice that sounds Mediterranean speaks on the other side of that curtain. "I think you'd better do as your partner says..." Then a familiar face pops in, brightening up the torture room. "...because flocks hate it when you wake their young."

The light from the other room blinds both postal inspectors as it always does whenever one of the harpies enters. However, this is no harpy that appears right before them. A sight for sore eyes brings Secoli more joy than reuniting with Chap as he blinks profusely, adjusting to the brightness.

"Zephyra?" Secoli says. "Is that really you, Ms. Klouví?"

She shushes and covers her nose before replying, "God, it smells much worse in here than out there. Yes. It is me." She quickly looks at both prisoners. "I see they took your pants and shoes. I wish I had brought extra clothes with me."

The harpy hunter heads toward Secoli and pulls out a bobby pin and a piece of metal. She then grabs Secoli's wrist and uses the pin to unlock the chains. She does her best to avoid stepping on his feces below him.

"How in the world did you find us?" Secoli whispers with utmost glee. "Everyone in town is dead," she replies while picking the lock. "I got out

without the harpies noticing."

"What?" Secoli asks, surprised.

"What did you say?" Pluck replies in complete shock. "Say it ain't so."

"It is true," Klouví replies. "The flock went on a full-on attack and spared no one.

Even the cavalry that came to the rescue died with all the women and children."

"My God...," Secoli mutters in disbelief as he stares into space. "The women...the children.... And the cavalry? We failed to save Point Postal."

"You mean to tell me no one survived?" Pluck asks, feeling perturbed. "No one." Klouví unlocks and frees Secoli's left arm. She then unlocks the only chain. "All except one soldier who survived. I told him to get more soldiers while I went after the nest. It took me a whole day to find this place. I understand why Margohot kept Inspector Pluck alive, but why did she spare you? You don't show any signs of having the harpy disease. Do you have desirable genes like him?"

Neither of the prisoners answers the harpy hunter's question. They both are stunned and appalled that the harpies have made Point Postal the next ghost town. Even when Klouví frees Secoli's other hand, he doesn't rub his wrist with relief. He falls on his knees and makes the thousand-yard stare over how egregious Margohot and her flock truly are. Even Chap, on the stool next to him, notices his master's disassociation.

"They also killed the cavalry?" Secoli mutters. "What chance do we have in taking those monsters down?"

Klouví leaves Secoli alone as she focuses on freeing the other postal inspector. Pluck is taking this sudden news as hard as his partner. Shivers come down his spine, and his jaw shakes over the thought that the women and children suffered a terrible fate. Once Klouví unchains Pluck's wrists, she catches him from collapsing. Despite losing so much weight while being held prisoner, he's still too heavy for the five-foot-three woman to carry to assist the six-foot Federal agent.

"Hey, you," Klouví whispers to Secoli, still on his knees. "Please help me.

He is too big and heavy for me to carry. I cannot carry him alone."

Secoli rises from his knees and wobbles as he stands. He takes a few steps toward the harpy hunter and his partner. It has always been dark in the torture room, but when he gets closer to Pluck, he clearly sees the horrible shape he is in. He carefully puts Pluck's arm around his neck and helps Klouví carry him. Despite how much his feet ache, Pluck walks with his carriers to make this escort more bearable. Before slipping through the curtain, Secoli grabs the injured Chap from the wooden stool, finally exiting the torture room.

As they leave the torture chamber, they find themselves face to face with a nest of harpy chicks. Klouví pulls the postal inspectors to the nest, and they all see the chicks asleep with the three eggs in the middle. They all grow uncomfortable seeing the next generation of harpies looking innocent yet aware of their capabilities. Pluck is horrified that the three firstborns very much resemble his little girls at home.

"How long have we been held captive?" Secoli whispers in horror. "The last we saw these bastards was when they were just infants. They've doubled in size."

"Harpies grow fast," Klouví replies quietly, "and in puberty, they go rampant. They become fully mature adults within fourteen years."

"My God," Secoli whispers. "And I heard from Margohot that she has lived over a century. How can they have such short childhoods and live twice as long as humans?"

"It is the human flesh that they feed on that's giving them extraordinary growth and a longer lifespan than any organism," the harpy hunter answers quietly. "While it's common for females to live up to two centuries, it's rare for the males to live that long since there's only been one male on record that lived that long."

"Goddamn," Secoli swears. "No wonder that freak Margohot prefers females. Those females are more beneficial to the species than just for reproduction."

"How is it possible for a female harpy like Margohot to bring this many children in so little time?" Pluck mutters.

"Unlike female mammals," Klouví continues, "eggs bear children at a much faster rate than pregnancy. Female harpies ovulate their eggs within four days after mating with a human male. It takes an additional four days for those eggs to hatch. And it takes six years for a hatchling to enter puberty."

"So what do we do next?" Secoli asks. "We can't just let them live, can we?" They all become silent over Secoli's words, knowing where this is heading. The idea of harming something so young makes all of them uncomfortable. It won't be the first for Klouví to eliminate a nest of harpy hatchings, but the postal inspectors are inexperienced. Both of them are uncomfortable with what must be done.

"You two," Klouví says slowly and softly, sounding more serious than she usually does. "Turn around and let me finish the job."

"Wait...," Pluck replies, pausing momentarily. "Let me do it. It's my fault that I brought these abominations into this world. And I need to undo what I've done."

Pluck removes his arms from Secoli and Klouví's shoulders and walks to the nest.

He looks at the ground and sees a rock with a pointy edge. He picks it up and stares intensely at the stone before glaring at his sleeping harpy children. He harbors a great sense of guilt and sympathy over the fact that they're so young. Even harder is that they all look like his little Janet when she was a baby. He's indecisive about committing prolicide, feeling the gravity of this situation that's making his stomach turn.

After much stalling, Pluck swallows and says, "I'm ready. Turn around, Louie. I don't want you to see any of this."

Secoli immediately does what he's been told and puts Chap next to his chest.

Pluck doesn't bother checking if his partner obeys him when he climbs into the nest. He takes a deep breath before holding one of the older ones down and stones the young one right in the skull. His lack of strength against the harpy's durability only wakes the toddler. She cries in a tremendous amount of pain, sounding like an eaglet. This only wakes up her other five siblings.

The two older ones wake up and analyze their surroundings. They look at what Pluck is doing to their sibling and immediately crawl out of the nest. The younger ones lie where they are, next to the eggs, and continue their birdlike cries over their rude awakening. Pluck becomes immobilized and stares at the baby he's holding down. He's in complete shock over what he has done. Already, he feels like a horrible father over something he'd never imagined he'd do.

Klouví notices the two older babies attempting to make their escape. She grabs a sizable stone lying next to her that requires both hands to carry and runs up to one of them, who's already climbing its way out of the nest. The escaping toddler catches a glance at the harpy hunter approaching her. Before it can react, Klouví stones the young one with the small boulder, splitting its skull open. Unlike Pluck, Klouví successfully kills the baby harpy and doesn't hesitate to go after the next one.

Pluck starts tearing up over killing something related to him. He still keeps the young one down on the haystack before giving it another stoning to the head. Blood splatters onto his face, but the young one is still alive. She struggles to free herself by slapping her wings and attempting to claw her biological father's wrist with her underdeveloped talons. It is pointless to tell Pluck to let go, as she will continue to be hit on the head.

Meanwhile, Klouví begins stoning the infants. The infanticide continues as she uses only half her strength to crush the infants. The only harpy chick still screaming is the one Pluck is struggling to kill. As Klouví crushes the last infant, she focuses on the unhatched eggs. She takes a deep breath before aborting the unborn baby harpies.

She stones the closest egg to her, and fluid splatters all over the nest. Klouví, Pluck, and his victim get soaked in the egg's fluid. The embryo from the egg slips out, allowing Klouví to crush it even though it's already dead upon premature hatching. She then cracks open the other two eggs, with even more fluid splattering out of the nest and hitting Secoli. Louie startles after feeling something wet and warm touch his back but doesn't dare turn around.

After the third egg is mercilessly aborted, Pluck finally ends his victim as she stops crying and moving. Despite the chick not showing any life, Pluck continues to stone it. He stares blankly and goes on autopilot as he continues beating the chick with the stone. It's like a man possessed where his body is still committing infanticide while his mind is thinking of the guilt.

Pluck continues to stare at the last one that Klouví stoned. He feels a tremendous amount of guilt that's weighing on his heart. He struggles to convince himself that none of these are his children, and he hasn't committed prolicide. But the damage he's incurred is so hard for him to fathom that he refuses to see the damage the harpy hunter has done to the rest of the nest.

Klouví sees Pluck traumatized over this ordeal, and Klouví gets in front of him and says, "Inspector, I know it is hard for you to take, but we can't waste another moment while we have the chance to escape."

"I can't believe I killed my children," Pluck mutters, staring into blank space. "What? No. You did the right thing. Those harpy babies would have just been—"

Crying in horror, Pluck interrupts the harpy hunter. "It just won't end!" Secoli finally turns around, hearing Pluck make his last scream after listening to the cries of chicks filling the room. Seeing Pluck covered in blood and fluid and crying over the murdered harpy children becomes another level of horror. Normally, he would immediately go after Pluck whenever he's in trouble, but the scene is so unsettling and revolting that he can't make another step closer to the nest. He places Chap back against his chest, unable to fathom how much worse it is than he imagined. Pluck's screaming goes on longer than

necessary, and Klouví has no choice but to slap him across the face.

"Get a hold of yourself!" Klouví shouts. "They are *not* your children! You understand? They are not human. They are abominations that do not belong in this world. You are not a murderer. You've done the right thing."

"Please, Jed," Secoli says, his eyes watery. "I don't want to spend another goddamn minute in here! I want to go home, but I can't do that without you!"

He offers a hand to Pluck. At first, Jed thinks it's a handshake, but now his mind is clearer. As soon as he gives him a handshake, Secoli pulls him up and places his arm around his neck. He then carries Pluck out of the nest room. Seeing how slow they're moving, Klouví places Pluck's other arm around her shoulders and helps them speed up. Pluck tightly closes his eyes, unable to look back at the genocide scene.

Along the way, the cave's stench changes from smelling like sewage to something fouler. Having both of his arms around his carriers' shoulders makes it impossible for Pluck to cover his nose. The most he can do is hold his breath as they transverse through the cave. Just when things can't get any more uncomfortable, he feels Secoli stop in his tracks as

Klouví continues onward. Pluck is caught in the middle of the two. Like a domino effect, the weight of the two men collapsing causes Klouví to fall to the ground with them.

He shouts in frustration, "What was that all about, Lou—"

He then stops himself when he sees that the series of macabre is still ongoing. Light from the ceiling reveals an array of dead human bodies, disturbing both postal inspectors. It's a pile of bodies that reaches six feet from the ground. Every one of the corpses is completely naked, exposing countless gashes and piercings over each body. In the pile of females and children with their faces sticking out, Pluck recognizes many of the women and children they left behind at Point Postal.

It becomes clear to him that they failed to protect this whole pile of Point Postal's citizens. Secoli and Pluck sit motionless, finding the deaths of the town's citizens far more terrifying than hearing the news from Klouví. The fact that all of them have ghastly wounds far worse than their scars shows how remorseless the harpies are. These once-living sentient beings are nothing more than stocked food. Since Pluck has lost the strength to scream, he instead pants and turns pale. Unable to stomach any more of the carnage, he leans forward and regurgitates the flesh the harpies fed him earlier.

Pluck's vomiting echoes through the cave, making Secoli stop being distracted by the pile of bodies. Secoli sees Pluck's regurgitation colored red as blood and filled with organs, haunting him over what they were fed, as it could have been the remains of anyone from that pile. The thought crawls under his skin, disturbing him so much that he can't make a sound. Instead, Secoli has his head down and throws up the same thing he's been fed with. His vomit is no more pleasant than what Pluck regurgitated.

"Pull yourselves together," the harpy hunter loudly whispers, pulling Pluck back up. "The harpies might return at any moment. We need to hurry." Secoli helps Klouví get Pluck back up, wanting to escape from the body pile. As Secoli helps the harpy hunter carry Pluck away, they can't keep their eyes off the pile of the dead. It makes it hard for Klouví to continue guiding the postal inspectors, who are deeply affected by the countless losses they have witnessed. All she can do is lead the men on the same path she came in, with no alternative paths or different ways of escaping. It becomes easier for her to continue leading the men to their escape once they bypass the pile and continue forward.

"Those fucking bastards!" Pluck cries, closing his eyes and catching his breath. "That damn Jezebel. They killed all of them. How could they be so cold-blooded?"

"Shut it," Klouví whispers right into his ear. "How many times do I have to tell you to be quiet?"

Pluck remains silent as he's being carried out of the cave. His feet hurt with every step he makes, no thanks to the ground getting rockier as they progress farther. He cannot get his mind off of how evil and powerful the harpies truly are.

As they progress, the cave's smell shifts from the corpses' odor to the harpies' stench. It still isn't pleasant, but it's preferable. The postal inspectors are still without pants, feeling the cold wind freezing their legs and groins. Both of them are shivering while Klouví is the only one fully clothed, although she's completely filthy since escaping from the jailhouse. Having traveled through the cave for a lengthy period, the escapees finally reached the cave entrance and came to a halt.

Both postal inspectors squint as they adjust to the bright sunlight and see that it is midday outside. The barren desert was just as desolate as ever.

"Okay," Klouví says. "It took me a long time to climb all the way up here.

I know it's asking a lot, but climbing down is our only option."

"No way in hell am I climbing down with my hand and wrist still in bad shape," Pluck responds. "There has to be a better way."

Secoli snaps his fingers and rushes behind them, saying, "I remember. The men and I left a rope here somewhere. I hope the harpies didn't find it."

Both Pluck and Klouví turn around and see Secoli get behind the stalagmites next to the cave wall. He pops out of stalagmites and pulls out the rope. "It's still here." Secoli laughs joyfully. "It's a miracle those dumb birds never found it. Here, let me wrap this around you, Jed, so Zephyra and I can help you down."

He then wraps the rope around the thickest stalagmite and firmly ties it. Secoli then grabs the other end of the rope and wraps it around Pluck's waist. Despite feeling so ill, he smiles at the thought of successfully escaping and returning home.

As Secoli continues to wrap the rope around his partner's waist, Pluck heads to the cave's exit. He gets his heels on edge, preparing to climb down. Before he starts descending from the plateau, Secoli hands him Chap and gives him a nod, trusting that he'll keep his muse safe. Secoli and Klouví grab the rope and lower Pluck down.

On his way down, Pluck keeps his eyes closed, afraid of heights. This becomes counterproductive as he struggles to use his feet to keep himself from hitting the wall. Not to mention that Secoli and Klouví are releasing the rope faster than he's going. But once he gets to the halfway point, he gets the hang of the pace of descending down without ever opening his eyes. He keeps walking backward, with his feet against the wall, until his heels hit the ground.

Once he gets both of his feet to the ground, Pluck unties the rope around his waist, then shakes it to signal the two above. His hands hurt so much, but he has to endure it. He looks to his left and almost forgets he's had Chap on his shoulder this whole time. This is the first time he's ever interacted with the budgerigar out of its cage, and he finds it therapeutic as he pets the injured bird. Pluck's so distracted with the bird that he doesn't notice that Klouví and Secoli have climbed down safely.

Secoli has his hands on his knees and makes a sigh of relief before saying, "I never thought I'd ever get out of there. Freedom never felt so sweet." He straightens his back when he sees his partner. "Oh, I see that Chap has grown fond of you. You two actually look adorable together."

"Now I can see why you keep this bird around." Pluck hands Chap back to his master. "We gotta keep moving before they find out what we did."

"On to the horse." Klouví stops herself and gasps over something she just remembered. "Wait. My crossbow. What happened to it? Don't tell me you two left it back up there."

"I'm sorry, Zephyra," Secoli replied, "Margohot grabbed it and destroyed it right in front of me. If only my men weren't so careless, we would have skilled the flock."

"Malakai," she swears in Greek. "Never mind. We can still kill them by luring them to the army. Come on. We have no time."

Secoli places Pluck's other arm around his neck and says, "How the hell did you find us? And how did you manage to get more than one horse with you?"

Klouví leads the two the way and replies, "After the harpies attacked the town, I followed them without being seen as they carried their victims back to their lair. As for the horses, luckily, they spared them all. I took one from town to get here. Along the way, I found another horse that was lost. I assumed it might be one of the horses you brought on your expedition since it carries a saddle. I thought I could bring it with me in case I found survivors."

"Thank you so much, Zephyra," Pluck says. "We're so grateful that you found us. Now I regret keeping you locked up instead of taking you with us."

YAZEEM AND MARGOHOT return to the plateau's cave after spending a day's work hunting and gathering. Even though they've hunted and brought in all the remaining people from Point Postal, there still aren't enough bodies to last through winter. As the season turns, the mother and her prince are dissatisfied, not having found another human to hunt and add to their resources.

Walking through the cave and approaching the pile of collected bodies, Margohot spots bloody liquid and organs on the floor and says, "Is that vomit I see on the floor?"

"Doesn't Rotzen or Ezio know any better than to waste food like that?" Yazeem comments. "Especially when we don't have enough to last the winter?"

The queen of the harpies gets closer to the vomit and smells it. "I don't remember your brother's regurgitation smelling anything like this, my prince."

"You recognize our regurgitations, Mother?" Yazeem asks, getting next to her.

"Of course I do," she replies in annoyance. "You know that whenever the babies struggle to chew their food, I can always smell you three making them fresh foie gras."

She stops herself as she hears the sounds of wings flapping, echoing from the cave's entrance. They turn just when Ezio and Rotzen approach in the air with fresh dead bodies in their talons, ecstatic over what they have caught.

"Mother," Ezio says with glee, helping Rotzen place the dead soldiers on top of the pile, "it took us all day to find fresh meat, but these two are filled with muscle that will surely make the young happy at tonight's meal." He then gets down from the pile and notices Margohot is upset. "What's wrong, Mother?"

"Where have you two been?" the harpy queen asks aggressively.

"We were out hunting," Rotzen replies. "Wasn't it our turn to hunt today?"

"You fools!" she shouts. "Did you forget that you hunted yesterday? That means my babies have been neglected all day. Has anyone fed them?"

"I'm so sorry, Mother," Ezio replies with his head down. "We left this morning thinking we were nurturing them. I don't hear them crying, so they must still be asleep."

"How stupid can you two be?" Yazeem says. "And you've wasted perfectly good food all over the floor here."

"You're blaming us for that?" Rotzen replies, looking at the vomit behind them. "Come on, Yazeem. Do you think any of us would ever waste food like that?"

"Then who did this?" Rotzen asks, pointing at the bloody vomit. Margohot doesn't say a word as she turns toward the nest room. She becomes anxious over how everything feels off, from the mysterious vomit on the ground to the complete silence in the nest room. Something ominous is coming right from that room. She heads to the nest room with her three sons following her.

"Babies?" Margohot anxiously calls out, rushing through the curtained doorway.

There's no response from the nest. She slows her pace as she gets closer to the haystack. Before seeing her young in the nest, she sees pieces of shells similar in color to her eggs and fluid on the floor. Margohot's heart is racing faster than ever before she sees inside the nest. Her sons behind her are equally concerned, unable to get any closer to the nest as Margohot looks into it.

In great horror, Margohot witnesses the mutilation of all of her daughters. The sight of her oldest daughters' heads split open, the newborns crushed like bugs, and unborns smashed open out of their eggs is enough to put her in complete distress. The mother of the flock sees herself now as a bereaved parent in the cruelest way possible. As the three brothers run up to see what she sees, they gasp over their sisters' remains. Margohot covers her ears, shrieking louder than she has ever shrieked in her life.

All her sons back away and cover their ears for dear life over her ear-piercing shrieks. She's so loud that the ceiling starts crumbling pebbles. If any of the young somehow survived, they would have been awakened by their mother's screeching. Alas, there is no movement from the fallen young. Margohot's shrieking continues to get louder and higher in pitch.

While Ezio and Rotzen struggle to protect their ears, they notice rocks falling from the ceiling, with some nearly falling on Margohot's head. Realizing that she's putting everyone in a dangerous position, Ezio runs up behind her and shakes her shoulder in an attempt to stop her screaming. He successfully makes her stop the deadly squawk, and the ceiling stops crumbling into pieces. When her only living children let go of their ears, Margohot turns around and gives Ezio a vicious roundhouse kick.

Rotzen sees his brother collapse to the ground and runs to his aid. As he reaches Ezio, he sees a gash across his cheek. It becomes clear to him that Margohot didn't just kick Ezio but slashed him with open talons. Before he turns to his mother, he feels sharp talons pierce his shoulder and throw him into the nest. Rotzen grabs onto his bleeding shoulder and sees his mother in a frenzy.

She runs up to him and grabs him by the ankles, piercing him harder than on the shoulder. Margohot then throws him back to Ezio, landing on top of him. Before either of them can get back up, Margohot jumps on top of them, continuously strikes them with her razor-sharp wings, and stomps them with her talons. She puts all her rage upon the two she holds responsible for her babies' deaths. Ezio and Rotzen struggle to escape her wrath, but every attempt has them pulled back.

After recovering from tinnitus, Yazeem pulls his mother from beating his brothers and pleads, "Mother, stop! Please! Please stop!"

Rotzen falls to the ground as his throat is freed from the choke. Margohot then slaps Yazeem's hand away from her shoulder. She kicks him right into the stomach, followed by a slash across his chest and a vicious wing slap across the face. Yazeem falls right into the nest, landing on top of his dead sisters. As soon as Margohot jumps on top of her chosen prince and gives him more of a beating, she pauses.

The left side of Yazeem's face is covered in needles from her feathers and dripping blood onto one of her dead babies beside him. Seeing her beaten son lying next to his fallen sisters is enough to cease her frenzy and stop her from inflicting any more abuse onto him or any of his brothers. She backs away from the nest, unable to take her eyes off the horrifying sight until she finds herself with her back against the wall. As soon as she sees her sons get back up, she falls onto her knees and sorrowfully cries out.

She turns into her human form as she covers her face and sobs. While Yazeem and Rotzen begin to empathize with their mother's grieving, Ezio rushes to the torture room. Despite being badly hurt, he makes it through the curtained doorway to find that their prisoners and the budgerigar have escaped. Ezio feels terribly ashamed as he slowly returns to the previous room and approaches the prince of the flock.

While Yazeem watches his mother sob, Ezio whispers into his ear, saying, "The prisoners—they escaped. They must have done all of this."

Yazeem closes his eyes and sheds a tear, doing his damnedest to control his fury against the humans. He knows he must remain strong while they're all in a flock crisis. The prince of the flock takes a sorrowful sigh before approaching Margohot at her most vulnerable.

Yazeem then hugs the queen of the harpies and whispers into her ear, "I'm so sorry, Mother. It's those damn humans. They're the ones who did it."

"I'm so sorry!" she cries louder. "I'm so sorry, my sons."

"It's not your fault, Mother. It's nobody's fault but theirs."

Yazeem lets go of his mother when he feels someone tapping him on the shoulder to see Rotzen handing him a coin. He takes it off him and looks at the emblem craving on it and recognizes the symbol of an arrow across a silhouetted harpy. At that moment, he knows who freed the postal inspectors and helped murder their young sisters. Margohot picks her head up and notices Yazeem holding the coin. Without saying a word, Yazeem shows her the side of the coin with the harpy hunters' symbol on it. The sight of that familiar Greek symbol infuriates the harpy queen.

Margohot shakes with rage while saying, "They did it again.... Those hunters just... won't...stop!" She gets back up. "Let's go, my sons. Let's kill all of them."

"You mean to kill Jed as well?" Yazeem says as she heads toward the exit. "The only man with the genes to help you produce more females to save our race?"

Margohot stops in her tracks and screams, "I don't care anymore! I want his head split open as he did to my daughters! As long as his penis and testicles are intact, I'll drain every ounce of his sperm to save our race! Now let's go!"

She's the first to slip through the curtained doorway, leaving the three brothers behind. All three of them are still hurt by her abuse.

"Thank you, Yazeem," Rotzen replies, holding the deep wounds on his neck. "I never thought Margohot would have been as cruel and abusive as our legitimate mother. I thought we were done for."

Yazeem doesn't say anything to his brothers. He knows it's all their fault for letting their prisoners escape and allowing them to destroy the nest. As much as he wants to scold them for it, however, he knows they've endured enough abuse. He looks at the new scars and bruises all over their bodies, then remembers some of the needles from their mother's feathers are still on his face. Then Margohot squawks from the other room for them to hurry.

They immediately rush out of the room to catch up to the queen of the harpies, who's waiting at the cave's entrance. Upon their arrival, she's holding a rope dangling outside the cave's entrance.

"How did none of us notice this when we made it back to the lair?" Margohot says, looking at her boys with much disappointment.

None of them can reply to her question, uncertain if it is rhetorical or genuine.

She drops the rope and flies out of the cave. The three male harpies follow her but cannot catch up with their mother, who is still hurt from the beating. None of them says anything, preventing her from getting any more enraged than she already is. If a female harpy wishes exact bloody revenge, it's in the males' interest to obey her at all costs, even at their own expense.

CHAPTER 18

Zephyra Klouví wastes no time riding her horse and leading the escapees across the Red Desert. The two postal inspectors ride on a separate horse, doing their damnedest to keep up and not fall off. Pluck is sitting behind Secoli, holding on to him for dear life. Secoli and Pluck are still without pants and feel the cold wind below their belts. Considering that Pluck is free from being sexually violated by the harpy queen, he is much more uncomfortable sitting behind Secoli on the same saddle. Though sex is the last thing on his mind, he's doing his best not to let his privates touch his partner.

Pluck is having a difficult time holding on to his partner with one hand and Chap with the other as their horse moves at top speed. His hands are still injured, making this circumstance one of the most uncomfortable he's ever been. While their horse is riding two people on top, it's in exceptional condition and can keep up with the harpy hunter and her horse ahead. Recognizing the distance between where they are and their destination from memory, Secoli realizes there's still a long way to go before returning to Point Postal. The three of them manage to get through the badlands and need to bypass a desert plain they're on before climbing their way up one more plateau ahead before reaching back to town.

The postal inspectors and the harpy hunter expect their predators to already find out what they've done to their nest. Though they've been on the run for a long while, the way back to town is much faster than when the expedition went to find the harpy's lair. Despite making good progress in this escape, Secoli senses exhaustion from his horse.

"Hey!" Secoli shouts at Klouví ahead of him. "We need to slow down. The horses are getting tired. They're no good to us if they become too tired to make it back."

The harpy hunter turns to him and shouts back, "No. We have to keep moving!"

"For pity's sake, we must give them at least a few minutes to catch their breaths. They've been trotting for so long, and they can die from exhaustion."

Klouví notices her horse panting harder than normal and replies, "You are right. Let's make a quick stop now."

Klouví is the first to pull the reins to make her horse stop in its tracks. Secoli didn't expect her to stop so soon. Several feet past her, he pulls the reins to stop his horse. As soon as his horse stops, both postal inspectors suddenly feel their horse go off balance and fall on their sides with their transporting animal. The horse finally takes a breather and finds comfort on the ground at the expense of hurting its two riders. Secoli slides his leg out from under the horse's side, but Pluck has a rougher landing.

The poor man cries in pain after the horse's hips crush his right ankle. It is such an excruciating experience that he drops Chap from his grasp and holds on to his thigh. Secoli attempts to pull his leg out, but it only makes Pluck cry even louder. Despite being in much better condition than his partner, Secoli is still too weak to help Pluck.

This is all happening so fast that both of them don't notice Klouví rushing up to assist them. With her help, they slide Pluck's right foot out from underneath the horse. Upon successfully pulling his leg out, Secoli and Klouví notice Pluck's ankle bending unnaturally. The experience is so excruciating for Pluck that he holds his breath while enduring this new position of discomfort.

The harpy hunter puts her attention on Pluck, who's still screaming in pain. He's making so much noise that it echoes across the desert. Klouví hastily takes off her only shirt and tears it into two. Secoli is confused about why she is topless. She then rips her shirt in half, places one half of her shirt to cover Pluck's mouth, and says to him, "Bite down. I'm going to have to bandage your foot. This is going to hurt you really bad. And please...do all you can to keep the noise down."

Pluck bit down on the cloth as hard as he could, bracing himself for the pain to increase. Secoli grabs his partner's arms before Klouví treats Pluck's ankle with limited resources. Pluck cries even more as the foot is bent back into place. Bandaging it with the other half of the torn shirt feels worse for him. Secoli struggles to keep Pluck from squirming and touching his leg as Klouví treats his ankle. Little does he know he is still hurting his partner by holding and squeezing his injured hands.

"Now then," Klouví continues, holding the other half of the cloth from his mouth, "since this single cloth won't do much in keeping your foot from bending, I'm going to have to take this and use it to bandage your leg up some more. I need you to let go of the cloth. You." She looks at Secoli. "I need you to cover his mouth to prevent letting the harpies know that we're here."

"Damn it," Secoli says. "I'm having a hard time keeping him from touching his ankle. Here..." Secoli removes the only cloth left and snatches the other torn cloth from her. "Use mine to bandage him up. He needs this thing to bite to endure the pain."

"But...you are naked," the harpy hunter replies. "You will be freezing."

"I don't care about that right now." Secoli raises his voice, tossing his shirt at her. "Jed is my partner. He needs this more than I do."

Klouví doesn't argue back. Instead, she uses Louie's shirt to seal up Pluck's injury. Secoli puts the torn cloth back in Pluck's mouth, and Pluck bites down again. Jed moans in pain as Klouví has Pluck's ankle fully bandaged with her and Secoli's shirts. Uncomfortable seeing Secoli naked and underweight, Klouví bandages up Pluck's ankle quickly yet tightly. As soon as his ankle is tightly bandaged, she gets up from the ground, crosses her arms to cover her breasts, and walks away.

Secoli doesn't take notice of how strongly she reacts toward walking away. Having grown men yelling at her in the nude gets her anxious, especially since she's physically close to them. From where she stands, she can hear Pluck calming down and breathing more slowly.

Before she walks farther away, she stops in her tracks when she hears Secoli say to her, "I'm sorry I yelled at you. Thank you, Zephyra. Thank you for all you've done."

Hearing Secoli's gratitude calms Klouví's anxiety. Hearing his gentle, softspoken voice behind her makes her a little more comfortable, realizing these Federal agents have no ill intent. She's caught off guard when she sees Secoli still by Pluck's side, holding on to his injured budgerigar. Somehow, the uncomfortable sight of the men being naked and angry turned into a wholesome sight of the three together. Though she keeps her arms crossed to cover her breasts upon turning back to them, neither man looks at her.

The unwanted sexual tension turns out to be misjudged on the harpy hunter's part. Seeing the scars all over Secoli's naked body more clearly in daylight shows that he's been through so much as the harpies' prisoner. She becomes more sympathetic toward these masculine figures, who are in the worst shapes of their lives. She then stares off in the direction where they came from, making sure no harpies are spotted.

While she pulls watch, she notices the postal inspectors' horse still panting from exhaustion. Then she sees her horse in front of her doing the same, lying on its side, trying to cool down from all that running. She feels guilty over pushing the two animals so hard, but everyone involved is in danger, and their only means of transport is getting them much closer to home.

Secoli takes a moment to close his eyes and dozes off from where he sits. He takes his mind off everything, even Chap, who's on his shoulder. Just as he starts passing out like his partner next to him, the cold wind wakes him up, chilling his naked body. Now he's reconsidering his choice in giving Pluck his only shirt to bandage up his injury.

"Oh, no!" Klouví exclaims. "We gotta get moving! They're here!" "What?" Secoli responds. "The harpies? How did they find us?" "No time. Hurry and wake him up. Help me get the horses back up."

Klouví runs to the postal inspector's horse and pulls its reins to get it back up. The poor animal is still tired and struggles to do as commanded. Meanwhile, Secoli slaps Pluck on the cheek to wake him up. "What?" Pluck moans. "What is it now?"

"Jed," Secoli says urgently, "we gotta get going. They found us."

Pluck opens his eyes and sees the flock approaching above the horizon and over the badlands they've come from. Three pairs of silhouetted wings are around a pair of crimson wings in the center of the flock, flying toward them. With only one good leg, he pushes back up with his left foot from the ground and has Secoli guide him back to the horse. As soon as their horse is back on its four legs, Secoli assists his partner back up, avoids hurting Pluck's ankle, and hands him Chap.

He then runs with Klouví to her horse and helps it get back on its feet. Her horse doesn't struggle as much to get back up, considering that it only transported one rider. As soon as Klouví gets on top of her horse, Secoli rushes back to his horse and gets on top of it with his partner. The horse falls to its knees as soon as he gets on top of it. Secoli immediately gets off the horse's back, noticing it cannot carry the same weight as before. The horse has no problem getting back up when he backs away.

Noticing the horse can only take one rider, Secoli immediately carries Pluck off the horse's back in a fireman's carry.

"What are you doing?" Klouví yells urgently.

"Our horse is too tired to carry two people." Secoli quickly places Pluck behind Klouví on her horse. "Jed has to ride with you. I'll follow you. Now get going!"

When she feels Pluck sitting right behind her, she whips the reins, and the horse runs for it. She grows very uncomfortable with Pluck pantless and sitting so close behind her. But now isn't the time to think about personal space when their predators are heading right for them. While her horse starts going up the hilly path that leads up the plateau, she turns to see how Secoli is already on his horse and catching up with them. It relieves her to see him caught up, but not so much with the flock drawing closer to them.

What took so much time for the escapees to make it across the desert plain and up the path to the plateau only now takes them less than half the amount of time for the flock to fly across. The flock leader makes an unworldly call for murder in a way that only a female harpy can. That familiar call from Margohot brings chills down the escapees' backs, feeling much anger directly from her. Even the horses recognize the harpies' call from all of their attacks in the town, making both of the animals put more effort into getting to the top of the terrain, hoping their riders will guide them to safety.

The escapees ride to the top of the alluvial fan, standing right next to the bottom section of the plateau. Their horses have never been so exhausted, yet their destination is below. What should have been a sight for sore eyes somehow brings an eerie feeling to the trio. Point Postal now feels ominous as danger pursues them, realizing how unprepared they were for how unpleasant it has become upon their return.

Secoli analyzes his surroundings and yells, "Zephyra, where's the cavalry?" "I don't know," Klouví answers anxiously. "That military leader said he'd

be here. I don't know where he is."

"Ah, shit!" Secoli swears, looking down at the desert. "Here they come!"

The flock doesn't waste time and soars up to the escapee's altitude. Both riders whip their reins, and their horses rush to the new ghost town. Secoli is right behind Pluck and Klouví, rushing down the landslide. Despite going as fast as possible, Secoli senses their horses aren't moving fast enough.

The feeling comes at the most inconvenient time for Secoli as he feels an instantaneous searing pain across his back. One of the harpies gave him a slash across his back, from his kidneys to the left scapula. It feels so overwhelming that he leans forward and holds on to his saddle to prevent himself from falling. Despite the urge to stop, he keeps steady as his horse moves forward.

When Secoli looks up, he sees one of the male harpies flying over him with his own blood on its talons. He then sees this harpy soaring directly to his partner and the harpy hunter ahead. They both turn behind them when they hear Secoli's agonizing screams. Pluck and Klouví see the same harpy that struck Secoli, pointing its talons directly at them. Klouví immediately pulls the reins to make their horse move left and dodge the incoming pounce. As soon as Secoli sees how she manages to dodge the fiend, he turns and sees Margohot attempting the same attack as her lackey.

A quick learner, Secoli immediately pulls his reins and makes his horse take an immediate right. He dodges the harpy queen's lethal pounce as she flies uncontrollably past him. Luckily, his friends ahead of him are so far left that they're out of the reach of Margohot, who's moving at top speed. With Margohot and one of her lackeys making a U-turn to give them another strike, Secoli looks behind him. The other two male harpies are nowhere to be seen. He then looks up and sees one of them attempting a diving attack right above Pluck and Klouví ahead of him.

"Look out!" Secoli shouts at the top of his lungs. "They're right above you!"

Klouví hears Secoli's warning, she pulls her reins and her horse makes an immediate right. They were mere inches from coming in contact with the male harpy's fatal drop to both of their skulls. It instead lands hard on the landslide, allowing the escapees to bypass such an attempt. Just as Secoli starts to wonder where the fourth harpy is, he looks up and sees the other harpy making the same maneuver toward him. He, too, comes mere inches from coming in contact with the harpy if it weren't for him pulling his reins and making his horse move closer to his allies. Like the last harpy, this one collapses to the landslide but rolls down the rocky slope.

After avoiding the fourth lethal attempt, the escapees make it off the landslide and into the desert sand. Just as they move ahead to their destination, Margohot and her lackey make a 180-degree turn and head toward them with their talons reaching out. Secoli sees Klouví move her horse to the left, changing direction. He does the same and follows her, hoping she has a plan. There's nothing ahead in this direction but sandy hilltops that are as wide open as ever with no points of interest to make a diversion.

What's worse is that he notices his horse is slowing down as Pluck and Klouví are riding faster than him. The poor creature didn't get enough time to cool down and is reaching its limit. Secoli desperately whips his reins and kicks the horse's sides to keep pace. He continuously kicks the animal and whips the reins harder to make the horse go faster but to no avail. The horse has had enough and collapses again against his rider's wishes. Secoli finds himself off his horse's back and rolling into the sand.

The sand touching his newly scarred back stings him so badly that it causes him to scream. Klouví turns her horse around when she hears him and sees him and his horse on the ground. Unfortunately for Secoli, the harpy hunter and Pluck are too far away compared to how close Margohot and her lackey are. As he gets up from the ground, Secoli sees the flock flying directly at him and Margohot's talons pointing directly at him. The once-bold postal inspector watches helplessly as he sees his life flash before his eyes. He wishes to end his further suffering by joining all those who have died, especially his Civil War comrades.

As the harpy queen comes closer to contacting him, Secoli hears gunfire and Reveille. An immediate thought comes to his mind, thinking his post-traumatic stress is bringing him back to his fight in the Civil War. After everything he's been through, his trauma from the war somehow turns into bliss. The tortured postal inspector wants to embrace what he struggled to escape from his whole life. For the first time in his life, he wants to relive his time of being shot at and finally come to terms with that major turning point instead of dealing with more pain from the harpies.

At any moment, Secoli anticipates reliving his battlefield experience and having his surroundings change back to what was once a horrifying time for him. However, his imagination isn't taking control over him. He still sees the desert and the harpies in front of him, flying backward and away from him. This isn't what he remembers, but for some reason, the firings he's hearing are unlike how it goes on repeat. What made him realize that what he's seeing is real is that the Reveille playing isn't the one he heard from his battles, but an entirely different bugle call.

It becomes apparent that a storm of bullets is flying over him, all hitting the harpies. Margohot collapses over the overwhelming amount of bullets she's taking, and even her razor-sharp feathers cannot shield her. Seeing how close they are to hitting him, Secoli ducks for cover on his stomach. When he hears the same bugle call playing, he peeks over his shoulder to see hundreds of cavalry soldiers riding their horses over the sandy hills and firing directly at the flock.

Secoli turns back toward Margohot's direction as she attempts to use her ear-piercing screeching as her last resort against the cavalry. However, the endless amount of bullets she's taking is so excruciating that she cannot use her deafening shriek. The male harpies aren't taking as many bullets as their flock leader, but there are too many for this small flock to handle. Seeing how close to death his mother is, Yazeem flies to her, carrying her away from the firing with all his might. The endless bullets hitting him prevent him from helping his mother flee.

Yazeem cannot save Margohot as the overwhelming amount of bullets he's taking causes him to collapse. His other brothers see what's happening to them and come to their aid. They grab their prince and queen's ankles and take them away from the ambush. Quickly, they fly over the plateau and make it out of everyone's sight.

The firing finally stops, but the sound of hundreds of horses galloping continues to be heard. Secoli finally gets on his knees from the cold sand and has the cavalry's frontline run past him. The frontline goes up the landslide from where he and his friends came from and goes after the flock. Secoli turns around and sees a couple of soldiers getting off their horses and helping Secoli up from the ground.

"Are you alright, sir?" asks the soldier carrying him. "None of us hit you, did we? Can someone hand this man some clothes?"

Secoli is so overwhelmed by the turn of events that he's unable to give the soldier a response. The soldiers assist him in bringing him to another soldier, who gets off his horse and approaches him. The soldier looks much older than everyone else in uniform and has a single star on his rank.

He stares intensely at Secoli before saying, "Are you one of the postal inspectors we've been searching for?"

Secoli nods and replies, "Yes. I'm Inspector Louie Secoli."

"Oh, thank heaven!" the soldier responds with much relief, shaking his hand. "I'm Brigadier General Timothy Griffin. We've been searching for you for weeks. We were given orders directly from Congress to pull out of our station in Kansas to look for you two. I didn't believe these monsters even existed until I saw four a moment ago." He turns around and points behind him. "Is that Inspector Jed Pluck over there?"

"Yes, General," Secoli answers. "Inspector Pluck and I and her are the only ones that survived against the harpy attacks that's been terrorizing this state."

"Hot damn, Inspector," the general responds. "So glad not to have a single United States postal inspector die in their line of duty. Not on my watch. How the hell did you three manage to survive all that? No matter. We've got to get

you three some clothes and get y'all taken care of. We'll take it over from here. We'll track those damn beasts down and regain control of Wyoming in no time." The general focuses on his subordinate next to him and calls, "Captain Neilson!" He waits for him to give him a salute before saying, "See to it that you give our postal inspectors and that lady over there some proper care. I'm assigning you to protect these three at all costs."

Captain Neilson remains saluting to his superior and responds, "Yes, sir."

The general salutes him back and is the first to put his arm down before the captain does. Neilson waits for his superior to get back on his horse before he follows the frontline with the chase. The captain then gets back on his horse, and the soldiers help Secoli up to one of their horses. Once Secoli gets on top of one of the cavalry's horses, he sees the horse he rode on still lying on the ground. Other soldiers pour water on the exhausted creature to cool it down and help it hydrate. Secoli is relieved that his horse is under the cavalry's care. The postal inspector has a blanket placed over his back, bringing so much comfort to Secoli. After being the harpies' prisoner for so long, the rough linen that only the military uses becomes the most comfortable thing Secoli has felt in a long time. He's almost in a trance over the sudden comfort he's in. He doesn't even notice the soldier who's guiding the horse to follow Captain Neilson on foot.

Secoli finally comes back to reality when he hears Klouví calling for him. He opens his eyes and sees Pluck being transported by another soldier's horse and also is wrapped in linen as well. Secoli looks down to see Klouví, with a towel to cover her top, walking next to Captain Neilson, who's leading the three to safety.

Secoli overhears the harpy hunter and says to the captain, "Thank you for saving us. Those harpies would have ended us if you didn't have this many soldiers to help us."

"Actually," Neilson replies, "it is you I need to thank. Everyone thought the postal inspectors were long dead. But what are the odds of you finding them? Speaking of which, did you find the harpies' lair?"

"I did," she answers. "As promised, I made sure to eliminate their nest and prevent any more harpy babies from coming into this world."

"Thank goodness for that, but they're still out there. We have to kill rest while Wyoming is still in danger."

The cavalry's camp is a long distance away from Point Postal. By the time they reach camp, the sun has set and torches are lit everywhere. The rescued are brought into a medical tent that's spacious enough to hold four cots. Several barrels have lamps on top of them. Soldiers assist Pluck to one of the cots, making Secoli nostalgic over being treated as a casualty during the war.

Secoli approaches a medic examining Pluck's condition and injuries and asks, "How does he look? Is he going to be okay?"

"This man has the most sickly spots I've ever seen, fractured hands and wrists, and a broken ankle," the medic replies. "I can treat his limbs, and hopefully, none of them will need to be amputated. But the skin, though—I think he's going to see a doctor who's an expert on skin conditions. That part is beyond my expertise.

"Excuse me." Captain Neilson pops his head in the tent. "Inspector Secoli. If you have a minute, I need to ask you some important questions about your case."

"Sure thing, Captain," Secoli replies.

Before Secoli heads out of the tent to inform the captain, he suddenly feels the blanket he's been carrying around being pulled. He turns around and sees his partner pulling for his attention. He can see in Pluck's eyes that he needs to tell him something.

Secoli kneels and asks, "Do you need something, Jed?" Pluck hands him Chap, who's now asleep.

"Oh, Chap. I almost forgot about him again. I'm sorry, but thanks for doing this for me, Jed."

"Louie," Pluck says, letting go of his blanket and clearing his throat. "You can tell them everything except what Margohot did to me. It's too embarrassing for anyone to know, especially for a man like me."

Secoli understands what he means and gives him a serious nod before returning his full attention to Captain Neilson. Though he witnessed Pluck getting violated by Margohot, he knows it's uncommon for a man to get raped as she did to him. In a man's world, there's an expectation that all men must be strong and fight off any problems. If only those same people in a man's world saw what Pluck suffered, they would understand it can also happen to even the manliest man. Nobody is untouchable. For the sake of Jed's reputation, and especially keeping his family back home from knowing any of it, Secoli gives a full report of everything they both have been through, except for that detail.

THE SOUND OF THE DOORBELL ringing in the Pluck residence so early in the morning is unusual. Usually the mailman or a telegram messenger comes knocking by sunrise during the weekday. But the weekend office hours begin much later in the day. Jessie is the only one up early in the morning and heads to the front door. The eldest daughter slowly opens the door and sees the local telegram messenger panting on the front porch.

"Mr. DuBois?" Jessie reacts with surprise, opening the door wide. "Why are you out here so early?"

"I'm sorry to bother you this early, Miss Pluck," the telegram messenger replies, catching his breath, "but we got an urgent message from Wyoming for your family. We don't normally deliver messages so early, but this is an urgent federal telegram." He passes her the telegram. "Have a wonderful day." "Wait!" Jessie calls out. "Aren't you forgetting to receive your payment?" "The government already covered the expense. Again, have a wonderful day."

Before Jessie can express her gratitude, the telegram messenger rushes off the porch and rides his bike back to his telegraph office. Jessie closes the front door and then reads the telegram. She intensely reads the message on repeat before she places her back against the door. The eldest daughter is so overwhelmed by what she's reading that it causes her to scream at the top of her voice. This wakes the whole family, and they immediately rush down the stairs and to the foyer.

"What's the matter, Jessie?" Julia shouts. "Did something happen?" "What's with all the screaming?" Allie asks. "Don't you know it's not even six o'clock yet?"

"What's that in your hand, Jessie?" Clara asks with concern, being the last family member to come down the stairs.

"Mother," Jessie cries, "it's Dad—he's alive!" "What?" Clara reacts with shock.

The mother tries her best to avoid bumping into any of her daughters in the way.

She immediately snatches the telegram from her hand and reads out loud, saying:

Cheyenne, Wyoming

Pluck family. After weeks of searching the state of Wyoming, we found Jed Pluck and his partner, Louie Secoli. Both are in critical condition since the harpies kept them as prisoners. The cavalry's medics did their best to treat them, but both required additional medical attention upon their return home. They're relieved from their duties and will take a train back to Boston tomorrow when one arrives.

"*Brigadier General Timothy Griffin, 12:10 A.M.*"

Clara puts down the telegram and sees Janet, Allie, and Julia getting teary-eyed. Clara, too, is overwhelmed by the sudden news that Jed survived but is saddened over whatever injuries weren't described in the letter, trembling with emotion.

"Is it true?" Janet asks. "Is Daddy really alive?"

"Mommy," Julia says, "critical condition means hurt badly, right? How bad is Daddy hurting?"

Clara is unable to give any of her daughters an answer. She's shaking and tearing up so much that she can only extend her arms to signal the girls for a hug. All four of her daughters head toward her for a big family hug. Clara cannot keep herself steady, so she gets on her knees. The daughters go down with her and start embracing.

This moment for the family becomes so overwhelming that they all cry together. Everyone's pajamas get soaked with teardrops. This is the happiest news for everyone, especially since they thought Jed was dead. Allie is especially happy, considering her birthday wish finally came true. She's just excited and joyful to know that her father is returning home.

Then, a thought enters little Janet's head, overthinking what her mother read aloud, leading her to ask, "What are harpies? Do you know what they are, Mommy?"

Clara lifts her head from crying on her daughters' shoulders and rereads the telegram. She makes an immediate change of expression over who held her husband captive. Clara doesn't know what to make of it as it's left more questions than answers. Though she's never heard of that word before, she can only imagine that it's some kind of typo. Even military leaders make mistakes. But if it isn't even a typo, she's got many questions for her husband that require explanation.

REVISITING POINT POSTAL is the least ideal as it has ever been. Plenty of memories and grief have been left behind in this town. Secoli needs to see the aftermath for himself and give proper respect to the people he failed to protect. He walks down the main road one last time, with a cavalry squadron providing him security. While the soldiers give him the time and space to grieve, they watch over him with intense care.

Given the time to reflect, Secoli looks around the town infested with the harpies' shed feathers from their frenzy. Unlike the other ghost towns he investigated, not all are silhouetted. The crimson ones that are in the mix are evidence of Margohot's involvement in the genocide. Even more disturbing are the bloodstains on many of the buildings' porches and damage he doesn't recall seeing when he left Point Postal.

As Secoli walks down the main road, he passes by buildings that once brought him joy, but now he can only imagine how each victim fell from the harpies' final invasion. It is difficult for him to remember the good times he had here. The row of buildings on his left doesn't offer as many good memories as he wishes it had. Instead, they all remind him of the regrets he and his partner have. Starting with seeing the jailhouse again, despite thinking about Sherriff Wood and Deputy Hall, he's reminded of his regretful decision of keeping Zephyra there instead of taking her with the expedition.

It's harder to look at the bathhouse again where Pluck had his extramarital affair with Margohot when everyone believed that she was the real Fiona Fletcher. The fact that it was the place that helped the harpies build their nest is enough to make him turn away and never look at it again. The building next to it, farther down, the trading post, is the hardest for him to look at, considering it was once used as a mortuary. He can smell the corpses of the townspeople he couldn't save, which is enough to make him look away and pay attention to the opposite side of the main road.

Except for the bank and the destroyed saloon, which he never had the opportunity to visit, the hotel and Town Hall remind him of everyone since it is where he got to know the townspeople more. He now considers it a privilege to have had the opportunity to be part of the community and get to know all the people in town. It sinks his heart to know how badly he wanted to have them all survive and live peacefully. Nearly every crucial moment that has happened in Point Postal always returns back to here when the town once was intact. The facility that kept church services, town meetings, and court cases is just as destroyed as the saloon.

Now that the building is demolished, Secoli can't remember what the place looked like but only remembers what he and everyone did when it was intact. The sight of the destruction of the most important building in town represents everyone he saw die, especially the body piles in the harpies' lair. Folks like Sheriff Wood, Deputy Hall, Mayor McLusky, Pearl Herbert, Annabelle Larson, Julian Cunningham, Angus McKinsey, and the rest are all those he wishes were still alive. Though they're all gone, he can only imagine hearing their voices with open arms like before.

He can't bear looking at the hotel where he slept during his time here. The memories of the place where he slept are overshadowed by the harpy queen who slept next door. The fact that she played everyone a fool gets him as angered as when he looks at the bathhouse across the road. Looking back, it makes sense that nearly every mystery about the harpies involved her. His hatred for Margohot overshadows everything good and not-so-good about the hotel.

The memories of everyone are getting him choked up. The destroyed Town Hall, the damage, and the bloodstains on the buildings are reminders of his failures in protecting the town. Going anywhere closer to the railway makes him think he brought doom to this town, and things continued to get worse each passing day, starting with the train crash that destroyed the saloon upon their arrival. Logically, none of the disasters and crises were Secoli's fault, but he feels a tremendous amount of guilt thinking he could have done more. After a long cry, Secoli notices Captain Neilson approach him with his partner on a horse. He wipes his tears quickly and tries to get his mind off the dead. He sees Pluck holding Chap with his hands fully wrapped in bandages. His left foot has wooden splints wrapped in linen, keeping his broken ankle steady while healing. Since the cavalry medical team doesn't provide crutches or wheelchairs, riding the captain's horse is Pluck's only other option as a means of transportation. What's worse is that now that he has had a clean shave, the spots on his face are noticeable in the distance. Secoli ponders how hard it will be for Pluck to avoid attracting attention to their

return to Boston.

"Pardon our interruption, Inspector Secoli," the captain says, pulling the reins to stop his horse. "We're ready to burn this town down. It will behoove you to continue grieving out of town, where it's safe."

"Are you sure you want to do this, Louie?" Pluck asks, handing him Chap from his horse. "I know I want to forget my time here, but I also know how attached you are to this town. Once we burn this town down, it will be taken off the map, and only we will know this place ever existed."

Secoli retrieves Chap from his partner's hands and sighs before saying, "I thought about it long and hard. This place should be forgotten. I failed these people. The least I can do for them is cremate all memories of them. Did your cavalry find the harpies' lair as we instructed, Captain Neilson?"

"I received a report that they did. The pile of bodies is as disturbing as you described. The men had no choice but to burn the bodies instead of taking each corpse down from the plateau's cave. And now we'll do the same thing for this town very soon."

"Excellent—and thank you," Secoli replies, failing at sounding cheerful while stroking his parakeet's scalp. "Any status on the harpies?"

"Negative, Inspector," Neilson answers. "My cavalry is still searching for them. We haven't seen them since we scared them off yesterday, and their lair is empty. Sorry, but shall we continue this conversation elsewhere? The fire is

about to start soon."

While the three make their way to the end of the main road, cavalry soldiers rush on foot with barrels of kerosene and pour them onto each of the buildings' interiors and exteriors. Both postal inspectors are impressed with how fast they move and how quickly they get all the town's locations filled with flammable material. Once all the buildings are covered in kerosene, the soldiers hurry back to the safe zone with the rest of the squadron. Neilson stops next to Zephyra, who waits in front of the safe zone.

Captain Neilson turns his horse around for Pluck to see the town's burning. The last two soldiers do the honor of throwing matches on the fluids and start firing up each building. They all rush closer to the safe zone as the buildings are engulfed in flames. Reveille is playing the "last post" in respect of the fallen. Everyone removes their hats and remains silent as the trumpeter plays the tune. Even though the town's burning is occurring in broad daylight, the heat from the fire fits perfectly in the cold desert.

Watching the scene, everyone can't help being mesmerized by how apocalyptic it all feels. Though the soldiers stand and watch, none of them can fathom what the two postal inspectors have gone through in trying to protect this town with limited help and resources. A simple and peaceful town such as this should never be subjected to so much trouble. It also makes him feel guilty that the other towns aren't receiving the same treatment as Point Postal since it is the only one where they get to know the residents. After the numerous funerals in this town since the postal inspectors' arrival, this is the last funeral the town will ever have.

The buildings that are standing start collapsing one by one. The ones that had already been demolished before being put into flames are cremating much faster than expected. The fire has gotten so high and widespread that the main road is caught with the fire. Somehow, the fire doesn't reach past the sands where the cavalry squadron is standing and watching.

While the burning takes place, Pluck leans over to the captain, taps him, and whispers in his ear while still on the saddle, "How are we going to get back to Boston?"

"We messaged the government and requested a train over here," Neilson replies.

"Do you think it's safe for train travel in Wyoming to reopen?"
"Wyoming is still restricted. And don't worry, our soldiers are all over this

state searching for the rest of those monsters."

Neilson waits for Pluck to respond as either a confirmation from him or further questioning. Instead, he hears a loud thump next to him. The captain turns around when Klouvís gasps for Pluck. Everyone sees Pluck just fell off of Neilson's horse and lying motionless on the sand. Neilson immediately rolls Pluck onto his back and sees him panting and making rapid eye movements.

"What's wrong with him?" Secoli yells, running toward Pluck.

"The harpies' disease!" Klouví exclaims, kneeling next to him and checking his pulse. "It is getting worse! That means Margohot is still alive!"

"How do we treat it, Zephyra?" Secoli replies urgently.

"There is no medicine to help him. The only cure for his illness is to kill Margohot. It is not just a disease but a curse."

"Wait a minute," Neilson says, "how do you know all this? How come Inspector Pluck has this disease, but you and Inspector Secoli don't?"

Before Klouví answers, Secoli gives her a stare and shakes his head. Immediately, she remembers the private conversation with Secoli last night over to keep Pluck's rape a secret with this subtle verbal signal.

Once she breaks eye contact with Secoli, the harpy hunter gets up and answers, "Louie here must have a good immune system, while Jed doesn't. Everyone's bodies react differently toward a harpy environment, and unfortunately, he caught the harpy flu that's contagious to those who aren't immune to such a disease."

"Why didn't you tell us that sooner?" the captain asks angrily.

"Your regime was supposed to kill the harpies in that ambush so Jed can heal right after they are taken care of," the harpy hunter replies. "We underestimated Margohot and her flock, so Jed's disease continues to kill him slowly. If you will excuse me, I have unfinished business with them."

"I'm sorry, Miss Klouví," Neilson replies, "but the Red Desert is now restricted. Only the cavalry and military personnel are allowed in there."

"But your men don't know how to kill a harpy properly," the harpy hunter says with irritation. "This man is dying, and they're still out there."

"Ma'am," the captain responds, "I understand you have expertise in fighting off these monsters, but Wyoming is now under military restriction until they're taken out."

Her irritation escalates to anger, and she raises her voice, "Since when?" "Since last night." Neilson places Pluck's head in Secoli's lap and gets up from the ground. "And by order of the United States Government, you're

going to Boston with the postal inspectors for your safety."

"You are making a big mistake!" Klouví then shakes Secoli's shoulders. "Please, Louie. Don't let them go after the harpies without me. Tell him to reverse that order."

"I'm so sorry, Zephyra," Secoli says, grabbing her wrist to stop her from shaking him, "but I'm powerless to reverse that order. I'm relieved from this case, and it's up to the cavalry to finish the rest of the job."

Klouví pulls her wrist away and lowers her head down before saying, "You don't know the harpies as I do. None of you do. Jed will die if we don't kill all of them soon."

"How much time does Jed have left?" Secoli asks, holding Pluck's head. "It is hard to tell when he got the disease," she replies. "The timeline

varies between people. Some die within a day, while the longest sometimes lasts two months. But he will worsen if Margohot is still alive."

"If what you're saying is true," Captain Neilson says, "I'll order my men to put double the effort into tracking and ending those harpies."

"You better," Klouví says, "or you and your soldiers will be remembered as being responsible for having the first ever postal inspector to die in the field in the American history books."

CHAPTER 19

Nightfall is always the most difficult time to search for anyone or anything. Even a regiment as populated and widespread as the 1st Cavalry Regiment still can't spot the harpies on the run. Tracking prey on foot is always easier for any hunter since they can follow their trail on the same ground that they both stand on. Tracking flying prey is the most difficult, as flying animals leave few traces and can easily hide in high terrain.

Greek harpy hunters are the only known specialized unit that tracks down these flying beasts using tools that the cavalry does not have.

The cavalry has been informed that Pluck's condition is worsening because the harpies' queen is still alive, so they are redoubling their efforts to find her. Now that the entire state of Wyoming is under military restrictions, there have never been this many military personnel guarding and searching such a desolate state. Out of all the locations in the world, the harpies underestimated migrating to the desolate state of America and hunting human beings as prey. They never expected to be on the run as if they were still in Greece and other European countries.

Margohot and her flock hide on a different plateau, farther away from where they escaped the ambush. All of them are recovering from their gunshot wounds; that's all over their bodies. They all managed to take all the bullets that pierced through their bodies and seal the opening wounds with mud. While they're in their harpy form, their feathers keep them warm from the cold temperature at high altitudes. What's worse is that the plateau where the flock is hiding is surrounded by many cavalry soldiers below. Amid the barren desert, countless torchlights are seen everywhere they turn, below the high terrain they're on.

Without a single cloud in the night sky, the moonlight gives enough light for everyone to see through the darkness. This scenario is most difficult for the harpies to be in, to the point where they can't escape without being spotted. From the peak of the plateau, the flock hears the soldiers' yells echoing throughout the badlands. None of them have decided to climb up and search the high terrain yet, but the harpies grow wary over how much closer they are. Rotzen, the flock member in better condition than the rest, analyzes their surroundings below.

"The American military has us surrounded," Rotzen says, returning to his flock, who are still resting. "There are too many of them everywhere."

"If only she and the other flocks were alive," Margohot says, lying still, "I would ask them why they decided to live all the way out here in a place that's so barren. If they'd known about other places in North America to migrate to, we wouldn't be in this mess." She turns around and looks at her sons. "Do you know how long it took me to find you boys?"

"I can imagine you traveled throughout the continent to find us," Yazeem says.

"That is exactly right, my son," Margohot says, turning her head back to face the night sky. "And this is why your old mother should have listened to me."

"Hey, Mother," Rotzen says. "Can you tell us about our old mother?"

"What is it that you'd like to know about Grettilla?" she replies. "Did she ever tell you anything about herself?"

"Not really," Ezio answers. "She was distant to us, favoring our sisters over us."

"Gather around, my sons." The queen of the flock gets up into the sitting position.

"Let me give you a history lesson about our bloodline."

The three male harpies eagerly gather around Margohot. Judging by their reaction, Margohot can tell that their old mother didn't tell them much. Deep down inside, she knows what she will share with her sons might be life-changing for them.

"So what do you know about the harpies' one true purpose?" Margohot says. Ezio replies, "Is it to serve Zeus and be his messengers?"

"Right you are, my son," the flock queen says. "And being messengers of Zeus is more probable if we continue to populate and expand. Zeus has had many followers, and all of them have either betrayed him, failed him, or faded into obscurity. We are the only species he trusts."

"If he's that powerful," Rotzen says, "then how come he's not doing all the messaging himself? Furthermore, what are we messaging from Zeus exactly?"

"Zeus is from an entirely different world, my son," she answers. "And if you're from another world, you cannot reach or speak out in the one we're living in. I don't know exactly why he hasn't returned to Earth, but he's relying on us to communicate with this world and do his bidding. The natural world is godless, and you can see humanity ruining the environment in its reign of dominance. Once we harpies are gone, there is no hope in reversing all the damage that humanic is causing."

"What damage have humans caused in the natural world, Mother?" Yazeem asks.

"Well, everything. They keep growing cities and society at the expense of destroying an environment created for other species. You smell the air, and it's all pollution. And the sea where Poseidon rules is turning into a cesspool. And worst of all is that they put so many species to extinction. And now our species is next in line to become extinct. Out of all the species that cannot afford to be extinct, it is us."

"Is there another species Zeus can communicate with to carry out our duties?" Ezio asks.

"If there ever was one, they would have been able to speak his language and do what he commanded by now. But this is the one thing that makes us harpies, Zeus's true servants. Did Grettilla teach you how to pray to him properly?"

"You mean just speak to him whenever we're alone?" Rotzen replies. "That's humanity's concept of prayer. It's a one-sided conversation from the one praying to their chosen god when, in fact, it's the other way around.

Unlike humanity's gods in the religions they've created, we actually hear Zeus directly from him." She struggles to get more comfortable. "This is what I want all three of you to do. Close your eyes and concentrate. Ignore the noise going on down below and clear your mind. You'll hear his voice only when you get rid of any thought."

The three male harpies do as she says by shutting their eyes and sitting with their legs crossed like Margohot. She watches her sons attempting the harpy prayer. Though none of them are peeking or disobeying her, the harpy queen notices only the prince of the flock is still while Rotzen and Ezio struggle to get comfortable and concentrate.

"I can tell by your fidgeting that you're not concentrating," she comments. "How do you expect Zeus to communicate with you two if you have distractions in your head?"

Rotzen and Ezio stop moving while they sit together. Margohot watches her sons closely and can feel them slowly drift into a trance. She detects no further movement from her boys and can sense they're having an out-of-body experience. It doesn't take long for her to only sense their breathing and heartbeats go on autopilot as their souls have departed their bodies.

Moments later, all three of them open their eyes and simultaneously gasp in shock. Yazeem puts his wings behind his back to prevent himself from falling backward. Ezio and Rotzen both fall forward with their wings on the ground. All three of them pant over how overwhelming this spiritual experience was for them. Margohot smirks over what she expects their reaction will be.

"So tell me," the harpy queen says, "what did you hear?"

Yazeem catches his breath, stares at the night sky, and replies, "I...heard... the most masculine voice I've ever heard. It was so deep, intimidating...and direct. He said, 'Save the harpy race, young one.'"

"That's what I heard," Rotzen says, catching his breath. "He said the exact same thing to me."

"I, too, heard 'Save the harpy race,' just like they described," Ezio replies, panting with his head facing the ground.

"How is this possible, Mother?" Yazeem asks, looking at her. "How did he speak to all three of us simultaneously?"

"That is the true power of a god, my son," she answers. "I had the same experience as you three when I prayed to him for the first time."

"What did he say to you in your first prayer?" Ezio asks, raising his head.

Margohot chuckles over his question before answering, "I remember him telling me, 'You're chosen to lead every flock, for I have chosen you to be the queen of the harpies.' When I told the flock I originally came from, my mother was happy to know I was the one he chose. My siblings, unfortunately, didn't take too kindly to it."

"What happened, Mother?" Yazeem asks eagerly while he and his brother sit down with their legs crossed again.

Margohot sighs before answering. "My siblings…tried to have me killed."

Her sons simultaneously gasp, sequentially, with Rotzen asking, "But why? Zeus selected you to lead our race. Why didn't they accept it?"

"They were jealous of me." She looks away. "I remember my older siblings waiting to be selected as queen of the harpies directly from Zeus. Since none were ever chosen, they attempted to have me killed. Little did they or I know the strength I was gifted from Zeus to fight off their ambush that day. I was winning my fight against all fourteen of them—until my twin siblings, Jazaline and Herlos, betrayed me. I don't remember any of my older siblings' names, but my twins I remember fondly."

"What happened to the flock you were born in?" Ezio asks. "Did your mother punish them?"

"When I came back to the nest after my siblings had left me for dead," Margohot continues. "I saw my mother slaughtered by their talons. My only guess is that they were jealous that I became her favorite child and killed her for it. After I found my mother lying motionless in the nest where all my siblings and I were born, I prayed to Zeus, and he told me to 'fly to the shores of Volos to see that I will lay my wraith for you.'

"So I flew to the location where he sent me. On my way there, it was a cloudy day. I saw lightning strike in the same location several times. When I reached where the lighting hit, I found all of them burned to death. None of them left, but their feathers burned. That's when I knew Zeus wanted me to witness my siblings' demise.

"It was harder on me to know my biological flock was not mine to lead." She puts her head back up and faces her sons. "I understand Zeus really wants me to be the harpy queen and lead all of them. But being a queen of our kind has its challenges. Too many of them continuously challenged my commands and questioned their loyalty to me. My eldest daughter has questioned her loyalty to the flock by creating her own separate flock from the one I have gathered and united. Soon, many more followed her influence. And because she and her siblings no longer believe I am the chosen queen and no longer pray to Zeus, we're on the brink of extinction."

"So what do we do now?" Yazeem asks. "Americans know of our existence and Jed Pluck is under their protection. Do we still need him to save the harpy race?"

"I cannot find another candidate for a potential suitor," Margohot replies. "I've been looking for one while I've been searching for the flocks in Wyoming. Plus, I can feel I'm reaching my limit from ovulating. A female harpy can only lay a total of sixty eggs in a single lifetime. The amount of sex and ovulation I've gone through is the most that I've ever carried out in a short period of time."

"How many more eggs do you have left to ovulate, Mother?" Rotzen asks. "Surely we can let Jed Pluck die and find you another suitor."

"I've counted fifty-four eggs that I've brought into this world in my lifetime, my son. I only have about six more eggs left within me. I cannot risk wasting my last eggs on any human male who doesn't possess genes as good as Pluck's. Since he's consumed so much of my disease during intercourse, he will die soon."

Margohot gets interrupted by a train whistle echoing through the badlands. The entire flock puts their attention in the direction where the noise is coming from. They see smoke coming from the other side of the other plateau, where Point Postal is.

"Where did that train come from?" Ezio comments.

"I remember Jed telling me the US Government seized all trains from coming to Wyoming," Margohot replies, getting up from the ground and walking toward the direction of the smoke. This could only mean he's evacuating the town." She turns to her human form and rushes back to her boys. "My sons. I'm too hurt to fly. I need the flock to take me to that train. We must hop aboard and follow Jed Pluck."

"But Mother," Yazeem says, "the moon is too bright. We'll be spotted until some clouds cover it and make it darker for us to make our move."

Margohot looks directly at the moon behind Yazeem. The flock soon looks in the same direction while she remains quiet. A giant cloud approaches and starts covering the full moon. Margohot smirks over this sudden turn of events. Once the moon is no longer seen, the Red Desert quickly becomes pitch-black.

"Zeus truly is on our side, my sons," Margohot says. "If that's not a work done by him, then it's surely another god doing us a huge favor." She turns to her sons. "Yazeem, turn into your human form. We're going to have Ezio and Rotzen fly us to the train."

Yazeem turns into his human form, allowing Rotzen to carry him in the air. Ezio gently holds Margohot's arms with his talons and follows his brothers back to Point Postal. Despite it being so dark, their eagle-like eyes have night vision, making flying around the badlands possible. The flock flies over and bypasses the hostile cavalry, searching tirelessly for them. It doesn't take long for them to return to the same location where they were ambushed.

Upon their return, they're all confused about why Point Postal is in ashes. They see cavalry soldiers pulling guard in the destroyed town. Past the remains of the town, the flock finds a locomotive connected to a long line of cars. There are a lot of torchlights surrounding the train, making it hard to enter any car without being spotted.

Margohot, in her human form, still possesses a bird's vision. She zooms her sight to the first-class passenger car behind the locomotive. She spots Pluck being carried by several men to the car's entrance, with

Secoli and Klouví entering with him. The sickly postal inspector is entirely wrapped in bandages, except for his face, which shows those sickly spots caused by her.

"Ezio," Margohot whispers, looking up at him. "I see Jed boarding that train. Take us to the end. That last baggage car should be our perfect hiding spot since there's no light coming from that direction."

He gives her a nod and proceeds in that direction. Rotzen and Yazeem can't hear what Margohot whispered to Ezio, but they nonetheless follow them to the end of the train. Upon arriving at the last baggage car, Ezio lets go of Margohot, and she gently lands on the ground. Margohot slides the baggage car open as soon as Rotzen and Yazeem join them. Upon entering the empty car, which was devoid of any baggage, crates, or barrels, they realized that they would need to be more creative in order to avoid being seen if someone walked in. Just as Margohot attempts to close the door, she stops immediately when she sees a light approaching in her direction.

She leaves the sliding door open and whispers to her flock to hide. The person holding the torch is wearing a conductor uniform and appears young. He scratches his head in confusion, wondering why the baggage car's slide door was open, before peering inside. He sees nothing in sight. The flock is hanging onto the ceiling of the car, doing their best not to get noticed. Margohot stares at the conductor while hanging, preparing to strike him before he yells for help if he sees them.

The conductor then slides the door closed, and the flock hears him whistle loudly at everyone ahead of him from the other side of the door. The locomotive whistles again, and the train starts moving. The harpies all get down from the ceiling and sigh over how successfully they made it on the train. Though it's so dark, there's nothing of interest in the baggage car. They have the whole place to themselves. When recovering from their injuries, the flock feels fatigued from pushing themselves to board the train.

Margohot cracks open the sliding door and peeks out to see the destroyed town. Even though she caused so much chaos and massacre here, a part of her will miss the good memories she had with the townspeople. The harpy queen knows it's an inescapable part of harpy nature to be so violent against humankind. As soon as the train moves past the remains of Point Postal and the camps, it becomes pitch black.

She slides the door closed and turns back to her sons. Before she says a word to them, she sees all three of them sitting with their legs crossed and in a trance. Margohot is happy that they're praying to her god and that she successfully made believers out of them. Without making a sound, she sits next to them, forming a circle, and joins them in prayer. The flock continues to listen to everything Zeus says throughout the rest of their trip until the postal inspectors make it to their transfer.

JED PLUCK IS TORMENTED by nightmares, both asleep and awake. He has not been able to sleep soundly since evacuating Wyoming and being relieved of his case, as his subconscious mind constantly reminds him of the trauma. In this repeated nightmare, Margohot appears in her human form and has consensual sex with Pluck in that bathhouse. In the middle of this extramarital affair, his memory of the event dramatically changes to being surrounded by eggs. Those eggs then hatch, and out comes those harpy infants that have mentally scarred him since he first saw them hatch. But the dream never ends here, and it transitions to a more horrifying experience.

Though he never witnessed how Point Postal fell, the nightmare takes him to the town's main road, where Pluck is standing still, naked. Everyone surrounding him is acting like business hours are open, not acknowledging him like he were a ghost. Then he hears the townspeople scream for their lives as the harpies swoop in to terrorize the town. But these aren't the male harpies that tormented him, but instead a flock of females that resemble his eldest daughter Jessie in her harpy form, pouncing, slashing, and abducting innocent citizens. The worst part is that Pluck remembers what the citizens all look like, and they're all victims of his harpy children, all grown up.

The nightmare escalates to having the harpy queen land before him and slowly walk up to him. Pluck cannot move and remains stuck like a sleep paralysis as she approaches him intimidatingly. She sticks out her talon and slowly pierces him in the sternum, stabbing his beating heart while giving him an unwanted, deadly kiss. This is where the nightmare ends, and Pluck wakes up screaming. Multiple times, he's been screaming about this repeated nightmare, making the travel back to Boston difficult for Louie Secoli, Zephyra Klouví, and an unfamiliar postal inspector escorting him.

Pluck awakes from the same nightmare once more, but to his surprise, he's no longer on a train or in a train station. He finds himself in a dark hospital room, lying in a bed next to a window. After catching his breath over how continuously overwhelming his nightmare is, he looks out the window and sees that it's raining. His foot hasn't recovered, so he sticks his chin up and recognizes the architecture through the glass window.

"We're in Boston," Pluck mutters with relief before lying back down.

Pluck tries wiping the sweat off his face but then finds his hands wrapped in new bandages; bandages also cover his entire face with only his eyes, nostrils, and mouth exposed. He takes off the blanket he's wearing and sees himself in a patient gown and completely bandaged. Seeing all this angers him for changing his clothing when he was unconscious and without consent. His temper quickly fades away when he remembers these doctors are doing their jobs to get him better.

Pluck looks away from the window to evaluate the room that he's in and sees Secoli is in a separate bed right in front of him, snoring ever so loudly. It becomes clear to Pluck that the weird green object next to him is Chap, sleeping on top of his master's pillow in his unique position. Even though the parakeet is still too hurt to fly away, he really does love Secoli to the point that he is inseparable from him.

While awake, Pluck looks at the room and finds himself in a hallway with a row of beds. Though it's a struggle for him to see where the hallway ends, he can tell with what little light is at the end of the room that all these already-made hospital beds are empty. He and Secoli are the only patients lying in bed in this dark hallway. As far as he can tell, the space between his and his partner's sides of the row of beds is quite narrow. He imagines how difficult it is for the nurses and doctors to see them at the end of the hall.

The sickness once again wears the postal inspector down, and the sound of rain outside lulls him back to sleep. A moment of relaxation is interrupted when Pluck hears someone or something breathing nearby. The traumatized postal inspector grows anxious, thinking it might be one of the harpies about to do him more harm. He looks out of the corner of his eye, on the opposite side of his bed where the nightstand is, and sees a vase full of flowers. He grabs the vase's neck and turns it upside down, pouring the water and flowers onto the stand.

He quickly jumps out of bed and prepares to hit the intruder with the vase. Suddenly, he stops himself from swinging and recognizes the person that's now in front of him.

"Clara?" Pluck mutters, feeling surprised.

Clara Pluck has been sleeping on the chair next to his bedside since he was taken to the hospital. Pluck finds himself dumbfounded to see her here, waiting for him to wake up. He wonders how long he has been unconscious since returning to Boston. Even with his vision disjointed, his wife is somehow more beautiful than he remembers. He gets carried away with how gorgeous she looks whenever she's asleep, and after he's been away from his family for so long, she's certainly a sight for sore eyes.

While he stares at her and lets her get some sleep, his bandaged hand is losing its grip on the vase. It slips out of his hand and crashes onto the floor. This wakes everyone in the room.

"What was that?" Secoli exclaims at the rude awakening, jumping out of the covers and getting underneath the bed.

"Oh, my Lord!" Clara gasps, her eyes wide open and mouth covered.

"Clara?" Pluck says, turning to her. "It's me. Jed."

Clara quickly calms down from the sudden noise that has startled her. When she looks at him, he notices her expression change due to being imitated by his appearance. He wishes to rip the bandages covering his face to show her what he looks like but then remembers that spots from the harpies' disease are still all over his skin. He doesn't know what to do or say now, knowing he has become a disgusting freak of nature. Jed starts getting teary-eyed over the fact that she might turn away at any moment.

"Oh, Jed." Clara's tears pour down. "I'm so glad you're awake."

She gets up from her seat and gives her husband the tightest hug. Jed feels so much pain caused by the slashes over his back and torso. He doesn't want to spoil this affectionate moment with his wife, but the pain is too much for him. Clara lets go when she hears him groan over the hug and helps him sit on his bed.

"Hey, hun," Jed says, relieved from being let go. "When did I get back to Boston? And how long was I out? What's today's date?"

"Today is September 10th, 1899, dear," she replies, caressing his bandaged hand. "You came back home two days ago, and you were in a coma on your train ride back home. The doctor said your sickness and the amount of pain you're dealing with is what contributed to putting you in a coma. Please, Jed. What happened to you? Tell me what's going on."

Before Jed can give her an answer, something that feels like a feather pokes an exposed area of his skin. This startles him so much that he leaps into his wife and hugs her tightly. Clara is taken aback to see him cry on her shoulder, a side of him she has never seen before.

"Help me, Clara," Jed cries quietly into her ear. "Help me. Don't let them take me again." He gets louder, crying for mercy. "Please don't let them take me again!"

"Who, sweetheart?" Clara asks. "Who's trying to take you away? Are they the harpies that hurt you?"

Jed takes his head off her shoulder and grabs Clara's shoulders. "How do you know about them, Clara?" He shakes her shoulders and continues to get louder. "How do you know who those monsters are?"

Clara continues crying out of fear of being shaken by the one man she's depending on. She is so frightened by how scared her husband is. He keeps shaking his wife out of desperation, demanding how she knows of the fiends.

"Jed!" Secoli gets out from under the bed, separates the spouses from each other, and stands between them. "Calm down. This is your wife. She doesn't know anything. I know you're scared, but she doesn't deserve this."

Clara covers her face, unable to look at her husband. She attempts to run out of the room until she accidentally kicks a big piece of the broken vase still on the floor. Everyone hears the piece being smashed and looks right at it.

"What's that on the floor?" Secoli asks.

"That—that was a gift from our girls," Clara answers, struggling to control her emotions. "We—we all missed you, Jed. After all you've been through, the girls and I just wanted to give you this thoughtful gift."

Pluck looks at the mess he made from one side of the bed to the other. He then realizes that what touched his arm wasn't even a feather. Instead, the tip of one of the flower petals all over his bed cover wounded him up. When he looks over the nightstand where he grabbed the gift, the letter still on top is soaked with all the ink splatter from the water. Pluck feels a great deal of guilt because he not only ruined the present from his family, but he also didn't get to see how the flowers looked or read the letter that came with them. He feels like he has let his family down.

This realization breaks his heart, and he feels like an awful father after going missing for so long. Jed is so guilty that he can't even look at his wife, who's weeping in Secoli's arms. His partner is the only one emotionally stable enough to calm his distressed wife. All Jed can do is sit on his bed with his head down, listening to Clara's cries echoing in the hallway. The three don't budge when a nurse barges into the hallway and rushes to their aid.

"What's going on?" the nurse says. "And why is there such a big mess on the floor? And look at your bed. It's all wet."

"It's all right, Nurse." Secoli lets go of Clara and turns to the nurse. "Both of them got startled and rudely awakened each other. Bumped the vase in his sleep, which started this whole ruckus."

"I'll take care of the mess. Can you please take care of Mrs. Pluck for me? She and her husband aren't in the right mindset to talk to each other right now."

"Sure thing." The nurse places her hands on Clara's shoulders and guides her out of the room. "Right this way, ma'am."

The two ladies head downstairs, leaving Secoli and Pluck alone. They can hear Clara continue to weep from the stairway, making Jed feel worse than he already does. Secoli walks back to his bed and takes Chap out from under the covers. "Are you still having nightmares about…you know?" Secoli asks, stroking his muse on the scalp. He waits for Pluck to respond, but he sits on his bed, dejected. Secoli looks out the window beside Pluck's bed. "You know, Jed. You and I are the same now. We're both victims of those traumatic experiences. You're not alone, pal. I, too, am having nightmares about them. I feel guilty of being more scared of those damn things than when I fought in the Civil War. Life truly is hell."

"I'm an awful father," Pluck mutters. "Excuse me?" Secoli turns to him.

"The vase. Abandoning my family. The affair…" Pluck covers his face. "All of it's my fault."

Secoli feels worse about seeing his partner in this awful state of mind. Even so, he can't come up with the words to cheer him up. Instead, Secoli lets him cry while he grabs a broom and dustpan to clean up the mess on the floor. It doesn't feel like Pluck notices that the mess has been taken care of. As he weeps in one place, Secoli sees his partner as a former shell of himself, similar to how he struggled with his own trauma.

Pluck's inability to deal with his trauma is just as bad as Secoli's when they first met. Secoli refuses to submit to create a pity party with him, considering that one of them must remain strong in these dark times. Secoli tries to take his mind off Pluck's crying and stares at his reflection in the window. Seeing him hold Chap in that reflection makes him think about how much he's grown from being triggered by the Civil War. Never would he have guessed that things could get worse.

However, his partner endured the same war and never broke down until the harpies came. The roles are now reversed between the two postal inspectors since they met. It was difficult to find a solution for

Secoli to cope with his trauma, but Pluck's is much more atypical and arguably more traumatic. Since they evacuated Wyoming, Secoli is out of ideas for helping his traumatized friend, considering that male rape victims are uncommon and not as vocal as they should be. If only more of these men were brave enough to bring this to the public's attention, there would have already been a subject matter expert Secoli could refer Pluck to for special treatment. Secoli feels hopeless hearing Pluck endlessly weep with no solution to his problem.

Secoli's moment of reflection ends when he gets interrupted by knocking coming from the window. It's hard to see through the pouring rain this late at night, but the mysterious figure leans closer to the window. Upon closer inspection, Secoli sees Klouví on the ledge wearing the same patient's outfit he and Pluck are wearing. Even more bizarre is that she's with someone he's never seen, standing on the same ledge as her. They both wave at him through the glass and point at the frame. Secoli then slides it open and lets both of them in.

Secoli glances at the person she was with. The mysterious figure is wearing a greenish cloak, similar to the one they had seen on Klouví at Point Postal, and brown gloves as thick as miner's gloves. He removes his hood and reveals his Mediterranean facial features, which are similar to Klouví's. He's half a head taller than Secoli and appears strong, with his chest sticking out. Secoli mentions Klouví's name, which makes Pluck stop his sobbing and quickly wipes his tears.

"Was going along the ledge necessary when you could have used the stairs and hallways to come and see us?" Secoli sarcastically asks.

"I am sorry," Klouví replies, "but the nurses won't let me leave my room. They think I might have the same disease as Inspector Pluck, but I keep telling them it is not contagious. But that's beside the point. We gotta get Jed out of here."

"What?" Pluck stops rubbing his eyes. "Why?"

"Because you're still in danger," she replies. "Margohot is here in this city."

"What?" Pluck exclaims, hiding under the blanket in fear. "Here in Boston? H-how do you know that? How's that even possible?"

"Because he told me." She points to the mysterious man standing behind her. "Allow me to introduce you to a fellow harpy hunter. This is Alistair Pantazis."

"Another harpy hunter?" Secoli comments. "So you're telling me he witnessed Margohot and her cronies flying around the city?" Secoli shakes his head in disbelief. "Mr. Pantazis, is it?" He offers him a handshake. "It's a pleasure to meet you."

"I'm sorry, Louie," Klouví interrupts. "He doesn't know how to speak English like I do. But I can translate your conversation for him."

She speaks to Alistair in Greek. The male harpy hunter shakes Secoli's hand and speaks in his foreign language.

Klouví translates, "He says, 'It's a pleasure to meet you, Mr. Secoli.'"

"Can you ask him how he managed to find us since you two got separated?" Secoli asks. "How did he manage to get here in Boston?"

"I can answer that, Inspector," Klouví says. "He told me he reached Ohio and realized I was right about the harpies creating a diversion to make us lose their trail. He immediately went after me in Wyoming. By the time he arrived in Lemonstown—I mean, Point Postal—he had arrived just in time to see me boarding the train that we all got on upon our evacuation from that state. He got on board unnoticed. When I had to remove myself from you two and the other agents to get some air alone, that's when Alistair and I finally reunited."

"Why didn't you tell us your fellow harpy hunter was on board our train?" Pluck interrupts while still wiping his eyes.

"Because those Federal agents would have arrested him when he was protecting us from any possible harpy attack."

"And how did he find out the harpies' whereabouts?" Secoli says.

Klouví turns to her comrade and asks him that question in her native language. As he speaks, she translates, "As he was hiding in the multiple trains we took, he noticed the same suspicious passengers getting on the same trains. They were always one train car behind the ones we rode on. After the third transfer and seeing them do the same thing, Alistair sat behind them and analyzed them.

"That is when he noticed the suspicious group overdressed like they were going to a theater, not for traveling. They must have gotten tickets themselves because as he kept an eye on them, they didn't cause any trouble to the conductors or anyone who sat next to them. However, their mannerisms, strange behavior, and stench resembled harpies in their human form."

"And why didn't you take those suspects out when you had the chance?" Pluck aggressively asks, becoming more paranoid.

Klouví brushes off Pluck's rudeness, asks Alistair his question, and translates, "He says because he only has one crossbow and two harpy arrows left." Alistair removes his cloak and shows his quiver and crossbow underneath.

There are as many arrows as he claimed.

"He used almost all of them when he fought harpies before we separated. Since he couldn't get harpy feathers, making more arrows as powerful as these is impossible. He said he did his best to lay low and only act if any harpies tried to attack us."

"Did those suspects attempt to strike during our ride to Boston?" Secoli asks, sitting on Pluck's bed.

"No," Klouví continues translating, "but upon our arrival at the Governor Michael S. Dukakis Transportation Center, one of them noticed his crossbow and fled before he could chase them down. Likewise, he also lost us as we were being transported to the hospital. He spent these last few days looking for the hospital they put us in."

"How can you be certain any of those suspects are harpies?" Secoli asks.

Klouví asks him his question and continues translating. "Because when he was searching for them in the station, this is what he found as evidence."

Alistair takes a crimson harpy feather out of his pocket and shows it to them. This makes Pluck's eyes widen, causing him to panic.

"No. No. No. No. She can't be here!" Pluck screams, getting out of bed, and has his back against the wall. "You're lying! Margohot isn't here!"

Pluck continues getting louder, banging his head against the wall. Realizing this escalation to hysteria is causing him to hurt himself, Secoli intervenes. He places Chap on Pluck's bed and rushes toward his partner. He struggles to hold on to Pluck's wrists, attempting to stop him from squirming and injuring himself.

"Jed!" Secoli shouts, struggling to hold on to him. "Get a hold of yourself!"

Pluck screams louder, forcing Klouví to run after him and cover his mouth before whispering in Pluck's ear, "Silence. We're trying to get you out of here." Alistair watches Secoli and Klouví trying to control Pluck, who's struggling to free himself. The traumatized postal inspector completely loses it and is hysterical. As the bandages on his face rip open from moving his head too much, Alistair sees Pluck's blue spots, causing him to immediately feel sympathetic. Despite the language barrier, he knows exactly what Pluck's going through. He's seen more than enough survivors acting and behaving the same way whenever they survived being raped by a female harpy. Just seeing Pluck's blue spots and hurting is enough for the harpy hunter to offer his help.

After a few steps toward the three, a loud shattering of glass is heard behind Alistair Pantazis from the window he came through. Before turning and seeing what created such a ruckus, Pantazis suddenly feels a sharp stab piercing his back. Next thing he knows, he's pushed across the hallway and crashes into one of the beds. Upon landing on one of the beds, he can feel whatever stabbed him hasn't let go. Pantazis tries reaching for his crossbow on his back, but it's nowhere to be felt.

Searching for his crossbow is no use, though, as Pantazis feels the sharp object go deeper. With all that weight on top of his back, there's no way for him to escape. The whole experience is so excruciating for the harpy hunter that he feels the tip of whatever is piercing him, poking his heart. All Pantazis can hear is the postal inspectors and Klouví screaming across the hallway. The pain is so overwhelming that he can't react, feeling his life slipping away.

Just as soon as Pantazis accepts his fate, he hears a clicking noise that sounds like a crossbow being loaded. Hearing this familiar sound from behind him influences whatever is stabbing him to suddenly let go of him and back off. As soon as the weight and stabbing release, Pantazis rolls on his back to see that a male harpy struck him. The black-feathered fiend focuses on Klouví aiming, Pantazis' crossbow at the harpy. Seeing the ripped strap on the crossbow, Pantazis realizes how he dropped the weapon.

Klouví takes a shot at the harpy. Somehow, the fiend quickly dodges the arrow and flies away from Pantazis. The arrow goes through the wall next to the bed Pantazis is on. The harpy crashes through the window behind Pantazis and flees from the hospital. While there's no danger to be seen, Klouví runs after her comrade, who's bleeding on the bed.

"The bastard got me in the back! Quick!" Alistair groans, rolling over to lie on his stomach. "Bandage me up before I bleed to death."

"Hold on," Klouví anxiously replies, getting up from the bed covered in his blood. "Hang in there. I'll get help." She then turns to the postal inspectors and shouts in their language, "Jed! Louie! I need assistance. Alistair is bleeding profusely." The two postal inspectors hide underneath separate beds. Secoli is the only one who gets out and rushes to help the hunters. Pluck remains hiding and is scared out of his mind. Once Secoli covers Pantazis' wound with a pillow, Klouví searches for bandages and other medical supplies in the cabinets beside the exit. She stops searching when she gets interrupted by the same nurse who took Clara away. As the nurse rushes through the door, she becomes shocked upon seeing Pantazis lying on a bloody bed.

"What in the world is going on?" the nurse exclaims. "Where did this guy come from? And what happened to the windows?"

"Miss…," Secoli hysterically replies, still applying pressure to the pillow onto Pantazis' injury. "This man has been attacked. He lost a lot of blood. Please help him."

The nurse turns to the cabinets next to the door and almost bumps into Klouví. Despite Klouví being in the men's hospital room, the nurse doesn't say anything to her. She knows saving this man's life is paramount and starts collecting the items in the cabinet Klouví didn't search. She fetches the medical supplies, and the nurse rushes back to treat the male harpy hunter's wound. Once Secoli releases the pillow from Pantazis' back so the nurse can do her job, she becomes disturbed by seeing how wide and deep the wound is.

"Please, Nurse!" Secoli yells. "He's dying. Let me help you. Tell me what to do."

The nurse shakes her head to stop feeling disturbed and says, "Right. Help me remove his coat and shirt."

Secoli does as told.

"Here. Place this pad on his wound and add pressure while I wrap the bandage around his abdomen." She hands Secoli the pad, and then she turns to Klouví. "You. Go downstairs and get the doctor on the clo—"

The nurse gets interrupted by a scream from the door where she entered. It startles the nurse, who drops the bandage roll to the floor. Everyone turns in that direction to see Clara has entered the room and is frightened by the gruesome scene. Frustrated, the nurse gets off the bed and searches for the bandage roll underneath it.

"What happened to Jed?" Clara cries. "Wait—that isn't Jed. Who's he?"

"Damn it," the nurse swears, searching under the bed. "Can someone take

Mrs. Pluck out of here? This isn't the right time for her to be—"

The nurse is interrupted again by another scream—but this one is much louder and coming from the same broken window the harpy escaped through. Though this is the first time the nurse and Clara have heard something so loud, everyone else in the room remembers it too well. Being the only two who've never heard anything so loud, they collapse to the floor and cover their ears for dear life. Secoli is forced to let go of pressuring Pantazis' back to hold on to his ears, like everyone else who's enduring the ear-piercing shrieks. Klouví is the only one with her ears covered with a pillow, which was unfortunately used to cover Pantazis' wound.

As everyone in the room covers their ears, Klouví is the only one to turn in the direction where the shrieking is coming from. A different black-feathered harpy has its head sticking in through the broken window and is making all the ruckus. The fiend cannot move while exhaling its deadly tactic toward everyone in the room. While the male harpy is in place, Klouví looks to where she dropped the crossbow and arrow.

She finally removes the pillow from her ears when she reaches the last arrow. The harpy hunter hastily loads the crossbow and takes aim. She struggles to hold the crossbow and load up the weapon as the shrieking continues. Once she suffers tinnitus, she finally takes proper aim before pulling the trigger. The harpy ceases its shrieking upon seeing an arrow hurtling toward it across the room. It sticks its head back outside and flies away before the incoming arrow hits it.

Despite knowing she missed the shot, Klouví is relieved the unbearable screams have ceased. A few more seconds of her ears unprotected could have resulted in permanent hearing loss. The harpy hunter sticks a finger in her ear and twirls it to regain her hearing. While she's attempting to stop the ringing in her ears, the others get back up and recover faster than her. Pantazis is the only one too weak to get out of bed, feeling colder from losing more blood than he should.

Klouví sees her comrade turning white as his head and arms lie on top of the bloody bed, looking like he's dying. She tells the others to help stop Pantazis' bleeding, but everyone else focuses on whatever is behind the harpy huntress. While she struggles to hear anyone or anything, she notices the nurse, Clara, and Secoli have disturbed expressions on their faces. Klouví turns around when she finally hears a sorrowful, manly scream through her tinnitus. Right behind her, she sees the bed that Jed hid under is now flipped over and on top of another bed. Red wings are raised above the sickly, terrified postal inspector.

With those wings flapping down, Margohot is revealed, glaring angrily at Pluck. The queen of the harpies has her eyes set on only one person and ignores the others in the room. She gets in midair and grabs Pluck's injured hands with her talons. Klouví hears Jed's screaming more clearly, having the same body parts being pierced again. While he's pulled up in the air, Klouví pulls out the quiver to take out another arrow.

After feeling nothing inside, she looks down at the quiver and remembers that was the last arrow she had left. Before she starts losing hope, she remembers that one more arrow is still in this room. She looks at the wall beside the bed where Pantazis is lying. The arrow that was supposed to hit the harpy that attacked Pantazis is still nailed to the wall. The razor-sharp feathers at the end of the arrow kept the arrow from going completely through the surface.

Klouví takes Pantazis' glove off one of his hands and wears it before getting on the bed. The glove is thick enough to hold on to the razor-sharp feathers attached to the arrow and pull it free. No one is paying attention to what Klouví's doing since they all watch Jed being abducted by Margohot in the most painful way imaginable. As soon as Klouví manages to take the arrow out, Jed is being carried out of the window on the other side of the room. Secoli and Clara run after Jed and watch him from the broken window as Margohot carries him away, flying with her flock.

"Jed!" Clara screams as she watches her husband taken away.

Klouví loads up the crossbow with the last arrow and rushes to the same window. She shoves Clara and Secoli out of the way and aims right at Margohot. The rain makes it difficult to see clearly, but the city lights make the harpy queen's red feathers stick out of the darkness. Another issue is the altitude that the flock is at, being that they're six stories high, thinking that Jed might not survive the fall if she hits Margohot now. Then she notices the flock is flying above a smaller building where he can safely land.

The ringing in her ears slowly recovers as she hears the rain, Chap's shrieking out of fear, and Jed screaming in front of her. Hearing him helps her tell how much farther away he is through the darkness. The harpy hunter then aims above Margohot and pulls the trigger. The arrow flies through the rain and moves at the right speed to prevent the rain from disrupting the arrow's direction. From the point where the arrow starts descending, it falls directly toward where Margohot is flying.

Out of the corner of his eagle-like eyes, Ezio catches a glimpse of the arrow falling directly at his mother. The arrow is going so fast that there's no time to warn his flock of what he sees. The male harpy pushes Margohot out of the way out of necessity. Then, the arrow hits Ezio in the back of his skull, sending him down to the rooftop below.

Margohot ceases flying farther away from the hospital, hovering above the small building where he landed, and exclaims, "Ezio!"

Ezio's brother swoops down to the rooftop to help him. Yazeem checks to see what's wrong with him while Rotzen panics behind his prince. He turns Ezio over to lie on his back and detects no movement from him. The arrow through Ezio's skull is evidence that the hunter shot him. The flock's prince gently places his foot on his chest and detects no heartbeat.

Yazeem looks up at Margohot soaring above him, still having Jed within her grasp. The prince doesn't say anything as they stare at each other, giving looks of despair. Despite still flapping her wings, she is on autopilot, stunned over this devastating turn of events. Not even Jed's endless screaming and shaking takes her mind off her fallen flock member. Her heart then breaks when she hears Rotzen repeatedly shout, "Ezio is dead!" Margohot glances back at the shattered hospital window through which they had escaped.

Before she attempts to go back to get revenge, she sees Klouví still aiming the crossbow at her. With so much rain in the way, she can't tell if she has another arrow loaded. Knowing who Klouví is and how great of a shooter she is, Margohot decides not to risk it while she still has Pluck. The addition of police firing their guns from below only adds to her anxiety.

The harpy queen continues fleeing and shouts in Greek, "We have to keep flying! Everyone has spotted us!"

Yazeem and Rotzen immediately fly away and follow Margohot. It breaks both of their hearts to abandon Ezio on the rooftop. While they wish to have more time to grieve their brother, they know this is their final chance to escape with Inspector Pluck. The flock flies around the buildings ahead and vanishes from sight.

Back in the hospital room, Klouví sighs with relief over successfully fooling the harpies into thinking she has another arrow while aiming at them. She sees Secoli retrieve Chap, who's been shrieking from all the chaos. However, she's still upset over not hitting Margohot and failing to rescue Jed. She turns around to see Alistair Pantazis sitting on the bed and raising his arms for the nurse to bandage his abdomen. Klouví's amazed at how much he's been pushing himself.

Clara then rushes to her, pulls her shoulder, and yells, "What in the hell was that? And where are they taking Jed?" She then hysterically shakes Klouví's shoulder. "Can someone please tell me what's going on?"

Clara gets interrupted by the police rushing into the hospital room. There are many of them filling up the room with urgency. A man in a gray suit and brown fedora is coming out of the crowd of policemen. It is a fellow postal inspector who escorted him, Jed, and Klouví to Boston. He has a square face and is a head shorter than Secoli.

"Inspector Charlie Duncan," Secoli says. "They took Inspector Pluck."

"Chief," Duncan turns to the policeman behind him, "have the whole Boston Police Department on the search for Postal Inspector Pluck. I'll be damned if a Federal agent dies under my watch. He's our biggest priority."

"Affirmative, Inspector," the police chief replies, then turns to his subordinates surrounding him. "You heard the man. Spread everyone all over the city. Keep an eye out for suspicious activity flying in the air, and don't hesitate to fire your guns if you spot one. Finding and rescuing postal inspector Jed Pluck is our number one priority."

All the policemen, except for the ones investigating the evidence in the room, head out the same way they came in. Klouví and Pantazis attempt to follow the police exiting the room until Duncan pulls their arms from behind. "And where do you think you two are going?" Duncan asks, squeezing their arms tightly. "And who is this guy? Why is he wrapped up in bandages?"

"Don't take it out on these two, Duncan," Secoli says, pulling his hands off the two harpy hunters. "Without these two, Mrs. Pluck and I would have been killed by those foul beasts. Besides, Klouví here shot one of the harpies lying dead outside."

"She did?" Inspector Duncan replies, looking at her still wielding the crossbow, then at Pantazis, shirtless but wrapped in bandages. "Show me where this dead harpy is. I'd like to take a closer look at this thing."

INVESTIGATORS CIRCLE around the dead harpy on the rooftop where it landed. So many photographs are taken, and everyone is wet from the pouring rain. Secoli, Klouví, and Pantazis are out of the hospital with umbrellas over their heads. The three changed their patient gowns to more appropriate clothing. They all closely examine this fallen harpy with the policemen, who will never know that his name is Ezio. To all of them, it's just a monster they're glad has been put down.

"How can such a thing exist?" Duncan says in disbelief. "It's so unreal to see a person with wings, feathers, talons, and sharp fangs."

"What's worse, Duncan," Secoli says, standing behind him, "is that they can change into looking like a human."

"Say what?" Duncan turns to him in shock.

"He's right," Klouví adds, who's on Duncan's other side. "These supernatural beasts possess the power to disguise themselves as human beings. They'll pass by everyone in the city as its citizens, meaning while your police force searches for them in the air, they'll actually be on foot."

"Gawddammit!" Duncan swears, crossing his arms. "Why didn't you tell me that before the chief sent every policeman out to search for them?"

Klouví remains silent, knowing she made a mistake in forgetting to share that information. Even Secoli feels disappointed in himself for not sharing that crucial detail. Duncan knows this mistake is irreversible; there's no point in sending back all those policemen when they're already on high patrol.

Duncan finally breaks the awkward silence and takes out his pen and notepad before asking, "So, how do we distinguish a harpy in disguise from a real person?" Klouví changes her mood and answers, "The only thing they cannot change is the shape of their feet, which are talons. So they'll be wearing shoes to hide that from everyone. While the males will be struggling to walk properly, Margohot, on the other hand, is used to walking with any shoes she wears. "However, their horrid stench is noticeable. They'll immediately have that strong smell when they grow their feathers and when they remove all of them.

Unless there's a shower within their reach to wash away their distinctive smell in human form, anyone with a sense of smell can tell."

Duncan finishes writing and asks, "Good. Anything else we need to know?"

"One more thing, Inspector," she replies. "Harpies have very thick skin, even in their human form. It's so thick that shooting bullets at them is like throwing rocks. It will only bruise them but hardly goes through."

Duncan puts down his notepad and pen and asks, "Then how the hell are we going to kill one of those damn things?"

Before answering, Klouví looks at Pantazis before they both look at the dead harpy. Secoli and Duncan see this as off-putting, watching both harpy hunters simultaneously staring at the dead harpy.

While staring at the corpse, Klouví answers, "You know that crossbow you confiscated from me, inspector?"

"Yes. What about it?"

"May we touch the dead suspect?"

Inspector Duncan looks at the one in charge of the evidence. He stops unscrewing the lightbulb on the camera when he sees the Federal agent looking at him. He nods to Duncan, making him answer, "You may."

Klouví speaks to Pantazis in Greek, saying, "Hand me your glove. I have to show them our secret weapon."

Her comrade takes off his gloves and hands them to her. She puts both of them on and kneels down to lift the harpy's head. Klouví then pulls out the arrow from Ezio's skull and shows it to Duncan.

"This is a harpy arrow," Klouví says. "It is a Greek invention designed to kill harpies. It's made of steel, and the feathers at the end are harpy feathers. Unlike bullets, the steel is durable enough to go through the harpies' thick skin, and the feathers are made with the steel to create impeccable speed and accuracy when shot by a crossbow."

"Okay, so I take it you need your crossbow back since you want to help us hunt down the harpies," Duncan says. "But you mentioned you're out of arrows. How can I allow you to fight those things off if you don't have any more of them?"

"Pantazis here can craft a bunch of small pipes to shape them into arrows like this one if you give us the time and resources. But thankfully, we have the most important thing to craft more arrows like this one."

"And what's that?"

Klouví grabs the harpy's wing and lifts it up. The glove she's wearing prevents any stabbing or poking from the razor-sharp feathers. Secoli and Duncan take the hint that they can use this harpy's feathers to create more ammunition against the harpies.

"So, how many arrows can you make by taking all the feathers from this harpy?"

"Based on my experience, a harpy carries around two hundred to three hundred feathers. With that many, Alistair and I can make around a hundred

or so arrows within a few hours—if we have the right resources."

"Officer Dundee," Duncan looks back at the policeman in charge of the evidence, "how many more pictures do you need to take?"

"We just finished photographing the evidence and suspect. We're wrapping things up."

"Tell your men to help these harpy hunters remove all the feathers from this dead thing. They will need every feather to create the ammunition to kill those monstrosities."

"Right away, Inspector," he replies.

"One more thing, Miss Klouví," Duncan says. "If the harpies aren't going to kill Inspector Pluck, why do they need him? And how much time do we have left before the disease he's carrying will kill him?"

Klouví briefly stares at Secoli standing next to the postal inspector in charge. Once again, he gives her that intense look and slowly shakes his head. She then looks back at Inspector Duncan before he notices what she's looking at.

"I don't know why they took Jed. But since he's been sick and is more exposed to where the disease came from, he only has a few more days until his sickness finally kills him. His life can be shortened since he's once again exposed to those harpies."

CHAPTER 20

After being kidnapped and having his hands pierced by Margohot's talons, Jed Pluck's hands have never felt as painful. Adding insult to injury, his kidnappers are flying at top speed through the pouring rain in his patient gown, which makes it unbearably cold. The flock is flying much farther away from the hospital and is taking him to a building with a water tower. As soon as Margohot releases Jed's hands, the postal inspector falls heavily to the roof and tries to crawl away. But every time he tries to escape in a certain direction, a male harpy lands in front of him. The only path that's open for Jed is heading under the water tower.

The rain stinging his pierced palms is preventing the kidnapped man from moving as fast. With no other choice to stop the pain, Pluck has to go under the water tower that provides shelter. Pluck, soaked to the bone from the rain, is trapped in the middle of the flock as they surround the water tower. He's shivering more out of fear than the cold at the sight of Margohot's presence. Just as Jed is about to scream, the male harpies grab hold of his arms and cover his mouth.

Margohot shushes her captured mate and says, "You'd better keep your volume down if you know what's good for you."

"Please, Margohot!" Pluck cries as soon as his mouth uncovers. "Please stop doing this. Please stop this madness. Please let me go."

"You're in no position to make any requests, Jed!" Margohot yells. "You have no idea what I've been through, coming all this way after you and your friends destroyed what I created." She looks away and cries, "First Ypsipétis. Then Barthas. Then, all my young daughters were in my precious nest. And now, Ezio. How dare you, Jed!" She faces him with tears pouring down her cheeks as she clenches her fingers into a fist.

"How dare you murder so many of my children! I should kill you right here where you stand. But I'm fighting this urge because I, unfortunately, still need to use you."

Pluck remains silent, knowing that any response he'll make will only escalate her resentment against him. The poor postal inspector is too terrified to make any movement or action, seeing how distressed Margohot is. All he can do is put his head down, unable to come up with a single response. Yazeem and Rotzen continued to hold Jed's arms firmly, even though he was no longer resisting or trying to escape.

Margohot wipes her tears and calms down before continuing. "Don't bother apologizing or making any excuses, Jed. No amount of either one of those will ever make me forgive you. Now then…" She turns away and transforms into her human form with all of her feathers removed. "It's time to rebuild what you destroyed."

"No, Margohot!" Pluck yells as he raises his head up and uses his last bit of strength from being pulled down by the harpies. "No more!"

"What did you say?" she retorts, turning back to him, surprised and offended.

"I said no more!" Pluck says, looking at her with blazing eyes. "I'm not going to allow you to violate me anymore! This ends now!"

She pauses over how intimidating he is, shocked to see him change so boldly. Out of all of her victims and after all that she has done to him, Jed still dares to stand up against her. Then she brushes off his attempt to take control when he groans over his arms being bent by her sons and remembers how weak he is.

"No, Jed," Margohot says, kneeling to his level. "You will do as I say and fornicate with me one last time."

"Stay the hell away from me, you rapist!"

Jed startles Margohot by spitting at her face. She gets up and steps back after feeling his saliva hit her eyes. Yazeem and Rotzen are offended by this and throw him on his back. They both kick and slash him with their talons. The postal inspector covers his head dearly, reconsidering his choice to fight back.

"Stop it, you two," Margohot says in Greek, wiping the saliva off. "It's just a pathetic attempt to make me scared."

Yazeem and Rotzen cease beating Pluck. Jed then lies on his side, holding on to his stomach from all the slashing the male harpies caused. While Pluck is panting, the male harpies tear off his patient gown. Once he becomes naked, Jed gets up and attempts to run for it.

The postal inspector doesn't make it far as he limps away from the fiends. Rotzen foils his attempt to escape by leaping toward him and landing on him. The harpy then grabs Pluck's broken ankle and drags him back underneath the water tower. Pluck is yelling from the pain and repeatedly says no.

As soon as he's dragged back under the water tower, Margohot says, "Get him on his knees, now!"

"Why, Margohot?" Pluck asks while being pulled by the male harpies. "Why is it that when a man violates a woman, everyone gives her support and protection? But when a woman violates a man, nobody gives a damn? That's a clear case of hypocrisy."

"Hypocrisy?" the harpy queen replies, stopping over his question while her sons struggle to get him to kneel. "Hypocrisy? I'll tell you what's hypocrisy, Jed. What about when a man has a say in deciding to abort a woman's child when she is the only one out of the two that has the power to give birth? What you did to my nest is no different than what you human males do to your females whenever it's inconvenient for a man to have a child she has to bear. How do you men have power over your women's bodies and determine if she can or cannot have a child?"

Pluck can't respond to her counterargument, seeing it as a conflict between men's and women's issues. As her son firmly holds him down and places him in the kneeling position, he feels utterly hopeless. He can't reason with a monster who only wants children from him.

"Since you brought up children," she continues, "I need to know something." Pluck only sees her turn around before his head gets pushed down. Margohot picks up a feather from the pile she shed upon transforming into her human form. She then snaps her finger at the feather's tip, and it slowly burns. A small flame ignites the feather's tip, and smoke comes out. She then places it under Pluck's nose. Inhaling the burning smell of the feather is unpleasant, making him cough, and immediately, his mood changes to neutral.

"Since you killed so many of my children," Margohot says, still keeping the feather under his nose, "I'm going to get a little payback. Tell me where your family is."

Pluck loses control of his mind and replies, "My family's residence is at 259 Brouse Avenue. It's located outside of the city heading north."

Margohot takes the feather away and throws it out into the rain. Pluck regains control of his body, shocked at what he had said to her.

"What did you do?" Jed mutters. "How did you do that?"

"A female harpy's feathers are capable of many things, my love. I made you tell me the truth by burning one of my own and making you smell it. Now that I know where they are, I will ensure that the only daughters you'll have are only harpies."

"No!" Pluck yells. "You leave my children alone, you bitch! They have nothing to do with this!"

"Neither did my children." Margohot snaps her fingers, signaling her two sons to place him on the ground. "But you took them away from me. It's time to get even. But first, let me put all my aggression onto you."

Pluck attempts to scream, but his torn patient gown covers his mouth. Once the male harpies get him to lie on his back, Yazeem places his left talon on top of Pluck's left arm and his right talon on his left foot. Rotzen does the same for Pluck's other limbs, making it impossible for the postal inspector to escape. The only movement Pluck makes comes from squirming his head and body.

Once Margohot slips Pluck's penis into her, she aggressively slams all her weight onto his lower body in the cowgirl position. On top of his already injured limbs being crushed by her sons holding him down and watching him be violated, Jed feels his pelvic bones crack. Whenever he makes any noise, Margohot chokes him and lets go of his throat to allow him to breathe. The harpy queen is remorseless about the number of tears coming from Pluck's eyes. Every fornication they both have together becomes much worse than before for Jed, and this one is the most mentally and physically painful, after knowing what she's going to do after she's done with him.

As his most horrific nightmare never ends, it escalates to a much more painful experience than ever before. Even if Margohot were human, she'd still be able to get away with what she's doing to him. Rapists who target males like her take full advantage of society's misunderstanding that nonconsensual sex is something only men do. Pluck is one of her many victims, and no one understands what a man like him is suffering through. Jed wishes he could be someone other than himself because he feels less like a man and more like an object of desire for a complete monster.

IT'S BEEN A VERY LONG night for Clara Pluck. The distressed wife has never felt so unsafe riding back home, although she's protected in one of the Boston Police Department's horse-drawn carriages. Even the barred windows—as well as the fact that she's sitting with Zephyra Klouví, escorting her back home— aren't enough to make her feel secure. Her life changed after witnessing the harpies and their capabilities in just a single night.

As soon as Clara sees them pass a familiar intersection, aware they're halfway to her destination, she breaks her silence and says, "You didn't have to come along and escort me back to my house, but thank you."

"Oh," Klouví replied, regaining her composure. "Well, you know, I don't want anything to happen to you on your way home. It's dangerous out there."

"So you're a harpy hunter, right? I take it that your occupation is self-explanatory. Why did you choose this profession?"

"That is not all we do. "Klouví struggles to get more comfortable. "We also nurture and protect those in need of our help."

"Just how many of you are there?"

"Thousands of us in Greece. We've been around for centuries as a part of Greece's military. My home country has been at war with the harpies that seek to overthrow the Greeks and make Greece theirs to claim. When the harpy population began declining, harpy hunters separated from Greece's military forces and went on hunting separately."

"Why do those monsters want to take over your country? And why are they here?"

"It is a bit complicated," Klouví answers, scratching her head. "There are two separate stories behind our conflict with those beasts. You decide which of them is true. You see, Greece used to worship in an old religion where the gods that created everything hated humanity. Legend has it that the titan Prometheus gave mankind fire, and the god Zeus is angered that mankind obtained such forbidden knowledge.

"Zeus, however, gave us mercy in exchange for worship. It wasn't meant to last since other nations stopped worshiping the pantheon and mistook him and the others as different godly figures for newer religions. We Greeks are the last to worship him. It was only a matter of time before Greece converted to modern religions like Christianity. As the deities either departed from the pantheon or faded into obscurity, Zeus's last resort was to send his most loyal followers, the harpies, to replace humanity and restore faith in him. Or that's what the harpies claim."

"And what does the other story say about men and harpies?" Clara asks. "Most Greeks today are Orthodox Christians. We believe our old religion

is nothing more than a mythology used for cultural identity. I am still unsure of what to believe, as it is difficult to fathom how harpies came into existence. It would take millennia for something as monstrous as a harpy to evolve. However, Christianity denies any scientific evidence of evolution, so I doubt God himself would ever create such monstrosities to slay his children if he is a loving god."

"But that still doesn't answer what those harpies are doing in America." Klouví looks away and replies, "After centuries of fighting off those monsters, hunters are responsible for the harpies' population decline. In Greece, for the first time having a full month with no harpy attack, we hunters discovered that they migrated. When we captured and interrogated one of them, it claimed that Zeus commanded the harpies to repopulate in the west. We're so close to putting the harpies to extinction."

"Are you sure these monsters you're chasing are the last ones remaining?" Klouví looks into Clara's eyes and replies, "Since we discovered the harpies migrated, we harpy hunters are scattered globally. If anything happens to me or I don't return within a certain time, more harpy hunters will come and take over my duty. Trust me—my organization is well organized and skillful enough to complete the job."

"So what's next after you killed all the harpies?"

"I...uh..." Klouví stutters, "I don't know. I...never really thought that far ahead. I've been fighting these beasts for so long that I never imagined doing anything else."

"C'mon, Miss Klouví," Clara says. "I'm sure you have other hobbies and dreams outside this endless fighting. Ever thought of starting a family of your own?"

The harpy hunter blinks profusely and looks out the barred window before replying, "I...am a widow, Mrs. Pluck."

"Oh," Clara gasps, leaning back in her seat. "I'm so sorry..."

Klouví chuckles at the remark, tears falling down her cheeks before answering. "The marriage? It only lasted a day. My husband died on our wedding day."

"Oh, my God," Clara gasps again, covering her mouth. "What happened?" Zephyra can no longer maintain her fake smile and closes her watery eyes before answering, "It was the harpies—Margohot. She took Milos away from me. She knew what he and I did to her nest and wanted revenge on my wedding. I should consider it a blessing that we both said 'I do' before..."

Klouví can't finish what she's saying. She covers her face and tries her best not to make any sobbing noises. Clara feels heartbroken over how emotional she has become. Hearing that the harpies ruined her dreams on the most precious day of her life is too much for her to hear.

"I'm...so sorry, Zephyra," Clara says, placing her hand on Klouví's lap. "I didn't mean to bring it up if it was that awful." She wipes her own tears. "Margohot—you mentioned it many times back in the hospital. Is she the same harpy we're chasing?"

Klouví nods and uncovers her face before saying, "Yes, she is the same harpy we're chasing...the one that ruined my wedding, but she didn't kill Milo."

"What?" Clara responds with confusion. "I don't understand."

Klouví raises her head to make a big sigh before answering, "She killed every one of our guests at our wedding. She thought she had me killed, but..." She takes another loud sigh. "She kept my husband alive to rape him."

"W-what?" Clara exclaims, covering her mouth. "Rape him? How? How is it possible for a man to get raped?"

Klouví wipes her tears and looks up at the carriage's ceiling. "Female harpies are the most dangerous of them all. It's their duty to build a nest and keep the harpy race from going extinct. However, male harpies cannot fornicate because they have no reproductive system. The females' only way to lay eggs is to have sex with human males. But since no man ever wants to fornicate with a harpy, they take the men by force."

"What happened? Please. Tell me what happened to your husband."

"When I regained consciousness, I saw myself surrounded by all the guests lying dead. I then saw Margohot raping my newlywed husband. I grabbed a crossbow from a fellow harpy hunter who was dead alongside everyone. Just before I had her, she heard me reload and moved away when I pulled the trigger. I missed her, but I shot my husband in the heart...I accidentally killed my husband."

"Oh, sweet Lord!" Clara yells. "Is that why they took my Jed?"

Klouví realizes she has revealed Pluck's secret. She sees how intimidatingly fearful Clara has become. The harpy hunter covers her mouth and quietly gasps. "What's going on down there?" shouts the police officer driving the carriage. "Please!" Clara cries, grabbing Klouví's hands from covering her lips and holding them tightly. "Say it ain't so! Tell me they're not raping my husband! Tell me they're not raping Jed!"

"Please, Mrs. Pluck," Klouví pleads softly, struggling to free her hands from Clara's tight grasp. "You're hurting me."

"You're lying, aren't you?" Clara cries even louder, squeezing Klouví's hands even more! "Jed is too strong to prevent anyone from ever harming him! You don't know how strong he really is. No way in hell would anyone ever be able to rape a man like him!"

The two police officers driving the carriage stop the horses from pulling the wagon as soon as they hear Klouví scream in pain. They get down from the driver's seat and rush to the back of the wagon. When they open the door, they see Clara stand over Klouví while the harpy hunter is still in her seat, struggling to get her hands off Clara's. The officers both get inside and help remove Klouví from the emotional wife. The harpy hunter rushes out of the carriage to recover from the pain in her fingers, and Clara calms by sitting back down. "What's the matter with you two?" asks the officer, stepping out of the carriage with Klouví. "Do we have to keep both of you separated while we're taking her home?"

Before the harpy hunter says anything, she gets distracted by bells ringing in the direction they're going. Klouví gets in the middle of the road and looks at what's making all that noise. Through the bleak road, she witnesses red carriages being pulled by white horses. The officer outside pulls Klouví back to the side of the road before she gets run over. She watches those red wagons rushing past her with multiple men on board wearing red hats. On board, each of those wagons has ladders and some sort of machinery that looks like steam machines seen in factories.

"Who are they supposed to be?" Klouví comments as the last wagon passes them.

"Those are fire trucks," the officer replies. "Something tells me there's a fire in the direction that we're going."

The officer and harpy hunter both turn to Clara, who's out of the carriage and scream, "Oh, my God! What's happening in our neighborhood?"

Everyone is out of the police carriage and sees heavy smoke over the buildings before them. A hellish-looking light illuminates the thick smoke, which is as dark as the night sky. The sight of so much smoke stuns everyone until all four of them simultaneously have a thought in their minds that it could be the Pluck's residence that's caught on fire. Without saying a word, the two women are the first to run back inside the carriage. Then, the officers return to the driver's seat. They urgently whip the reins, and the horses hitch onto the carriage and move hurriedly.

Urgently continuing in the same direction clouds Clara's mind with anxiety.

There's that unwanted feeling that something happened to her home where she last left her daughters. Once they enter the neighborhood, she sees through the barred window that the fire is much closer to their destination. It continues to get uncomfortably brighter as the carriage approaches the Pluck's residence. As soon as they round the houses leading up the hill to her home, Clara's worst fears are realized. Not only is Pluck's residence engulfed in flames, but it has already collapsed. All the neighbors are in front of the burning house, helping the firemen in any way they can. Despite hosing the fire, they're far too late to save the house. While the carriage's door is unlocked, Clara wastes no time jumping out while the vehicle is in motion.

She rolls on the road and cares little about getting hurt, landing on the concrete. Clara repeatedly yells, "Jessie! Julia! Allie! Janet!" as she gets up and runs toward the arson crime scene. Klouví gets out of the carriage on time and catches up with her to pull the distressed mother from getting any closer to danger. Just as it becomes too difficult for the harpy hunter to keep Clara away from her burning house, neighbors come in to successfully take her away from harming herself. Clara collapses as they place her in the crowd, making the loudest, most heartbreaking cry of her life.

Everything she and Jed built together is burning before her very eyes. Her husband's kidnapping and her home's arson couldn't have been done by anyone else but the same monsters. No mother should ever deserve such cruelty, but Clara is unfairly chosen to endure the harshest turn of events. Everyone surrounding her witnesses how awful it is to lose an entire family in the comfort of the American suburbs.

Clara grieves so much that she starts hearing her daughters cry in her mind. The sound of Jessie, Julia, Allie, and Janet crying with her is the worst part of the whole experience. Just imagining how they all suffered burning with the house is too much for her. Clara cowers and holds on to her head after being unable to control the sound of their voices appearing in her head. The moment she moves her hands to cover her ears, her children's crying suddenly becomes quieter.

Noticing the sudden change, she uncovers her ears and hears their voices get louder than covered. She then feels a hand placed on her shoulder and hears one of her neighbors saying, "Clara. Your children are over there," bringing her back to life.

The same person then helps the mother back up and takes her to where the loud crying is coming from. After passing through the crowd to the other side of the front yard, Clara sees a sight for sore eyes right before her.

Jessie, Julia, Allie, and Janet kneel on the grass, hugging each other and crying as if Clara's the one caught in the fire. There are no signs of burns or anything out of the ordinary from any of the girls. They're all in their pajamas and grieving like Clara was a second ago. The realization that all her children are safe couldn't be more relieving.

She takes a deep breath before saying "Girls" to grab their attention.

All four simultaneously turn to their mother and immediately get up from the grass. Clara opens her arms wide and gives them all a family hug. Feeling all of them once again ensures that this isn't her imagination. Rather, it is a sheer miracle and an act of mercy from God. The family keeps holding each other tightly and much longer than they normally do.

Clara cries, "I thought I lost you. How did you manage to get out of there?" Clara asks, tears pouring down her face. "A fire like that could have gotten you killed."

"I'm sorry, Mother," Jessie speaks quickly, shaking her head. "You didn't come home for days, and taking care of my sisters became too much for me to handle. I had to get Jacob to help me, and he gave me and the girls a place to stay in his house. I'm so sorry, Mom. I didn't mean to set the house on fire."

"Slow down, Jessie," Clara says. "I'm not mad at you. I'm just happy that you all are alive. All four of you are priceless compared to all that we've lost." She hugs her eldest daughter. "And you said Jacob gave you a place to stay? Where is he?"

"Right here, ma'am," a voice replies right behind Jessie.

Clara raises her head from Jessie's shoulder and sees the young blond man. Remembering that this is the same young man, Jessie always runs off to change her perception of him. When this family needed their father the most during his absence, Jacob selflessly took the responsibility to protect her girls. Somehow, she sees her eldest daughter's boyfriend resemble Jed when her husband used to be young and available.

"Thank you," Clara says, still hugging Jessie. "Thank you so much for protecting my family, Jacob."

Jacob nods to his girlfriend's mother, allowing her to continue holding Jessie.

Jessie pulls herself out of her mother's grasp before replying, "Where's Daddy? Aren't you supposed to be with him until he gets out?"

Clara looks at her daughter, unable to give her an answer. How should a mother explain the awful truth of her father's kidnapping and his kidnapper doing unspeakable things to him? Although she has never lied to her family before, she doesn't wish to damage her husband's reputation, especially when all her daughters look up to him. Feeling helpless in this situation, she looks around to find Klouví. Once she finds the harpy hunter in front of her, Clara gives her a sorrowful look in the distance.

UNLIKE PREVIOUS OCCASIONS when he woke up from those recurring nightmares, Jed managed to wake up quietly. He finds himself still lying underneath the water tower and freezing naked. Jed is tempted to shake and shiver from the cold air caused by the drizzle surrounding the water tower. However, knowing the harpies might still be around, he pretends to still be asleep. He struggles to keep still from feeling so cold, but his time in the United States Army taught him self-discipline.

Pluck finds himself in a similar situation of pretending to be dead upon an ambush in one of his battles in the Civil War. While reminiscing about that time, he remembers how difficult it was to act lifeless and as still as the dead comrades he was surrounded by. That moment in his life was frustrating, but he was fully clothed to endure the cold weather, and while his comrades were dead, they had some body heat to help him cope with lying in the snow. Now he's in the poorest shape of his life, has nothing to keep him warm, and has been violated again makes this situation much direr.

While lying still on the concrete, Pluck examines his surroundings. He sees a couple of bricks lying next to him, and past his foot in front of him are three large eggs on top of a small haystack. Remembering how long it takes for Margohot to ovulate after fornicating with him, he realizes he must have been asleep for a couple of days. The sick postal inspector is so disturbed by the sight of the three new eggs in front of him that he's tempted to pick up a brick and use it to destroy them before any more abominations are born into the world. However, his hands are too hurt to lift a single brick, and his only good foot has been crushed after he was stood on during his last rape. Even if he could, he'd rather pretend to be still asleep than get caught by the flock if he failed.

Remaining still and struggling not to react toward the cold is all he can do as he catches a glimpse of one of the harpies coming by. Two black-feathered harpies get under the water tower where he lies, take the eggs off the nest and bring them to the mother who bore those eggs. Yazeem and Rotzen walk farther from the water tower, where Pluck is. They place the three eggs on the ground and shelter them with their wings. Margohot can barely stand still, considering she's recovering from recently ovulating those eggs, but she has something urgent to tell her remaining flock members.

Margohot kneels to her eggs, kisses all three, and says, "My sons, I have a very important task for you. Our race is on the brink of extinction once again. I won't leave my babies unsupervised, nor will we raise them in a hostile environment like this place. That's why each of us is going to carry one of these eggs and start raising them on our own to increase our chances of saving our species."

"What?" Yazeem says with surprise. "But Mother, you said individuality and dividing the flock prevent harpies from expanding. Why would you ever consider that?"

"I know what I told you, my prince," she replies. "But whenever one of us as a flock makes a mistake, it costs us greatly. It's best to lower our chances of extinction if we separate and raise each of them on our own. If one falls, the other will continue soaring and carrying out my legacy."

"Are you sure about this, Mother?" Yazeem says. "What you're asking us to do is be kings of our flock. You, above anyone else, know that's forbidden and will never work. I know these eggs will guarantee daughters, but I'm unsure if these chicks will ever obey Rotzen or me without a female harpy to help us take charge."

"Yes, Yazeem," Margohot replies. "I'm very sure about this. I'm fully aware that only a queen can control a flock. And I'm even more aware that female chicks will inevitably go through their rebellious phase, and you two will see the worst in them. But we have no other choice. Zeus told me to divide this flock, or we will all fall together."

"He did?" Rotzen asks. "Who did he say which of us will fall?"

"He didn't," she answers, "but I would rather have these three eggs be as far away from harm as possible than to have them end up killed like the last nest we built. Rotzen, I want you to take one of these eggs and fly west until you find a wilderness to perfectly hide the egg and build a nest there.

"Yazeem, you'll fly south, far away from this city, to build a nest for one of my babies. I know you've always wanted to live your own life outside of the flock. This is a chance of a lifetime for you to live your own life and raise one of my chicks."

Yazeem pauses by overthinking this decision before replying, "I don't know, Mother. No female harpy has ever listened to me, and I don't know if one of these soon-to-be-born chicks will ever be easy to control. I'm too scared to raise this child to become anything but a strong and outstanding harpy."

Margohot smiles and places her hand on his shoulder before saying, "I understand your concern, my prince. But my only advice in parenting your egg of choice is to never give up on your authority when it's being challenged. You will not be a father nor king to any of my chicks. I want you to remain as their brother and build a strong bond with them at an early age before they enter puberty. Once they're ready to lay eggs, you must do your damnedest to watch over your sister to continue the legacy."

"Right," Yazeem comments. "Do you want us to make sure that they only mate with males who guarantee daughters?"

"I wish there was another way, but only having grandsons means we cannot continue our bloodline."

"Then how do we even know if the human male they chose as a mate is suitable enough to grant her daughters? How will we know if anyone, like Jed Pluck over there, possesses good enough genes and guarantees daughters?"

"I'm leaving that up to you, Yazeem." She takes her hand off his shoulder. "Since you're very worried about raising one as a child, how about this? If we all make it out alive, I'll find you two, and we can reunite as a flock and grow even further to create a harpy paradise, the one thing we've been at war with the humans over."

"Okay," the prince of the flock replies, putting his head up. "I assume that since Rotzen and I are carrying one egg each, you'll carry one of them as well?"

"Yes," she replies. "As soon as I conceive with Jed for the last time, I'll kill him and take the egg north and build a new nest before I lay my final four

chicks."

"That sounds like a good plan," Rotzen says, impressed with her idea. "Before we go and carry out this duty, how will you find us?"

"Don't worry about that. I will find you as long as you stay close to your nests, and I'll pray to Zeus for directions. I did, after all, find this flock when you were all in the desert. It won't be as difficult if you stay in one place." Margohot hugs Rotzen. "Take care, my son. Choose your egg, and her name will be Tycherós."

Rotzen picks up one of the eggs with his talons, flies up in the air, and says, "So you want to give them the names of our lost sisters, Mother?"

"Of course," she answers, then gives Yazeem a big hug. "Goodbye, my prince. Select your egg, and you shall call her Sýnnefo when she hatches."

"I will, Mother," Yazeem replies as soon as she releases the hug. He picks up one of the two eggs and flies up from the ground. "I take it that the egg that you'll be taking care of will be named Dóro?"

"Yes, son," Margohot says, bringing the last egg to chest level. "Take care of my daughter. I'll find you both before they're old enough to fly. Go now." Yazeem and Rotzen fly off in their separate ways while holding the eggs.

Margohot continues watching them fly away until they are both out of sight. Though worried about her sons raising her children, she never disobeys Zeus's commands. Deep down inside, she wants to receive more answers for the future than what her god told her. Despite so many turns of events and constantly having things taken away from her, all she can do is keep faith in him and hope for the best.

Margohot goes under the water tower and puts the egg in the small haystack. She stares at the egg intensely, thinking about how important this one is in saving the harpy race and carrying out her legacy. She pats and rubs Dóro as if she were already hatched and needs comforting. Already, she imagines how much she'll spoil this one once she hatches, but she's even more excited to ovulate the last three eggs within her.

The harpy queen turns to Pluck, who's still lying motionless. He isn't as attractive as before now that he's so sickly and underweight. Margohot is more than willing to get this last fornication over with and kill him where he lies so she can raise her last children in peace. She stands over him and closes her eyes, imagining he's the same handsome and healthy postal inspector when she first met him before going down and grabbing his penis. She feels something very hard hit her cranium prior to putting his genitals into hers, knocking her down to the column shoe of the water tower's leg.

While Margohot is dazed upon getting hit in the head, Pluck drops the brick he hit her with and does his damnedest to get himself back up. He hops in one place with his only good foot and sees the only egg in the nest. Seeing that this is the perfect opportunity to smash that egg, he picks up the egg, and with all his might, he slams to the floor with all his strength. Upon impacting the ground, the egg shatters into pieces, the fluids pour all over, and the embryo slides off. Seeing the embryo look like a tiny miniature of Janet leaves him perturbed while standing over the dead fetus.

As he hears Margohot groan and sees her getting up, Pluck hops out from underneath the water tower and heads toward the hatch that leads to the access ladder. After lying down for so long, he realizes his only good foot is asleep. Pluck has to fight himself from allowing the numbness to slow him down. The rain gets heavier as he approaches the hatch. The dire situation continues to get worse for him when he attempts to open the hatch and discovers it's locked.

Out of desperation, Pluck leaps toward the slanted wooden door and uses all his weight to break through. As soon as Jed hears Margohot sob through the rain, he does it again out of desperation and crashes through the hatch. The postal inspector finds himself landing hard on the floor of a hallway, with pieces of the hatch falling on top of him. While recovering from hurting himself, Jed realizes he's in an apartment complex when a few residents come out of their rooms down the hallway to see the commotion. Jed wastes no time getting himself up and tries to ignore that he's scaring the witnesses with his nudity and exposed skin condition. The runaway is far more concerned with escaping from the harpy queen than exposing himself to all these strangers.

"Somebody call the cops!" Pluck shouts. "There's a killer on the loose!"

All the witnesses hurry back inside their apartments as he approaches them. Jed sees the stairway upon making it to the end of the hallway. Before going down, he checks the hallway to see if Margohot is chasing him. The only thing out of the ordinary is the rain pouring down the access ladder and pieces of the hatch, as well as the trail of his blood, smeared all over the walls he's been leaning on.

Pluck slips down the stairs and feels his broken ankle banging against each step as he rolls down the stairs. Jed stops rolling when he lands on the quarter, landing between floors. His first reaction after rolling down the stairs is to grab hold of his broken ankle. The splint that kept his ankle steady snapped, and the bandage wrapped around it could only do so much to keep the foot from bending again. He cries briefly over how badly it hurts until he hears Margohot screaming in the hallway he just came from.

This immediately makes Jed stop focusing on his severe pain and crawl his way down the stairs. Still soaked, Jed uses this to his advantage by slithering down the concrete stairs. The amount of anxiety the postal inspector feels makes him ignore the physical punishment. He slides down the stairs so fast that he's getting dizzy from losing count of how many quarter landings and doors he passes through. Although the pain and dizziness don't stop the naked postal inspector from escaping, his lack of stamina can only take him as far.

Pluck finally makes it to another door in another hallway and stops to catch his breath. He has never dragged his body over so many stairs and is fatigued from pushing his body to its limit. He looks before him, seeing there's another floor to go. The floor farther down is much darker and colder, making Pluck feel weird, wondering if he went past the lobby and is already in the basement level. Before he continues farther down, the door next to him opens and bumps his side.

Jed looks at the door open and sees an old couple, wearing coats and holding umbrellas, standing over him with the same expression as the witnesses on the top floor. They both back away from him and then run out of the entrance. Pluck catches a glimpse that he's on the first floor as they both exit the building's front door. He grabs the door from closing, crawls to the lobby's hallway, and goes in the same direction the couple went. There's no one in the hallway, and he sees the rain through the entranceway.

Pluck finally has had enough of crawling his way out of the building and gets himself back on his only good foot. However, his broken ankle having no splint for support makes him move much slower than before. Pluck takes much more time than necessary to walk down the front steps past the apartment building's front door before finally making it to the street. Upon getting soaked again, Pluck sees the same old couple from earlier talking to two police officers sitting on a horse-drawn police carriage. The old lady covers her face, seeing Pluck again, and the rest stare at him with disturbance.

"That's him, Officers!" the old man says, shaking his index finger at Jed. "That's the nutjob who's streaking in our apartment and disturbing the peace."

One of the police officers blows his whistle and hops out of the driver's seat. He and his partner approach Pluck and grab him by the wrists before saying, "All right, fellow. I don't know what kind of stunt you're trying to pull here, but you can't be doing this in Boston. Where are your clothes?"

"This might be the postal inspector we've been looking for," the other officer says, examining Pluck as they handcuff him. "He fits the description of having blue spots."

"Yes, it's me!" Pluck yells with apprehensiveness. "I'm Postal Inspector Jed Pluck! The one who was kidnapped! The one who took me is still in the building! You gotta get me out of here before it's too late!"

"Hold on, Inspector," the same officer replies. "We've been searching for you all over the city. It's been nearly a week since the whole department began looking for you."

"Did you say that the one that kidnapped you is in the building?" the other officer asks. "He's still there?"

"She's still there," Pluck replies, struggling to stand on one foot. "And she's gonna kill us if we don't get out of here."

"Wait a minute," the same officer replies, "how did you let a woman kidnap you and..." He briefly looks down at Pluck's lower body. "...do all this to you?"

"Weren't you paying attention to our briefings, Franklin?" the other officer interrupts, holding on to Pluck's cuffed wrists. "It was a bird-woman who took this poor man away, for God's sake. She's dangerous, and we're advised

to use excessive force to take her down."

"Please, I'm begging you," Jed says with a lower volume and a serious tone. "If she catches me out here, we're through. You have to take me away from here." The police officer holding the postal inspector's wrists uncuffs him. He removes his own raincoat and covers Jed with it. He then assists Pluck to the wagon and helps him hop aboard the back, where the windows are barred and heavily secured. After the carriage's door is locked, more officers arrive at the scene. Pluck can't make out what the officers are saying to each other as he looks through the barred window. While all the others enter the apartment building, the two officers approach the carriage Pluck is in.

"Don't worry, Inspector," says one of the officers, looking at Pluck through the barred window, "we'll take you to the Boston Police headquarters right now. Your friends and family are waiting for you there."

"My family? They're still alive?" Pluck asks, putting his hands on the bars. "Wait! You're not sending all those officers in there, are you?"

"Not to worry, Inspector." The officer climbs into the driver's seat. "They're highly trained professionals who can handle any criminal that sets foot in Boston."

The officers whip the reins and the horses to pull the wagon. Pluck sits on the carriage seat and stares at the apartment building through the door's window. Despite being in the carriage, having the windows barred, and being taken away from the crime scene, he still feels unsafe. He could envisage the dreadful fate that awaits the policemen who are pursuing Margohot in the building. This makes him feel just as terrible as being unable to save the people back in Point Postal.

Jed, however, quickly realizes that none of the officers in that building will be facing Margohot. While watching through the window on the carriage's door, he sees a figure with crimson wings jump off the building's rooftop and fly toward his carriage. What's more terrifying is that despite the carriage moving at high speed, the figure is flying much faster. It doesn't take long until Pluck sees Margohot approach him with her talons pointing directly at him. No matter how many times he feels like there's a sign of hope for him, Jed continues to find the harpy queen tirelessly going after him, just like in his nightmares.

CHAPTER 21

Losing their home and having Jed go missing daunts the entire family. They should count their blessings that he works as a Federal agent, which has made the entire Boston Police Department give them the best protection at all costs. However, Clara and the girls aren't allowed to go anywhere since they're all still in danger. Spending the last couple of days under the protection of the Boston Police Headquarters has been a grueling experience for Clara and her daughters. Even with the commissioner's office for them to sleep in isn't enough hospitality or protection in the world that can calm Clara's nerves. The harpies still haunt the distressed mother.

This is the first time Clara has felt unease over the rain, which used to calm her nerves. Even with her daughters fast asleep on the same couch, all sitting together, she feels incomplete without Jed. Spending another day at the police department leaves her to sit on the commissioner's chair, weeping alone every morning before breakfast is brought to them or one of her four daughters awakens. She then stops crying when hearing numerous people yelling outside the office.

"Mother," Julia whispers, waking up. "Why is everyone yelling?"

Clara quickly wipes her tears and continues listening until everything gets immediately quiet before replying, "What's going on out there? Wait here, I'll be back."

The second-eldest child slowly gets out of the couch from waking her sisters and whispers, "I'm coming with you."

Clara doesn't object as she gets up from her seat and says, "Stay close to me, Julia. A police station is no place to wander around."

As Julia and her mother head out the door, Jessie is the next to wake up and whispers, "Where are you two going? The police said no one is allowed to leave this office unless we have to go to the bathroom."

"I know, but this is just one time," Clara replies, opening the door. "We'll be back soon. Watch Allie and Janet while we're gone, okay?"

Julia and Clara exit the office and slowly close the door, keeping the two youngest in the family from waking up. As they walk through the office floor, no one, not even an officer, is sitting in their office space. This is a first for the mother and daughter to step out of the commissioner's office and not see a single police officer in sight.

"Where is everybody?" Julia comments.

"I don't have the slightest idea," her mother replies.

Clara leads Julia through the desks and toward the stairs. As they get closer, they hear many shouts echoing down the stairway from the floors below. The mother and daughter are uneasy over how aggressive the commotion sounds. They make their way to the floor below, unable to understand why there's so much yelling. They both make it one floor down and still hear the commotion farther down.

Julia stops when she notices her mother is distracted by the door to the second floor, which is cracked open. Clara and Julia peek through to see they're on the jail floor where the inmates are held. Surprisingly, all of them are silent, and there isn't an officer watching over them. A thought comes into Clara's mind over how incompetent it is to leave the jail door open and neglect the inmates on this floor. After glimpsing over the first jail cell with an intimidating figure inside, Clara pulls Julia's arm and continues leading her down to the next floor.

Clara and Julia both make it to the lobby floor and see that all the officers are making the noise. They both exit the stairway and walk toward the front desk, where all the officers are gathered around the headquarters' main entrance. Upon closer inspection, Clara can see over the officers' shoulders that a carriage has crashed through the front entrance and is lying on its side. The horses drawn to this police carriage are detached, and more officers outside the main entrance are holding their reins. Clara and Julia walk past the main desk and around the officers and see the carriage soaked in blood, as well as numerous scratches and holes on the back and top. The carriage must have gone so fast that it was able to go up the entrance stairs outside and crash through the giant front door and windows, where shattered glass is now all over the floor.

The mother and daughter both see Inspector Secoli carrying Chap in his new birdcage and the two harpy hunters helping the police attempt to open the back of the carriage. None of the officers notice Clara and Julia as they all focus on the police carriage in the lobby. Everyone is having trouble opening the carriage's door, considering that the officers assigned to this carriage have gone missing and no one has the keys. The mother and daughter arrive just in time to see the officers use bolt cutters to break the lock and take whoever is inside out. When the lock breaks and the officers pull out the passenger, Clara and Julia are shocked to see Jed being dragged out.

The poor postal inspector is in much worse shape than when Clara last saw him. Jed is much thinner than before; his right ankle is bending in an unnatural position, and the blue spots all over his skin are much darker and larger. Julia is the first of her sisters to see her father unbandaged, exposing his skin condition. It horrifies her to see her father naked, grotesque, and looking barely alive.

"Daddy!" Julia exclaims.

All the officers next to Julia turn in her direction before Clara shouts, "Jed!

What happened to my husband?"

"Ladies," says an officer beside them, attempting to pull the mother and her daughter away, "you're not supposed to be here."

"I have every right to be here!" Clara exclaims. "That's my husband!" She pulls her wrist away from the officer's hand and runs toward her sickly husband, who's been placed on the floor. She kneels next to Jed. "Is he all right? What happened to him?"

"One of our patrols found him," says an officer next to her as Clara watches another officer check Jed's pulse and the rest of his body. "But witnesses said some kind of giant bird chased this carriage down. We don't know what happened to the patrol officers who drove this carriage, but whatever caused their disappearances certainly did a number on this vehicle and freed the horses drawn to it." The officer turns to the other policemen. "Somebody get an ambulance. He needs medical attention."

"Clara...," Jed mutters, as his naked body is covered by a spare coat. He barely looks alive as he turns to her, his eyes half open. Despite his best efforts, his weak voice can't be heard in the loud lobby.

"What is it, darling?" Clara leans closer to her poor husband, placing her ear next to his dry lips.

Pluck speaks as loud as he can but still is too quiet. "Run—we're all in danger." Clara slowly pulls away before Secoli asks, "What did he say, Missus—"

Secoli is interrupted by the familiar noise that instantly makes him hold on to his ears. The same ear-piercing shrieking is coming from outside the Boston Police headquarters, and it gets louder as the shrieker approaches. All the police officers hold on to their ears for dear life as they all are now experiencing the harpy queen's most painful tactic. While Jed and Clara cover their ears like everyone in the lobby, Secoli pulls Clara up and leads her out of danger. Klouví immediately picks Pluck up from the ground, places his arm around her neck, and helps carry him away, following Secoli and Clara ahead of them.

Secoli does his damnedest to endure the shrieking, as he has his hands full by pulling his partner's wife and carrying his birdcage. In front of them, as he's helping Clara flee from danger, Julia is in their path. The poor child cannot bear the noise, covering her ears and cowering from the excruciating experience. Secoli hastily places the birdcage underneath his armpit and uses that hand to grab Julia and lead her to safety. The postal inspector is determined to keep Jed's wife and daughter from danger even if the harpy blows out his ears and makes him deaf.

Even though he has endured the same tactic from the harpies numerous times, he cannot endure any more shrieking for this long. The farthest that Secoli can take the mother, her daughter, and Chap is near the doorway to the stairway. His ears start ringing, and the two ladies he's pulling away to safety are unable to continue moving. Both of them start weighing Secoli down, adding to the dire situation they're all in. With no other choice, Secoli kicks the door next to the stairway, throws the three in there, and finally covers his ears.

While Secoli holds on to his ears, he stands in front of the men's room, guarding the three in there. He pulls out his handgun and returns to the lobby. To his surprise, he sees Klouví carrying Jed to safety. He sees Jed is still naked and limping with his only good foot. Klouví is enduring the shrieking with her ears uncovered much better than Secoli ever could.

"Klouví! Jed!" Secoli shouts as loud as he can. "We gotta get you two outta—"

Klouví interrupts Secoli by pushing him so hard that he falls inside the men's room with the three. The harpy hunter does this to allow himself to hide safely with the other three while she takes Inspector Pluck up the stairs. While trying to avoid landing on the ladies, who are lying on the floor with their ears covered, Secoli trips over, hitting Julia's foot, and lands on top of the birdcage. Secoli's weight separates the birdcage's bars and base with the grille upon impact. After nearly a month of healing, the budgerigar can fly again, fleeing from the noisy environment.

Chap flies around the room, looking for a place to hide or find a way to flee from the unbearable noise. The bird sees a window above one of the toilets where all the glass is shattered from Margohot's screeching, and it flies out of the police headquarters. He flies farther away from where the shrieking is coming from. While he flees for safety, the bird sees a red-feathered harpy standing before the headquarters' entrance. Seeing the harpy queen again is enough to make Chap fly farther away from her.

Back at the entrance, Margohot continues shrieking as she slowly heads up the stairs and walks through the entrance. She catches her breath after screeching for that long. Upon entering the lobby, a couple of policemen grab their guns and open fire at the harpy queen. Feeling bullets hit her but none pierce her skin infuriates Margohot.

The situation reaches a boiling point, and Margohot enters a frenzy that she desperately tries to control. Instead of shrieking again, the harpy queen starts slashing and killing everyone in her way. One by one, the officers are outmatched by the harpy's claws, razor-sharp feathers, and talons. So much blood, guts, dismemberments, and beheadings. The still-alive policemen continue to fire at her but to no avail.

Alistair Pantazis gets up from the ground and sees Margohot slaughtering all the policemen. While his ears ring, he can see the lobby is rapidly filled with crimson as the harpy queen continues her onslaught. The harpy hunter knows too well how dangerous it is to have a female harpy go into a frenzy. There were around fifty officers in the lobby, and now they're losing each of them by the second. Feeling everyone else's blood and organs land on top of him is enough to make Pantazis stop staring at the slaughtering.

Pantazis immediately pulls out his crossbow and aims it at Margohot, who still has her attention on the officers. He then remembers that he doesn't have an arrow loaded or any in his possession since all of them are kept in the evidence room. The harpy hunter looks around to see if he can spot the officer who holds the keys to all the doors on this floor. It doesn't take long for him to find that officer lying dead on the ground with his guts exposed. Pantazis doesn't waste any time crawling over to the corpse and snatching the keys off his belt.

The harpy hunter then picks up his crossbow from the ground, rushes past the front desk, and toward the evidence room. His tinnitus subsides, and he hears the policemen screaming, guns firing, and bodies ripping apart. Pantazis doesn't dare to go back to where the massacre is occurring as he makes it to the door to the evidence room and tries each key on the keychain to unlock the door. Upon attempting to unlock the door, he notices the guns stop firing. As Pantazis hears the last man scream for his life before becoming the next victim, he crawls under the nearest desk.

While he's hiding underneath the desk, his tinnitus quickly disappears. He can hear the blood drops leaking, talons stomping on the floor from the entrance, and Margohot's heavy breathing. Pantazis holds his breath to prevent any noise as Margohot walks around the front desk and heads toward the stairway. The ringing in his ears is completely gone as soon as he hears her slowly walking up the stairs. He waits a few seconds for her to proceed to the next floor before he can breathe again, then opens the evidence room's door.

Right before him are both his and Klouví's quivers filled with all the harpy arrows. The harpy hunter takes one of the arrows out of the quiver and loads his crossbow. After getting his weapon loaded, he straps both quivers on his back and follows the harpy queen up the stairway. When he gets out of the room, he sees Secoli with Clara and Julia exiting the men's room. Pantazis is confused over why the postal inspector is holding an opened birdcage and looking distressed.

"Alistair?" Secoli says, wiping his tears and dropping his empty birdcage. "Is it over? What happened? Have you seen Chap? Where is my bird?"

Pantazis shushes Secoli as he approaches them, and with limited English, he tries telling him, "You...quiet. Margohot...up there."

"What?" Secoli replies. "She's still here?"

Alistair then gets interrupted by more screaming and the sounds of bodies tearing apart coming from upstairs. His immediate reaction is to point his crossbow toward the doorway to the stairs. The sounds of the massacre echoing through the stairway are enough to give all the survivors in the men's room goosebumps.

Clara and Julia are oblivious to the violent noise happening upstairs, unable to hear a thing. As they're recovering from tinnitus, their attention is drawn to the blood trail leading to the front entrance. The mother and daughter slowly walk back to the main lobby. Secoli and Pantazis turn back and see them turning to the bloody crime scene and run after them. Julia and Clara are perturbed to see every surface of the room covered in blood, with organs all over the floors, walls, and ceiling.

There isn't a single officer making any movement, nor one that isn't soaked in blood. Staring at everyone's remains while hearing the massacre coming from upstairs adds to how demoralizing all this is. Clara has seen the harpies in action once, and what she's been informed about them is much more terrifying in practice. On the other hand, Julia couldn't grasp how dangerous the harpies were until now. They all remain silent and perturbed by what they see until a dismembered arm falls from the ceiling.

Seeing that separated body part land on a pool of blood is enough to make Julia faint. Even her mother breaks down and screams over witnessing that much blood and gore. Despite how much anxiety is flowing through his veins, Secoli has enough inner strength to grab Clara from behind and cover her mouth, preventing her from grabbing any attention from upstairs or other harpies who might be outside. The postal inspector pulls her back to the men's restroom while Pantazis picks up the passed-out daughter from the ground and follows them. Upon returning to the men's room, Clara cries uncontrollably with her mouth covered as Julia is gently placed in the corner.

"Please, Clara," Secoli gently cries into Clara's ear, still covering her mouth and holding her upper arm. "I'm scared… I'm so scared of those harpies, just as you are."

Clara finally calms, hearing his gentle voice, feeling how terrified he is as she feels him trembling.

"The last thing I ever want is for you, Jed, or any of your daughters to end up like the rest of their victims. I've endured so much from those goddamn monsters. They did much worse to your beloved husband—and made me watch."

Clara can feel Secoli's tears drop on her neck and shoulders. He is filled with so much terror that he's unable to let go of her. She still feels him shaking more, and he's panting much faster than she is as the screaming from upstairs continues.

"I hate them," Secoli continues whispering in her ear, feeling more emotional over the echoing screams coming from upstairs. "I hate all of them so much." He sniffs the mucus coming out of his nose. "Nothing scares me more than them. I'm asking you to do one thing for me while I do my damnedest to protect you, Clara. I need you…to be braver than I am. I can feel I'm about to lose it now that Chap is gone, and I'm seeing everyone around me die again because of her." Secoli clears his throat and sounds more relaxed. "Please. Be brave for me. For your family. And for the fate of everyone."

Secoli feels Clara nodding before he finally lets go of her. Secoli collapses on the floor, and Clara tries to help him back up. Pantazis doesn't understand what Secoli has said to her and is confused seeing this turn of events. Likewise, the harpy hunter is relieved to see the mother finally calm down and decides to head upstairs.

Over Secoli's shoulder, Clara sees Pantazis stepping out of the room and says, "Wait. Where are you going?"

The harpy hunter turns to her and shushes her before replying, "You all... stay. I go up..." He raises his leaded crossbow. "...and kill...with this."

"Please," Clara says softly. "My family is upstairs. Please save them."

Pantazis only understands what "family" means and gives her a nod before closing the door and heading up the stairs. He quietly yet quickly heads up to the second floor, where all the noise comes from. The door to the second floor leads to the jail floor and is cracked open. The harpy hunter peeks in and sees the jail bars bent open and blood everywhere. The inmates are left defenseless and abandoned to Margohot's endless killing.

He sees Margohot farther down a couple of cells, tearing apart a couple of captives and convicts in there. From where he's standing, Pantazis can't get a good shot at the harpy queen with so many bars in the way. He senses that now isn't the perfect time to strike her, even when she least expects it. Even if he gets to shoot her, the harpy arrow won't penetrate deeply with her in her hysteria; Margohot's blind rage strengthens her durability against projectiles until she gets exhausted from pushing her body past its limits.

Since it's only recently that the harpy queen has entered her frenzy, Pantazis must abandon the inmates. He hates that they all have to be sacrificed to tire Margohot out. This won't be the first time he has to do that to her victims when she's in such a state, and he hopes this will be the last time he ever has to do such a thing. He slowly closes the door and locks it. Pantazis can still hear the inmates screaming for their lives, trapped in their cells.

He has no doubt that Klouví has taken Inspector Pluck to the next floor up. Every harpy hunter's tactic is to make it to the rooftop to fight off the harpies invading a building. Knowing that Margohot has kept herself busy with the inmates, Pantazis sees she hasn't caught up with Klouví, Pluck, or his family upstairs. He continues his way up the stairs and does his all to ignore the abandoned inmates left for slaughter. As Pantazis heads up the stairs, he feels conflicted about rescuing everyone upstairs over those beyond saving below.

JESSIE, ALLIE, AND Janet do as they are told and remain in the commissioner's office. Despite being kept in the headquarters' most prestigious room, the three sisters are in danger, and they know it after enduring the ear-piercing screeching from outside. These girls had never heard anything so damaging to their hearing—something that caused all the windows to shatter. The three sisters are all on the floor, covering their ears and enduring the ringing in their ears. Allie and Janet are so terrified that they refuse to move, nor do they wish to uncover their ears.

Jessie lets go of her sisters, shakes their shoulders to get their attention, and says, "Allie. Janet. We gotta get out of here. It's not safe."

Her little sisters pick their heads up, and Allie is the first to say, "What did you say, Jessie? Speak louder."

Janet responds in the middle of what Allie says. "What is it, big sister?"

Jessie can hear both of them through her tinnitus. However, both of her sisters can't understand a word she's saying. The eldest sister panics over both of her of her sisters' deafness.

"Allie!" Jessie shouts, shaking her shoulders. "Can you hear me?"

"Stop playing around, Jessie!" Allie shouts back, pushing her arms away. "And why are you shaking me? Don't you know I hate it when you pretend you're mute?"

"Jessie," Janet says, pulling her sister's sleeve. "How come I can't hear my voice when I speak?"

"You too, Janet?" Allie yells after seeing her baby sister's lips move. "You two better stop pretending you're mute, or I'm telling—" Allie stops when she notices she, too, can't hear her own voice. "What's happening to me? Where's my voice?"

Jessie is frustrated over their communication, so she leans toward her ear and shouts, "We gotta get out! It's dangerous."

The only word that Allie can make out through the tinnitus is "out."

"Out?" Allie replies, rubbing the ear that Jessie yelled into. "What's out there?"

Losing patience, Jessie grabs her sisters' wrists and pulls them to the door. Neither of them understands what Jessie is doing and is worried about being unable to hear anything. Jessie opens the door and is shocked to see someone in front of it.

She falls over at the sight of Klouví carrying a naked man covered in blue spots. Allie is also disturbed by the sickly man and runs behind Jessie on the floor. However, Janet is the only one out of the three who recognizes her father and isn't disturbed by his appearance upon closer inspection. The look of exhaustion on this man's face shifts to one of joy. Seeing the three as a sight for sore eyes fills him with energy.

"Daddy!" Janet shouts, running toward him and then hugging his leg. "It's you!" Jed does his best to ignore that she bumped into his broken ankle and kneels to give her youngest daughter a hug. He's in so much pain that he can't say her name. The father then gives her a big hug in exultation. Jessie then recognizes her father and rushes toward him to join in on the hug. Despite how much pain Jed is in from enduring their hugs and how uncomfortable his broken ankle is, he cries in both pain and joy.

Allie is unable to recognize her father right in front of her. While recovering from her deafness, she's confused as to why her two sisters are hugging this sickly, naked man. She steps back until her back hits the commissioner's desk.

Jed looks up after hearing a bump on the desk and says, "Allie...." He groans as Jessie lets go of him. "It's me. It's Daddy. Don't you recognize—"

Allie screams as her father reaches out to her. She has no idea how loud she is.

Klouví immediately rushes toward her and covers her mouth. Realizing everyone is still in danger, Jed lets go of Janet's tight hug and gets up to close and lock the doors. He then limps to the wardrobe to finally put on some clothes. Before opening it, he notices a jar filled with water on a coffee table next to the wardrobe. He hesitantly grabs the jar's handle and drinks the whole thing before putting on whatever clothes he pulls out.

"Where are your clothes, Daddy?" Jessie says, struggling to cover her baby sister's eyes. "You don't look so good. What's going on?"

Their father wraps the belt around his waist and takes a spare shirt before replying. "I escaped from my kidnappers, Jess. And now they're after me and want to take you away from me."

"Who's trying to take us away from you?" Jessie cries, getting emotional as she lets go of Janet's eyes. "Where's Mother and Julia? And where's the police?"

"Oh, sh—" Jed stops himself from swearing in front of his children. "Oh, no. They're still downstairs. Stay here. I gotta go get them."

"Stop," Klouví interrupts before he heads out the door and lets go of Allie's mouth. "You're putting yourself in danger if you go after them."

"Daddy?" Allie says, recognizing her father now fully clothed. "Is that you?"

"Of course, it's me," her father replies. "It's what your sisters and I have been sa—"

Allie doesn't let him finish as she runs toward him with tears and hugs him. Jed kneels before she hugs his leg, preventing her from hurting his ankle again. He's much happier now that all his daughters recognize him.

"Okay, Allie...," Jed attempts to break free from her tight hug. "I gotta get Mommy and Julia."

Allie refuses to let go.

"Hey, didn't you hear what I just said?"

"Daddy...," Jessie interrupts. "She can't hear you. That loud sound from outside hurt our ears. I'm the only one who can hear. Janet and Allie can't."

"What?" Jed immediately takes Allie off him and shakes her shoulders. "Allie.

Speak to me, darling. Can you hear me?"

"Daddy? What's wrong with me? Why can't I hear you or my sisters? And how come I can't hear my voice?"

Jed cries again out of hopelessness and looks up at Klouví. "Zephyra? How did she—how can we help her get her hearing back?"

"These three were nowhere as close to Margohot's shrieking, so I say they have a better chance of recovering their hearing than anyone alive downstairs. It's nothing—"

Klouví is interrupted by a loud knock on the door. Jed immediately grabs Allie and pulls her behind the couch. Jessie does the same for Janet and joins them for safety. Klouví leans against the door and pulls out her crossbow, strapped around her back.

"Who goes there?" Klouví shouts.

A familiar voice replies through the door, saying in Greek, "It's me. Alistair."

The harpy hunter opens the door to let the other harpy hunter in. After Pantazis slips in, Klouví locks the door and gives her partner a quick hug.

"Sorry," Pantazis says. "I forgot to tell you I came up here to bring you ammunition. Your crossbow is useless without them."

"Thank you for coming all this way to give this to me." Klouví receives her quiver filled with arrows. "Are there any survivors?"

"Inspector Secoli, Mrs. Pluck, and his daughter are the only survivors.

The police—they fought well, but Margohot is in a frenzy right now."

"Damn it," Klouví swears. She turns to Jed and his daughters peeking out from

behind the couch and switches to English. "Good news. Alistair confirms that your daughter and your wife are safe, Jed. He came to help us make our escape."

"What a relief," Pluck says, stepping out from behind the couch with his daughters. "What's the plan?"

"Daddy...," Janet nervously interrupts. "What is that?"

Everyone turns to Janet's direction, who's standing in front of the window. Peeking through the broken window from outside is a pair is demented, yellow eyes staring right at the youngest daughter. The moment they all see crimson wings raised in the air, the adults know who exactly it is. The two harpy hunters then pull out their crossbows and fire at Margohot. Having predicted they'd use harpy arrows against her, the harpy queen dodges them by descending.

While Klouví and Pantazis quickly reload their crossbows, Jed runs after Janet. He calls for his younger daughter, but Janet doesn't hear him. She continues staring out the window. Before Jed can grab hold of his daughter, a talon goes through the broken window and grabs Janet. Margohot is merciless in grabbing little Janet as her talons pierce the girl's shoulder and pull her out of the building.

Everyone hears Janet screaming in pain, something a six-year-old should never have to endure. Jed is screaming no repeatedly, unable to fathom seeing his youngest daughter being carried and tortured in the air. Never has he ever heard a girl her age scream in pain as she is now. Margohot flies past the window where Jed sticks his head out and takes Janet with her to the building. His youngest daughter is still crying on the roof, making those painful cries a father never wants to hear from anyone in his family.

Jed immediately changes from being fearful to incensed. Enraged that the harpy queen is hurting his youngest daughter, Pluck limps as fast as he can out of the office and heads directly to the stairway leading to the rooftop.

As the father barges out the door, Klouví runs after him and shouts back, "Alistair, I'll go to the rooftop and try to stop her! I need you on the ground outside and be prepared to shoot her from below when she flies over the roof." Klouví then helps Jed up the stairs while Pantazis moves down in the opposite direction. Jessie and Allie cannot stay in the commissioner's office any longer. They then decide to follow their father up the stairs and help save Janet while they still can. Jed is so blinded by hatred that he doesn't command his other daughters to stay out of danger. Fully knowing how remorseless Margohot is, he won't allow his tormentor to do the same to anyone in his family. In Jed's eyes, little Janet is the last person to ever deserve such treatment.

CHAP DIDN'T FLY VERY far from the Boston Police headquarters. Since the parakeet hasn't heard any more shrieking from Margohot since he escaped, he remains sitting on the ledge of a rooftop across the street from where he came from. Already, the poor bird is reconsidering his decision to fly away and abandon his master and friends. The intelligent bird already has abandonment issues being apart from Secoli and still remembers how dangerous it was the last time he separated from him.

Chap has been examining the police headquarters' exterior since he escaped. The only thing out of the ordinary is policemen from other stations arriving at the crime scene, confused over why everyone surrounding the headquarters below has yet to enter the building. It's odd for the intelligent bird to see human beings as always being willing to help each other, yet these people out there are delaying the inevitable.

It takes a while for Chap to see someone coming out of the entrance with a crossbow. Upon closer examination, the budgerigar recognizes that Pantazis is exiting alone, and policemen approach him. Knowing he's one of the humans following his owner, he's confused about why Secoli and the others have yet to exit the building. All these things are making Chap frustrated and lose more patience. Just when he's about to swoop down to Pantazis, he catches a glance of the same crimson figure getting up from the rooftop.

What's more worrying for the parakeet than seeing Margohot again is Janet being her captive. Chap hears Janet crying from that direction, making painful screaming that he has never heard from a human child before. The intelligent bird understands that the little girl, who he used to play with and who took care of him when Secoli had to leave him in Boston, is in danger. Knowing how violent Margohot has been toward the postal inspectors makes Chap fearful for the little girl's life. Seeing that no human has yet made it to the rooftop to save Janet is enough to make Chap go after her.

The morning rain is much lighter, making flying back much easier for his small wings. Since the building that the parakeet flew off is roughly the same height as the headquarters building, Chap maintains the same altitude and doesn't worry about using more of his strength to go higher. Despite wanting to save the little girl, the intelligent bird doesn't have any plan to save Janet from her kidnapper. The budgerigar lands on the edge of a window frame right underneath the ledge Margohot is standing on.

Chap managed to get there without anyone noticing. From where the parakeet can see, he sees Margohot standing above him with her back turned away from the ledge. Now that the budgerigar is closer to danger, he can hear Janet crying in pain and fear. Chap desperately wants to help rescue her, but what kind of improvising can the tiny bird come up with to go up against such an indestructible being?

As Chap awaits Margohot's next move, the harpy queen waits for Jed by using his youngest daughter as bait. While facing the only door to the stairway, Margohot has her left wing placed on Janet's back and her right on her front. Little Janet has little room to move, feeling Margohot's razor-sharp feathers poking and peeling her skin and dress whenever she makes sudden movements. The six-year-old so desperately wants to hold on to her pierced shoulder due to how excruciating it feels, but she feels pain all around her whenever she moves. Never in her life had she ever been so scared or felt this much pain.

Janet's father barges through the stairway's door with Klouví carrying him. The harpy hunter immediately lets go of Jed and aims her crossbow at Margohot.

"Let her go, harpy queen!" Klouví shouts in Greek, keeping her aim at Margohot. "You've done enough already. Harming the little girl is a new low, especially for you."

Margohot laughs before replying in the same language, "That's rich coming from you two. Do you know how hypocritical you sound after you massacred my babies and aborted my unhatched children? You'd better put that crossbow down because if I clap my wings together, this little bitch will be crushed like she's in an iron maiden."

"Firing this crossbow will kill you before you attempt such a thing."

" Go ahead and do it, Zephyra!" Margohot replies. "Let's see if you'll hit

me or hit her just like you shot your husband on your wedding day."

Klouví is fighting that urge to pull the trigger after hearing that remark. The history between the two is long and too personal. She knows that even if the harpy arrow hits her, Janet won't survive with that many sharp feathers contacting her body. Klouví remains silent but keeps her aim at the harpy queen.

"Janet," Jed cries, trembling while standing on his only good foot, "if you can hear me, everything is going to be alright, my darling. Daddy's here. I'll take care of everything. Okay?"

"Da–daddy," Janet nervously replies, trying to control her volume to prevent her from making sudden movements while feeling her kidnapper's deadly feathers. "I-I can hear again. I can hear my voice, too. I'm hurting, Daddy… I'm hurting really bad."

Jed can't stomach looking at his baby girl suffering right in front of him. The sight of the blood pouring down to her feet as her body is covered by Margohot's wing is too much for him to bear. Seeing that Margohot is so close to killing someone so dear to him brings him an utter sense of powerlessness and hopelessness. The father falls on his knees and weeps in front of his daughter and the harpy queen.

"Please, Margohot!" Jed cries, putting his hands together as though in prayer. "I admit that what I did to your daughters—"

"*Our* daughters," Margohot loudly interrupts, offended that he refuses to acknowledge the biological truth.

"What I did to *our* daughters," Jed corrects himself nervously, "was wrong. It is my greatest sin against you and your fami—flock." He puts his head down and cries louder. "I committed the most unforgivable sin—by not only favoring my human children over our own but deciding to kill them without your consent as the mother. I admit it all! But please...let my child go! Leave her and my family out of this mess." He places his forehead on the ground and puts his hands back together. "I'm so sorry."

Margohot watches Jed in the pleading position, looking weaker than ever. She has never seen Jed look so helpless, even comparing him to his captivity. The harpy queen is fighting the urge to kill Janet but keeps her alive for a reason.

"Thank you, Jed," Margohot says, "for acknowledging and admitting that everything you've done is terribly wrong. I just want to let you know that you didn't just kill our children, but you're killing my race. My species. My given bloodline. Do you know why every species in this world wants their kind to exist for many years?"

Jed raises his head from the ground and shakes it in a nonverbal response. "Because extinction is the worst defeat of them all," the harpy queen continues. "If there were more harpies than there are now, I would die happy knowing that my kind will continue my legacy, grow our numbers, and get stronger. Everything my dead children, my ancestry, and I have built is to prevent the next generation of harpies from suffering the same thing everyone is dealing with now. If only our reproductive system didn't breed with the same species we eat, it wouldn't be so fucking complicated and difficult to manage. What would you do if the roles were reversed and humanity was on the brink of extinction? Would you want the human race to go extinct once you die?"

Jed nervously shakes his head again.

"No species in existence wants to be at the end of the line until they go extinct," she continues. "Humanity is fully responsible for every mass extinction, and none of you can ever be satisfied with how many have overpopulated the earth. It's unfair that organisms like me deserve to exist, but your species never played fair!"

Janet interrupts by screaming from feeling the tips of Margohot's feathers pierce her back and the front of her body. The harpy queen notices she's getting too emotional and calms down. In a better state of mind, she puts her wings a little farther away from Janet, already demonstrating how much danger the little one is in. As Jed screams over Janet's suffering, Jessie and Allie, eavesdropping from the stairway, run toward their father. Jessie gets on their knees and gets in the same begging position as Jed. Allie gets behind her father and hugs him for dear life.

"Girls!" their father shouts. "Stop! Get back downstairs!"

"Please stop hurting my little sister!" Jessie exclaims with tears coming down her cheeks. "I beg you. I love her very much. If you take her away—"

Jessie can't develop the words to make a good argument against the harpy queen.

She's too young and naive to persuade Margohot to let Janet go and leave her family alone. All the teenager can do is cry in front of Margohot, hoping she can make the harpy queen sympathetic. However, Margohot's heart is filled with too much hatred to reconsider. She finds it empowering to see Jed's family kneeling in front of her.

"Isn't it nice," Margohot comments, "to see the Pluck family reunited?

How come my stupid sons couldn't kill all of you as weak as you all are?"

"That was you who burned our house?" Allie replies.

"No, you idiotic child," the harpy queen rudely answers. "I said it was my sons—but no matter. If you want the job done right, you'd better do it yourself."

"Stop, Margohot!" Pluck shouts, getting himself up and releasing himself from Allie's grasp. "It's me that you want, right?" He quickly limps toward the end of the roof and gets on top of the ledge. "I'll kill myself if you hurt Janet again."

All his daughters gasp at their father's suicidal tendencies.

Jessie exclaims, "No, Daddy! Don't do it!"

"Please, Daddy!" Allie loudly cries. "I don't want you to die!"

Margohot doesn't flinch at his suicidal threat and replies, "Oh, please, Jed. Do you honestly believe I won't be fast enough to kill little Janet here and catch you before you hit the ground?"

Jed remembers how fast Margohot can fly and realizes this is a bad idea. He hops back onto the rooftop. Feeling more hopeless, the father falls back to his knees and has both hands on the ground. He struggles to look at Margohot or his daughters.

"Then what do you want me to do?" Jed screams. "What can I do to make you stop hurting Janet? I'll do anything—anything for you to let her go! Even if it means taking me away to give you more babies! Then get it over with! Let her go!"

"Speaking of which," Margohot interrupts, "I did come through all this trouble because you owe me an egg—a whole nest even. I will free Janet." Pluck puts his head back up and replies, "You will?"

"Sure, I will," Margohot says. "I still need to mate with you one last time to lay my last eggs. But we're not going to do it where we're alone. I'm going to make your daughters watch how we do it together."

Pluck is repulsed by her request. "You're sick. That's absolutely—sick. Why the hell would you ever make me do that in front of my children? That's going way too far!"

"Then say goodbye to Janet, Jed." Margohot moves her wings away from Janet a little and is about to clap them together.

"Wait!" Jed exclaims, straightening his back while still kneeling. "If it's daughters you want..." He rips his shirt open, exposing his spotty chest. "... then it's daughters you'll get. Now release Janet!"

"Not so fast!" Margohot interrupts. "Zephyra is still pointing that crossbow at me. You..." She turns to Klouví. "...unload your crossbow and arrows and throw it to me."

"What?" Klouví hesitatingly responds.

"Now!" Margohot shouts. "I won't tell you again!"

Klouví can see that Margohot isn't bluffing. They both give each other an intense stare for a couple of seconds before the harpy hunter gives in. Klouví stops aiming her crossbow at her and removes the arrow loaded on the weapon. She puts the arrow in the quiver with the rest of her ammunition before throwing the crossbow in front of Margohot. Klouví throws the crossbow first, then the quiver right lands next to the harpy queen's talons.

The quiver goes a little farther and lands on the ledge. Though the quiver doesn't fall off, arrows land on the rooftop's surface and fall off the roof. The two arrows falling off the ledge startle Chap, who's been hiding underneath Margohot this whole time. It spooks him so much that he jumps out of the window frame and hastily flies up to Margohot's level. The budgerigar flies so fast that he ends up hitting her face.

This causes Margohot to raise her wings, freeing Janet. Despite her pain, the youngest in the family runs as fast as she can toward her father. Chap improvises by gouging one of Margohot's eyes with his talons. This becomes very effective considering that not only is a harpy's eye very sensitive, but with long-distance vision like an eagle, it's difficult for Margohot to tell where Chap is so up close. Chap keeps holding on to her right eyeball with both of his talons despite getting hit by her deadly wings. The tiny bird holds on to the eye until Margohot smacks him for the fifth time, causing Chap to lose his grasp on her eye and collapse on the ground next to Allie's foot.

Allie is the only one who notices where Chap fell as everyone focuses on Janet and Margohot. When she picks up the parakeet, she sees Chap's green and yellow feathers covered in blood and still breathing. Allie clung to Chap for protection, as did Jed to Janet. Margohot's right eye was clearly blinded and bleeding profusely. The harpy queen is entering a frenzy over her damaged eye. She tries looking for the budgerigar but discovers Klouví right below her with a loaded crossbow pointing at her.

After all this time feuding with each other, it is at this moment that Klouví finally has her. The harpy hunter pulls the trigger, sending an arrow through her chest. Finally, a projectile pierces Margohot's body. While Margohot writhes in over the pain, Klouví wastes no time grabbing an arrow from the ground, reloading her crossbow, and firing another on her left wing. Now that there's an arrow through her elbow, the harpy queen cannot fly away. Klouví does it again and shoots at her neck.

It doesn't hit her in the throat, but the third arrow hits Margohot in a sensitive part of the neck. She loses her balance and falls off the ledge of the three-story building. She's in so much agony that she's unable to fly. Margohot crashes through a spare police carriage with no horses hitched to it. It scares the other horses drawn to the other police carriages nearby. The public surrounding the Boston Police headquarters rushes toward the harpy to get a closer view of the monster.

Photographers from the newspapers are the first to reach Margohot and take pictures of the barely alive harpy. In each picture they take, they quickly change lightbulbs. The flashing from the cameras gives the harpy queen a splitting headache, making her wish she were dead already. The photo-taking doesn't last long as the police interfere and push the public away from the culprit. The next people approaching her are the police commissioner, Inspector Duncan, and Alistair Pantazis.

Lying motionless on the damaged carriage, Margohot stares at them before saying, "It's not fair...that he gets to keep his children...and I lose all of mine." Pantazis has waited a very long time for the harpy queen to finally fall.

He has mixed feelings about the bad shape Margohot is. She looks much more defeated than he could imagine, and he takes some pleasure out of putting her out of her misery. He can feel history being made as he slowly points his crossbow to her mouth and pulls the trigger. An arrow goes through Margohot's mouth, and there is no more movement from the harpy queen.

Pantazis sighs with relief and puts his crossbow down before saying in English, "It is over. It is over." He sheds tears of joy. "It is over."

The officials do not object to Pantazis' decision to end her life, knowing how dangerous it is to keep humanity's greatest threat alive. They're even more aware of how long Pantazis and Klouví have been looking forward to ending the last female harpy and preventing any more harpies from coming into this world. Now that this long journey is completed, the only ones who are upset are the media, which wants to make their story more interesting by keeping Margohot alive.

ENDING MARGOHOT ISN'T as celebratory as anyone hoped it would be. The lack of policemen on duty makes controlling the crime scene more difficult than it needs to be. News reporters and photographers attempt to trespass in the aftermath of Margohot's doing and have many unanswered questions. It doesn't help that her body has been taken away by mysterious men wearing identical black suits and sunglasses and placed the harpy's remains in a semi-truck before driving away. Even the Boston Police Department is uncertain about who they are and where they're taking the harpy queen.

Many citizens are attracted to the damage and violence caused in Boston's most feared location. With so much pandemonium, it makes exiting the police headquarters more frustrating than it needed to be for the Pluck family, harpy hunter, Secoli, and Chap to get transported on the ambulance wagon. Jed lies restfully on the stretcher, listening to Janet and the rest of his daughters crying. Janet has never felt anything so agonizing, and no six-year-old should deal with this suffering and trauma.

Jed's relaxation gets interrupted as he feels the paramedic touching his ankle and says, "Ouch. Hey, Nurse. Don't worry about me. Please check on my daughter. She needs more medical assistance than I do."

As soon as the paramedic focuses on Janet's injuries, Jed looks at his daughters in tears.

"Hey, girls. Don't worry. We're safe now."

None of his girls can stop crying, even when he's using his gentle voice. If only Jed weren't hurting so bad, he would get up and hug all of them. He looks at the wagon's other side and sees Secoli next to Klouví, petting his muse. Just as much as he worries about Janet's injury, Jed equally worries about Chap's condition. It breaks his heart to see the poor parakeet not so green and looking barely alive. Jed empathizes with Louie, who looks so sorrowful over his bird's condition.

"Hey, Nurse," Jed interrupts the paramedic while checking Janet's gaping shoulder. "After you're done helping her, can you check my partner's parakeet? Chap is just as important as anyone in here. He did save my little girl, after all."

"Jed, now is not the time," Clara irritably says while hugging Janet.

"It's true, darling," Jed replies as the paramedic checks Janet. "This bird really did save Janet while she was held hostage. Zephyra over there wouldn't have been able to kill Margohot if it weren't for this brave bird helping us. How else did Chap end up in such a terrible state?"

"It's true, Mother." Jessie nods. "Chap came out of nowhere and got that harpy in the eye. The bird was so brave to risk his life to save Janet."

Secoli lifts his head, overhearing all this about Chap. They smile at each other, understanding that despite how unimportant the bird is to the paramedic, the Pluck family sees value in the small bird. Chap is a hero who more than deserves proper treatment after helping to take Margohot down.

"Thanks, Jed," Secoli says, fighting himself from crying in front of everyone. "Don't mention it, Lou," Jed replies, lying back on the stretcher and passing out from exhaustion. He closes his eyes, trying not to let his girls' crying get to him. "He's just as much family as the rest of us."

"Jed, your skin—" Clara says, waking Jed back up. "Those blue spots— they're— disappearing. How are you getting better all of a sudden?"

"He is?" Klouví gets out of her seat, kneels to Jed, and grabs his arm for closer examination. "He's getting better because Margohot is dead. We finally cured Jed before the curse could kill him."

"So she's really dead?" Jed asks, his voice filled with hope.

"You couldn't get any better if she were still alive," Klouví replies.

The father can't be any more relieved that his tormentor is gone and his skin is getting back to normal. This puts Jed to rest peacefully, knowing that the harpy queen is permanently gone. Once all the blue spots have vanished, the Pluck family is delighted to recognize their father, who rests on the stretcher.

Then a thought comes into Secoli's mind, and he says, "Hey. What about the other two harpies? Please tell me you found and killed the rest of them." Klouví turns to him, shakes her head, and replies, "We only saw Margohot. They must have run away since they didn't want to die with her. At least we killed the most important harpy. With the last female harpy out of the way, they'll never repopulate." She pauses, then turns back to Jed. "Hey, Jed. When the harpies kidnapped you, did you see any eggs?"

Jed opens his eyes and replies, "I did. Before I escaped, I made sure that I destroyed that one and only egg in that nest."

"Are you sure you only saw one egg?"

"I'm positive. There was no other egg in that nest."

"What a relief. Margohot must have only laid one egg this time. You did the right thing in destroying it and preventing any more from coming to this world."

Hearing even more good news puts Jed in peace of mind. He finally passes out, knowing that he can't be in a safer environment.

"Hey, Allie—" Louie faces the girls sitting across from him. "I want to thank you for saving Chap back on the roof after he saved Janet. This bird could have died after that monster attacked him, but you did a great job in rescuing and keeping him alive."

"Mr. Secoli just thanked you, Allie," Clara says, nudging her by the elbow. "And what do you say when you're being thanked?"

Allie can't say a word. She's too emotional about her family still hurting. "Thank you, Louie—and especially you, Chap, for saving my daughter."

Clara adds, hugging Janet, "I really hope Chap gets well soon, Louie." When Secoli nods at Clara in gratitude, he shifts his attention to Janet, who's still crying in pain. Secoli's heart is saddened that this incident will affect her for the rest of her life. This family crisis has left a permanent mark on them, and none deserve it.

The bird owner then looks up at Chap, resting on his palms, as the budgerigar gradually opens his eyes. It is a grave disappointment for Secoli that Margohot disguised herself as Fiona Fletcher and nurtured Chap only to nearly kill him. Secoli feels guilty for putting Chap in a life-threatening situation and does not want Chap to have to live like that for the rest of his life.

Secoli looks at Allie, being comforted by her two older sisters. Jessie and Julia cannot control her emotions, no matter how much they caress and comfort Allie. It's traumatizing enough for a nine-year-old to have her father miss her birthday and now witness her youngest sister hurting. Remembering when Jed mentioned that he wanted to get Allie a budgerigar on her birthday gives him an idea. It's something he's been conflicted with since the case began, but it's time for him to concede.

"Excuse me, Allie," Secoli says. "How long ago since you turned nine years old?"

Allie is too emotional to answer the postal inspector's question. Normally, she would answer immediately, but she's not in the right mindset.

Julia, the least emotional of all her sisters, answers, "Over a month ago, sir."

"Her birthday was August fifteenth, wasn't it?"

"Yes, sir," Julia continues. "It was. Why do you ask, mister?"

"Because I've got a belated birthday present just for Allie."

Secoli presents Chap to the girls sitting before him. They immediately cease feeling emotional and become wide-eyed over what Inspector Secoli is doing.

"Chap is all yours now."

"Mr. Secoli," Clara says. "That won't be necessary. Chap belongs to you."

"I thought long and hard about it, Mrs. Pluck. Our time in Wyoming made me realize I've put him at too much risk. Today is the closest I've come to almost losing Chap. I can't bring him with me anymore. He deserves a more stable and loving owner, one who will keep him in a safer home."

"Do you really mean it, Inspector Secoli?" Jessie asks, wiping her eyes. "Are you really letting us adopt Chap?" Julia adds.

Secoli nods before saying, "I'm certain about it. Chap is very easy to take care of. Just keep him in a cage with a bird swing in it, give him plenty of water and bird seeds, clean up his mess, and let him out once in a while. You'll never find a smarter or more loyal bird than a parakeet. Chap's going to make your lives a lot more homey."

"Well, go on, Allie," Jessie says, gently shaking her shoulders to make her feel more joyous. "You wanted a bird just like Chap. Mr. Secoli is giving him to you."

Jessie and Julia help Allie up from her seat. The nine-year-old slowly walks toward Chap. She then opens both her palms, and Secoli gently places him into her hands. As Allie keeps the bandaged parakeet lying on her palms, Jessie and Julia get up and look over her shoulders. Julia then sticks her index finger on Chap's head, and the parakeet, in return, rubs his head on the tip.

Allie's mood changes, and she laughs, feeling the feathers tickle her hands as Chap moves. Thankfully, she's stable enough to keep her hands still to prevent sudden movements that would disrupt the injured bird.

"What do you say to Mr. Secoli, Allie?" Clara asks.

Allie looks at Secoli and replies, "Thank you, Mr. Secoli. Thank you so much. This is one of the best gifts that I've ever received. I'll take good care of him. I promise."

"I know you will," Secoli says with glee.

Secoli isn't feeling at all anxious, nor does he sense any triggers kicking in. There may be a reason for this, such as Chap being in his presence or the fact that he did a good deed by giving the girls a new addition to their family. How will he cope when he separates from him and his trauma causes him to hallucinate? As Secoli thinks about it, he's prepared to have it happen again but wants to be able to fight it off alone instead of letting it overtake him.

Though the postal inspector is still a work in progress, at least he knows he's still progressing in his mentality and overcoming these emotional shocks. Secoli's most important goal is not to let them take over his life so he can have full self-control without depending on anyone or anything.

CHAPTER 22

Boston Police Headquarters Massacre & the Wyoming Disappearances Connected by Harpy Attacks September 26, 1899

The Boston Police headquarters massacre and the discovery of the harpy are the biggest headline news. What was once Greece's secret enemy is now public knowledge that harpies exist. Since the species originated in Greece, the world demands to know why the Greek government has kept their existence away from the world. However, the prime minister of Greece, Georgios Theotokis, has yet to answer. Greece's failure to respond has tarnished its reputation, leading to doubts about its relationship with the United States.

The news media have engaged the public with the harpy story. There are clarifications that the same culprit connects the Wyoming disappearances and the Boston Police headquarters massacre. Despite revealing so much detail about the harpies and their actions, the United States Postal Inspection Service leaves the mystery of why they chased and kidnapped Inspector Jed Pluck. Pluck is the only survivor as the harpies' captive being kept secret created a lot of suspicion and conspiracies among many captivated by the story. As of this report, Inspector Pluck's whereabouts are kept secret.

Another mystery is the whereabouts of the harpy's corpse. Inspector Pluck and his partner, Inspector Louie Secoli, were the last to see the dead harpy before mysterious men in dark suits took the corpse away. Where its remains are is a mystery.

Despite having many pictures of the harpy in print before its disappearance, the fact that no one knows its whereabouts makes many conspirators believe this is a work of fiction by the media. With so many secrets kept from the public, it only makes the public more engrossed, and discussion of the harpy will continue for years. The fact that such a species is as violent and nearly indestructible has brought a new paranoia to Americans everywhere near the end of the nineteenth century.

Never before has the Boston Police Department suffered this many casualties. The memorial for all those seventy-two brave who died at the hands of the harpy will be the largest the city of Boston has ever held. Many of the officers' loved ones will attend the memorial to mourn and pay their respects to those massacred in their line of duty. That is not counting the inmates whose loved ones blame the Boston Police Department for neglecting them and leaving them for dead. This situation is a similar argument as to why US President William McKinley did not retaliate when the same harpy slaughtered all of Wyoming's population. Despite how the inmates at the Boston Police Headquarters and Wyoming casualties' loved ones feel, the public is much more sympathetic toward the officers who died that day.

The memorial will take place outside of the Boston Police Headquarters. Police officers from other stations will perform a police parade from the city center to the police headquarters as part of the memorial. The stage will have a wall full of framed photos of the fallen officers. Mayor Henry L. Pierce predicts that this memorial and parade will gather a large yet peaceful crowd and hopes it will not be as chaotic as when the harpy was put down. There are assigned seats for loved ones, and those who want to attend without a seat assigned will have to watch the memorial from behind.

Mayor Pierce predicts that many people will attend the event because of their fascination with the harpy mystery and not out of respect for the fallen police officers. Since yesterday's report of a harpy slaughtering an entire police station, the masses demand more answers. Wary of another attack by another harpy due to the possibility there are more of them, Americans and the rest of the world are concerned. However, time alone will tell if the United States Government, the Boston Police Department, or the United States Postal Inspection Service will reveal more information about this new and dangerous species.

THE PLUCK FAMILY ISN'T able to attend the memorial. They're all in the hospital since two family members are receiving medical attention. However, Inspector Secoli and the two harpy hunters do attend to pay their respects. Except for a few familiar faces, the three don't know any of the officers who died in the Boston Police Headquarters massacre. Despite how much mourning he did in Wyoming, being surrounded by grieving widows and children breaks Secoli's and the hunters' hearts.

Secoli especially feels guilty for not getting to know a single officer whose picture is displayed on the stage. He's lucky to have been given an assigned seat and to be able to watch the commissioner, mayor, and fellow officers give their speeches. With the thousands in attendance, the ones giving their speeches speak loudly for all to hear. The memorial concludes with a firing squad shooting in the air in memory of their fallen comrades. Everyone gets up from their seats, and everything becomes noisy. While Secoli speaks to one of the mourners beside him, he notices Klouví and Pantazis leaving.

He follows the harpy hunters, trying not to bump into anyone in his way. Walking through a row of chairs is challenging for the postal inspector, considering how narrow the rows are with everyone getting up. Judging by how fast the harpy hunters move, Secoli senses they're leaving without saying goodbye.

He stops in his tracks when he bumps into a family before he sees them enter an alley. Secoli doesn't shout at them or tell any officers nearby to stop them.

It's a struggle for the postal inspector to get through the crowd. It takes him much longer to reach the alley they went to. Secoli sprints and frees himself from the cluttered crowd. He then slows down when he sees Klouví and Pantazis waiting for him not far from the alley's entrance.

"Why are you two running?" Secoli asks, approaching the two hunters. "You do know that you have to go back to Greece soon, right?"

"We're not running away," Klouví replies, leaning her back against the wall with her arms crossed. "But we're not going back to Greece just yet." Klouví walks toward Secoli. "Have you forgotten there are two harpies still out there?"

"Shit! How did I forget? But at least we took care of Margohot. Without any female harpies, there's no way they can repopulate."

"Not so fast, Louie. Jed claims he destroyed the last egg, right?"

"Right. Where are you going with this?"

"I do not believe Margohot laid only one egg in her last ovulation."

"How can you be so sure? He would never leave an egg if there were more."

"After we dropped Jed to the hospital, Alistair and I went to the apartment building where she kept Inspector Pluck. We did our own investigation under the water tower, and we did find one smashed egg. However, we found the spot where Margohot ovulated. Though it was dry, the remains show that it had a bigger puddle of wet fluid. There's no way a female harpy would spill that much amniotic fluid with just one egg."

"Jesus...wait. It was raining that day, wasn't it? How do you know if it wasn't the rain that caused it? And how is that fluid still there and not dried up? Or maybe there was a leak from the water tower."

"The puddle was in the middle under the water tower, and it was the only wet spot in that dry area that they used for shelter. What makes the harpies' amniotic fluid different from water is they make the surface sticky if they are not washed away. We saw the evidence. There is no doubt that her goons took those eggs away from danger."

"My God...," Secoli interrupts. "That means those eggs will guarantee female harpies. Son of a bitch." He kicks a trashcan near him. "That bitch is so smart and fooled all of us again. That means the harpy race has a chance to repopulate from near extinction if they're born female. Please tell me you know where those harpies went."

"Not a single clue. But this is between us, okay? We received a telegram from the Greek government that Prime Minister Theotokis sent hundreds of harpy hunters to America to track down the last harpies. We're acting now to fix our country's mistakes of not killing all of them sooner."

"Really? So we're increasing our chances of putting those demons to extinction while they're on the run with those eggs?"

"That's the plan. Our mission is to finish what we started, and we don't want the public to know that harpies are still out there. While they don't know that more of us will be coming, we'll follow them before they fly away."

"Are you sure about that? I can inform Congress of your involvement and help your fellow harpy hunters increase your chances against those runaways."

"That won't be necessary. The police and government's involvement will only alert everyone that more harpies are still in this country. We must keep the public from knowing so Margohot's sons won't expect us to come for them."

"So what can I do to help?"

"There's nothing you can do, Louie. Just let us handle it, and I swear that after we eliminate all the harpies in this country, we'll evacuate back to Greece immediately."

"I don't know, Zephyra." Secoli looks away, shaking his head. "I know this case is closed as far as the Postal Inspection Service is concerned, but they're still out there."

"Just trust us, Louie," Klouví says, grabbing Secoli's hand. "Compared to Margohot, those harpies are barely a challenge for us. You've seen what we do. Since many more of us are coming, we'll overwhelm the rest of those harpies. Now, we have hundreds arriving as we speak. I need this to be kept secret, and we'll do the rest."

"Fine," Secoli replies, pulling his hand away and pointing to her. "I'm going to let this slide. After today, however, I'm powerless to help you out."

"Powerless?" Klouví asks. "What do you mean?"

"I'm heading back to Maryland today and requesting to be relieved from my postal inspector position. I'm leaving the Postal Inspection Service."

"You are?" She shakes her head in disbelief. "Why leave so soon? Is it because Chap almost died?"

"I've had enough of getting traumatized in this job. I just want to do something that will finally make me happy and move on from the unnecessary danger. As for Chap, he deserves a better owner by being with the Pluck family instead. I realize how cruel and unfair I've been in getting him involved with everything."

"So what will you do now?"

"I've saved up more than enough money to open an aviary. I've been thinking about how I'll cope now that Chap has been adopted by Jed's daughters. Since I've always found birds so therapeutic, why not surround myself with birds of all kinds?"

Klouví smiles at how smart Secoli sounds before saying, "An aviary sounds like the perfect fit for you, Louie. Seeing how well you treated Chap, I can tell you'll be doing great business taking care of those birds. I must admit, seeing you stand on your own without emotional support is kind of a turn-on."

"It is?" Secoli replies, his face turning red.

"Of course it is. You keep improving yourself, and you'll no doubt find a bunch of girls who'll love visiting your aviary and help build those nests with you," Klouví winks at him and walks away. "Take good care of yourself, Inspector."

Secoli blushes over the harpy hunter's flirtation. Though he has no personal feelings for her, hearing it from her gives him more self-confidence. This is validation he wasn't seeking, but since receiving it, it flatters him. He watches her walk away until Klouví stops in her tracks as soon as she sees Pantazis not moving. Her partner pulls out an envelope and gives her a smirk. She retrieves it and turns back to Secoli.

"Oh, I almost forgot," Klouví says, handing Secoli the letter. "This is for Jed. We don't have the time to say goodbye to him, so we're giving him a farewell letter."

"That's very thoughtful of you," Secoli replies, taking the letter. "I wish you two a safe journey."

Klouví gives him a nod, and she continues moving down the alley with Pantazis. Secoli watches until they're both out of sight. He genuinely hopes they both will be safe as they continue the endless hunt for harpies. Though completing his last case as a postal inspector didn't turn out how he intended, at least it's a bittersweet closure for him. He finally finds a sense of peace now that he's more appreciated. After going through so much hell this past month, he's ready to move on from his trauma.

IT'S BEEN DAYS SINCE Margohot ordered her sons to separate and for each to carry one of her eggs. Both of them obeyed her orders by flying in the directions she instructed. Yazeem brought his egg to Mississippi and settled in the wilderness next to a camp of railroad workers. He has never lived so close to human society before, but he always has wanted to experience living among human beings, like how Margohot did in Point Postal. Changing into his human form allows him to socialize with his new friends.

Luckily for him, these railroad workers are Greek immigrants who are there to build railroads through the forest. Yazeem has no intent to follow them as he has an unhatched sister he needs to keep secret. Yazeem doesn't see these Greek immigrants as prey since they speak the same language, and he fits right in. It still is a struggle for him not to act upon his indulgences and learn to eat the food they cook, which is barely edible for him. As long as Yazeem wears clothes suitable for the occasion and keeps his talons hidden by wearing boots, he can get to know these people.

On the third day after settling in their camps, Yazeem sees one sitting on the log and reading the newspaper. He sees a photo on the cover of Margohot lying dead. He immediately snatches it from the reader's hands and examines the printed photo.

"Hey," the one reading the paper yells in Greek, "I was just reading that!"

"I'm sorry, but can you tell me what this says?" Yazeem points to the article with Margohot in the photo. "I don't read English, and I need to know what this is saying."

"Haven't you heard about the harpy? The story has been in every newspaper, saying the disappearances in Wyoming and the massacre at the Boston Police Headquarters are connected. Damn it, moving to America was too good to be true."

"Tell me what happened to her. The harpy in this photo."

"She massacred a police station, and they retaliated by killing her."

"What?" Yazeem exclaims, dropping the newspaper and grabbing the man's collar. "You're kidding, right? Tell me they didn't kill her. Tell me that's all a lie."

"Don't take it out on me, Yazeem," the man replies, putting his hands up for mercy. "I didn't come up with the story. The ones who printed the story did."

Yazeem takes a deep breath and lets go of the man.

"What's gotten into you? You should be glad that a harpy is taken down. Don't you remember them terrorizing us back in Greece?"

Yazeem looks at the newspaper on the ground. He stares at the same photo of Margohot lying dead with an arrow through her mouth like she's a dead animal. He recalls her saying that one of them will perish. Now that it happens to be her, he fights his urge to cry. Yazeem doesn't say anything and heads back to where he left the nest.

Upon returning to the nest, he notices railroad workers surrounding the tree where his nest is located. They attempt to take the egg down from the tree using sticks and throwing stones at it. The nest is so high up on top of the tree, yet the egg is so huge that it's noticeable. The Greek immigrants all know exactly what that egg is and want to destroy it. Yazeem sees his unhatched sister in danger and runs after the intruders.

"Stop!" Yazeem exclaims, running after them. "I said stop! Don't harm that egg!"

"Get out of the way, Yazeem," says one of the attackers. "That's a harpy egg."

"If you're really from Greece, "another in the group says, "then you know how dangerous that thing is!"

"How do you know?" Yazeem yells. "How do you know if it isn't an egg from a rare bird species?" A rock strikes his head. "Ow. What is that for?"

"That's for saying the stupidest thing that I ever heard coming out of a Greek's mouth," says one in the group. "You wouldn't be saying that unless you're a harpy."

"He's right," said a man behind him. "Take off your boots and show us your feet."

"What?" Yazeem blushes, unable to control his sudden shaking. "Don't be ridiculous. I don't need to show you my feet."

"I knew it," says the man who had his newspaper snatched by Yazeem. "You're one of them, aren't you? You're the spawn of that female harpy from the newspaper."

"You're crazy!" Yazeem exclaims. "I'm just as human as all of—"

Yazeem gets interrupted by another stone hitting his head. He finds himself leaning against the tree and covering his head as he feels more stones thrown at him. None of them hurt as much, but it doesn't change the fact that it reminds him of all the times he got shot in Wyoming. His traumatic experience of remembering how merciless the humans are triggered him.

Soon, more people from the camp join in the stoning, causing more pain to Yazeem. These Greek railroad workers are aware of the existence of harpies and hold prejudice against them. This is where Yazeem realizes that Margohot was right about harpies being incompatible with befriending their only food source. So many stones are hitting him that he can't take it anymore.

Yazeem transforms into his harpy form. His razor-sharp black feathers tear his shirt apart, and his talons break free from his boots. Everyone who hurt him runs away for dear life. However, they all just angered the beast. Yazeem looks at his nest above his head and remembers his promise to his mother.

He leaves the egg alone one last time to ensure there are no survivors. Yazeem slaughters the camp, and nobody can fight back. It breaks his heart that he has to kill all those he wants to make friends with. However, they are a danger to his unborn sister, and he is unwilling to risk her and the harpy race's future.

After Yazeem kills every one of the railroad workers, he comes back to the tree and rests from all the slaughtering. His moment of peace doesn't last as he detects movement from the nest above him. He flies to the nest to see what's happening. The male harpy stands on the tree branch and sees that Sýnnefo is starting to hatch. Yazeem is excited and anxious that his sister is about to arrive soon. Seeing the egg shaking and then noticing everyone he killed below convinces him that harpies and humans cannot coexist together. Yazeem is no longer concerned about finding someone to connect with after realizing that his mother gave him the companion he had always wanted.

EVERY UNBORN CHILD always starts their existence in darkness. Whether through pregnancy or in an egg, a natural birth always begins by seeing the light after the infant's development. Female mammals must push their children out of their wombs, while species born in eggs must exert more effort. Unlike mammals that can consume whatever their mother eats in the womb, those that came from an ovulated egg aren't fed during their development from fetus to infant. The first sense of starvation motivates the baby to use all of its strength to hatch out of the egg, hoping something outside can stop the hunger.

For harpy chicks, there's an expectation for them to be gifted with immense strength to crack open their rock-hard eggs. Being born out of a harpy egg is either a life or death situation for the unborn harpy. Their hatching time means they only have a few hours to last, or they'll starve to death. Once they successfully hatch out of their egg, they require immediate nourishment to survive on their day of birth.

Margohot's unborn child has outgrown its egg and is now starving due to lack of space. Realizing she has no more use remaining inside, the chick wants to break free. It is grueling for her, considering there is little room to move her wings and talons. All she can do is use her weight to roll the egg around. As the unborn harpy does that, she can slide her limbs from being curled up and put them to good use.

The unhatched chick is dizzy from making the egg roll around and starts kicking, smacking, elbowing, and headbutting the egg's interior surfaces. No matter how hard the chick tries, no progress is being made. If only she had more wiggle room, hitting harder would be much easier. On top of her already feeling fatigued, breathing albumin does little to restore her stamina. Still, the yet-to-be-born harpy wants out.

She tries again to break the surfaces until she feels a soft spot. Hatching out of a harpy egg's tough, thick shells requires intelligence and strength. Feeling an area of the egg that's less rigid than all the areas she hit is the most crucial part of the hatching process. The intelligent chick uses her talons and stomps the egg's weak point. She does this repeatedly until she finally sees the light.

Her first-ever exposure to light blinds her. Despite hurting her eyes, the sudden brightness compels the unborn chick to see the world outside. Being able to move her body with little room makes her familiarize the structure of her body by feeling the length of her wings to not feeling anything at the tip of her talons. The intelligent chick kicks the same area several times and slides her talons between the cracks. She then pulls the crack apart, adding more cracks to more areas of the egg's surface.

The unborn harpy then uses her wings and head to break through the other surfaces of the interior. Little by little, the interior of the egg gets brighter and brighter. She continues doing this until her index finger on her wing becomes the first body part that makes it out of the egg, and a beam of light hits her eyes even more. She feels it's much colder outside, but she's too curious about what's out there.

The hatching child feels the albumin spilling outside the egg and the cool air coming in. Knowing her entire world is changing, she keeps kicking and smacking the cracks, which are getting easier to break. More albumin is pouring out of the egg, and with her nose and mouth exposed to oxygen for the first time, she takes her first breath. Inhaling and exhaling the air entering the egg recovers her stamina and makes it easier for her to crack the eggshell.

Now, she pushes away the shell pieces and has enough room to stick her head out. The newly born harpy tries to get used to the light so she can see her surroundings. She sees herself surrounded by haystacks with a giant figure staring at her. Like all hatchlings, the first organism she sees is what she'll latch on to, and this one sees one of her kind for the first time.

The hatchling sticks her head out even more and hears her first words in Greek. "Welcome to this world, Tycherós. I'm Rotzen. I'm your brother." He then tosses a separated arm into the large nest. "Here's your reward for making it out of the egg."

The carcass in front of the hatchling catches her eyes and makes her stomach rumble more. Tycherós slides out of her cracked egg and crawls toward the arm. Once she reaches it, she starts biting and chewing on the forearm. Tasting human flesh and blood satisfies her craving. Since she hasn't grown her teeth, she does the smart thing by scraping the separated body part with her nails and then swallowing the pieces.

Rotzen watches Tycherós enjoy her first meal and sees her feeding herself. The guardian doesn't do any traditional harpy calling or rituals that his old flock used to do whenever there's a newborn. He takes full advantage of finally being in charge and making up the rules. The male harpy then looks around and likes the interior of the barn he's in. He enjoys the company of the barn animals sharing the same space.

Despite sparing the animals, he took pleasure in killing the farmers who owned them. He looks behind him to see the entire family of farmers he killed piled up, thinking he has enough to feed Tycherós for a while. Flying to Iowa this time of year and building a nest for his newborn sister might not have been a good idea. He wishes Margohot had told him to fly south instead, where Yazeem and Sýnnefo are now. Unlike Yazeem, Rotzen already knows that humans are a grave threat to his kind and doesn't hesitate to kill any for his and Tycherós' survival.

Watching Tycherós continue eating makes Rotzen wonder how Yazeem and Margohot are doing with their new hatchlings. He has a funny thought about how Yazeem will be doing poorly as Sýnnefo's guardian. Then he thinks about how much he's already missing him, thinking that it is he who fell after Margohot told them Zeus said one of them would die with their egg. Since it has gotten colder, Rotzen won't take a chance carrying Tycherós or expecting her to fly to a warmer location anytime soon. He was told to find a territory to claim and wait for Margohot to find him. Disobeying her order will only make it harder to reunite as a flock once more. Little does he know that his mother is dead. While waiting for the false hope that Margohot will return to him, he sticks with his decision to live on this farm and raise Tycherós with all the farm animals.

ALTHOUGH THE FIGHT against Margohot is finally over, the horrible memories of her feel endless. Being a survivor of someone as evil and pitiless as her can damage any strong soul. Those who have dealt with the harpy queen's brutal and degenerate ways have always been permanently scarred for life. In Jed Pluck's situation, he's witnessed her death but will be forever traumatized by all she has done. Despite having no longer carried her disease, he sleeps with the same repeated nightmare.

Filled with sweat and panic, Jed wakes up from another repeated nightmare. Upon waking up, he looks around for Margohot but finds himself in a small hospital room, lying in bed. He sees his broken ankle in new bandages, propped up on a pillow. When he reaches for his foot, he discovers both hands are fully wrapped in bandages, with only the fingertips revealed. The traumatized inspector continues panting until he sees his youngest daughter sleeping beside him in a separate hospital bed.

The father's panic is calmed by watching little Janet sleep peacefully. He has forgotten how innocent and precious she looks with her eyes closed. Seeing her shoulder and arm wrapped in bandages breaks Jed's heart. The fact that he almost lost one of his own children shows how consequential that extramarital affair was before it all became beyond his control and consent.

Jed wants to approach his daughter and give her a hug, but he's in too much pain to get out of bed. The father is filled with so much guilt that he breaks down into tears. Even after coming out victorious over the harpy queen, there is no resolution for the postal inspector. It is despairing for Jed to learn that everything is irreversible and no one is untouchable.

He cries alone, quietly enough to keep Janet asleep, until he hears a knocking on the door. Jed hastily wipes his tears with his blanket and pretends to be asleep. The door creaks open, and he keeps an eye barely open to see who stepped into his hospital room. His eyes immediately widen when he sees Secoli entering the room. "Sorry, Jed," Secoli whispers, startled by Jed's sudden awakening as he places his hat on the table between their beds. "I didn't mean to wake you up. I didn't want to leave Boston before saying farewell."

"You're going back to Maryland, I presume."

"Yes. As soon as I file my report, I'll resign as a postal inspector."

"You're really going to leave the Postal Inspection Service? It's not because you gave up Chap to my girls, right?"

"To be honest, I'm not meant for this job, and I've put that parakeet through so much that I'm guilty of relying on him to do my job. Plus, this case...broke me."

"Same here," Pluck sighs, holding the bridge of his nose. "I can't do this anymore. I'm responsible for everyone's deaths and putting my family in danger."

Secoli sits on his bed before whispering, "No, Jed. You know exactly who's responsible for everything. And I sure as hell know it isn't you. It's those damn harpies."

"I know, Louie." Pluck starts tearing up, struggling to control his volume. "But I committed that affair, which escalated this whole mess. I even brought that jezebel here and almost lost my little girl."

Louie glances at Janet and interrupts by whispering, "Hey. Hey. Hey. It's alright, Jed. Your family is still alive, all things considered. Count your blessings that Janet and the rest didn't end up like everyone else."

"That's what's eating me up, Louie," Jed sniffs, trying to keep his volume down. "I've never seen a child suffer like she did. Hearing her cry when Margohot hurt her and held her hostage is the worst part of this experience. Can you imagine how much worse it was for the women and children I failed to protect in Point Postal?" He places a hand on his forehead and trembles. "I can't get it out of my head. I can't get it out of my head, Louie. What am I supposed to do? Those harpies are still out there."

Seeing his partner still suffering gives Secoli watery eyes. Deep down, he wishes he could see the same stoic Jed he used to look up to. The harpies put him through made Jed the opposite of who he once was. All Secoli can do is silently acknowledge Jed, listening patiently as he lets it all out. Jed's psychological challenges break Louie's heart, making him feel guilty for being the strong one out of the two.

Secoli slowly reaches Pluck's hand to show some compassion. Upon touching the exposed fingertips, Pluck instantly places his head on his partner's chest and hugs him tightly.

He continues letting Jed cry on him for a while, then says to him, "I'm so sorry, Jed. I'm not qualified to help you when I'm still trying to help myself." He feels Jed's grasp around his stomach loosening, allowing him to help him lie back down. "You can't give up on your wife and daughters. Even though all the harpies are dead, I don't want this family to break apart like Point Postal did when we failed to protect them. They need you more than anything. Get well soon, Jed."

"Are they really dead?" Jed asks, with his head down.

"Yes. They're all dead. Oh, I almost forgot." Secoli takes out the envelope. "Here's a farewell letter from Zephyra and Alistair. They couldn't say goodbye since they're being deported back to Greece. But they want to wish you the best in spirit." He hands Jed the letter. "Goodbye, Jed. I'm going to miss you, pal."

Secoli extends a handshake to Pluck. Despite feeling hopeless, Jed shakes his hand, even though his hand is still injured. Pluck can see Secoli's eyes getting watery, realizing he's holding back his tears. Despite being the strong one between them, Jed can tell he's receiving sympathy from his old partner. As soon as they release their handshake, Secoli heads out the door.

Jed finds himself alone despite Janet sleeping in the same room. All he can do is watch his youngest child slumber, hoping to leave with her soon. Jed has developed a phobia of staying in hospitals, no thanks to the last time he got kidnapped. He wonders how he can get better after what Secoli told him. Fathers must always be at their strongest when their family needs them.

How is he in any position to continue raising his family if he's in such a bad mindset? His moment of pondering gets interrupted by Clara entering with a flower bouquet.

"Hello, hon," Clara whispers, placing the flowers on the nightstand between them. "The girls and I brought you two flowers. How are you two doing?"

Clara caresses Janet's forehead and checks her shoulders. Her touch is so gentle and soft that it keeps Janet sleeping comfortably. Watching his wife nurturing their daughter fills Jed with so much guilt. Noticing her getting teary-eyed makes him feel like an even worse husband. Jed ends up dropping more tears than his wife. Upon hearing her husband lightly weep Clara attends to him.

She sits on his bed and strokes her husband's left hand while his other hand covers his eyes to hide his tears. Clara attempts to intertwine her fingers with Jed's, but the bandages wrapped around his hands prevent her from making the romantic gesture they both love. It's so easy for Clara to have emotional conversations with her female colleagues, but she has no idea how to cope with her husband's emotional damage. Men have always hidden their emotions from the world, and her heart cannot fathom that her husband is the first man she's ever seen to break down in front of her.

"It's all right, Jed," Clara whispers, touching his shoulder. "Everything will be fine. The Postal Inspection Service is giving you as much time as you need to recover."

"It's not that," Jed interrupts, looking at his wife. "Clara. There's something I need to tell you."

"Oh, hon. I know about your situation. Zephyra told me everything. You got raped many times. Tortured to death. Almost died from her disease, but you look so much better now that you're cured. I know how badly she hurt you and Janet. But she's gone, and you and everyone are safe."

Jed stutters with anxiousness, frustrated by not being able to come up with the right words. "No...I... it's not that." Confusing Clara more, he shakes his head. "You don't understand. I'm so sorry. I'm truly sorry, Clara."

"Then what are you crying about?" Clara asks with tears coming down.

Jed takes a moment to catch his breath to keep his emotions intact. He knows the truth is the only way for him to stop feeling this way. Keeping a secret from her is going to make him start up over again. She deserves to know. All spouses do.

"I have a confession to make," Jed says softly. "Clara, it's true that all those sexual violations were never within my consent—except one. The first one."

"What?" his wife replies in shock, pulling away from him.

"It's true. I had an affair with…Margohot. She had all of us fooled that she was a human being. She seduced me after I told her no. But she never took it as an answer and somehow convinced me to change my mind.

"This is all my fault, Clara. I let her have sex with me. She killed all those people in the town I was supposed to protect during my captivity. And I brought her here when she was still chasing after me and nearly killed our children."

Jed shuts his eyes, unable to look at his wife's distraught expression, and continues, "I understand you hate me for it. I'm not expecting you to forgive me after all the stress this travesty caused you. I faced my punishment, and you deserve to know why I'm still facing the consequences of that affair. I'm so sorry for what I did to you…did to us…did to our girls.

"You've done so much to keep this family together, and I've been away from you and our children for far too long. I'm a horrible father and a worse husband. Clara…" He takes a deep breath. "I'm so sorry."

Jed doesn't dare open his eyes. As he sits on his bed, he can feel his wife's rage filling her. He then stops sobbing and moving, feeling intimidated as ever. The cold shoulder is enough for him to understand how Clara feels. The lack of anything from either of them is an awful sign that this affair has permanently damaged their marriage.

After sitting on the bed for a while, Clara gets up from his bed and slowly heads out the door. There is no sound of aggression when she slowly leaves the room. Even when she opens and closes the door, she does it so gently and manages not to wake Janet. Jed refuses to pick his head back up even though she's gone. All he can do is leave Clara alone and remain in his hospital bed with his youngest daughter. After staring down at his blanket for a long while, he notices the letter from Klouví and Pantazis is still beside him. He takes a deep breath to get his mind off his wife and attempts to open it. He bites the corner of the letter and rips it open. It says:

Hello, Jed,

Sorry we couldn't say goodbye in person. I wish we didn't have a language barrier that prevented us from getting to know each other. I'm using Zephyra to translate what I need to tell you, hoping it might help your situation.

When I first met you in the hospital the other night, I realized you're traumatized in a way only rape victims can be. I've seen it so many times from both women and men. It hurts me more that your child almost got killed because those same violators refused to stop tormenting you. I wonder why God allows such cruel and evil individuals to exist.

I'm reaching out to you because seeing you break down when we mentioned your rapist reminded me of when I was like you. I know what you're going through because I, too, am a victim of rape. It wasn't the same individual, but my rapist is similar to yours. What I'm going to share with you isn't going to make things better because my road to recovery took so long for me to solve.

People associate rape as exclusively a woman and child issue, but you and I know it happens to men too. It's quite uncommon for rape victims to be fully grown men, making society not informed about it since many, like us, keep it hidden because we're afraid to be seen as weak.

We, men, are expected to endure pain and suffering, but no one can ever expect what is so sexually overpowering that it severely damages a man's resiliency and functionality. It even breaks my heart that other men don't help male rape victims like us because they expect all men to be self-reliant. That mentality is why the healing process takes longer than it should.

Rape is evil like no other. We live with it worse off because it destroys our dignity and self-respect. Worst of all, it stays with us for as long as we can remember. Despite moving on from it, I still remember mine like it's happening all over again. Indeed, we don't get pregnant from it, but it doesn't excuse the fact that those violators used us for their self-gratification, and we weren't treated like humans. Rape is evil. And since it happens to men, too, it's clear that evil has no gender. But thankfully, neither does good have a gender.

You're going to be alright, Jed. We've taken care of your rapist together, which took great bravery. Now, it's up to you to find your healing. You faced an individual who had as much strength as she had evil intentions, and she used it against your will. I cannot give you the healing you need. What worked for me may not work for others because everyone's need for help differs.

Your time is precious. The rapist's bleak future should not be your focus any more than our bleak past was theirs. Our future as survivors should be seen as bright. Not because we're past it but because you'll eventually find more like us where you'll be the light in their dark times. Your family is dealing with very dark times, but they're looking up to you as their only light.

You're so blessed to have a healthy family. Being surrounded by positive people is a great start to your recovery. Let their time with you be treasured. Avoid staying lonely because it will make you remember those awful times. I'm certain you'll overcome this whole experience and be the postal inspector you once were and even a better father.

Take good care of yourself,

Alistair Pantazis

Jed can't cry quietly anymore after reading the letter. It is more than a thoughtful letter. He needed to know that someone understood him and reached out. Although his marriage is broken and Clara might never come back to him, he feels a sense of hopefulness, something he hasn't felt in a while. Pantazis' message affected Pluck to the point that he believes in second chances.

The reward of this whole journey wasn't to solve the case or end the harpy queen but to have another chance to be a good father to his wonderful girls. There's no way that Jed could ever be a father to the harpies that are related to him. He was always meant to be a father of daughters of the same species as him. Jed's crying is so intense that it wakes up Janet.

"Daddy?" Janet says, getting out of bed and pulling her father's sleeve with her only good arm. "Why are you crying? Did the doctor hurt you?"

"Janet?" Jed responds, wiping his tears, "I'm sorry, baby. Did I wake you?"

"Why are you so sad? Is it because I'm hurt?"

Pluck holds on to her good hand, looks her in the eyes, and says, "Yes... and I'm sorry that I brought those monsters here and that they hurt you."

"Daddy, you're silly," Janet says, smiling but not understanding what he meant. "You didn't bring those monsters here. They followed you and caused too much trouble."

Jed doesn't have the mental capacity to explain it to a six-year-old. Despite his foot recovering, he picks his girl up by the hips and makes her sit on his lap. He immediately gives her a hug and cries on her shoulder. Janet doesn't understand what her father is truly thinking about while being embraced by him. To her, having her father back home is as good as it gets.

Moments later, a knock is heard on the door. Jed is in shock to see Clara make her return after his confession. A tearful expression appears on her face, not the one he thought his wife was showing earlier.

"Jed. I can't stay mad at you, hon," Clara says. "You've gone through enough. I forgive you…I miss you. I miss you so much that I can't stay mad at the father of my children." She turns to the door she came through. "Girls. Your father and little sister are ready to see you."

Jessie, Julia, and Allie enter the ward with joyful expressions. Allie is carrying a birdcage with Chap in it. Despite being wrapped in bandages, the little hero appears healthy and looks as alive as ever. Seeing everyone and the new family member with the father is the second chance Jed thought impossible. Everyone joins the family tradition by getting in on the giant family hug. Allie is the last to join the hug, making Chap join in while still in the birdcage.

Jed notices Chap's cage touching him in the family hug. Seeing Secoli's old muse again makes him guilty that he adopted his parakeet into his family. The budgerigar seems happy to bump into him again as his new master. If there's ever going to be a nonhuman that could be a member of the Plucks, Chap is the best choice for the family. Most importantly, the father is back and ready to be a parent again.

Before Jed closes his eyes and gets lost in the family hug, he sees Louie Secoli returning to the hospital room. He's retrieving the hat he left behind but returns at the perfect time to see the Pluck family and his old muse in on the family hug. Seeing Jed in a better state of mind and having Chap close to him puts a huge smile on his face, knowing his job here is done on much better terms. While the other family members don't notice Secoli returning, Secoli quietly puts his hat back on and waves goodbye to his old partner before exiting the room. This is a much-preferred way for the two postal inspectors to part ways than how they last said their goodbyes.

With Secoli finally gone, Jed is finally lost in the family hug. This family hug is the most meaningful they've had together. There are no dry eyes in the room. After all he's been through, Jed is treated like a decent human again. At that moment, he realizes what being the light in the darkness truly means. A good and redeemable father is key to restoring a broken family. He promises to himself that he will never let this light go out again now that he's been given a second chance to make it brighter than before.

About the Author

Keith Melo was born in a US Naval Hospital in Okinawa, Japan, in 1990.

He is American by birthright and ethnically Filipino Caucasian. He spent his entire childhood as a military brat, accustomed to diverse cultures, and has been voted the best artist in many of his classes growing up in DoDEA Pacific Schools, where art isn't as valued. With several degrees, two of which are artistic degrees, and as a United States Army veteran, he spent a lifelong journey understanding the world.

Tragedy and xenofiction are what he specializes in, having a new aspiration of telling good stories that are not always exclusive to humanity but sentients at large. Keith's transition between industries presented challenges, but he ultimately discovered a fresh avenue to express his creative freedom.

He strives to read and write more after finding inspiration from Michael Crichton, Guy Gavriel Kay, Harlan Ellison, Robin Hobb, and Richard Adams. Inspiring himself to create a bibliography of meaningful nonhuman characters and unique points of view, he no longer fears his dyslexia, which he has been battling his entire life.

Read more at https://www.keithmelo.com/.

Milton Keynes UK
Ingram Content Group UK Ltd.
UKHW031152251124
451529UK00001B/109